I0726459

CHILD OF KITARRA

THE SANARII CHRONICLES

BOOK I

ANDREA GIBB

www.andreagibb.com

To Melissa, Lesha, and Sonya.
For helping me fall in love with
adventures in the forest.

And to Quinton.
Because you are my favorite adventure.

THE LONG ILSES
KITARRA
WITHE
THE WANDERLING MOUNTAINS
PINNAE
THE FERRY
WINDEKEEP
KITARRA PEAK
ATTINGARD
KILEV
STANDING STONES
THE TARM
ALLATI
TAYEH'S VALE
MAHLAS
LITTLE HILL
THE MIDLANDS
STONYHILL
THE GREAT FOREST
OLD ROAD
THE KEEP
FISHTOWN
DWELLER'S KNOLL
CAER ANDRI
JULLAYAH
ULLIAN
CARTENEL
ALDERRIDGE
THE GREAT BAY

Those who were strong are now weak,
With healing hands, the babes will speak
Light turns to dark and colors shift,
Two rivers join when two lovers rift,
Watch for the child of two thrones,
Born with magic in his bones,
A child lit by the stars,
Watch for him, for he shall be ours.

TAYEH

"TAYEH OF KITARRA, what are you doing in my forest?"

"And a good day to you, Lulanan of the Forest," Tayeh said without looking up. He continued the slow, meticulous preservation of his blade, a Kitarran latha, running the soft leather rag over the bright steel. It would irritate the Forest Guardian, but Tayeh could not resist irking the fickle creature. He felt a smile grow across his face.

"There is a girl in Jullayah. You know her. You have watched her parents. You have watched her as a babe," Tayeh told the other Guardian. "She is important to us."

"'Us'?" The statement was punctuated with reluctance and a chill like hoarfrost on a midwinter dawn.

"We must work together, you and I," Tayeh raised his eyes to meet hers. Her fair face was reminiscent of someone eating - and then spitting out - sour prickle-berries. The Forest Guardian was a *velidar*, but no one remembered the old word anymore. For the moment she looked like a young, human woman. Mostly. Her hair was red as autumn leaves and nearly as tangled. Not a speck of clothing covered her moon-pale skin. But it was her eyes that betrayed her true nature. They were orange and wild, filled with a luminous glow no living thing possessed. Tayeh knew his own pointed irises would reflect the same unearthly glint.

"Why would a human girl be important to us, Warrior?"

"I don't know exactly. Yet. I just know that she is important." Tayeh would not lie to her; there was too much at stake. Suddenly he felt impossibly old and impossibly tired for an immortal.

"You came all the way out here, abandoning your people, without knowing why?"

"You must have a little faith, Lulanan."

"Faith!" The word was bitter. "Sometimes it is hard to remember why we are here," Lulanan said settling on the moss, looking rather small. She exhaled long and slow. "I have sensed something troubling. The feeling grows stronger with every turning of leaf and wind, but I can hardly credit myself these days, everything is so clouded."

"I know." Tayeh's voice sounded sad even to his ears. "Something dangerous approaches. A poison I cannot see. The Allmakers have gone deep - I feel their fear. The cendari trees blossomed in winter. Their blooms withered in the frost. I fear unless we intervene, your realm, and mine, will be lost."

"This girl - this human - is the key?"

Tayeh nodded. "One of them." It was an ambiguous answer, but his companion didn't seem to mind.

"Crea will not like it, not at all."

"Crea is not one of us, not really." Tayeh stopped his careful movements across his blade, turning his attention to the intense little woman. "The Crow cannot reach the Forest. That is why we must bring the girl here."

Lula looked dismayed. "How will we do that, Cat-man?"

Tayeh smiled. "We must reveal ourselves to her. Show her the secret way into the Forest," Tayeh said fingering the cendari-leaf pendant hanging around his neck. Lula watched him with a frown.

"The portal?"

"The portal."

"The Crow really will not like that." But she smiled wickedly.

CHAPTER 1

EVA

SOMETHING WAS UNSETTLING about the village. Nothing in its outward appearance struck her as alarming. The provincial houses and barns were unimposing and exactly what Eva would have expected, and the people were friendly, genuinely honored to welcome Lady Clarette of Ullian and her niece, a favorite of the king, betrothed to the prince. No, the strangeness was a taste in the air, a feeling in the trees, a sharpness along the edge of her nerves making her skin prickle. She could not identify the cause, but it made her want to watch her back. That was it - she felt watched, like prey, like something was slavering, crouched, waiting for her to dart.

But then she stepped inside the inn and felt the warmth on her face. The kitchen-y smells greeted her like lost friends and the innkeep put a steaming cup of tea in her hands, making her incapable of thinking beyond the drink heating her from within and the warm fire thawing her without. Eva looked down at her fingers to make sure they had not melted.

Her journey had been thoroughly miserable so far. Wretched weather. Muddy roads. Flooded bridges. Five years Eva had made the journey from the Keep to the king's city with her aunt, and in those five years, she could not remember a spring so cold. Riding had been tolerable, but her hands and toes were numb from it. Sleeping in a tent had not been so tolerable, with the cold penetrating her bones, even with all her furs. It felt… disturbingly ominous. She pushed the dismal thoughts away, leaning over her tea, allowing the steam to fill her mind instead. Maybe its warmth would reach her heart.

By all accounts, they should have arrived in Caer Andri a few days ago. They should be settling into their court chambers, the ills of the cold melting away by warm fires, lavish blankets, and soft beds. But the winter snows had turned into spring floods, and along with chilly spring rains, the bridge at Barrowsby had flooded, forcing them to turn north, hedge along the Great Forest until Dweller's Knoll. Only then could they redirect back to the south to the king's city.

Part of Eva was thankful for the delay. With Clarette's news, Eva was hesitant about arriving in Caer Andri, afraid of the changes she would find there.

Eva would have enjoyed the detour if it weren't for her worries and the damp, biting cold turning her into a whiny, spoiled brat and therefore a hypocrite - she had promised herself she would never become that kind of noblewoman. She had never been north along the border of the Great Forest, and usually traveling by horse and tenting at night was not as discomforting. But the rain, oh the rain, was so cold it was almost snow. Arriving in Dweller's Knoll was a relief.

"There you go, my Lady, are you warmer now?" The innkeep was a sturdy sort of woman with a round face and round eyes and a round tummy all of which added to her motherly demeanor. The arrogant merchants and shopkeeps of Caer Andri could learn a thing from the kindly peasant.

"I am. Thank you so much," Eva replied, smelling the hot potpie placed before her. Her stomach had been moaning for hours. Clarette was in her room, changing out of her traveling clothes, but Eva had decided to eat first. She could change and bathe later. An excellent decision based on the plate steaming before her.

The small common room was empty. Clarette's men were out seeing to the horses and wagons. Eva guessed not many traveled the northern road along the Forest. Jullayans were too superstitious. Besides the doting matron, Tarek was Eva's only companion for the moment. And he stood silent and still, her perpetual shadow, always ready to leap between Eva and whatever danger might present itself to a young noblewoman.

"Please, bring some food for my guard," Eva asked the matron.

"He may look as impenetrable as an oak, but I can see the hungry glint in his eyes."

The woman eyed the tall, imposing guard with a sullen, uncharacteristic wariness. Tarek instilled mistrust in people. It was his job to glower and look menacing, to keep nosy lordlings away from Eva as she grew from an impressionable young girl to an eligible young woman. Eva knew it was not an act. He was a deadly weapon, a skilled fighter hired by Clarette to guard a then eleven-year-old Eva. For five years Tarek and Mahone had been a constant presence, watching over Eva day and night. The matron gave an unconvincing smile and headed back to the kitchen.

The room was too quiet. Usually Eva wore quiet like a soft, warm blanket on a winter night, but the air stirred uncomfortably, reminding Eva of her unease as they approached the village, the off-ness of the tall woods and the drab stone buildings cowering under the heavy clouds. The awareness was still there, still watching her. She looked around instinctively, but it was just a simple room. The shadows held no warnings, the gray daylight tried to penetrate the shuttered windows, but failed. The fire crackled amiably, an ignorant beast. Tarek looked unperturbed, but Eva was the first to admit she was lousy at reading her impassive guard. Eva tried to shake off the feeling. Likely, it was just her dour mood exaggerating her fears. Maybe all she needed was rest after the long ride.

"Tarek, stop glowering and come sit with me. You must be as cold as I am," Eva observed, taking a bite of her pie. "And this is as delicious as it smells."

The energy in the room shifted as Tarek came over and sat with her at the small table. He still glanced at the door, to the corners of the room, as was his habit.

"Mahone will not forgive me for eating without him," Tarek said. Mahone had obviously drawn the short straw. He was out in the cold with the horses, unloading Eva's things into the inn room. Tarek smiled as the innkeep brought him his own pie. The woman tried not to stare at Tarek's face. Even with his cordial smile, the crisscross of old scars on Tarek's once-handsome features gave him a nightmarish appearance. "This is divine," Tarek mused, ignoring the woman's shifty stare.

Eva looked up to see her aunt step into the common room, freshly dressed, prim, poised. Clarette glanced at Tarek sitting at Eva's table, her eyes narrowing, but only for a moment. Eva marveled, not for the first time and surely not for the last, how her aunt looked fit to dine with the king in such a short amount of time. Her dress was immaculate, detailed, the embellishments and deep red color only enhancing the older woman's beauty. Once, Eva would have felt like a slug in comparison, wearing her dirty riding clothes, her cloak hemmed in mud and her boots scuffed, a dress the furthest thing from her mind. But she no longer cared. And neither did her aunt. Clarette had long ago accepted that Eva could look and act like the perfect young noblewoman when needed, but only when required. Eva was more comfortable in leggings and a tunic with a dagger attached to her belt and her riding boots on her feet. Clarette dressed with such opulence because she loved it.

Tarek rose and saluted the lady and went back to his watching. Clarette took Tarek's place. She took his fork and began to eat Tarek's leftovers without a moment's thought in a most un-lady-like fashion.

"Maybe we should stay here until real spring arrives. This dish is amazing," Clarette stated. "This cold is atrocious. Never have I been happier to be in an inn!"

"I don't know about staying too long, my lady," Darys said coming in, hanging up his wet cloak, his grizzled face red from the chilled air. "I was talking with the stable boy. He says there have been some odd happenings of late. Bandits, they think. Not a place I want to linger with you fair womenfolk," he added with a wink. "I then spoke to the village elder and told him when we reach Caer Andri, we will tell the king - or rather the prince - of their local troubles."

"Great. Bandits. That is just what we need," Clarette moaned.

"Raiding bandits?" Eva asked calmly. Her intuition was screaming at her.

"Something of the sort. Raids. Attacks. The people are scared and uneasy."

Bandits were uncommon in Jullayah. Thieving was a rare occurrence beyond the slums of Caer Andri, and rarely accompanied by violence. Sometimes the border towns between Jullayah and the Midlands saw raiders from that lawless place, but Dweller's Knoll was far away from the Midlands. King Rhais kept a peaceful realm. Harvests were plentiful, food and wealth were not hard to come by. The peasants were happy. Maybe news of King Rhais's failing health was already causing trouble. Eva's food suddenly tasted like ash in her mouth.

The little round matron had come back with more food. More meat pies and bread, cheese, ale. Wine for the lady. Overhearing Darys, she said, "Not bandits. Forest Folk." Her voice was stern with controlled emotion. The woman was afraid too, Eva could see it now.

"Forest Folk? That is impossible," Eva scoffed.

"Not impossible, begging the lady's pardon," The innkeep continued. "I have seen them with my own eyes. When I was a child, I saw a woman turn into a wolf."

"A wolf?" Clarette gave a patient laugh. "Eva, you have lived under the shadow of the Great Forest all your life, have you ever seen the Forest Folk?" It was a measure of Lady Clarette's practiced air that the innkeep did not hear the derision in the noblewoman's voice.

"Of course not," Eva lied. Lying was not one of Eva's strengths. However, Clarette, who was good at sniffing out lies, was so sure of the ludicrousness of the woman's statement that she did not sense it. "And besides, if there were Forest Folk, why would they attack Jullayans? Those stories are centuries old."

"The woman who turned into a wolf was sent to the Black Goddess. No one ever heard from her again. Maybe they want revenge?"

Something about her tale unnerved Eva. Perhaps it was merely the mention of the Black Goddess.

"Well, I am not concerned. My men are the best trained in all of Jullayah. Eh, Darys?" Clarette turned to her captain. Darys raised his ale and took a sip.

"Not to worry, my lady," Darys said. "But I will post extra watches. But by the Black Goddess, it will feel good to sleep indoors tonight!" He turned his roguish grin to Clarette.

The ale went to Eva's toes. The fire was hot on her face, melting her resistance to the fatigue that pleaded for sleep. So when the door opened with a blast of cold air and shouts, she jolted from her daze feeling irritated.

"Captain, something is afoot." It was Mahone, his graying black hair whipping around his face adding to the frenzied look in his gray eyes. Tarek was at Eva's side in an instant. There were shouts from the street outside. The shouts turned to screams. The sounds of blades and fighting broke out.

"What -?" Darys shushed Clarette, taking her by the arm, guiding her forcefully into the back of the inn and relative safety. Mahone, on the other hand, did not usher Eva into the depths of the inn. He tossed Eva a sword. She caught it easily. It was not her sword, and it was heavy and short, not her ideal weapon, but it would do. She gritted her teeth. She had been forced to leave her sword at the Keep because women were not supposed to know how to defend themselves, and Clarette, who suffered her niece's unsuitable hobbies tolerably, did not want the court to find out exactly how eccentric the daughter of the late Lord Finnan really was.

"She should stay back with Clarette -" Tarek growled at his partner.

"No. I can fight," Eva interrupted Tarek.

"We need her. Eva is as good as any of us. And half of Clarette's men are down already," Mahone hissed, his eyes wild. Eva had never seen him in such a state.

"How -?"

"Shh. They are coming," Mahone said in an urgent whisper.

Eva shifted the sword in her hand, trying to sort through Mahone's ambiguous warnings. Bandits couldn't make quick work of Clarette's men. And Forest Folk would never attack Jullayans.

Would they?

She hardly had time to think when the heavy wooden door to the inn was hit hard by something, someone. Someones. Plural. Eva felt the pounding of it in her ears, rattling her nerves. She could fight, and fight well, but it was all in practice. Countless winter days spent with Tarek and Mahone in the great hall or her father's abandoned council room, sparring and practicing. She had never killed a man.

Even with Mahone and Tarek pressed against it, the door was forced open. The wood broke and splintered, the latch bent. Writhing bodies poured inside, but Eva was not sure she could call them men. There was a bestial madness about them that seemed unreal. The violence and malice were palpable. Spit flew from their mouths.

Their hands were bloody to the elbow, like they had ripped apart their adversaries with their bare hands. They were wounded, some limping obviously, and yet didn't seem to register pain. They came in like the plague, a hoard with nightmarish intensity, their eyes glazed but intent, shouting incoherent, inhuman noises. Their hands held crude weapons, kitchen knives, clubs. Mahone was dazed, knocked aside when the door burst, bleeding from a long splinter that cut his scalp. Tarek struck man after man, limb after limb.

Somewhere behind the fray, Eva heard the innkeep shrieking. Eva lunged and swung, hitting bone and flesh, feeling hot blood on her skin, the smell of iron in her nose. She concentrated on each thrust, not the death that came at the end of her blade. She thought only of her guards, her friends. She saw Tarek take a hard hit as he deflected a man from coming at her. The man went down, but another took his place. Mahone had recovered from his daze and was attacking with equal madness, but it was focused madness. The efficiency of his blade was a force.

Within moments, Eva was able to drop her sword arm. No more were coming. The foe had not been a cohort of warrior. Their strength had been in their madness and their numbers, and in the end they fell easily to the superior skill of Eva and her guards.

The room was transformed into a mass grave. Eva counted twenty men and then gave up. There was so much blood. Eva felt sick, unable to tear her eyes from the scene of violence. She knelt beside a man who died with his eyes wide, his mouth open in a scream of defiance or madness, she could not tell. Something drew her to his face, his eyes glazed and dead. She touched his skin and felt - magic. But it was not like her magic. It was bitter and rotten and empty like a starless night, but alive, writhing within the death-encapsulated body. It reached for her. She withdrew her hand like she had been stung, backing away from the dead men.

Mahone had gone out into the street, coming back after a moment with several battered Ullian guards, reporting that the threat was over. No more bandits.

Bandits. The men they had killed could not be bandits. They had been too crazed, drunk on blood-lust and violence. They had been touched by magic. But a magic unlike any she had known existed.

Eva blinked. She felt unsteady, like she had slipped into a long-forgotten tale. Her memories twisted awkwardly around what she knew about magic, about dark magic. She couldn't remember anything that made sense or connected to the dead men before her.

The world became instantly upright when she saw Tarek slumped in a chair, his breathing ragged. She flew to his side, ripping his shirt to see the extent of his wound. His head was red with blood from the contusion he had suffered, but worse was the gash in his stomach. Blood bubbled out of his mouth indicating that he was bleeding internally. A mortal wound.

"Eva. No, you can't," Tarek said in a weak, wet voice, correctly reading the determined look in her eye. "Your secret -"

"Secret be damned, I will not let my friend die!" Eva said, putting her hands on his skin, the blood on her hands mixing with his. She hadn't been able to help the king, but, by the Guardians, she was going to save Tarek. She reached for her *sanarii* magic, for the river within her, within every living creature, and touched it, drawing its strength, pouring it into her friend, mending his hurts, knitting his skin together, healing the bruised flesh. Tarek was a strong man. He did not scream, even when the pain of Eva's healing magic on top of his wounds must've been almost unbearable.

"Eva," Mahone's voice was loud in her ear. Her eyesight blurred. She could no longer feel Tarek's body beneath her hands. Her connection to her magic was weakening. The *simul rami* was leaving her. She could feel the precipice beside her that warned she had almost gone too far. She couldn't focus her eyes or her mind. She sank into darkness, unable to contemplate the consequences of what she had just done.

CHAPTER 2

EVA

EVA WOKE SWEATING, HER HEART POUNDING from the nightmare that had been more vision than dream. It took a moment for her to remember where she was. Dweller's Knoll. The inn. The attack. Tarek.

Tarek. His wound had been dire. Had her magic done enough?

It was night. The inn was soundless. Well, not quite soundless. Eva could hear footsteps in the hall. A steady, pacing patrol. She stood up, then sat back down on her bed, dizzy and weak. She waited for the feeling to pass and tried again, with more success. She made it to the door, grasping the handle to keep from falling.

"Darys?" Eva opened the door and whispered into the hall. Darys was at her door in an instant.

"Eva, are you all right?" Darys asked. "You should be resting."

Eva shook her head, dismissing his concern. "Where is Tarek? Is he all right?" Eva needed to know.

Darys fixed his steady eyes on her for a long moment. "Yes. Yes, he is. Thanks to you, missy. He is resting in the room next to yours."

Relief was not enough to melt the icy fear in Eva's stomach. "What did my aunt say?" She also needed to know.

"She bound us all to secrecy. You know what would happen if they found out about this, right?" Darys asked quietly.

"They" were the Black Goddess's people. "This" was Eva's magic, a legacy passed down from a mother Eva hardly remembered. An Allati woman who beguiled Lord Finnan with magic and set the king against his sister, nearly causing a rift within the aristocrats of Jullayah. Or so Eva had been told.

"I couldn't let Tarek die."

Darys's face softened. "Of course not, my dear. You did the right thing. But Clarette is worried for you. Now that King Rhais is weak and Prince Caeris is king in all but name, things will be different. Caeris is not his father."

The wave of grief welled up within Eva. The king. Her dear king. Winter had gripped Jullayah like a tale of old, with ice and snow and wind that howled like haunted spirits. The unusually harsh season had brought a sickness that took old and young and healthy and strong. Many had died, choked by an invisible foe, burned by an invisible fire. Some had recovered, but many had been taken by the raging sickness. Only the Keep, isolated by ice and forest, had remained untouched by it.

Over winter the sickness had nearly killed the king. With sadness, Clarette had told Eva how the sickness had left him an invalid, no longer fit to run his realm. Eva could hardly imagine King Rhais reduced to a bedridden husk of a man. How could it have happened? If Eva had been there, she could have healed him. King Rhais was like a father to her. Her inability to save him felt like a betrayal.

"Rest now, Eva. We can talk more in the morning," Darys said kindly. Darys too was almost like a father, or a big brother. Eva smiled, feeling a rush of gratitude for the people in her life. Her childhood loneliness still lurked, eager to greet her when her insecurities surfaced, but it came less and less.

With a "good night," Eva closed the door so Darys could resume his watchful pacing. Eva was thankful for the captain's reassurance, but she still needed to see Tarek with her own eyes. And she was reluctant to go back to sleep. Her nightmare hovered behind her eyes, eager to consume her rest.

She knocked softly on the door that joined her room to the room Tarek and Mahone shared. Being bodyguards to a soon-to-be princess had its luxuries; they never had to sleep in the stables.

Mahone opened the door, letting her into their shared room. Tarek lay on the bed, asleep. Eva leaned over him to make sure he was breathing and all in one piece. "He will be fine, thanks to you, Eva." Mahone spoke softly as not to wake his fellow guard.

"A relief," Eva said. Regardless, she put her hand on Tarek's forehead and sent a small pulse of magic through him, just in case there was still bleeding or infection. But no, he was good. Weak, but healed. Mahone gave her a sideways look that echoed Darys's comments about Eva needing her rest. "I had to know."

"It was a risk, Eva. Your secret is no longer safe," Mahone said.

Eva sighed.

"Caeris is more zealous than you think," Mahone told her, his deep voice soft and reassuring despite his words. He sat down on his bed, gesturing for her to sit next to him. "If he finds out about your magic, he will send you to the Temple."

"I am his betrothed - he would never!"

"You were his father's choice for him," Mahone reminded Eva. It was a redundant reminder. In the two years they had been betrothed, Caeris never let Eva forget that she was not his choice in a wife. He showed her little attention and no affection. Theirs would be a marriage of state, not of the heart. Eva doubted Caeris would ever even attempt to love her.

"I know. I know," Eva complained sharply. Her head hurt from fatigue. Her romantic heart hurt from Caeris's continual detachment. She leaned against Mahone's broad shoulder. "What was wrong with those men who attacked us, Mahone?"

"They were obviously mad, but we don't know exactly. We hope to find out more information in the morning," Mahone told her. "Go back to bed, Eva."

Eva nodded, feeling heavy. Mahone took her arm and gently steered her to her own room and her own bed. Eva lay down and closed her eyes, but all she saw was the nightmare that had somehow crept into her reality. Crazed men with strange magic in their eyes and hideous markings on their skin. And the ocean, vast and unyielding, its frothy waters a chasm of mystery and haunting promises.

Eva stood on the edge of the village, looking up at the cliff face that rose like a wall from east to west along the border of Jullayah. The top of the cliff was crowned with trees so big they stood like a second tier, reaching up to brush the clouds. A breeze picked up and the evergreen boughs danced. Eva had the strangest feeling they were dancing for her, for who loved the trees more than she did? It was difficult to imagine evil magic coming from the Great Forest.

But the magic had come from somewhere. Something.

The morning had not brought answers, only more confusion. The dead men were identified as folk who lived just outside the village. Simple people who lived with the land, tending their various livestock. They had lived well. The earth was fruitful. The warm summer often brought an abundance of crops. They had no reason to turn vicious and attack the village.

Clarette's beautiful face was harsh, like a long-forgotten queen, an effigy of stern grief and leadership. Twelve of Clarette's men had died, and she wanted answers. Twelve young, able men had been swept away by the raw violence of the crazed men.

Eva spent the morning listening as Darys and Clarette spoke to the village elders and those from the surrounding areas, contemplating what would drive good men to attack without apparent cause or goal, hardly a warrior between them. Some of those men Eva had killed, blotting out their souls from the earth, taking them from their families, their simple lives. She could not even recall their faces. She would never know their names. All she would remember was the feel of their blood drying on her hands.

The villagers spoke of Forest magic. It was hard not to believe them.

The breeze became fervent, pulling at Eva's long, pale hair, biting the exposed skin of her face. She shivered. She felt watched, but the feeling did not come from the Great Forest. She looked into the forest of normal-sized trees that hemmed the village, but the brown, tangling depths held no answers. No eyes, no persons looked out at her. Not even an owl or robin. And it was silent. No birds or frogs lifted their voices to compete with the cold spring breeze.

"Do you believe it, my lady?" Tarek asked, breaking the unsettling sensation. Mahone stood beside Tarek and Eva sighed with guilt-ridden relief that she was not subjected to the same grief as her aunt. Her heart ached for Clarette. They had been good men.

"There is something - odd - about this place," Eva mused, turning toward the inn, away from the trees, squeezing herself between the two guards and linking their arms in hers. "But I can't believe it comes from the Forest."

"But there are so many stories about the Great Forest and its Folk," Tarek pressed.

"Yes. But they are just stories. We can't know what is truth," Eva told Tarek. Oh, how she regretted not being able to tell her loyal guards what she knew about the Great Forest, but some secrets she could not share. "Maybe magic was not even involved," Eva said, not believing it, but she really didn't want to talk about the Great Forest and its mysteries. "Maybe they ate something that made them mad. Or tainted water. It is not unheard of. Maybe a strange disease."

Mahone grunted. Tarek was silent.

Clarette's men were buried without answers. Clarette did not weep, but she did let Darys, her captain, keep his arm around her shoulder as she spoke of her men and their loyalty. The widow of Ullian, with her beauty, her kindness, her way of making the haughtiest of noblemen listen to her, a woman in a world of men, was a precious treasure to be protected. Clarette was a goddess to her men. It was no wonder the guards of Ullian were renowned for their loyalty.

Eva doubted she would ever inspire such devotion. She was too - something. Growing up running wild in the Great Forest had encumbered her ability to develop the subtle skills of a powerful noble-woman. Instead Eva was a pretender, forced to hide her true gifts. Gifts that she would never be able to use for the greater good, gifts that would forever be set apart from those around her.

The villagers dealt with their dead, but by then Eva and Clarette were on their way to Caer Andri once more.

"The *simul rami* has a strong hold on her," Lula said.

"Yes," Tayeh agreed.

"What is it, Warrior?"

"Something has shifted. Have you not felt it?"

"I feel a lot of things. My Forest is alive, growing, changing."

"Not in the Forest. In Jullayah. I think a vercuri has been awakened."

That made Lula's fox-eyes sharp, the glow brighter.

"How can you be sure?" Lula's voice was tinged with fear.

Tayeh gave the fox-woman a level look.

"Don't look at me like that," Lula warned. "I do remember one of our tasks is to find the vercuri. But to be fair, they haven't been seen in an age. For all we know, time has destroyed them."

"I have held a vercuri. I know what it feels like," Tayeh reminded her.

"What will you do?"

"For now? Wait."

CHAPTER 3

EVA

THE UNSETTLING FEELING of being watched followed Eva to the outskirts of Caer Andri. And the questions circled in her mind like flies over a corpse.

The land dipped down to the plain where the king's city had been built hundreds of years ago. Before the road descended in gentle arcs one could look down from Thieves Hill to where Caer Andri lay glistening like an agate in the sand. The palace gleamed at the city's center, the flag of King Rhais fluttering from the towers. Eva could see the Temple of the Black Goddess, identifiable by the surrounding gardens, visible even at a distance. It looked tiny and harmless. Like the Temple gardens, the farmlands around the city were already bright green. Spring was always eager to come to the royal city.

Eva loved the lookout from Thieves Hill. The great expanse of air was alive with the *simul rami*. The wind was calling to her, and she could not ignore its summons. She breathed it in and let the vision unfold before her.

The vision showed her boats. Their tall masts boasted fanciful, exotic sails. Altos had her memorize all the holdings of Jullayah, great and small, the standard adorning the boats was not one she could not place: a golden flag bearing a rose-like flower in white. The ships were grand, unlike any Eva had even heard of. Among the sailors were people much more impressive than the elegant ships: Kitarrans. Of course.

She knew Kitarrans loved the water and were great boat builders, great masters of current and tide. These Kitarrans looked much like their Guardian: tall, strong, with their fierce feline faces. Their bodies were covered in fur of many different shades and patterns. Their fingers ended in claw-like nails. They stood strong and balanced, their long tails holding them against the pitching of the boat. Somehow Eva knew they were coming to Jullayah.

The vision faded. Eva shook her head, bringing herself back to the present, feeling her horse shift beneath her weight, eager to move on; her aunt's entourage had trailed ahead.

"You all right, Eva?" Mahone asked, always close by, always observant.

"Of course," Eva replied smoothly, her mind still focused on what she had seen.

Kitarrans. Coming to Jullayah. It had been ten years since their last visit. Eva had been a child then, immured with her mother at the Keep. But she could still remember the night her father had returned and told her the tale of their visit.

Kitarrans were proud warriors, but they were coming in peace. War had not been mentioned between Jullayah and Kitarra for hundreds of years, not since before the time of the Guardians. A time when the arm of the Kitarran king stretched far and wide throughout the realms, far enough to influence the humans of Jullayah. Or so Tayeh told her in his stories.

Eva was ever curious about the Kitarrans, and to meet others like Tayeh would be exceptional. She hoped they would arrive at Caer Andri within the summer so she would have a chance to see them with her own eyes.

Still, there was always the chance that her vision was of the past, not the present. Though Tayeh told her the wind mostly brought visions of the present, carried on its back like the scent of a delicate flower. Her mentor also taught her to look for clues in the vision, a telling of the season or weather, the fashion of a cloak or dress to help her decipher the past from present. She was learning, and her scope of the world was still narrow, but she couldn't shake the certainty that the Kitarrans were coming soon.

Arriving in the king's city, Eva promptly forgot her excitement about the Kitarrans, even with Caeris's formal announcement about their upcoming visit. She forgot about the warmth of spring and the beauty of the palace gardens.

The king lay in his bed. He smiled to see her. Eva sat at his side, gripping his hand, trying to keep her tears from falling. His grasp was weak, and his dancing green eyes had faded. His skin was thin and pale. It could have been a different person than the man Eva had said farewell to only a few seasons ago.

"You will need to take Path through his paces now," Rhais said, his voice catching. "That horse needs a firm hand. I know you can handle him."

"I will. Of course I will," Eva assured him with a little, wet laugh.

Rhais rubbed her tear away with his hand. "And you will come visit me? You won't forget about me up here?"

"Never," Eva vowed. She held his hand in both of hers and reached out with her magic. But there was nothing to heal, the damage had been done. The king's body would never regenerate from the sickness that took his strength, nearly his life. It was everything she had feared, and it broke her heart.

The Kitarrans came with little ceremony, but everyone knew instantly of their arrival. They stood out like a fox in a hen-house. Eva was not fortunate enough to be present to see their parade through the city. Though not a grand event, it attracted multitudes of bystanders none-the-less. Lady Alline told Eva about it later. Alline had heard about it from her sister, who heard it from some lord, who claimed to have seen it all. Eva had been with the king, reading to him, trying to bring back the glimmer of life to his eyes.

The Kitarrans came on foot. They were tall, with long limbs, and lithe tails, their strong muscles completely covered in short fur. On their backs they wore broadswords. Some carried bows or elegantly carved staffs. Some carried a weapon unlike any used in Jullayah. They wore armor made of hardened leather braided with metal. Their expressions were at odds with their menacing appearance. They smiled and admired Caer Andri with as much curiosity as the Jullayans admired them. And there were humans with them. It had been surprising to learn at first, but then Eva remembered Tayeh had mentioned that many humans lived in Kitarra.

A grand, welcoming feast was being prepared for the Kitarran delegates. Eva resigned herself to wait until then to get a glimpse of the Kitarrans. It would be no good to be found snooping around the quarters assigned the foreign visitors. Eva bridled with impatience. Only the fear of her aunt's disapproval, and Caeris's, kept her from sneaking around.

"You're a bundle of nerves," Tarek noted as she stuck her head out the door for the third time in an hour.

Eva scrunched up her face. "I know, it's ridiculous."

"Well, if your aunt doesn't show up in a quarter-hour I will take you down myself," Tarek assured her. "Though Caeris should be the one escorting you."

Eva ignored his comment. It hurt to think of Caeris's aversion. "Thank you," Eva said, flashing him a half-hearted smile.

After what felt like hours (Tarek assured her it was only several minutes), her aunt did appear, and Clarette ushered her quickly downstairs. Clarette was also excited about the grand feast and meeting the prince's guests of honor.

The main hall was lit and decorated for the occasion. Courtiers were already milling about. The airy room was alive with the talk and light laughter of people anticipating an enjoyable evening.

The Kitarrans were already present. Eva could barely see them surrounded by a crowd of people, but their height was unmistakable. As she moved closer, she noticed an uneasy gap between the Jullayans and the Kitarran warriors - as if the Jullayans were afraid to get too close.

The king's advisers were making introductions between the Kitarrans and the king's court. Prince Caeris stood beside them, bright-eyed and slightly flushed. Beside him stood a tall, remarkably handsome man. His long, black coat was elegant with black feathers stitched along the shoulders. A man of the Black Goddess if she had ever seen one. But Eva had never seen him before.

Eva dismissed him, her attention on the seven Kitarrans. Only seven? There were also three men dressed in a fashion not typical to Caer Andri. The humans from Kitarra, Eva assumed. Such a small group. She had expected more.

Her eyes were drawn to the smallest of the Kitarrans, a woman. She was slight but surveyed the room with both ease and wariness. Her fur was black as pitch. Her eyes were the color of a perfect autumn sky, almost an unreal shade of blue. She was beautiful. She was a warrior, her stance, her armor, her weapons, all spoke to it. It was a bold statement to send a woman who was not just a warrior, she was obviously the leader of their group. Eva had never wanted to meet anyone so badly.

Caeris, a tall man, was dwarfed by the huge warrior he was talking to. He saw Clarette and caught her eye, waving her forward. Eva scrambled to catch up, desperate not to be left out of the introductions.

"My Lord Susor, this is the lady Clarette of Ullian and her niece, Lady Evangeline of Cartenel," Caeris said.

Susor's yellow-brown eyes looked over them thoughtfully, resting on Eva. She couldn't help smiling up at him. He was so much like Tayeh. They even had similar markings along the jawline. Susor held out his hand and Eva put her palm against his in the Kitarran greeting she had learned from Tayeh. But this Kitarran was no spirit. He was flesh and blood and fur, his hand warm against hers. Caeris looked astounded by her gull, or perhaps by the Kitarran's interest.

"I did not know Jullayah was home to any Allati," the Kitarran named Susor said in a voice like velvet.

"Jullayah is not, my lord," Caeris corrected him, looking somewhat sourly at Eva and her pale, almost white hair. "Evangeline is the daughter of the king's late captain, Lord Finnan of Cartenel. She is also my betrothed."

"Then you are a fortunate man," Susor said with a smile Caeris did not share.

Eva looked at the floor, wishing Caeris could at least pretend he wanted to marry her. From the corner of her eye, she saw the man in black watching her with a hard expression. She felt a light touch on her arm and looked up to see Susor's eyes had turned sad. "I met your father on our last visit ten years ago. I am sad to hear Captain Finnan has passed. Where is your mother, child?" he asked.

"She is also dead, my lord."

"An orphan." Despite the pity in his eyes, his expression was mottled with intense interest, as if Eva held a puzzle he could not quite solve. Eva was probably reading him wrong. It made no sense. She was no one special, despite being betrothed to Caeris.

"You must meet Emri." At the sound of her name, the Kitarran woman turned toward them, excusing herself from whichever nobleman she was talking to. "This is Princess Emri, the First Defender of Kitarra and Captain of the Peace Guard, wife to our prince." It was a long title. Eva's tongue was silenced under the woman's gaze. She looked young for such responsibility. "This is Lady Evangeline of Cartenel. Soon to be Princess Evangeline."

"My lady." Emri's voice was rich and sweet. She gave Eva a slight bow in greeting. "I am pleased to meet you." She gave Susor a look Eva couldn't read. After being introduced, Clarette said some elegant and suitable words. Eva had nothing to add. Her words would never come out as dignified as her aunt. Others were eager to meet the Kitarrans Susor and Emri. It was not polite to keep them.

"It is nice to meet you Lady Evangeline. I am sure our paths will cross again before we leave Jullayah," Emri told Eva with a smile.

"I hope so," Eva replied, hoping she didn't sound like a love-sick puppy.

Eva should be sitting at the head table with Caeris and the Kitarrans, but she was placed with Alline, and several other highborn young women. In two years Caeris would be her husband. Her place was at his side to help him with his duties, to ease his worries, not across the hall.

Eva shook off the grumbling thought, noticing she wasn't the only one stealing glances at the head table where the guests sat with the prince. She thought several of the Kitarrans cast curious looks her way, but she discarded the thought as altruistic.

She watched the man in black who sat beside Caeris. The Goddess's man. She thought of Dweller's Knoll, and the inscrutable force that had turned good, simple men into monsters. Was that why the Black Goddess hunted those with the slightest tendency toward the uncanny? Eva rubbed her hands; they itched as if still covered in blood.

The feast highlighted the many wonderful varieties of dishes of Jullayah. The guests were well pleased. After the final round of little cakes, the Kitarran travelers stood to acknowledge their host, offering gifts of goodwill from their queen to Caeris, and speaking with grief and regret that King Rhais was too ill to join them. It was concluded very amiably by Caeris who spoke with a maturity that surprised Eva. Caeris was only a few years older than she was, and she had never seen him address the entire court before. He was being very brave, she realized. What happened to Rhais and taking over his father's place so unexpectedly must be very difficult for him. Rhais had been a strong man, a good king. Caeris was hardly more than a weedy youth.

Caeris turned to the musicians and told them to strike up a tune and let the dancing begin.

Eva found she had many willing dance partners, some old, some young. One young man asked for a dance, introducing himself as Eyri, his accent marking him as one of the humans from Kitarra. Eva put her hand in his and was whisked off to the dance floor. He promised a dance with Alline next. Eyri was like sunshine, cheery, eager, humorous. He didn't stop talking the whole time they danced, and most of what he had to say was amusing. Eva found herself laughing, held securely against his person.

"May I?"

Eyri paused in his tale about waves, seagulls and a silly bet between sailors as a man cut into their dance. It was the man with the black cloak Eva had seen next to Caeris earlier. He was clearly at ease among the lords and ladies. With his wavy almost-black hair, lean build, and captivating smile, he was the most beautiful man she had ever met. His deep blue eyes were sharp, curious, and intriguing.

"Of course, I have kept Lady Evangeline far longer than intended." Eyri bowed away to fulfill his promise to Alline.

Eva took the mysterious man's outstretched hand.

"My lady."

"My lord?"

"Serac." He smiled in an apologetic fashion, as if it was his fault she did not know his name. Eva recognized the name instantly.

"Lord Serac, Prince Caeris's cousin?" Eva knew his name and that he was married, but that was all. She could not remember the name of his wife who did not appear to be at court with her husband. Not that it mattered.

"The very same."

Serac had never been to court before. Which was strange, since he was Rhais's nephew, after all, the son of Princess Fara. Eva found she didn't want to be impertinent and ask why. She had an irrational desire for him to like her. Eva smiled up at him. She could hardly take her eyes off his as they danced. Eva could find no fault in his partnering. They danced until the music changed, but he retained her hand, pulling her to a bench along the wall. She was perfectly happy to accept the unspoken offer to catch their breath together.

"Why is it I have not met you before?" Eva asked.

"I am a man of the Goddess. I have spent most of my time traveling, doing the Goddess's work. I was recently nominated by Caeris to be the next Temple Master."

Eva's smile slipped. Not just a man of the Goddess, but *the* man of the Goddess.

He asked if she had ever been to the Temple. She said she had not.

"You must come with me sometime," Serac offered, his handsome mouth twisting into an eager, equally handsome smile that made Eva's next words painful.

"I can't. I am sorry."

Serac was understandably perplexed by her answer. Before he could convince her otherwise, Eva stood and quickly thanked him for the dance. She had an immeasurable desire to see him again, but she couldn't go to the Temple.

The Guardians had warned Eva of the Temple and the Crow. Could Crea really be as dangerous as Tayeh and Lula said? And if she went to the Temple, she might learn something about the magic that had turned those poor men mad.

Eva turned, opening her mouth to rescind her refusal, but Serac was already dancing with another woman, well and truly distracted. The opportunity was lost. Relief and disappointment waged war within her; she wanted answers, but she couldn't ignore the wisdom of her spirit mentors.

CHAPTER 4

EVA

THE MID-SUMMER MARKET was one of the highlights of every summer at court. Merchants came from all over Jullayah to sell their wares, everything from spices, exotic cheeses and wine to tapestries, tools, and horses. Eva loved to peruse the horse stalls. Not that she ever found a horse better than her beloved Lily, but still it was fun to look. There were some beauties, like the little gray pony perfect for a young nobleman's son, or the pure white stallion, beautiful but with such a foul temper, no one wanted to get close to his paddock because he would bite.

Next to the horse stalls, Eva's favorite place to visit was the swordsmiths. Their tents were decorated with their wares, swords new and old, some made of weak steel but priced accordingly, some too pretty to use for combat. There were daggers, throwing knives, arrowheads, armor. Eva was always forced through that part of the market quickly. Alline, her usual companion, grew bored and insisted loudly that there was no use looking at weaponry.

Alline loved to look at the silks and other fine cloth from the east. She swooned over the variety of textures and colors. She could rarely decide which to purchase, complaining it was far too overwhelming. They were beautiful. There was some credence to Alline's plight.

Alline moved on to another booth. Eva was still admiring a fine bolt of amber-colored fabric. It was gauzy and held the light with a glow that reminded Eva of the eyes of her spirit mentors.

"That is beautiful," came a soft voice beside her. Eva turned to see Emri, the Kitarran, inspecting the booth, admiring the same cloth. Lord Susor was at her back and another Kitaran was not far away.

Eva's own guards were not far either. Both Tarek and Mahone insisted on following her around the market.

The Kitarran woman wore a short, flowing emerald-green dress that made her look less like a warrior and more like the exotic princess she was. Though she did wear two daggers in her belt, Eva noticed. Emri was taller than Eva, though not as tall as Eva remembered. She wore a friendly smile which Eva returned.

"Princess Emri," Eva said with a slight bow. "Yes, it is beautiful, but not very practical."

The Kitarran laughed. It made her sound young, almost like a girl. "No, not at all, but I think Queen Arrah would like it."

"Here." Eva handed her the light bolt of fabric. There was not much left. Emri took it and ran her hand over it.

"It is delightful. Were you going to purchase it?" Clearly Emri wanted to buy it, but there would not be enough for two dresses.

"It is really far too impractical for me," Eva told her. "Please take it for your queen."

"Thank you." Emri handed the bolt to Susor who went about the transaction with the merchant.

"I don't like haggling," Emri confided in Eva. "Susor would never forgive me if I paid full price, so I'll just let him get on with it. He enjoys it, the old tooth. Will you walk with me? I would be glad of your company."

Eva nodded, hardly believing her good fortune. Emri was like the heroines in Tayeh's stories; she was even married to the Kitarran prince.

"May I ask you about Cartenel?" Emri asked as they strolled further down the isle of fabric booths.

"You may, though I don't know how much I can tell you. I have never been there," Eva told her.

"Really? Was I mistaken? Did I not hear that you were Lady of Cartenel?"

"No, you heard correct. I am the only living heir to Cartenel, but my father was War Commander and Lord of the Keep, a fortress in the mountains. I grew up there." Eva did her best to explain.

"So you will have two sons, one to inherit the throne and one to inherit your grandfather's estate," Emri deducted with a smile.

Eva's grimace did not go unnoticed.

"Yours is an arranged marriage," Emri stated correctly.

Eva nodded.

"It is hard for a Kitarran to imagine such a thing. Without love, true love, a Kitarran cannot, well, you know - be intimate," Emri said the last part in a whisper much more suited to a girl trading secrets than a warrior princess. She looked behind her to make sure Susor had not heard.

"Really?" Eva found herself asking. Tayeh never mentioned anything about that, Eva thought with a silent laugh.

Emri nodded with a knowing smile.

"You must love your prince very much then," Eva said. "You must miss him."

Emri's eyes glowed, but behind the glow was a sadness so deep Eva felt it pierce her heart. "Yes. I do. But - we lost our baby. A little girl who would have grown up to be queen. She was born dead. I just needed some space. To get away from Kitarra for a time."

"I am so sorry. That is unimaginable."

"It happens often to Kitarrans. Children are a great blessing. Too many of ours are stillborn."

"That is awful," Eva said softly.

"Yes. But Arrain will be waiting for me when I get back. I really do miss him," she added smugly. Eva smiled, feeling Emri's obvious joy in her husband.

"These are beautiful as well!" Emri exclaimed over a collection of scarves in bright colors. "More practical," she added with a smile. "Would you like one?"

"I love the gray and green one, with just a hint of gold, but you needn't pay -" Eva said when Emri picked up the scarf in question and handed it to Susor. "I have my own coin."

"A gift, Eva," Emri said, shaking her head. There was nothing Eva could do. Emri had the scarf paid for from Susor's pouch. Eva took it, knowing she would treasure it always.

"So Evangeline, if you do not live at Cartenel, tell me about your home. I know so little of Jullayah!" Emri said as they moved on.

Eva smiled and told her about the Keep. About the ancient fortress built against the cliff, close enough to almost touch the Great Forest.

The hot pools and the great hall and the simple people who lived there now, since Rhais never appointed another War Commander. His grief over the loss of Lord Finnan, his dear friend, had been too great. Eva saw Emri smile as she told her in great detail about the trees and moss.

"Your Keep sounds similar to Kilev, the royal city, built against a great mountain and a wild forest, though not the Great Forest by any means," Emri said with what sounded like relief. "It is beautiful. There is a winding creek that comes down from the mountains that is hot just like your pools at the Keep. The water is heated from the depths of the earth. Arrain took me there once. A good trek up the mountain, it was." She looked into some far-off memory. "I didn't grow up in the mountains. I grew up in the islands with the wind and the sea, the smell of salt in my nose and fish on my hands. The trees of the islands are crooked and stunted but full of character. Further inland there are proper forests, but I always loved the beach, the salt water, the predictable tides. Someday you should come visit me in Kitarra," Emri declared suddenly.

Eva laughed. "Ah, I would love that, were it possible," she added. Her heart did desire to see Kitarra, but it would be impossible. When she turned eighteen, she would marry Caeris and she didn't think she would make it to Kitarra before then.

"When will you be wed?" Emri asked, as if following the line of Eva's thought.

"Two years, after I turn eighteen."

"You could come back with us. I could stow you away in the boat!" Emri teased with a light laugh. Eva laughed with her. "Arrain would adore you. He could teach you all about the trees and the plants and all the wild things in Kitarra."

"No, I could not leave without my raven or my sword!" Eva said with humor, thinking of her old nurse forced to look after Calypso indefinitely. Poor Calypso. He did not deserve it.

"Your raven? You have a pet raven? And I thought Jullayan women never learned to fight," Emri asked, eager to know more.

"No, they don't, but I grew up with a bunch of boys and I learned how to fight with a sword. And I found a baby raven in the forest and nursed it back to health. He has been around ever since." It was the short version, the explainable version. Emri would never believe the truth.

"Amazing! I think a raven would make a great friend. They seem clever and full of personality."

"He is."

"Arrain has a pet fox. He found the pup abandoned and raised it, feeding it milk until it could eat alongside the palace dogs. It is adorable. Even now it follows him around the palace. It nips quite a bit though, just in play, but you have to watch your fingers."

Eva laughed, delighted by the idea, though she had her own fox friend that was far from a pet.

"Princess Emri -"

"Just Emri."

Eva smiled. "Emri, may I ask you a question about Kitarra?"

"Of course. Ask away!"

"Is there magic in Kitarra?"

Emri's brilliant smile faded, replaced by a more shrewd expression. "Magic? What do you mean?"

Eva bit her lip. "A few weeks ago my aunt and I were attacked by men, farmers who had gone mad, turning them violent. I can't help feeling magic was involved, somehow. It was so strange," Eva said, waiting for Emri to give an uncomfortable laugh and brush her aside to seek out a less crazed companion.

But she didn't. "You had to kill the men, didn't you? I can see their deaths in your eyes."

Eva nodded because she could not speak.

"There have been - instances - in Kitarra," The air around them felt cooler as Emri spoke. "Unexplainable violence. Parts of the forest rotting away from a strange disease. But the sickness doesn't just affect the trees and plants, it also affects the minds of any who stray too close. But is it magic? I do not know. Arrain has been studying it for years but has not found answers."

"I wish I could speak to your Arrain. He sounds intriguing."

And the air warmed once more as Emri laughed. "Intriguing? His head would swell to an unhealthy size if he could hear you. Arrain is a dear, but he could spend three weeks in the archives and think it was only an hour."

Eva smiled, but her stomach tingled with possibility. Caer Andri had its own archives, why hadn't she thought of it before?

"I like your pendant, by the way," Emri noted.

"It was a gift," Eva mentioned, fingering the leaf-shaped necklace she wore always.

"I could swear it is shaped like a cendari leaf!"

A gentle rap on Eva's door tore her from her daydreams. She gave the ceiling a last lingering look, wishing it was green bows and leaves above her head instead of carved beams and honeyed wood. She turned her attention to the door, which opened almost without a sound to reveal Tarek.

"The prince is here to see you," he announced.

Eva sat upright, all thoughts of the forest washed from her mind. Caeris rarely took the time to speak to her. She couldn't imagine what he wanted to talk about. Her heart fluttered with a futile hope that maybe her betrothed had finally decided she was worthy of his time.

Caeris entered and Tarek left, closing the door behind him, effectively trapping Eva with Caeris. Caeris's lips were in their accustomed position, a thin line that turned his handsome face serious, and almost mean. The wings of her heart faltered and fell.

"Eva, what is this business of you asking about the archives?" Caeris asked, his voice laden with irritation.

"I - I am looking for something," she replied.

"Looking for something? Who do you think you are, a scholar?"

"I want to know if what occurred in Dweller's Knoll was an isolated incident. If it wasn't -"

"Dweller's Knoll?" Caeris interrupted.

Eva felt sick. How could he forget about Dweller's Knoll? "The men who attacked my aunt and I. The men who went mad."

"It's none of your concern what happened in Dweller's Knoll," Caeris barked.

Eva wanted to argue that it was damned well her concern. Instead, she bit her lip and looked at the floor.

"I'm sorry. I know it must have been terrifying, hiding from those men, hearing the battle, not knowing if you would be safe," Caeris said. So he did remember. He just didn't have the right facts.

Eva tasted blood in her mouth where she bit her lip.

"There is no need for you to worry about Dweller's Knoll. There is no need for you to go to the archives," he continued.

Would Caeris change his mind if he knew she had seen the madness with her own eyes and taken the lives of the madmen with her own sword? Eva doubted it. Caeris didn't care about her emotions. He only cared that she didn't embarrass him with her odd, un-lady-like behavior. If he only knew.

"I want to find answers." Eva tried to explain.

"Enough, Eva. Leave it alone. The archives are no place for a woman," Caeris said. "Really, it's embarrassing that I have to remind you how to behave like a noblewoman. You are not a child; by the Guardians, someday you will be queen! And my wife." Caeris spoke the last two words as if they tasted like sour milk.

"But -"

"Leave it alone, Eva," Caeris commanded.

Eva continued to stare at the floor as Caeris left, afraid that if she met his eyes he would see her outrage and find some way to punish her for it.

The Kitarrans only stayed in Caer Andri for one short week before following the current of the river back out to the sea. The journey to Kitarra was a long one, and they didn't want to chance the autumn gales that would force their ships upon the cliffs that lined the coast between Kitarra and Jullayah.

Court slowly returned to normal and the summer passed by with a swiftness born of busy days and short, warm nights. Eva tolerated court and grew tired of the parties, the people. She half wished she had taken Emri up on her offer to stow away on their ship. Not that it had been a real offer, but sometimes Eva dreamed of a different life, a different land.

Summer came to an end. Visiting vassals departed to return to their estates to oversee their harvest or prepare for the winter. Eva's thoughts turned to fall and returning to the Keep. And Dweller's Knoll was often in her mind, and in her dreams.

In the evenings she would grab a cloak and take a walk along the palace parapet to catch a glimpse of the great mountains to the north.

At their roots her home lay waiting. Just knowing the Keep was there, waiting for her return, dispelled her homesickness a little. She was counting the days until their departure.

That night the sunset was minimal, hidden behind a ceiling of low-lying clouds hinting at rain. The wind picked up, pulling Eva's hair, making her tug her cloak tighter around her.

"Do you want to go in, my lady?" Mahone was standing several paces behind her.

"Not yet," Eva replied, turning her head so he could hear her voice against the wind.

Mahone said something else, but Eva didn't hear him. The wind called to her and she answered it without hesitation. Every time the wind called to her, she hoped it would bring a vision that would give her answers. Or at least clues. What she really wanted was to spend more time with Tayeh learning better control of the *simul rami*.

The vision was of a familiar place. The king was in his study, a room Eva had been in a handful of times. Clarette was with him. It was King Rhais Eva knew before the sickness took his robust features, his mischievous eyes, his strong, determined jaw. A vision of the past.

"Rhais." Clarette said the king's name with unusual affability, her voice soft and vulnerable.

"Clare," Rhais said in the same tone.

Clare?

"I think you know what I am going to ask you."

The king sighed, his face suddenly lined and old.

"You know she can't marry him." Clarette's voice took on an uncharacteristic plea; Lady Clarette of Ullian did not beg.

"I know."

"Fara has been dead these past four years. Surely the betrothal cannot stand. No one but you and I and your sister knew of it."

"I believe that to be the case."

"Please. It will be the death of her."

"I know."

"She has Allati blood, my king. We must protect her."

The king nodded and continued to nod, his eyes distant, until Clarette grew petulant.

"Caeris. She should wed Caeris," the king said.

Clarette adjusted her expression to hide her relief.

"They can have many children, one to be heir to the throne, and one to be heir to Cartenel. Yes. I would like Eva as my daughter, very much. I hope I live to see my grandchildren." The old man looked like a kitten in the cream.

The vision was gone as quickly as it came.

Eva shivered.

The king and Clarette spoke of a betrothal that must be broken to protect Eva. Fara was the king's only sister, Serac's mother. Why would they need to protect Eva from Serac?

Eva drew a sharp breath at the thought. Serac. His beautiful, compelling features. His clever wit. A pang of regret pierced her heart. Yes, he was a man of the Goddess, but at least he showed an interest in her. Caeris had never looked at her twice.

Foolish thoughts. If Clarette and Rhais felt Serac was a threat, then Eva would be a fool to see the vision as anything but a warning. She wanted to go to the Temple with Serac to seek answers, but the ominous clattering of her heart made her knees wobble thinking about it.

"Should we go down?" Mahone stood at her elbow.

Eva nodded. She took Mahone's offered arm as they went down the narrow steps into the depths of the palace followed by her unanswered questions.

CHAPTER 5

COTOCH

THERE WERE TWO PRISONERS beneath Cotoch's house.

It was an old, old house. Ancient. It had been abandoned for an age before Cotoch's father came across the sea, made it his home, and birthed the town of Mahlas around it. Cotoch was not clear on its ancestry. It was not obviously Kitarran.

The original wing of the house was entirely stone, with tall arching ceilings, damp clinging to the walls. The new additions were finer, warmer. Wood, harvested from the mountain forests, had been paired with cob to create an impressive architectural feat. Not as elegant as the buildings of Kilev, but Mahlas did not have the advantage of Kitarra's generations of craftsmen.

The crypts were part of the original building, ancient tunnels that wove beneath the house toward the roots of the mountains.

Cotoch had first discovered the crypts when he was five, hiding from his father. The round doorway had been almost impossible to see at the end of a particularly damp, dingy corridor. His five-year-old self had felt his heart beat in his palms as he pushed it open, putting all his hope into the workings of the door. Relief flooded the poor boy he had been. The door opened. Beyond lay darkness. But Cotoch had apprenticed to the dark. He welcomed it. Embraced it like the mother he had never known. Darkness was preferable to his father's wrath.

Of course, as a five-year-old boy he thought the secret of the crypts his own. He did not know then, as he sought to hide in it, that his father was already master of the twisting recess beneath their house.

He would never forget the encompassing blackness of those twisted corridors, the thick smell of waste and death and terror. There

Cotoch-the-boy realized he was not the only thing his father tortured. There were others - men, criminals, women, old whores long past their beauty. Hopeless creatures that called to him with voices hoarse from screams and tears.

His father found him within the hour but left him to think on his sins along with the walking dead. Two days later his father came back for him. Or so he was told - it felt like he had spent years crying in the pitch-black.

It was the first time his father left him in the crypts, but not the last. His father left him locked in the depths for longer and longer depending on Cotoch's misdeeds.

It didn't take Cotoch-the-boy long to learn tears were useless.

He learned to disregard his father's victims. They were meat. They would die under his father's hand as he took their will, their hope, to feed his sorcery.

Cotoch knew, even as a youngster, the source of his father's magic. Surrounded by the dark, Cotoch felt the air become electric with the *varing*. The magic leaked out through the misery and pain of others. It made Cotoch stronger. His father did not know Cotoch was stealing it - could steal it. Bit by bit he absorbed the remnants of his father's work. It didn't take Cotoch long to realize someday he would be a better, stronger sorcerer than his father.

The irregular stones of the floor became his map, the muffled sounds his eyes. His father had not built the crypts. He did not know their secrets. Cotoch did. The crypts began to yield their treasure to his searching hands.

One day his hand touched something. A stone, as large and wide as his hand and twice as long, not a blade, but sharp. A stone was not unusual - the tunnels were birthed from stone - but this stone hummed in his hand, and Cotoch knew it was special. Cotoch hid it in his dirty pants.

When his father allowed Cotoch to come back into the world of light, Cotoch looked at his treasure properly. It was not stone as he first thought, but wood that only felt like stone. There were strange designs carved on one side and it had a small hole Cotoch could thread with a piece of leather. He wore it under his shirt.

The amulet called to the *varing* and the *varing* answered. As Cotoch grew older, stronger, wiser, he realized the power and advantage the amulet gave him. The amulet revealed another secret hidden in the crypts.

Cotoch would always hate torture, but he loved power. Power gave him the tools to protect his people, his town. Mahlas, the people of the Tarm, had no one else to care about them. What was a little torture compared to the livelihood of hundreds? The people of Mahlas had become his responsibility after his father's death.

His father had been dead for years. In life, he had been an exiled sorcerer prince from across the sea, sent from his birthright in a boat with three slaves and a solid gold basin. Cotoch had never seen Rodan, his father's homeland, in the flesh, and he doubted he ever would. Not that he wanted to. Rodan held no pull for him.

His father had accomplished one thing in exile: Mahlas. Mahlas had been sown in the dirt of his father's leadership, but Cotoch was the sunlight that made Mahlas thrive. Cotoch was the leader his father had tried to be. Cotoch would make Mahlas into a city equal to Kilev or Attingard. And now he had ties in Kitarra - legitimate ties.

Cotoch smiled, thinking of his wife's curvaceous figure and amusing appetites. He had expected the task of finding a wife to be more difficult, a wealthy, well-known merchant's daughter, preferably. A young woman willing to leave Kitarra for the Tarm to be his lady. He had found Sandra. Her father, a merchant with ties to the palace, was well connected in Kitarra, if not superfluously rich. She was perfect and Cotoch felt his body grow hard remembering hers.

Torture. Right.

Cotoch became lord of Mahlas after his father's death. He also became the master of the dark. He also received an unusual visitor. She came with a flush of feathers and the smell of licorice and a sanguine smile made for seduction. Crea, the Black Goddess, she called herself. Others knew her as the Guardian of Jullayah. She knew about Cotoch and his magic. She knew about Cotoch's family across the sea, his cousin the sorcerer king. She wanted a deal. She offered Cotoch a kingship. How could he say no?

Torture. Right.

The crypts were a cage. The only way out was at the end of a knife. Cotoch didn't really mind if the person was a monster. A child rapist, for instance, was almost pleasurable to kill slowly and meticulously. Not that he came across too many of those. His father had killed a child once. Cotoch swore he would never do that.

His first prisoner was Kitarran, a spy from the queen. Cotoch was not pleased he had to kill the man. The queen would be suspicious when he no longer reported back to her, but she would have no proof Cotoch was behind his disappearance; the Tarm was reputed as a dangerous place, after all. The man had to die. There was no way around it; he had seen too much. And if he had to die, Cotoch might as well harvest what he could from him. The *varing* was calling to him - he could not refuse.

Cotoch did it alone. He wanted no witness to his ceremony.

The Kitarran was pallid with fear and smelled of urine and hope.

"I don't like this, you know," Cotoch said as he started. The man screamed. They always screamed. Cotoch hated it. Really hated it.

The *varing* pulsed. Cotoch closed his eyes as it overcame him. He felt strong, he felt nourished, he felt unstoppable.

The second prisoner wept.

"Oh, Cotoch, what a mess."

"You're a Guardian, use your immortal powers to clean it up," Cotoch told her.

"That is not how it works," Crea said. Cotoch noted that her black wings glistened in the lantern light like the blood pooling around his feet.

"What do you want, Goddess?" Cotoch asked. He twisted his neck trying to work out the kinks that irritated him almost as much as his unwanted visitor. He liked to work in private.

"You know what I want," Crea crooned. "I want Kitarra dead and destroyed." Then she sighed. A sound like wind over ice. "But that will have to wait. There is a man. I tried to kill him once, but unfortunately, it didn't take. Humans can be overly compassionate when babies are concerned."

Cotoch didn't have any idea who she was talking about, and he didn't really care. His acquaintanceship with the spirit woman had taught him not to ask too many questions - she wouldn't answer them anyway.

He still didn't entirely trust her. And he wouldn't, he decided, not until he was sitting on Kitarra's throne as she had promised. But he didn't need to trust her - and so far she hadn't asked him for anything he could not give.

Her cold smile remained fixed in place as she continued. "Southern Jullayah has forgotten its Goddess. I want Imal to send his warriors to attack it. Kill or take everyone, I don't care. Destroy it - make the people run to the king, to the Temple, for solace."

"I thought you wanted a man dead, not a realm," Cotoch mentioned.

"One in the same," Crea said with a wave of her hand.

"I thought you wanted Kitarra."

"Of course, I want Kitarra! Did you not learn patience down here in the dark when you were a child? Or when you were waiting for your father's death so you could take over this paltry city? There is time. You are a young man - strong, virile." The way she said "virile" sent an uncomfortable shiver down Cotoch's back. "There is time," she repeated, touching his cheek with an insubstantial finger.

He was fairly certain the spirit woman was addled in the head. But he didn't care, so long as he got what he wanted. A throne. Power. Control. To never spend another day in the dark cultivating fear and pain like a farmer grows wheat.

"The time will come, Cotoch. Revenge is the reward of the faithful," Crea said fading into thin air like a fragment of Cotoch's imagination. Cotoch really hoped he was not the one going mad.

CHAPTER 6

EVA

SAYING GOODBYE TO RHAIS was the hardest part - perhaps the only hard part - of leaving Caer Andri. Eva kissed his brow and squeezed his hand and assured him she would see him in spring.

"We will see," was the king's soft reply. Eva almost didn't hear it.

After escorting Eva to the Keep, Clarette would travel home to Ullian for the late harvests and winter season. Once home at the Keep, Eva could soak in the quiet and simple life of living in an almost abandoned fortress. Eva could not think of a place she would rather spend her winter. Though she fervently hoped the coming winter would not be as cold and oppressing as the last.

Over summer, the bridge at Barrowsby had been repaired. Eva was thankful there was no reason to go back to Dweller's Knoll. The town was an ashy smudge in her memory, like she had stumbled into a bad dream from which she abruptly woke, the strangeness of it fading into lingering grief. She told herself again and again that killing those men had been unavoidable, self-defense from a foe both mysterious and evil. She had trained as a warrior; what had she expected?

Calypso the raven met Eva just outside the Keep, his raucous voice music to Eva's homesick ears. She stroked his smooth, glossy black feathers and whispered greetings into his ear as he rubbed his long beak against her chin like a cat. The raven had been a fixture at the Keep for years, and no one blinked an eye to see him. It would have been more out of place if he had not come screaming his raven greeting. Only one person at the Keep disapproved of the resident bird, and Eva had long ago accepted that Wilanna was incapable of love. Devotion, yes, for she stayed on at the Keep with her husband, the steward in memory of Lord Finnan, but she was a cold woman and always had a few nasty words for the big bird.

Eva looked up at the cliff and the trees and the Keep with a satisfied sigh. She was home.

Yes, she was home, but her heart felt more twisted and sad than content and relieved. What had changed? She had questions and wasn't sure how to ask them. Caer Andri had had no answers for her.

She felt the guilty weight of the handkerchief in her pocket. She was rather pleased with her subterfuge, stealing the token from right under Serac's distracted nose. As soon as Tarek and Mahone relaxed their zealous watchfulness, she would get away into the Great Forest and seek what answers the old spirits might have for her.

But the hot pools called to her, and Scrub had made a delicious feast, combining his love of impressing Lady Clarette with his passion for creating culinary feats, so Eva did not find herself alone until the sun had almost set.

Pleading exhaustion, Eva went up the long flight of stairs to the highest wing of the Keep. She went past her little pragmatic room to the council room that had once belonged to her father. Now, officially it belonged to no one, but Eva felt like it was hers.

Eva pushed her shoulder against the door to shift the heavy wood into compliance. The door groaned like an old man. Without a fire, the room was dark, but Eva knew it intimately. She moved past her teetering stacks of books, her favorite chair, the long-neglected council table to the small door that led to the strange courtyard. She winced as she stepped outside into contrasting green light that drenched the little walled courtyard. The stone was almost indefinitely covered in moss. Hardly any of the carved stone showed through. Only Eva knew the secret it held.

She took a moment to breathe in the damp, earthy smell of the dew-covered moss and to run her hand along the fern-clad wall, stopping only when her fingers felt the rough edges of the picture carved in the stone. She traced the line of animals where they formed a circle surrounded by ferns and berry bushes; at the center was a fox. The fox was small, but all the other animals in the carving were looking at it, waiting for it. Its eyes were two tiny amber-colored agates set into the stone. Eva put her finger on the little pointy face.

A soft thud and a creak echoed from the stone wall, followed by the appearance of a crack. The crack continued as a fine line making a perfect circle. Then it moved. The wall appeared to tilt toward Eva. She smiled, remembering as a child how fearful she had been of the wall collapsing on her, imagining its crushing weight. Of course, the slab of rock did not fall. It swung slowly on hinges revealing a door, round as a full moon and just the right size for Eva-the-child to walk through. Now, as a grown woman, she had to bend considerably. Beyond were the familiar uneven steps cut into the cliff face. A path into the Great Forest. Her path.

A white head appeared at the top of the steps between the birch trees. A black nose twitched. Amber eyes watched. A fox. It moved a step closer and sat on its haunches, waiting.

Eva grinned. "Hello, Lula."

As soon as Eva was within an arm's reach of Lula the fox, Lula stood and bounded away from her into the Great Forest. Eva laughed, rushing to keep up with its playful leaps. Lula had quick little feet. Every time Eva thought Lula had abandoned her, there she was, just ahead, a white beacon in the forest of green.

The fox slowed and stayed close to her. Almost close enough to touch her long, graceful tail - if Eva dared.

"Eva." The voice was like a familiar dream.

Eva looked up from the Forest Guardian to see the sunlit clearing. As her eyes adjusted to the bright light, she saw him. He was tall. She was always surprised how tall. His shoulders were broad, accentuated by leather armor. Behind him, slowly moving side to side like a snake, was a long, furred tail as beautiful and graceful as the fox's, only sleeker, with the same black stripes as his face and arms. His face was cat-like, terrifying, fierce, yet his eyes were kind and his mouth held a slight smile. As always, there was something about him, something unreal, something that spoke of magic.

"Tayeh." Eva said his name as a sigh.

"Evangeline. Welcome home," the Guardian said, his smile growing.

"It is good to be home," Eva said, feeling the peace of the Great Forest, the wisdom of the trees, the agelessness of the earth soak into her bones and seep into her heart. She rushed to Tayeh and he wrapped his long arms around her like the father she had lost years ago. His embrace was always strange, not quite warm, not quite real, tactile, but unlike anything she had felt before, like touching sunlight. "It's been an interesting summer."

Eva told the two Guardians about Dweller's Knoll and the attack, the Kitarrans coming to Caer Andri, which disappointingly Tayeh had hardly a comment. He was the Guardian of Kitarra, after all - shouldn't he show more interest in his people? She told them about the vision of King Rhais and Clarette deciding her fate.

"I want to use the gold bowl," Eva stated after she had finished her tale.

"Why?"

"I want to find answers about Dweller's Knoll. And about Serac."

"The Crow's man?"

"I guess you could call him that."

Tayeh looked uneasy, but he reached into his pocket and took out the little bowl made from gold, a tool used by the *sanarii* magi of old.

"Thank you," Eva said, taking it in her hands, feeling the weight of it. It would be heavier after she filled it with water from the hot-spring creek nearby. When Eva returned, bowl filled, years of experience keeping the water from sloshing over the brim, Tayeh looked even more grim. Lula was in her womanly form, naked, her expression equally stern. Eva took out the handkerchief marked with the black feather of the Goddess.

Tayeh took out his knife and cut a piece from the stolen cloth and placed it in the water where it sunk to the bottom of the bowl.

Tayeh had taught Eva as a child to use the bowl to find clarity within the flood of visions in the *simul rami*. It was a tool to focus her magic, and combined with an item, could be used to focus on a particular subject. Serac was the object of Eva's curiosity for the moment. She needed to know why she had been forced into a loveless union, forbidding any chance of love. Over summer, observing Serac, dancing with him, Eva could only feel bitterness that their secret betrothal had been dissolved. If he was evil, she could not see it.

Eva looked into the bowl. Or the bowl looked into her - she couldn't tell which. The bright ripples of the *simul rami* disappeared, replaced by thick, black smoke. It twisted up into her nose, her eyes, between her teeth. She was sinking. She couldn't speak; she could hardly breathe.

A brilliant gold flash dissolved the ominous murk instantly. Something hot and wet hit Eva's hands. Tayeh had knocked over the bowl, spilling the water onto the moss and Eva.

"What was that?" Eva asked, taking a deep breath.

Tayeh looked … afraid. Deeply afraid.

"It is what I feared. Do not go near that man," Tayeh whispered loudly.

"Tayeh, what kind of magic was that? It felt like - it felt like the dead man in Dweller's Knoll."

Tayeh shook his head slowly.

"We will not speak of it."

"But why? I need to know - the magic - it's not like mine," Eva implored.

"No, Eva. Somethings are best left unspoken. Somethings are best left buried," Tayeh said. "Forget about Dweller's Knoll - and stay away from Serac."

And for the first time, the tone of his voice made Eva fall silent. Her desperate questions died upon her tongue, but inside her apprehension writhed like a caged beast. Tayeh was her teacher, her mentor. She respected him with a depth that put the ocean to shame. She would abide by his command.

"She has a strong hold on your heart, does she not?" Lula asked when Eva was gone from Tayeh's sight.

Even in her human form, the Guardian of the Great Forest was still slight. Her nakedness gave her the appearance of fragility, like a skeleton leaf. She wore only twigs, leaves, and the mane of orange-red hair falling about her thin frame. Yes, she looked fragile, but she was as fragile as an eagle, or a bear. She was tough, enduring. Tayeh had known the Guardian of the Great Forest for a long time.

"No more or less than she has upon your own heart, fox-girl," Tayeh answered with a smile.

Lula growled a little in her throat. Perhaps it was the nickname, or perhaps the insinuation that she cared for the human. Lulanan was

not fond of humans as a rule, although Tayeh knew of several exceptions, even if she would not admit to them.

"I cannot see her path. What happened in Dweller's Knoll …" Lula
did not elaborate, hugging herself against a chill even if she felt none.

Tayeh shrugged. "I have felt the stirrings of evil, and the Allmakers' fear, for a long time. Now you cannot deny it. We cannot wait
much longer. I will not leave my land defenseless. Someday she will go
to Kitarra - for the good of my realm and yours."

"Perhaps you should tell her the truth."

"She is not ready yet."

"Or is it you who is not ready?"

CHAPTER 7

EVA

TAYEH'S SILENCE ON THE MATTER of the weird smoke-like mist in the bowl was unsettling. He told Eva to stay away from Serac, which wasn't going to be too difficult, really. Serac was married. Eva was betrothed. She had no right to his attention. She was like a leaf pushed around by the wind. Like a nobody. A woman with half a lineage and no voice. What she wanted she couldn't have, and what she had didn't want her. Tayeh wouldn't answer her questions and she had nowhere else to find answers.

But Dweller's Knoll still haunted her.

She tried to use the *simul rami* to find visions that would offer her answers. But it was difficult. The *simul rami* was a river of magic, connected to every creature and plant, past and present. She was not skilled enough to find what she was looking for.

And then nightmares began to plague her relentlessly. Haunting, unimaginable offenses filled her nights. She dreamed of Serac. In her dreams he hurt women in ways most vile, ways Eva could not even begin to fathom. Then the dream changed to choking black feathers. Then monsters in the guise of men.

The first time she saw the strange men in her dream, she thought it was just a strange figment of her imagination, a concoction created by her troubled conscience. A remnant of what had happened in Dweller's Knoll. But it was so real, her doubt grew, feeding on her fear.

The dream began peacefully, a quiet village by the sea, bathed in the peace of simple things, mending fishing nets, children collecting shells along the beach, a small fishing craft bringing in a fine catch. Then strange boats approached, unlike any Eva had seen or heard of.

Long ships with many oars, the rowers held to the deck with shackles and motivated by the whip. The villagers stared as they came ashore. Wonderment quickly turned to dread as a hail storm of blazoned arrows dehisced from the boats. People screamed. Children cried. The arrows were followed by a mob of strange men. Their skin was rent with strange markings, like someone had drawn upon their skin using a knife instead of ink, leaving red, scarred welts behind.

They quickly darkened the beach with their presence. Their weapons raised, strange nerve-shattering cries upon their lips. They chased and hacked at the poor villagers showering Eva's dream with blood and death and pain. Flames engulfed the village and Eva woke.

The strange cries rung in her ears and the sight of blood hovered before her eyes. She knelt over her chamber pot, waiting for the sick to come, cold sweat beading on her forehead. Her breathing calmed, her stomach roiled, but not enough to purge itself. She lay back down on the bed telling herself it was just a dream. Dreams had no power over her. It was not real. She begged for it not to be real.

Eventually, she fell back to sleep and if she dreamed again, she did not remember it upon waking.

The next night she had the same nightmares, filled with the same terrible men. They were creature-like in their feral ferocity, but unlike a wild creature, their eyes were ablaze with greed and blood lust. Their merciless expressions, marred by the terrible scars, were terrifying. They killed men and children, the old and weak, but women they took. If the young men fought, they were killed, sometimes slowly. Torture squashed any attempts of resistance. They corralled all the women and raped them.

Another village. Another onslaught of arrows, fireballs designed to alight houses and men alike. After the arrows, they would descend, and the air would be thick with the screams of the dying and the cries of the innocent and the smoke of burning lives.

"You don't look well, Eva." Lula made the effort of changing into her womanly form to comment, her fey eyes regarding Eva with concern.

"My dreams have been terrible lately," Eva told the Guardian, rubbing her temple. She had been mid-practice with Tayeh, but had dropped her sword in frustration. The lack of sleep was getting to her.

"More nightmares about marrying the prince?" Tayeh teased with a smile. The Guardians were pleased with her betrothal. She often voiced her misgivings, a subject Tayeh loved to tease her about. Lula too had contributed to the subject, but her advice, though well meant, had only added to Eva's nervousness about marriage. Lula, apparently, was an expert on certain aspects of making love and felt it was her duty to absolve Eva's fears by a very thorough and detailed discussion. Tayeh had been absent that day.

Eva shot Tayeh a scathing look.

"No, actually," Eva replied sharply. She told them about her dreams. "They are just dreams, right?" she asked when they didn't say anything, merely looked at her with identical expressions of concern.

Neither of them volunteered a comment.

An icy fear plunged like a knife into Eva's belly. "I used the *simul rami* to try and find answers about Dweller's Knoll. You warned me - I - I did it anyway … They have to be dreams," Eva went on. "If they are visions, I would see them in the wind, or water, or fire. But I haven't." She was trying to convince them, and herself. If the dreams were visions, of real men and real victims, that meant her dreams of Serac could be visions too. She remembered the dream of Serac with a young woman who looked a lot like Eva's friend Alline, taking her from behind, her tear-stained face, his guttural grunts and lust-filled eyes. It could not be real. But how could her mind create something so vile on its own? She felt sick.

"Describe the men again?" Tayeh asked.

"I still am not sure if men is the correct term. They look like men, but they are so full of hate, so full of blood-lust. They crave it. I can see it in their faces. They thrive on cruelty and pain, monsters in the guise of men. Their hair and beards are long and matted. They have etchings in their skin. They do not speak a language I am familiar with - it sounds like gibberish to me."

"I think these are not dreams, Eva, but visions. My guess would be if you looked into the water or wind or flame, you could search these visions out. It is your sensitive consciousness that is keeping them at bay until you are asleep and your barriers are shut down," Tayeh told her, his mouth a thin line.

"If it is true, then something terrible is happening. Somewhere people are falling to this cruelty," Eva exclaimed feeling the weight of the abhorrent possibility. Her eyes pricked with tears. She could not mention Serac. She was afraid of that truth and what it meant. "It is like the men from Dweller's Knoll, only worse. So much worse."

"It is not the same as Dweller's Knoll … The men could be from the Forgotten Lands," Tayeh mused.

"Forgotten Lands? Explain, please," Eva asked.

"An age ago, humans came to this land from another. They made peace with the Kitarrans. It is even said some of them were favorites of the Forest Folk. Legend suggests that is how the Allati got magic in their blood." Lula ignored Tayeh's sideways glance spectacularly. "The Forgotten Lands is a place the Allmakers abandoned long, long ago. It was lost to darker forces, a place desperate humans fled to come here."

Eva shivered. It wasn't the cold in the air. Her cloak was lined with thick wool, her boots made of thick leather. Tayeh put his large, furred hand upon her shoulder, and she felt the darkness lift, ever so slightly. His touch was like light. A small seed of peace settled in her stomach.

"Are your dreams of Jullayah?" Tayeh pressed.

Eva thought about the visions, reaching back into her memory, back to the details that would reveal the location of the evil men and their victims. Mostly she could only recall the blood, the terror, and yet -

"I think it must be Jullayah. I saw in one vision a statue of Crea, her black wings broken by a thrust of a club. But it must be in the south. The trees are different, leafier, brighter flowers. The land is emptier, rolling hills of grass, but the uplands are barren, dry."

Lula nodded. "That would make sense that they would come from the south, from across the sea."

"It will be all right, Eva. You must be strong, steadfast. Your heart will guide you," Tayeh told her, keeping her locked in his intense gaze, his amber eyes bright.

"Can't you do anything? You are Guardians after all," Eva pleaded. "Your job is to protect us. Can't Crea do anything?"

Tayeh's nose wrinkled at the mention of Jullayah's false goddess. "We cannot directly intervene. We are not like you, not made of flesh and bone. We can only inspire the hearts and minds, teach and love.

Crea could do it. She could bring the people together to fight this host, but her motives are selfish. Caeris's army is weak because of it. The men have lost their love for the land, for their people. They have lost the concept of unity and think only for themselves."

"What will happen?" Eva asked, feeling as though her stomach had melted and then solidified into ice.

Tayeh shrugged. If he knew, he didn't want to tell her. Eva wanted to yell and scream and demand answers.

Instead, she sighed. Follow her heart was what Tayeh always said in times of indecision. It meant she should trust her instincts.

"Come now. Let's practice with that blade. It won't be long before the snow falls thick about us, making these sessions more difficult, or should I say more challenging?" Tayeh said, smiling suddenly, read-justing his stance. Eva remembered a time when she practiced with a wooden blade - not that she could injure someone who was not really alive - a time when magic was a lesson and death a concept instead of a tool.

Eva shot him a challenging look, but she could not quite manage a smile. Her heart was too heavy for it.

Only weeks into fall, and the first snows came. The snow had barely melted when another storm came, wrapping the mountains in ice and fog. Eva wondered if another hard winter was upon them. What if another sickness came? If it did, Eva feared for the king. She doubted he could survive it.

She took the Guardian's advice and sought her visions out rather than letting them come unabated in her sleep.

She stood on the highest parapet of the Keep. The wind whipped into her hair and her eyes, pulling at her clothes, tugging at her like an insistent child. The stone fortress sprawled down the cliff face before her, the bare forest at its ankles. A thin, gray ribbon of road wound through the brown trees leading out of the mountain foothills, gently making its way to Caer Andri.

It all disappeared as the wind blinded Eva to her surroundings, but she could still see. A great vastness opened before her. Out of it emerged burned villages, bodies lying in their own blood, eyes life-less, mouths curved in a final portrait of their last terrible moments. And the creatures - she could not bring herself to call them men - rummaged through the villages, taking anything of interest. A shiny necklace, a young horse, a young woman left alive, or barely that. They hacked at the dead limbs as if for something to do. Eva could not count the dead or the devastated villages and farms. There were too many.

Eva came to herself sick and dizzy from grief. She fled from the parapet, vowing never search out the visions again. It was too awful.

But they came in her dreams instead. She could not escape them.

She could hardly eat. She could hardly sleep. Her troubles did not go unnoticed. Tarek and Mahone begged her to tell them what was wrong, vowing to fix it, a promise beyond their abilities. Eva had been a lonely child when she first confided in her guards about her magical abilities. As a woman grown, she spoke of it less and less, and she had not wanted to burden her friends with her violent nightmares. But as she told them about the attacks, the slaughter, her voice broke with sobs, and they held her close and dried her tears. She was thank-ful for their friendship.

At midwinter, a break in the weather brought a messenger with the dire news Eva had known for months: Jullayah was under attack. The prince was riding south with his army. Winter did not grip the south like it did the north and Caeris was hopeful his army would strike the invaders dead in their path.

On the day they received the message, Eva was floating in the hot-test of the Keep pools. She swirled the water around with her hands, watching the small eddies and waves ripple across the water. Steam was thick in the air, the product of the hot water and the piercingly cold air. Ice crystals grew in her hair. She looked into the steam and saw a face staring back at her. She didn't seek the vision, but when two elements combined, it was almost impossible to keep the *simul rami* from touching her mind.

The face was familiar, a face Eva had seen many times. His severe mouth almost curved at the edges, almost ready to smile. He was thinner than she had last seen him. There was no softness to his face despite his lilting, determined smile. His forest-green eyes were shadowed with something she could not quite put her finger on. It was Caeris, but it was not Caeris.

The vision changed to another village, another raft of burning arrows, the enemy's death-heralding call, but this time it was not followed by cries for mercy or screams of the dying. There came an answering call of arrows, an answering cry of challenge. The creatures looked on in surprise, then pressed forward with more enthusiasm. But the defenders were ready and waiting.

The defenders fell back. The monsters chased them, sensing victory. The defenders led the enemy to a field. A trap. Waiting for the creatures was a long line of men on horseback. Their horses were tall and lithe, bigger than any Eva had ever seen. The riders were grim, the set of their faces fierce in their determination. Their tall spears were tipped in bright, deadly steel. Other weapons glinted at their backs: swords, long daggers, maces, and cudgels.

Caeris, on a tall black horse, stood before them all. He turned to his men and roared a command. In reply, the Jullayan host gave a cry more terrible than the cry of the monsters. It was wild, rooted in desperation and revenge. The line of riders pushed their horses into a canter, a gallop, Caeris at their head, a great wave of men and horse-flesh, strong and immovable. The vision faded like the invaders under the hooves of the southern host.

Eva floundered out of the pool in her haste, splashing Calypso. The raven had been sitting on the edge of the pool playing with pebbles. He scolded her noisily. She ignored him. He would forgive her, especially if she stole him a couple of tidbits of meat at dinner.

It was cold. Eva flung a robe across her shoulders, not bothering to change. She did put on her slippers, but her hair was wet, clinging to her back as she ran up the steps.

"Tarek! Mahone!" Eva shouted, wondering where her guards were. She needed to share her excitement. If she didn't, she might burst with it. The prince was fighting back, victorious.

Tarek and Mahone relaxed their rules considerably when at the Keep. They still refused to let her leave the fortress without them, but they didn't shadow her constantly like at court.

They were not in the kitchens. Or in the main hall, where Altos and some of the other men were playing chess, keeping warm next to the large fire. She asked if they had seen her guards and they said no, but Tarek had mentioned something about chopping firewood. Well, Eva was not about to run outside to the stables in her robe and wet hair. So she set off to her chamber to change into something suitable to search the cold crags of the fortress.

Once dressed in warm, dry clothes, with a cap about her ear and her favorite scarf around her neck, she made her way to the old council room. Sometimes her guards were there, relaxing in front of the fire. It was the coziest room in the Keep.

"Tarek? Mahone?" Eva pushed the door open with a creak.

The room was empty, but there was a fire in the grate. In her mind, Eva could still see her father beside the huge fireplace, a book in hand, cradled in his favorite, padded leather chair, and her mother sitting with her back to the flames, working on a piece of embroidery, humming a song or telling a tale. As a child, Eva had sat, enraptured by her mother's tales. The little, felted creatures she once played with, the deer, the mountain cat, the little fox, still sat unused on the edge of the broad hearth. Years of dust had faded the colors to gray.

Eva was about to close the door when she noticed the small door to the courtyard was open a crack. They must be in the walled garden. Why else would the door be open?

Mahone and Tarek were in the garden.

Kissing. Her guards were kissing. Like lovers. Lip to lip, body to body, skin against skin, hands - hands in places she had no business observing. And yet she could not find her feet. She was struck by their harmony, by the love and tenderness in their expressions, in their intimate gestures. She had little hope Caeris would ever look at her the way Mahone was looking at Tarek, like he was his whole world.

They had not noticed her, and no wonder, they were thoroughly engrossed with each other. She regained her composure enough to slowly back away.

"Eva!" Tarek said, suddenly aware of her presence. Mahone said something as they disassembled instantly, their faces identical in their petrifaction.

"I'm so sorry -" Eva stumbled, her face burning like the summer sun. She turned away from their mortification.

"Wait!" Mahone cried, promptly following her through the door, grabbing her arm. Tarek followed, shrugging back into his shirt. Mahone's eyes, fearful and pleading, stopped her in her tracks. The hand on her arm was soft, not threatening. "Please, don't tell anyone."

Eva had never seen fear in Mahone's eyes. Caution, yes, but not fear.

"I wouldn't tell anyone. Ever," Eva assured them. The thought had never crossed her mind. "How dare you even think I would! You two are my family. I would never! I don't know why two men - or women - can't be together. I know it is forbidden in Jullayah, but the way you looked at each other just then, the way you - were… how could that be wrong?"

The fear dissolved from their expressions. Their shoulders relaxed. Mahone smiled and wrapped his big arms around Eva. Tarek wrapped his arms around them both and Eva closed her eyes, engulfed in their bear-like embrace.

They stepped back. Tarek shared a secret smile with Mahone. Eva realized she envied the warmth they turned upon each other, their masks cast aside.

"We thought you were bathing," Mahone said after the moment had passed.

"I was bathing, but -" Eva's face slid into a wide grin. "They are fighting back, and winning! Caeris was at the head of a strong host of men!" she said, remembering why she had come racing to find them in the first place.

"The prince's army? Couldn't be. It is a long ride to the south of Jullayah," Tarek mused.

"Come to think of it, I don't know if it was the prince's army. I couldn't see any standards or flags, or fancy armor. It must have been though. Caeris was there," Eva said. Now that she thought about it, it was strange that the prince's men were dressed as commoners, with barely a helm between them. But did it matter? They were victorious!

"Maybe you were mistaken? It couldn't have been Caeris," Mahone said, echoing his lover's statement. Lovers. By the Guardians, she had been blind.

"Maybe you are right," Eva said, rubbing her head with her hand. "Why didn't you tell me you were lovers?"

"We wanted to. But - it is hard. We have heard - and witnessed - too many stories," Mahone said sadly.

Eva nodded. She had heard of the awful things people did to those like Tarek and Mahone. Cruel, ignorant people who would never know true affection if it spit on them.

"Does anyone else know?" Eva thought she understood better the reasons why her guards respected her secrets.

"No one else knows. But I think Clarette has a suspicion. Why do you think she picked us to be a young, impressionable noble-woman's bodyguards?" Mahone huffed.

"We have been very careful not to arouse any suspicion," Tarek added. "We even fooled you."

Eva ignored the jibe. "So you have never been with a woman?"

They both shook their heads.

"You have never wanted to be with a woman?" Eva couldn't help her curiosity.

They both shook their heads.

"I guess, from now on, I should take longer baths?" Eva asked with a grin, pleased to see that Tarek's scars went bright red, but Mahone winked at her.

☾

Caeris stood before a man. A man that was more creature, more monster, than man, the same height as the prince. His hands were bound. His hair was long and matted with braids woven with beads and bones and trinkets of obscure and fathomless symbols. His face was lined, aged. The raised scars crisscrossed wrinkles. An alarming pattern, intricate and ominously deliberate. In the center of his forehead, the scars drew a picture of flame. Blood dripped from the corner of his mouth.

As unnerving as the man's appearance was, his gaze fixed on the prince was more so. It was mocking and dangerously void.

Caeris looked at his prisoner, and his green eyes were tired. A wealth of sorrow was in his gaze as he raised his knife threateningly toward the prisoner. The knife was not metal or iron. It was dirt brown and strange markings flashed in the light as it moved. The prisoner smiled as his throat was cut. He stood until his body could no longer hold him, eyes locked on Caeris's. His body collapsed as his blood pooled and stained his feet. His eyes were the last to leave.

As the man's eyes glazed, black smoke came from his fatal wound, sliding out from his body like the birth of a nightmare. The smoke grew thick as blood and rushed into Eva's mind, filling her with insatiable fear.

Eva woke coughing, gagging. The taste in her mouth was tangy, like iron. She shook in her bed. Terror woke her. Terror made her sit up straight and search her room as if expecting to see the nightmare smoke all around her. There was nothing except a haunting familiarity. She had felt the darkness before.

Calypso had woken on his roost and crooned sleepily at her.

"It's all right, Cal, it's nothing. It's nothing."

It took her several lifetimes to find sleep.

Since Eva's vision of black smoke and terror, all she could sense when she reached to the *simul rami* was muddled fog. Not black and evil, just obscure. The wind would not part with its secrets. Neither would the water. Earth was always the trickiest, so she didn't even attempt to use it. And fire - well, she had a complicated relationship with fire. The *simul rami*, the elements, would not answer her. Neither did it call to her.

At first, the vacancy of her mind was welcome. The evil visions had disturbed her for long enough that the respite was intensely welcome. There was no way to erase the memory of the visions, but at least she could push those remembered images from her mind with effort. She slept deeper, longer.

But what if she could never use the *simul rami* again?

Relief turned to worry, which turned to desperation. What was Eva without her magic? Without her connection to the *simul rami*, she was just a pawn, a young woman with nothing but a loveless betrothal and her dead father's inheritance.

It was cold in the Great Forest. The still, damp air crept into Eva's lungs. Her toes ached after a few steps across the snow-covered moss. Something caught her foot, and she fell into the soft snow. The icy dust managed to get into her gloves and down her neck, trickling down her back as it melted. She cursed, kicking the root that had tripped her. But that only made her toes hurt more.

"Damn you, Allmakers," she muttered. "Why won't you give me answers?" Her voice grew louder. "Where are you, spirits? Show yourselves! Tell me what is happening! Tell me what I need to do to see! To understand. Give. Me. Fucking. Answers!" Her voice rang through the silent Forest. She waited. But there was nothing. Even the trees were silent.

She trudged toward the glade where Tayeh and Lula were always waiting. She wondered if they had heard her shouting. Her face grew warm thinking of it.

Tayeh and Lula said nothing when she arrived damp from the snow and red-faced from irritation. She told them about the black-ness and fog and her muddled connection with her magic. They hid their unease well, but they were hiding something from her. Eva did not press them. They told her to be patient. They told her the visions, although not apparent, were meant for her to see. Perhaps the lack of sight was also for her benefit. Perhaps it was to protect her.

"You mean, what I see is only what I am meant to see? How can that possibly make sense?" Eva asked pacing in circles around the little glade. Lula and Tayeh watched her with identical, patient expressions that made her want to smack something.

"Everything we do in this life is what we are meant to do," Tayeh began. "What you see is what you are meant to see."

"But that doesn't make any sense! To say that is to say I have no choice in my own destiny, no control over my own actions." Eva waved her hands in irritation.

"No, Eva, our choices govern our lives. It is as simple as that," Lula told her solemnly.

Eva groaned. "That still makes no sense. You're saying I have no choices. Everything that happens is meant to happen, but at the same time my choices decide the direction of my life? A contradiction."

"Not exactly." Lula's mouth twitched into a half-smile. "Some things in life happen and there is nothing you can do to change them, but you can always choose how you react to those happenings. No one person or thing, not Tayeh or myself, can make those decisions for you."

"So my visions are meant to influence my decisions?"

"Perhaps," Tayeh mused.

Eva groaned again, pressing her palms into her forehead.

"What you see is the history of the world. It is the old magic still alive in the elements, hidden from all but those who know how to see it," Lula reminded her. "Don't curse your gift, even if you don't understand it."

"Magic is forbidden in Jullayah," Eva said, feeling a sudden chill.

"Yes, it is. Crea fears and desires magic. There is not much of it left outside the Great Forest, but every once in a while, she finds some and uses it for her own - or destroys it." Tayeh's words were ice in Eva's heart.

"I am going to be queen!" Eva said. "What will happen if they find out?" It was something she thought of more often than she cared to admit.

"They will never know. Some will remember you are half Allati, but that doesn't mean they think you have magic in your blood. It is not as well known for magical abilities to manifest in women. And Clarette has worked hard to help people forget who your mother was."

Eva bit her lip. "Why, if this gift is usually only in men, do I have it?" Eva said, still angry. At whom, she didn't know.

Tayeh sighed. "You are special, Eva. Perhaps your mixed blood makes the magic stronger."

"But why don't I see things from other lands? Why don't I see anything from Kitarra? Or from my mother's land?"

Tayeh shrugged. "Perhaps it is not time."

Eva sighed yet again, rubbing her eyes, feeling like a lost child.

"You must wait, Eva. In time you will see," Lula said. The Guardian was in the form of a woman, but she had an unreadable fox-like expression.

"It's cold. I'm going home," Eva announced. She wanted to be alone. A warm soak in the mineral baths might pull her out of her dour mood. Perhaps she should hibernate like a squirrel.

"Poor child. Don't worry, spring is on its way," Lula said with a delicate laugh, changing in the blink of an eye to a bounding fox whose springs and leaps echoed her laughter.

Spring made a slow entrance. The days remained cold, the nights colder. A frost lingered in the shadows and coldest nooks and crannies of the Keep. The frost melted quickly when the sun dared to come out from behind the cool mist. Even if it was a cold spring, Eva was determined it was still spring. She spent her days riding in the forest, fishing in the little lake, visiting the Guardians.

Eva's visions still did not return. Her dreams were often nightmares, but they were so incoherent and abstract, she knew they could not possibly be real. Still, she would wake flustered, covered in sweat, her heart pounding.

No official messages arrived concerning Caeris. The old men of the Keep ruminated on the possibility that Caeris had died in battle, that the creatures were on their way up from the south, that soon they might reach Caer Andri. It didn't sound plausible. Eva didn't think Altos really believed it. Surely they would have received a message if the prince had died. Altos still had many friends at court.

Lady Clarette arrived, and it could barely be called spring. The delicate snowdrops were relentless and stubborn, blooming even in the frost, but the crocus' were barely poking their green heads above the ground.

"It's been weeks, my lady. Have you any news?" the steward asked the evening of the lady's arrival.

"No one has heard anything, Tudos. Perhaps it is a good sign. If the army were failing, the prince would call for more men," the lady said at her most sympathetic. Darys at her side nodded in agreement.

"It is troubling, Steward. We hope to learn more when we arrive at court," Darys confirmed. A conversation ensued about the prince's campaign, a conversation Altos and Tudos revisited so often Eva could recite it in her sleep. Sometimes Mahone added his own thoughts and opinions. They were all eager for a new voice to be added to the debate. Clarette had her own opinion, which surprised no one.

Eva closed her ears to it. In two days they would leave for Caer Andri, and they would learn, for good or ill, the fate of their prince.

CHAPTER 8

COTOCH

THE GOLD BASIN GLITTERED. Long ago Cotoch's father had used a special water to enhance his visions, a solution involving ground minerals. Cotoch needed nothing of the sort. The *varing* in his blood, the amulet, were all he needed.

After torture and death, Cotoch was strong, potent. The vision he wanted came instantly.

Jullayah was bleeding. The south had been ravaged by the invaders from Rodan. Imal's warriors were ruthless. Cotoch wished he could reap the *varing* from the pain they created. Part of him abhorred it. A small part, apparently, because he felt no guilt.

He wondered if Crea's plan had worked. He had not had a visit from the goddess for sometime. But then, it was not uncommon for months to go by without her making an appearance.

The Jullayans were fighting back. A pathetic attempt with swords and horses and cunning courage. Perhaps not so pathetic. Another vision came, and Cotoch saw the invaders cringe and begin their defensive - and lose.

It was irrelevant. The damage was done. Crea had her hurting realm, and if her man wasn't dead, Cotoch was sure the conniving spirit would find another way to deal with him. And more importantly, Imal would be pleased. Cotoch had fulfilled his side of the bargain. He had shown Imal the way across the wide sea, the hidden island where his ships could take water and stock. Imal's warriors had taken what they wanted from Jullayah, enough to satiate any man's greed, even a sorcerer emperor.

Cotoch reached across the sea and felt his magic stretch like a sail in the wind. He loved the feeling. He called Imal to him, and in a moment Cotoch was back in his body, looking into the gold water.

A face, not unlike his own, looked back at him. Black eyes, dark hair, sharp nose, decisive brows. Cotoch thought they resembled brothers more than cousins.

"Cotoch," Imal said tersely. "The first ships have come back. Your word was true. It was more than I hoped for." A grin stretched across his lips.

"Are you ready, dear cousin, to put our fathers' past behind us and embrace each other as *candarii* allies and kin?"

"Yes." It wasn't until Imal acknowledged him that Cotoch realized how much it meant. A ripple of joy and pride flowed through him. Cotoch was so much better than his father. Mahlas, his people, were fortunate indeed to have him as their lord, their protector. "Our alliance will bring you your kingship, and me more wealth." Imal had a laugh like a dragon. "I am sending one of my daughters to you," Imal went on "You can teach her, use her as you see fit. She is a good, clever girl."

Cotoch wasn't sure he needed an apprentice. He hoped to teach his own children, someday. Sandra had yet to quicken with pregnancy, but someday. However, the girl could be useful if she was what her father said. Cotoch was ever a strategist. If not, he could send her back, or find some other use for her.

"I will watch for her."

Imal inclined his head, his eyes flickering with suppressed anticipation, and the *varing*. He faded into glittering gold.

Cotoch shivered. He didn't like looking into his cousin's eyes. They were predatory and too much of a mirror. Cotoch knew his own eyes would seem as sharp and electric, the shadow of his magic. Sandra liked it. But she was an odd woman, even to Cotoch's standards. Not that he minded.

CHAPTER 9

EVA

"IT'S OVER. You were right, the rest of them scattered into the hills -" The man speaking halted and inspected the condition of the man spoken to. Blood covered the other man like a second skin. His short hair was matted with it, not his own blood, but still, it was shocking. He buried his face in his hands, long, dirty fingers nearly pulling his hair out by the roots. His body was hunched, emanating despair.

"You okay?"

The answering nod was unconvincing.

"He didn't come," the other said, his face still hidden, his grief raw through his gruff, hoarse voice, almost a sob. The voice of a man who has been stretched to his limits, physically and emotionally. The voice of heartache and endurance beyond comprehension. "I can't believe he didn't come."

"Well, we didn't need him, did we?" This was followed by a mirthless laugh.

The man standing held a flask in his hands. He took a swig before handing it to the man sitting, who reached up for it. The sitting man took a long drink. He coughed. His eyes were red, his face unshaven beneath the layer of blood and battle grime, but he was still recognizable.

"Their leader is dead, their boats burned. Soon the last of the cowards will be dead. We will track each one." The standing man's voice was tired. There was no satisfaction in his words.

"We could have saved so many men, Kaile," the prince said. "More will be dead by morning as they succumb to their injuries."

"They knew they were going to their deaths," the tall man named

Kaile said, his voice barely audible. "We all prepared for that. We followed you regardless, we believed you could do it, my lord - and you did."

"Don't call me that."

The vision left as abruptly as it came. A vision. Eva's magic had not abandoned her after all.

The cold wind was the only sound in the silent forest. It slid through the silent trees, creeping over the moss carpet white with the heavy morning frost. Eva could see it swirling her breath, pulling the heat away from her body. It seemed to echo the message of death and despair. The Forest had never felt so forbidding, so empty, so forgotten. Winter hung onto the land with desperate, cruel fingers. The tiny new leaves had shriveled with the unexpected frost. But there was hope of a thaw. The prince's campaign was a success. The monsters who hadn't died on the battlefield disbanded and fled.

The image of Caeris's face, lined and distraught, stuck with Eva. Clearly he was reeling over his losses. Eva's heart was heavy to see the blood of Caeris's enemies and men upon his clothes, his skin, to imagine his fear and violence. So many injured and dying. Eva was a healer, but she could not help. Caeris was her betrothed, and she could not comfort him. She would have held his hand as he wept. She wondered if he would have let her.

Her footsteps were loud on the frost as she continued on her way. She hardly noticed. For the first time she could imagine herself as Caeris's wife. The wife of a man who knew humility, who was selfless and inspiring. The man in her vision. She yearned to hold him, to comfort him.

Eva only had a short time to bid her farewell to the Guardians. Tarek and Mahone would be looking for her soon. Already they were saddling her horse, loading her things into the wagon, preparing to leave for Caer Andri.

Eva paused on the edge of the clearing. The little break in the Forest was bathed in sunlight, the only place that seemed to encapsulate even a small amount of spring. The frost had melted. The moss was bright green. The wild crocus had agreed to open their shy blossoms, their leaves untarnished by the frost.

Tayeh was there. As usual, he looked set apart from any effects of the season. He was never cold, never wet. He was like a stone, unchanging and unaffected. Eva didn't see Lula at first; then she noticed the white fox at the Kitarran's feet, soaking in the sun. They knew she was there. They sensed her presence the moment she stepped into the Great Forest. Perhaps they were always aware of her, even when she was far away at court. They were Guardians, after all. They only turned to smile in greeting when she stepped across the threshold of sunshine.

"Cold morning for spring," Tayeh noted.

"You have no idea. The Keep is covered in an inch of ice, I swear it."

"All the steam from the hot pools."

Lula stood up and began an epic stretch that only ended when she touched her black nose to the back of Eva's hand. Eva smiled. Lula was generally a shy fox. She rarely came over to let Eva run her hand along her soft fur. Eva scratched her behind the ears.

"It's the last summer," Tayeh said thoughtfully. "This time next year you will be saying your farewells to this place forever."

"Surely not forever?" Eva lamented. "I am sure I will come back to the Keep someday."

"I cannot stay here once you are gone."

"You are leaving?" Eva asked. The thought of coming to this clearing to find it empty filled her with a cold dread.

"Don't worry about that now, Eva. It is not for a whole year," Tayeh said dismissively. "Now, by the light in your eyes, I can tell you have good news to tell us." He leaned back against the great tree, arms crossed over his massive chest, a warm smile dancing on his gray lips.

Eva smiled, settling on her cloak in the sun, and told them what she had seen moments earlier.

"I am glad your visions have returned," Tayeh said. "But who was the other man in the vision? I don't remember you ever mentioning a man named Kaile close to the prince," Tayeh pondered. Lula looked disinterested and curled up beside Eva.

"I don't know him either. He did seem close to Caeris though - perhaps a southern lord?" Eva offered.

Tayeh nodded in agreement, but Eva could see that the idea didn't appease his curiosity. He was still pondering it. "You said the prince was covered in blood?"

"Yes, but most of it was not his."

"Was he wearing the royal crest?" Tayeh asked. "Tell me again what he said." Eva repeated the fragment of the conversation from the vision.

"I don't think he was wearing his crest. In fact, he looked quite ordinary. His armor was leather, worn and oldish. It was not his usual armament," Eva told him. It did seem odd that Caeris had been dressed decidedly un-prince-like. And before, when she had seen him in the vanguard, he had worn no helm.

Tayeh was nodding thoughtfully like there was a puzzle he was trying to solve. Then he shook his head in dismissal. "Never mind," he said, noticing the odd look Eva was giving him. "Eva, I have a task for you."

"What kind of task?"

"There is an artifact. In the wrong hands, it could be very dangerous."

Tayeh had her full attention.

"An artifact? What does it look like?" Eva asked.

"I don't know. It could be anything. An amulet, a token, a dagger. I need you to keep watch for it."

"How can I look for something if I don't know what it looks like?"

"Your magic will sense it," Tayeh assured her.

Eva bit her lip. "You are just trying to distract me," she grumbled.

"Maybe. Maybe I am trying to kill two birds with one stone," Tayeh said. Lula growled softly in response to his idiom.

"But what does it do? Is it dangerous?" Eva asked.

"To some. But not to you."

"Why not?"

"Because you have your own protection." Tayeh tapped his long, clawed finger on her pendant.

"My necklace is magical?"

"It protects you from the effects of the vercuri," Tayeh told her.

"The vercuri? The artifact?"

Tayeh sighed. "A long time ago, an evil spread through the land, threatening to destroy the *simul rami* -"

"And then it was stopped, and the Allmakers created the Guardians - yes I know this story," Eva folded her arms over her chest.

Tayeh fixed her with a patient stare before continuing. "Yes, but exactly how the evil was thwarted is much debated, even among us Guardians. There is a tale that an old spirit, even older than the All-makers, who created the vercuri from a fallen cendari branch. She used it to balance the magic, to bring peace and light back to the *simul rami*. But the artifacts were lost, It is believed that in the wrong hands, they could be dangerous."

"There are more than one?"

"There are nine."

"Nine? But you are just looking for one?"

"For now."

"Do the vercuri have anything to do with Dweller's Knoll?" Eva asked.

"Shhh." Tayeh's amber eyes flashed in alarm. Lula's ears had gone tight and pointy, her eyes wide. "Do not speak of it. Not here. Not in the Forest."

"But - why?"

Tayeh's face softened. "To speak of evil is to invite evil. We must be cautious, especially here in the Forest where the *simul rami* is most delicate." He put his hand on Eva's shoulder. "Please. If you want to help, look for the vercuri."

"I will try." Eva sighed. She would do anything for the Guardians.

It was always hard to say goodbye to her mentors. Eva missed their wisdom, their lessons, their stories. Tayeh embraced her like a daughter and sent her on her way. He always left her with the same piece of advice.

"Remember to follow your heart, Eva," he would say, and this time was no different. She looked up into his amber eyes, noticing this time he said it with more ferocity than usual.

"I always do try, Tayeh," Eva replied, and Tayeh smiled. She pulled her cloak around her shoulders once more and stepped out of the sun into the cool shadows of the Forest.

Lula would follow to the hidden door. On days of farewell, the Forest woman preferred to stay in her fox shape, but she always remained close until the last possible moment. Eva knew the sincerity of Lula's devotion to her.

Eva was almost at the door, inches from the Keep, but she knelt and wrapped her arms around the little furry spirit creature. Eva pulled back, and Lula stopped her with a paw resting upon Eva's chest, just over her heart. The look in the flame-light eyes was just as fierce as Tayeh's had been.

"I'll remember," Eva assured the fox-woman.

With Caeris and most of his councilors gone, court seemed almost empty, quiet. The ladies complained about the lack of society. Eva found the silence enjoyable. She enjoyed the empty hallways. She didn't miss the throngs of girls and women whispering in corridors or playing nuanced games in the gardens. The lack of overly grand dinners and dances did not faze her, nor did she harp over the canceled games and races. She had plenty of time to go out riding with Mahone and Tarek. She often visited the king at his bedside, or when the weather was warm she sat with him in the rose garden, if his physicians allowed it.

Rhais always enjoyed her visits, but his heart was heavy with grief for his hurting realm. He worried about Caeris, his only child. Eva wished she could tell him what she had seen, but she couldn't seem to find the right words to tell him of her secrets. The king would know soon enough.

Finally, a message came from the south. The campaign had come to an end. The foe was defeated, and Caeris was on his way back to Caer Andri. One turning of the moon and he would be home.

His victory would be cause for a summer-long celebration. There would be games, and crowds, and endless parties and all the things that made court chafing. But it was a mere trifle on Eva's troubled mind. She arrived at the palace and immediately felt the stirrings of unease - and she had not even begun her quest for the vercuri.

A vicious rumor circled court concerning Alline and Lord Serac. The scandalous story told of an affair, ending with Alline running off, shamed and pregnant. No one had seen or heard from her in nearly a month. Eva could not credit the rumor. Alline was a romantic girl who longed for love and had often swooned regretfully over the already wed Serac. With Serac's wife not at court, many of the young women felt emboldened to flirt with the Temple Master. But Eva could not imagine Alline as Serac's mistress. Alline was too traditional and proper.

The king's councilors and their families still gathered for formal dinners on occasion, at least those who were not away on their estates or off to war with the prince. Upon their arrival, Clarette and Eva were insisted upon to join the hearty meal. Lord Serac sat opposite Eva.

Eva looked at Serac as if for the first time. She watched the way he conversed with his peers. The sharpness she had once admired seemed more arrogant than witty. What she had once thought was cleverness was supercilious. She lost something suddenly. She knew she could not trust Serac.

"Where is Lady Alline?" Eva asked cordially, her voice sweet, a practiced tone. "She is my friend and I heard you and she formed something of an alliance?" It wasn't proper etiquette to ask, but Eva found she didn't care.

Serac did not answer. It was evident he had no intention of answering.

After the feast, Eva waited in the hallway for him, hoping he would not ignore her again.

"Serac, a word, please," Eva asked. He swept over to her, glancing at her guards a few paces away. Eva saw Caeris in his dark, brooding gaze. Cousins indeed. "Where is Alline?"

"Lord Barim's pretty daughter?" Serac drawled.

"Yes. I heard you had an affair with her. And now she is missing."

Serac's eyes focused on Eva.

"That is no concern of yours."

"She is my friend. It does concern me. Is she ill? There were rumors she was pregnant."

"Pregnant. No."

"Tell me, please."

Serac smiled. A serpent's smile. Eva heard a muffled scream of anguish in her heart.

"Oh, Eva, so contrite." Was he mocking her?

"Serac. I won't let this go. Where is she?"

"I can see you won't. You have no common sense. No wonder Caeris finds you so vexing, you are so -" He sneered looking for the right word. " - Importune."

His crescendo of condescension cut her like daggers.

"She is my friend, Serac."

Serac's sneer twitched back into a graceless smile.

"Since you asked so nicely: Alline ran away. She was embarrassed."

"You are lying."

"And what makes you think that?"

"You hurt her," Eva said, feeling the truth of it in her bones. Serac's eyes glinted with interest.

"And how is it you think you know me so well?" Serac said moving closer to her, his finger lightly brushing her neck. There was a coldness in his touch. And a promise. "Alline is gone." The finality of his voice made Eva shiver. "Keep your thoughts on the matter to yourself. No good will come of wandering tongues."

Was that a threat?

"Anything else on your mind?" Serac asked in a bland tone as if she suddenly bored him more than a recount of Jullayah's kings.

"Good night, Lord Serac."

Eva turned away from him, uncomfortable in her own skin. His words were worms and she was a rotten apple.

Eva wanted Serac to be innocent of the crimes her instincts warned her of. She wanted her dreams to be just that - dreams. But she felt the niggling of distrust. She could not discount the foul mist in the bowl that continued to hang around him like sticky spider silk.

She might be able to find the truth with her magic. But she didn't want to. Instead she allowed herself to believe Alline had run away, traveling far away from Caer Andri to find love and peace somewhere else, away from pernicious, gossiping noblewomen. Maybe hope was safer than truth.

The vercuri was often on Eva's mind. But she had no one she could trust with questions about a magical artifact. Caer Andri was filled with devout worshipers of the Black Goddess, and Eva would not risk more attention from Serac.

Another message came from Caeris. He was expected within a fortnight. Soon all of Caer Andri was swarming with excitement like a beehive on the first warm day of spring. Soon the lords and vassals were making their way to court to join the celebrations.

Once more Eva was constantly bumping into people in corridors. The gardens were overflowing with courtiers. Groups blocked doorways as they stopped to talk to one another, sharing yet another piece of information about the prince's campaign.

Eva secluded herself with the king as he awaited the return of his son. Rhais was growing more frail every day, and Eva feared for his health. She held his limp hand in hers, once so strong and calloused from use. The king had been a man who lived in constant motion. Now his body was soft and almost lifeless, the veins and bones clearly outlined underneath his pale skin.

The news of his son's impending, victorious return roused him. The hint of color in his cheeks was a gift.

Caeris returned on a gray summer day at the head of an exhausted but strong, spirited army. Cheering Jullayans lined the streets of Caer Andri. The beaming faces of wives and children awaiting the return of beloved husbands and fathers shone out in the crowd.

With the prince's officers tasked with disbanding the army, Caeris returned to the palace where his court was waiting for him on the steps in front of the grand doors. Eva smiled as she watched him dismount, hoping to catch his gaze. His body showed no sign of weariness, but Eva could see the lines of fatigue on his face.

He greeted his councilmen warmly, clapping Lord Serac on the back affectionately. Hasty greetings exchanged, Caeris hurried off into the palace. He said something about speaking to his father immediately and in private. He took Serac with him. He didn't even spare a glance in Eva's direction.

She stood on the steps watching the tall back of him disappear into the palace, biting her lip, unable to tear her eyes from the door he had just disappeared into. She didn't meet the eyes of her aunt, or Darys, or any of the other courtiers. She took a deep breath and stood up straighter. She should have worn her blue dress. Caeris liked blue. He might have noticed her if she had worn blue.

The victory feast was magnificent. The grand hall was decorated with more splendor than usual. Rumors said that fresh water lilies were brought from the great lake to the east, more than twenty miles away. Sure enough, great bowls filled the fragrant, exquisite flowers sat upon the tables. Eva had never seen them before and marveled at their delicate, almost translucent petals.

Wine was opened from the king's personal wine cellar and the oldest and rarest vintages were served aplenty. Tales of the prince's victory were told. Eva heard a myriad of different stories and events. Some quite unbelievable, some not fit for delicate ears - the prince's men were quickly in their wine.

The resounding story was that Caeris really had little to do with the actual battle. By the time the prince and his army arrived in the south, the fighting was over, the enemy leader dead, the last of the evil men running for their lives. All the prince's army did was chase after them and eliminate any chance the invaders would have to retaliate.

This recollection of events warred with the truth Eva had seen. It felt all wrong. She had lived the vision of Caeris fighting with his army. The *simul rami* could not lie.

Briefly, one of the prince's captains spoke of a brave young man, a peasant, who created an army, defeating the barbaric invaders with bravery and cunning.

Caeris shot the man a silencing look and no more was said. He was hiding something. He was not telling his court the whole truth, not by far.

Eva wondered if this man, this mysterious hero, could be the one from her vision. Kaile had been his name? She remembered the strange conversation she had witnessed. It still did not make sense. She had not seen him ride up with the prince's men. He was nowhere to be seen in the grand hall. Surely a hero would be offered high honors from the prince and king before the entire court.

Eva's curiosity was not appeased. However, she did notice one newcomer sitting at the prince's table: a young, comely woman with long, shining brown hair and a curvaceous figure. The strange woman toyed with her meal as if she had no appetite, looking nervous, rarely gazing up from her plate. When she did, her brown eyes darted around like a wary animal. Once, Eva caught her glance and the girl immediately found something very interesting on her untouched plate, a faint, uncomfortable blush rising to her cheeks.

It was odd behavior. Eva wondered who she was. No one had thought to introduce her. Eva had a suspicion, from the way the young woman pulled at the frills on her gown and often ran a hand down the silky fabric, that she was of low birth, no noblewoman. It was probably the first time she had worn such exquisite fabrics and eaten in such intimidating company. Probably a mistress to one of the prince's men found in some small town and brought back to court. Mistresses flitted through court often enough. When their men tired of them, or they got with child, they would be lucky to leave to some undisclosed place with a small income of their own.

At the other end of the table, Lord Serac sat surrounded by his returned peers. He looked as handsome as ever in his black state coat. He caught Eva's eye, nodding to her. He was genial, but Eva felt chilled.

The feast was followed by music and dancing. The courtiers mingled and laughed and gossiped. Eva was short of breath from a lively dance with young Lord Westin, a boy of fourteen, who always had a cheery, harmless smile. She hadn't seen Serac approach but managed to hide her dismay and fear as he cornered her.

"Lord Serac."

"Lady Evangeline."

Eva bit her tongue against the words she wanted to pelt him with. The accusations.

"Caeris has informed me that you have not yet been to the Temple." Serac's voice was smooth, as glossy as his handsome features. Why did he have to be so beautiful? Why couldn't he be ugly and utterly repulsive, like a rat, or a slug? No, that wasn't quite fair to the slugs.

"Why is it any concern of yours?"

"I am the Temple Master, and you will be queen. Your duty is to be a good role model for all Jullayans. We should be allies, you and I."

Eva said nothing.

"Come with me tomorrow. You can begin your duty to the realm, and to the Goddess."

"I will not."

Her answer seemed to infuriate him, and please him. The juxtaposition was unnerving.

"Eva, I am only trying to help you," he said, his voice honey once more. "Caeris expects you to be dutiful. I will fetch you at second quarter."

"I will not come."

"Oh, I think you will."

"Then you are delusional."

"Me? Look in a mirror, my lady."

Serac left. Eva watched him go, seething. Her distrust turned to hatred and her hatred turned to fear. She now believed that the Temple was dangerous. She had been wrong to doubt Tayeh's warnings. But Serac was right. She was going to be queen - it was expected of her to visit the Temple and worship the Black Goddess. Caeris expected it of her. She needed to ask the Guardians' advice, but they were not around.

She met Mahone's eyes where he stood in the shadows, watching, guarding. His gray eyes flashed, mirroring her unease.

CHAPTER 10

EVA

THE FOLLOWING MORNING, Eva received a bossy note from Lord Serac informing her that he had to leave on an urgent errand for the prince, and very sadly, he would be unable to escort her to the Temple. Eva swooned with relief. But the message held a promise for the day after his return. He did not specify when that day would be.

It seemed the entire court knew of Serac's mysterious departure. No one knew what the errand entailed, but naturally, rumors abounded, circling court like carrion crows. There were other rumors as well, one rumor Eva did not like in the least. The talk concerned her more than the disappearance of Serac, prince's errand or no. It was about the young, nervous lady from the feast.

Her name was Unalla, and she had come up from the south with the prince's men. She was Caeris's mistress, and she was pregnant with his bastard child.

Eva often spent time in the garden, being social with the other court ladies, practicing for when she would be queen and such appearances would be a necessary part of her life. The women talked about the strange, southern beauty in hushed voices, trying not to be obvious, but their voices pitched so Eva would overhear them. It would be extremely poor form for them to speak outright of Caeris's mistress to Caeris's future wife, but evidently, they wanted her to be informed. How gracious of them.

Informed she was. She found a polite exit from the group in the garden and made her way to a secluded corner of the park. There were tall, shading trees surrounding the little man-made pond. She was not entirely alone; Mahone followed her silently.

She sat down next to the little pool and looked into the water, the bottom filled with little stones and leaves. It did not reflect the sky, only her face. Her long tendrils of pale hair dipped into the water. Concentration was the key. Eva blocked all thoughts and sounds.

She rarely summoned a specific vision. It was difficult and taxing. The rumors the court women spoke of, the possibility that Eva's future husband would never be faithful to her, never love her, tormented her. She had to know the truth.

It took a long time for the vision to come. Eva's fingers started to itch. She ignored it, digging deeper, trying to connect with the *simul rami*. She concentrated on the little nuances around her - the smell of the earth, the faint fragrance of a plant she couldn't quite name, the smell of the water itself, not wholly clean, not rightly unpleasant, the rough edges of the stone under her palms. Her breath became loud, and she slowed and nearly silenced it. Soon it was just her heart punctuating the stillness, beating slow and steady. Finally, there was the vision.

Unalla, smiling shyly as she brought a basket of fresh bread and spring berries to the prince's camp. She took the basket to the prince's tent. Caeris sat at his campaign table, thinking hard, surrounded by his advisers. She wore a simple dress, her long, curling hair unbound and shining in the morning sun, a perfect specimen of young, feminine beauty. She looked under her lashes at Caeris and offered him fresh fare from her village as a small token of their devotion. Her eyes held an unspoken message the prince read clearly. The vision shifted showing Caeris and the woman making love on a pile of pillows and travel blankets. They were smiling, laughing, enjoying each other completely. The vision faded and Eva cursed.

"He loves her, Mahone," Eva said as she stretched, her neck stiff from the prostrate position.

"Who and who?"

"The prince and his pretty mistress," Eva told him glumly, wondering how he could have possibly missed that rumor.

"Ah. You look upset about it. You shouldn't be."

"And why is that? He has gotten her pregnant, Mahone! I thought I was supposed to have the prince's children? I thought I was supposed to share his bed as his wife? How can I do that if I know that he is planting his seed all over the country?"

Mahone regarded her with a piteous look. "Eva, I am sorry. This is nothing new. The prince has had many mistresses. This is just the first one that he has - err - flaunted a little."

Eva was dumbfounded. Then she felt like a naive idiot and groaned, slumping against Mahone's strong shoulder. He stood as still as a statue and Eva wondered why he wasn't putting his arm around her shoulders like he often did. Then she remembered they were not at the Keep but in the middle of the royal gardens. The last thing she needed was the whole court thinking she was having an affair with her bodyguard. A man could have a mistress, but a woman, a young engaged woman destined to be a virgin bride, could not. The thought made her furious.

She pulled away from Mahone and stalked out of the garden kicking her feet into the soft grass forcefully, knowing she was reacting in a most un-lady-like way.

Disappointment. Jealousy. Eva knew courtiers did not marry for love. Caeris did not love her. She knew she had a duty to the king and Jul-layah. By betrothing Eva to Caeris, Rhais and Clarette had saved her from a terrible fate. Yet watching Caeris and his mistress was intolerable.

Eva went riding. She rode the king's old, piebald horse. Poor Path did not get the attention he deserved with the king frail and bedridden. Path was as eager as Eva to get out for a ride.

Away from the palace, Eva felt her spirits lift. Without the deco-rum of court hanging over them, her guards could once more be her friends. They could laugh and make comments they wouldn't dare if there was a chance of being overheard.

They took the king's discreet path through Caer Andri and out into the countryside. Eva and Rhais had ridden the path countless times before he took ill. The king's friendship had made court bearable for the homesick little girl Eva had been.

The summer sun beat down with an uncharacteristic vengeance. They rode through the shaded, leafy woods with no other object than to find a lake to cool off in. Eva wanted nothing more than quiet woods where there was no one to judge her.

The lake they found was small, but well shaped, a rocky beach at one end where the water gradually deepened. They sloughed all but their small clothes and spent a luxurious time cooling off in the water, then lounging on the beach, then once again swimming in the cool water.

Eva sat in the shallow water, the sun warming her bare back. Mahone and Tarek lounged on the beach, half-asleep.

She swirled the water with her hands, watching the silt rise slowly, then fall like an exhale. The ripples of sunlight grew - the *simul rami* called to her. In her mind, Eva spoke the word vercuri.

In the vision, Eva's hand was green and covered with moss and twigs and mushrooms. She reached down and picked up a fallen branch, its bark smooth and hard as stone. The vision shifted into darkness so absolute Eva felt panic slide down her back like ice. But it was not the obscuring nothingness from when the *simul rami* would not answer her call. It was only the darkness of a stone passageway devoid of window or torch. Damp air filled her lungs. Cold stone permeated into her toes. A hopeless longing clutched her chest.

Eva opened her eyes. The emotions she had felt in the vision faded like a dream upon waking. The lake was still bright and blue before her. She could not imagine how the two images intertwined. She wanted to scream or weep in frustration, but all she did was take several long, deep breaths. Tayeh had taught her that controlled breathing was essential to a warrior. It was like she was at war with her unanswered questions - and losing.

When they returned to the palace stables, it had been full dark for nearly an hour. Eva was surprised the stable boys were still about, but she was glad she didn't have to see to her horse herself.

The hallways of the palace were filled with shadows. Only a few waning sconces still flickered. Tarek and Mahone followed close behind her. Tarek held a lantern to illuminate their way. He could always be counted on for such practicalities.

The dampness of Eva's hair, which had been refreshing, was chilly in the cool marble hallways. She wished for a cloak. She walked faster, eager to be in her bed and under warm, comforting blankets.

They turned a sharp corner, nearly colliding with three men walking the halls in equal silence. Eva swayed back on her heels. Tarek's hand fell on her shoulder ready to pull her from danger. His other would be on his dagger. Neither hand moved when he recognized the man Eva nearly collided with. Eva stood paralyzed under Lord Serac's gaze. His eyes were black and powerful in the torch light.

"What are you doing wandering the hallways at such an hour? You look like some sort of street rabble," he muttered in an amused voice, his eyes raking over Eva in callous inspection. He was probably right. Eva doubted she resembled a high-born lady. She had discarded her long riding dress in favor for leggings and a sleeveless tunic. Her shoulders were bare and tanned from the sun, and she had braided her hair without the aid of brush or mirror. Not that she cared.

Her eyes darted past Serac to see Caeris, who avoided her pleading gaze. The third man standing beside the prince did not hail her attention, his features obscured by the long shadows beyond the torchlight.

"Not your concern, Serac," Eva said, surprised her voice sounded calm when her heart was pounding in her chest. She made to push past him, but somehow he was taking up the entire hallway. As she made to move his arm shot out and grabbed hers tightly. Eva tried not to flinch and betray her unease. Something in his eyes made her shiver.

"Tomorrow we will go to the Temple. I will let you know when."

She glared up at him. Caeris coughed lightly, as if to remind his cousin they had some pressing matter despite the late hour. The lord swept past them, stalking down the hall into the dark, his cloak billowing behind him like a raven taking flight. Caeris and the stranger followed in his wake. The men were blessedly unaware that Tarek had drawn his knife.

The whole thing was peculiar.

"Tarek," Eva said in a whisper as they continued walking. "I think that man, the third one, was Kaile."

"The man from your vision?"

"Yes."

"That is odd."

"I'm worried, Tarek."

"Hmm?"

"I can't go to the Temple. It is dangerous for me."

"Eva, don't worry. He can't hurt you. We won't let him hurt you."

Despite her fatigue from the previous day, Eva was up early and insisted on going riding again. She wasn't going to be around for Serac to snatch her up and whisk her away to the Temple. He would be angry, but she would be queen. How much power did he really have over her? But the thought didn't make her feel better.

Mahone took her down to the stables. Tarek, who had been up all night on guard, stayed behind, leaving Eva under his lover's care for the day.

The stable boys were hard at work putting fresh hay and water in with the royal horses, mucking out stalls, polishing saddles and harnesses. The sun was just high enough to stream in through the open windows, promising another hot day.

Eva did a double take as she walked past two stalls with new occupants. They were two of the biggest horses she had ever seen, though not quite as tall as draft horses. They were tall and lean, with beautiful lines and proportions. One was black from his ears to his flocks - a stallion. He looked a little uneasy in his new surroundings, pawing at his bedding, and he had not yet touched his hay. Eva reached out her hand to him. He sniffed it cautiously before huffing indignantly. The second new horse made Eva grin in delight. He was beautiful, a gelding. Not as tall as the stallion, but he was a muted, dappled gray, with a dark muzzle and mane, a coloration Eva had always found most attractive in a horse. His ears perked up as he munched his hay. He reached out his nose to smell her as she walked up to his door.

"Whose horses are these?" Eva asked a boy passing by with a wheelbarrow of hay.

He shrugged. "Not sure. They came up with some southern fellows last night. I heard someone say they were for the prince."

Eva nodded. The boy continued on his way.

"Well, you would be wasted on Caeris," Eva murmured, patting the dapple gray on his velvety nose. "He hates riding for fun, and you look like you like having fun," Eva said with a smile, unlatching his gate.

"You're taking him out?" Mahone asked.

"Yes. Isn't he lovely?"

"Yes, but you don't know anything about -" He stopped, rolling his eyes, knowing further argument was a waste of breath. "I will see if there is a saddle for him," he said instead. Without moving out of earshot or line of sight, Mahone found a stable boy who fetched all the right-sized tack for the bigger horse. Eva saddled the gelding herself. He was very well trained, standing patiently. He didn't even flick his ears as she tightened the girth.

The new horse was a complete pleasure to ride. They took the back way out of the palace again, the King's Track, Eva called it. Soon they were on the track proper, and Eva could take the new horse through his paces. He flew over the obstacles she set before him. He was exceptionally trained. Not exactly easy to ride - he was very sensitive, so she had to be conscious of the signals she was sending him lest he get confused. Soon they moved in harmony together, and Eva knew she would be at Caeris's feet groveling for him to gift her with the horse. He would still have the stallion after all. The king, who loved horses where his son did not, would help her with her case. Eva couldn't wait to tell King Rhais about the gelding.

They came to the little lake once more at the hottest time of the day and ate from the small pack they'd brought. They took off the horses' saddles to help the hot beasts cool down and let them find what they could among the dry summer grass. Eva was surprised when the gray gelding waded into the lake up to his knees to drink. She remembered he was from the south, and no doubt used to hot weather and cooling off in lakes. She wondered if he would swim and let her ride on his back. She shed down to her small clothes and wandered out into the lake, pulling gently on his rein, talking sweetly to him in a calm voice.

The water deepened gradually with a nice, firm, sandy bottom, no tangling weeds or muck. Mahone lounged on the shore eating an apple, mostly at ease, one eye always cautious. He was caught between laughter and concern when he realized what Eva was trying to do.

Eva ignored her guard. The horse continued to walk into the water, ears perked forward eagerly. He was almost up to his withers when Eva hopped on his bare back, and together they went into the water.

Eva laughed in delight as he began to swim happily along, his feet kicking gently off the bottom, stirring up a silt into the clear, blue water. After a while the horse made for the shore. Eva let him, clinging to his back as he gave a little shake. She dropped to the ground to rummage through her bag for an apple. The horse deserved a reward for such admirable behavior. Eva wished she knew his name. She was tired of calling him Mr. Gray, or Big Boy.

She had the apple in her hand when Mahone suddenly went still. Eva met his worried gaze. She heard it too. Someone was calling them, already getting quite loud.

Mahone relaxed, slightly. "It's Tarek," he said. "Wonder what he is doing here." He grabbed Eva's shed clothing and threw it at her. "He might not be alone."

Eva blushed thinking of what would happen if someone saw her alone with her bodyguard in her scanty undergarments. A person would jump to conclusions.

She hurriedly put her clothes on, but it was no small feat because she was all wet from the lake. She froze in mortification as Tarek came into view from the undergrowth into the little clearing at the lake edge.

He wasn't alone.

Caeris was with him, riding the black stallion, and she was exposed with her tunic barely covering her small clothes. She had not even gotten to her leggings. Caeris saw her instantly, his green eyes brimming with anger.

CHAPTER 11

ILLIAH

WHEN THE SUN FINALLY FILLED THE ROOM with its first light, Illiah was already wide awake. Well, he hadn't really slept. He had tried. He had closed his eyes hoping for sleep to claim him, but something always pulled him from the comforts of sleep, making him toss, making his thoughts circle relentlessly. Reluctant, yet relieved to see the day, he sat up in his bed. His fine, feather-cushioned bed.

Never had he slept - or not slept - on such an exquisite piece of furniture. The mattress was filled with goose down, the blankets thick and silky, woven from a material so fine he slept naked to enjoy the feeling against his skin. His embroidered pillowcase depicted a scene of a hunt: horses, men, and dogs. Illiah fingered it under his thumb, wondering at the hours it had taken some noble lady to create.

He had grown up accustomed to an ample living. His family - his foster family - was wealthy enough to have a comfortable home. But nothing like the palace. It was nothing short of opulent. Illiah wasn't sure how that made him feel. After months of war, and then travel, sleeping on the hard ground, exposed to the elements, he was torn between enjoying such frivolousness and feeling guilty since so many he knew had lost house and home.

Did he deserve it? He pulled his little dagger from under his pillow. He never slept without it close. He turned it over in his hands, feeling the smooth, stone-hard wood, cool and soothing against his rough skin. He could sense the magic in it, reminding him of a slow, resting heartbeat. The dagger looked more blood-red than brown in the morning light. It didn't feel sharp, or lethal, but Illiah knew it was. Oh, Eelan, why did you give me this? The question was not a new one.

He shook his head. He was over-thinking. And he didn't want the guilt to surface. Guilt led to grief that led to pain and he didn't want those thoughts and memories to raise their ugly, carnivorous heads. Over and over he shoved them down deep, into what he imagined was a light-less prison in his mind. But he knew his thoughts were canny criminals. They would always find a way to escape and haunt him.

With the memories of war a distant, albeit sour, tune in his head, Illiah turned his thoughts back to the night before. A much more pleasant memory. He admitted to himself he had been thinking about it all night, replaying the conversation, the expression on the king's face, on Caeris's face. He wanted desperately to believe they were both honest in their affirmation of him as their kin. But he knew, now, how the dagger worked.

Regardless of his doubts, Illiah smiled to remember the day less than two months ago when he met Prince Caeris, his brother - his brother! - for the first time.

The last battle had ended. The invaders had scattered into the hills where they would become trapped between Illiah's army and the sea. Their boats had been burned or sabotaged by Illiah's men before they met in that last bloody battle. The leader had just been captured and killed by Illiah's own hand. His dagger drunk evil blood that day.

Caeris had been two days too late for the last and bloodiest battle. Two days. Illiah had been heartsick over it, but he had hardened. He could not change the past. But a niggling voice in his head, similar to a crying child, kept reminding him that if Caeris had come before that last battle, Illiah would not have needed to sacrifice so many of his men.

Illiah's makeshift army had prevailed despite being made of farmers and merchants and the odd man-at-arms. Yet their losses had been great. Caeris's army would have won with fewer casualties; having better armor and weapons would have ensured it. Instead, Illiah walked the paths through the makeshift camp of wounded, comforting those he could, holding a hand here, wiping a brow there. When Caeris arrived, he brought skilled surgeons, but for most it was too late. Infection and fever had already set in. Not even the most skilled healers could help them.

The prince arrived in all his state, wishing to meet with the leader of the southern army - a great hero, they called him. When Illiah entered the prince's camp, he couldn't ignore the strange looks, tongues muted in blatant disbelief. Only when Illiah saw Caeris and they stood face to face did he begin to understand the odd behavior of the men from Caer Andri.

A full minute - the space filled with the eerie silence of complete and utter astonishment - the two men looked at each other, and it was like looking into a polished mirror.

At first Illiah thought it was a hallucination born of too little sleep and improper rations, perhaps a little too much of Kaile's home-brewed drink. Caeris recovered first and waved everyone else out of his tent, his face pale. Not a hallucination then.

"I can't believe what I am seeing before me," Caeris said. "What is your name, your place of birth?"

Illiah stumbled over words as he told the prince about his family, horse breeders, the finest in the area, though they were not his family by blood. He told the prince how he had been found as an infant along the road beside the dead body of a peasant woman. No one knew where he had come from, or the dead woman, but his foster mother, who at the time was due to have a baby within the month, wanted to adopt him.

Caeris listened intently, his eyes glinting. Illiah fell quiet, eyes still locked on the prince, his mind so shocked he could barely compre-hend the situation. He looked at the other's eyes. They were the same green. There was the same nose, the same lips, the same brown hair so dark it was almost black. They stood the same height, the same stance, the same, the same. Even their hair was cut in the same short style Illiah found best suited for camp living.

"Come. Sit," Caeris offered, gesturing to a travel stool. Caeris sat on another stool, opposite him at the camp table. There was a bottle of wine. He poured them each a cup. Illiah took only a little, having already drunk a little more than was good for him earlier that day - and the day before. He took a sip of liquid courage. It was very good wine.

"It is well known that my mother gave birth to twins," Caeris said in a quiet, thoughtful voice.

Illiah almost choked on his wine. It caught like fire in his throat. Even a hero couldn't spit wine all over a prince.

"My father told me one baby died. Could it be possible that it didn't die? Could you be that baby? My brother? My twin?" Caeris's voice barely hinted at the awe shining in his eyes.

"Ah." Illiah was at a loss for words. The prince thought he was his brother? A long-lost twin? It was a likely explanation. It also explained some other things. But at the moment he couldn't mull over the possibilities. His stomach roiled. He felt almost ill. Too many spirits - damn you, Kaile - too many emotions.

"There can be no other explanation," the prince said. "We must ride home, quickly. You must meet my father. We must ask him what he thinks, although I can see no alternative. Surely the woman you were found with must be connected to our parents somehow. Already my mind turns to reasoning. A midwife perhaps, who stole you for her own? Someone out to enact revenge upon the king? Or my mother?" His words tumbled as his thoughts overcame him.

Illiah pinched his eyes shut. The precipice of sanity and decrepitude closed to a narrow gap he was suddenly thrown across. It was like the crash at the end of a long battle, when all the adrenaline has gone, leaving tears and weakness behind. He thought he had already experienced that. It was threatening to overwhelm him again: the feeling that pushes one to give up, to crawl into a hole and never come out. However, people called him a leader, and leaders don't run.

Instead of dashing from the tent into a fox-hole, he took a deep breath and embraced the logistics of his situation. "I can't. The hills are crawling with the invaders still, their leader is gone, but still they must not be allowed to regroup. We must go after them."

Caeris nodded. "Of course, of course. How long do you think it will take?"

"With your army? A week, maybe less."

"Good. We can ride in one week."

"My prince. I must go home, talk to my family. We have been through a hard time."

"Of course," Caeris said again. Illiah could see the excitement in his eyes; Illiah could feel the faintest echo in his.

That day had been the beginning of his new life.

He had always wondered about his real family. Ever since the day his father told him exactly how he had been found and adopted. Although he wasn't by birth a son of Devlin the horse breeder, he had always been loved and accepted as part of the family, a son in all but blood.

Now he was in the house of his birth-father, the king of Jullayah, who had acknowledged him with open arms, wishing to grant him lands, titles, anything his heart desired. In a matter of hours, he would be publicly announced before the entire court. He was to be granted the title of Lord War Commander since he had absolutely no desire to challenge Caeris for the throne. He didn't want an estate. He didn't want riches. He knew they could all be his, easily. He could just reach out his hand and take them. And the dagger would help him. No, he didn't want that life. He just wanted to protect the people, to make sure what happened in the south never happened again. It was why he kept the dagger after all. At least that is what he told himself.

No one would argue over his right to the title. It was impossible to dismiss that Illiah was the son of King Rhais. Even without Caeris as proof, there was a strong resemblance. He still wondered why no one had noticed it over the years. The story of Queen Mellya's twin boys was well known. The heartbreak of the queen was a common tale between empathetic wives. It was something he and Caeris had wondered over on the journey north. He supposed the reason no one had noticed his identical resemblance to the prince was that people from the south rarely went north. And besides his family wasn't that well-to-do. They had no connections with court. Illiah always avoided his foster mother's fancy parties, the only place there would have been a sliver of a chance his likeness to the prince might have been noticed.

The day had barely dawned over Caer Andri. A city unlike any Illiah had seen, or imagined, with its tall walls and righteous architecture. He had only seen it at night. He could only imagine how the city came alive during the day.

Caeris suggested Illiah stay away from the public until the announcement, for obvious reasons. No use confusing the people of Caer Andri needlessly. Though there were sure to be rumors; Caeris's men had seen them side by side. There were only so many tongue-silencing threats to go around.

Illiah didn't want to stay abed until the announcement. He was anxious to check on his horses. They had traveled a long way in a short time.

Caeris had been impatient for Illiah to meet their father. After a brief explanation and good bye to his family, Illiah had come north with only Kaile and a small contingent of Caeris's men. Even Tarran, his young ward, had stayed behind. The poor boy had longed to come along, all but begged. Illiah had hardened his heart and told him he would see him soon enough. Illiah's men would come north soon. He needed them.

Illiah dressed quickly and splashed some cool water on his face to clear his head. He had bathed the travel sweat and grime from his person before seeking out his bed the night before. When not under his pillow, his dagger took residence in his boot. When not in his boot, it was securely fastened to his hip. It was a boot day. The dagger looked pleased as Illiah slid it home.

It was a large room. He counted fifteen paces to the door. He had been assigned a guard by Caeris, not for protection, Illiah could protect himself, but for assistance. The palace was a big place and Caer Andri bigger still. The old guard was a tough, burly fellow with tight lips. He nodded in greeting.

"I need to see to my horses. Can you take me to the stables?"

A grim nod. Illiah had yet to see the seasoned guard smile or look anything but menacing. But he obeyed Illiah's request, and Illiah followed him through the palace, down the winding passages of carved marble, past curved, ornate windows letting in the first rays of morning. It was going to be another beautiful summer day.

He had only seen the palace by night, outlined by lanterns and shadows. It had been beautiful then, the fine craftsmanship clearly visible. Now, in the light of day, it took Illiah's breath away. He had never seen anything like it. Some of the rich villas in the south might have some similar features, but he had only seen them in the war - broken, burnt-out husks, their finery looted or destroyed.

The palace was all but empty. Only servants were about, making their way quietly here and there. Too early for courtiers.

Even the royal stables had their own practical beauty. Illiah inhaled the smell of good hay and well-kept leather. The smell of the oils filled his nose, reminding him of a childhood of cleaning saddles.

He grinned at Penn as the large black stallion stuck his head out of his stall, giving a friendly albeit demanding nicker. Illiah reached up and gave the horse's ears a good scratch. He looked in the box and saw plenty of water and good bedding. It had already been mucked out Illiah noticed approvingly.

He looked next door expecting to see Sasha, but the stall was empty. Dismay filled him suddenly.

"Ah, horsemaster?" he hailed. "Where is my gelding? Has he been moved?" Illiah asked in a rather demanding tone.

The man turned and bowed. "My prince! I don't know where he has gone, but I will ask the stable boy."

"If he was stolen -" Illiah warned, angry. This was the royal stables. He had been assured his horses would be well looked after. Perhaps someone took him for a ride. The thought was just as irritating. Sasha was young, still being trained, training that could be damaged by an inexperienced rider.

The horsemaster gave a nervous bob as he ran off calling the name of the stable boy. They both returned within minutes.

"Tell the prince where his horse is," the horsemaster demanded, glaring at the young boy as if it was his fault that the horse was missing.

"Lady Evangeline took him out," the boy said, wincing as if he expected a blow.

Illiah cursed. A lady. The name sounded vaguely familiar. A noblewoman Caeris had mentioned, no doubt. A noblewoman who assumed she could take out whichever horse pleased her. His irritation rose.

"It's all right, lad, not your fault," he added, seeing the look the horsemaster was giving the young boy. "Where did she go?" It would do no good to ask the horsemaster who this lady was. Surely Prince Caeris, whom they thought he was, knew every lady in court. Especially from what Illiah had seen of his brother's habits with women.

"I don't know, my prince," the boy said shaking his head. "It was the lady and her guard, Mahone. Tarek, her other guard, might know. I can fetch him if you like?" he offered.

"Yes. Thank you," Illiah said, wondering what kind of fine lady requires at least two personal guards.

"My lord, there is no time," Grim-face reminded Illiah. Illiah gritted his teeth. He couldn't run after his horse. The assembly. The announcement. He had to prepare himself, dress appropriately. He couldn't run off into the unfamiliar countryside. He was about to be acknowledged as royalty.

"Fine. After the assembly then. Young horsemaster," the boy preened at the title, making the old man frown. "Can you find Tarek for me and bring him to Grim - err Hapti here?" He nodded to his guard.

"Of course."

Illiah nodded his thanks and went moodily back into the palace to dress for the assembly.

He was irked about his horse. But after breakfasting with Kaile on fresh fruit, pastries, and anything they might wish for, he found himself distracted. He was glad his foster brother had agreed to come with him. Kaile was a humorous man and kept him from being overcome with nerves.

Illiah found a box of clothes in his room. Clothes fit for a prince. He wondered if they were from Caeris's own closet because conveniently they wore the same size. Illiah had to admit it felt good having a real brother. Not that he didn't love Kaile, his foster brother who was almost like a twin, they were so close in age, or his other foster brothers. But Caeris was his brother by blood, and that meant something too. And already the warmhearted king loved him like a son.

Illiah dressed. The pants were loose. He pulled the belt tighter. It was one difference between himself and his brother. He had a little less meat on his bones. Skinny, he had been called, but wiry was more apt. He had spent the better part of the last six months in the fields of war living on harsh rations when he had an appetite to eat them. Caeris was used to a much more comfortable existence. Illiah wouldn't hold it against him. His light weight made him light on his feet and had saved his skin many a time.

His father, was waiting for him just outside the great hall where the court gathered in expectation. Caeris had explained to Illiah how their father had taken ill a few years back. He had almost died and now was not a strong man. The shortest walks tired him. Illiah was secretly touched the king made an effort to walk with him into the assembly.

He leaned heavily on a sturdy staff, grinning as he saw Illiah, his eyes crinkling.

"You look just like Caeris! If it weren't for the lack of a few pounds around the middle and that beard of yours, I would have to ask who was before me now," the king said with a proud guffaw. Illiah fingered his short beard. Caeris had asked him to keep it. Caeris was shaved - this way his subjects would be able to tell them apart. Illiah grinned back at the king, taking his arm without hesitation.

"Thank you, my son," King Rhais added smugly. Caeris was already in the great hall before his court. The prince would stand before his court, announce Illiah, and only then would the king and Illiah make an entrance. Illiah found his stomach a knot of nerves. He had prepared for countless battles, but this was different. Facing one's death was almost easier. He said as much, making the king laugh.

"Court is never easy. They will judge you, hate you, love you. Just ignore them and get on with what needs doing," Rhais said reassuringly.

"With your permission, I intend to."

"You are already a hero, and a prince, even if you forgo the title. You can do no wrong. Shall we go down?"

Illiah nodded, taking a deep breath. The king spoke more truth than he would ever realize. Illiah could do no wrong, not while he possessed the dagger. So why did he feel like a swarm of catterflies was feasting on his innards? There was no turning back.

Illiah didn't hear what Caeris said as his nerves muffled his ears, but the king led him onto the dais in front of the entire court in the great hall.

A sea of people, rippling colors of finery, swayed before him. They were silent, probably in shock. They recovered quickly, and hushed voices filled the air. Illiah guided the king to his throne before standing beside his brother. Caeris was grinning proudly. Beyond him was Kaile, and Lord Serac, looking more haughty than normal. Illiah had spent some time with his cousin, Caeris's closest adviser, when Serac had been sent to escort him. Illiah was not impressed with the man who was his kin.

"Kneel for Lord Illiah, my twin brother," Caeris said, his strong, vibrant voice echoing through the hall, rising above the drone of excited voices. Illiah bowed formally before them, a smile dancing on his lips despite his nervousness. "Lord War Commander and Lord of the Keep," Caeris continued. "In honor of this day, the king and I have a gift for you, brother."

Two men brought out a long box. They placed it at Illiah's feet and opened it. Behind a layer of velvet lay a longsword. Illiah picked it up, pulling it from its sheath of etched leather. Was that Kitarran steel? The craftsmanship was exquisite. He held it in his left hand, his sword hand. For the length of it, it was remarkably light. For all its shining beauty, Illiah knew it was a weapon of death, crafted for the battle-field. What he wouldn't have given to have had it six months ago.

Illiah slipped the weapon back into the sheath and turned to his brother, his hand over his heart in gratitude. He was at a loss for words, but gave his prince a bow. His eyes were prickly with unshed tears.

The crowd erupted with cheers. Illiah was suddenly being patted on the back, his hand grasped. Everyone wanted to see him up close, see him next to the prince. Illiah followed Caeris's lead, nodding politely, shaking a hand here, saying a friendly word there. Caeris introduced him as the people came again and again. Illiah would never remember all their names. He stopped trying almost right away; time for that later.

"This is the Lady Clarette of Ullian," Caeris said, introducing Illiah to a middle-aged woman of exceptional beauty and bearing. Illiah would remember her. She had a sharp intelligence about her, scruti-nizing him in a way that made him feel naked, reminding him of his foster mother.

"My lady," Illiah took her hand in what he hoped was the right fash-ion. He had no training for such etiquette. His foster mother, if she could see him, would be caught between shameful tears and amused laughter, all her lessons in manners blatantly ignored.

"My lady, where is your niece. Where is Eva, my betrothed?" Caeris asked the lady. Illiah could hear the edge in Caeris's voice. Eva. Evan-geline. The prince's betrothed - of course, that is where he heard the name. Eva the horse thief.

Clarette looked nervous. "I don't know, my prince. Evangeline is out riding, I think. I was told she left just past daybreak." Her voice was laced with exasperation. "It was such a sudden announcement, the assembly. She is always up earlier than the rest of court. Tarek had no time to fetch her. Please forgive her."

Caeris gave no answer but it was clear to even a lady like Clarette that she was dismissed. Illiah found himself wondering about this young woman betrothed to his brother who had stolen Sasha. He wanted nothing more than to find her and get his horse back. The great hall, even for its immense size, was getting stuffy. Even Caeris felt it. He called an end to the assembly, assuring the courtiers who had not yet had a chance to meet the new prince that a grand feast was planned for the evening. Caeris gestured for Illiah to leave. He took the king's arm himself and they exited the room.

Illiah excused himself, making his way back to his room. He changed into his riding clothes, kept the new sword at his hip, his dagger stayed in the boot.

There was a knock at his door. He opened it to see a tall, muscular guard dressed like a man who doesn't want to draw attention. His face was a criss-cross of aged yet nasty scars. The man was formidable even without the scars. He had that look about him that screamed skill and subtlety. Illiah knew this was a man who could easily disappear into the shadows and take you out with his knife in an instant.

"You must be Tarek," Illiah said, already walking down the hallway toward the stable. Tarek fell in step beside him. "Lady Evangeline stole my horse." Princes had no need to mince words.

"My lord, ah, I am sure she had a reason for doing so. She could not have known it was yours. She had not even met you or known of your existence," Tarek said in a surprisingly smooth voice.

Illiah looked at the guard with more perception. "Didn't I pass you last night in the halls? You and another man, and a young lady - that was Lady Evangeline?" Illiah said, realizing it to be the truth. He had seen her last night. At the time he had thought it odd for a young lady to be running around close to the dead of night with only her guards. It had been a fleeting thought. He had had others to distract him. Now he remembered the encounter clearly. How Lord Serac had stopped her, grabbed her arm in a forceful manner. His cousin had obviously been annoyed with her. Poor girl, she was not making any friends with her antics. Illiah tried to recall her face to mind. All he could remember was that she had striking pale, messy hair.

"Do you know where she went?" Illiah asked Tarek.

"I think so, my lord," Tarek replied in a guarded voice.

"Good. Take me to her."

They saddled up. Penn was eager to get out of the box, which didn't surprise Illiah. Tarek saddled up his own mount, a dun charger as rangy as he was.

The hills around Caer Andri were quaint, with little forests and villages, farms and inns. Not all that different from the south, but even in midsummer, there was still so much green.

From a rise, he could see the river beyond the city. He could look to the south where far away his home had once been, where his foster family, like so many others, were starting the hard work of rebuilding their lands. The south was home no longer. Now Illiah was a man of the north. He looked north to the mountains where he had been told his new home, the Keep, lay hidden, almost secret. Soon he would go there to start his work as War Commander, but not yet.

"This way," Tarek said, urging his mount onto a path that was hardly even that. It wove through a forest thick with logs to jump, ditches to climb. Illiah fretted over Sasha.

They rode until the city and palace were in the hazy distance. They crossed fields and more woods, over little winding creeks. They came to another more densely wooded area and rode under the trees for a time. Tarek called out as the trees thinned.

Illiah could see a small lake through the remaining trees. The water was startlingly blue. Tarek slowed his pace and called out again. The trees disappeared into a clearing where grass grew plentiful, turning to sand as it met the lake: a picturesque place. Illiah could see two horses. Sasha stood placidly, coat gleaming in the sun, wet from being in the lake. Illiah grumbled. Then his attention was drawn to the girl standing beside his horse. She stood clutching her clothes to her chest, her tunic becoming damp beneath her long wet hair.

She stared at him with wide, anxious eyes. He seemed to be interrupting something. A man had been lounging on the beach, his tunic undone, his feet bare. He stood up quickly with the agility of a fighter. Her other guard, Illiah supposed.

"What is going on here?" Illiah asked.

Her hair was still messy, a strange shade, almost white. Her eyes were large and green-blue, the same color as the lake behind her. She was not tall, nor soft, but Illiah couldn't help but admire her contours, exposed as they were. She blushed prettily. Illiah almost felt guilty he had embarrassed her. Then he remembered he was angry with her.

The second guard approached him saying something. Illiah realized he was staring and turned away from her to her guard, whom Tarek introduced as Mahone.

"This is not what it looks like, my lord," Mahone said, concerned for the lady's reputation. Illiah knew things were more traditional in the north, but didn't Caeris insist on parading his mistress about? From the very little Illiah knew about Caeris's betrothal, it was an arranged marriage. Caeris had told him he did not love the woman his father had chosen for him. What this woman did with her own lovers was none of his concern.

"No! No," the girl said rather loudly. "I was just swimming." She looked terrified. Of course, she thought he was Caeris.

Illiah looked back to the lady briefly. His face twitched into a smile before he looked expectantly at Tarek.

Tarek cleared his throat. "You were missed at court this morning, Eva. The prince called an assembly. He had an announcement to make, a rather important one at that. It's a long story. He told it this morning to the entire court. In summation, it turns out while Caeris was in the south campaigning he came upon his long-lost twin brother: this is Lord Illiah," Tarek explained. "My lord, this is Lady Evangeline."

Evangeline looked at him dumbly. He couldn't blame her; it was a shocking way to find out.

"You're saying this is not Caeris?" Evangeline repeated.

Tarek nodded.

"This is his brother?" Another nod.

"Queen Mellya had twins, and one died," she was saying, almost to herself. Her eyes held an eerie, faraway look.

"He didn't die," Tarek said.

"He was stolen. I'm right here," Illiah said, feeling ignored. He dismounted, tired of feeling like he was looming over everyone from Penn's high back. Tarek had dismounted as soon as he had come into the clearing.

Evangeline turned her beautiful eyes onto him, her expression assessing. Illiah could see her mind working in her gaze and wondered what she was thinking.

"You look just like him," she said quietly, taking a step closer to him. Now that he had dismounted she no longer had to crane her neck upward to look at him. She still had to tilt her head, because, like Caeris, Illiah was tall, a good head taller than she. She studied him, her eyes searching. Illiah held her gaze, saw the briefest of shadows there, curious about what caused them.

"Are you done inspecting me?" he asked with a hint of humor. The girl cleared her throat and turned away.

"Sorry," she said, still holding her leggings over her barely clothed body. "Can you let me finish dressing?" A deep blush returned to her cheeks that made her look like a young girl. It was really very hard to stay angry with her.

The three men turned and waited until she had shrugged back into her clothes. She was pulling on her boots when she gave them the okay. "It was you last night wandering the halls with Serac, wasn't it?" she asked as she pulled at her wet hair, braiding it quickly down her back.

"It was," Illiah replied. "I won't ask what you were doing at such a late hour."

"I am fond of riding. We were out all day," Evangeline replied fiercely, also reminding Illiah of his foster mother, or perhaps his sister - both women with a reputation for fiery tempers.

"I see that. You stole my horse," Illiah said not bothering to hide his exasperation. "I went to the stables this morning as soon as I could to check on them, but Sasha was missing." His voice sounded stern. Good.

"They are your horses?" the girl replied, eyes down, fingers fiddling with her necklace.

"Yes."

"I thought they were gifted to Caeris," came the glum admission.

"The prince doesn't really enjoy riding. My father, my foster father, that is, wouldn't exactly give his horses away to a man who does not value them, even if he were the crowned prince."

"Have you met the king? Your real father?" Eva abruptly changed the subject. She didn't seem to be deflecting. She sounded genuinely curious.

"Of course. I met him last night. I was on my way there when we ran into you in the hallway."

"What did he say?" Not that it was any of her business, but he answered her anyway. He couldn't help but smile at the tone in her voice.

"He remembered when we were born, Caeris and I. The midwife told him that one baby died. The king told me how the queen was heartbroken. He never saw the dead baby's body. He just accepted that he - I - had died, which happens often enough. He thinks now that the midwife stole me. She disappeared from Caer Andri soon afterward. My foster father told me I was found along the roadside, next to the body of a woman who fit the king's description of the midwife. Even after twenty-one years, he still remembers that night clearly. Incredible, isn't it? He was naturally overjoyed to meet me, as was Caeris."

His brother's betrothed looked thoughtful.

"I like the name Sasha," she said changing the subject once more, turning to the big gray horse standing still beside her. She patted the horse's neck with affection. Illiah stiffened, indignation rising once more.

"My lady, since you are my brother's betrothed, I am compelled to forgive you, but please do not ride my horse again," he told her sternly. The look she turned on him was nothing short of a challenge.

"How am I to get home then?" She demanded with a flash of anger. "Clinging to the back of one of my guards?"

"It doesn't look like you would mind that," Illiah replied lightly, teasing her. She took it too seriously. She had a murderous glint in her eye. Illiah couldn't feel guilty about it. She was a bit irritating, confident, opinionated, rash.

"Don't insult me," she snapped.

"Don't worry, your secret is safe with me," he said, still smiling. He felt the steely gaze of her two guards. He didn't take his eyes off the lady, but he knew if he were not a prince, he would be treading dangerous ground by antagonizing her.

"I rode him here, I can ride him back."

"He is still being trained. I don't want his careful training ruined by a heavy hand."

She opened her mouth to say something but closed it promptly. Perhaps his stern expression stopped her tongue as she conceded. Illiah could feel her anger radiating. Perhaps it was her sense of injustice halting her words. She truly believed she was a good enough rider. Not even Illiah's own sister would be allowed to ride his horse, and Freya had grown up in the saddle.

Evangeline saddled up Sasha with a deftness that surprised him, not that he would admit it. When she was finished, she handed the reins to Illiah meekly enough, but her eyes were still sharp. Illiah watched her mount up behind Tarek, looping her hands through his belt.

"Take us home. As fast as possible," she muttered to Tarek, giving Illiah one last, reproachful look.

Tarek muttered something about not wanting the new prince to lose his way. He was expected at the grand feast after all. The guard's sincerity was questionable. Well, it was heartening to know his magical dagger didn't influence everyone.

CHAPTER 12

EVA

"EVA! WHERE HAVE YOU BEEN? Out riding? You are incorrigible," her aunt said as soon as Eva stepped into their shared apartment. "Did Tarek fill you in? Do you know what Caeris announced this morning?"

"He told me. I still can't believe it."

"Just wait until you meet Lord Illiah. He looks just like Caeris. There can be no arguing that they are not brothers - twins!" Clarette said.

Eva didn't bother to correct her aunt that she had already met the new prince. The less said about that, the better. She still felt riled after her brief encounter with the Caeris impostor. She still wasn't sure if she believed it. Not until she saw them side by side would she really believe it.

Clarette insisted on dressing immediately for the grand, celebratory feast planned for that evening. She wanted the prince's betrothed to make a good impression for her soon-to-be brother-in-law. Eva thought glumly that the new prince had already seen her twice at her very worst. Once in her small clothes! She shuddered and went red at the thought.

"Why does he go by Lord Illiah, instead of Prince Illiah?" Eva asked as the thought occurred to her.

"Apparently, he prefers 'lord.' The prince thing is too strange to him. Plus he has no interest in being a candidate for king. Maybe he dislikes titles. He grew up practically a peasant. Caeris has made him War Commander, so lord is just as appropriate."

"My father's old position?"

Clarette nodded. Eva groaned inwardly. More unfavorable changes in her life.

"Yes, Lord Illiah is the great war hero from the south, the one man who gathered farmers and arborists together to fight off the invaders! Great things are said about him," Clarette said excitedly, a flurry of fine fabric following her around the room.

"Honestly, Auntie, where do you find these things?" Eva said as her aunt laid another new dress on her bed. The dress was quite demure, in light creams, greens and lavenders. Usually, her aunt picked bold colors, reds, yellows, blues. The fabric was heavy with laces up the bodice. Eva didn't relish the thought of being tied into the dress like a prisoner of war.

Clarette smiled. "I know you have next to no interest in picking out new dresses, but that doesn't mean I can't have my fun. I had Corianne sew this one up for you. It was exceedingly fortunate that it was ready yesterday. I can't believe the good timing," she added with a smirk. Eva rolled her eyes at her aunt's fondness for looking beautiful.

An excessive knock came at their door making them both jump. Mahone's hand leaped for his belt knife. He opened the door, revealing an uneasy-looking messenger. Eva saw the black feather on his shoulder and knew the boy was a servant of Lord Serac. Fear cascaded across her gut for an instant before she mastered it.

"Lord Serac wishes to speak with Lady Evangeline. He is waiting in the council room," the boy announced. "He urgently requests that you come."

"What could Serac want that is so urgent?" Clarette chided.

The boy stood there with no answer.

"I just got in. I will change quickly, and then you can take me to Lord Serac," Eva replied, shutting the door. She exchanged a worried look with Mahone before retreating to her private room to change.

She picked out a fine dress a deep plum color with red embroidery. Eva knew it was striking. She finished combing her hair and left it down. Her reflection in the polished mirror was regal. She wanted Serac to remember she was betrothed to the prince. She was untouchable. She had no illusions about the reason for the summons. She slipped a discreet knife into her soft leather boots.

The boy was still waiting, still nervous. Mahone was waiting on her as well, grim, ready for anything.

The reason for the messenger's agitation became apparent when they entered Caeris's council room. Serac all but pounced on her with thinly contained fury. He was like a wild cat yearning to sink his claws into her.

"Where were you this morning, Eva? You were not at the assembly. The prince's betrothed! You mock your duty. Disgraceful." Something in his eyes terrified Eva. Instinct made her seek out allies. Caeris sat at the council table watching the vehemence of his councilor with a slight expression of surprise. Coward. Couldn't even berate her himself. He let Serac lash into her instead.

Standing beside Caeris was his brother Illiah, his eyes narrowed. So there were two of them. If Eva hadn't been in the process of being wrangled by Serac, she would have been lost looking between the two brothers trying to spot any differences between them. Neither of the princes said anything or made a move. They looked irritatingly, identically remote.

Well, she had no allies except Mahone, and he could not speak up for her. It was her battle. Eva recovered slightly from her shock and tore her eyes away from the brothers to face Serac's volatile accusation. She straightened her back, meeting his gaze levelly.

"You accuse me of lack of duty? I left before any mention of an assembly was made. It was too sudden. You cannot blame me. And what about your duty, Serac? What about your duty to Alline?" Eva replied with as much calm as she could muster. It took all her will to glare back at the haughty lord, suppressing her fear as best she could.

Serac pressed his lips together in an angry line. He grabbed Eva's elbow in one hand, his grasp firm. She wouldn't give him the satisfaction of knowing that it hurt. He all but pushed her into a seat at the table. He didn't sit; he paced, glowering at her. Eva realized she had misjudged Serac badly. He was a soulless wretch. It made her sick to think she had once been angry with the king for dissolving their secret betrothal.

"Do not speak of her." Serac took a deep breath, but his attempt at calm was unconvincing.

"Why? Are there truths you would rather not have known? I know what you are, Serac. I know what you did to her." Now she was the one losing control. Her voice rose in pitch and anger. She could feel the brothers judging her. "You thought you could just take her? You don't deserve anyone." She didn't spit in his face, but she wanted to.

Serac raised his hand to strike her, but Mahone intervened and had a knife poised below Serac's ribs instantly. A shout came from across the table, and Illiah too was poised to stop Serac, his hand on his sword. Caeris remained sitting. His face was stony and unreadable. Eva stood before another word was spoken and stalked out of the council room with her fists clenched at her sides, Mahone close behind her.

Well, she was really making some great impressions.

"I heard you had an altercation with Lord Serac this afternoon," the king said in a soft voice as Eva sat at his bedside, taking his hand in hers. He often sounded so weak, but Eva was heartened by the sense of peace about him. She thought it had something to do with Illiah. She had watched the king at the grand feast just hours earlier. He had attended for a short time, even though it wore on him. He had watched his two sons, identical, already forming a bond of brotherhood.

"He accused me of not doing my duty."

The king's face darkened. Eva wished she had not spoken of it.

"I fear Lord Serac is a man with a festering sliver in his soul. Fara, my sister, was not a good mother to him. I should have helped him, summoned him to court as a child. Not that Fara would have allowed him out of her sight. She was always ... difficult. Controlling. Just ignore Serac. Time will set him right. Caeris is a good influence on him."

Eva worried the king had it the wrong way around.

"You will be a great queen. You look lovely this evening, my dear," Rhais noted, fingering the soft embroidery on the cuffs of her new gown.

"Thank you."

"Now I have two sons and a daughter," he said closing his eyes, savoring the thought.

"We aren't married yet, my king," Eva reminded him with a light laugh.

"Soon enough. Soon enough. Just think of all the grandchildren

I will have! I hope I live long enough to meet them," he said with a snort of laughter. Then he became somber. "Mellya always wanted lots of children. She adored them." He spoke looking into a far-off place, a place he once shared with his true love and queen. "She was so happy when she found out she was pregnant. I remember the day she told me she was positive there was not one baby, but two dwelling inside her body. She was so happy. Fearful too, for childbirth is tricky, but she was such a brave, stubborn little thing." He was silent a few moments. "I remember when she told me one of the babes had died. She was holding Caeris, all wrapped up tight, her face a tragic combination of love, happiness, and dreadful grief. She had one beautiful baby, but not two. Days later, I remember her telling me she felt the other baby was still alive. Somehow she had a strange notion. It haunted her until her death. Turned out she was right. A mother's love knows all. Oh, how I miss her." The king's eyes were wet and bright. He squeezed Eva's hand.

Eva smiled at him, hoping it was comforting.

"But never mind my mutterings. This is a time for action. Illiah has agreed to take on the post vacated by your father, my dear friend. It heartens me greatly. I know he will be a great asset to the strength of Jullayah, and to Caeris. So I have told Illiah he should come to you with all his questions regarding the Keep. I know he will have many, as he will be selecting men to accompany him there this fall to help with the building. No one knows that crazy place like you do."

Eva found she had lost her voice.

"What do you mean, 'building'?" she asked when she was once more able to form coherent thoughts.

"For the men who will go there to train. They never rebuilt the barracks after the fire, remember?" the king said quietly.

"I know. I just - of course, it makes sense - I just didn't think ...," Eva stammered, envisioning the influx of men and commotion in her private, comfortable home of homes. She shook her head. "If Illiah has any questions, of course I can help him."

The king smiled patiently. "Did you enjoy the feast?" he asked, yawning.

"I did, but I am not sure I will enjoy the rest of the summer with all the rumors and conjuncture surrounding your new hero of a son. I can just imagine the ladies going on and on," Eva replied with such honesty, it made the king laugh.

"Yes, I can imagine," Rhais said with a twinkle in his eye. "He seems much more approachable than Caeris. The ladies will find that quite tantalizing, I imagine. But then, what do I know of the ladies these days?" he said with raised brows, his eyes laughing.

More than a month passed since Caeris acknowledged his long-lost brother. The city was still full of impromptu celebrations in the new prince's honor. They loved him instantly. Illiah could be seen everywhere, telling stories of the war, talking business with the lords, walking with his foster brother Kaile in the gardens with a flock of silly young women. Honestly, if Eva heard the name Lord Illiah one more time, she would scream. Lord Illiah did this. Lord Illiah thinks that. Argh.

Eva was invited to a party hosted by Lord Barim in the Temple District. She couldn't rightly say no. She declined the last invitation she had received, and her aunt reminded her she could not avoid every party.

Lord Barim's house was large, a stately, sprawling expanse thick with courtiers. Every hallway and nook hosted its own group of whispering women and scheming men. Lord Illiah was the guest of honor. Thankfully he didn't speak to her or acknowledge her. Eva smiled and danced and pretended interest in things that did not interest her.

She left early. No one noticed.

Caer Andri was a beautiful city. Eva couldn't help but admire the architecture illuminated by shadows of the setting sun. The red light glared off the glazed windows like fire. A fiddler on the corner played a slow tune that was joyful and sad all at once.

Eva crossed the Temple Square, blissfully empty but for several lingering nobles. The market was closed, the stalls hooded and the wares locked away. Eva heard a metallic clang that almost sounded musical. She turned to see the gates of the Temple had closed. The sun had gone down. She shivered. The Temple wall was gray and ominous without the sun to warm it. The gate was solid and awful.

Eva continued on her way. Tarek and Mahone stayed close. A breeze picked up, tossing a piece of crumpled parchment across the cobbles. The breeze tickled Eva's face and pulled at her hair.

Eva heard a scream, faint and utterly heart-wrenching. She stopped so suddenly, Tarek and Mahone almost clipped her heels.

"Did you hear that?"

"Hear what, my lady?"

"I heard a scream."

"Are you sure?"

"No." Eva listened. She heard it again, but not just a scream, a cry, a plea for help. Words.

Please stop, please stop … Please, please.

Eva could feel the magic of the *simul rami* tangled in the words. Her heart leapt. A vercuri? Eva spun; the wind circled with her. She stopped, facing a narrow alley. Twilight had descended, the sun had relinquished its hold on the world, and the shadows grew. Something was in the darkness, something more solid than shadow. Eva reached down and put her fingers to it.

"Mahone, Tarek, this is blood," Eva whispered.

"Blood?" Mahone was instantly to her side. Tarek took up the position of sentinel.

Eva rubbed the blackish smear between her fingers, gritting her teeth. She gathered her strength, following the trail to a hooded doorway. Twilight had fled the spot early, swallowed by the shadow of the wall. She saw something - someone - crumpled on the ground. A still figure swamped in fine fabric, a lady. Not a vercuri.

"Mahone," Eva called loudly. "Here. It's a young woman. She is unconscious. We must get help." Eva felt for a pulse, kneeling beside the lone figure, cupping the pale, blood-smeared face in her hands. The heartbeat was weak under her fingers. "You must carry her."

A tangle of black curly hair fell around Eva's fingers, smelling of sweet herbs and - other things. Eva bit back a curse. Mahone shot her a glance filled with trepidation.

"Look at her arms." Eva took a slender arm carefully in hers, the skin marred by deep, purposeful cuts, blood trickling like tears from the clefts.

"Eva, I think she is -" Tarek started, glancing at the girl Mahone was carefully lifting off the dirty ground.

"What? A prostitute? Probably," Eva agreed sharply. It was a logical conclusion. The young woman's dress was fine, but the bodice was roughly laced, like she had dressed quickly. Her attire was far from suitable at court, the bodice cut too low, her shoulders bare. Eva balled her hands into fists to stop them from shaking. "She needs help. It doesn't matter who she is."

"No one will take her. She is as good as dead." Tarek's voice was sad.

"We will take her. I will heal her myself," Eva retorted acidly.

Her guards were silent a moment.

"Fine. But best be discreet about it. Lady Clarette won't want this to touch her," Mahone cautioned. Eva nodded.

Stealth was something Eva had worked at over the years. She had managed many times to sneak away from her watchful guards at the Keep when she wanted to get into the Great Forest.

They were not far from the palace, and Eva knew the king's secret ways. They moved carefully. Mahone carried the girl, Eva and Tarek on guard for anyone, servant or courtier. They must not be spotted. Eva was thankful most everyone would still be distracted by Lord Barim's party.

Even without Mahone's reminder, Eva knew the girl was not welcome in polite society. Polite society indeed. A society that masked cruelty and violation with pretty words and titles. It was no coincidence they found the girl in the richest district of the city.

When they reached the rooms Eva shared with her aunt, Eva breathed a sigh of relief to see Clarette was not in residence. With her aunt's guards attending their lady at the party, it was easy to sneak the girl into Eva's private rooms.

Eva instructed Mahone to put the girl on the couch in Eva's bedroom. Eva pulled off the girl's cloak to see her dress was ripped in places and smeared with blood.

The girl had two long cuts, one down the length of each arm. They were too perfect, too sharp to be caused by some accident. Someone had tortured the poor girl. Eva ground her teeth and continued her assessment.

The fair skin was a mass of bruises, her skirts soaked with blood from wounds not obvious to Eva's eyes. The girl's face was pale. She had large shadows below her eyes that fluttered open, her mouth moving. She was trying to say something, but nothing came out. Eva hushed her, putting her hand upon the girl's brow, putting her into a deep sleep with her magic. The girl went limp.

Eva hovered over her, making quick work of her bruises, cuts, and other small abrasions. They all but disappeared under Eva's touch. Eva placed her hand just below the young woman's navel where the worst of the girl's bodily harm lay hidden. The injury was not as severe as Eva though the strange girl had lost a lot of blood. It would leave her weak for a few days. The emotional scars would take longer.

The young woman's injuries were healed, but Eva sensed something else. A subtle ill, a taint with tendrils secured within the woman's whole body, clinging to every fiber. Like a snake, hidden but deadly. Eva tried to pull it from her body, but it flared like a fire in the wind, tearing through the poor girl's body, demanding, coercing. Eva drew back from its intensity, afraid it would pull her in too deep. She turned to Mahone who was watching her with concern.

"There is something here I cannot fix," Eva said, shaking her head. "I don't know what it is."

Mahone didn't have anything helpful to say.

"Mahone, this girl is dying, and I can't fix her!" Eva wailed, pushing back a tear.

Mahone knelt down beside her, next to the sick girl. He pulled back the long, black hair, exposing the girl's neck. Just behind her right ear was a tiny mark etched into the skin. A tiny flower, like a lily, the size of Eva's thumbnail.

"That is the mark of a culla girl. Her body is going through withdrawal from the drug."

"A what? A drug?"

Mahone looked grim, his eyes black.

"She is a slave. Some man found her, drugged her, made her dependent on the drug - a potent herb - to control her. To go more than a day without a dose of culla would most likely cause her death. Not many live through the withdrawal. There are men in the city who have harems of these women they have enslaved. They force them to work as prostitutes. The drug makes them loyal, dependent. Those girls only live a score of years before their bodies waste away," he explained. "By the look of her, she is rather expensive to hire. That dress was very fine. She is young, pretty. She probably hasn't been a culla girl long. That makes her fresh, more desirable, and therefore more expensive. Her patron must have paid an enormous sum for her since he had no intention of returning her alive."

"How can the king allow this to happen?" Eva whispered. It was horrible.

Mahone sighed. "It's hard to control. It has been going on for a long, long time. The king just doesn't have the enforcement. Most of the girls are orphans or runaways, doomed from birth. Many of them go into it willingly, thinking it better than a life on the streets."

"That doesn't make it okay, not nearly so."

"I know," Mahone agreed sadly. "There are many patrons right here at court. If the king could enforce the laws against it, he might wake up one morning with a knife in his back."

Eva was shocked to hear it. Was not King Rhais loved and respected? It had never dawned on her that the loyalty of his subjects was bought, not earned. It terrified her to think of one of his vassals wanting him dead. Caeris would retaliate; they would kill him too. Without a king, chaos would reign in Jullayah. Was a peaceful realm worth the cost of the girls' lives?

"So, what happens now? She dies unless she gets another dose?"

"She is too far gone now. Not even another dose would save her. The drug is leaving her body, her blood. She might die from it or she might be one of those rare, fortunate souls strong enough to live through the withdrawal. Either way, we'll know by morning."

Eva nodded, feeling suddenly overwhelmingly tired. Healing was always draining. She studied the young woman's face, beautiful now that the blood was cleaned away and the angry bruises gone. She had well-shaped features and long, curling black hair, delicate skin with a hint of freckles. She looked asleep, but her face was far from peaceful. The gray circles were still heavy under her eyes. Her skin was clammy and had a waxy sheen.

"You don't look so well yourself," Mahone said.

"I'll be fine. I just need to lie down."

Mahone nodded. "When Tarek comes back, he can help watch over the girl."

"Thank you, Mahone. I just hope we can keep this from Clarette. You are right, she wouldn't approve. I guess just try to keep her out of my room."

"I am the soul of discretion. Tarek too."

"Thank you. I am lucky Clarette found such loyal bodyguards for me." Eva had never spoken more truth.

CHAPTER 13

EVA

"WHAT DO YOU WANT? Why am I here? Where is Lord Serac? Where is my sister?"

The girl's voice shook as she shivered. She was very much awake, her eyes darting around the room. Eva approached the young woman with a caged, wild animal in mind.

Serac. An image flashed in Eva's mind of the girl as Eva found her - the cuts, bruises, the lacerations to the young woman's sexual organs. Her mind created the picture of Serac looming over the girl with a knife, her own blood dripping from the blade. The girl cowering in pain and fear, her eyes glazed by the drug. Serac's other hand untying the laces of his pants. "I own you, culla girl." Serac's voice echoed in Eva's mind amplified by her pounding heart. He was a monster.

Eva found her voice with difficulty. "It's okay. You're safe. I found you. You were hurt. I brought you here so you would be safe."

"Why? Why would you do that? So Serac can have some more of his fun?" Her voice was weak and strained, but the anger was clearly audible.

Eva frowned. "No, of course not. I brought you here because you were hurt. I would hope that if I were in your situation, someone would stand up to help me. I am a healer, of sorts."

Now the young woman was afraid she told a secret not meant for telling.

"You don't have to worry about Serac. Serac cannot hurt you anymore. I am Lady Evangeline. You have my protection. These are my guards. They are loyal to me. They will keep you safe."

The girl's eyes briefly took in the two guards in the shadows before she narrowed her eyes at Eva. "You are betrothed to Prince Caeris. Caeris and Serac are kin."

"I speak the truth. You are safe here," Eva repeated. "Yes, I am betrothed to Caeris, but I know what kind of man Serac is. The only favor I would do for that man is give him a swift death."

The girl looked eager to believe it, but her eyes were still haunted. She lost focus. "He has been - worse - lately. Serac is a patron of mine, he bought me - and my sister." Her face was hollowed and pale. "She is only ten." Large crystalline tears trickled from her eyes. Eva felt a hard lump in her gut. Ten years old. A child. Damn Serac.

The girl noticed her arms devoid of cuts or scars.

"What did you do to me?" she asked in confusion, her voice shaking as her shivers turned into convulsions. She retched, but nothing came up. Eva put her hand to the girl's brow to calm her, wishing she could draw out the effects of the drug like any sickness.

"Hush. I told you I was a healer. You need to sleep, conserve your strength. The culla is fighting your body for control. Only one can win, you know this," Eva said, not unkindly.

"Murryn, my sister. My little sister," she muttered as Eva forced her into sleep, hoping it would aid the girl's fight.

Eva looked to Tarek. His eyes were dark, dangerous.

"We need to find her sister," Eva told him.

Tarek didn't nod, but his face was grim.

It was a long night. Eva slept for part of it, but fitfully. Mahone left to take what sleep he could. Tarek was there, silent, watchful, a reassuring figure in the still night. At dawn Mahone came in to spell him, waking Eva from a disturbing but forgetful dream.

Eva tensed with apprehension when she noticed Mahone was not alone - Darys was with him. The captain of Ullian looked across the room at the girl and back to Eva.

"Don't look so hostile, Eva. I'm not here to berate you," Darys said quietly, a smile in his voice. "I can help, if the girl lives. Mahone told me she is doing well, considering. That would be thanks to you, I imagine." Eva's heartstrings warmed once more toward the captain.

Eva grimaced. "I can't get rid of the culla."

"Don't beat yourself up about it. You have done more for this girl than anyone else would."

"That's part of the problem."

Darys nodded in agreement, glancing at the still figure on the couch. "Lady Clarette dislikes the use of culla girls. She will not exactly object to this. However, she will worry about her reputation if it is learned she is harboring prostitutes. So I suggest if this girl lives, we pretend she is Tarek's sister and bring her back to the Keep. She can be your lady-in-waiting. I think Clarette will approve of that."

Eva rolled her eyes. As if she needed a handmaid. But it was a good plan, and Eva told him so. He nodded curtly in acknowledgment, looking at the girl one more time, his jaw tight. Eva could feel his anger and outrage echoed in her heart.

"I'll inform Clarette about our guest myself if she lives," he continued.

"She has a ten-year-old sister. They were both sold to Lord Serac," Eva told the captain.

Darys's sharp indrawn breath told Eva of his shock.

"What are you going to do?" Darys asked Eva.

"I am going to bring her here."

"How are you going to achieve that, missy?"

"I don't know yet."

Darys nodded. "You are a clever girl, with strong, clever guards."

"Thank you, Darys. For everything."

"Not a problem." He flashed her an easy smile as he left.

The next time Eva examined the young woman, it was clear she had been through the worst of the withdrawal. Her face held more color, her breathing easier. Eva thought she would live.

"I think she will sleep for a while longer. I am expected at breakfast with Lady Brenah," Eva told Mahone.

"I'll send someone to get Tarek so he can accompany you," Mahone said sternly, leaving the room to speak to one of Clarette's guards.

"Poor Tarek," Eva crooned when he walked into the room hardly five minutes later. He didn't really look tired, but Eva knew he had had only a couple hours of sleep. She began to regret the necessity for breakfast.

"Nonsense. I hardly need to sleep," Tarek assured her looking glum.

"Send someone for me if she wakes," Eva instructed.

After a perfectly dismal breakfast with Lady Brenah and her daughters, where the Lord Illiah's chorus was sung in tuneless, exaggerated fealty, Eva was back in her room.

She closed the door behind her, leaving both Tarek and Mahone on the other side so she was alone with the girl. The mysterious young woman was standing, gazing out the window, a blanket pulled around her shoulders. She heard Eva enter and swiveled around, her eyes fearful. She relaxed slightly as she recognized Eva.

Eva gave her a little smile. "Good morning. Are you hungry?" Eva gestured to the table of uneaten food Mahone must have brought her.

"No, thank you, my lady," she added, looking down at the floor. "My stomach still feels uneasy," she said awkwardly. "My name is Mila, by the way. And thank you for saving my life." She smiled weakly, her voice riddled with tremors.

"You're welcome. Call me Eva."

"You have been exceptionally kind, to help me like you did, my lady, but I must leave now," Mila said taking the blanket off her shoulders, folding it neatly, and placing it on the back of the couch.

"You need to find your sister."

Mila nodded. It was clear she could not speak. Her eyes were wet and bright.

"We will find her together. And, once she is safe, you are both welcome to come with me back to my home as my ladies-in-waiting. If you want. My home is the Keep. It's in the north, against the mountains. It is an old fortress, but it is a good place with good people. You could start a new life there. There would be good, honest work."

Mila put her hand over her mouth to stop her lips from quivering. Her deep blue eyes were tight with longing. A great sob came out, racking her lithe frame. She wrapped her arms around herself to regain her composure.

A scuffle came from the other side of the door. It opened and in came a haggard Darys carrying a large bundle. It took Eva a moment longer than Mila to recognize the bundle as a girl of about ten. Eva noticed the shocking red hair first, then skinny arms and legs.

"Darys!" Eva exclaimed. Mila sobbed in relief. The girl scrambled out of Darys's arms into her sister's. Her face was pale, not just from her complexion. Her eyes were rimmed with red from crying. Her face was like a doll's, just as pretty as her sister, except where Mila had black hair, hers was a vivid red.

"Murryn. Murryn…" Mila chanted her sister's name over and over.

Eva pulled Darys away from the heart-warming scene to berate him.

"Darys!" Eva began. Then she noticed Darys's labored breathing was not just fatigue. "Darys, are you hurt?"

He opened his cloak, and Eva saw a crimson blossom on his gray shirt.

"Heroic fool," Eva muttered as she peeled back his ripped shirt to see a decent stab wound. It must have just missed his lung. She put her hand over the wound and took a deep breath. She knew it would leave her weak and sick, but she had to help him. Selfless man.

When Eva woke, she was on her bed. The two girls sat beside her. Murryn smiled at her while Mila handed her a cup of weak tea.

"Are you okay?" Mila asked.

"I will be fine. Sometimes I faint when I use my - my magic."

"Murryn? Go get some pastries from the table," Mila told her sister. Her sister obliged, moving conveniently out of earshot.

"Is she okay?" Eva needed to know. Murryn looked fine. She skipped to the table with no sign of injury or taint.

Mila nodded, unable to speak, her eyes brimming. "She is fine. He had not touched her - yet."

Mahone came over to Eva.

"You okay?"

Eva nodded, taking a sip of the sweet tea.

"Is Darys okay? Where is he? I want to know what happened."

Mahone grinned. "Of course you do. Darys is attending his lady."

"Did he tell you what happened?"

Mahone nodded.

"Well?"

"Darys broke into Serac's house and found the girl. One of Serac's guards caught him and Darys killed the man. No one else saw him. He has vowed us all to secrecy - to the grave," Mahone said, looking to Mila.

"Serac will know who we are," Mila stated.

"He will blame me," Eva said.

"But he can't say anything. He won't want to announce that he bought two young women. Hiring culla girls is one thing, but keeping them to torture is another," Mahone assured her.

Eva agreed. Serac would be a fool to make it known that he used women the way he did. He was not entirely immune to justice, or at least she hoped.

"Darys, where did you find these?" Eva asked the captain the next morning when he arrived with an armful of dresses.

"Never you mind, missy," he answered with a grin. He put the dresses on the couch. "They are for the new ladies."

Mila and Murryn were happily ensconced in the bath.

"I told Lady Clarette. She is anxious to meet Tarek's sisters, and pleased that you have finally agreed to take on some proper hand-maids," Darys told her. Eva wondered who her improper handmaids were. "She is in the garden waiting on your pleasure."

"Thank you, Darys. Please tell Auntie we will be out shortly."

Murryn was thrilled about the new dress. She held it to her chest and twirled. Mila tried to hide her apprehension.

"Eva, what if someone recognizes me. What if Serac sees me?"

Eva had the same concerns. "I try to avoid Serac as much as pos-sible," she said lightly.

Mila pulled back her hair. "This would prove that I am not who you say," she said, showing the little tattoo.

"I have an idea about that - an unpleasant one, I'm afraid," Eva told her. "I could use a sharp blade, cut back the skin. I have the ability to heal flesh - it would only hurt for an instant. There would be nothing left but a scar, probably not even that."

Mila looked pale. "Are you serious?"

Eva knew it must sound quite mad.

Eva called Tarek and explained what she wanted Tarek to do. Tarek didn't hesitate. He took his sharp dagger from his belt, slid it across the back of his hand, making a perfect cut. Instantly blood started to ooze. Eva wiped it away, placed her hand upon his, and when she withdrew, there was no cut, not even a line on the skin to show where it had been.

Mila's eyes were wide with disgust and shock.

"Best if you don't mention it to anyone," Eva said. "Not very many people know I can do that."

Mila nodded. "Okay, do it."

They went over to the bathing tub. Tarek held Mila's hair; Eva held the dagger. It was very sharp, one quick cut, or more like a slice. Mila's quick indrawn breath was all that told of the sudden pain she felt. Eva pressed quickly on the wound. It was gone almost instantly, just like Tarek's.

Mila looked in the looking-glass. There was a scar - Eva had to cut deep to remove all the ink that was under the skin. It was a faint ragged circle in the soft skin on her neck. A person would have to be very close to see it. A slow smile spread across Mila's lips. Her eyes were wet with emotion.

"Thank you, my lady," Mila said in a quiet voice. "That is a precious gift. I remember the day I got that mark. It felt like a brand, a chain. Now it is gone forever."

"It is nothing. Now let's get dressed and go to the garden with the other ladies, Auntie wishes to meet my new ladies-in-waiting," Eva said with mock enthusiasm.

"Auntie, I want to go back to the Keep."

Eva could see the faint trace of pity in her aunt's steady gaze as she looked over the rim of her teacup. Clarette put the cup down, taking a moment to answer.

"I know things have not been easy for you," Clarette said. "I see how you watch Unalla and Caeris. I know you have a romantic heart." Clarette put her hand on Eva's and gave it a little squeeze. The older woman sighed.

"It's not that," Eva lied. "It is the last year I spend at the Keep, and soon enough Lord Illiah will assume his position there, and it will never be the same. There will be no more quiet."

Clarette smiled. Eva didn't think for one moment her aunt was fooled by her lie, but Clarette was a wise woman and said nothing more about the prince and the woman who carried his bastard child.

"All right. Go. Take Darys, Tarek and Mahone, and your ladies. Spend some time in your beloved Keep before the onslaught of young men descend - Goddess forbid," Clarette told her with amusement.

"Thank you, Auntie, thank you."

A great weight lifted from Eva's shoulders. For the first time in weeks, she felt truly happy, excited.

A wave of guilt swept over her. She had not forgotten Tayeh's task. But she had not felt any pull toward any objects, no sense of otherness. What had Tayeh been thinking? It was impossible to look for something when one doesn't know what to look for. And she needed to be home. She needed to be at the Keep. That was what her senses were telling her.

She could almost smell the musty smokiness of her father's council room. It would be hers only for a little longer. She would soak in the peace and memories of the room while she could, the smells, her father's lingering spirit. Soon enough it would belong to Lord Illiah. And soon enough she would be married to Caeris.

She had hardly spoken three words to Lord Illiah since the first day she'd met him. She still admired his horses whenever she went to the stables or when she passed the practice ring and saw him putting his stallion through his paces, something he did regularly, it seemed, between befriending ladies and communing with lords.

She had seen him the day before with Sasha, his beautiful gelding. She couldn't help but watch. The horse's movements were music personified, the harmony between rider and animal enchanting. She found herself drawn to Illiah's technique, his quiet, capable manner.

At the tourneys held in his honor - that she had been obligated to attend - she had seen him compete with a skill she had never witnessed before. His fighting technique was unique. He beat his adversaries easily. Rumors abounded that the competition had been rigged. Unlikely. Illiah was War Commander for a reason. He had defeated a fearless enemy. He was barely in his third decade. Only a fool would think him unexceptional.

She was tempted to ask him about his technique, but anytime she happened to be in his proximity when he was disengaged, her mind was consumed with reminders of their first encounter. Her face flushed, her voice suddenly abandoned her. It was irritating. He was irritating.

Illiah broke his concentration with his horse and looked in her direction, as if sensing her haughty deference. She held his gaze briefly. She hoped he knew she had not forgiven him his slight to her horsemanship. His insult. It irked her further to see him smile at her. She continued on her way, her face hot.

Darys started preparations for their departure almost immediately. Murryn and Mila prepared eagerly for their journey away from Caer Andri. Eva went to see the king and told him of her plans to leave court early without her aunt.

Rhais looked frailer than ever. Part of Eva recoiled to see the shadow of the king's former self. The light regained in his eyes since Illiah's arrival had dimmed. He had overexerted himself, trying to spend time with his new son and his vassals. He even attended the tourney to watch Illiah compete. Eva knew why the king had gone; the pride in his eyes as he watched his second son was telling enough.

The king was resting, but not asleep when Eva went to him. The smell of lilies was strong in his room, which helped hide the smell of the infirm and sick of the room.

Eva sat beside the king and took his hand. Rhais opened his eyes and gave her a weak smile.

"My lady." The king's familiar voice was soft.

"My king."

"You look like you have news for me. Your eyes look lighter than last time I saw you. What is it, my dear?"

Eva was surprised the king had noticed. As much as she loved him, she believed his intuition lacking.

"I am leaving court early. Tomorrow we will be on our way. I came to say goodbye."

"Your aunt is leaving too?"

"No, just me and my guards and ladies."

"It has been a busy summer. No wonder you are aching to get back to your bit of forest." The king's eyes crinkled in humor.

"And I can help prepare my people for Lord Illiah's arrival, and the arrival of the new recruits. There is much to be done."

"Of course. You are a capable woman."

"Thank you, my king."

"Farewell, Eva. I imagine you have much to prepare. Leave me now. I am quite tired," the king said regretfully as he lifted his hand to pat her cheek. She held his hand there for a moment. Rhais closed his eyes, and Eva left.

That evening at the feast, Eva told herself over and over that it was the last time. On the morrow she would be traversing the northern road. It was the last feast surrounded by dozens of babbling courtiers. The last time sewing herself into fancy, impractical dresses. The last time sitting still for far too long letting Mila do up her hair. The last time in the presence of Caeris's mistress. The last time making small talk with the lords and ladies pretending to be amiable and sweet. The last time for over three seasons. Once she was eighteen there would be no escape. In three seasons she would be forced to accept her fate as queen and give up daydreams of escaping into the wild woods. But until then, she would dream of days under leafy trees.

After the feast, servants moved the tables aside, and the dancing began. Not every feast was followed by dancing, but tonight it seemed that the courtiers were in a particularly boisterous mood and the music was lively and merry.

Eva danced with Darys and several other noblemen, trying to keep a pleasant smile on her face and exude gracious comments to her partners, and trying desperately to avoid Serac. As soon as she deemed acceptable, she pled exhaustion. She took a seat at one of the benches that lined the hall for those wishing to observe rather than participate.

Eva sighed. The dim corner was welcome. The candle nearest to her flickered a little. Eva felt the familiar touch of the *simul rami*, but she hadn't called for it. Something felt odd, like an invisible pulse in the air. It faded and then was gone. She must have imagined it.

She noticed a man sitting close by in pensive silence. She knew the prince's profile, but it was surprising to see Lord Illiah alone for once. Perhaps no one knew he was there.

He caught her eye. Eva looked away, feeling a familiar vexing blush in her cheeks and wished she had sat somewhere else. She took a deep breath and turned back to Illiah, determined to get over her silly reaction to his company.

"You are not dancing tonight, my lord?" she asked him, hoping it didn't sound like an invitation.

"No. I have discovered, over the course of the past few weeks, I am not such a fan of dancing as I first thought."

"So you seek the shadows? Are you escaping from your vassals?" Eva teased him.

His little smile did not reach his eyes.

"The king told me that you are leaving Caer Andri tomorrow," Illiah said.

"Yes, I am." Why the king was discussing her with Lord Illiah, she didn't care to know.

"Do you have some time in the morning, before you go, to discuss the Keep with me? I am told you are an authority on the place." He smiled again, and this time it brought a touch of warmth to his expression.

The Keep. Of course, that made sense.

"We plan to leave early, but if you come to my chamber at first quarter, we can talk."

"Thank you, my lady. I will."

Eva nodded graciously.

"Good night, Lord Illiah," Eva said rising from her seat.

The air around her pulsed slightly, but it faded almost instantly under the heat of her blushing cheeks.

CHAPTER 14

ILLIAH

FIRST QUARTER WAS EARLY. The knock on the door woke Illiah from a light sleep. He had ordered his borrowed serving boy to wake him just before the bells tolled. He hadn't been asleep, not really. His mind was absorbed lately, leaving sleep short and tentative. He welcomed it. Less sleep meant fewer nightmares.

"I'm up! Thank you," he said loud enough for the boy to hear beyond the heavy door. "I'm up," he muttered to himself unconvincingly, rubbing his eyes.

The sun was not yet over the horizon, but the clouds were pink in preparation for a fine day ahead. The air wafting in through his open window smelled of the palace garden where the roses were still in bloom. His mother's roses, he had been told.

He dressed without much care, for once. Strangely, he didn't feel his meeting with Lady Evangeline warranted his best coat and boots. He mulled the thought over, wondering why he felt no need for formality with the future princess. Perhaps it was the begrudgingly early hour. No, that wasn't it, Illiah decided. It was because he had never felt the same judgment from his brother's betrothed that he received from the other court ladies. Evangeline seemed, well, different. He had heard Caeris use the term, without much fondness, for the woman he would marry. Illiah agreed there was something about Evangeline that set her apart from her peers. Something besides her oddly pale hair, a shade of starlight he had never seen before. He couldn't put his finger on it.

If there had not been the incident with her stealing his horse and finding her swimming nearly naked in a secluded wood (he couldn't imagine the other ladies he had met doing so), he might assume she was just like the other court women - poised, beautiful, but a little useless and uninteresting. Lady Evangeline the courtier, the fine lady betrothed to the prince, was quiet and beautiful, like a painting. But Lady Evangeline the horse thief seemed assessing in her own right. Keen intelligence, not judgment, lurked behind her penetrating gaze.

The playful smile she had shown him the night before made him think she may have forgiven him for their first meeting. Unless it was the charm of his dagger swaying her judgment of him. It was not his intention, but he couldn't trust the dagger to be innocuous.

His own anger toward Lady Evangeline had faded quickly. She was not deserving of it. He saw the way she watched Caeris and his mistress. He could see the hurt Caeris inflicted upon his betrothed. Oh, the tender hearts of women.

Court women were odious. He was tired of them. The men as well. He was tired of deciding if their endless attentions and affections were honest or feigned, influenced by the dagger, or just their own agendas. The king and Caeris both tutored Illiah on which men were allies and which warranted watching. Illiah didn't trust his brother's advisers, but he didn't have the authority to advise his brother on such matters, yet. Time would be his ally. He had the dagger, after all. He would observe those he didn't trust from a distance and watch his back.

He wondered what he would do if he had to live at court all year round. Each and every day followed and beleaguered by fussing ladies and questioning lords. He was fairly confident it would drive him mad.

He was told his new holding was secluded. The Keep tugged at his curiosity, kept his mind roving and planning as he lay abed trying to find sleep, trying to keep away the dark.

Illiah gave himself a last cursory glance in the mirror before gathering up the maps and drawings that littered his table. He stepped into the silent hallway to make his way to the apartment of Lady Clarette and her niece. The stone halls were chilled from the lingering night air. The torches had long burned out, and the only light was that of the pale and optimistic dawn.

There were no guards outside Lady Clarette's door, though Illiah's soft knock was answered by the large man Tarek. So it was not exactly unguarded. Not that the women were in danger, but courtiers valued their privacy.

Tarek nodded in acknowledgment, admitting Illiah into the lavish apartment. Illiah faced a large dining and sitting room. Tall windows let in the morning light, tall doors led off on either side to the private rooms. It was all very pretty, a fitting room for two of the king's favorite noblewomen.

The wealth and luxury of the court nobles still took getting used to.

"My lady," Illiah said with a nod to Lady Evangeline - Eva - where she sat at the long polished table with her two ladies. Well, one of her ladies-in-waiting was still a girl. There was a simple breakfast. Eva was pouring steaming tea.

Her appearance surprised him. Her hair was pushed back from her face, coerced into a tidy braid. With the absence of her tumbling hair, the contours of her face looked stark. Her simple woolen tunic covered by a leather jerkin that was too plain for the opulent room. His brother's wife-to-be appeared very young, almost girl-like, her cheeks rosy. But Illiah couldn't help noticing the curves of her body under her tunic belonged to a woman. Her ladies were dressed similarly. He nodded to them in greeting as he took a proffered seat. As he sat, they rose and went to work packing.

"My lord, have you eaten? Please, help yourself," Eva said, gesturing to the table before them.

"Thank you. Call me Illiah, please."

"Sorry about the early hour, but we are hoping to be out of the city within the hour."

"No, it's fine. I have been up early these days, pondering, making plans." Illiah gave her a small smile which was met with her wide, watchful eyes. "I brought these drawings of the Keep. I was hoping you could explain a few things to me."

"Sure. Let's eat first," Eva suggested. "Then we can clear the table."

Practical enough suggestion. The girl was quiet as they ate and Illiah didn't know what to say to her. Her guards were watchful from where they worked with the woman and girl packing as if they didn't trust him.

Illiah didn't know much about the two men, Tarek and - Mahone. He recalled the name of the older, long-haired man after a moment. Neither had participated in the tourneys. He had no idea how skilled they were. Some of Clarette's other men had done well. He had attempted to recruit several for the king's guard, but none were willing to leave their lady's employ. He would expect the same loyalty from these two, even if they weren't exactly part of Clarette's household guard.

Eva finished eating quickly and pushed her plate aside. She picked up one of the drawings, a sketch of the Keep as an artist would draw it, rough gestures and thick lines. Illiah found it with the architect's plans drawn up years ago under the order of Evangeline's father. Her face softened as she studied it.

"Do you miss it? The king told me you spend all winter in that place, that you grew up there."

She looked up at him. "Yes, I miss it. It is my home. Do you miss the south?"

Illiah shook his head. "Not yet. The south can be unbearably hot this time of year."

"You may miss the heat when it is winter and the snows are up to your knees," Eva told him with a smile.

"Yes, I assume it gets cold in the mountains. Strangely, the south can be cold too, at least inland from the ocean."

"Let me see those other drawings."

Illiah laid them out for her and asked her the questions he had been left with after studying them. Her answers were helpful, giving him a better picture of the place, the rooms available, what they would need to do in preparation for the arrival of near one hundred new residents.

"That many?" Eva looked surprised.

"We will begin work almost immediately on the new wing to house the recruits. We will need to get provisions from the nearby villages and farms to store for the winter. You said the store rooms are not used to capacity?"

"The store rooms at the back of the Keep." She pointed to a space behind the kitchens that was not on the plan. "They're huge and hardly used. The spiders will not be pleased to be evicted," she remarked dryly.

"I think we can handle a few spiders."

"We? I don't do spiders," she said with a snort.

"They don't bite, do they?"

"I never give them a chance to find out."

Illiah grinned at the tone in her voice.

"I would like to repurpose these rooms here to accommodate some of my southern men who are coming with their young families," Illiah said, gesturing to the rooms she told him were unused. They were on the main level, just beyond the great hall and kitchens.

"My aunt usually stays here." She tapped one of them. "And these at the back need a lot of work. And if you are going to bring recruits, you are going to need to work on the armory and the practice yard - it was converted into a pig pen."

"Great."

"Altos tries to keep the armory in good condition, but it has been hard to keep up. Some of the swords have turned rusty."

"What about defenses? I don't see any guard posts on any of these maps."

Eva pointed to the tower and tapped it. "The tower, of course. There was once a guard post here - old records tell of it." She pointed to an area not far from the little squiggly line that marked the road. "I have hiked that hill, but if there was a guard post, there is no sign of it now. There is a creek here -" She moved her finger a smidgen. "You would have to cross it. It is substantial enough that it would be better to have a bridge. The view from the hill is exceedingly good, better if you can fell some trees."

Illiah nodded, pondering. He wanted a guard post. Not that he feared approaching danger, being so far north, but he wanted a post for his recruits to guard, to learn the tedious nature of it, and the importance. Already he had thoughts about mock ambushes and battles. It was one thing to face an enemy well rested and well fed and another to spend night after night on watch, in all weathers, and then face an opponent staunchly.

"Anything else?" Eva asked him.

Illiah shook his head slowly.

"When do you expect to arrive at the Keep?"

"I don't know," Illiah replied. He was half ready to ask her to wait another day, another few days, and then he could travel with them.

But he didn't think she would entertain the notion. She had no reason to do him any favors. "Well, thank you, my lady. Your insight has been most helpful," he told her, hoping it was the right thing to say. He thought he was getting better with formalities.

Eva helped him gather his maps into a pile he could carry in the crook of his arm. He took his leave, nodding to her guards. The young girl with fiery-red hair smiled at him sheepishly and Illiah grinned at her, wishing he had been introduced. She would be about the same age as Tarran, he decided, around ten or eleven. It would be good for the lad, who was still traveling up from the south, to have someone his age around. A pretty girl would be a good distraction for his ward.

The palace was still quiet as he made his way back to his rooms. In his mind, he was writing a list of all the things he needed to prepare. He sent his borrowed serving boy to find Kaile.

Kaile could read and write, plus Illiah enjoyed being able to lord over Kaile, literally. It brought him a certain amount of satisfaction. Not that Kaile would let Illiah get big-headed.

Kaile was not long in coming. He looked sharp enough for the early hour that Illiah decided he must have had an early evening, without company. Kaile was enjoying his new popularity. He was far from royal blood, but he was Illiah's foster brother. Court loved him nearly as much as its new prince.

"Good morning, brother-mine," Kaile said, sitting down at Illiah's table, pouring himself a glass of stale water from the pitcher. "Where's breakfast?"

"I ate already," Illiah told Kaile remorselessly.

"Where?" Kaile's eyes narrowed with humor. "What early morning trysts were you conducting already this day?"

"I wanted to meet with Lady Evangeline about the Keep. She is leaving this morning to return there. I had to meet her at first quarter. She let me eat at her table." Illiah ignored his brother's innuendo.

"Too kind of her," Kaile drawled. "How did that go? Lady Evangeline seems -" He paused for the right word. "Unpredictable. I haven't been able to figure her out, and the courtiers are all divided on their opinion of her. Some think her wonderful, well suited to being queen. Others think that she is too young, too strange - too something."

"It was fine. Lady Evangeline seems perfectly suited to her role at court." Once he said it, Illiah realized it wasn't true. He wasn't sure why. "She answered my questions and helped solidify my plans. I need you to write a list."

"Ah, so this is why I have been summoned." Kaile looked amused as he found a parchment and pen. He turned back to Illiah expectantly. Illiah was ever thankful Kaile never pressed him about his inability to read and write. As children, they had been tutored side by side. Illiah had tried endlessly to learn his letters. Kaile had watched silently as Illiah cried tears of frustration and failure.

Illiah prattled on and on, pausing now and then to gather his thoughts and make sure Kaile hadn't missed anything. It took most of the morning, but finally Illiah felt that his wishes had been put on paper, leaving his mind less plugged than before.

"I need you to get everything ready for when Will and the rest come. Along with the recruits. We have already selected them - just make sure they are ready."

"And where will you be?"

"I am going to the Keep."

"When?"

"Today."

Kaile rolled his eyes. Illiah ignored him.

"This is far less than you can handle. I am needed there, not here."

"Agreed, I can handle this. It is just an abrupt decision. The court-iers will miss you so," Kaile said with a teasing smile.

"Yes, their poor, aching hearts."

"Oh, the lasses will miss having you to bother over."

"They will still have you. I am sure they will manage."

"That they will," Kiale muttered smugly.

"You really should be careful, Kaile. You are going to end up with a mule-load of bastards."

"What's one or two bastards? They would be well looked after. Even if you had several yourself, they would be loved and adored. Bastards of the hero prince." It was a conversation they had revisited several times, and still differed on.

"Maybe, or I will be forced to wed a woman because her lord father demands it. Mum always said, 'Don't sleep with a woman you can't imagine as your wife and mother of your children - it only takes one time.'" Kaile laughed at Illiah's depiction of their mother. They were both quiet for a moment, thinking with fondness of her, miles and days and weeks away in the south.

"Fine, noble words until -"

Illiah closed his ears. He didn't need to hear about the fine, perfect pair of pale breasts that belonged to lady-so-and-so, nor the warm cleft of the merchant's daughter. He sent his foster brother on his way and assured him he would find him once more before he left.

Suddenly, the idea of leaving court was tantalizing. Arriving in the grand city of Caer Andri - what was it, two months ago? - had been exciting. Now leaving was equally as appealing. A new adventure. Even better, he could put his plans and effort to work. His plans would see the Jullayan Guard restored, his realm fortified. Should there be another attack, they would be ready. It was the reason he hadn't abandoned the dagger when he learned what it could do.

It was tempting to pack his bag and rush off to the stable, departing immediately, but he knew that was unacceptable, as appealing as it was. He needed to see his brother, the prince. He needed to wish the king goodbye.

It was late afternoon before he had his bag packed with his meager travel things, his farewells said. He changed from his court clothes to his drab travel attire. His cloak was thick, far from opulent, but it would keep him warm and dry if the weather turned and at night it would serve as a blanket. He had disposed of his old travel clothes long ago. They had been patched countless times. His old boots had been resoled so many times, they were held together with a wish. His new boots were stiff, but they would wear in soon enough.

He fastened his new sword to his new belt. The only thing he had from his old life was his dagger, his gift from his mentor years ago. At least Illiah liked to think it had been a gift.

Illiah fastened his pack onto Sasha, who was first to take his turn as pack horse. Penn snorted and pawed at his stall, eager as ever to be moving, running, anything to get out. Illiah saddled the big black brute and mounted up. By the Crow, it felt good to be in the saddle.

The shadows were lengthening as Illiah rode past the outer walls of the city into the tame countryside. There was still plenty of light left for his journey ahead. He was confident he would catch up to the lady's group before night descended. If not, there would be the moon. Only a thin scattering of clouds dotted the sky. It would be a bright night.

Illiah passed fields and farms and little towns until all there was for company was the long, lonely road ahead of him. It wound through docile hills, blotched here and there by little woods and lakes. The sun set and Illiah still had not caught up with Lady Evangeline and her troop.

As true night fell, he came to a town that boasted an inn. He called for the innkeep to ask if Lady Evangeline was there.

He was welcomed generously and told the lady was not in residence. The innkeep told him if Lady Evangeline was heading to the Keep, she was no doubt camped along the road, as was her custom in good weather.

Illiah was offered a hot meal and a warm bed, but he declined. It was with some difficulty that he got back on his horse. The innkeep was overly eager to have the new prince under his roof for the night.

The moon had not yet risen. Everything was darker than Illiah had anticipated. The trees were tight to the road and darkened it further. Illiah was surprised and vexed that he had not yet caught up with his quarry. He grumbled to himself a little and ate some roasted nuts as he rode.

Another hour went by, and the moon rose, nearly full. The light of the moon was reassuring. Illiah could hear night insects humming and chirping, frogs too. Now and then an owl. He breathed in the damp night air with relish, looking forward to sleeping under the stars and waking with dew on his blanket.

He paused, listening past the frog song. He heard a sound that did not belong in the night forest beside the frogs and crickets. It belonged in his nightmares. His hand moved to his sword. He dismounted and followed the noise, drawing his sword, the sounds of clashing steel came faster and more urgent.

As he approached, he could make out the glow of a fire a ways off the road. Someone's camp was under attack. He only hoped it wasn't Lady Evangeline's.

Illiah crept through the forest, staying to the deepest shadows, keeping away from the firelight. The trees were thick, with sizable trunks and long arching branches making it hard to ascertain the situation and how he might help. An opening in the trees illuminated the clearing and he felt instantly foolish. There was a melee, and although it was strange, there was no danger.

Eva's handmaids were seated by the fire along with Darys and Mahone. Tarek engaged someone, their bout taking up the rest of the small clearing. The horses were tied beyond the firelight, placid eyes reflecting the scene.

Illiah stepped into the firelight, sheathing his sword quickly. The melee stopped, and Illiah stared. Evangeline had been sparring with Tarek. She stopped, facing him.

"What are you doing here?" she asked, her voice uneven from exertion, but he could still hear her displeasure.

"I decided, after our talk this morning, it would be worthwhile for me to go to the Keep sooner rather than later. I thought I would catch up with you before nightfall."

She did not sheath her sword, he noted. It was no practice sword, he also noted. Short and rather wide, but better suited to her small frame than a longsword like his own. Damned strange thing for a woman to fight with a sword.

"Hungry?" Darys asked, throwing Illiah a cheery smile. Illiah liked the captain of Ullian. At least there was one friendly face. "It might be a bit cold, but it will fill your stomach."

"Yes, thank you." Illiah tethered his horses before settling before the fire.

The bowl Darys handed Illiah was filled with stew of some kind. It smelled good enough. "Good evening," Illiah said, nodding around at the others who regarded him with little more warmth than their lady.

"Tarek and Mahone," Darys introduced the guards once more. They were stoic, as usual, which, at the moment reflected the expression of their lady. "This is Mila and her sister Murryn."

"My sisters," Tarek added.

"My ladies," Illiah said, inclining his head to them. The girl, Murryn, grinned at the title; her older sister was wary, her eyes suspicious. Not the warmest greetings he had yet received. Nor the coldest.

"My lady, you were sparring?" Illiah turned to Eva. He couldn't dismiss his curiosity.

"Eva. You can call me Eva," she surprised him by saying.

"Eva. I am sorry I interrupted. Please don't stop on my account," he added. She tossed her head a little, not unlike an unruly horse, as if he had challenged her in some way.

"You did not interrupt," she said, shaking her head and sitting down, the look of challenge replaced with something different, something friendlier. "I am out of practice. My arms are tired. There is little time for such things at court," she noted quietly.

Illiah didn't comment. He couldn't imagine there would be any time for a lady to practice swordplay at court. It just wasn't done. Even from his backward end of the realm, it was unheard of. He didn't think it would be wise to insult her honor by mentioning it. Personally, he thought it was a good idea. He had seen women suffer horrific fates. Perhaps they would have had a chance if they had learned to fight and use a blade.

"Did your father teach you?" Illiah asked her, distracting himself from the nightmares threatening to wake from his line of thinking.

"No." She huffed a regretful sigh. "I was only seven when he died. I learned a little from Altos, an old guardsman. He taught the boys at the Keep, I tagged along. Tarek and Mahone have been excellent teachers as well."

"Would you spar with us, my lord?" Tarek asked. "When you have supped, of course."

"I would gladly," Illiah replied, eager to find out finally what the two mysterious guards were made of.

The stew was cool, as Darys promised. Not exactly a meal to relish, but welcome nonetheless. He finished quickly and stood, eagerly drawing his blade. "I didn't see either of you compete in the tourneys. Darys, you won a round, did you not?"

Darys grinned. "Aye I did, and a nice purse went with it. Not too bad for an old man."

"You aren't old!" Murryn piped up from where she sat at the captain's elbow. The captain ruffled the girl's hair. Her pretty sister watched, but the corner of her serious mouth lifted a little.

"Well, old enough to be your father, and then some," Darys chided.

"We have no interest in tourneys," Mahone replied in his quiet, strong voice.

Illiah's stomach was satisfied with the stew, but his fingers were itching. He met Tarek's eyes and smiled a challenge that the other man met.

The tourneys had been tolerable. His participation resulted from the king's insistence - how could he say no? His adversaries had been trifles really, leaving him with scant confidence in the abilities of the royal guard. These two men would be different. There was a rawness, an uncultivated aspect to them that Illiah expected to translate in the way they fought.

Tarek was exceptional - Illiah was not disappointed. He was pleased his instincts continued to serve him well. Tarek was a dangerous man. He was big, strong, yet fast and light on his feet. He knew his weak spots and protected them. Illiah was soon tight-lipped, concentrating on every sinew of his body and his breathing. Yes, Tarek was fast, but Illiah was faster, and intuitive. It didn't take long to learn the weak spots in his opponent's technique and manipulate them. The dagger at his belt hummed for his ears only, and he felt it lend him strength. Illiah pressed Tarek harder in a series of offensive strokes that left Tarek scrambling and wide-eyed. Darys called it as Illiah feigned a blow to Tarek's neck.

"Illiah got you," Darys said. Illiah wished they wouldn't praise his technique. He wasn't trying to show off. Yes, he was good. The best. He had the dagger. But what right did he have to praise when so many of his men had died?

He nodded and shook Tarek's hand. He caught a glance from Eva. She was smiling shyly. His pride swelled. His cheeks felt hot suddenly. The dagger quieted. He sat down at the fire, taking a swig of something Darys passed his way. He coughed.

"Strong stuff, Darys! Fine, but strong," Illiah managed once his throat eased.

Darys laughed.

"I'm done," Illiah announced as he stifled a yawn. "Mahone, tomorrow night we are on, deal?"

"Aye, my lord," the other guard said. Illiah saw a flash of his teeth in the faint light. "Eva, Tarek and I will be on watch," Mahone said to his ward. The two guards stood as one and dissolved like smoke into night.

On the edges of the firelight, the women laid out their blankets, and the sisters settled under the heavy furs. Eva wished them a good sleep and came back to the fire. Illiah watched her tuck her cloak under her bottom to protect her from the damp earth. Darys had gone to check the horses. Illiah was left alone with his brother's betrothed. She seemed like a different creature surrounded by the forest, in the wild with only the fire to cast light upon her features, which seemed less fine and fair, and more wild and mysterious.

"You are an exceptional swordsman," she said, her eyes trained on him. Eyes full of secrets, of knowing.

He shrugged.

"Who taught you?" she asked.

"A traveler, a nomad who stayed at my father's farm for a few seasons. Strange man, but a good teacher."

"You use your left hand."

Illiah looked at the appendage in question. "Yeah, I started training with my right. It felt weird, then I tried my left and everything was easy after that."

"You can fight with either hand?"

"Aye, though I am much better with my left."

She held up her left hand and flexed it, then flashed Illiah a bemused smile. "I can't even imagine using my left arm!"

Darys returned and sat down with a grunt and a yawn.

"The girls did well today," he said to Eva.

"They did better than I expected. And Mila is a wonder at organization, bless her," Eva said with a little laugh.

"Well, I am off to bed, my lady. I suggest you do the same. It has been a long day, albeit a pleasant one," Darys said, giving Evangeline's shoulder an affectionate squeeze.

"Good night, Captain." The title was full of fondness.

Illiah wasn't sure if he would sleep if he lay down. His body was tired, but his mind was full.

"Illiah," Evangeline said softly, her voice tentative. "I would appreciate if you would not speak of my swordsmanship with your brother. He would not approve." Her expression hardened, though her eyes were beseeching.

"He doesn't know?"

She shook her head, looking into the fire. "His opinion of me is already jaded. I don't want to be a further disappointment." She sounded more angry than hurt. Illiah felt a rush of frustration toward his brother.

"Why do you do it, then? Do you enjoy the knowledge that you could gut a man?"

She bit her lip. "No one likes to feel vulnerable," she muttered. "And I will not stop merely in the hopes it will appease the prince."

Illiah hid a smile. The woman was all pride and prickles. No wonder his brother was not in love with her. Caeris liked submissive women. Obedient, meek women, good for warming his bed and looking pretty on his arm. This woman was none of those things - except for the pretty part. Illiah was torn between amusement and horror that his brother was stuck with this woman and that she was stuck with Caeris.

"I will not tell him. You have my word."

Evangeline yawned and stood up.

"Good night, Illiah," was all she said before leaving him alone with the dying fire.

Illiah tried not to watch her as she tucked herself under the furs she shared with the other girls. He went to check on his horses before he too spread out his bedroll and laid his thick woolen cloak about him.

It was a warm night so he kicked off his boots and settled on his back with his dagger under his makeshift pillow. He looked up through the leafy branches where the moon shone down upon the camp, its light lost in the red light of the fire. He fell asleep thinking of Caeris and his brother's pregnant mistress.

CHAPTER 15

EVA

THEIR SMALL GROUP TRAVELED quickly compared to Eva's aunt's entourage. The weather remained tolerable, allowing them to camp under the stars rather than the hassle of pitching tents or the slow business of inns.

Illiah often looked on the cusp of stepping in to assert his authority and ideas. He had been in charge of an entire army. He could effortlessly lead their small group. But he held back. Eva suspected it was with effort.

At first it had been disconcerting to see him barge into their camp, arrogantly inserting himself into their party. Immediately she assumed their pleasant travels were at an end. She had been wrong. Illiah was an easy traveling companion. Sometimes he was quiet and thoughtful. Other times he was loud and entertaining. He got along well with Darys and even won praise from Mahone. She forgot he was irritating. She forgot he was the new prince.

Until they arrived in Barrowsby.

The little town was at the edge of the forest, nestled in the foothills before the land rose up with more fervor to meet the Great Forest and the northern mountains. They crossed the bridge and Eva's gaze drifted to the fork in the road. Left would bring her home to the Keep via a narrow road of steep ravines, rocky hills and hollows, and small but torrent creeks. Right would take her to Dweller's Knoll.

"What are you looking at?" Illiah's voice broke through Eva's troubled thoughts.

"Nothing," replied Eva.

"Hmm. You looked like you were seeing ghosts," Illiah muttered before pressing his horse onward.

Barrowsby had suffered from the death of Lord Finnan in a similar fashion to the Keep. There were fewer merchants, less society. Neglected buildings scattered the town, dilapidated homes for rats and owls. The people who stayed were tough and unrelenting, willing to work the earth and travel to barter for other luxuries.

The townsfolk trickled from their houses to stand along the street, eager to catch sight of the new prince, the new War Commander and Lord of the Keep. His presence meant soon their village would bustle once more as people traveled regularly from the Keep to the royal city.

For the first time, Illiah asked to impose his wishes upon the small group and stay a night in the village. He wanted to meet the townsfolk personally.

Eva wanted to be home. The Keep was only two days away. For a brief moment, she decided to go without Illiah. But she remembered she had promised to show him the lay of the land as they rode, and she wanted to see his face when he saw the Keep for the first time.

Illiah exuded endless patience as he greeted the villagers and endured their questions and concerns, some poignant, some trivial. He answered them as best he could with equal concern. His friendly smile resembled the sun, lighting the faces of all who looked up at him. Illiah was new at being royalty. He had grown up a modest villager like them. It made him better at it. The people loved him already. Eva read it like writing on their faces.

Watching the instant devotion of the townsfolk toward Illiah was unsettling. The pang in her gut was envy. When she became queen, she could never inspire the same level of loyalty and admiration. Not even Caeris loved her the way the people loved Illiah. She should have ridden on.

The morning came soon enough. They left to a fanfare of well-wishers, little boys and girls chasing them down the road. Soon they were secluded in the woods, beyond the view of the waving townsfolk. Illiah was riding next to Eva and exhaled deeply.

"That went well, did it not?" she stated.

"It did. I just can't seem to get used to it."

"Used to what?"

"The people, their admiration, the faith they put in me! As if I could solve any of their woes with a snap of my fingers. It's a lot of responsibility."

He sounded bereft. Eva pitied him a little.

"The people need you, Illiah. Everyone needs hope."

"It's starting to rain again," Murryn piped up in a pitiful voice. She sat bundled up on Illiah's big gray gelding. The poor girl was tired. Eleven days was her limit it seemed. And the last few nights, since leaving Barrowsby, had been cold and wet.

Eva could hardly blame her. Murryn had been stalwart every moment since being rescued from Serac. She had braved her new life with courage and a maturity beyond her years. But cold and wet were miserable companions for a girl in her eleventh year.

"Don't complain, Murryn," Mila chided her sister in a quiet voice.

"We are almost there," Tarek assured the girl.

"Think of the warm baths!" Eva said in an attempt at encouragement.

Eva peered ahead through the mist up at the trees. The hills were getting steeper and the forest denser. Everything was shrouded in cloud, but they were getting close. The difficult terrain made the Keep seem even more remote and desolate. The lingering mist and moss-clad trees only intensified the feeling of otherness.

"We should be there today. Once we get to the marker trees, Tarek will ride ahead to announce our arrival. There will be warm food waiting, warm beds, and a hot bath will put you right."

The girl nodded, pulling her cloak tighter around her face. She looked plaintively at Illiah, the woe-fixer. His expression was patient. He gave her a little smile.

Illiah let Murryn ride Sasha as a bribe to raise her spirits. Illiah was fond of the girl and felt sorry for her. When he suggested it to Murryn, her face lit up with one of her captivating smiles. Illiah missed it. He was watching Eva, waiting for her reaction to the offer. Eva ignored his bait. She hadn't asked, but Illiah dropped hints about not letting anyone ride his horses. Usually these remarks were in Eva's hearing, usually accompanied by a mischievous look that made Eva smile, even though she felt compelled to smack him.

The rain was disparaging, but Eva could ignore it. She was almost home. Nothing could dispel her fond thoughts of the Keep. The pools, Calypso, the Great Forest, Lula and Tayeh - she had missed them all.

They rode forward in silence as the steady rain fell. The forest was hushed; only the predictable sounds of the horses' hooves on the road broke the silence.

"There are the marker trees I told you about," Eva said, breaking the silence, gesturing to the two grand evergreens appearing out of the mist before them. The two trees stood like solemn statues on either side of the road. Their girth was greater than any of the other trees in the forest, though they were nothing compared to those of the Great Forest. Still, they were grand trees. The Keep was only a few more miles ahead.

"Those would make great beams for the new build," Illiah mused, pulling Penn up beside Eva's horse. Eva was filled with horror at the thought. She turned to Illiah and her fear turned to annoyance. His lips twisted in a provocative smile, obviously pleased he managed to rile her.

"You are not serious." It was part statement, part question. She needed to make sure he was teasing.

"They would yield a lot of useful lumber," he said gazing up at the splendid trees.

"Tell me you are not serious," Eva pleaded again.

"Well ..."

"Illiah!" He was so difficult she wanted to punch him, but she was smiling. Why was he as amusing as he was irritating?

"Calm down. I'm not going to cut down your precious trees. They would likely be too cumbersome to manage anyhow."

"Uh-huh."

Jesting aside, Illiah craned his neck gazing up at the trees, exclaiming that he had never seen the like of them before. Eva was satisfied. She told him the trees in the Great Forest looming over the cliff at the edge of the Keep were much taller and wider, with roots the size of mature evergreens.

"At least there is no shortage of wood for this cold winter you warn me of," Illiah said, smiling.

"That hill over there is where the old guard post is marked on your map." Eva ignored his remark and pointed to a place above them. The hill was covered in cloud. "Believe it or not, you can actually see the road quite well from up there."

"On a clear day, maybe."

The persistent rain was dampening, and not just literally. They were all anticipating the end of their journey.

The cloud and wet didn't affect a raven. The faint sound of wings cutting through the air came just before a rough call echoed in Eva's ears as a black-feathered bundle landed on her shoulder. Calypso gripped into her tunic with his talons and squawked an enthusiastic greeting.

"You ridiculous bird!" she chided, transferring him to her forearm. He was a big bird and didn't fit well on her shoulder, especially when he was off balance with excitement, not to mention his loud voice right in her ear.

Mahone and Darys laughed. Illiah looked stunned, trying to control a jittery Penn who was not pleased by the flapping, noisy black bird who was bigger than any raven had the right to be. Murryn looked out from under her wet cloak, her eyes enchanted. The girl seemed to love all animals. Mila grinned, but winced against the noise.

Eva shushed the bird. Eventually he fell silent with one last croak. Eva praised him, stroking his soft, glossy, damp feathers.

"That's a good boy. I missed you," she whispered.

He hopped back to her shoulder and settled there, looking smug.

"Why doesn't it surprise me that you have a pet raven?" Illiah stated.

"He is not a pet!" Eva retorted. "Only cruel people keep birds as pets. He's a friend."

"Uh-huh."

"He missed you!" Murryn said. "Can I hold him?"

"Give him some food and he will be your friend for life," Eva suggested. Murryn looked in her pockets and found a little bread. She held it out to Calypso who made a little happy noise, inspecting Murryn with one black eye before hopping to her knee to take the treat. "Greedy bird," Eva muttered as they moved on.

The rain stopped just as the forest opened. Before them lay the Keep, nestled against its cliff, skirted by the simple pastures that fed the Keep's little farm.

"It looks more formidable than I imagined," Eva heard Illiah murmur.

Eva tried to imagine her home as he saw it for the first time. The tall walls, built of huge slabs of stone, the inner buildings, all stone. The tall tower resembled vertebrae along the cliff face. The Forest at its back hovered like an overbearing mother. An impenetrable fortress with no hint of softness, no complacent marble and glass to tame its outward appearance. It was nothing like the palace in Caer Andri. It was wild and ruthless. Eva loved it.

A flag atop the watch tower drew Eva's eye, a blazing silver sword on a crimson field. A flag that had not been raised for a long time. The War Commander had returned.

The raven took off just before they reached the gates, which were open. Eva couldn't recall if the gates had ever closed. The huge hinges were likely rusty from disuse. Illiah would have them oiled and brought to life in no time.

They passed under the shadow of the wall so thick, the passageway was a tunnel. On the other side, the courtyard seemed bright, even under the cloudy veil.

The people of the Keep were waiting, a small assembly in the airy, stony expanse. The steward and Wilanna stood side by side. Altos leaned on the crooked staff he kept mostly for company; his knees were strong as yet. Wilanna looked nervous, but the steward and the others looked eager, excited. Even Scrub had crawled out from the kitchens to greet the new lord. He still wore his apron though, still covered in flour.

Illiah dismounted immediately and greeted the people with a friendly, open manner. He asked their names and occupations. Justyn the elderly stable master spoke with enthusiasm about Illiah's horses and offered to see them to the stables.

"Wilanna," Eva addressed her former nursemaid. "This is Mila and her sister Murryn, my new ladies-in-waiting. Could you please show them to a comfortable room and make sure they have everything they need?"

Wilanna's brows rose. She nodded tersely. Wilanna had never been a warm woman.

"I am glad to see your aunt has finally talked some sense into you.

I always said it was proper for a lady to have servants," Wilanna said.

Eva bit her tongue from an angry retort. Mila caught her eye and gave her a sympathetic look.

"She has not suffered from a lack of handmaids from what I can tell, is she not a fine lady and betrothed to the prince?" Illiah came up beside the steward's wife. Wilanna froze in mortification.

"My lord is right, of course. All I meant was that it is nice to have female companionship," Wilanna said, ushering the newcomers inside as an excuse to leave the scrutiny of her new lord.

As satisfying as it was to see her old nurse put in her place, Illiah had no right to insert himself into her life. She didn't need protection from Wilanna. Eva was used to the old woman's ways and had long ago become adept at ignoring her intended and unintended slights.

"My lord, should I show you to your apartments?" Eva asked. Illiah might want to change and bathe. She was desperate for it herself.

"You may, if you quit calling me 'my lord,'" Illiah said, smiling. Illiah had a good mouth for smiling. Eva found herself drawn to it a little too often. Luckily, Altos interrupted promising Illiah a mug of fine ale and an earful of tales when he had righted himself from his travels, so Illiah didn't see her burning cheeks. Illiah grinned and nodded at Eva's old tutor before turning back to her.

Illiah shouldered his heavy pack of belongings. "Where's Tarran when I need him?" he muttered under his breath as he followed Eva deeper into the Keep.

"Who's Tarran?"

"My page."

"I didn't know you had a page."

"I do. He is about the same age as Murryn," he told her. "I'm never going to remember all these names. I shouldn't have left Tarran with my men. He was always good at remembering everything. Kaile too."

"All these names? All twenty of them? Didn't you meet scores of people at court?"

Illiah looked hurt. "Yes, but I had Kaile. He is good with these matters."

"Why don't you write them down?"

"No good - can't write or read," Illiah said even though he knew she was teasing.

Often peasants and farmers couldn't read, but royalty? Then she remembered he was a farmer, of sorts.

"Come. I'll give you a quick tour first. It wouldn't do if the lord got lost in his own Keep," Eva told him. Illiah said nothing, content to follow her.

"Where are your guards? It is strange to see you without their hovering presence," Illiah murmured as they walked.

"The Keep holds no threats to my person."

Illiah accepted this without comment.

Eva led Illiah through a small courtyard into another passageway. There was a stone antechamber with marble accents. Some parts of the Keep hinted at more grandeur than the stone allowed.

Eva pointed as they went. Guest chambers, kitchen, storage rooms. Down another spacious hallway, through an arched doorway into the wide, open courtyard to the hot mineral baths.

"Just stick to the staircases that have newer torches, fewer cobwebs, and are generally well worn, and you shouldn't get lost."

"Sure."

Next, they went up. And up. Eva could pick her way down the stairs in at night without a candle and still know when to expect the stair that was uneven or the one with the crack that tended to stub her toes. But it must seem like an endless climb to Illiah. It really wasn't, once one got used to it.

"Are we there yet?" he asked, shifting the weight of his pack slightly.

"Nearly."

They were. The stairs gave way to a smooth stone floor and a rounded hallway lit by narrow windows. Eva caught Illiah peeking out the window from the corner of her eye.

"This is my room." She pointed to the first door. "This is where Mahone and Tarek sleep," Eva said, pointing to the door next to her own room. "These are unused. Down that hallway is where the steward and Wilanna, my old nurse, have their room." They walked a little farther. "This is the lord's apartment." Eva stopped in front of his heavy oak door. The door was carved with symbols of the forest - a fox, a squirrel, trees of all shapes and sizes, a stag hidden among the pines. "But first let me show you the council room."

Illiah dropped his bag and followed her as she continued down the hallway.

Eva pulled the lever, and the door groaned, forcing the old hinges into use. Home. It was her home. Was. Had been. It was Illiah's now.

Wilanna had been in the room. The protective tablecloth was gone, and the wooden table shone with fresh oil. No dust lingered. Eva's books had been piled neatly to the side, out of her particular order. The hundreds of books that lined the walls in curved shelves looked untouched. Pity Illiah could not read.

"Where does that door go?" Illiah asked perceptively, pointing to the small, narrow door at the far side of the room. Eva walked over to it and opened the door into the little garden. She explained that it couldn't quite be called a garden - it was walled in against the cliff itself. More like a little bit of forest rather than a purposeful collection of flowers and herbs. She didn't draw his attention to the wall carved with animals that held Eva's most carefully guarded secret. Tayeh and Lula would be waiting for her in the Great Forest. She had so much to tell them.

Illiah was inspecting the small, green space. His expression was hard to read. "It looks like you could almost jump the wall here and run off into the Forest," he said. Eva put her hand upon the mossy stone for support. How could he be thinking thoughts that paralleled her own?

"Right," she scoffed to hide her unease. "That is the Great Forest. Go there only if you want to court the consequences of raw magic."

"Those look like plain birch trees to me. Raw magic? I have never given much thought to magic, if it exists." He did not believe his own words. Odd, Illiah did not strike her as a dishonest man.

"Magic is real. The Allmakers are real. Raw magic has no rhyme or reason. And it does not tolerate trespassers." Or so Tayeh and Lula had warned her.

He turned a skeptical eye on her. "Allmakers? Don't be ridiculous."

Eva shrugged. Let him believe what he would. As if she would make these things up.

"Come. I'll show you your apartment now," she said, walking past him back into the council room.

Eva opened the door to the lord's chambers with a deep breath. She had only been in the room a handful of times since her parents' death. The place held many fragile memories. Each time had been like visiting a tomb. She didn't know what she would find or feel.

It was apparent someone, probably Wilanna again, had been in the room. Everything was cleaned and dusted. Fresh fall flowers exploded from a vase on the table. The hearth was clean and fresh wood was stacked next to it in preparation for cool nights. The furniture was not as Eva remembered at all. The bed was different. The blankets were new and neatly laid out. The tapestry she remembered as a child hanging above the fireplace was gone. Maybe Wilanna put it in the storeroom. Not that it mattered. The room no longer pulled on the delicate threads of grief in her heart.

"I think you will find this quite delightful," Eva said, leading Illiah into the bathing chamber. His brow furrowed in confusion.

The lord's privy was large and freshly cleaned. Eva led him through another small door and into the lord's private walled garden. It was similar to the bit of forest off the council room, only this one was smaller, made completely of stone, no moss anywhere. In the center was a sunken pool cut into the rock, just large enough to fit a grown man or two. A tiny stream came from a crack in the rock and trickled into the pool. Steam rose lazily into the air.

Illiah gave a shout of laughter, feeling the hot water. "This is too perfect!"

"I'll leave you alone, then."

"Thank you for the tour," Illiah's words chased after her.

"Not a problem," she said, closing the door, her heart a jumble of mixed and contradictory emotions.

Naturally, Scrub made a feast. Wilanna, surly as ever, fetched Eva from her bath, but she didn't mind. Her stomach growled thinking of Scrub's honey cakes. Except for the two conversing figures of Illiah and the steward making their way slowly to the table, the assembled were already seated. Illiah too had been fetched from his bath. He was freshly dressed, his short hair gleaming damply, his beard short and trimmed neatly. They were still talking when Eva approached the table and caught their attention.

"You are wearing a dress," Illiah stated, one brow arched.

Eva deferred not to comment. Illiah grinned at her non-reply and Eva felt her cheeks stretch. Was she really smiling back?

Illiah took his seat by the steward. Eva was pleased to see everyone smile at Mila and Murryn, a gracious nod here and there. She had no doubt the pretty young woman and her sister would have no trouble settling in. The sisters went to the other end of the long table to sit with Tarek as was appropriate since they were supposedly his kin. Eva sat opposite the steward beside her nurse.

The spread made her mouth water. Numerous dishes of summer squash, delicious sauces with wild berries, fresh bread, rolls, cheeses, and a roasted goose. The steward brought out his finest wine, telling Illiah proudly of its origins, pouring a small glass for each of them. Tudos made a toast to the new lord. Illiah looked sincerely touched and drank the wine with animated relish.

Eva told Scrub his honey cakes were better than Eva remembered. He beamed proudly at her, his face rosy from the wine. Illiah was asked to recite tales from the war. He did, but not enthusiastically. Still, the table was enraptured by them - he had a good strong voice for speaking.

Dusk was several hours away. Eva wouldn't be missed if she left. A question poised by Altos caught her attention before she could slip out unnoticed.

"How is it you became the one to lead the southern men? Surely there were older, more experienced men at arms, captains of some household guard that would have stepped in. I mean no disrespect," Altos added quickly, "but still the question intrigues me."

Illiah smiled, but it did not reach his eyes. He looked down at his hands as if pondering the question and what his answer might be. From the hesitancy of his small movements, the tightening of his handsome features, Illiah was uncomfortable recounting the events of the war.

"The village of Alderidge had been burned, a sizable establishment, close to the Great Bay. Most of the inhabitants had been found dead, some - mostly young women - were missing. We didn't know at that time what was going on. We thought perhaps there was a thieving band marauding the countryside, though the carnage ..." Illiah's body language indicated the violence was beyond the abilities of a band of thieves. "We didn't think it was invaders; they hadn't yet been spotted. A council was being formed to which we were invited. We rode out, my brothers, my father, several of our neighbors and their elder sons. We saw smoke on the horizon, toward the place where the council was to be. We knew in our hearts it boded ill. As we approached we could smell it. Death. Father bid us to go back - he was scared. But we had to know. We had to see for ourselves what was going on. We went onward, slowly, cautiously, our blades drawn."

Illiah gave a mirthless guffaw. "My blade was sharp and well honed as was my practice, but my brothers were not so studious. My father had only a boot knife. I also had my bow and a clutch of arrows. Just Kaile and I went forward, on foot, as careful and silent as we could. We heard the cries of the dying before we saw them. The invaders were still there, and it was clear they were not from this realm. It was obvious they felt no threat from us, for none stood guard, no look-outs. They went about their abhorrent business without fear. They were right. We knew it and it made us sick. We were no match for them. We watched them for a short time, and what we saw I will not tell, as it is fit for no person's ears. There are no words to describe the anger I felt. It took a great deal of strength not to leap from my hiding place and charge them down. Kaile too felt the same. In fact, I had to grab his shoulder and pull him back, or he would have charged to his death, albeit a valiant one, right then.

"We crept away, and our pale faces told our companions all they needed to know. Father was terrified. He wanted to go home. We bid him go, as he was not a fighter. Others left in fear as well. Father begged us to come - he pleaded, terrified for our lives, but Kaile and I could not ignore what we had seen. Several of our neighbors stayed, feeling the same need for action as we did.

"When we gathered to plan our action, they all looked to me. I don't know why. I had never thought of myself as a leader before. As Illiah, the son of Devin the horse breeder, my name was well known in our part of the south for my aptitude with a blade. I had a bit of a reputation. There was an incident, previously." He did not elaborate. "And clearly, they were all ready to follow me, which was just as well. I already had a plan."

A chill made Eva sit straighter, a warning, a sense that Illiah was withholding something. Omission was a form of lying, and lying suited Illiah as well as a broken wing suits a bird. His eyes were vacant as he retold his story.

"Basically my plan was to take them by surprise. We had horses, big horses - the invaders had none. We could rely on speed and surprise and brute force. Simple really. That is what we did. Our blades added more blood to the soaked earth that day. We were too late to save the village, and more people were missing, many dead or beyond our help. We felt no satisfaction. There was no easing our need for vengeance that day. We knew there were more, somewhere. Those we destroyed that day could not be the whole of them.

"Word of that day spread quickly. People came to me whether I asked them to or not. Before I knew what my role was becoming, I had over a hundred men camped with me - volunteers, kin of those killed or missing. We tracked the invaders. I spent much of my waking time strategizing and molding farmers into warriors, teaching them to fight from horseback, using my old mentor's techniques. I was harsher. Though. We had so little time. A message was sent to the king, of course, but I knew we couldn't wait on him. To answer your question, Altos, I stepped up before anyone else could, and no one ever challenged my leadership."

Illiah stopped and took a long drink of his ale. All were quiet, contemplating his experience. Altos gripped Illiah's shoulder in wordless affirmation. Illiah avoided the other man's eyes. Altos had some specific questions about Illiah's strategies. Illiah appeared more eager to talk strategy than retell painful memories.

Eva watched Illiah thoughtfully. Her heart was heavy for him, for what he had witnessed and endured, a heavy burden for anyone to carry. She had seen it in her visions. But Illiah had lived it. Maybe the ill she sensed was just the lingering awfulness of the war tainting Illiah's words.

Eva had heard enough of war for one day. She needed moss beneath her feet and forest-damp air in her lungs. She whispered reassurances to Mila about meeting later in her room. Her friend nodded absently; like the others, her attention was on Illiah. Eva left quietly.

She climbed the many steps to her room, grabbed her warm outdoor cloak and boots and headed out into the little mossy courtyard. She took several long strides across the little forest garden, pausing a moment to take in the familiar sight of the place, the quiet stone walls and narrow windows looking down as a raven would, from a great height. The moss was thick and pale from the summer's warmth, but the air was cool. The sun was going down, and long shadows stretched out toward the tall trees of the Great Forest above her. Eva walked to the wall and fingered the little fox carving in her specific way. The hidden door creaked open, and Eva went through the circular door.

Before Eva was the familiar winding path, like a passage into another world, as if the Keep disappeared into her fantasy and the only reality were the trees before her. Eva closed the door, concealing her secret and crept up the little path.

At the top, she was instantly enclosed within the dense hush of the Great Forest, cradled by the ancient trees. Eva smiled and breathed in deeply. The smell of the moss and dirt and summer air made her feel instantly at home.

There were no coherent paths in the Great Forest, just small crisscrossing tracks made by animals, and those would disappear and reappear at any given place. The track Eva had worn to Tayeh and Lula's glade had grown over since spring, but she would not get lost.

Her Guardian mentors were waiting. They always knew when she crossed the border of the other realm. She smiled at them and ran down the little hill into the familiar glade.

"Well met, my dear," Tayeh said, towering over her, his arm rested on his massive weapon as if Eva just interrupted his practice. His Kitarran face was turned up with a feral grin, sharp teeth exposed. He looked unworldly and fierce, but Eva wanted nothing more than to hug him. Lula was in fox form, as per usual, but she too was happy, wearing a foxy grin and dancing around Eva's ankles like an excited puppy. Eva laughed.

"Well met indeed," Eva echoed, patting Lula on her black nose. Tayeh took Eva's hand and kissed the back of it in a Kitarran sign of love and respect, a gesture more heartening than any embrace.

"You are home early this year. Tell us what is going on in the court of Caer Andri these days," Tayeh said, sitting down, getting comfortable for her tale. Or more aptly, her report.

Eva's smile dropped from her lips. She started to pace. "So much happened this summer - now that I think it over, it seems unreal." Eva's tale of Serac's misdeeds and cruelty caused Lula to finally sit still with a grave look on her canine face. Tayeh too was grim-faced. She told them of Mila and Murryn, safely at the Keep, away from their past life, her dear friends already.

"Serac scares me," Eva said with a shudder.

"Don't worry about him, Eva. His words can't hurt you. He is a scarred, empty man. Pity him for his choices, but do not think of him," Tayeh said with a wave of his big hand.

Eva sighed. Could it be that easy? Pity him? Yes, she could almost pity a man who made his life out of pain and misery. But pity didn't bring justice for Mila.

She told them about Caeris's return from war, victorious, with a pregnant mistress hanging from his arm. Tayeh and Lula exchanged unhappy glances. Eva passed over the subject quickly and told them of Illiah, the shock his appearance made at court, how happy the king had been when he discovered he had two sons, how eerily identical the two brothers looked. Eva described Illiah's personality, his slight, but substantial differences from his brother.

"What?" Eva asked. Tayeh had the most peculiar expression on his usually controlled face.

"You are telling me that all this time the prince's twin, his brother by blood, has been in the south making himself into some kind of hero?" Tayeh repeated.

"It's not like you to be redundant, Tayeh."

Then Tayeh surprised Eva by laughing. He clutched his cuirass as the loud guffaw shook through the Forest. Eva had never heard him laugh in that manner before. Lula had no explanation. The fox gave a human-like shrug that looked odd on the Forest creature, but something in the fox's eyes sparkled with amusement and insight.

"He is at the Keep now. Caeris appointed him his War Commander, my father's position," Eva went on, not sure if her mentor was still listening. "They are going to make the Keep back into a proper military fortress."

Tayeh asked question after question about the new prince until Eva grew quite hoarse and the sun descended below the horizon. She wasn't surprised by the Guardian's interest. Everyone was interested in Illiah. She told Tayeh about Illiah's skill with the sword and how she could personally attest to it.

"You like him?" Tayeh asked, startling her.

"What do you mean?"

"You trust him? You think he is a good man?"

"Yes, I trust him. Yes, he is a good man. Better than his brother anyway," Eva replied caustically.

Tayeh nodded, finally appeased.

"I should get going. The sun has set. I promised to show Murryn and Mila around the Keep."

"Of course," Tayeh said with a gracious nod. "It is good to have you home, Evangeline."

"It's good to be home, Tayeh."

She walked back to Keep with the white fox to guide her. Lula's bright coat was luminescent against the darkening hues of the Forest, like a lantern bobbing here and there under the ferns. Eva wished the fox good night. Lula disappeared into the Forest, and Eva disappeared inside the Keep.

Eva paused in the mossy garden. Tayeh had not asked her about her task.

CHAPTER 16

EVA

TAYEH HAD NOT ASKED her about the vercuri. He couldn't have forgotten. Guardians don't forget. Not that Eva had anything to tell him. She hadn't sensed anything that might be a magical artifact. What a hopeless task. What had Tayeh been thinking?

Eva yawned. She was ready for the day to be done.

After several steps, the warm air of the council room consumed her. The evening air was cool for the end of summer. Perhaps there would be an early winter.

"What are you doing here?" A sharp voice came from the chair before the hearth. It was Illiah. Eva hadn't seen him, and her heart lurched.

"What are you doing here? You scared me half to death!" Eva exclaimed, her heart rate slowing a notch.

"You? What of me? What were you doing out there in the courtyard all this time?" Illiah said, his eyes narrowing. His face looked oaken in the firelight. Deep lines framed his reddened eyes, his mouth a grim line.

"I like it out there," Eva told him lamely, studying his face as she closed the door behind her, locking out the cold.

"It's much warmer in here," Illiah muttered, turning back toward the fire. He slouched in the chair, his head resting in his hand. Eva had seen him in that stance before, slumped under a tree, covered in blood, crying about lost men and a prince who didn't bring his army on time.

She could almost feel her heart fracturing with pity. She wanted to see the hopeless shadow in his eyes disappear. She imagined wrapping her arms around him, whispering words of comfort in his ear. The thoughts shocked her. Instead, she sat down heavily in the chair opposite him.

"The steward announced that he is relinquishing his post," Illiah told her. "You missed his formal announcement at the feast."

Eva bit her lip. It seemed important announcements were often made in her absence. Illiah appeared to follow her train of thought because he smiled slightly, muttering something about her talent for disappearing at critical moments.

"He is returning to his hometown. They are making preparations now."

"That means Wilanna is leaving too," Eva said. She should feel something in regards to the news. Happiness, sadness. Her nurse had never loved her, never understood her. But the steward and Wilanna were the closest thing Eva had had to proper parents since she was seven. Eva felt nothing. They held no place in her heart after all, for good or ill.

"When do your men arrive?" Eva asked.

"Not for another month or even two." He met her eyes, and Eva was glad to see his inner storm had dissipated slightly.

"Well, I know as much about this place as Wilanna. I am sure we can manage without them. Mila is a capable woman as well." Mila had proved that on the journey north. She had a natural efficiency, from plucking the grouse Darys took down along the road, to tending the horses or campfire. It astounded Eva, but then she admitted to not being the most practical sort. Eva would make a disappointing wife for a farmer.

"Yes, Mila will be an asset," Illiah agreed thoughtfully. "Isn't she supposed to be your lady-in-waiting?"

Eva gave Illiah a disbelieving look. "Do I look like I need a lady-in-waiting? Actually, don't answer that," she added as Illiah opened his mouth. The look in his eye was pure mischievousness. She was willing to forgive him - mischievous was better than the hopeless grief that had been there moments before. "Anyway, speaking of Mila, I was going to show the girls around their new home."

Eva was exhausted by the time she finally crawled into her bed.

Her feet felt like they were carved from rocks, her legs, wood. She banked her fire to keep the cold shadows from taking over her room. Cold, creeping shadows like the cold, creeping memories she had seen obscuring Illiah's hope.

In the dead of night, Eva woke from a startling dream. Her eyes went wide before she rubbed them in confusion. She was highly suspicious the dream had been a vision.

The vision had been of Illiah. Illiah, and a woman. He had his short, well-trimmed beard so she knew it had not been Caeris.

The two lovers were ensconced in what could only be Illiah's chambers at court. The room and furnishings were grand, opulent, the perfect place for a prince to woo a beautiful lady into his bed. The young woman was from court, but Eva could not put a name to her face. They were naked. It was horribly clear they were enjoying each other. Thoroughly.

Eva shut her mental eyes and willed herself back to now. Her cheeks burned with embarrassment. Thankfully, there was no one but the night to bear witness to her deviant magic. What a strange, useless, irrelevant vision to come past her barriers. What a deeply personal, intimate thing to see.

Embarrassment was a passing thing, but the stabbing, gutted feeling left behind could only be jealousy, and it lingered like a horrible stench. As hard as she tried to cast it aside, she could not. Whomever Illiah - Eva's mind whispered the word *fucked* - was no concern of hers. Absolutely no concern. None of her business. So why did she feel so heartbroken and upset?

She turned in bed and put her face into her pillow, pulling her blanket over her head. If she could block out the physical world perhaps, it would make the images in her mind disappear. Nope. It didn't help. She still felt a desperate longing she didn't quite understand.

The sunlight made a funny black shadow dance across Eva's floor. Calypso was perched on her window ledge, soaking in the sun, ruffling his feathers. A typical morning at the Keep, a routine she had missed dearly. The raven didn't look eager to come in. He was just letting her know he was about and when she was ready, his presence required some acknowledgment.

The sun beckoned Eva from her bed to the forest. The wildness was waiting. But Eva didn't want to get up. After being awoken by the arbitrary vision, a scene both primal and beautiful, sleep had been elusive. After the deviant dream-vision, she had other dreams. In her dreams, her hands were tangled in short, dark hair. Fingers touched her lips, her throat. The touch was a fire that begged her to leap into its flames. The flames became familiar forest-green eyes that devoured her. Or maybe she devoured them. In her dream she tried to douse the fire, but Illiah was the water and it poured over her like sweet summer rain.

Ridiculous dreams. There was no place in Eva's mind or heart for such carnal notions.

The giant raven, grown large on Scrub's cooking, gave a huge, raucous caw. Eva glared up at him. He regarded her with one large, obsidian eye.

"All right, all right. I'm getting up, you ungrateful, feathered bell," she mumbled, pulling on her stockings. The floor was cold. Her fire had long spent itself, and the sun had not yet warmed her room from the silver-clad night. She washed her face in the basin of cold water and dressed quickly.

She made her way down to the kitchens with heavy steps, trying to distract herself from her tantalizingly sweet dreams. She berated herself the whole way. She was a foolish girl. Illiah was the brother of her betrothed. And he was irritating. Bossy. Arrogant. At least most of the time. Even if ... No. No ifs.

It wasn't as late in the day as she had originally thought. In the kitchen, Scrub was still hard at work making the day's bread, kneading a huge ball of dough on the wooden counter. He paused just long enough to wish her a good morning and hand her a steaming bowl of porridge, tossing her piece of bread from the day before. She thanked him and started into her breakfast.

She hadn't been so distracted by her visions since the disturbing night visions of the war. And that just made her think of Illiah again. Damn.

"Good morning, my lady, Scrub," came an all-too-familiar voice. Illiah walked purposefully into the kitchen. When Illiah called her "my lady", he managed to make it sound respectful and teasing at the same time. He looked sharp and well dressed like he had slept well, a contrast to how she had seen him the night before.

Scrub offered him a warm greeting and handed him a heaping bowl of porridge and grumbled apologetically about the bread not being ready yet.

Eva's face flushed as Illiah flashed her a warm smile. The warmth from her face licked down to her toes, lingering in the region between her legs. She looked down and continued eating. At least he would never know her thoughts.

"I thought you might have time today to show me the lay of the land? The mist is gone," Illiah asked, sitting down next to her on the long bench. There was plenty of room, but Eva's thumping heart was acutely aware there was hardly a finger's breadth between them.

"Only if you let me ride your horse."

Illiah scowled. "You have your own horse."

"I have the king's old horse. He can't keep up in these woods."

"What happened to little Lily?" Scrub interjected. "She was such a sweet little mare, sure-footed."

"I gave her to Mila," Eva replied. Illiah seemed impervious to her withering glare. "Well? Are you going to let me ride him or not?"

"Fine. You can ride Sasha."

"I have to check on Mila and Murryn before we leave," Eva added, feeling the satisfaction of a sweet victory.

"If you two head southwest, keep a lookout for those late-summer basket berries. They would make some lovely tarts," Scrub mentioned.

"I'll keep that in mind, and bring a basket," Eva assured the cook.

☾

Illiah winced as she mounted up. Eva ignored him. He was just being overly dramatic in an attempt to irritate her. Sasha was a tall horse, but Eva refused the leg up offered, managing to land gracefully in the saddle. Her belly twisted with excitement, similar to the first time she had ridden Sasha. Illiah sat astride his stallion in an instant. Penn stamped his foot, eager to be moving.

"Lead on," Illiah encouraged.

They did go southwest - the forest was more open, drier, with less moss on the ground. The birch leaves showed a hint of golden, their trunks white against the fading summer cascade. Eva kept to the ridge so that whenever they had a slight vista she could point out landmarks and directions. Always to the north were the looming mountains and the dense trees of the Great Forest.

"This looks like an old road," Illiah said, pointing north. It ran down along a shallow dell. Eva was surprised Illiah noticed it, for it was indeed an old road, an ancient road, but it was almost impossible to see it without some imagination. Eva had learned about it from the Guardians.

"That path leads to the bottom of a large cliff, at the very edge of the Great Forest," Eva told him. "Do you want to see it?"

Illiah nodded, and Eva pushed Sasha into a canter. The path, overgrown as it was, was flat. Cantering along it was highly enjoyable. Penn easily caught up, and Illiah kept them at a pace side by side.

Eva had no need to reign Sasha in to halt when they approached the border between Jullayah and the Great Forest. The horses could sense the otherness about the place. They slowed and came to a stop without the need for their riders' command. Illiah's expression didn't reveal much. Sometimes his face was expressive to the point of hilarity. Sometimes he was impossible to read. He looked ahead of him at the Great Forest with a calm, unreadable expression that reminded Eva of Caeris.

The great cliff that ran along the border of the Great Forest and Jullayah gave way to a chasm perhaps fifteen paces wide. The Forest spilled out from the chink, the only place in Jullayah one could stand next to a giant tree of the Great Forest, a tree as old and wise as the earth itself, steeped in time and ancient magic. If ten men linked hands and encircled the tree, they might reach around it.

"I think here, at one time, long, long ago, there was a road that ran through the Great Forest linking Jullayah with the realms beyond. No one goes that way now. No one dares the Great Forest anymore," Eva told him in a hushed voice. Not since the magic became fickle and wary. But she wasn't about to mention it.

The whole place was quiet, hushed, as if every living creature who lived in the shadow of that place knew silence and reverence were required, as if the trees demanded it.

"I never imagined a tree could grow so big," Illiah remarked. His voice sounded unusually loud in the still air that haunted the gateway to the Great Forest. Maybe the trees remembered some ill of long ago, still and silent, sentinel guards. Eva always felt that if a great danger came, the trees would move and close in to protect the Forest. There was a watchfulness about them, a knowing. They groaned and squeaked, but there was no breeze. Lula once told of a time, before she was a Guardian, a great evil came to the Forest, and the Allmakers went deep into the trees. Since then, the Great Forest has been forbidden to humans and Kitarrans alike - with some exceptions.

Eva dismounted. She had nothing to fear from the trees; she who loved the Great Forest. She didn't think she could visit them without taking a moment to touch one. They knew her. She placed her hand upon the surprisingly warm bark and felt the tree's quiet energy, its lifeblood, its slow and steady heartbeat. She didn't talk to the trees anymore, but she could almost hear their whispers. Eva smiled to herself. She relinquished the touch and turned back to Illiah, catching his eye. He had that look again, questioning and amused. She didn't offer answers.

"I think we'll find some berries over that next hill. And there is a good lookout that would interest you," Eva told him. He nodded and gestured for her to lead once more.

They found a whole hillside of basket berry bushes loaded with plump, ripe berries. Another week and the berries would be too far gone to be of any use to Scrub. They let the horses graze on the sparse tufts of grass while they picked.

"Tarek and Mahone certainly followed you with a high degree of circumspect at court and the journey here, and yet they did not ride out with us," Illiah mused.

Eva smiled. "They get tired of chasing me around. Keeping track of me in the forest has always been a hopeless task. Don't tell my aunt," Eva said. "And besides, today I have you. And Calypso is around here somewhere, even if he hasn't made an appearance. He always keeps an eye on me and alerts me to any trouble."

"The raven?"

Eva nodded. "You're supposed to be picking those, not eating all of them." Eva swatted his hand as he popped another berry into his mouth. He grinned rebelliously back at her.

"How did you ever train a raven?"

"I didn't. I saved his life when he was a hatchling, and he has stuck around ever since."

Illiah fully accepted this. Eva felt a pang of regret that she couldn't tell him how Calypso had been her first lesson using her healing magic. She remembered the bent, almost dead bird Lula had found abandoned in the Great Forest. It was near impossible to accept that the handsome raven had grown from the poor, helpless bundle of gray skin and pin feathers. Giving the little bird a chance at life and realizing the possibilities of her magic had made that day one she would never forget.

"So, how come you left Caer Andri early? I thought you always traveled with your aunt?" Illiah asked.

Eva was quiet, trying to decide how to answer, if she wanted to answer. But she liked talking to Illiah. Honesty was something that came easily between them. Mostly.

"I left because I don't like court."

Illiah shot her a surprised look.

"Why would I?" she retorted. "I grew up here in the forest, surrounded by quiet and simplicity, people I knew and trusted, more or less. There is nothing of this at court."

"I thought maybe it had something to do with Caeris parading his pregnant mistress around," Illiah said after a moment.

Eva sighed. "Caeris will never love me," she murmured, throwing the berries into her basket with a little more fervor.

"Do you love him?"

Eva turned to look at him directly, shocked by his bold question. Then she laughed softly. "Arranged marriages are never about love."

"No, I guess not."

A thought occurred to Eva. She felt bold enough to voice it. "Did you leave a betrothed behind to come to court? I imagine such things are much the same in the south."

Illiah scoffed. "No. I was never betrothed. And yes, some things are the same everywhere. My family - my foster family - is not well enough renowned to be sought after for alliances, allowing such simple people the simple pleasure of marrying for love. My sister, though, was betrothed to a man, before the war," he said, trying to keep his voice devoid of emotion. "This man sought the marriage not based on alliances, although he was very fond of my father's horses, but based on my sister's fair looks. My sister is young. She didn't love him, but she saw that he was a wealthy man, and kind enough. My father could hardly refuse, so my sister agreed. But that all changed after the war. My father would never force her into marriage. My sister might never marry." His voice was sad.

"What happened?"

"She was captured by the invaders." His voice grew heavy and his brows furrowed, a shadow falling around them. "Most women would not have survived what she had to endure before we got to her. Many do not have the strength of character or heart."

Eva didn't ask for details. The visions of rape and abuse of women, young and old, from the war were never far away. She couldn't help but think of Mila, who suffered the same at the hands of someone all too close to home. At least the invaders had been punished. Mila would never receive justice for her hurts.

"My brothers and I avenged her. Our retaliation on the invaders was harsh and merciless. I suppose revenge is a comfort to some, but not for me," Illiah went on, echoing Eva's thoughts.

"How many brothers do you have?" He had mentioned it, but she couldn't recall what he had said. It had seemed like a lot.

"Counting Caeris?" Illiah asked with a twisted smile.

"Not counting Caeris."

"I have three brothers still living, and our youngest brother Aralis died in the war. He was only seventeen," Illiah went on. "Kaile is my age. We are only a month apart. Lindin is next, a year older than Kaile, then Evyn who is the eldest. He is married with two young children." Illiah smiled fondly. "Freya is my sister - she is sixteen, although she has aged years from her experience."

"You must miss them."

Illiah shrugged. "Kaile is here, and Lindin will come soon. Yes, I miss them, but I was not meant for farming and raising horses and little children. Don't get me wrong, I love my nieces, but I always knew I would leave home, seek my fortunes away from the estate. I just didn't think that my fortunes were already made for me," he added with a grin. "This basket is full. We should have brought another."

Eva looked down. The basket was full, brimming with the purple and red berries.

"I guess so. Maybe Murryn will want to come out tomorrow with me to pick some more."

"I'll come out with you again. We could look for the guard post from the old map," Illiah said eagerly.

Eva smiled. Her stomach flipped over with a joy that was juxtaposed by her unease.

CHAPTER 17

COTOCH

SOMETIMES Cotoch had strange dreams.

For a long time, he thought they were just that - strange, repetitive, perhaps they held a deeper meaning lost to him. Then one day, he figured it out. He understood. They were not dreams. And they were not his.

He dreamed of a tall forest. The trees opened into a clearing of tall grass, dry, not unlike the Tarm in autumn after the hot summer sun baked the green to golden. In the center of the clearing was a pool of water. And, in the manner of dreams, it was difficult to tell if it was small like a puddle or vast like a lake. The water was deep and dark and filled with tiny pricks of light. It was the night sky reflected in the water. But it was not night.

Cotoch heard whispers. He cringed like an intruder, a thief. When he saw no one, he stole a glance at the water. The stars disappeared, replaced by knowledge.

A girl with pale hair sat beside a Kitarran made of sunshine and memories. The water flickered and flashed and rippled. The girl again, but this time as a woman. She had grown into a beautiful creature and Cotoch felt something tighten within him: longing, lust.

Kitarra, she must go to Kitarra … Her son … Her son will be a force. He will restore what is lost and broken … He will …

The whispers were thick and old and steeped in a magic he almost knew. They spoke to the Kitarran that seemed made of light. Neither saw him.

Cotoch did not hear the rest because he woke.

The angry shudder flickering through the *varing* made Cotoch realize it was not just a dream, not just his own imagination. His prisoner was reacting to the intrusion into its thoughts, its dreams. The result of Cotoch's *candarii* magic.

He wondered if Crea knew. Crea had destroyed half her realm to kill a man and now there was a woman the Kitarrans wanted. He wondered if he should tell her what he had seen. What would the Goddess do? He had stumbled across Kitarra's hope. The young woman and her someday child. Crea would want the woman dead. Cotoch wanted the woman for himself.

Ideas and plans wove an abstract map inside his head. He didn't know where the young woman was, but he would find out. He never backed away from a challenge. He had the power of the *candarii* at his fingertips.

Cotoch grinned and stretched and laughed. It was a beautiful morning.

CHAPTER 18

EVA

EVA WAS LEARNING that when Illiah got an idea, life could not continue until it was explored and thoroughly exhausted.

Illiah was adamant about the need for a guard post. He admitted his dislike of the deep valleys and hidden hills. He wanted a guard to be able to watch the road. He reiterated how it would be a necessary experience for the recruits. Eva told him he had mentioned it several times already.

So they went scouting.

The hill where the map marked the guard post was through a rough patch of forest, and then there was the creek. They tethered the horses and followed the creek until they could cross without getting wet over their ankles. The water was frigid even for the tail end of summer.

The rocks were slippery. They argued over the best place to cross. If Eva was stubborn, Illiah was more so. He picked a spot that was proving trickier than first anticipated. To get to the little beach on the far side required a series of carefully placed steps using the exposed yet still slippery rocks. The wrong step would land them in the cold water and leave them with chafing, wet shoes. In spring, under the influence of the winter thaw, it would be impossible even to contemplate.

Illiah chose the placement of his feet wisely. Eva chose her own rocks to serve as steps. She would have to jump the last bit because her legs were shorter, but it was not beyond her ability.

"Here, take my hand," Illiah said, standing on the beach, leaning out over the creek toward her, his hand outstretched so she could grab it.

"No, I'm fine. I can make it," she told him, gauging the jump, her arms out for balance as she stood on the precarious rock. She was about to take the leap when he took her hand and pulled her onto the beach, his grin triumphant.

"I didn't need your help!"

"Yes, you did. You almost fell."

"No, I didn't!"

"Just let me be chivalrous for a moment, won't you?" he demanded with a grin. Eva was grinning right back and tried unsuccessfully to school her face. Only then did he let go of her hand, as if he just realized he was holding it a little too possessively. "I guess a bridge might be in order if this place works out."

"It would be easier," Eva commented.

They hiked in companionable silence as Eva steered them in the direction she remembered from the map. The track up the hill was a scramble. When they reached the top, even Illiah was short of breath. Illiah cut off his commentary about precipitous, pathless hills and took in the view of the southeast. They could see the Keep, the mountains, of course, and parts of the road winding through the forest to the south. Far to the south was a pale haze where the hills became less mountainous, and the forest gave way to farms and fields.

Illiah was thoughtful. Then he disappeared up a large evergreen with the formidable ease of a weasel. Since when did princes climb trees? After a moment he informed her that he could see the road, and with an ax, he could fell enough trees for it to be a good guard post. He looked pleased when he finally came down, brushing the dirt and sap from his hands.

"Tomorrow, we build a bridge!" he announced.

"We?"

"Sure. You look capable."

"Thanks," Eva drawled. She wasn't sure bridge building was an occupation she wanted to indulge in.

"What was that?" Illiah's expression lengthened alarmingly.

Eva heard it too. The horses. Rasping squeals punctuated by snorts. Not the sound of happy animals.

"The horses," she said.

Illiah nodded, his tight mouth mirroring Eva's unease. They

scrambled back down the way they had come, the sounds of the pan-icking animals urging them onward.

"Grab onto the ferns. They have deep, sturdy roots - no, not those ones! These ones," Eva coached as they made their way down the steep slope. This time Eva took Illiah's helping hand to cross the creek.

Penn and Sasha were still tethered where they had left them. The poor animals were clearly agitated. Penn stamped and tossed his head. The whites of Sasha's eyes were visible. They snorted and huffed. Eva took Sasha's bridle and spoke soothing words to him.

"Something spooked them," Illiah said, looking at the forest.

"Obviously. I wonder what it could have been. There have been no bears or wolves or mountain cats seen in these parts for decades."

The forest seemed to hold its breath. No birds sang. No leaves rus-tled. Even the clouds above seemed to pause in their traverse across the sky.

"There is something out there," Illiah said, pulling his sword from its sheath.

"Where?" Eva followed Illiah's gaze but saw nothing.

"I don't know. I just saw a shadow. I couldn't tell what it was. I don't think it was a person. An animal, maybe?"

Eva stroked the soft fur of Sasha's neck. The horse drew short, panicky breaths, but he was calmer than moments before. Eva's eyes raked the forest around them, as did Illiah's. The stillness transformed the forest into something other.

From nowhere, a thing collided with Eva's face. A cool and black silky thing. Sasha reared in alarm, pulling the rein from Eva's hand. It was a mercy she didn't lose her balance.

The thing was Calypso. The raven managed to anchor himself onto her shoulder with his clawed feet. She began to berate him for his carelessness and scaring her half to death, but she stopped. She could feel him trembling as he pressed close to her neck.

"Calypso is terrified," Eva said, trying to get the raven onto her forearm. He optimistically tried to hide in the crook of her neck. What did he think he was, a sparrow? But he wouldn't budge. He put his beaky head under her chin, his claws digging uncomfortably into her shoulder. "What scared you, Cally?" He didn't even give her a croon. "I don't like this," Eva told Illiah.

"Let's get back," Illiah said. "It was probably just an animal of some kind."

Eva agreed because logic outweighed doubt. But she felt watched. More unsettling was the familiarity of the watchfulness. Like it had seen her before. Like it knew her and wanted to reach into her head and soul and pick out the tasty bits to eat. For a fleeting moment, the dead faces of the men from Dweller's Knoll blotted out the sun. She would never forget that day. But beyond her memories, there was nothing to see. And yet her unease did not leave until they were within the walls of the Keep.

Illiah was unperturbed by the strange incident. He didn't wait for the next day to start his bridge. He went out that afternoon with Tarek. They took saws and axes and came back with the twilight, exhausted from an afternoon of felling trees. Eva didn't like it. But what could she say? In her mind, every reason to keep Illiah inside the Keep sounded paranoid and controlling. And she wasn't his keeper.

Calypso was still terrified and unusually quiet for an opinionated bird. He only moved from her shoulder to Murryn's. That night he slept on Eva's bed in a most un-raven-like fashion, snuggled on her pillow next to her head, like a cat.

The next day Tarek and Illiah went out again. Eva was busy all day helping Mila, who had many ideas about reorganizing the Keep for the influx of people. Mila had talked to Illiah about her ideas, and he had given her the new position of head stewardess. After learning that several of Illiah's men who would be residing at the Keep had wives, even babes on the way, Mila was eager to make some rooms available to them, but it required some cleaning and energy.

Mila took to her new position like a hummingbird to a flower, surpassing even Wilanna's expectations. When the steward and Wilanna said their farewells, it was with glad hearts that they were not abandoning their beloved Keep to careless hands. They had kept the Keep as well as they could in memory of Lord Finnan.

Tarek returned to the Keep as the sun was getting low, just in time for the dinner that Scrub had prepared. Illiah was absent as they sat down to eat. Tarek told them Illiah planned to be along shortly. He was just finishing something. They had orders not to wait.

They ate, and Illiah still didn't come.

Eva offered to find their tardy lord. The sun was a burning sliver above the horizon. Soon the forest would be bathed in a brief twilight before night descended. Eva had borne witness to Illiah's navigation skills in the forest and wasn't convinced he wouldn't get lost. And she couldn't forget the strangeness of the previous day.

She threw her cloak about her shoulders. The air was chilled without the sun to warm it. Calypso perched on her shoulder, almost his old self again. His wings brushed against her face as he flitted off into the trees, seeming to know the direction she sought.

Eva found Illiah at the creek consorting or arguing, it was hard to tell which, with his new bridge. He had shucked his shirt and didn't seem to care that his feet and legs were soaked to his knees. His pants were rolled up around his thighs, his boots discarded in a pile with his shirt and cloak. He was pulling a large piece of lumber across the breadth of the creek to form another spine of the bridge.

He lurched when he noticed her silently studying him. A blush rose to Eva's cheeks as she realized she had been staring. She looked away from his neatly muscled frame crosshatched with old and new scars, some still red and distorted. She forced herself to inspect his construction instead.

Tarek and Illiah had spent their time making lumber. There was a stack of neatly trimmed beams, similar to the one Illiah was wrestling with. Eva was pretty sure the wood was winning. And Illiah knew it.

"It's getting dark," Eva told him.

"A good observation," he retorted acidly.

"Why did you send Tarek back if you didn't mean to come yourself? It looks like you need help. You shouldn't be out here alone," Eva observed, crossing her arms.

Illiah glared up at her from beneath the heavy beam that looked less like lumber and more like it was trying to escape back into the forest to rejoin its brethren. His eyes were dark and desperate and stubborn. Then he looked like he had a thought.

"Come here. You can help me get this across."

"You're jesting."

"Nope, get over here." He gestured for her to come.

"My shoes -"

"- will dry. We have to get this across." He saw she wasn't coming.

"Why does it need to happen right now? Can't you get Tarek and come back tomorrow?"

"No. I got it this far, I could do the rest myself, but it would be faster if you helped me." He looked impatient. "Please," he added softly.

"You are so stubborn." Eva threw off her cloak in consternation. "Fine, I'll try."

She tucked her long skirt into her belt and took off her boots and socks before stepping into the water. It was cold. Her feet would be numb within a minute. She took the opposite side of the beam and at Illiah's signal pulled and lifted. It moved, a little. Illiah was encouraged.

"You're stronger than you look," he noted between pulls.

Eva resented that she was unable to spit out the retort on her tongue because it took all her strength to lift the great piece of wood. After a few more pulls, Eva's retort became a curse. She almost dropped the log on Illiah's foot, but they made it to the far bank and plunked it on the spot Illiah had prepared for it. Eva's breath was ragged. She glared at Illiah, hopping back across the creek for her warm shoes. Her feet were aching from the chill of the water.

"Thank you," Illiah said, holding out her cloak for her. "Not many girls would do that."

"Not many men would ask." It wasn't meant as a compliment.

A week later, Illiah had finished the bridge and made good headway on the trail to the bluff. Of course, he couldn't devote all his time to the creation of the guard post. He was the lord of the entire Keep.

Eva could not fathom how the Keep had managed for so many years without him. If there was a problem, he found a solution. Or he was the solution. If a difficult job needed attention, he appeared from some dark corridor and proceeded to apply himself to it effortlessly. In the evenings he relaxed in front of the fire, discussing some fine point of swordsmanship with Altos or played a quiet game of strategy with whoever would take him on, usually old Enid. His patience with the old geriatric was a marvel.

Usually at some point every day, Tarek, Mahone, Darys, and Illiah convened for a practice, either outside in the recently reinstated practice yard (the pigs evicted) or in the great hall. Altos would sit on the sidelines and scoff at them. He dismissed any offers to spar complaining over his old bones.

Cooler weather came with the onset of fall, and more practice sessions happened in the great hall. However, Illiah did insist that practices should not always be so comfortable. Rain, wind, and mud were important ingredients for building endurance. He said this while sipping hot cider, stretching out his long legs on the table after a particularly grueling bout with Mahone, who was determined to best the young lord at some point. It was just after the midday meal, a brief time of rest for the bustling residents.

Eva looked up from the book she had been reading to catch his eye, giving him an amused and disbelieving look.

"At least the young recruits will need to believe that," he added with a laugh.

"Tell me about these recruits," Eva asked, putting down her book.

"Caeris is sending a rabble of his guards for some hard training, the beginning of a long chain of young men who will be coming to the Keep to train. His army has been given too much slack in the years since your father died. The palace guards have grown soft," Illiah told her. "I think Caeris's men will be doing as much building as learning how to defend themselves and their men against an enemy." He paused, taking another sip from his mug. "We need the manpower to expand. Kaile is bringing the architect with him when he comes."

Eva nodded. "The old dormitories burned down."

"I know." By the look in his eyes, he knew her parents had died in that fire.

Eva turned back to her book.

"You read too much." He tugged playfully at her book. She pulled it back, protecting it from his coarse hands.

"Just because I grew up actually enjoying books, instead of running around, grubby-handed, roping horses and catching rabbits with my teeth, don't hold it against me," she shot back at him.

She had been surprised at his inability to read. It seemed impossible that Lord Illiah could have any failings, he was so irritatingly competent. He explained that it was no fault of his parents. They had tried to educate him, hiring tutors, which his father had paid handsomely to teach his young boys and small daughter. Illiah told Eva how frustrating and discouraging it had been for him. He just couldn't grasp the written word. After a while, he had refused to participate. There had been no threat his foster parents could come up with - and were willing to see through - that would make him keep at it. Eventually, they gave up. Eva rolled his eyes. He could be so stubborn.

Illiah laughed. "Nah, the rabbits were too fast."

Altos was also laughing from where he sat engaged with old Enid in a game of cards, listening to their conversation. He gave Eva a cockeyed look.

"I seem to remember a certain little girl who was off with the boys, catching fish in the creek with her bare hands when she forgot her pole," he said, a twinkle in his eye.

"Nonsense," Eva said, turning back to her book. She looked up under her brows at Illiah to see that he was grinning at her. She hid her own grin behind her book.

A loud patter of feet echoed through the hall making them all turn their heads. Murryn was running across the vast, nearly empty room. Her red mane of hair streamed behind her, her pale skin flushed from exertion, a wide smile on her face.

"Illiah!" the girl exclaimed, coming to a dramatic halt before him. "A scout wearing Lady Ullian's colors is on the way here! I saw him from the east tower!" Illiah stood instantly, making his way outside, thanking Murryn for her prompt report. She grinned up at him proudly.

The scout wore Lady Clarette's colors, but he told Illiah that a host of southern men were riding with the lady and expected to reach the Keep by nightfall.

Illiah's southern men, Lady Clarette and her entourage, and a slew of royal guards arrived with the setting sun to a welcome song sung by a raven. Calypso's voice was almost impossible to hear over the din of the courtyard: horses hooves on the cobbles, the voices of relieved travelers finally arrived at their destination, the shouts of men reunited with their beloved leader. The courtyard was bursting.

Illiah's men worshipped him, and Illiah obviously loved his men. It was visible in the meeting of eyes, a grinning face, a silent look here, a hand grasped there, a shoulder given a slight shake. They had all been through terrible hardship, bled and grieved together.

Orders were given. Horses needed to be stabled, wagons needed to be unloaded, rooms and beds needed to be found. Eva was suddenly tripping over her bodyguards. Too many new faces and names. Part of her wanted them to leave. They were too noisy. The Keep was meant to be quiet and safe.

She took a deep, reasonable breath and went to greet her aunt, picking Clarette out of the throng of people easily. The rose among the wildflowers. Duty fulfilled, the rose on her way to her room to rest, Eva scanned the crowd for Illiah. He was talking to Kaile and another man who must be his other brother, Lindin. The man looked very much like Kaile, though not as tall. Seeing Illiah standing beside them made Eva smile. The resemblance he shared with his foster brothers was striking, even though they shared no blood. They all had the same black-brown hair, the same tall, lean build, the same well-defined features of face. Only Illiah had green eyes where the other two had eyes of deep blue.

They said something to Illiah that made his brows pull and wrinkle. He searched the crowd with intense scrutiny. He shouted a name Eva couldn't quite catch. The host of people paused to follow Illiah with their eyes as he cut a path through the crowd toward a young woman.

Eva walked forward, anxious to see what was happening. Her breath caught in her throat as Illiah gathered the young woman fiercely into his arms. Eva felt like she was falling, a fool dancing too close to the edge of a cliff.

The young woman was tall and slim, her long, wheat-blond hair escaping from several long braids cascading down her back. She was startlingly beautiful, with fine features and large expressive eyes. Eva needed to hear their exchange.

"What are you doing here?" Illiah demanded as he released the strange beauty ever so slightly from his embrace.

The girl stepped back and stood up straight, giving Illiah a stubborn look. She reached behind her for something, someone. A man stepped forward and took her hand in his. Illiah stared the man down with an expression Eva had never seen on his face. It was clear the two holding hands were lovers. The man was tall, young, handsome in a pretty way. The way he stood spoke of arrogance, his chin tilted up, although he quailed under Illiah's anger.

"Talamir!" Illiah hissed. Illiah's hand went for his belt knife instinctively. Eva had never seen Illiah act rashly, and going for his weapon was surely a rash act. The girl stood in front of her lover.

"Illiah, don't you dare!" the girl shrieked angrily.

"What lies have you been telling my sister to make her follow you across the realm? She should be home with Da." Illiah's voice was cold steel.

Illiah's sister. The oppressive weight constricting Eva's breath released.

"Illiah, stop. I couldn't stay behind without my husband," the girl pleaded. She looked too young to own the words "my husband."

Illiah seemed to agree. He looked from the girl to the man called Talamir in disbelief. He struggled to control his features and calm his voice. "Now is not the time, but I want a full account from you Talamir," he said, pointing his finger at the man. Talamir nodded, not meeting Illiah's eyes. The couple disappeared into the crowd, out of their lord's sight, quickly and quietly.

"My lady," Eva realized Kaile was addressing her. He was looking around the Keep with a shrewd eye.

"Kaile. How was your journey?" Eva asked pleasantly. She didn't know Kaile, but Illiah spoke of him often and with fondness.

"Easy," he replied.

"I am glad for that. Welcome to the Keep."

"Thank you. Lindin, this is Lady Evangeline," Kaile said, introducing his brother at his side.

"My lady," Lindin said with a slight incline of his head, which Eva returned. Kaile continued to introduce her to Illiah's men. Eva tried hard to catalog the names and new faces, but she would have a hard time remembering them all. She was a hypocrite for teasing Illiah about it. She could remember and name any plant in the forest, but people for some reason always eluded her, much to her aunt's dismay.

Eva went to find Mila to ask if she needed any help. Mila looked thankful for the offer and set Eva to work immediately. Together they figured out where everyone would sleep. Murryn bobbed about like a puppy, so Mila sent her off to help Scrub in the kitchen. He would no doubt still be flustered about what to feed all the people, cursing that he should have had more notice, that half a day was not enough to get a feast ready - and Scrub did love preparing feasts.

Eva noticed Mila, once or twice, pull her hair closer around her neck, conscious of the scar that was once her tell tale tattoo, the sign of a culla girl. The young men stole glances at Mila. Eva was unsurprised. Her friend was a beautiful, young, obviously capable woman - naturally they would look at her. But they said nothing rude or inappropriate. Eva would expect no less from Illiah's men, or Clarette's. Also, everyone thought Mila was Tarek's sister. No one in their right mind would want to cross the intimidating bodyguard.

"So, I think that covers everyone," Mila announced happily. "And no one will have to sleep in the stables after all."

"I think you can relax, Mila. Everyone seems happy enough," Eva said, looking about the great hall.

"I think you're right." Mila sank onto the bench beside Eva.

They were wrong. The crowd of Illiah's right-hand men wanted for something apparently, because Illiah came over to them, wearing his most charming smile.

"Do you think you two girls could run into the cellar and grab some of those bottles of blackberry wine I saw down there the other night?" Illiah asked.

Eva regarded him evenly, but she was already standing up. "And what were you doing scrounging down in the cellars?"

His charming smile became an impish grin. "Never you mind, young lady."

The Keep cellars were dusty but well stocked. Scrub liked to collect wines, although there were rarely occasions to drink them. The result was an ample stockpile, some bottles dating back at least ten years. Mila and Eva grabbed as many bottles as they could carry.

"I know Illiah said blackberry wine, but this white looks wonderful. I think I can make out something on the faded label. Peach, I think it says. Must be from the south. You and I can share this one," Eva said. Mila grinned back.

They deposited their load before Illiah. His men praised them loudly for their efforts. Wine was poured. Many toasts were made. Eva and Mila found themselves at a different table, joined Freya, Illiah's sister and her husband, Talamir.

Talamir and Freya were quiet, sitting close and holding hands under the table. Freya's glance shifted to the other men at the table. Eva remembered what Illiah had said about his unfortunate sister. He said she would never marry, that she had been taken and abused. But she had married, and yet her brother was unhappy about it.

Murryn came out, followed by Scrub and a young boy Eva had not seen previously. All three were carrying platters heaped with hot and savory food. They deposited them on the tables, promising more to come, so Eva and Mila got up to help them.

In the kitchen were more platters. Eva gave Scrub high acclaim for making such an extravagant meal in such a short time. Scrub was still in a tiff and was not accepting of her compliments, saying that he could have done so much more with just a little more time.

Eva learned the young boy was Illiah's page, Tarran. She remembered he was the same age as Murryn, making him the youngest member of Illiah's crew. The Keep was a long way from the young boy's home.

Tarran was a thin boy, small for his age. He reminded Eva of a street urchin, even though his clothes were fine and well made, marking him a servant to royalty. He had a tussle of golden-brown curls and nutty-brown skin. His eyes were wary, though he went about his task with confidence.

The meal was delicious. Scrub really was a master at what he did. The little fruit cakes weighed heavily in Eva's stomach, at odds with her head, which felt a little light from the sweet wine.

Illiah and his men grew louder the more wine they consumed. To everyone's surprise, Scrub produced a barrel of honey-gold ale. Where he had kept it hidden, no one knew. Illiah was amused but gave him a hard time about his secrecy.

Some of the men procured musical instruments and lively music ensued. Eva was delighted. She had not expected such talents from Illiah's warriors. Several of the men had wonderful voices and added their skills to the festivities.

The ale and noise flowed generously and the celebratory atmosphere became boisterous. Mila and Murryn opted to retire. Eva decided to join them. The three walked up the long flight of stairs together. The silence was welcome, a stark contrast to the boisterous hall. An indicator of the days to come.

The sisters had moved upstairs to the steward's old chamber. The girls didn't mind the climb. Eva and Mila were quiet, listening to Murryn's litany about the newcomers. She knew all their names already.

Eva bid her friends good night as they continued down the hall to their room at the end.

Eva changed her destination and decided to go to the council room. Now that Illiah's men had arrived at last, the room would truly be Illiah's. To be used as it was designed, for council. A little voice in her head whispered that the council room had never been meant for her. It was a room for men and leaders, not for a young woman with hopeless dreams.

Eva sighed as she opened the door. It was empty, exuding solitude and peace. She knelt down to make a fire, waiting as it caught and lit up the room, warming her face instantly.

Once it was burning reliably, she curled into one of the chairs and sat waiting for it to warm up the room. The flames danced and grew and stretched. Her book lay open on her lap, but she did not pick it up.

She shivered. A great change was taking place. She felt it in her bones, in her heart. Something was stirring and she didn't like it. She didn't want to say goodbye to her home, her quiet places. She didn't want to lose Illiah. The presence of all the men meant Illiah wouldn't have time to go out riding with her or welcome her into his council room. She would be a hindrance, a distraction. There was the training. The new barracks. Illiah's beloved guard post. The prince's architect had made the journey and would be spending the winter at the Keep overseeing the ambitious new build. Yes, Illiah would be too busy to spare time for her.

Eva's thoughts dissolved with a sudden bolt of surprise as the heavy wooden door creaked to life. Illiah. He saw her and nodded. He looked grim, followed by a glum-looking Talamir.

"No, you can stay for this," Illiah said, raising a hand as Eva started to stand, mumbling about excusing herself. "I saw Mahone out in the hallway. I figured you were in here. I noticed you left the hall earlier. I knew there was a good chance you would be here, hiding from the rabble," Illiah explained, the corner of his lip curving with a smile. It was gone the instant he turned to Talamir.

Illiah's perception made her feel better than it should have.

"Besides, this won't take long. Sit," he commanded his man. Talamir sat at the long lord's table, looking like a fish in a barrel. Illiah did not sit. He paced. Like a wild cat.

"Does my sister know, Talamir?"

"Know what?"

"Don't you dare play coy with me."

Talamir winced. "Yes. I told her."

"You told her about all the women? You told her about Fillias?"

Talamir's wince deepened at the name. "She knew about Fillias already."

"And what did she think about it?"

"She thought my actions were despicable, which they were."

"Talamir, Freya was raped. She was traumatized. What were you thinking? She is not one of your whores."

"I love her, Illiah."

"You love her? Do you even know what love is?"

"Do you?" Talamir raised his voice before remembering to whom he spoke. Why was Illiah making the man suffer? "I love Freya, and she loves me. She accepts my past, because it is just that - my past. She knows me. She knows that a person can change from their experiences. Have you forgotten that?" Talamir's voice was quiet and calm. His words took a slice out of Illiah's pride. "I know you worry about her," Talamir continued when Illiah said nothing. "I know you would do anything to keep her safe, but that is my job now. And I am honored by the trust she has put in me. And it would honor me - us - to have your blessing."

That undid Illiah. "Of course you have my blessing, Talamir." Illiah placed his hand upon the other man's shoulder. "But as her brother, I warn you if you break her heart and are unfaithful, it will take much more than an oath of loyalty to sway my hand. And I am a prince. No one will stand in my way."

"I will prove my worth for your sister, my lord. Do not doubt me," Talamir said with a bow.

"Off with you, then," Illiah said with a wave of his hand. Talamir nodded, his handsome eyes bright. He left, no doubt to climb into the arms of his waiting wife. A lucky man.

Illiah sank into the chair opposite Eva and regarded her with a faint smile.

"Do you feel like, perhaps, you overreacted a wee bit?" Eva ventured.

Illiah ignored her implication. "It mystifies me. I never thought Talamir a man to settle down with one woman. I have even heard him swear to it. He is a good man, but if he is tethered down, he will run wild. And the women! There have been many. He convinced Fillias he loved her and would marry her only to get into her bed as part of a bet. And Freya, what possibly could she see in him? I certainly would have my reservations about a woman who spreads her legs as eagerly as Talamir is - was - to be in them," he stated, then had the decency to blush at his coarse words.

"They seem happy. They certainly look handsome together."

"Hmm. But he is such a scoundrel and she has always been so inno-cent. I don't understand."

"She is your sister. Thinking otherwise is unnatural. Perhaps she needed something from him. Perhaps she needed reassurance after what she went through that she could love a man and not be afraid. That she was in control of her body, her choices." Eva was glad of the dim light, her face flushed. "Then perhaps it blossomed into some-thing quite different."

Precisely one of Illiah's brows arched. "What exactly are you suggesting?"

"I'm not spelling it out for you, Illiah. Besides, she is your sister, after all. I imagine one does not think of a sister in that way. Forget I said anything about it!" Eva could no longer look him in the eye.

"You're saying a man like Talamir might have something to offer a woman? What about a man like Tannin?" Illiah ventured. Eva could feel his gaze burrowing into her.

"Tannin? Why are we talking about Tannin? What do you even know about him?"

"Your aunt's man." His voice was a thunderstorm of implications. "I saw the way he was looking at you."

Eva narrowed her eyes at him, shaking her head slightly. "You really think I - Tannin - really?" She couldn't even.

"That wouldn't be a good idea."

"Really?" Eva rolled her eyes. "What would you know about what a woman really wants from a man anyway?"

"Excuse me?" Both brows were up.

Eva couldn't believe she was having this conversation with him. It was something women talked about only among themselves, conversations she had had with her aunt or Mila. Plus, she could hardly contribute her knowledge to actual experience.

"Men don't usually pay much attention to what a woman wants." Did she really just say that?

"Except someone like Talamir?"

"Well, from what you said, he is very popular with the ladies, or was. That must be attributed to something." Eva fixed her eyes on her book so she could ignore the amused and slightly uncomfortable look Illiah shot her way.

"That's not true, what you said about men not caring," Illiah murmured. "I can't imagine you have knowledge of these matters, even with Tannin flitting about." His hand took off into flight for a moment.

"I am not simple and ignorant," Eva said, glaring at him.

He laughed at her. "You were the one insulting my gender, and now you feel slighted because I gave you a compliment?"

"I suppose it is a kind of compliment. After all, my virtue is apparently important," Eva said sarcastically, forgiving him instantly. "And you're right. I don't have any experience in those matters. I get my information second hand."

"Ah."

"Why are you looking at me like that?" Eva asked. Illiah's eyes glinted mischievously.

"Remember the first time we met?"

Eva groaned. "Unfortunately, I have not forgotten, not for lack of trying. I nearly ran away that day, never to return to home and duty," she said, covering her eyes.

"So how do you suppose I assume that your virtue is still intact?" He grinned at her obvious discomfort. Eva's cheeks were on fire.

"I don't know. I admit the circumstances could have been misconstrued."

"At first I assumed what anyone would assume, but then I spent some time observing your two bodyguards, and I came to a reasonable conclusion."

"And what is that?"

"That Tarek and Mahone are, in fact, lovers," he said, pausing for dramatic effect, leaning forward in his chair to enjoy her reaction.

"First of all, they are not." Lying was not one of her strengths. "Second of all, don't you have better things to ponder?"

He ignored her second point thoroughly. "They are. I am not a barbarian. Whatever goes on behind their closed door is their business, not mine, or anyone else's, for that matter." He looked well pleased with his deductive prowess, like an otter with a trout. "So the fact that they are not attracted to the opposite sex makes for a more relaxed environment."

"Very eloquently spoken, my lord," Eva replied caustically. Then she said, "Do you think others will notice?" Not everyone was as commendable as Illiah.

Illiah shook his head. "Don't worry about it, Eva. They keep it well guarded, as many do."

"How did you find out?" Eva was still perturbed he had guessed at something she had been ignorant of for years.

"I have known men like them before. There was something familiar about them. It took me a while to figure it out. Your obvious ease with them solidified the notion."

"You don't think I would be that comfortable with my guards if they were attracted to women?"

Illiah shrugged. "You're not that comfortable around me."

Now they were treading into a mud puddle of a conversation Eva didn't want to have with any man, much less a man she respected greatly. A man she could trust with all her secrets if she wanted to. A man she would have liked to meet under very different circumstances.

"I need to go to bed," she said, making an excuse to get up. She made for the door, but he caught her by the arm lightly, halting her. His warm touch moved through every part of her. The air felt alive; she could almost hear her body humming. He only held the contact for an instant before releasing her, muttering something about a good night's sleep. And then she was alone in the hallway, making for the solace her own room. But her heart was wandering, lost in the dark hallways.

CHAPTER 19

EVA

INSTEAD OF VANISHING over night as Eva had hoped, the ominous sense of change only intensified, and it invited resentment to join the dance.

Eva rose early to combat the plague of people that threatened her secrets and therefore her happiness.

After the copious amounts of spirits consumed, Illiah had announced a day of rest for the Keep folk, new and old. But Eva did not want rest. She wanted to be out in the Great Forest.

She wished she had an accomplice. Her younger self had but one challenge, to avoid her guards long enough to slip out of the portal door. Now she not only had to elude Tarek and Mahone, she had to evade a Keep full of people.

In the kitchens Eva found she was not the only one awake at an early hour on a rest day. Scrub was making bread, covered to his elbows in flour. But the cook never slept. He survived on flour dust, broths, and herbal teas. Illiah sat at the wide informal table, bright-eyed despite his late, boisterous night with his men. Likely he survived on witty comments and brooding silences.

Illiah was talking to Mila who sat beside him on the bench. They were talking quietly, but with animation. Mila laughed in her light, tinkling laugh, a rare sound for the usually quiet girl.

Eva's morning darkened.

She wished them a good morning as they glanced up from their breakfasts to welcome her. Illiah moved closer to Mila to make room, but Eva shook her head, grabbing a bun and an apple before hurrying out of the room again. She had places to be. And they looked perfectly happy, just the two of them.

The air was cold as she stepped out of the council room into the open air. It started to rain lightly as she made her way through the Great Forest to the little clearing.

Tayeh gave her a little grief about her long absence. She guiltily told him she had been busy. It was a weak excuse.

She told them, between taking bites of her meager breakfast, about the arrival of Illiah's men. She told them everything. About Illiah's sister, his displeasure in her choice of husband, his brothers, her aunt's behavior toward the young lord, about Mila and Murryn, how Mila was wary and about Murryn's boundless benevolence.

The rain came down with more determination and Eva was thankful for the thick boughs of the giant evergreens that sheltered her while she ate. Once finished, she stripped off her cloak and pulled out her sword. She wanted to spar with Tayeh. The Guardian was the best sparring partner she could hope for. With him, she was completely devoid of inhibition. She could push herself past any insecurities. And he always had something new to teach her.

Eva put all her frustrations into her practice. The physical exertion was a release. The rain turned from benign to thunderous, soaking her through to her small clothes. Still she smiled at Tayeh, challenging him. He answered with his fierce amber eyes and his latha.

A Guardian is not a person, not in the same sense that Eva was. They are not affected by cold or wet. Tayeh had not a hair out of place, not a drop on his gleaming fur, not a burnish or mar on his impeccable armor. Lula too was impervious. Not a drop chilled her flawless skin. She looked like a woman today, leaning from a branch in the tall tree beside the clearing. She leaped down with the grace of a sparrow, calling a stop to the practice.

"You are drenched, Eva," Lula said, shaking her head. "You must go home before you catch an ailment."

Eva opened her mouth to speak.

"Oh no, you know that healing yourself is not possible," Lula added in a more severe, almost maternal voice.

Tayeh laughed. He also enjoyed a grueling practice. "I have almost forgotten what it is like to be wet."

"Do you remember anything of when you were alive, Tayeh?"

Eva had asked the Guardians many times about their lives, but there was not much they could - or would - tell her.

"A little, but it was long, long ago," was all he said, but he was still smiling. "Lula's right. Off you go. Run home to some dry clothes and a hot bath."

Eva shivered. The mention of a hot bath must have reminded her body it was actually cold and protesting.

"Good match, Eva. If you were a Kitarran, you would be almost ready to take your iudarii trial," Tayeh mentioned.

"My what?"

"I'll tell you about it another time," he said. "Off with you."

Eva put her cloak around her shoulders. It was damp and far from comforting.

By the time Eva sneaked back through the round door into the walled garden, she was fully drenched. She grinned; she had made war with the rain and returned victorious.

Thankfully, the council room was empty. If Illiah had been in council with his men, she wouldn't have had a ready excuse to offer him. The thought hadn't occurred to her before. She almost stopped in her tracks. She had prepared to leave the Keep unseen, but not thought of returning unseen.

She wondered if Illiah would find it odd if she asked him for a schedule of his councils. No doubt he would answer with some prying comment. She couldn't tell him where she was going; he would think she was really insane.

"Where the blazes were you?"

The voice behind her was familiar and oozed with amused contempt. Eva was almost at her door, Illiah just down the hall outside of his. He gawked at her wet attire, her wet boots and dripping hair tangled with leaves and brush from the many times she had been knocked to the ground by Tayeh's defense. She assumed she looked quite a mess.

"I was outside."

"Really?" The sarcasm was tactile.

From behind Illiah came Mila carrying a basket of sheets and bedding. She met Eva's gaze with a slightly flushed expression. All the elation from Eva's morning excursion fled, leaving her feeling empty and crushed. Illiah looked behind him at Mila, but offered no explanations.

"Here, Mila, I'll help you with those. I am heading down to take a bath anyhow," Eva offered, pushing her reckless emotions aside.

"Thank you, Eva," Mila said, walking past Illiah, who was immobile for some reason, to hand Eva some of her overflowing load.

"Thanks for the help, Mila," Illiah said, leaving the two women to their chore.

The laundry rooms were adjacent to the bath yard. Eva was cold and wet - the hot pools called to her. It was a day of rest, after all.

Bathed, her innards warmed, Eva was surprised to find Tarran waiting outside in the arching hallway to the main Keep telling her Lord Illiah desired her presence. His hair was limp and heavy from the rain.

"I'm sorry, Tarran, I didn't know you were here waiting in the cold."

He shook his head. "My lady, it is my duty."

His voice was noble and full of said duty. Eva hid her smile in case her amusement hurt the boy's pride.

"Where is Illiah?" Eva asked as they began meandering through halls.

"He is out in the practice yard."

Eva followed the boy silently as he fulfilled his duty. He was filled with such purpose that she couldn't just dismiss him, as she would any other messenger - she knew how to get to the practice yard.

"I think that door is the one we want to take," she said when Tarran paused, looking a little lost. Her suggestion caused him to deflate slightly.

"Murryn told me there was a shortcut," he said, trying not to sound woeful.

"Murryn is not always reliable." The girl had probably played a trick on him. There weren't any shortcuts in the Keep and Murryn could be a tease. Illiah was a bad influence on her sense of humor.

"I had a feeling something might be up. She looked like she was trying not to laugh when she told me, then she ran away. She sure is weird," Tarran said looking so annoyed that Eva laughed.

"Here we are," Eva said as they followed the hallway outside into the yard. To the right were the stables and holding paddocks, in front of them a large paddock Illiah had converted into a practice yard.

In the yard, men practiced in pairs. Many of the men from the royal guard were inferior in skill. Eva didn't know if it was from the late night or just general incompetency.

"My lord, Lady Evangeline is here," Tarran announced formally to Illiah who was standing at the fence, spectating. Eva suppressed another smile. The boy was trying so hard it was endearing. Illiah turned to Eva.

"You're still all wet," was the first thing he said, pointing to her hair.

"Thanks for noticing," Eva returned dryly. He grinned. "Can we go inside? I'm cold," she said, trying not to shiver, thinking of her outdoor cloak hanging to dry.

"Of course."

Illiah gave a meaningful nod to one of his men beside him as they left. Eva couldn't remember his name, but he was a big fellow, with long, blond hair plaited down his back. His features were so starkly recognizable that she had no excuse not to remember his name.

"Carltin," Illiah murmured in her ear as they left, reading her thoughts. "He is downright mean with an arrow. Best archer I have ever encountered."

"I thought today was a day of rest?"

"Yes, but some of us get restless. The ones who can take their ale better," he added with a wink.

"Caeris's men weren't doing so well were they?" Eva asked as they made their way back into the Keep and began the long climb up to the council room. Funny, they both knew and accepted it was their destination. "Is that from the ale or neglectful training?"

Illiah frowned. "They are slightly indolent, compared to my men. They will get used to our methods soon enough. Tarran, would you go fetch something to eat from Scrub? I haven't had lunch and I doubt Eva has either."

"Lunch? Isn't it closer to dinner?" Eva asked.

"The boy needs something to do," Illiah muttered after Tarran went on his way.

"He is very eager, and sweet," Eva noted. "You should get Altos to tutor him."

"Yes. I was thinking that myself. I noticed his little lessons with Murryn. I already mentioned it to him."

"He agreed?"

"Of course. Altos is happiest when he is lecturing."

Eva laughed.

Illiah led her up the long flights of stairs to the council room. The fire was in need of encouragement. Illiah bent to the task efficiently, and soon it was raging once more. Eva settled herself on the chair she liked to think of as hers.

Doing so, she couldn't help but think fleetingly of their conversation the night before. She pushed it from her thoughts as quickly as it rose. Illiah pushed his sleeves up to put one last log on the fire, exposing the fine shape of his wrist where it met his cuff and his long, well-shaped fingers. One hand, just below his thumb, was wrapped in a bandage.

"What happened to your hand?" Eva asked. He was favoring the hand slightly.

"Just a little scratch." He dismissed it with a shake of his head.

"Let me see it. I have some skill with healing." Eva held out her hand.

Illiah looked at her stubbornly, then crouched down and placed his hand gently in hers for inspection. His skin was rough, a consequence of his industrious personality, but his long fingers were warm and comforting.

She busied herself unwrapping the expert bandage, ignoring the warmth from his hand moving up her arm, evolving into a different feeling entirely. Her ears buzzed faintly.

Without the bandage, a deep, nasty cut was exposed along his wrist toward his thumb. The gash no longer bled, but the torn flesh was ragged and begged for comfort.

"What did you do?" Eva ran her finger along the edge of his hand. He stiffened, inspecting his hand subjectively.

"It was embarrassing - I fell onto a rock."

Eva's eyes shifted from his hand to his eyes. "You fell onto a rock?"

"Yeah."

Eva shook her head in disbelief. He had better reflexes than anyone, an amazing sense of balance. How he could fall onto a rock was beyond her.

"That is embarrassing. I hope no one saw you," Eva said, laughing at him. She continued to run her finger over his hand, around the ugly wound, gently over the broken tissue. Illiah settled into a sitting position, happy to leave his hand in hers even though he had no idea what she was doing.

"Only Kaile. Probably the worst person to bear witness. He is still laughing about it. And now you are too." He was amused, but his features sharpened. The lancing pain that accompanied Eva's healing magic was settling in his wrist.

"I would never!" Eva assured him, not at all sounding sincere. Eva inspected his hand knowing the fiery pain would be gone. Her magic had done its work. There was nothing but a thin red line, and that too would disappear by the end of the day. She reluctantly dropped his hand.

Illiah looked down at his hand, meaning to wrap it up again. He paled.

"What did you do?" he asked in an expressionless voice.

"It is not a skill I use openly," Eva told him. Illiah's eyes narrowed with displeasure. She despised that expression on his handsome face. Her innards turned icy knowing she was the object of his disapproval.

"You spoke of magic. Legend says the Allati are people of magic. I guess it is true." He ran his finger along the minute scar, then gave a small, mirthless laugh. When he spoke again, his voice was thick with emotion. "I have watched men die in the arms of their comrades. My little brother took his last breath as I tried vainly to hold him together. And you heal my hand with a simple, deceptive touch in the space of a few heartbeats." His voice was anguished. "Where were you?" It was an accusation.

Eva sat up straighter, her eyes narrowing in turn. She had seen exactly what he described, in her dreams, visions born on the wind, in the water, in the heat of the fire. She had yearned with a trepidatious desire to help those lost souls, to heal the wounded, to bring comfort to them in any way she could. To know with certainty of its impossibility caused her more grief than he would ever know. Who was he to judge her? She had shed a river of tears over those poor souls. Tears that once more pricked at the back of her eyes.

"And how would I accomplish that?" Injustice welled deep within Eva like a burning fire, making it impossible to remain seated. "My life - my whole life - is not mine to control. Do you think the decisions made for me are mine to make? Is this the life I would have chosen for myself? To be sitting here waiting, waiting to be the wife of a man who doesn't love me? Who will never love me? I don't think so, Illiah. And I would have done anything to save those men, and women, and children. I see their faces in my dreams." She left the council room with the subtlety of a waterfall.

Tears streamed down her face and she hated Illiah for making her feel weak and raw and exposed. She didn't listen as Illiah pleaded with her. She closed the door in his face as forcefully as the old door would allow.

Once alone, Eva managed to halt her tears and take a deep, calming breath. She was overwhelmed by guilt; she had clearly overreacted. She felt foolish. And angry. Mostly angry. But that anger was fading.

Allowing Illiah's opinion of her to rule her emotions was just stupidity.

Illiah's ignorant words had been cruel, but he spoke from a place of deep hurt and unimaginable grief. She couldn't really stay angry at him when she knew the pain that haunted him. Getting angry and storming away wouldn't make either of them feel better.

A knock came at her door. She opened it hopefully, but found it was only Mahone asking if she was all right. She nodded, hoping he had not overheard her argument with Illiah.

She took a deep breath and slunk back to the council room.

Illiah was standing in front of the fireplace. He turned to her when he heard the small thunk of the door as it hit home. He must have oiled the creaky hinges. She hadn't noticed when she tried to slam it in his face.

"I'm sorry," he told her, straightening his back. It was the apology of a leader who doesn't apologize often. He looked uncomfortable and applicably guilty, his eyes begging her to accept it. Eva's heart melted, the last residue of anger and injustice dissolving.

"Me too," Eva replied. "I should have told you."

Illiah shook his head. "I was shocked. I shouldn't have spoken like that to you. It was unacceptable." His sincerity warmed the room. "On the fields of battle, and after, there were many times I wished so fervently that I could heal with the touch of my hand or something like it. I never guessed that it was actually possible for someone to do."

Eva nodded. She understood.

"So why did you want to see me?" Time for a change of subject.

"Right," Illiah said, sitting down heavily in the chair opposite hers. "There was a message that arrived with one of the guards. One of Caeris's advisers is planning to make a visit before winter sets in, to bring a progress report back to the prince."

"Who?" A cold knot of apprehension tightened in Eva's belly.

"Lord Serac," Illiah told her. The cold knot twisted in her gut like a steel knife. Illiah was watching her thoughtfully, digesting her reaction. "I want to know your opinion of Serac, my cousin."

Illiah valued her opinion enough to consult her? She had not expected it. If she told Illiah her misgivings, would he take her seriously? Perhaps he would not and his good opinion of her would be lost. But her happiness and Illiah's opinion of her did not need to coexist.

"What is it?" Illiah asked as she hesitated. "Are you afraid of Serac?"

"Yes." Eva drew a deep breath. "Serac is behind the disappearance of my friend Alline. I don't know how or why, but I think he hurt her."

"Disappearance? You think he killed her?"

"I don't know. I hope not. I pray to the Guardians that it is not so. But he is cruel - he can't come here." Eva sat down, feeling the blood drain from her face, fear crawling up her spine like spiders. The fear was not for herself. Mila was Serac's victim, his conquest. Perhaps Eva had been naive, imagining she could protect Mila and Murryn from Serac. She had made a promise to Mila - what if she couldn't keep it?

"What else did he do?" Illiah's eyes were electric with some rage or hate that lay low, waiting. A monster building its strength from darks deeds and dark memories. Illiah could be cruel too. He was a killer. The difference was he abhorred it.

Monster or not, Eva could trust Illiah. She had already placed one of her carefully guarded secrets in his care. This secret was not hers to tell, but she would if it meant protecting Mila. She couldn't seem to keep secrets from Illiah.

"If I explain, you must promise never to repeat it to another soul. Ever," Eva told him. "I wouldn't even think of telling you this, but I know you have a good heart and can see the best in people."

Illiah inspected his roughened fingers, rubbing a callus absently. "Thank you."

"And Mila would never tell you herself."

"Mila?" His eyes were bright.

Eva cursed. "I shouldn't be telling you this. Mila doesn't want anyone to know. She is terrified that everyone would treat her differently, ostracize her. But you would understand. You would still be her friend, no matter what?"

Illiah looked confused and wary, but he nodded.

Eva took another deep breath, the breath before the plunge, and told him.

Illiah's inner monster lurked and paced behind his eyes as he listened. His fists and jaw were clenched by the end of her retelling. A boiling silence filled the room. Eva waited anxiously for Illiah's thoughts.

"Thank you for telling me, Eva," he said at length. "I wouldn't let any harm come to Mila or Murryn." The sincerity in his eyes was a flood of relief. Her faith in him, her trust, was not misguided.

"If Serac sees her, he might try to humiliate her, or intimidate her, or worse. He is - unstable. I am afraid he will try to take what he thinks is his," Eva told him. "Plus ..."

"What else?" Illiah's eyes flashed.

"Serac thinks I am a disgrace to Caeris. I think he hates me."

Illiah's brows jumped onto his forehead. He shook his head slowly. Eva wished she knew what he was thinking.

"I will have to think on it. Whoever it is will not be arriving for a month or so. Perhaps I should travel back to Caer Andri myself with the report," he pondered out loud, but with resolve. "You healed Mila, saved her life, didn't you?"

"I tried, but in the end there was nothing I could do to rid the culla from her veins. It had to run its course. Either it would be flushed from her body or she would die from lack of it. In the end she was lucky."

"There are some things you can't heal, then," he said slowly.

"Many things." The realization was a constant one. "Thank you, Illiah. Thank you for having a good heart. I trust you to keep her secret safe."

Illiah gave the slightest of nods.

"Just so we are clear, are there any other strange things I should know about you? I don't like surprises," Illiah asked with a hint of his usual mirth.

Eva gave him a ghost of a smile, but didn't answer. She left the room, letting him ponder her response.

CHAPTER 20

ILLIAH

THE BOY WAS TOUGH, yet still so vulnerable. Illiah questioned his judgment harshly. He should have brought Tarran with him on his expedited trip north. He should not have left the boy behind. It had done Tarran no favors.

At the time, Illiah thought it best for the young lad to stay back with his men. The hard ride north would be taxing, and Tarran had been through so much. But seeing Tarran in the courtyard of the Keep, riding straight and proud on his petite mare, close to tears with relief, his small frame stiff with anxiety, Illiah realized he made the wrong choice. He should have kept Tarran close. He was all the boy had.

Lindin confirmed that Tarran had been withdrawn the entire ride north, reporting that the boy had seemed anxious, not himself. Lindin had been worried, at least until they arrived at the Keep. Tarran saw Illiah and brightened like a candle in the dark. Illiah had embraced his young ward and felt tight little arms grasping his middle like Tarran would never let go. Illiah wasn't leaving the boy behind again.

Besides his disinclination to leave Tarran behind, the boy was the right choice for a companion. Once on the road the boy's somber, quiet facade dissolved into a boy who loved to laugh, a boy who kept up a running commentary on just about all things and loved to tell tales. Illiah was never bored with Tarran around. And Tarran's unusual abilities were always an asset.

Traveling to Caer Andri had been an obvious choice. It would appease his brother, make Serac's visit obsolete, and please his father, the king. Win, win.

Kaile heard about Illiah's plan to travel to Caer Andri and decided to come as well, making their party three. They could leave the recruits in the capable hands of Lindin and Will and the others, for a time. The trip would be quick; they would be back at the Keep before the worst of the winter weather, when the moon began to wax once more.

Upon arriving back at Caer Andri, Illiah immediately sought his father. The king was eager for news of his son's endeavors. His face cracked into a wizened grin to see his second son pull up a stool and settle beside his bed. But the old man's face was pale, and despite his obvious pleasure, there were deep shadows beneath his eyes. Clearly the king had ailed from such an engaging summer.

"Illiah," Rhais said in a weak voice. "What brings you back so soon? I did not expect you."

"Caeris wanted a progress report, so I thought I would come myself. But I cannot stay long, less than a week."

"Tell me of your Keep. The times I spent there as a young man ..." The king's voice trailed off as Rhais was lost in fond thoughts. Illiah filled the silence with his own experience and impressions of the place, the Keep's wild beauty and surprising comforts.

"Yes, it is a wild place," the king said wistfully. "How is Eva? She fares well? When she came to say goodbye, she looked ill at ease, but I couldn't get her to admit it."

"She is well," Illiah told the old man. "She has been a great help to me."

"Excellent. I miss her," the king said softly. Illiah was surprised by the affection in his voice. He knew the king was fond of Eva, but he hadn't realized the depth of it. So Illiah told him about Eva, about hiking in the forest, finding a good spot for a guard post. Illiah explained the need for a guard post was more for practice than necessity; the men needed to know the feeling of sitting at attention for days on end with small comforts and much boredom. Had he mentioned that already? It made the king laugh regardless. A weak laugh, from shallow lungs.

"Oh, Illiah. We were robbed of so much," the king said as a sigh, gripping Illiah's hand in his.

Illiah's tongue stuck in his mouth under the throes of an emotion he couldn't name. Regret, maybe? He had been cheated from a childhood with his father. But he loved his foster family dearly. He couldn't say if he would trade his memories of growing up as Illiah, Devlin Horsemaster's adopted son, for memories of Illiah the prince - or whatever his name would have been. Luckily, he would never have to make the decision.

"I hope Caeris is a good husband to Eva," Rhais mused in a quiet voice, almost to himself. "Eva will be a great queen. I just hope your brother can see that."

Illiah agreed with both sentiments but had nothing to add. He rarely heard Caeris talk of Eva. He had no true inkling of what his brother really thought of his bride-to-be, only what he had gathered from observation and palace gossip. But he did know his brother did not love Eva in the way the king hoped.

The king's eyes were heavy, his breathing long and slow. He looked ready for sleep. Illiah bid him good day, but wasn't sure his father heard. A maidservant came to see to the king's comfort and Illiah left his father to his restive sleep. The maid in her deep-yellow serving gown reminded Illiah of another question he had for his brother.

Caeris was walking in the garden, his pretty mistress on his arm, her rounding figure no longer hidden by her heavily bustled gown. It was impossible to keep the secret that she was expecting a baby come winter. Illiah could not remember her name. Besides her pretty face, he didn't think there was anything remarkable about the young woman. A typical camp follower. She could have been in dozens of beds before she found her way into the prince's. Camp women were not worth the hassle, although Illiah couldn't find it in himself to banish them. Many men were lonely and ill at heart from the war. A woman was a small comfort in those times.

Whatever the woman's charms, she had entranced the prince. Caeris looked at her with a smile in his eyes. What did Caeris find in this girl that he couldn't find in his betrothed? Eva was smart, kind, and more beautiful, if in a different way. Eva was strong-minded, but was that really a curse? The southern girl seemed docile. She gave Caeris an accepting smile as the prince dismissed her, seeing Illiah coming across the garden.

"Brother!" Caeris said with a tight-lipped smile. His brother did not show his emotions often or freely. Not that Illiah considered himself to be overly emotional. Surprise, surprise, he had something in common with his twin. "What brings you back to Caer Andri?"

"Some questions. Also I know you wanted an update, so I thought I would come myself."

"Excellent."

They fell in step together as Illiah began his report. For a warm autumn day, the garden was blissfully empty of overly affectionate ladies.

"Another thing, Caeris. We need servants at the Keep. The place has run itself sufficiently since Lord Finnan died, but now it is just not practical," Illiah told his brother.

Caeris nodded. "I can talk to Linea. I am sure she will have some people for you."

"Thank you. Do you think they will be ready to return with me in a week's time?"

"I don't see why not."

"Good."

"What do you think of the Keep? I haven't been there since a young child."

"I like it. Secluded. Dark hallways. Thick forests. The hot pools. Endless things to do and plans to make."

"Our blood does not stagnate well, does it?"

Illiah laughed. "No. Eva has been a wonderful help. She is never afraid to lend a hand. She showed me the lay of the land, the forest. I let her ride my gelding. She looks like a child on his tall back. But she can jump him over almost anything. I wouldn't tell her this, but she is a very capable rider."

Caeris looked displeased.

Illiah wished he hadn't mentioned Eva at all.

At least he hadn't mentioned the sword fighting. But he remembered Eva had made him swear against it. And he certainly couldn't mention how he longed to spar with her. He had a strong desire to test her limits. The way she rose to a challenge was endlessly amusing to him. For some reason.

"Will you join me at the Temple this afternoon, before dinner?" Caeris asked.

"Unfortunately not. I have some other tasks to see to today. Perhaps tomorrow." The latter was to appease Caeris. The Black Goddess made him uneasy. He found no solace in the Temple. He had no desire to be in the domain of the Goddess who allowed a man like Serac to be her eyes and ears. He occasionally went to make his brother happy, but this was not one of those times.

Caeris nodded. "I will see you at dinner, then." Illiah gave a short bow and left his brother to collect his mistress and head off to the Temple. Illiah was also headed into the city. He needed to find a blacksmith who was also a swordsmith - he needed weapons.

There were several smithies and metal shops in Caer Andri. Illiah sought each out with Kaile at his heels. Walking into a shop was still an interesting experience. The demeanor of the shop owner would change from genial to venerating when they recognized him as the new prince. He despised the title, but he couldn't let on, or Kaile would call him by nothing else. Tarran told him it was what they called him in the city, despite his title of War Commander. Tarran was about the city too, doing what he did best, though Illiah didn't know exactly where.

Illiah skirted around the small talk and told the shopkeep blatantly he was looking for a smith to move shop and live at the Keep and take charge of the armory. He asked to see their best work, and if they had a young journeyman that might be interested in relocating.

They were all interested, mostly to keep face in front of their prince. Illiah looked over their work and found much of it lacking. He needed someone who could create weapons unmatched for quality. Someone who could train others to do the same, but also attend to the many other tasks of a smithy, making tools and such.

"I need swords like this," Illiah said, taking out his blade, his gift from the king, his father. He placed it on the counter for the blacksmith to inspect. The blacksmith's brows rose in appreciation for the fine weapon.

"That sword is a rarity these days. Forged by a legend, it was. Germain is dead this past twelve years," the man told him sadly.

"Surely he trained others?"

The man nodded thoughtfully. "Hemly, down in second quarter, was one of his apprentices. Germain didn't take on many."

"My thanks," Illiah said, clipping his sword back onto his belt.

He had already been to Hemly's shop. The smith had obviously not picked up his mentor's skills.

Illiah did not find a blacksmith he was willing to bring back to the Keep, but not for lack of volunteers. He mulled it over as he sipped his ale at dinner.

Dinner was a small, informal party. Illiah was much aggrieved to learn Lady Catalina had remained at court with her father. She was batting her eyelashes at him, hoping to get his attention. Her father, Lord Henway, was a fool. Illiah had learned Henway's only purpose at court was money - he had a lot of it. He was not all that intelligent, nor a good strategist, nor conversationalist. He preferred gossip to anything of interest. Lord Henway was also hoping to find a husband for his daughter. What man wanted a wife who spread her legs for anyone? Illiah regretted the night he spent between them. His body, however, decided to remind him of Catalina's alluring chestnut-hair and smooth, creamy skin. Even so, Illiah found her less attractive than he had two months ago. Her hair was too brown, her figure too rounded. She didn't have Eva's athletic form; she was too soft and meek.

Illiah ground his thoughts to a skidding halt.

Why was he comparing all these women to Eva? Ridiculous.

Illiah didn't want to wed a woman like Catalina, which meant he needed to stay out of her bed. He shuddered to think of being tied to her because he got her pregnant. What would a woman like her do in a place like the Keep? Only an odd noblewoman would willingly be the lady of that place - even if in recompose she had a prince for a husband. He didn't need a wife. The Keep didn't need a lady. They could manage quite nicely on their own.

Caeris was on his left, flanked by Lord Serac whom Illiah was trying hard to ignore lest his temper outweigh logic. Serac might be kin, but Illiah yearned to bring the man to some kind of justice. He was too damned untouchable. For now.

Kaile nudged Illiah's right shoulder. Trust Kaile to distract him.

"Catalina is trying hard to catch your eye," Kaile said in a low voice for Illiah's ears only. "I think she wants an encore."

"I don't think so. You can have her this time."

"Too kind. The prince's seconds."

"Shhh." Illiah leaned closer to Kaile. "We shouldn't talk like that. We are better than those boys making fun of whores and bastards."

Kaile sobered, then shrugged. "I don't really mind your seconds." He took one last mouthful of ale and made his way over to Lady Catalina where she sat with her father, oblivious as always to her pursed lips and sly eyes. Illiah rolled his eyes. His foster brother was just as much of a whore.

"I must thank you, cousin," Serac said, coming to sit in Kaile's vacated seat. "Your arrival has saved me from several weeks of cold, miserable travel. But tell me, how does life fare at the Keep?"

Illiah shrugged. "The Keep suits me well. There is plenty of work to be done, good men to do it. It is not as luxurious as Caer Andri, but the Keep is not without its comforts."

"Comforts indeed. Tell me, how is Caeris's betrothed? Is Eva well?" Serac asked. His voice betrayed some innuendo Illiah did not quite understand.

Illiah ignored it. "Lady Evangeline is well."

"Is she happy at the Keep?"

Illiah felt the bristly chills of his internal alarm. "I do not know the lady well enough to offer a comment on her happiness," Illiah lied.

It was Serac's turn to shrug indifference.

"My prince has informed me that you are looking for servants to come to the Keep," Serac went on. "I would like to offer you one of my acolytes. The Keep needs some presence of the Goddess, and my girls are very capable in all domestic matters."

Illiah wasn't sure which was more irritating: that Serac offered him an acolyte, or that Caeris felt the need to inform Serac of their every conversation.

"That would be welcome," Illiah lied again. He didn't want a single one of Serac's people at his Keep, but he couldn't think of an excuse to say no. "Tomorrow I was hoping to come to the Temple with my brother. Could I meet the girl you have in mind then?"

"Yes, of course. I haven't chosen one yet for the task, but perhaps you can help me with that," Serac suggested, obviously pleased. "I have several in mind."

"Excellent." Illiah hoped his voice sounded enthusiastic.

His dagger was in his boot, pressed against his ankle. He let his thoughts flow into it. Friend. Kin. He focused its magic at Serac. The dagger hummed for his ears only.

Illiah wanted Serac to trust him, to believe him a fool. And, one by one, Illiah would get his claws into Serac. The dagger would help him. He couldn't look at Serac without the images Eva's story created floating forefront in his mind. From the first, Illiah knew Serac warranted watching. Eva's tale solidified the notion.

Tarran appeared at Illiah's elbow, washed and cleaner than any eleven-year-old boy had the right to be. He was wearing Illiah's colors, with his sigil, a sword on a field of deepest red, upon his shoulder. He stood on alert like any young page, as if he had been there all evening. From the look in the boy's eye, he had something to tell Illiah, likely for Illiah's ears only.

"Excuse me, brother, cousin," Illiah said with a bow.

Illiah waited until they were in the privacy of his own rooms before he turned to Tarran expectantly.

"Well, what did you discover?" Illiah poured some juice from a pitcher on his table; the lad was still too young to hold his ale. "You're not hungry?" Illiah asked as Tarran opened his mouth to talk.

"No, I ate," Tarran said with a grin. "Those cakes look very tasty, but first I'll tell you that I found a blacksmith."

Illiah raised his brows as he settled into one of the padded chairs, waiting for Tarran to go on.

"I found this blacksmith, well, really a swordsmith. She is said to be the best."

"She?" Illiah asked, slightly incredulous.

"Yes, that's why she is not well known. No one wants to go to a woman, but her swords really are the best. She used to apprentice under Germain the Swordmaker. Then she went to work for Hemley, who gave her no credit at all. She got pissed-off and left, starting her own shop, but despite her skill, she has a hard go of it because she is a woman."

"Interesting."

"Yes. I went by her shop to feel her out. She is a prickly one. Maybe she just doesn't like little boys."

"I'll visit her tomorrow."

Tarran nodded.

"And the other thing?"

Tarran nodded again, his amber eyes pointy. "I snooped around Serac's house, and the Temple, but nothing was out of place. Just big, scary guards. Serac likes them mean. They most certainly do not like little boys."

"I don't want you risking your skin. Don't go near them again. You remember that, Tarran," Illiah said sternly. "Maybe I shouldn't have asked you to look into it."

"Sir, I can look after my skin. Don't worry," Tarran told him with his street urchin grin. Tarran was young, but he was no child. The poor boy had seen more than any boy should. Illiah didn't wish to involve him any more than strictly necessary.

"Okay, good work, Tarran, but I don't want you going back there again. I mean that," Illiah said, pushing the plate of cakes toward the youngster. Illiah's insides pinched thinking of Tarran coming to harm under his command. A cruel man would think nothing of hurting an orphan street boy.

The next day, Illiah donned his "prince clothes." They were finely made, colorful, embroidered by artisans. Just the long-sleeved doublet had taken weeks to tailor. He had stood still on three separate occasions to be measured, pinned, and generally subjected to boredom. He had learned what a tabbard was. He wore the clothes only when he needed to appear as an equal to his brother, who always dressed in such finery.

He would never miss the opportunity to remind Serac he was a powerful man too. So when dressing to go to the Temple alongside Caeris, he wore the clothes that made him feel like a cocky rooster. His dagger looked primitive compared to the clothes. Illiah slipped it into his boot, right where it belonged.

He walked through Caer Andri with Caeris, Caeris's guards trailing along behind them. The sun was surprisingly bright and warm for autumn, a fair day for walking.

The Temple was an imposing, sprawling structure built of hard, cold marble, surrounded by beautiful gardens and a wall. The wall was not tall, just high enough a person could not scale it, even with a reasonably sized ladder. Beautiful images were carved into the stone - lots of birds, many pretty maidens. Windows pocked the wall, allowing a peek into the world of the acolytes, the girls and women who served the Goddess. All one would see were pretty black-haired girls tending the garden, or singing. No mysterious rituals or ceremonies. The windows were hardly more than slits; not even a child could slip through. The only way in or out of the Temple was through the gate.

The gate was taller than the wall, built to look ornate, but the steel was tough and thick. Illiah wasn't sure if the gate was to keep threats out or keep something in. It was locked every night until daybreak, barred with a massive beam lowered by a pulley. Only a siege-scale battering ram could bring the gate down after it was closed and latched. It must have cost a fortune.

The goings-on of the Temple were a mystery to Illiah. He doubted even Caeris or the king really knew what the Goddess required of her acolytes.

The Temple had the illusion of openness, as ornate as the wall that circled it, the pillars an example of exquisite craftsmanship. It was as fine a thing as the royal apartments of the palace. Inside, the illusion of openness dissolved into a labyrinth of hallways and doors, hidden passageways, and rooms beyond the access of anyone besides Serac or the acolytes.

The mysteriousness of it irked and unsettled Illiah.

Singing drifted over the lawn. Caeris paused to savor the sweet feminine voices. Lord Serac came out to meet them just as they began to carry on. He greeted them with a bow.

"Come this way, my liege and lord. A quick service is prepared and then we shall speak with my girls," Serac said leading them inside the Temple briskly.

The service would be in the sanctuary, the only part of the Temple Illiah had seen that spoke of more than pretty girls and sweet singing. The temperature always dropped the deeper they went into the stone building. The sanctuary was the coldest.

In the center of the round chamber was a statue of black marble, standing upon a dais. It was of a woman, young and virile, with a beautiful face and shapely form. Two great wings spread from her back into the room, feathered like a raven. Or a crow. The Crow. Illiah hoped the Goddess could not pluck the obloquy from his mind.

The service was an appalling ritual. But he knelt below the statue of the Black Goddess in a fair imitation of Serac and Caeris. The cold stone soaked into his knees. The hair on the back of his neck rose as it usually did in the Goddess's sanctuary. His head was down, his eyes locked on the floor. The vulnerable position made his palms itch.

In the presence of the statue, Illiah always felt watched. His skin prickled. Somewhere inside his head he heard a woman laugh, a gaudy sound. Perhaps it wasn't in his head after all. Not for the first time, his eyes caught a flash of something black and feathery. Not stone, it was real, soft. He had seen it - her - before and knew it would go away if he pretended ignorance and waited for Serac to finish his litany to the Goddess.

Illiah's dagger thrummed, just a little. It was not the first time the dagger reacted to something beyond his thoughts. It was not the first time he wondered why. A sense of remembering trickled over him. A void fell before his eyes. Stars. A pool deep as the night sky. Loss. Longing. He reached out to grasp the memory, but it fell through his mind like it had never been.

Illiah's thoughts drifted back to the Keep. He felt an acute home-sickness. Which was interesting. He never yearned for his home in the south. Was it possible, in his heart, he had already made the Keep his home? In his homey picture, complete with cliff walls and tall trees and long stairways, was a young woman with bright hair, like starlight. He could not picture one without the other.

Serac finished the ceremony with his usually gravity and emotional rectitude that caused Illiah some degree of discomfort. The man was far too caught up in his role, like a bad actor in a street-corner play. Serac reached his hands up to the statue like a forgotten lover, his eyes closed, his face contorted as he begged to satisfy the Goddess.

Finally Serac stood and Caeris and Illiah were free to do the same. Caeris and Serac looked like they had risen from something as simple as a pleasant meal. Illiah tried to hide any sign of how much Serac's ritual irritated him.

He followed the other two into the royal solar, a comfortably furnished room looking out onto the garden, a room Caeris used when he spent time at the Temple.

A lovely young woman named Deotha, one of the senior acolytes, greeted them. Illiah remembered her from another time at the Temple. Beside her stood four girls in a row. Well, they were women, but very young women. Not one looked to be older than fifteen. They all had long black hair and were all exceptional specimens of the female kind. They stood silent and obedient, their eyes shining with an eagerness that made Illiah suspicious. He was beginning to wish he had said no to Serac's proposal.

"These are the junior acolytes who qualify as servants of the Goddess. They are each good, capable women who will bring the presence of our Goddess to that back-of-the-woods place." They each gave a delicate, practiced bow as Serac spoke their name. "So which one will be the lucky girl to accompany you back to the Keep?" Serac asked Illiah, his face genial, but his eyes were icy.

The girls looked harmless. The little voice in Illiah's head - the one that kept warning him Serac's "girls" could be part of a violent plot against his person, or Eva - threw its hands up. Not one of them had the physique of a fighter. They were soft from youth and days devoted to the Goddess. He doubted their perfectly tailored facade hid a killer. Serac said they were capable, but Illiah couldn't imagine them scrubbing dishes or dressing game. They were all long fingernails and polished hair, immaculate dressed, plain as they were. There was a sameness to them that was unnerving. They could not be sisters, yet they had the same features. He shook his head.

"Whichever your lordship chooses, for I can not," Illiah said, hoping he had not just made a grave mistake.

"Very well. Simirri will go with you," Serac said easily with a wave of his hand. "You may go prepare, Simirri." The girl whose name was Simirri looked to be the youngest of the four. She nodded eagerly, her eyes bright. She was followed out by the other girls.

"Deotha, bring her to the palace in three days," Serac told his head woman. The woman nodded and left. "Simirri is young, but she is capable."

That word again. Illiah hoped Serac's idea of capable and his idea of capable were somewhere in the same realm. He was already thinking over the disadvantages traveling with a girl who would slow them down. He had never seen an acolyte ride. There was no stable at the Temple. It would take them longer to get back to the Keep, which he regretted.

"Before you leave, Lord Illiah, do you have any further need of the Goddess? I can arrange a private ceremony with one of the acolytes?" Serac always asked the question after a service. Illiah wasn't sure what he meant by it, and he had no desire to find out. As Illiah held the man's icy-clear gaze, all he could think of was Mila. He shook his head slowly.

He extricated himself from the Temple and made his way through the city. He was hoping to speak with the blacksmith Tarran spoke of. To work as a blacksmith, she would have to be the complete opposite of the women he had just met. She would be tough, unrelenting, confident to a fault.

Finding the woman's shop was tricky, even with Tarran's directions. The outer district of the city was less familiar to Illiah. He went down another wrong street and began to regret not taking Tarran with him from the outset. Instead, foolishly, he had told Tarran to meet him at the swordsmith's.

A passerby saw Illiah, recognized him, and guided him in the right direction.

"I don't know why you would want to see Kota. Her swords are sharp, but her tongue is sharper," the merchant told him.

Illiah laughed and thanked the man with a silver piece for his trouble.

The shop was behind some other shops, accessible only through a narrow, dead-end alley. The buildings surrounding were tall; not a pinch of sunlight penetrated the wayward street. There was no sign to indicate a place of business. The building appeared to have been a stable, awkwardly converted into a smithy, but the red glow of the coals and the huff of smoke told Illiah he was in the right place.

Illiah watched the smith wipe her brow with her sleeve and settle back on her heels, taking in her morning's work.

"Good morning," Illiah said casually. The woman was brawny enough in her leather apron, her shirt ripped up to her shoulder, her muscles showing, overly large for a woman, the sign of her demanding profession. She looked up at him with scrutinizing light-blue eyes that narrowed as she recognized him.

"My lord. You are unexpected." She made it sound as though he was unwanted as well. He ignored the tone.

"Two things," Illiah said. The woman looked short on patience and would appreciate brevity. "Firstly, I am looking for a sword. I am told you apprenticed under Master Germain. Do you have a shop?"

"I did. I do. This way," she said, putting her rag down on her bench with her hammers.

She led him through the smithy to a room at the back. The small room served as shop, bedroom, and kitchen all at once. Illiah ignored her sheepish look about the state of her shop, having to share it with her living space.

He inspected the swords displayed in rows along one wall. They were of many sizes and shapes - some long, some wide, some long and wide, some sharp and narrow. Each lethal and polished to perfection. Illiah smiled when he found what he was looking for: a small sword about the length of his arm. He picked it up. It felt too small in his hand, but that was the point. It was for a hand much smaller than his. Its balance was exquisite, the metal of superb quality. It was perfect.

"How much is this sword?"

"That sword? That 'tis a boy's sword, or perhaps a woman, my lord," she said awkwardly.

"I know. How much?"

"Fifty." It was a fair price. Illiah was glad that she hadn't offered him a deal nor overcharged him, both which were the norm for a prince looking for a purchase.

"I'll give you fifty-five if you put a design on the hilt for me and have it ready in three days," he said, handing it over to her.

She took it expertly and nodded. "A finer sword I have never made. The heart is of Kitarran steel - and you know how hard it is to find reputable Kitarran steel. I would keep it myself if I knew how to wield it," she told him. Illiah couldn't help but smile. He had an idea. But first, he explained the design he wanted with the aid of her charcoal and a flat piece of wood.

He paid her half, as was customary, telling her she would receive the rest when she delivered the sword to the palace in three days.

"You said you had two things, my lord. What is the other?"

Illiah smiled. She was perceptive.

"My Keep does not have a smith. We are in dire need of good weapons for training and to build up the armory. Are you interested in the position?" he asked her outright. She stared at him in surprise, her mouth slightly agape. "It is an isolated place, very different from Caer Andri. You would find it easier, I think, to apply your trade without prejudice. Also if you did want to learn to wield a sword, there are women who could teach you." Well, one woman, but others were learning. Murryn was a promising student. "Please think on it. I leave in three days. I would like your answer by then."

Illiah left the shop with the smith still in stunned silence. She would think about it - Illiah knew she would. He would buy the other swords from her as well. They were good weapons. His brother was a fool not to use her weapons. His guards should all be wearing such fine swords at their hips.

Back in the dim alley, Tarran was nowhere to be seen. The boy was supposed to meet him. Where was he? It was unlike Tarran to be tardy.

Illiah walked toward the bright square flooded with sunlight, eager to leave the dim alley. The contrast was not lost on him.

"Lord Illiah." A soft voice made him spin back toward the gray light of the narrow alley. A woman stood not far behind him, her head cocked sweetly to one side. Her hair was light blond, her pale skin exposed, the swell of her breasts pronounced. Illiah tore his eyes from them to see her pretty face. A country boy he may be, but he knew a rent girl when he saw one.

"I have something for you." She smiled and handed him a folded piece of paper.

Illiah took the paper and felt his cheeks glow red. "I cannot read this. Please, tell me what it says."

She was beautiful for a whore. Her delicate brow rose, and she smiled in a false, simpering way.

"It says your boy Tarran is in trouble and unless you come with me, they will kill him."

Illiah's stomach slid into his toes with a torrent of fear and anger. His lost boy, his ward. Following the woman was as dangerous as following a rabid bear into its den. But he would do it. He would do anything for Tarran.

CHAPTER 21

ILLIAH

"ARE YOU COMING?" the rent girl asked.

"Come here first."

The woman did as Illiah commanded, her curvaceous body so close she almost pressed against him. Proximity was nothing to her. She smelled nice, clean, floral. Illiah pushed her long pale hair aside to see the tattoo below her ear. The little innocuous flower told him they had a mutual friend. And by friend, he meant serpent.

"Take me to Tarran."

The culla girl nodded.

She led him down the alley away from the sun, away from the tame streets of the city. The tips of the tall buildings were cast in the red light of the dying sun.

Illiah did not know Caer Andri intimately, but he wished he did. He was quickly disoriented by the uniformity of the buildings, the crisscrossing of alleys, the narrow streets.

The woman paused before a door that looked like a dozen they had already passed. There was nothing to mark it as extraordinary. She knocked lightly. It opened, sucking the dim light of the alley into its dark abyss.

"Come, dear lord," she said, her voice as sweet as violets.

Illiah was a fish set on a hook but could see no way to tear the line. He followed her into the gloom.

The room was small. The rent girl saw the two men a second after Illiah did. Her demeanor suddenly changed, any trace of sensuality mutated into terror. The transition was disturbing. She turned to escape out the door. One of the big brutes leaped across the room in a huff, lunging into her with his elbow. Illiah moved to place himself between the two, but the second man was in the way. Illiah heard a sickening crack. The girl was on the floor, blood pooling from her head.

The assault took an instant, and Illiah needed less to draw his sword.

"Put down the sword, or the boy dies," the man said. The second man cut the throat of the girl before dragging her lifeless body into another room. Illiah was always disgusted how silent and slick death was.

Illiah couldn't see Tarran, but he put down his sword. The man took it. Illiah connected his mind to the dagger. Felt it warm beside his ankle. He used his will, hoping to make the two brutes back down. He saw their expressions flicker. It was working, but would it be enough?

"And the dagger." The man's chin made a gesture toward Illiah's boot. Nope, not enough. Illiah had not mastered its magic. The dagger did not transfer Illiah's will fast enough.

His dagger. Illiah didn't fully understand the nature of his little wooden weapon, but he knew handing it over to the man was the worst thing he could do. But it was the only thing he could do. He pulled it from his boot. The man grabbed it, securing it in his filthy hands.

"This is it? Looks like something a boy would whittle out of wood," the man sneered.

And with that ignorant remark, Illiah knew what it was all about. The dagger. He didn't question why; he questioned how. No one knew about it. Not even Tarran or Kaile.

"What do you want?" Illiah asked, hoping to distract the man.

"A good steak and a fine woman," the swine answered.

"Your friend just killed a beautiful woman. She was probably willing enough, even for an ugly brute like yourself."

"Nah. I like them a tad less pale and fragile." The man's voice was thick as sludge. "Besides, it's just business. Leave no witnesses, he said."

"Who?"

"The lord. Not sure why I am speaking to a dead man - Lug!" The man called to his companion before approaching with the wariness of a badger. Illiah had done a mental search of the room upon entering, looking for allies among the structure and items. Nothing spoke of opportunity.

Panic crept over him, slowly, but panic nonetheless. He had lost the dagger. He was nothing. Death was silence. Death was an instant. Death was a promise.

Tarran was likely dead. They would have killed him immediately, like the girl. Leave no witnesses. Illiah was a fool for believing otherwise. He could imagine the boy with a puddle of blood below his head, his throat a jagged maw. Illiah shivered and felt sick, but he was not ready to die.

They came at him with daggers. The room was too small for swords. Illiah put the backs of his hands out to protect his wrists. *Keep your back to the wall, Illiah.* Eelan's voice was in his head.

Illiah sidestepped the men. The wall was a comforting presence behind him. The men had to avoid hitting each other as their trajectory weaseled out from under them. Illiah trapped one dagger between his crossed hands. A little twist sent the dagger to the floor - helpful. But it was out of his reach - not so helpful. Still with the man's hand locked, Illiah propelled the man's face into his knee before shoving him into the second attacker. The second man swerved and swung at him. Illiah blocked, and blocked again. He couldn't land a decent blow. He couldn't reach the door. If he moved away from the wall, a dagger would be in his back, across his neck. The visual did nothing for his heart rate. Cold steel cut into the backs of his hands and arms as he sacrificed them to keep the blades away from his body. He couldn't keep it up for long. Swerve. Kick. Block. His arms hurt.

Illiah heard the door open, and a small shadow convalesced into the form of a boy. Tarran was small and quick as a viper. His child-sized daggers, one in each hand, were poison. Before the two men knew what the intruder was and what the intruder could do, they were down, bleeding their strength onto the stone floor.

Every time Illiah witnessed Tarran's abilities, he was astounded how much deadly skill was contained in the body of such a young boy.

Tarran didn't like to talk about his past, but Illiah knew enough that he could speculate with horror the circumstances for one so young to be an expert in murder.

"Sir," Tarran said in a small voice, rushing to Illiah, his twin daggers hidden once again in his trousers.

"Tarran," Illiah breathed, his eyes raking over the boy. Tarran had a black eye and a cut eyebrow, but Illiah could see no other hurt. Illiah slumped down. His hands and arms felt leaden and fiery. Blood dripped from his arms onto the earthen floor. Dripped, not sprayed - his arteries were intact. Lucky that.

Tarran took off his tunic and wrapped Illiah's wounds.

"You saved my life, Tarran."

Tarran grinned.

"I thought they killed you. They told me they had you." Illiah could hardly talk. His lungs almost forgot to breathe.

"They did. I got away. I would have come sooner, but it took me a few minutes to figure out where they took you."

Illiah crushed Tarran to him, breathing in the sweet scent of relief.

"Let's get out of here."

C

A predictable buzz of contention moved through the palace and Caer Andri once the attack on Illiah became known. Illiah would have preferred that the attempt on his life remain a secret, but Caeris preferred an inquiry be held. So an inquiry was held. The city was searched with the intention of rooting out the culprit.

Illiah nursed his hurt pride and his hurt hands in pensive silence. He knew who the culprit was. Caeris sent men to the building to retrieve the bodies. None were found. The room was cleaned of blood, any sign of struggle and murder erased. Only Illiah's mangled hands and Tarran's fading bruises were evidence of Illiah's tale. Illiah knew it had been Serac. Without proof, confronting his cousin was a politically fatal errand. Illiah knew trapping a monster involved cunning and patience.

C

Illiah's relief to see the back of Caer Andri was almost eclipsed by the pain in his hands. Almost. But by the Crow, his hands hurt. Perhaps being a prince was making him soft. He exhaled a long breath, watching his troop trail behind him. An icy breath it was; the weather had turned cold.

His troupe had grown by twelve, mostly women of varying ages. The servants, which he had selected from the list Linea provided, turned out to be a capable lot - the kind of capable he approved of. He had questioned them thoroughly, wary of another attack on his person, or his loved ones. He was mostly certain not one of them was an assassin. Simirri was wane and soft, and if she was hiding her ruthlessness, she did it very well.

Illiah was pleased to learn Kota had agreed to come to the Keep, even with only three days to close up shop and finish commissions. It helped that Illiah offered to help pay her way out of her contracts. She had had only two, so it had not been difficult or expensive.

Along with the twelve additions were two wagons. One belonged to Kota and held her entire smithy; Kota would not leave her anvils behind. She didn't trust that the Keep had sufficient tools and Illiah didn't have the knowledge to assuage her fears. He knew little of blacksmithing. He didn't know what a critical eye would make of the old smithy at the Keep, and Kota seemed a woman of exacting demands. The second wagon carried the meager belongings of the servants and the Temple acolyte.

Kaile, Tarran, and Illiah were the only ones with experience riding, so the going was slow. They found sturdy horses for those not afraid to travel in the saddle, inexperienced as they were. The rest rode in the wagons and endured the bumps and cold as best they could.

The servants kept mostly to themselves. Kota kept to her wagon and her tools. Simirri was the one who was out of place. She had the attitude of a noblewoman and turned her nose up at riding in the back of the wagon, but looked terrified at the thought of riding one of the placid horses Kaile had mustered.

Illiah was saved some exasperation as Kota offered the girl a seat next to her where she drove the wagon. Simirri gave Kota an assessing look, but climbed beside her without another word. The two women were an odd pair - Kota was fierce, her face was not beautiful. It had lost a little of her feminine fairness over the hot fires of the smithy. Simirri next to her was like a spring flower, delicate and beautiful, her skin creamy and unblemished. Her expression was nervous where Kota's was confident and determined. Kota drove the wagon like she was born to it. Simirri clung to the bench over the bumps, clearly uncomfortable.

Kaile flirted with both women. He wasn't serious about it. He was just bored. Kota ignored him. Simirri batted her eyelashes at him prettily.

Tarran avoided Simirri, but he liked Kota instantly - a good sign. Tarran had good instincts and an infallible intuition.

Illiah was thankful the Temple girl kept her obvious misery to herself, hugging her black cloak around her in silence instead of whining and complaining. Illiah didn't think his patience would last if he was surrounded by whining women - or men - and he considered himself a patient man.

His hands hurt. Luckily Penn did not need a heavy hand for the slow traveling. He thought of Eva and her healing magic with the longing of a sober drunkard.

After a few nights of camping, Illiah began to regret his decision to bring so many people back home with him. Illiah was used to the cold, uncomfortable nights that accompanied sleeping outdoors, but the servants were not. Neither was the smith nor the Goddess's acolyte. The first night Simirri looked at him with wide eyes, honestly surprised that they were not making use of an inn. He was a prince; money was not a concern. The cold ground was horrid to her.

Kota rolled her eyes and asked the girl if she had never spent a night outdoors.

"Of course not!" she replied, stricken.

In the morning Simirri looked terrible. Shadows haloed her eyes, her long, black hair tousled as if her misery kept her from combing it. Illiah felt a pang of guilt on her behalf, but only for an instant. However, when they came to the next little town he announced they would sleep in an inn for the night. Simirri all but jumped for glee. Illiah didn't bother reminding the young woman that for the last few days of travel, there would be no inns.

The inn was comfortable. Perhaps Simirri had a point. Not that Illiah would admit it. His hands ached. His temper was on a short leash. He ordered the best room in the establishment, unabashedly enjoying the benefits of being a prince. He also ordered a late bath after dinner. If he was going to be warm, he might as well be luxuriously warm.

The previous night he had been visited by nightmares. All day the images, memories really, lingered and danced in front of his eyes, leaving him tense. He wasn't constantly plagued with nightmares, but every once in a while, they returned unbidden, if not entirely unexpected. A hot bath helped dissolve the tension in his body.

He regarded the minuscule tub and realized he was in danger of becoming spoiled. At the Keep, he could gaze up at the stars, the trees, hear the birds, frogs, all while soaking in a perpetually hot bath with no fear of the water turning cold. It was no small luxury. He would be lucky if half of him fit in the small brass contraption.

He said nothing, of course. He would not allow himself to be that pompous. The servants who laboriously filled his tub were the same people who owned the inn. They filled the tub with the hottest water, leaving him fresh soap and clean linens. They were as considerate as their means allowed.

Illiah thanked them when they were done, waiting until they had left to shuck his clothes and climb in. The water was hot, tingling his cool skin. He kept his hands and arms above the water. The water would sting his wounds and make a mess of his bandages. The heat was soothing, but he knew it would cool all too quickly.

Maybe he was becoming a spoiled bastard. A spoiled bastard prince.

He fit in the tub better than expected. He could almost stretch his legs out, and his chest was mostly in the water. He could lean his head back and rest it on the edge. He closed his eyes and imagined he was back at his Keep, in his pool, with his trees bending overhead, the rustling of the wind in his ears. The raucous call of that rascal of a raven. Calypso always seemed to know when he was bathing, and always came to investigate, hopping across the stones to inspect Illiah's hands for treats. What kind of lady has a raven for a pet? Ravens were carrion birds. They picked at carcasses for fun and ate maggots. A hawk or a kestrel was very ladylike; even more so a finch or dove. But a raven? He found himself smiling as he drifted off.

He was half asleep as he lay in the tub, thinking thoughts that were most unbecoming to him. Thoughts he would never allow if his mind had been fully conscious. Thoughts of warm skin and bright hair and blue eyes tinged with mossy green. He felt soft, searching hands slide down his shoulders onto his chest, down his body. A heavy wave of hair cascaded across his brow. Lips touched his jaw, tentative, unsure. His body responded appreciatively. She smelled of licorice. That was wrong. Eva smelled of lavender and dirt.

He opened his eyes, fully alert. He grabbed the hands that encompassed him, pulling the woman around to see her clearly, ignoring the pain in his hands and arms lancing up into his shoulders and neck. He splashed a fair amount of water in the process. Simirri let out a small cry as he wrenched her wrist. He let her go instantly, but with malice. The force of it made her stumble backward.

"So Serac sent one of his whores to sneak secrets from my bed. Or are you here to kill me?" Illiah accused angrily. His eyes flickered to the dagger on his bed.

She shook her head. Her face drained of all color. Her shock was absolute. "No! No, I would never hurt you! But please," Simirri begged, kneeling, hugging her arms around herself. "Please, he told me it was my duty, that it was the will of the Goddess that I lay with you." Her eyes glinted with fearful tears. "You are angry. I am not worthy of the Goddess," she said, looking dejected and oh so young. And terrified.

Guardians help him! Illiah ground his teeth.

"Don't send me back. I can try again. I can please you, I am sure. Just don't send me back to Lord Serac," she pleaded when he said nothing. She looked genuinely terrified of displeasing the Temple Master. Illiah was forced to wonder how the psychopath punished his girls.

"I don't want to lay with you, Simirri, not now, not ever. And if you ever come into my private chambers again unbidden, there will be consequences," Illiah said sternly. "Since you are coming to live at my Keep, you should know I do not follow the Goddess like my brother, and neither do my men. You will not have relations with them. I will not have a common whore under my roof, and that is what you will be if you do that. The Goddess is not welcome at the Keep, but you will be if you follow my rules and work hard like everyone else." He paused to let her absorb his words. She looked confused. "What did Serac tell you your duties included once you reached the Keep?"

"The will of the Goddess," she told him, sitting straighter. "He instructed me to please you, and your men, and teach them the generosity of the Black Goddess, to guide them to her."

"With sex?" Illiah asked, incredulous. Simirri winced.

"That sounds vulgar." Her voice was very small. "What we do is lead the way to the Goddess," she said redundantly.

"How many men have you 'Led to the Goddess'?" It was certainly none of his business, but he asked it anyhow.

"None. I have only just earned my position as an acolyte with Lord Serac's guidance and tutelage." Simirri's posture was proud, but her eyes were wary as she mentioned Serac's name. Illiah felt sick.

"Did you enjoy this tutelage?" Illiah heard himself ask.

"N-no. But that is to be expected. I am just learning," she said, regaining her composure, slightly.

Illiah closed his eyes thinking of all the girls at the Temple, the women, being used by Serac as pawns for him and the "Goddess." His hands shook, he was so angry.

"Remember what I told you, Simirri. No exceptions or I will send you back to Caer Andri. Leave me."

He was done with the Goddess and her pawns. He couldn't wait to be home. The cuts in his hands throbbed in time with his anger.

CHAPTER 22

EVA

EACH DAY ILLIAH WAS GONE felt like a slow loss. Strangely, Eva's days passed by with a catalog of things she thought Illiah would find interesting or things she wanted to share with him. His absence was a hole in her life she hadn't noticed until, thinking of him, she stumbled and fell into it. It was a deep hole, she discovered.

Despite his absence, Illiah's ambitious project was taking form. Trees were cut and harvested, shaped by steel and strength into beams that would form the skeleton of new barracks. The barren plot of land that held the ashes of Eva's parents became once more a place of industry. The progress was astounding; when Illiah returned, he would be pleased.

Winter was in the air. Frost covered the ground in the mornings. The first snows could be seen dusting the pale mountains to the north. The cold did not deter Illiah's project, nor did it stop Eva from standing atop the watchtower.

She gazed out over the naked forest. The cold, damp wind whipped her hair around her face, making her nose numb, threatening to pull her over the precipice beyond her high perch. Calypso was gliding along the thermals beside the cliff, making daring aerial dives and swoops, clearly enjoying himself.

Showoff. Eva wondered if his face was as cold as hers.

"Ready to go in yet?" Mahone shouted from where he stood beyond the reaches of the wind, tucked in beside the wall.

"You can go if you want. Clarette left weeks ago. Your presence is hardly needed," Eva said, laughing at him. "Don't you have something better to do?"

"Not really. Lindin is recruiting every able-bodied soul to help put up the beams today."

"So you are hiding from work?"

"Nonsense. This is just so much more rewarding," he said with heavy sarcasm.

Eva turned back into the wind.

Illiah was late.

Illiah, Kaile, and Tarran should have arrived four days ago. Illiah had promised his return within the turning of the moon. An ambitious plan, no wonder he had overstepped it. Eva hoped that no ill had befallen him, another reason she stood against the cold wind desperately searching for a vision.

But mostly Eva just missed him. It bothered her.

How could he have ingrained himself into her life so quickly? She hardly knew him, yet she felt she had known him forever. She felt homesick, but she was home. She wished she had better command over the *simul rami*. She would welcome any vision concerning Illiah. She yearned for it as parched earth yearns for rain.

She told herself over and over that Illiah was not for her, could never be for her. Her foolish heart would not listen.

Calypso landed on the stone wall just beside Eva, startling her. She cursed him but fed him a treat from her pocket, which he gobbled up with pure greed. She stroked the back of his neck with her hand. His feathers were cold, smooth. He crooned in delight and bent his head so she could better administer her affections. She laughed at his endearing arrogance. How she would miss him. All too soon, she would leave the Keep. The thought was putrid.

Eva's ears and head were wrapped in a fur-lined cap to keep out the wind, but her face was burning from exposure. She liked the gritty, almost painful feeling. It ground her to her own inescapable reality. The small hopes and sweet dreams that entered her subconscious and crept into her waking thoughts would never come to pass. She knew this. Her future was like the cold, bitter wind - inescapable.

"Eva," Mahone said, startling her because he was suddenly beside her on the parapet. "Look." He pointed to the south watchtower. They were raising Illiah's flag, a sign his scout had been spotted.

Calypso took off and rode the wind to the south on a scouting mission of his own.

Eva couldn't help but laugh. What a useless gift her visions were. She had spent all morning in the cold and hadn't been able to foretell Illiah's arrival. Maybe she needed more practice.

Defeated, Eva relented to the cold and went inside to her room where it was cozy and warm. She was thrilled Illiah was almost home. She was terrified Illiah was almost home. She wanted to run down to meet him in the courtyard.

But she had no place there. She was not his lady. She was not his anything.

A while later she heard Calypso's welcome-home song. It sounded a lot like any raven caw, but Eva could hear the difference. Illiah was home.

She imagined him riding into the courtyard, tired, cold, but clad in the triumph and authority he carried with him like an invisible shield. He would smile his handsome, crooked smile at the sight of his gathering comrades. He would ask after the build and give a tight nod of approval for their expedient progress.

He was close, but a realm away. Her warm thoughts were treason. Her duty was to his brother, and to the king, who loved her like a daughter. Treason and duty aside, Illiah would never want her, no more than his brother did. Wasn't she difficult and odd like he always told her? Likely Illiah, the Hero Prince, the great Fixer of Woes, had a girl at court he pined after. Eva had seen them together; maybe that was another reason he had been eager to go back. Of course it was.

The realization forced an old loneliness to surface. From somewhere hollow and haunting and never forgotten came a little girl crying out for her dead parents. A girl who was all alone, bereft. A girl who was only seven and had not yet met the Guardians who would shape her into the woman she would become. Thoughts of the Guardians calmed her, steadied her. They cared for her. They loved her. They treasured her. Eva had Tayeh and Lula. At least for a little while longer.

An indeterminable amount of time later, a knock on Eva's door startled her. She opened it to see Illiah standing in the hall carrying a long box. The familiarity of his face was hot tea on a cold morning, the smell of baking bread, the twinkle in a raven's eye.

"May I come in?" he asked politely. Eva caught Tarek's eye where he stood behind their lord.

"My lady, it is not fit to see a man in your chamber alone -" Tarek stated formally, the hint of a glower in his eyes.

"Tarek. It is just me, don't be ridiculous," Illiah said with a laugh.

Illiah closed the door on Tarek, placed the box on Eva's bed and held his hand out to her.

Eva wondered what he was doing. Then she saw the ugly red cuts and half-healed welts on his hands and wrists and drew a sharp breath in alarm.

"What happened?"

"A common enemy."

"Serac?"

"Nothing can be proved. Or even formally speculated. There was no evidence, but for my hands and Tarran's bruises."

"Tarran? Is he all right?"

Illiah nodded in his assuring manner.

Eva traced his mostly healed cuts, but Illiah winced. Riding must have been agony for him. She soothed the wounds with her magic. Soon the stitches were unnecessary, the puckered, angry skin placid once more. Eva went to her bag to get a pair of tweezers and a small knife and went to work pulling the bits of twine from his healed skin.

"That tickles." His fingers twitched.

"Hold still. Tell me what happened."

He did. Eva didn't like his tale, not that she expected to. Tarran's role in the story was surprising. She could hardly believe it, but why would Illiah lie?

"I brought back servants. Mila is already giving them orders. And a swordsmith. Her swords are excellent. I will have to find a good source of steel, though. If only we could get Kitarran steel."

"Kitarra is a long ways away."

"I also brought back a Temple acolyte."

"A what?" She must have heard him wrong.

"A woman of the Black Goddess."

"Why on earth would you do that? After Serac trying to kill you?"

Illiah shrugged. "She is harmless."

"How do you know that?"

"I just do. When you meet her, you can judge for yourself."

"I trust your judgment." Eva could feel Illiah's gaze on her face. "Why do you think Serac wanted you dead?" she asked.

"I don't know."

Eva met his eyes, waiting for him to elaborate. He didn't. She held his eyes a little longer to let him know she suspected he was hiding something. Illiah was easy to trust for someone steeped in secrets.

"Thank you," he said when she finished. "Why does it hurt when you heal? It feels like bee stings," he asked as he flexed his hand.

"Because of your stubborn personality."

He rolled his eyes, sighing as he reached for the box beside him and handed it to her.

"I wanted to give you this. I saw it and thought of you."

Eva looked up at him skeptically. A gift?

"Call it a birthday present."

"My birthday isn't until late spring," she stated as she undid the latch.

"Yeah, well, no one has ever described me as punctual," he told her with a grin.

Eva opened the box. Gleaming in the torchlight lay a sleek, slim sword. Its proportions were perfect to hers, but even for its small size it looked dangerous in the velvet.

"It's as functional as it is beautiful," Illiah said. "Like you."

Eva's brows rose at the strange compliment, but she said nothing as she lifted the sword by the handle, taking it out of the box. Its weight and balance were perfect. Her hands shook as she moved the blade through the air. Her stomach twisted in delight.

"Thank you," she said. She wished she had some way to return the kindness, and told him so.

"You already have." He waved ten newly liberated fingers.

Eva inspected the detail on the pummel. The leaves etched into the steel disappeared beneath the leather grip and reappeared on the cross guard. The design was of the same leaf as her pendant.

"These leaves are cendari leaves ... Where did the sword come from?"

"I don't know what a cendari tree is. I asked Kota to add them. The sword is one of hers. I drew the design from memory. I know you wear that pendant all the time."

"How can I accept such a personal gift?" she asked him, putting the sword back in the box. "It should have been from your brother, not you." She put her hands at her sides. "I can't take this."

Illiah was silent.

"Just take it."

Eva wanted the sword. She wanted everything that came with it. She wanted his admiration, his friendship, his affection more than anything. The desire to kiss him was like standing at the top of something really high and fighting the irrational desire to jump.

She took the sword.

A thin film of snow covered the towering trees. An ear-splitting cry pierced the quiet of the woods. If there were words in the cry, Eva couldn't make them out. But it was human, high pitched like a girl or young boy.

Then she saw it. Blood streaked and splattered across the snow marring the perfect sylvan landscape. Eva saw the lifeless body first. It was small and tattered, lying limp, deep gashes drawn in jagged lines across flesh.

A second person stood over the lifeless form, taut and feral. A young girl. She brandished a sword too heavy for her, shrieking at the top of her voice, baring her teeth to her attacker.

The attacker was - wrong. Just wrong. Arms and legs covered in short, mangy fur. A torso hollowed like a starving animal. Stark ribs moving with every obvious breath it took.

Its hands and feet and face were human. Almost human.

The long, broken nails were red with fresh blood. Its eyes were human. Its mouth was red and dripped blood. It licked its human lips with a long, inhuman tongue. It paced, wary of the steel blade aimed at it.

The girl screamed again, waving the sword, stepping forward. The thing flinched and turned on its heel, scrambling away on all fours like a beast.

The vision faded like the thing faded into the undergrowth of the forest.

Eva fought for balance against the wall. She had disentangled herself from the *simul rami* too quickly. Mahone was by her side in an instant.

"What is it?"

Eva spun too fast and nearly fell. Her head was dizzy, her body weak. She knew better. Emotion rattled her senses. Mahone caught her elbow.

"Illiah, find Illiah! Tell him Tarran and Murryn are in trouble - now!" Eva commanded when Mahone hesitated. She pushed him toward the door, yelling at him to go. He read the desperate nature of the vision in her eyes and obeyed her frantic commands, leaving her alone.

If the vision had not been so clear and concise, Eva would have passed it off as a hallucination. Or a dream. But she could still feel the lingering connection to the *simul rami* like the shape of a bright light stuck in her vision. It had not been some mad dream. It was real. It was now.

Eva had to tread the stairs carefully with her head spinning. She could not risk her own neck or Tarran and Murryn were as good as dead.

Tarran, poor Tarran. He was such a sweet-natured boy, and so good. She prayed to the old spirits he would still be alive when they found him. She would not allow herself to think of the possibility that he was already dead.

The thought gave her feet momentum. She crossed the yard, looking hopefully for Illiah's tall form, for Mahone or Tarek. She didn't have time to wait for them. She had to get to the children. She ran to the stables, unlatching Sasha's stall door, grabbing the gelding's bridle. She didn't have time to saddle him. Thankfully, her sword already hung from her belt. Illiah's gift rarely left her side.

Eva was thankful for her detailed knowledge of the surrounding forest. She knew every cliff, every hill. She recognized one particular tree from the vision, an ash, rare in this part of the forest. Even in the twilight of the year, it feebly held onto several clumps of red berries, making it unmistakable. The rest of the forest was white with recently fallen snow.

Eva pushed Sasha faster than she ever would under normal circumstances. Reaching Tarran as quick as possible was the only chance to save his life, and Murryn's.

Unless the creature came back before Eva reached the children.

Sasha slowed, tensing, snorting loudly in alarm, his steps hesitant. Eva was close. Perhaps Sasha could smell blood in the air. Eva listened to the forest. It seemed - normal.

Eva spun slowly this way and that, discerning the direction she needed to go. The light was fading fast. The weak winter rays hardly penetrated the layers of branches covered in snow.

Eva gave a call. There was no answer. She was almost to the ash tree. She dismounted, leaving Sasha nervously tied to a tree. She pressed on cautiously, trying to keep her footsteps as light as possible through the crunchy snow. She called out, then strained her ears for an answer.

A sound came from behind her. A growl. Wind in the trees. Death's whisper. It was hard to tell which.

Eva spun to see a mottled form outlined by white snow. The creature. She met its human eyes. Long, gangling arms reached almost to the ground ending in claws. She couldn't tell where the human and the animal intertwined, but the essence of both was so wrong and evil, fear threatened to root her to the forest floor. It stood hunched, its animal legs awkward, wrong. Something emanated from its being, something not unlike Eva's own magic, but twisted, obscure. Hauntingly familiar. Her sword was a reassuring weight in her hand.

The creature darted forward, toward her, striking out with one of its human hands. Eva sidestepped, deflecting it with her blade. The creature was too fast, slipping out of her reach. It paced, playing with her. She needed to kill it. Tarran was dying - he needed her healing magic.

Eva stepped toward it purposefully, her blade seeking flesh. The creature darted behind a tree. Eva followed.

"Eva!"

Illiah's voice came from behind her. She was loath to turn her back to her prey, but she couldn't see the creature. Maybe it had run.

"Illiah, go find Tarran! I'll -" Eva froze, looking at Illiah. Illiah was not looking at her. His gaze was fixed on the creature that had reappeared a short distance away, its disturbing form hunched and intense. Illiah lowered his sword, all intention gone from his usually determined mien.

"Illiah. What are you doing?" Eva shouted. Illiah took a step away from her, toward the thing. Something was very wrong. Eva grabbed Illiah's sleeve, pulling him back toward her. He shrugged her off with enough force that she almost fell. Illiah's eyes focused on hers, but they were no longer his. They were hard and empty, like his soul had been eclipsed by a moonless, starless night.

He raised his sword. Fear cinched around Eva's heart. He swung at her. Eva had watched Illiah spar; she knew how good he was. And how fast. His sword grated against hers, steal screaming against steal. His strength nearly pushed her to the ground. Her feet slipped on the snow. Her arms burned. She forced herself to breathe, to find calm. She ducked, moving under his arm, toward his back, keeping her sword between her and him. She knew the creature was some-where behind her, but before her was a man gone mad. She had killed madmen in self-defense before, but she knew in her heart she could not - would not - kill Illiah.

"Illiah. Stop!" she begged, her voice ragged. "Illiah! Please."

Illiah lunged at her again. His sword was almost twice as long as hers, his reach twice as great. Tayeh had taught her to build on her strengths. She would never be stronger or taller than a man, so why try to fight like one? He had taught her stealth, feints, to keep secrecy in her movements, to find strength and flexibility where she could, to find the perfect moments in a fight to use all of the above to her adversary's disadvantage. But she could not keep her pace up forever.

A sound like the end of the world exploded around them. It was primitive, raw, and terrible. Something was fighting for its life - and losing. From the corner of her eye, Eva saw them: a grey mountain cat and the creature. The large cat had the ugly beast in its teeth, dragging it into the blur of trees and snow. Illiah's arms went slack, the fight gone from him.

Shouts came from behind her, Mahone and Tarek.

"Illiah!" Eva shouted in Illiah's face, resisting the urge to slap him hard. Illiah's eyes were closed. When they opened, they were green and alive and his once more.

"What happened?" he asked, dazed.

But Eva had no time to explain, something faint but unmistakably girl-like greeted her ears. She wanted to stay with Illiah, but she had not forgotten Tarran. Eva saw a shift of movement through the trees - the children. Murryn crouched over a heap of tatters that must be Tarran. Please, Eva pleaded to whatever spirits might be listening, let him be alive.

Eva shook her head before running to Murryn and Tarran. Mahone was with the children already, his arm around Murryn. Murryn was kneeling on the ground, sobbing, cradling a lifeless figure in her arms. Both were covered in blood.

Eva inspected Murryn quickly. The girl was beyond strained and pale. Eva asked her briefly if she was all right. Murryn nodded, though her hands were scratched. Eva snapped orders to the men.

"Help Tarran, help Tarran," Murryn repeated between sobs.

Eva did. She took Tarran's head and shoulders across her lap. Some-one grabbed Murryn in a tight embrace, wrapping her in a warm cloak - Mahone, because Illiah was beside Eva, fighting to control the sob of grief that came over him.

Eva spared Illiah no thought. Tarran was a mess. She placed her finger to his throat, feeling for a heartbeat, hoping for a heartbeat.

She found one.

It was slow and extremely weak. Tarran's skin was cold, like ice. Murryn had tried desperately to keep him warm, giving him her cloak and wrapping him as best she could. Smart girl.

Tarran's clothes were saturated with blood, making it impossible to decipher ragged cloth from ragged flesh. He had lost a lot of blood. It had melted the snow and soaked into the ground. Murryn had attempted to bandage Tarran's wounds to stop the bleeding. Eva unwrapped the makeshift bandages. The wounds were long and deep and many. Some raking gashes from the creature's claws, others deep punctures and rents from its teeth. Eva shivered thinking of the crea-ture and its human teeth on Tarran's flesh. Tarran must have fought back. She could smell the iniquitous magic on Tarran. A sour and ashy stench.

Eva's assessment took seconds. She opened Tarran's shirt and placed her palm over his heart, over a deep, shredded wound. The blood was sticky on her skin and hot against the cool air. His wound no longer bled. Not good. She thought she could see the pale white of bone in the well of the wound, but she ignored it. It didn't matter. Her other hand she placed upon his brow and closed her eyes.

His body was weak, tenuous, but his spirit was strong. She could almost hear his spirit screaming out for help. He didn't want to die, and he didn't want to give up. That was good. If the spirit gave up, the body could never hope to recover.

Eva started with his heart and gave it strength. It pulsed stronger. He still had enough blood left for it, but barely. Next, she worked on the injuries to his tissue so he would not lose his precious, remaining lifeblood.

His wounds were a maze. Slowly Eva worked over him, and by the last one, her strength was almost lost. Tarran's head had also taken a brutal hit, likely the reason for his unconscious state. She soothed it and healed what damage was beneath his thick skull, which luckily had not cracked. Beyond his lacerations and concussion, the rest of his body was merely bruised and weak from blood loss.

Eva took her hand away. Tarran's breath quickened and his body stirred ever so slightly. The burning pain of her magic would leave him instantly. She doubted he had even felt it. He would need time to regain his strength and ease his bruises. A couple of restful days would see him right.

Eva allowed herself a sigh of relief. She didn't want to open her eyes, she was so tired. Something cold impacted her shoulder and head. The ground, she supposed numbly.

She heard a voice shout her name. Illiah.

"Mahone, what's wrong with her? Help her!" Illiah shouted. His arms came around her, pressing her limp body to his. She wanted to tell him she was just tired, she just needed a rest, but she couldn't. She could hear Mahone's reply, but not make sense of it.

Then she fell into a senseless sleep.

CHAPTER 23

EVA

THE LAST THINGS Eva remembered were cold snow on her face and Illiah's voice calling her name and the smell of something woodsy and untouchable surrounding her like a warm blanket.

She was in her bed.

She didn't remember how she got there.

A fire burned in the hearth, the only light. Eva's stomach growled. How long had she been asleep? It was surely the middle of the night.

She stretched carefully, her muscles sore and stiff. Calypso was on his roost and unfolded his head from under his wing to look at her. He crooned softly at her before fluffing his feathers with contentment.

An unknown presence sat in the corner of her room. Eva's stomach lurched before she acknowledged that it was only Illiah. Only Illiah.

And it came back to her. The ache in her arms told her the nightmare had been real. She remembered the creature with all its wrongness and Illiah striking at her with his sword and all his skill, intent on killing her.

Illiah heard her quiet movement and looked up, the fire brightening his features. His eyes took a moment to shift from whatever faraway scene had captivated him. He didn't smile, but his face flooded with relief. Then he stood and had the grace to look abashed. Eva should be terrified of him after what happened, but all she could feel was relief.

"Tarek and Mahone insisted on watching over you, but they were beyond exhausted. I am just here to spell them," he explained, examining his hands with uncharacteristic diffidence.

"Illiah, do you remember what happened in the forest before we found the children?"

"What kind of question is that? Of course I remember," Illiah stated softly.

"Do you? You attacked me, Illiah. We fought. You almost killed me," Eva said, her hands shaking. "There was something in the forest - it was waiting for you. Something evil. I think -" she spoke as the thought occurred to her. "- it attacked Tarran to get you into the forest, and then it took over you. There is magic here that you can't understand - I can't understand."

Illiah was silent, his expression controlled, an admission of his unease. "You think it was a trap? For me?"

"Yes. If the creature had not been attacked by that mountain cat, I think you would have killed me."

"It wanted you dead?" Illiah looked like he might vomit.

"Or it wanted you under its control."

Illiah was thinking. No, he was searching. Illiah was a fixer. He was already looking for a solution.

"I - I actually believe you," he said after swallowing hard.

"You do?"

The Illiah that regarded Eva was the Illiah she had seen in a vision of war and blood, drunk on exhaustion, sharpened by worry and doubt. "I would never hurt you, Eva."

"I know." And she did. With every fiber of her body, she knew he would never harm her. "It wasn't you. It was that thing that attacked Murryn and Tarran. It had a face and hands and feet like a man, but the body of an animal, covered in mangy fur ..." Eva fell silent, looking at the shadows of the room, feeling them grow. A prickling of unease crept down her spine. She swallowed the words she was going to say. Tayeh was right. To speak of evil would invite it into her space, into her light.

"What, Eva?"

Eva shook her head. "We should not speak of it here, in the dead of night."

"I can't help but agree with you," Illiah said in a quiet voice.

"I know I must sound mad."

Illiah didn't assure her otherwise.

"I - I want to tell you - there are other forces in the Great Forest - in the world ... I am worried for you, Illiah," Eva said.

"I thought we weren't going to speak of it?" he said sharply.

Eva nodded. But she couldn't eclipse the memory of Illiah, his eyes void of his soul, and his mouth tight with anger.

"Do not worry for me, Eva. I can take care of myself. You, on the other hand ..." Illiah gestured to her bed ridden state.

"How long was I asleep?"

"Asleep?" Illiah repeated. "I wouldn't call what came over you sleep. We couldn't wake you, or get any response out of you. If it weren't for your steady heartbeat, I would have thought you dead. It is a relief to see you awake. It's been three days, Eva."

Tarran must have been teetering close to death to take so much strength from her, she had never been gone for that long before.

"Tarran is all right?" she asked. "And Murryn?"

Illiah nodded. "He is fine. Back to himself, I daresay, at least more or less," he added thoughtfully. "He has some interesting scars he is a little too proud of. Murryn is good, a little shaken up. She has some scratches on her hands, but she will recover quickly. Thank you for saving them." Illiah tilted his head, his lips softening.

"What time is it?" Eva asked. "I'm so hungry my stomach hurts."

"It's the middle of the night, but I can get you something to eat," Illiah said, leaving without so much as a by-your-leave.

In the silent moments while Eva waited, listening to her growling stomach, she realized she was all but naked under her blankets, in nothing but her small clothes and a thin shift. A blush rose to her cheeks. She searched about for the nearest article of clothing. Her robe lay close by. She made to stand up and grab it but underestimated her strength. Three days abed and no food had weakened her. Her legs nearly gave way. Her head swam. She could not stand much less reach her robe. She gave up and pulled the blanket closer around her.

A wave of panic came over her. Her neck was bare. She fingered the red welt where her pendant should have been. She searched her sheets, her clothes, under her pillow. She didn't find it. She started the search again.

Illiah was not gone long. Eva heard the click of the door and reassembled herself on the bed, her blanket secure about her person. He had a basket full of smoked meats, cheeses, and bread, and a pitcher of cool, clean water. He placed it on the bed in front of her, then settled himself at her feet like a very big cat.

"My necklace. Do you know where my pendant is?"

"I'm sure it's here somewhere," he said looking around, moving the robe she had been unable to reach aside. "Ah, here it is." He picked it up off her little table.

"Thank you." Eva sighed as it settled on her chest.

"Did that belong to one of your parents?" Illiah asked casually, handing her a cup of water. She shook her head but didn't elaborate.

Eva found her mouth dry, thirsting for the water. She downed the full cup. It hit her empty stomach heavily. She helped herself to the bread and cheese with relish. Illiah picked at the food too, taking a bite here and there.

"How do you feel?" he asked after she had eaten enough to feel comfortably full.

"Dizzy."

"Is that normal?"

Eva shrugged. "It's probably because I have had no nourishment for three days."

Illiah nodded.

"How did you know about Tarran and Murryn, Eva?"

Eva had expected the question. Illiah's tone was level, but Eva could hear the hint of a command. It made her smile. The Lord of the Keep did not like secrets or surprises.

Eva looked into the bottomless pools that were his eyes. Calm, inky black pools promising trust and loyalty and protection. The eyes of a hero.

"I see things, visions, I guess you would call them. Things that have already happened or are happening. I cannot see the future. I saw Tarran lying in the forest, bleeding his lifeblood into the ground. I saw Murryn standing over him, waving a sword. She was very brave." She paused. "I can also look into the past. Some things are so subjective that I have no idea what they are. Others are more clear, obvious. Sometimes I can seek a vision out, about a person or place, but that is - difficult." Eva almost added that she was still learning, but that would risk exposing her teachers. And that was a secret not hers to tell.

"Allati magic again," Illiah said after a moment.

Her mother's heritage was not something people spoke of, but Eva supposed the physical characteristics were hard to ignore. She did have the unmistakable silvery-golden hair of her mother's people. "I am a *sanarii*," Eva told him.

"Never heard of it. Did you ever see me?" he asked quietly.

"Yes," Eva replied honestly. Illiah would know if she lied to him. He had a knack for it.

"Really?" Illiah said with a small sideways smile, relaxing on the bed.

Eva settled herself cross-legged, drawing her blanket up under her arms so she could take a little honey cake from the basket. She took a bite before answering.

"Don't look so pleased. I said the visions are mostly random. I have never sought you out," she clarified. "I saw you a year ago, but I thought you were Caeris."

"That would make sense."

"But it didn't!" Eva exclaimed. "I saw you, or at the time I thought you were Caeris, talking to Kaile, but the words just didn't make sense. You didn't act like Caeris, and of course Kaile was a stranger to me."

"You hear what is spoken in the visions too?" he asked, slightly alarmed. Eva nodded. "I don't like it," he stated.

"I can hear, I can smell, the visions are real to me, like standing in that place as a silent observer. Why? Do you have anything to hide?" Eva countered with a smile.

"No. But still - it's unfair."

Eva shrugged.

"So how do you know it wasn't actually Caeris you saw?" Illiah asked.

Eva sobered, remembering the vision she was relating. She had seen many visions of Illiah, but one, in particular, was engraved in her mind. Illiah pressed her softly for an explanation.

"It was before you even met Caeris, before you knew who you were born to be. It was after a great battle, the last battle, I think. You were upset. I have seen Caeris upset, but you were - different. Honest. Hurting, if that makes any sense."

"How much of that time did you see?" he asked, alarmed once more, but for her sake.

"I saw a lot of the war. The visions haunted my dreams for months, even before we northerners knew about the attacks in the south. Everyone I saw was nameless to me, but it was terrible, awful. What the invaders did to the women, what they did to the children was especially ... difficult."

Illiah regarded her with an expression she couldn't decipher. Pity, perhaps.

"What else have you seen?" he asked, obviously curious. "About me?"

Eva pressed her lips into a line. She could not speak of the man he had killed with a wooden dagger who had oozed black, choking smoke along with his blood. Even as a memory, the evil of it made her skin crawl and the night creep into her heart. Why did the strange magic follow Illiah like a perverse shadow? And then there was the vision of Illiah languishing, naked, with a high born woman whom he was possibly in love with.

"Nothing really," she said looking down at her hands. She couldn't look him in the eye. Not that it mattered. He sensed her hesitation and pounced on it.

"What else?" Illiah asked again, a smile turning up the corners of his mouth, enjoying her discomfort.

Eva squirmed.

"You're the one who invaded my privacy with your strange Allati magic - this *sanarii*. The least you could do is tell me," he chided in an amused tone.

"I didn't see anything about you intentionally! I told you I cannot really control it. I would never pry."

"What did you see?" he asked again in a wheedling tone, his smirk growing irresistibly.

"I'm not saying," she said. Her cheeks burned. Betrayers.

"Please."

The look in his eyes was an effective form of torture.

"Fine!" she said, rolling her eyes in defeat. "I saw you with a woman." She said it in such a way he could not misconstrue her context. "At court. It was summer time. There were not many blankets." Somehow it was easier to bring up a sensual liaison than a cold-handed execution involving magic.

"Ah." He didn't look embarrassed or uncomfortable, as she obviously was. "I wish you hadn't seen that," he merely said.

Eva had to agree with his statement, but she didn't say anything. She was tempted to ask him who the woman was, if he loved her, if they had shared a night or a relationship, did he still love her, had he seen her again at court? But she couldn't. It wasn't her business. But still, she had to bite back the questions begging to leap off her tongue.

"You all but forced me to tell you," Eva retorted instead. Illiah offered her a little smile for her exasperation.

"Could you always do this? Even when you were a child? I imagine such a gift would be very strange for a young girl to comprehend."

Eva thought of Tayeh and Lula, the two Guardians that had been just that, her guardians, her mentors since the death of her parents. Perhaps if her mother were alive, she would have taught her daughter about the magic of her people. Eva wouldn't have needed the Guardians.

"I have had these gifts since my parents died. By then I was already much older than my seven years," she said to appease him.

Illiah narrowed his eyes slightly, effortlessly discerning she was withholding the full answer to his question.

"All right then, my mysterious lady," he said, standing up with a bone-popping stretch. "I am off to my own bed, now that you are on the mend. I am sure Mahone and Tarek will be here first thing in the morning to make sure that you are still breathing. Tarran too will be eager to see you."

"Thank you, Illiah," Eva said. "And goodnight, I guess."

He hesitated at the edge of her bed. His expression, all dark eyes and trust and heroics, made something inside her chest hurt. He nodded and disappeared with ease into the blackness outside her door. Eva's heart pattered in her chest. It would be so much easier if Illiah were more like his twin brother.

CHAPTER 24

ILLIAH

THE DAY HAD BEEN every bit the winter Illiah had been warned of. Cold. Windy. Snow making every chore frustrating and difficult. Calling a half day of rest had been the right choice. The men had been relieved, thankful. It was a fine line between taskmaster and tyrant, he didn't want to be known as the latter.

Besides the challenge it brought, Illiah found he didn't mind the snow. The south was not known for cold, hard winters. If snow fell it only lasted for a day or two. Here it came in drifts, blanketing everything. It was beautiful, peaceful. Quiet.

Lovely as the quiet was, it also fed Illiah's misgivings. Eva had warned him about the magic of the Great Forest, but he hadn't expected it to spill over into *his* forest.

Eva had been wrong. The beast had not been after him. It had been after his dagger, using it against him, somehow. The first time Illiah realized he could use the dagger to take over another man's mind, it had been accidental. The second time had been entirely intentional.

Bren had been about to abandon the front line. Terror at the enemy and looming battle had taken his courage; he had begged Illiah to leave. But Illiah had needed every able-bodied man he could muster, and Bren had been a big man; a swing of his ax could take out two men easily. Illiah couldn't afford to let him go. So he had used his dagger. Bren had fought like a man enraged. He killed dozens of men that day, but lost his leg for it. And Bren had never been the same since.

So, for the moment, Illiah forbid anyone from venturing out into the forest alone. But he couldn't bring himself to discard the dagger. .

Illiah paused in the hallway to his chambers. He heard footsteps from the dim stairwell behind him. Deciding to wait, he peered out the window into the night. The view was mostly incomprehensible; only the faint red light of the minuscule torches highlighted the contours of the Keep. Still, it gave him a feeling of satisfaction. His home. His people.

The treads grew louder. Illiah deciphered it to be a man's footfall, not soft enough for a lady. Tarek emerged under the torchlight in the narrow hallway. He came to a stop, evidently wanting a word.

"My lord," Tarek said in his soft yet strong voice, "I was hoping to catch you in private before you went to bed."

"What is it?" Illiah asked, his voice a little sharp. He was weary.

Tarek was a quiet, secretive man, yet Illiah could not guess what he had to say that needed the absolute solitude of the hall, shrouded by night and stone.

The guard looked uncomfortable. "It's about Eva." He took a deep breath. "Mahone and I are concerned for her."

"Why?" Using her magic to heal Tarran had been taxing, but that had been seven days ago. Eva seemed a bit subdued since the incident, and they hadn't spoken of it since. Illiah kept expecting her to bring it up, but she hadn't. Maybe she was ill. Maybe using her magic had weakened her more than she let on. Cold fingers of concern clutched his gut.

"You, my lord - it's you." The big guard hesitated, then the words came faster, an awkward jumble. "We are afraid Eva has feelings for you, sir. We don't want her heart to get broken. She is betrothed to your brother, after all. And her reputation is at risk. Even some of the men have mentioned it, in private."

Illiah's heart beat faster. He willed his face to remain a mask. "I assure you her reputation is intact." He did not bother to soften his voice.

Tarek's scars were starkly outlined in the lantern light, the worry in his eyes clearly visible. "Sir, please, I am afraid she is falling in love with you. I've known Eva since she was a girl. She's something between a sister and a daughter to me. I know her heart. Please, listen. Her mother was ostracized because she was the reason Lord Finnan broke his engagement, a stray Allati girl plucked from the forest with no name or status. Everyone hated her mother for breaking that alliance. Lady Jaia was never accepted because she was the reason Lord Jonsef disinherited Finnan. There were rumors Jaia was a sorceress. Some demanded she be sent to the Temple for judgment. Eva doesn't deserve the same fate. It will be hard enough for her to wed your brother. Please don't make it doubly so."

"Are you suggesting I have been encouraging her?" Illiah asked, wondering if it were true.

"You do seem to enjoy her company."

Illiah had never paused to think about it before, never allowed himself to think about it. He did enjoy her company, more than he had any right to. Eva entered his thoughts more than any other. And then there were the dreams. Dreams he would barely acknowledge. The dagger could have used his thoughts, his desires, even without his consent. He cursed inwardly. He needed to put a stop to it instantly. Yesterday. Eva was to wed his brother in summer. How could he allow this to happen? Something hard lodged in his heart, cold and unsettling.

He gave Tarek a curt nod.

"Perhaps you are right, but I did not mean anything by befriending Eva," Illiah heard himself say. "She just seems lonely sometimes, but I will keep my distance." The words were bile stuck in his throat. To dismiss her friendship felt wrong. Part of him already hurt for the absence of it.

"Thank you for understanding, my lord," Tarek said. They parted ways at the top of the stairs. Illiah sought his room, feeling wretched. He closed the heavy door behind him and leaned against it.

He was too busy to spend time with Eva anyhow. There was the build - when not impeded by the weather - the training of the recruits, matters of the Keep to address, messages from court to attend to. The safety of Jullayah was his responsibility, after all. He hardly had time to sit still, much less indulge in frivolities like riding in the forest with Eva, or sparring with her, or inventing outrageous things to irritate her with.

He felt like a child denied a coveted treat. He loved her challenging smile, her determination, her stubborn, righteous will. She wouldn't let him get away with anything. It had brought him a strange satisfaction. Until now.

But it wasn't real. Eva's affection for him was just the influence of the dagger. Her actions did not reflect her true feelings. He had wanted to believe the dagger was a gift. He realized it was a curse.

Frustration welled within him. He pulled out his sword. He forced himself to calm his breathing as he moved through his routine. It came without thinking, the very first routine he had learned from his old mentor, the wandering warrior. Damn you, Eelan.

His body moved without his mind because he couldn't get her out of his head. The more he thought about the circumstance, the more anger he felt, the more it hurt. It occurred to him that he could use the dagger to influence his brother. He could make Caeris love Eva. He could give Eva the happiness she deserved. He could use his curse to do something worthwhile.

He would go back to court, back to his father and brother. Lindin and Will were more than capable of overseeing the build and the recruits. He had business in Caer Andri besides. He would be gone for a month or two; Eva would be leaving for court in spring, shortly after. Once she was wed, he would hardly see her but for feasts and other formal occasions. In time she would become the kind, wise queen he knew she would be. She would give Caeris his legitimate children, a son with bright hair and green-blue eyes. Illiah had no doubt she would be a wonderful mother.

That night he had nightmares. Haunting dreams were not new to him, but this time they were different. Eva was there - so was Caeris, Illiah's living reflection.

In his dream Caeris took Eva, pushing her over, her long skirts pulled up roughly, exposing her fair skin. The prince raped her from behind again and again. The dream changed and Illiah was in the war once again, surrounded by villages stripped of goodness and beauty, leaving only carnage. Eva was still there, but this time it was one of the barbarous invaders over her, his hair a mat of braids and dirt, his beard long and full of grime, his face etched with scars that told the tale of his monstrousness. A sword covered with dried blood and other unmentionable things in one hand, the other held Eva's fair breast as he crushed her to him, thrusting and thrusting. She was already dead.

Illiah woke up with a yell, covered in cold sweat. His hand held his dagger. He paced the room, opening the window, letting the piercingly cold air penetrate his lungs, freezing the drops of sweat on his skin. He started shivering almost instantly, but it took his mind off his evil dreams.

He went back to bed. He pulled the blanket over his head, as he had done as a child when he had been afraid of the dark. Only there was no one to comfort him, no mother, no brother, father or sister. Illiah had never felt so alone.

Lulanan stepped into the light. The Forest was bright. Snow blanketed the ground and crept up the trunks of the trees. Winter birds chirped encouragement at each other in their endless search for seeds.

"Lulanan." The voice was deep, almost like a growl, but smooth and easy.

"Timur."

The man had white hair and pale skin and eyes green as pond weed. Today his green eyes were narrowed, his jaw set.

"We found another wanderer. It was beyond the Forest. If the raven hadn't found me when he did, your girl would be dead."

Lula felt a cutting fear she had hoped would never return. Fear. And sorrow. A sorrow deep and pungent, tinged with failure. Her people. Hers to protect. She had failed. Again.

"Did you kill it?" she asked.

"We had no choice." The man cocked his head. "I did not know a Guardian could cry."

"I will search the Forest," Lula told him. "There may be more of them. Something is happening. I don't know if I can stop it. A wanderer senses its master's magic. Let us hope it is still too weak to spread beyond our reach. But … this is the second one in two years. Two years …"

The man nodded, his face less proud and more tired. The Forest shivered - only Lula could see it - and the man was a mountain cat. His long, lean body was covered in white and gray fur, his paws big and padded. The tip of his tail flicked, and his gaze shifted from her into the Forest.

Lula took a shuddering breath even though there was no air in her lungs. There was only light, and it was threatened by shadow.

CHAPTER 25

EVA

ILLIAH LEFT FOR CAER ANDRI at daybreak. He didn't tell Eva he was leaving - he was just gone. Part of her ached that Illiah left without saying goodbye. Part of her was just relieved that he was gone, away from the threats of the Forest.

Eva went to the Great Forest for answers.

She spoke with Lula and Tayeh about the creature. A wanderer they called it. They told her that it was dead. The Guardians were immune from time and the elements, but they were not immune from grief. Whatever the wanderer was or had been, its death saddened Lula deeply. Her fox eyes were dulled, her ears limp.

"Please," Eva said. "The wanderer took Illiah's mind, made him into a monster - just like the men in Dweller's Knoll. He would have killed me if it hadn't been for that mountain cat!" Eva exclaimed. "What if it happens again?"

"The wanderer has been killed, Eva. There are no more." Lula said, her voice paper thin.

"But are you sure?"

"Eva," Tayeh's voice was as old and wise as the trees. "Come sit. I think it is time to tell you something."

Tayeh was finally offering her answers, but all she felt was fear. She sat down beside him with her legs crossed, just as she had as a child when he told Kitarran legends.

"The balance is teetering," he began. "The wanderer was a sign that dark magic is poisoning the *simul rami*. But there is a prophecy. There is hope.

Those who were strong are now weak,
With healing hands, the babes will speak

Light turns to dark and colors shift,
Two rivers join when two lovers rift,
Watch for the child of two thrones,
Born with magic in his bones,
A child lit by the stars,
Watch for him, for he shall be ours."

Eva let the words sink in. A child born of two thrones.

"Your mother was descended from the royal Allati bloodline, Eva," Tayeh told her.

Eva's emotions writhed as she tried to wrap her numb mind around the significance of it. "That means the child of the prophecy - that could be my child - with Caeris." The Guardians had always been encouraging about her betrothal. "Why didn't you tell me?"

"I wanted you to live your life free from this knowledge. Free from the responsibility it brings. Sometimes it is harder to make good choices when the weight of the future hangs over us. The future is not set in stone. Even a prophecy may not come to pass."

"But the wanderer ... Dweller's Knoll."

"Yes. It is happening faster than we anticipated."

"Then I will do my part. I will do whatever I can," Eva said. The men she had killed deserved no less.

After one turning of the moon, the Keep waited expectantly once more for Lord Illiah's return. He was due any day. Then a message came from Caer Andri: Lord Illiah would be staying longer in the royal city. The king's health was ailing, and Illiah wanted to stay close to his father for a while longer.

The news was upsetting. The king. Eva's dear friend. She wished he was not quite so far away and the winter was not quite so cold. Her heart ached with the possibility that she would never see him again.

Eva sought Illiah in the *simul rami*. She saw him looking pensively into the fire, his eyes filled with troubles, the firelight casting shadows on his skin, tingeing his hair and beard red. He was beautiful - and lonely. Eva forbid herself to seek visions of him again.

Days and weeks passed. The snow melted, the sun held a touch of warmth, and the earth soaked up what little heat it could. Finally, six weeks after Illiah's departure, the first blossoms of spring came to the forest and the first intrepid new leaves.

It was dinner hour and the great hall was filling with the hungry. Eva almost tripped on her slippers when she recognized a tall, dark-haired figure talking to Altos.

Eva drank in the sight of him. Illiah looked tired. His cloak was travel worn and stained, his beard thick, his hair cut ruthlessly short.

Sometimes Illiah had uncanny senses. He must have perceived her gaze because he turned to face her. His green eyes looked almost golden in the torchlight, crinkling at the corners as he smiled tentatively at her.

Words could not express her happiness in seeing him. She wanted to run to him and throw her arms around him, lay her head against his chest, feel his strong embrace surround her. But she didn't - couldn't. Illiah excused himself from Altos to greet her.

"I didn't know you were back. Cally didn't warn me," she told him. Eva didn't remember crossing the hall, but suddenly she was standing before Illiah, her heart thrumming in her ears.

"Lazy bird," Illiah noted. Then Illiah was giving her the king's kind regards and Eva was telling him everything that had happened the last two months. Two months wasn't enough time to create any real drama. The recruits were well behaved. There was news that one of the other married couples were expecting a baby.

"That's not surprising," Illiah remarked at the news. "I guess there will scores of babes around soon. If Freya and Talamir don't have one soon, I will lose all my faith in the man's abilities." Illiah rolled his eyes.

"You'll be an uncle!" Eva said, confident Illiah's mischievous nature would only endear him as an uncle.

"I am already an uncle." Illiah gave her a sideways look.

"Caeris's mistress had her baby?"

"A month ago," Illiah said. "A baby girl. I can't remember the name. I didn't meet her. She was born early - I heard she was very small."

"Is she okay?" Eva asked, thinking of a tiny helpless baby, struggling for life.

"I think she will be. Mother and babe were sent to live at the Temple. Caeris believes the Goddess will take care of her," Illiah stated.

"Oh," Eva said. She remembered Tayeh and Lula's constant warnings about that place and the self-proclaimed Goddess. Would a misguided spirit like Crea take the time to spare a small child? Tayeh's opinion would be certainly not.

"I do not share my brother's devotion to the Goddess," Illiah told her with a shrug.

"He does seem slightly fanatical."

Kaile came up behind them and handed Illiah a mug of ale. He made a rude sound. "The acolytes are a pretty bunch, though. All glossy black hair and pale skin. What's the name of that girl who always dotes on you whenever we go there? She is-"

"You've been to the Temple?" Eva cut off Kaile.

"Many times, have you not?" Illiah asked, equally surprised.

"No, never."

"Huh. I would have thought Caeris would have taken you many times."

"Caeris doesn't like to take me anywhere, and besides, he knows I won't go there."

"What is it?"

"The Temple is dangerous," she told Illiah quietly.

He didn't say anything.

Kaile tugged Illiah away, speaking of Linden and the recruits and the build and the countless other things needing Illiah's attention.

Eva shivered as Illiah dissolved and shifted before her eyes from her friend into her lord.

With Illiah's arrival came a strange storm. Winter, being so fond of mountains and damp valleys, decided to grace the Keep and the Forest with one last visit. In the morning, a fresh layer of snow covered everything. Eva frowned. She pulled on her thick woolen slippers she had hoped not to use again until next winter. She remembered she would not see another winter at the Keep. Her frown deepened. With that morose thought, she traded her slippers for woolen boots and grabbed her thick cloak, resolved to make the most of the beautiful snow, unwelcome as it was.

She sneaked out of her room, down the passage to the council room, and quickly out through the little garden into the ancient forest. Her tracks were already melting in the spring air as she walked under the trees. Birds flitted around from branch to fern to root, their voices mingling pleasantly.

The sun was just rising over the horizon, shining timidly through the boughs of the tall evergreen trees. The air glistened under its warm caress as the snow melted with crystalline drips. The Forest was bejeweled, transformed, almost like a dream. Eva knew it was beautiful, but the beauty did not soak into her soul.

Lula fell in step beside her. The small white fox shook her fur as if to dispel the water drops, but nothing touched the Guardian. Lula paused in her tracks, her nose up high, sniffing, her stance attentive. Quick as a swallow, she was scurrying through the Forest, gone from Eva's sight.

Eva shrugged and continued without her companion. Lula was a fickle, playful creature, not unlike a real wild fox. Tayeh would be waiting regardless of what the other Guardian was doing.

Tayeh stood in the glade with his back to her, his stance reminding Eva of the parting look the fox had given her.

"What's wrong?' Eva asked, making him turn around. He flashed her a patient smile.

"Nothing, child." His expression was serene, trustworthy as always. Eva relaxed. "Come, walk with me."

"My legs will never grow longer. Slow down!" Eva begged as they walked.

"Are you happy, Eva?" Tayeh startled Eva with his abrupt question.

"What do you mean?"

"It's a simple question."

Eva didn't need to think about it, but she was reluctant with the answer.

"I thought not," Tayeh said sadly. "We have noticed you looking increasingly unhappy this past year. Lula is worried about you."

Eva pressed her lips into a thin line. "Life isn't about being happy.

The wanderer … the prophecy … the futile search for the vercuri … do you wonder why I am not happy?"

"Life is challenging, but there should also be happiness, joy."

Eva shook her head, wondering what Tayeh was getting at.

"Eva, to be happy, truly happy, you must follow your heart. Not your desires, but your heart of hearts that knows what is right and what is wrong." Tayeh stood before her, placing his clawed finger on her chest bone, right above her pendant.

Eva sighed. "You speak as though I have a choice. I don't. People make my choices for me. You tell me my child is destined - what choice will he have?"

Tayeh gave her a glower. It was only due to her close relationship with the Guardian that it didn't cause her to cower in fear. "You always have a choice."

"I can't see it, Tayeh."

"Eva," Tayeh said again. "You always have a choice."

Eva sighed. Sometimes she wished Tayeh would be less cryptic.

Tayeh came to a slow halt in the sunshine, stretching his arms out, pulling his long latha from its protective sheath to watch it gleam as it unfolded in the light. Eva always marveled at his weapon. It was unlike any she had ever seen. With a mechanical click, the two blades unfurled like wings of a bird about to take flight. Holding it in one strong hand, he completed the picture of a battle-seasoned Kitarran warrior.

"Ah, sometimes I can feel the sun," he said closing his eyes. Eva smiled. The sun on her face was glorious.

"Eva!" a faint voice came from behind her. She must have imagined it because it was Illiah's voice. But he could never be in the Forest. "Eva, wait." It came again, louder.

Eva spun to peer into the dim Forest. Past the sunlight was Illiah, walking through the thin skiff of snow. He was following her tracks, his faced flushed, but underneath he was pale, his green eyes as wild as the Forest around him.

"Illiah, what in the three realms are you doing here? It's not safe for you to be here!" Eva exclaimed once she pulled her tongue out from under her shocked silence. How did he get into the Forest? Without the sequence that opened the secret door, it was impossible. Could she have left it open?

Illiah was staring at Tayeh beside her. Not everyone could see the Guardians - only those granted permission by the Guardians themselves. Did Tayeh want Illiah to see him?

Illiah had the appearance of a person who had received a very terrible fright. Eva was strangely satisfied his heroic cloak had been torn from his shoulders. She thought it, and then felt guilty.

"What is going on here?" Illiah finally managed.

Tayeh regarded him patiently, still holding his latha. "I am Tayeh, Guardian of Kitarra," he said in his deep, ageless voice.

Illiah nodded. "I think I understand now." His eyes flicked to Eva, then back to Tayeh, wary. He cleared his throat, but he was at a loss for words.

"Why are you here?" Eva folded her arms.

"I saw you head into the garden - then you were gone. It was disconcerting. I thought there must be a secret door hidden somewhere, but all I could see was the carving. Then I looked closer, and one of the carvings looked like the white fox I often see staring at me from up on the cliffs. I always had an uncanny feeling about that creature. It couldn't be a coincidence, so I touched it, and the door opened. I want to go home, Eva." Illiah was nervous. Eva could see his fear. Wasn't there some idiom about prying into secrets and getting more than one bargained for?

"I am not the first Guardian you have seen today," Tayeh stated in an amused voice. "I hope Lulanan was kind to you."

Illiah's cheeks reddened. He twitched, flustered, a state Eva had never seen him in. What had Lula said, or worse, what had she done?

"Come, let's go home," Eva said in a voice she would use with a startled child. She grabbed Illiah's sleeve, leading him homeward, but not until she said a quick farewell to Tayeh. He gave her hand a kiss in typical Kitarran fashion. Illiah watched in continued surprise.

Once they were out of earshot of Tayeh, Illiah leaned close to her. "You didn't tell me you were a ward of the Guardians."

"A what?" Eva asked. "No one knows about this," she added with a look that meant it better stay that way.

"A ward. Someone chosen by the Guardians, someone who is close to them, can see them, talk to them, touch them," he went on.

"How do you know of such things? You can't even read."

A ghost of a smile returned to Illiah's pale face. "Freya had a book when she was a child, about the Guardians, with pictures and stories. She was obsessed with it for a long time, reciting it regularly. The stories became part of our lives for a time. I always thought they were just stories, for silly children." His voice drifted into silence.

"You see them. How is that possible? Or are you a ward of the Guardians too?"

"I'm a prince of Jullayah," Illiah told her with fictitious arrogance, his usual humor puncturing his wariness.

Eva rolled her eyes. "Being a prince can't have anything to do with it."

"I didn't believe the old stories until I saw magic for myself," he went on. "I mostly have you to blame for that."

"Have you seen Crea?" she asked in a different tone, ignoring his bait.

Illiah nodded. "A glimpse, but she didn't seem to notice me."

"Does Caeris see her?"

"He claims he does. So does Serac."

"But you don't think they really do?"

Illiah shrugged. "I don't know how it works, but the Guardians terrify me. They look right through me like they know my soul, my thoughts, my deepest desires - and find me lacking." Eva had never heard him sound so bewildered.

"Crea isn't really a Guardian, nor is she a Goddess. I am not sure what she is. Lula has never told me her story, but I know she is an evil, selfish creature," Eva told him. "You met Lula?"

She didn't get an answer to her question. Illiah was in front of her on the narrow path, his face hidden from her. Eva hadn't wandered far into the Forest with Tayeh and they were already at the steep path leading down the cliff to the Keep. On either side, the birches grew tight, creating an illusion that the branches would catch her if she stumbled and fell.

Illiah stopped, turning to her as if to say something. She nearly fell into him. Their eyes locked, his face level with hers and oh so close.

The kiss was quick. So quick and sweet Eva didn't have time to react. Only the burning of her lips, the warmth flooding through her body, told her it had happened.

Illiah kissed her again, as if the first was not enough. Not nearly enough. This kiss was not the quick kiss of a timid sweetheart; it was full and thick. She wound her hands around his neck. She never wanted to let go. Illiah's arm came around her waist and pulled her close. Eva lost something in that kiss, in the sweet pressure of Illiah's lips against hers, the taste of him on her tongue. Something fell out of her heart into his. She knew in that moment her heart had always belonged to him and no other.

Their bodies touched. For one moment Eva was whole and perfect. A sound escaped her lips. Illiah stepped away from her, dropping his arms, shaking his head. The moment was gone, murdered under his shuddered breath.

"Forget I did that. I am so sorry." His words tumbled awkwardly in her ears. He turned away from her. He would not look at her, would not speak to her when she called his name. He stumbled into the Keep garden, making the distance between them gaping.

Eva touched her fingers to her lips as Illiah disappeared into the Keep.

CHAPTER 26

ILLIAH

ILLIAH WAS SHAKING as he closed the door to his room. Eva was close, just outside in the hallway, perhaps making her way to her own room or down the long stairs to the common area of the Keep.

Foolish. Idiotic. Illiah couldn't believe he had just kissed her. Twice. The second kiss had been - Twice, really?

His mind was reeling with logical and illogical thoughts, but his heart was bleeding. His body ignored both, filled with desire, lust, led on by that witch woman in the Forest. Lulanan. That is what the Kitarran had called her. She hadn't given him a name when he met her.

Illiah had been amused and pleased he had discovered Eva's hidden door. He had walked up the narrow steps under the birch trees to the Great Forest, expecting to see Eva at the top, expecting to catch up with her easily.

That girl was full of secrets. He was not surprised she had somehow found a way into the Great Forest, a place she had warned him about. He had been eager to see the look of surprise on her face as he discovered yet another of her secrets, this time on his own.

When he reached the top of the steep, rocky steps and stood surrounded by the hushed Forest, he could not see Eva anywhere. The trees were huge and daunting, glowering at him like the intruder he was.

The hair on the back of his neck stood on end, reminding him of when he visited the Temple and felt the presence of the Black Goddess and saw a flash of black feathers from his peripherals. Only this was more potent, like something was pulling him, calling his name, but he couldn't hear the voice.

He turned to see Eva watching him.

Where she had come from, he didn't know. Before he had been alone; now she was right before him. He could have brushed his body against hers with one simple move. All he had to do was lean toward her.

Her beautiful blue-green eyes were filled with love and devotion, making his body stir from his fingertips to his … other parts. She reached her hand up to his face, outlining his jaw with a smooth finger. He thought he would drown in her eyes. His heart had never felt so light. Her touch was pure magic.

At the time, Illiah had been too absorbed with his body's reaction to say anything or move a muscle. Like one of his sweet dreams, not quite real, not quite safe. This dream-Eva had smiled at him, running her finger lightly down his throat to rest just below his collarbone. It tickled in a really good way.

"Do you love her?" a voice asked inside his head. Not Eva's voice. This voice was quiet as a breeze and sweet as honey and not entirely human.

"Yes." His response was instantaneous. Eva vanished. Before Illiah was a woman wearing nothing but her own long, red hair, and her milk-pale skin. She was beautiful in the way hoarfrost was beautiful. Or a forest fire. Her deception made Illiah angry and ill.

What surprised Illiah was that he knew her. He knew her from a picture in a long-forgotten book, a story told to him by a little girl.

"Illiah," said the Guardian of the Great Forest in the same honeyed voice that had been inside his head. "The Lost Prince of Jullayah. A hero, a strong man. A man who has felt the pain of the body, the pain of the heart. One who has seen death and defeated it. You have made good choices, brave choices. Do not doubt yourself."

Illiah was immobile. The creature before him sparked every sense he had honed. His instincts were screaming out in alarm, warning him of the danger he was in. The dagger in his boot was fire next to his skin. Her words were kind, but he remembered her deception.

"You do not trust me?"

"I cannot. You deceived me. You pretended to be someone you are not," he told her.

"You are angry because I exposed a weakness within you, and you are a man who can not afford weakness." She was smiling at him now. A predator's smile. "It matters not. You learned something and so did I. Keep it hidden - the dagger, not your heart," she said with a parting smile. And then she was gone, a white fox, darting through the Great Forest with the speed of the wild.

He watched her go until he was sure she was truly gone. He shook his head, unsettled, hoping the real Eva had not befallen any ill. He searched the ground until he found her tracks in a lingering patch of snow. It had been easy to find her after that.

What he hadn't expected was another Guardian. The Kitarran Guardian had sent fear through his vitals. He was a power. Eva seemed immune to it. She looked up at the feral being with devotion and respect. But it made a kind of sense that this Guardian had mentored her, taught her how to wield a sword, to find her strengths, to be a *sanarii* - whatever that meant exactly, beyond healing wounds and snooping into memories.

Illiah had no way of knowing what the Kitarran thought of him. Tayeh of Kitarra was not outspoken like the Forest woman.

Back in his own room, beyond the uncanny forces of the Great Forest, Illiah poured himself a drink from his bottle of fire wine he kept in his chambers for emergency purposes. He was not one to go to the drink for solace - he had seen what that could lead to - but he found it settled the shaking in his hands that came over him sometimes.

The Guardian's interest in Eva was strange. He couldn't understand it. She was part Allati, not Kitarran, and the Great Forest was a long way from Kitarra. He took another drink.

His mind was full of what Lulanan had said, or implied. Could it be true that he loved Eva? He knew nothing of love. He had been with women, not many, and he was convinced he had never loved them. And yes, his body seemed to find Eva desirable. Even now, shaken as he was, it still betrayed him. If he did love Eva, if the fox-woman spoke true, it was a cruel truth.

CHAPTER 27

EVA

ILLIAH BARELY ACKNOWLEDGED EVA. When duty necessitated he speak to her, he was cold and expressionless. Perhaps she had dreamed the kisses. It was certainly not uncommon to find herself kissing Illiah in her dreams.

Eva didn't mean to, but she found herself watching Illiah, drawn to him with the fatal futility of a moth to the flame. He stole glances at her as well. Eva saw his fist tighten, his jaw clench.

Whatever his reason for kissing her, whatever his reason for ignoring her, it was making him deeply unhappy. His attitude was sharp with his men. Training had become even more of a grueling practice. Illiah snapped at the recruits often. His patience, which had always been steadfast, was thin, even with his brothers. Lindin and Kaile exchanged worried glances behind their foster brother's back.

Less than two short months and Eva would be married. She tried to prepare, pack her things, expecting her aunt to arrive at any time as the weather grew fair. But each time Eva opened her traveling chest, her heart grew taut, her body shivered, tears pricked her eyes, and she didn't have the strength for it. Her heart cried out in protest. She heard Tayeh's words in her head: "Listen to your heart." He had told her so many times, and yet, how could she?

And she had barely thought about the vercuri. Thankfully, Tayeh had not mentioned it either. Eva wasn't sure she could tell him what - or more like who - had been distracting her from that hopeless task without melting into an anxious puddle. Maybe Tayeh had realized what an impossible task it was and had given up; Eva did not know the Guardian's mind.

The memory of Dweller's Knoll, the wanderer, and Illiah consumed by violent madness were enough to stop her hands from shaking. She would marry Caeris and fulfill the prophecy as Tayeh hoped. But a small voice in her mind whispered there was another child who would fit Tayeh's prophecy. Her child - and Illiah's. But Illiah didn't want anything to do with her. Not anymore. Not after that day in the Forest. Tayeh had mentioned that Lula had spoken to Illiah; what had the Forest Guardian told him?

Her sweet dreams did not last. Nightmares of the war invaded her sleep. She hadn't had such dreams for nearly a year. She wondered why she was suddenly overwrought by the disturbing scenes. At first, she was terrified the invaders had returned, but she saw quickly it was not so - Illiah was often prominent in the dream-visions.

Her dreams were memories. Shadows and echoes. Often it was the same vision of a young man hanging dead from a tree. He had not been dead long. His flaccid limbs resembled a cloak hung from a hook. His body was a crisscross of bloody wounds, several of his fingers were missing, his tongue had been cut out, blood seeped from his gaping mouth. His had been a hard death.

As he was lowered to the ground, it became horrifically apparent he was not dead. Illiah was there, a silent cry on his lips as he gathered the broken body into his embrace. Life clung uselessly to the young man, a boy, really. He looked into Illiah's eyes as if his spirit had been waiting for that moment to release, that moment to give up its terrible struggle. He died in Illiah's arms. Illiah broke his shocked silence and screamed and wept and cursed.

Eva woke shaking and sick to her stomach, her body covered in cold sweat. She could only imagine Illiah's anguish. The real memory was his.

Eva was compelled to seek out the Guardians, hoping they could tell her why she was dreaming of the war again. To do so, she would have to make her way through Illiah's council room, a place she avoided because of Illiah's desire to ignore her. But it was the only way to get into the Great Forest, so she kept checking to see if the room was empty.

She would peek silently through the small crack to see or hear if anyone was inside. The door was rarely left wide open. Several times she had seen Illiah, sitting alone before the comforting fireplace, his head in his hands. She had to fight a strong desire to come up behind him and wrap him in her arms, cradling him and his woes. But she couldn't.

Another time she heard voices and couldn't help but listen, peeking through the crack.

"Illiah. Lindin and I are downright concerned. We thought you were over this," Kaile was saying. Eva could see him hand his brother a little glass of something amber colored. A strong drink perhaps.

"The dreams, Kaile, I can't stop the dreams," Illiah said sharply. "I can't sleep. Even if I don't dream of Aralis, it's always-" He cut off, not wanting to say what was on his mind.

The momentary silence was heavy and full of grief.

"I remember when you brought his body back to camp. You didn't want me see to him," Kaile said, his voice gruff.

"They left him hanging in that tree as a message to us, to me-" Illiah said in a stony voice. "We thought he was dead. Gods, he wasn't dead ... if I had been there sooner -"

"Illiah, please don't," Kaile said. "Don't speak of that day."

Illiah was silent. "When I caught their leader," Illiah went on, "I didn't even have the heart to do to him as he had done to our brother. Our brother! I had planned to cut out his tongue, write my name in his flesh, but in the end, a clean death was all I could give him. Does that make me weak?"

"Illiah." Kaile gave a bear-like sigh. "You doubt yourself needlessly. You don't need to revisit this. You are an admirable man. People follow you, respect you, love you. Aralis, like any of us, was honored to die for your cause because it was a noble one. His soul lives on someplace, you know that. He would not want you to destroy your life with grief and guilt."

Kaile said something else, but Eva had already pulled away. Illiah dreamed of a young man with his tongue cut out hanging from a tree. It was the same dream she had over and over. Why would she share his dream? She felt wretched. Her heart ached for Illiah. It had not been some nameless young man, but a dearly beloved brother. His younger brother, his to protect.

The next time she ventured to the council room, if Illiah were there, she would just go in, face him, talk to him. She began to hope for it, but he wasn't there.

The room was empty. Only coals slumbered, glowing red in the grate. Eva took a deep breath to dispel her disappointment, making her way to the secret door.

The Great Forest was now alive with spring, but Eva hardly took stock of her surroundings. Her only thoughts were the questions mulling around in her head. The Forest held no peace for her.

Tayeh smiled his toothy, fearsome smile to see her. Lula was dozing in the sun. Eva hadn't been pleased with the fox-woman after she had rattled Illiah's nerves. But Eva didn't have the courage to ask Lula about it.

"Tayeh," Eva said. It was a sigh of relief. She immediately burst with her questions, describing the dream, Illiah's poor state, her unease. She could hardly finish without tears making her tongue thick and stinging her eyes. Tears for Illiah and his grief, tears that she no longer had her dear friend. Tayeh regarded her patiently, looking as though Eva should have figured this one out for herself.

"I don't understand, Tayeh. It's as if there is some connection between Illiah and I. I don't understand," Eva said, trying to keep a whine out of her voice. Tayeh didn't offer suggestions, as was his way sometimes. Sometimes he was a wealth of answers, but other times he left it for her to figure out. Usually the latter meant the answer was close, but she couldn't see it. Well, perhaps she could, but what she saw was impossible.

"Eva."

"Yes, Tayeh?"

"You know where the answer is: here." He put his finger on her heart.

"That doesn't help, Tayeh. How do I make it stop? How do I stop this hurting?" She wrapped her arms around herself.

Tayeh took a deep breath and released it. "Follow your heart, child," he said kindly.

"I was afraid you would say that."

Lady Clarette arrived. Eva made an effort to seem happy and excited. She wondered how convincing it was.

A feast was held in her aunt's honor. Wine was poured for the head table only; Illiah was still short with his recruits. He would not allow them the privilege.

Illiah drank more than usual. He was pensive. Not even Kaile, with all his charm, could rouse Illiah from his black mood.

Clarette was unperturbed by Illiah's demeanor and lightened the hall with her witty tales of her winter, her harvest, and the goings-on in her land to the east. She swooned over little Oryn, Will's baby boy, who was smiling and cooing away at her. Eva had not known her aunt was fond of babies.

Eva listened with little interest. Her aunt's affairs had always sounded dull to her. She was glad to see Darys again. The captain poured her a glass of something fine.

"To our young Lady Eva, soon to be married, I drink to your health," he said, his eyes twinkling. The captain was deep in his wine as well.

"Thank you, Darys," Eva said, drinking up. It was good stuff. It gave her an illusion of happiness and fed her courage. Perhaps with a deep enough cup, she could forget that she was leaving her home. Forever. The Forest, the Guardians, the Keep, dear Calypso, secret paths and pools. They would be taken from her. She took another drink.

After dinner, there was music and dancing. Illiah's men were good musicians and knew the best tunes for dancing. Darys offered his hand for a dance - so did Tarek, Lindin, and Kaile.

Illiah watched her as she danced. If he was trying to hide his emotions from her, he was failing miserably. His carefully constructed mask was slipping with every glass of wine he consumed. His eyes were a black abyss calling to her with the promise of wings. She knew the look. She had seen it when he kissed her under the birch trees. She had felt it. It was longing. Want. Need. Eva was a healer and Illiah was still broken.

Dancing was a welcome distraction. Somehow, Eva's feet moved along with her partner as her mind and body recoiled under Illiah's gaze. Next time Eva looked, she could not see Illiah anywhere. Eva forbid herself from seeking him out.

Eva's chest was tight. She was suffocating in the great hall. Too many people. She needed space. She needed to wander the stone corridors of her home alone. She needed to say goodbye and soak in the dark hallways, the sound of the wind on her windowpanes, the smell of the forest air from the watch tower.

She went up to the parapet and walked along the outer wall, watching the shadows of the forest. She didn't know if Mahone or Tarek followed her. She didn't care.

The night was crisp and clear and thousands of stars pricked the black sky. She watched for an unknown amount of time. The cool night air filled her lungs with the smell of starlight. She heard an owl in the distance, the fluttering of wings in the blackness.

Far below she could hear the rustling of people milling around the Keep, seeing to the evening chores, or finding their way to their beds. Music rose from the great hall to quietly greet her.

Eva began to shiver from the cold. The beauty of the night offered no immunity from the chill spring air. She bid the stars goodnight and went to her room. She made a fire and opened the window a crack for Calypso to hop in if he wished. She had a pocket of treats for him from dinner - roasted nuts, a few pieces of hard cheese. A raven wasn't picky.

She changed into her nightgown, wrapping her thick robe around her thin one. She sat in her chair and gazed into the fire. She wondered if a vision would come and hoped it would. She wasn't tired. She yearned for a distraction from her thoughts.

She couldn't forget Illiah's eyes. Her tongue felt thick. Her body was restless. She could see his finely shaped hands in her mind and imagined them on her skin. Her lips remembered the taste of his. She felt dizzy. Too much of Darys's wine.

She wanted to be with Illiah. Just once. One night.

Once the idea crept into her mind, it took root, its vines consuming any other thought. She pictured Illiah as he prepared for sleep, imagining the outline of his work-hardened body against the light of the fire as he undressed. She wondered if Illiah was in bed already. He worked his men hard during the day and most were abed early, including their lord, though Eva knew sleep often eluded him.

She found herself in the hallway. She was alone. Tarek and Mahone would not be far, but she didn't see them. She tiptoed down the hallway to Illiah's door, ears strained for any sound. Her guards would stop her if they knew what she was doing. They were sensible creatures, and it was their duty to protect her from interfering lordlings. Their trust in her was obviously unfounded.

The latch was cold on her palms. The door opened silently. She slipped inside, closing it behind her. Not even a squeak escaped the old door.

But he heard her.

Illiah was awash with red light where he stood before the fire. His gaze sharp, his eyes glinted as he regarded her. She bit her lip. Her back was to the closed door. She didn't know what to say, what to do. Her wayward heart had led her, but her mind and tongue had seemingly abandoned her. He could probably hear the pounding of her heart from where he stood.

"Eva," Illiah said softly. Then he shook his head. "Am I dreaming again?"

"Yes," she answered. Choices were simpler in dreams.

Illiah was drinking something. He took a quick sip and placed the cup on the table. He took several careful steps toward her, as if expecting her to transform or disappear.

His eyes lingered over the loose laces of her thin nightgown. Eva's body simmered under his intense gaze. Grief and emptiness and insecurity were forgotten. All that was left was a rightness. An exhale.

Illiah closed the space between them. He was a head taller she was, forcing her to tilt her head up to look at him. He was beautiful in the dim light. The proud angles of his face were carved in the warm light, his green eyes deep and luminous and heady. Her heart faltered and flew.

He kissed her, lightly at first. He tasted fiery and sweet, like sunlight. Sunlight that flooded her mouth, her tongue, and seeped under her skin. He was warm and real. Every touch, every contact between their bodies spoke and sang of his need for her. Of her need for him. It was the searching and finding, the breaking and healing. There was only his lips, his hands, the pressure of his body against hers, her hands on the soft skin of his waist, his back, his neck, along the curves of his hard muscles.

They paused for to grin at each other as friends, lovers.

Eva took Illiah's hand and pulled him onto the bed. Then some words were necessary because Illiah was having issues with his shirt. Eva laughed softly and helped him pull it over his head. He laughed too.

She had always admired Illiah's body, the way his muscles lay beneath his battle-worn skin. Now, she had the chance to do something she had always wanted to do. She stroked his soft skin, admiring his strong, lean frame, drawing a line with a delicate finger down his myriad of scars. She smiled as he shivered under her touch. Her hand lingered at his belt, and she looked up at him with a smile.

"Don't tease me, woman!" he whispered, pulling back, taking her nightgown with him. He sat and gazed at her vulnerable nakedness, only for an instant. It seemed he would much rather see her with his hands.

Then there was nothing but their bodies, their hearts and their complete willingness to love each other in that perfect moment.

ILLIAH

WHAT WAS HE DOING? By the Kings-Who-Were-His-Ancestors, what was he doing? The question surfaced, struggling for breath, then sunk, drowning under the waves of Illiah's heart.

ILLIAH

IT WAS MIDMORNING when a knock came at Eva's door. Tarek didn't wait for her answer and poked his head inside without hesitation.

"Eva? Are you all right?" he asked in a tight voice.

Eva rolled away so he couldn't see her tear stained face, her puffy, red eyes. "No," she told him honestly. "But tell Aunt I am ready to leave for court whenever she is."

Eva didn't want to stay in the Keep a moment longer. The sooner she was on the road, away from Illiah, the better. She would not dwell on things that could not be. She had known the impossibility of her actions. In her mind she had known, but her heart and mind were rarely in accordance.

By-the-old-spirits, it hurt.

Tarek left without further question or comment.

Loneliness and grief greeted Eva like long-lost friends. How had she managed to suppress them for so many years?

She shivered. Her room was cold and inescapably lonely. Like the day her parents died, her body ached and ached. Grief was a huge, gaping hole torn anew in her chest.

She pulled her blankets and furs around her, but it didn't stop the tremors that coursed through her lamenting body. What was worse was that she knew she had brought it upon herself. She was a fool. An ignorant, romantic fool. Of course her heart had been broken.

"Don't let me go," she had pled in a soft voice.

She had lain nestled beside Illiah, his skin against hers, her cheek resting on his shoulder. His face rested on her forehead. The bristles of his beard tickled her skin. The words came from the silence without forethought, born from her heart.

The hours of the night had deepened. They had made love until their bodies lay quiet. Then they had laughed, teased, and talked about nothing and everything until silence fell between them. Illiah had been tracing lazy circles on her arm, but when she spoke, he stopped. He pulled away.

In that moment, Eva's heart left her. She knew it was still there, with Illiah.

"Eva." Her name had been his reply, but the tone was one she knew well. It was uninviting and left no room for questions - the tone of a lord. Yet his eyes told her what he could not - would not. They were full of pain, full of longing, brimming with impossibility.

She understood his unspoken words. He wanted her but would not fight for her, could not fight for her. He would be loyal to the prince, to his brother. It had been clear in his expression, in the way his body language changed. She had been mute with hurt and anger, most of which was toward herself.

She had turned her back to Illiah, ignoring the grief in his eyes, ignoring his soft plead, or had it been an apology? She wrapped herself in her robe, scooped up her nightgown, and left for her own room. The hall had been vast, empty. No one bore witness to her deviance.

She had curled up on her bed and wept.

Anger still lingered, mingled with her grief. She couldn't forgive Illiah. He should have turned her away. She couldn't forgive herself. She shouldn't have gone. Yet she could not bring herself to regret her actions. She could not regret that night.

Eva regarded the cold ashes of her fire, the stack of logs beside it. If she wanted warmth, it would be up to her to create it. At Caer Andri there would be servants to light fires. Servants to bring her warm water for washing. She would be rid of the cold, damp hallways and endless stairs.

When Eva roused herself from her warm furs, it was with an angry resolution. She washed her face, combed her hair, found a clean dress and small clothes. She bound her hair down her back in a loose braid to keep it from her eyes. She then spent a furious hour cleaning her room, packing her things, throwing things into her trunk in a temper. She was ready. A new life awaited her at court: the wife of a king. Honor. Riches. Her and Caeris's child would bring balance to the *simul rami*, to the magic of the world. Marrying Caeris would keep Illiah safe.

But the thought did not absolve the tearing pain in her heart.

How would she face Illiah? How could she go downstairs knowing he would be there? How could she look at him? Her skin still hummed, the sensation of being with him still lingered in the depths of her body. She could not look at him without remembering his caresses, his lips, the sensations he had coaxed from the fractures of her existence unlike any she would ever know again.

Tarek gave her a searching look when she finally emerged from her room. She straightened under his scrutiny.

"What did Clarette say?"

"She said if you are ready, you will leave tomorrow." His narrowed eyes took in her fine dress, but he asked no questions of her.

Eva nodded, picking up her flowing, impractical skirts to walk down the stairs. Her stomach rumbled, but she had no appetite.

Because she intended to do what was required of her, she found some breakfast. The great hall was busy, so she ate in the kitchens.

The kitchens were always warmed by the big cooking hearths, but Eva couldn't dispel the dampness in her gut. Scrub was cheerful, handing her some tea, telling her he was planning a goodbye feast for her. Her face must have shown her dismay because his brows furrowed.

"You know I don't like a big fanfare, Scrub. Just give me a hug tomorrow and let me be on my way."

"I'll make those honey cakes you love so much too," he said with a consolatory wink.

"Thanks."

"Our little Evangeline, all grown up, going to get married. Next time you come here, you will be a princess, soon to be queen, perhaps with some little ones running around your feet," Scrub said with a toothy smile.

Eva tried to smile for her friend's sake. He meant well by it.

Illiah was out in the practice yard; the council room would be empty. Eva hardly cared who saw her steal away into the Forest. It would be the last time. The Forest and the Guardians had salved her soul once, but they could not help her this time.

As she walked the Forest path, her breath caught like fire in her throat as she tried to keep the tears away. She was sobbing before she came to the glade.

Lula and Tayeh were waiting. Lula was in the form of a woman, her amber eyes pitying, her arms outstretched. Eva let them embrace her. The Guardians felt like clear skies and cherry blossoms in spring.

"Why are you so sad?" Lula crooned.

"I don't want to go, Lula. My heart screams no." Eva didn't mention Illiah. How could she breathe his name? "I am trying to be brave, but I feel like everything is broken."

Tayeh and Lula exchanged a look. For once they had nothing to say. The only comfort they gave her was in their embrace.

"I leave tomorrow. This is goodbye. Will I ever see you again?" Eva asked, breathing deep, trying to stop the shivering. She had known this day would come, the day when she would say goodbye to her mentors. She knew it would break her heart, but she didn't know her heart would already be in pieces.

"Perhaps. Just remember what we have taught you," Tayeh said. He put his big hands on her shoulders and kissed her brow.

"Eva," Lula said, cupping Eva's head in her pale hands. "I want you to know that he loves you. He truly loves you. With all the depth of his heart, but he is afraid."

Hot tears slipped down Eva's cheeks. Lula wasn't talking about Tayeh. "If Illiah loved me, he wouldn't let me go."

Again, they had only silence for her. Another hug from Lula, a warrior squeeze from the Guardian of Kitarra, a kiss on the back of her hand, and then Eva left, to go out of the Forest, perhaps forever.

Lula paced with the ferocity of a mountain cat.

"Are you sure about this, Kitarran?" she snarled. "Humans can be such fools."

"Obviously," Tayeh said. Despite his previous confidence, he could hear the worry in his voice. He could feel it edge around his heart, hinting at black, sickening things.

"What if this all goes wrong?"

"Plans change, Lula."

"Things are worse than we imagined. The wanderer - beyond the Forest. Despite what we told Eva, there may be more. We need that man. He is part of this," Lula said.

Tayeh shrugged, unconvinced. "I don't know, Lulanan. Perhaps he is not needed after all. She may be all we need."

"If she weds Caeris, part of Eva will die forever. She has a strong will, a strong heart, but not that strong. How can we let that happen?"

"What happens will happen. Perhaps we are wrong to put our faith in Illiah," Tayeh admitted sadly.

"Wrong. This has gone all wrong."

Tayeh had never seen his fellow Guardian so concerned, so unsettled. A wanderer was a Forest creature polluted and rotten, tainted by dark magic. No wonder the Allmakers were so fearful and desperate. If there were more … Tayeh would not admit that it was too late.

"We cannot force them. We can guide them, love them, but in the end, it is their choice," Tayeh told her. "How often do mortals make the wrong choice? As often as the rains fall," he said, answering his own question.

Lulanan's glare was scathing. She ran to the edge of the cliff where they stood and peered down past the border of her realm to the fortress, as if she could see through rock and decipher the goings-on below. As if the walls might part with the answers she sought. She looked poised for flight. If she were mortal flesh and blood, Tayeh would be concerned she would fall.

"Can't you do something?" Lula begged, feebly.

"No."

Even the Guardian of the Great Forest could not argue with the finality in Tayeh's tone.

CHAPTER 29

EVA

EVA DID NOT EXPECT Illiah to be in the courtyard to say farewell. Some duties, apparently, the Lord of the Keep was not bound to.

The day dawned gray but warm. The green of the forest was blinding against the gray clouds. The blossoms were heavy on the trees, threatened only by impending rain. Eva stood beside her aunt in the courtyard, making ready to leave, her trunk of belongings packed in the wagon, her goodbyes said to everyone except one.

Eva looked at the long line of ready horsemen: Lady Clarette's household guards plus half of the recruits deemed fit to return to duty with their new training completed.

"Where is Lord Illiah? He should be here to see us off," Clarette said to no one in particular with a touch of agitation.

Eva was wrong. He came as if he had been waiting for the lady's call. He was leading Sasha, fully bridled and saddled. For the briefest moment, a thin ray of hope - she thought he meant to come with them. He placed Sasha's reins in her hand. She met his eyes for a second and saw his grief, turmoil, longing, and last of all, resolution.

"A gift, my lady," he said, his voice quiet but strong.

Eva stroked Sasha's soft nose. Not trusting her voice to speak, she nodded her thanks.

"My Lady Clarette, it has been an honor. I look forward to seeing you later this summer at court." Illiah offered Clarette a little bow, and she beamed at him, holding her hand to assist her onto her horse. Not that Clarette needed the leg up - she was merely overly fond of custom. Eva was not. She could not bear it if Illiah touched her. She swung herself up into Sasha's saddle, full skirts and all.

Somewhere past her silent grief, she felt the significance of the gift. Another time she would have been giddy. Illiah's guilt must be extreme for him to give her his horse.

Mahone and Tarek flanked her instantly, looking as grim as she felt. Some of their broodiness was directed at Illiah. She wondered what they knew, or perceived.

Eva dug her heels firmly, yet gently, into Sasha's flanks and they were off. Something bumped her leg. She looked down at her stirrup, which was knowingly just the height she liked and saw her sword hanging next to her saddle bag. The sword from Illiah. She couldn't bear to pack it and had left it in her room. If she couldn't have Illiah, she couldn't have the sword. He must have found it.

She wouldn't bring herself to ponder why he had been in her room. She pushed Sasha from a trot to a canter, Mahone and Tarek beside her. She didn't look back. She kept tall, hoping her tears would fall unnoticed. Behind her came a raven's call, long, rough, and lamenting.

When night fell, they made their first camp still surrounded by mountains and forest. Eva was alone in her tent, nestled in her blankets, listening to the rain beat down upon the canvas. Her hand went to her neck out of habit only to find her pendant gone. She searched the tent front and back, but she couldn't find it. Somehow, somewhere, her precious gift had come off its chain. It was just one more reason for tears, but Eva promised herself in the morning, no more tears. She hated how weak it made her feel. She would bear her grief in stony silence. She would marry Caeris to keep Illiah safe. She would not shed another tear.

The journey passed in a haze. Eva was tired, body and mind. She slept poorly. She still shared Illiah's dreams. Distance was no hindrance to the eerie, magical link she shared with him. She dreamed of the dead every night. Some nights it was his dead, tortured brother. Some nights, it was men she did not recognize. She would never know their names, but they all had one thing in common; they had all died terrible, painful deaths. The invaders had been fond of torture and mercilessly employed it.

Every night was haunting. Every night she woke in a cold sweat, her heart beating in her ears. Did Illiah wake with a silent scream on his lips, his heart pounding, his cheeks wet with tears? Eva pushed any thought of him from her mind. Her longing for him was a restless beast she was forced to chain. She thought of nothing: the road, the clink of armor, the steady plodding of horse hooves on the dirt road, the smell of spring blossoms, her wedding. It was an exhausting practice.

Darys, Tarek, and Mahone tried to pull her from her state of desolation. Nothing worked. By the time they arrived at Caer Andri, they had given up. She didn't think less of them for it.

Darys and Clarette said it was just the homesickness that came with leaving home. Clarette went on about how she had missed her home dreadfully when she left to marry Lord Lagdon. She had only been fifteen. It had been traumatic, and Lagdon had been so much older. Clarette reminded Eva, with a little pat on the shoulder, that it would be all right. Eva was not going somewhere strange - Caer Andri was a second home to her already, and Caeris was not a stranger.

The white walls of the palace were before them. Eva blinked against the bright sun and tried to remember how she got there. She could hardly recall. Her mind was foggy and uncooperative.

She let Clarette lead her to her rooms. In the back of Eva's mind, she felt guilty she had not seen Sasha to the stables. Illiah's voice scorned her for not taking care of his horse. Then her anger overrode her guilt. Served him right.

No, she was the architect of her unhappiness. She had gone to his chamber. She received exactly what she wanted - one night in Illiah's bed. Blaming Illiah was unfair.

She flopped onto the bed.

"At least take a bath, dear, before you fall asleep," her aunt clucked before leaving her in peace. It was sensible advice.

Eva asked for the tub to be filled, watching idly as the palace maids went about her bidding, filling steaming bucket after bucket into the big tub. Then she immersed herself, letting the maids wash her hair, scrub her back. She had never let a servant assist her before, but it was their duty, after all. She might as well get used to being a proper lady.

They placed clean night clothes on her bed and combed and braided her hair. Once she was clean and dry, the sun had sunk below the horizon. Twilight washed away the colors of the day. She wondered if she should seek out the king. She had missed him, but she was so very tired. Her lids grew heavy as soon as she lay down, eclipsing coherent thought.

A knock came at her door. Eva was lying awake in her bed, listening to the morning birdsong wafting in from the garden. It was a peaceful sort of music and Eva was loath to be disturbed.

The knock was followed by Tarek's deep voice. Eva rose reluctantly to open the door. Tarek announced that Caeris wished to see her immediately. Tarek's expression was worried. Normally, Eva would have asked him what was bothering him, but she found she didn't care.

"Let me dress and then I will come."

She looked at the gowns laid out for her to choose from. From the pale lavender one to the one of green, to the crimson red. All were beautiful. All were fit for her station in life. All were dresses she would never wear at the Keep. She chose the red one. She wasn't sure why. Out of habit, she tucked her little knife into her right boot.

Her neck felt bare without her necklace. But she was glad she had lost it. She didn't need the constant reminder of her old life. She would never see Tayeh again.

Mahone escorted her to Caeris. Her guard looked sharp in his uniform, newly shaved, gray eyes bright, but still grim. He led her to Caeris's personal study, not a room she had frequented. Previous visits had left her with an impression of starkness. The marble was beautiful, but there was not even a rug or tapestry to soften the sounds. This visit was no different.

Caeris stood with his back to her, by the fireplace. He resembled Illiah so much, Eva's heart leaped foolishly in her throat. He turned to her, dissolving the convincing illusion. Caeris was rounder in the face, his eyes missing Illiah's hint of humor and wit, his face devoid of Illiah's short, well-trimmed beard that framed his laughing mouth. The crowned prince looked grim as he assessed her silently. Another figure emerged from the shadows. Eva's heart hardened. Her spine prickled with unease.

"Lady Evangeline," Lord Serac said in his smooth, glossy voice, wearing his smooth, glossy smile. His eyes glinted with triumph. Eva's blood went cold. "You have been called here to account for your disgusting wanton, disregard for His Majesty the Prince. Did you, or did you not, adulterate with his brother, Lord Illiah?"

Eva didn't know what showed on her face: terror, truth, anger. She couldn't think of a reply, but apparently, Serac didn't really want one because he kept talking, his voice becoming more accusatory, more degrading.

"You are a disgrace to your late father and grandfather. You are a slut like your Allati mother. Don't deny it, Evangeline. I have seen the truth. The Goddess has shown me the truth," he said in a righteous manner, his eyes shining.

Eva swallowed hard, turning to Caeris. He was waiting for her answer, an impatient look in his eyes.

She straightened under their scrutiny. "I love Illiah. I can't deny that."

Serac looked delighted, which terrified Eva more than anything. Caeris looked angry, his face reddened by it. Hypocrite.

"My men came back with rumors that you and Illiah were on friendly terms. Serac told me what he had seen, but still I could not believe it - didn't want to believe it," Caeris spat at her. "My own brother? Eva, how could you do this to me?"

What right did Caeris have to be angry with her? He had mistresses - why shouldn't she be permitted the same accordance? No, she had chosen his brother over him. He felt slighted, inferior. She could see it now, his brother the hero, his brother whom everyone immediately admired and respected, and now even his betrothed had betrayed him.

"Let me speak to the king. Let me explain to your father," Eva pleaded with the two men. King Rhais might understand. He might find some way to ease the hurt in the situation. He understood love. Caeris shook his head slowly, his eyes shadowed by sadness.

"My father's condition has worsened over winter. Even over the last several days, he has become very ill. He is still ailing. He has no strength of mind to hear of this betrayal. It would break him. Already, he walks with one foot in the grave." Caeris's mouth was tight.

Eva felt the blood drain from her face. Rhais, her beloved king, was dying. "Please let me see him. I can help him."

Caeris laughed at her, a sick, mirthless sound. The sound of a man who doesn't know how to laugh, who only laughs when it is at the cost of another. "Oh no, my dear. You are not going to see the king. Our betrothal is broken. You are stripped of your father's status. You are nothing, no one."

His words hit her like an avalanche. She had made a terrible mistake. The prophecy. She already knew she was not carrying Illiah's child; if she didn't marry Caeris … It was over. The dark magic would grow, poisoning the *simul rami* until the river of life-magic was black and rotten.

"There is only one place for you," Caeris said. He looked to Serac and the reason for Serac's strange levity became apparent with his next words. "Serac will take you to the Temple. Perhaps the Goddess will help you repent your wrongness." He waved his wrist with a final gesture of dismissal. Eva let out a final plea, but Caeris had turned away from her. He didn't care.

"Come with me." Serac outstretched his hand, an invitation. As if she would take it.

Bright steel flashed. Mahone's sword was between Eva and Serac. Mahone grabbed Eva's hand. She needed no encouragement to let him pull her through the door. They ran down the cool corridor, heedless of Serac's growl of outrage behind them. Her long skirt and tight bodice made Eva feel close to drowning as they ran.

Before they could exit the hallway, the sounds of boots clicking on the marble indicated their way would soon be blocked. Mahone and Eva spun, but behind them approached Caeris and Serac, flanked by another group of guards. Eva and Mahone were well and truly trapped. Mahone pushed Eva behind him, against the wall, his sword ready, his stance protective.

"Take the girl, kill the guard. You know what he is," Serac ordered, his mouth twisting as if he had eaten something foul.

"My lord?" the guard paused. He would not look at Eva.

"Did you not hear? Kill the guard. Get the girl."

"No!" Eva screamed.

The guards moved toward her and Mahone from either side. Mahone could not keep them back. He tried. With every ounce of his strength, he tried.

Eva's arm burned, torn from Mahone's protection. She kicked and screamed and managed to lodge her elbow in the ribs of one of her attackers with all her force. It was to no avail. There were too many. Mahone took out two with one fast, capable stroke. But the next stroke against flesh was not his to claim.

Eva's hands were held fast. She could not reach her boot knife. Her heart hammered like a war drum in her chest, anger radiating like acid in her blood. She paused her struggling.

"Caeris!" she called in desperation. He could hear her above the melee, she was sure, but he didn't acknowledge her.

Eva bit the arm that held her. A roar of pain rasped in her ear. She tried to claw her way to Mahone, but the royal guards held her tight. The other guards swarmed over Mahone, a mass of bodies and armor and weapons. It was not a battle - it was an execution. Twenty against one. The hallway was narrow, closing in like a vice. Mahone, for all his skill and strength, stood no chance. Eva caught a glimpse of him through the press, swinging his blade with a fury that made the guards stand back for an instant. It looked as though he could fight them.

"Fools! Get him, now!" snarled Serac.

Serac was suddenly beside Eva, his voice ringing clearly in her ears. The guards straightened their shoulders and attacked again. This time there was no hesitation.

Eva screamed and screamed. Her throat burned. She fought the two men holding her with fists and kicks. A hand came over her mouth. She sank her teeth into it. She couldn't see Mahone, the bodies were too thick in the confined space.

"Stop."

For a moment, Eva thought someone had come to save them, but then she realized it had been Serac's command. The guards obeyed. Eva still couldn't see Mahone. Serac grabbed her firmly by her wrists wrenched behind her back. He leaned so close to her ear that every breath she took was filled with his smell. He smelled like her tears.

"Look what you have done. Look what your deviance has cost you." The men stepped aside, revealing Mahone's broken and bloodied body. A mountain cat could not have done worse. His limbs were a mess of cuts and gouges. His clothes were slick, dark, his lifeblood pooled silently onto the marble. Even she couldn't hope to piece together his broken body, not with all the magic she possessed. He was alive, barely. His breath came in ragged, liquid gasps. Blood bubbled from his mouth. Mahone was a strong man. Death did not come easily to him.

"Let me go. Let me go to him," Eva begged. Her voice was cracked and rough and quiet. "Please. Please." She didn't expect pity, but she asked for it anyway. She was pulled away and could no longer see Mahone. Tears streamed down her cheeks. She heard herself wail in great heaving sobs.

Serac shook her and slapped her cheek. Eva turned to him. Her heart solidified in her chest, and hate filled her with a white, fiery rage.

Serac was saying something. His mouth was moving, and the words drifted to Eva, past the choking grief and rage. "Although with his sickening appetite for men, it is nothing but a fitting end."

Then Serac was dragging her away, down the hall. Someone put a gag over her mouth. She screamed through it, muffled as it was. She used all her strength, all her skill against them, but with so many men, she had no hope. They were forced to carry her through the back ways of the palace and out into the city.

CHAPTER 30

COTOCH

"WHAT IS IT, love?"

Sandra's croon was as comforting as freezing rain.

Cotoch struck the gold basin hard. The soft thud of it hitting the floor was disappointing. Water splashed his feet. Sandra raised her brows and went to pour him wine. A good, dutiful wife she was.

"Meddlesome whoreson," he hissed. "Fuck his manhood: may it go limp and wrinkle and fall off."

"Who is it this time, darling?"

If Sandra really expected an answer, she wasn't the good wife she thought she was.

The greedy lordling just ruined Cotoch's plans. Cotoch had already decided Eva was his. His prize. His treasure. And Serac took her. Foolish son of a bitch.

"Should I send for Yeri?"

Cotoch took a moment to appreciate his wife's offer. Here he had believed her indifferent, maybe even jealous, of his mistress. He shook his head. Then nodded. Sandra gave him one last pitying look before leaving him alone.

"Crea!" The frustrated roar tore from Cotoch's lungs, echoing in his empty chamber.

Cotoch didn't expect the woman to answer, so he was surprised when she appeared before him, folding her wings like a contented vulture. The shock only made him more irritated.

"What is the matter, Cotoch?" The Guardian asked.

"You took something of mine."

"Oh? How is that possible? Mahlas is a long way from Jullayah."

"The girl. The Allati girl. Your cock-sucking man has taken her. She will not survive the Temple's hospitality," Cotoch said through gritted teeth.

"How did you know about her?"

"I saw her in a vision."

His anger grew as Crea grinned. If she were flesh and blood, Cotoch would have hurt her for that smile.

"The girl is mine. She has Allati magic in her blood," Crea told him.

"Is that why they call you the Crow? Because you hoard treasures you can never use? You are not even alive! You can't use the *varing*. If you could, you wouldn't need me," Cotoch growled.

Crea's eyes flashed, her smile swallowed by her indignation. But Cotoch was not afraid of her. She couldn't touch him.

"You need me. Give me the girl," he demanded.

"It's too late. Serac has her."

Cotoch was silent but inside his angry beast roared and paced.

"Cotoch, don't be a fool," Crea crooned. "Don't lose sight of what you really want - Kitarra, a crown. The woman can be replaced."

"Fuck you," Cotoch said with slightly less fervor. He took a sip of his wine.

"Forget about the girl. She is insignificant."

"You are wrong. The Kitarrans want her. In the vision I had, there were whispers about her child, a boy who will restore what was lost and broken," Cotoch said. Something twitched in Crea's expression. "But you already knew that, didn't you?"

Crea did not defend his accusation. "And you want her child to be your child? A son destined for greatness?" Her eyes lit up with amusement. "Fool. That spirit woman you keep down in the crypts is getting inside your head, filling it with silly, boyish dreams. Her kind does that, you know. Men are so fucking predictable," Crea muttered.

"Impossible," he said. "She is too weak. She can do nothing but sit in the dark and hope she does not hear me coming for her."

Crea shrugged. "Regardless, the Allati girl is mine now, and the Kitarrans are right and truly fucked."

CHAPTER 31

ILLIAH

ILLIAH WATCHED THE LADY OF ULLIAN and her entourage ride
away from his Keep. Away from him. His throat tightened with emotions trying to escape and wreak havoc like the criminals they were.

After all the grief he had suffered, he should have been immune to
the wretched way it enveloped his heart and soul. But watching Eva
ride away with her aunt was like a knife in his gut.

He had planned to be absent at their departure. He didn't care if it
wasn't proper custom. He didn't fear Clarette's disapproval.

He had been sulking (admittedly) in his room. Suddenly the overwhelming memories of Eva and that one night made his bed too big
and empty. The linens still smelled of her.

The night before, as he lay in an almost sleep, he could almost feel
her beside him, her soft skin under his hands. His mind had slipped
into dreams that were both blessing and curse. He woke alone, and it
was agony.

He should have sent her away that night. An honorable man would
have sent her away. He should never have taken her into his bed. He
had betrayed his brother. The prince. He was selfish. He had always
been selfish.

He had left his room planning to seek out the practice ring, to
lose himself in physical exertion, but he found himself in Eva's room
instead.

The room was bare. The sheets folded, the blankets tucked neatly
away in the wardrobe, the window closed tight, Calypso's roost secured
in Murryn's room. Eva's room held her essence in its eclectic nature: a
wall painted with ferns and delicate leaves, a comfortable chair by the

fire, discarded books on the shelf. On the naked mattress was a box. Illiah recognized it immediately.

He opened the box. Inside, Eva's sword was an exile wrapped in velvet. The steel almost glowed, shining in the dim room. The sword was part of her fierce nature; it belonged with her. He caressed the handle, the little leaves, with two fingers. After how he had treated her, why would she want to hold onto such a gift? She had given him everything, and … and it wasn't his to keep. Eva would forget about him. He would use the dagger on his brother. Caeris would fall in love with her. They would wed and be happy. It was a good plan. An honorable plan.

A niggling thought made him scoop up the sword and run to the stables. He took Eva's saddle and Sasha's bridle. Dressing the horse quickly, he attached the sword to the saddle, under the saddlebag, where she wouldn't immediately notice it. He patted his horse, smoothing the hair on his neck. Sasha turned an intelligent eye on his master.

"You take care of her now, young man," he told the horse. "Since I cannot."

Eva's expression was unreadable as he gave her the reins, all but forcing them into her hands. She looked numb, but he could see the pain and hurt in her eyes, even if no one else could. Her beautiful blue-green eyes, usually so full of intelligence and kindness, were dulled.

In another life, he would have whisked her off her feet, leaped onto Sasha, and rode off into the sunset with her. Isn't that what always happened in the old stories she was so fond of reading? But it wasn't real. None of it. It was just the dagger. Eva didn't love him, not really.

Illiah made a formal goodbye to Clarette and wished them an easy journey. He didn't mention a wedding, but he would see them in summer. His voice was steady and clear. Then he watched them leave. Eva did not look back. Not once.

He turned back to the Keep. Mila was saying something in her calm, commanding voice, a tone everyone, including himself on occasion, hastened to obey. She was ordering the people back to work. Thankfully, he wasn't the only one who had to deal out orders around the Keep.

Roughly half the recruits from the royal guard were leaving with

Lady Clarette. Fifteen remained, the men Illiah deemed in need of further training. Some might be trained as captains - time would tell. Another group would come soon. Illiah was looking forward to the smaller group of people. It would be quieter, the work harder.

With the new barracks nearly finished, Illiah hoped by next winter they would be able to house more people, more recruits. They also needed to expand the farming section of the Keep to feed the residents. Mila was organizing some trade with the farmers of Borrowsby. The girl was beyond resourceful - Illiah didn't know what he would do without her. Eva had been just as helpful, in a slightly more melodramatic way, but she was gone now.

That night, after a quiet dinner in the great hall, the only raucousness caused by young Oryn's cries of hunger, Mila approached him.

"So, who do you think we should promote to Eva, Tarek, and Mahone's old rooms? With a shortage of rooms, it only makes sense to move some of the permanent residents into them. Lindin perhaps? Tarran?" Mila suggested. She was trying to sound nonchalant. Illiah knew Lindin fancied Mila, but he hadn't thought she felt the same way.

The thought of filling those empty rooms was distasteful, and the last thing Illiah wanted to think about. He washed the distaste from his mouth with some wine. "I don't know, Mila. Let me think on it," Illiah said, sounding more curt than he meant to.

She nodded. Another good thing about Mila - she never took anything personally. Eva had been like that too, most of the time. He appreciated it in a woman. Freya always took everything personally, but then she was his little sister. Too much history, he supposed.

Empty rooms, empty places at the table.

Even through his effort to reverse the effects of the dagger, he had failed. Eva had always been close, yet not close enough. For a time he was sure it had worked and the attraction between them, those foolish kisses, were like they had never been.

He had been wrong.

She had come, like a dream thing, to his room. How could he send her away? The memory of her creeping silently into his room, her nightgown partially unbound, exposing the gentle curve of her breasts, her eyes bright with desire, desire for him, filled him with longing and despair. He had dreamed of her more often than he cared to admit. He had even imagined what he would do if she came. And then she did. His dream became real. And now she was gone.

He tried to feel shame for what he had done. He had betrayed his brother. His brother whom he loved. But he felt nothing. Only sorrow that Eva was gone, that she was not his, that he had no choice but to send her into the arms of a man who did not love her.

He rose, no longer feeling fit for company. His men wished him a goodnight. He scarcely heard. He did not reply.

The solitude of his room gave his thoughts wide pastures.

He was a fool. Even if he loved Eva, even if he wanted her as his partner, his wife, mother of his children, what right did he have? What if, over time, the dagger stopped working and she knew she had been tricked, coerced? That was evil. What he did was bad enough, letting her into his bed knowing that her desire for him was a figment of his lust. He was selfish, and he hated himself for it.

As Illiah fell asleep, a small voice asked a question: What if Eva really loved him? What if he was wrong about everything?

That night he dreamed of Aralis - again. Of Culi. Of Gera. Then another man whose name, to Illiah's great shame, he could not remember. All had died on his command, tortured by the enemy beyond endurance. Men he could have saved. He could have said no, not today. He could have told Aralis to stay home with their mother to guard the farm.

He hadn't.

He woke with cheeks wet from tears and muscles strained from being clenched tight. He forced himself to breathe deep. He rubbed his aching back, flexing his fingers where they had been fists. His nails dug creases into his palms.

He rose and opened the window. The cool air caressed his face. He pulled his sword from its scabbard and began one of his routines, a newer one, his own creation. It was still a challenge. His blade hummed through the air as he concentrated on the tricky combination of footwork and posture. The actions usually calmed him, helped him clear his mind. He continued until his muscles burned, his breath came quick, and his heart pulsed loudly in his ears. Then he repeated the routine, but instead of his sword, he held his dagger.

Still the feeling of unease refused to lift. Illiah threw the dagger against the stone in frustration. He lay on his bed staring up at the ceiling and waited for morning to come.

The practice was not going well. Illiah's jaw ached - he realized he had been grinding his teeth. The men were working, they were trying, even he could see that, but they were not doing it right. He had corrected them over and over, but still their strokes were too heavy, their balance off. He started to open his mouth, but Kaile interceded by putting a hand on his shoulder.

"What are you doing, bruh?" Kaile said, using their childhood nickname.

"Working my men."

"Oh?"

Illiah shrugged off his brother's hand and moved toward the trainees. Kaile grabbed his arm.

"Do you need a whip to go with your tongue?" Kaile quipped.

"Shut it, Kaile. This is my Keep. My men. My command."

Kaile held Illiah's eyes in a long, searching look.

"Why don't you take the morning off?" Kaile said, his voice softening. "Figure out what is eating you this time. Come back when you can deal with your men like the leader I know you are, instead of this -" He gestured to Illiah. "mess."

"What are you saying?" Illiah wanted to hit him. Hard.

"Illiah, you are being unfair. The boys work hard, they try only to please you. Give them a couple days, come back, then reassess them," Kaile suggested. "You know it is a good suggestion. And you know I am a good teacher. You don't have to have your hand in every pie."

Illiah glared at Kaile, but his anger was sloughing.

"Fine," Illiah said stalking off.

He spent the morning brushing down Penn. The stallion was shedding from the change of season. A puddle of black fur formed in the horse's stall, milling around his hooves. A chore Illiah's father had always made them do as a punishment. "Go brush down ten horses!" he would order his errant boys. The ache in their arms would remind them of their misdeeds, or so his foster father had hoped.

He passed old Path in his stall, the old horse Eva inherited who had once carried a king. The piebald horse was starting to look his age. His muzzle was bleached with white hairs. His eyes had lost some of their luster. Illiah suggested to Justyn that they put him out to pasture since Eva was no longer around to dote on him.

Illiah was leaving the stables when something caught his eye. Later he would wonder how he had ever seen it, small as his littlest toe, gray-brown like the dirt floor, shaped like a leaf. Eva's pendant, lying in the dirt.

He picked it up. The little leaf with its precise detail, the venation, the odd pattern to the edges unlike any leaf he had ever seen. Eva would be missing it dearly. She was overly fond of it and wore it always.

A smile turned his lips as he remembered it around her neck, nestled between her naked breasts. It had been her only adornment. She needed no other. Naked, she had been the most beautiful thing he had ever seen. She had been perfectly at ease with him, allowing him to admire her. They had lain naked together after, entwined. He had torn his eyes and hands off her to inspect her token. She had scolded him, telling him how precious it was to her. She told him the things she would do to him if he broke it, not so horrible things, really. As a retort he told her how tempted he was to break it, just to see what exactly she would do. They had laughed, and she had shown him anyhow.

He held the pendant tightly in his hand. His chest was tight, restricted. He knew in that moment he could not, would not, live his life without her. He needed her with every fiber of his body. He needed her body, her council, her kindness, her love, her wisdom. A thought struck him with the subtlety of a spooked horse: his recurring dreams, his memories, were of decisions he would give anything to change. An arm. His dagger. His life. But he couldn't change the past. Learning from his mistakes was the only way forward. But he hadn't. This time it was his life he was discarding.

Relief was a heady thing. He almost burst out laughing. He could fight for Eva. He would earn her love - without the help of the dagger. He was a selfish fool and a coward, but he could do better. He vowed to make things right.

He almost gripped the wall, afraid he would lift into the air from the lightness radiating from his chest. His path was suddenly obviously, painstakingly clear to him. He prayed Eva would forgive him for not finding it sooner.

CHAPTER 32

EVA

EVA NO LONGER had the strength to fight. They bound her hands tightly with rope. The rough edges burned, rubbing her skin painfully. She didn't care; physical pain was nothing next to her grief. Her guilt. Her heart screamed out for Mahone, for Tarek. Her mind begged for Tayeh's forgiveness.

She was roughly lifted in front of Serac on his tall horse by two of his guards. Serac's body pressed against hers. His breath on her neck woke her from her numb grief, making her skin crawl.

They rode through the back ways of the city without ceremony. One small blessing, she thought abstractly. They didn't plan to publicly humiliate her, though she doubted such a debacle would bother her. How could anything affect her anymore? Her king was dying. Mahone had been butchered. She would never see either of them again.

Serac was right - her actions had caused Mahone's death. A truth she would live with for the rest of her life. And what of Tarek? She feared Caeris had arrested him and had him killed too. If he had escaped, wherever he was, he would be a broken man. He had lost his best friend and lover. No, Tarek was likely dead too. He would not run when his lover had been brutality and unjustly murdered. He would be cut down by their efficient cruelty.

"Ah, look at it," Serac whispered in her ear, almost joyfully. The Temple of the Black Goddess loomed before them. They approached from the side by way of the alley, but the Temple was no less menacing, no less beautiful. "The Goddess will be delighted to meet you. All these years she has sensed you, sensed your magic, but you never came

here, would never come here. She had no way to get to you, until now."
Beyond Serac's voice, Eva could faintly hear acolytes singing.

They followed the wall and passed under the archway into the Temple
courtyard. Eva had passed the Temple many times. She had admired the
gardens and the beauty of the place as one admires a poisonous flower.
It was beautiful, but no less a prison. Even the acolytes fit into the picture of captivity with their controlled sameness, their plain gowns, black
hair and pale skin, young and old. They all wore the heavy manacle-
like bracelets around their wrists as if bound by invisible chains to the
Temple, the same bracelets Simirri wore. Eva had never seen the acolyte
without them. Eva had never asked Simirri about life at the Temple. She
had not managed to befriend the Goddess's woman - hadn't wanted
to. Eva knew nothing about their doctrine, only that the acolytes were
born into it, children born from the spring ceremony to the Goddess.

Serac pulled her off the horse. A young woman came to take the
beast away. The woman looked at Eva with round eyes that relayed not
a hint of curiosity. Serac took Eva by the arm, making a pleased remark
about how she had seen reason and subsided.

She no longer struggled to fight free, it was true. She was thinking of
the little knife still hidden in her boot. Serac made no move to search
her. Her wrists were still bound, but she could be patient.

The interior of the Temple was cool and smelled of licorice root.
Countless passages wound this way and that, filled with girls of all ages
going about their business, some silent, others singing softly in fine
voices.

Serac led her down what appeared to be the main corridor, through
a set of doors into a tall, domed room. In the center was a statue of the
Goddess carved from black marble. Kneeling before the statue, a row
of girls sang a lilting, lethargic song that sounded beautiful enough. Eva
didn't have the energy to decipher the lyrics.

She gazed up at the statue, her skin prickling with unease. The stone
Goddess was tall, thin, her face serene, her body clothed in a thin,
form-fitting shift, her breasts protruding, jutting forward arrogantly.
On her back, spanning almost the length of the room, two enormous
wings sprouted from her shoulder blades. There was no softness to the
effigy.

"Leave this room. No one will enter," Serac shouted to the girls who stopped their song instantly. They all hurried out of sight in an orderly manner, their fear and apprehension palpable.

The last of the girls exited and the doors closed. When they were alone, Serac came around Eva's back, pressing close to her as he untied her hands.

"There is no escape. No door will open for you," Serac told her. He lingered behind her, pulling a long strand of her hair to his nose to inhale her smell. Then he turned his eyes on the statue.

A figure emerged. The real Crea, an almost flesh-and-feather version of the statue. Her eyes were black and bitter and cruel. And sad.

The almost-Guardian who called herself a Goddess sauntered up to Eva, placing one obscenely long fingernail under Eva's chin. The sensation of Crea's fingernail on Eva's skin was vague and unsettling. Tayeh and Lula felt like sunlight. Crea's touch was much different, not exactly cold, but not warm either. It felt … hollow.

"So this is Tayeh's brat, Lulanan's toy," Crea said in a strange voice pitched somewhere between feminine and masculine, with an overtone of arrogance. Or perhaps it was bitterness. "Tayeh and Lulanan tried to keep you for themselves. Tayeh wants you for his own, but look who is the victor now." Crea looked into Eva's eyes and reached into her soul, turning it around, picking it apart. Eva backed away instinctively.

Crea turned to Serac, who looked like a puppy bringing its master a bone.

"She is of no use to me like this, Serac," Crea said with a wave of her hand, her expression formidable. "You must break her. Then bring her back to me. She must wilt and crumble. Only then can I take her magic. Only then can you learn to control her. She will learn that Tayeh and Lulanan will not save her. She must accept that the man who was her demise has truly abandoned her, casting her aside as a boring plaything. Then she will be ready."

"My Goddess, it will be done," Serac said, his face twisting in a strange, enlightened smile. Eva eyed the doors, her instincts begging her to flee, but Serac's closeness transformed her courage to despair. She was trapped. Crea dissolved once more into her statue. The room was empty except for Eva and the Temple Master.

Serac pulled Eva urgently by the arm toward one of the doors.

"You see, you and I have something in common, Eva," he said - gloated - as they walked. "We are both blessed with magic in our blood, blessed to see what others can not. The Goddess shows me visions, things to make me excited, things to make me terrified, things to use to achieve her desires. She showed me you, sneaking into Illiah's room like a cheap rent girl. I knew if Caeris knew the truth, he would never want you. Illiah doesn't want you. But I do. We are destined to be together. Oh yes, Eva. Rhais and your cunt of an aunt thwarted my mother's wishes. We were betrothed before we were conceived, and they broke it. Rhais made a promise to my mother, his dear sister, when he allowed Finnan to dissolve their betrothal to wed that witch-woman who was your mother. Finnan agreed that his daughter would wed Fara's son, so consummating the agreement your father loathed to. Your father sold you to me before you were born. This is how it was meant to be, Eva. This is what your parents wanted.

"When I told Crea about you, she agreed that I should have you. She knows the value of your Allati blood. Crea's own blood runs in mine. Our child will be a true child of the Goddess. You are strong-willed, arrogant, not unlike my dear mother. But she was cruel - the world made her bitter and diseased. She was a terrible mother. I will make sure you do not make her mistakes. I will teach you."

Serac was Caeris and Illiah's cousin. He was of royal Jullayan blood. If Eva bore Serac a son, the child would also fit Tayeh's prophecy. But Eva could not imagine a son of Serac's growing into a man who would fight for peace and balance and light. He would be poisoned, like his father.

Serac's eyes were filled with lust and hatred, and the juxtaposition terrified her. Eva thought of Mila and she couldn't stop shivering. Serac's smile widened.

Serac led her down an empty hallway. There were no windows. He pushed her through a small door into a small room, only one narrow window shed light upon them.

He closed the door behind him, locking her in with him. She backed instinctively into the corner, but there was only a small bed. Nowhere to run, nowhere to hide.

"You are very beautiful, but you will be prettier on your knees," Serac said, leering over her, pulling at the laces on his pants, his smile feral and evil.

Eva prided herself on her quick reflexes. She pulled her knife from her boot and plunged it deep into Serac's vitals. His flesh rent under her knife before he pushed her violently onto the bed, making her hand slip from the small dagger.

His eyes widened with shock and outrage; pain didn't seem to register. All he did was back up a step and pull the blade out, the steel red and dripping. Eva had hoped for more, but the knife was small, the blade sharp but short. His hand came across her face. Pain blossomed on her cheek. Spots danced in her eyes.

"You will pay for that," was all he said, his voice an icy promise. He left the room awkwardly. She heard the lock slide home behind him. There were drops of blood on the whitewashed floor.

She picked her feet up and tucked them under her on the bed. The pounding of her heart filled the small room. The walls, too close and too many, snagged her breath from her lungs.

She wrapped her arms around her knees and searched for comforting thoughts. Illiah's strong embrace. The smell of his bare skin. The touch of his short beard under her fingers, against her lips. Serac could not take her memories.

Crea's words hung heavy in Eva's mind. She hated herself for giving them credence. A discarded plaything used to satiate Illiah's lust. It couldn't be true. But she had misjudged Serac once. Maybe she had misjudged Illiah too.

No. Only love left a pain unlike any other. Only love could drown her soul and burn it all at once.

Tangled in her thoughts of Illiah was Mahone, his craggy, often stoic face lit by subtle humor. Her confidant, her friend. Every memory, every thought was tainted by blood and pain. Her fault. It was all her fault. There was no thought, no memory strong enough to keep the horror of his death at bay.

She knew bone-deep she was undeserving of those precious moments she had spent in the arms of the man she loved like no other. That night had been bought by blood, only at the time she had not known the cost.

Eva was dozing when the door opened, waking her abruptly. She scrubbed a hand across her face absently. Her skin was wet with tears. Her eyes would be red and swollen. Her cheek was tender where Serac had hit her.

Serac loomed inside the threshold. He stood bent, slightly hobbled. Unlike a wild beast, his injury made him appear less threatening. At least that gave her some time - time for what, she didn't know.

Three women came into Eva's room, making it feel tight. They stripped her of her gown, the empty chain around her neck. They even took her small clothes.

Eva ignored Serac as his eyes raked over her naked body. The girls were businesslike about the process, which Eva appreciated. They clothed her quickly in a plain, white shift. Then they left, the girls without a word, Serac with a parting sneer.

Eva grew hungry, but no food came. She lay on her bed and tried to dream of Illiah, but all she saw was Mahone, lying broken and bleeding on the floor. In her dream, he called her name.

Breakfast came the next morning, a meager affair, hard bread and a glass of goat milk. It seemed they didn't mean to starve her to death. Eva had never been fond of goat milk, but she drank it all the same, too famished and thirsty to care. The girl who brought it looked no older than twelve.

"Serac is not here this morning to torment me?" Eva asked the girl, not expecting a response. The acolytes looked obedient to a fault, and Eva doubted Serac would want them fraternizing with her.

The girl gave her a look that meant Eva best keep her mouth shut. She placed the tray on the bed, took the chamber pot, and left the room.

The next woman who came was older than Eva, but not old by any means. Her hair was straight and black and shone in the light. She wore a dress of pale gold. Eva wondered if it was a symbol of status.

"Come with me," the woman said, her mouth a thin line. When Eva didn't, the acolyte bridled with impatience. "Don't be difficult," she warned.

Eva stood, more out of curiosity than obedience. She would welcome a break from her little prison.

"Don't try to escape. There is no way you can get out of the Temple, so don't even think about it," the woman said simply. Eva glanced down corridors. Guards dressed in black dotted the halls, swords at their sides, black bows on their backs, a quiver of arrows at the ready. Were the guards on her behalf or were they to keep the placid acolytes in line?

The woman led Eva to an inhospitable bathing room. A dirty drain was inlaid in the center of the stained tile floor. A cold draft came in the only window. A tub sat in the middle of the room filled with water. It didn't look warm or in the least inviting.

The woman gestured for Eva to undress and get in. Another three women entered, each carrying something, though Eva didn't know what.

The bath was far from warm. She refused to get in. If they assumed she would not make their task difficult, they were delusional.

The golden-garbed woman gave her a look of disgust and called a guard. The guard was tall and burly, his eyes neither clever nor kind. Eva recognized him. He had spent the winter in the Keep, one of the royal guard. She couldn't remember his name. He showed no sign of recollection.

He struck her face, the same cheek that was still swollen from Serac's abuse the night before. It stung, and Eva tasted blood. She silently cursed the guard and Serac and Caeris. She threw Illiah in her curses too.

Eva reconsidered her options and took off her shift before getting into the tub.

The guard left, but only after an unsettling look as he took stock of her naked body. Eva glared at him as he left, wishing looks could kill, or at least maim.

The girls washed her. They scrubbed until Eva's skin burned and she was shivering from the cold. They ordered her to get out but didn't offer her a towel. They sat her on a cold chair and made her lean her head back.

They went to work on her hair, combing it before applying

something foul smelling. Inky black water made little rivulets toward the drain. They were dying her hair black. So that was why all the acolytes had black hair.

Finally, her neck aching from the awkward angle, they were done. They rinsed her hair before combing and braiding it neatly. They told her to dress. The other girls left. Eva was left alone with the senior acolyte, who was regarding her, assessing the handiwork of the women. She was frowning.

"Do you have a mirror?" Eva quipped.

"You need to adjust your attitude. Around here, those who are loose with their tongues pay for it," she said. "And you are already in trouble, after what you did to the lord." Did Eva detect a hint of, what, pity in her voice? She couldn't admit it didn't scare her.

"How is the 'lord'?" Eva asked in a mocking voice despite her fear.

"He'll live. He has been told to stay a bed, lest he get an infection."

"That would be terrible."

"I warned you," the woman said with a shrug, leading Eva back to her prison. "If I were you, I would be terrified. You don't know what that man is capable of." Again, the pity, or fear, was apparent.

"I do know."

"Then you are stupid to antagonize him. Just be nice to him, and he will be easy on you. Do what he wants, and he won't hurt you, much."

"You speak from experience?" Eva said unkindly. She might detect pity from the woman, but it didn't mean she had to like her.

"The lord beds whichever acolyte he chooses. It is an honor for us since he has been chosen by the Goddess. It is her will, her blessing," the woman said. Eva wondered if the acolyte believed her own words. Eva didn't comment. It was too awful a thought.

"Does he mean me to be an acolyte?"

"Of course," the woman said with a cold smile. She opened the door to Eva's prison, gesturing with her eyes for compliance.

Eva spent the day wishing she had used her knife with more accuracy.

CHAPTER 33

ILLIAH

KAILE HAD THE AUDACITY TO LAUGH. The bastard.

"I can't believe you didn't do something weeks ago. It was rather obvious you fancied her. This is what has been eating you and sending you nightmares? You are a foolish bastard," Kaile told him.

Any witty and scathing comment Illiah usually reserved for his brother was lost in his surprise.

"Thanks," was all Illiah came up with.

"You see, Tarran," Kaile turned to the boy who was watching the exchange with wide, curious eyes, "when a man loves a woman, sometimes it is hard to control -"

"Kaile," Illiah interrupted. The boy did not need details.

Kaile grinned triumphantly. "So, when are we leaving?"

And so, with Kaile and Tarran accompanying him, Illiah set off in an attempt to reclaim his heart. Or at least beg Eva's forgiveness. He wouldn't blame her if she didn't want him.

He was glad of their company. They forced him to rest, to make camp for the night, or stay in an inn if one presented itself. He was compelled to get to Caer Andri with all haste. He would have ridden nonstop, buying a fresh mount as he went, but Kaile was the voice of reason reminding Illiah that the wedding wasn't for another six weeks. Surely that wouldn't change without his notice. Illiah reluctantly agreed, but something nagged him. Something was pushing him to find Eva, something desperate and intangible. He found himself fingering the little leaf pendant. He kept it on a new chain close to his heart until he could return it to Eva.

They made good speed over the land, their best yet on the journey they had made several times.

It started to rain, spring rain that was good for the newly planted fields, but uncomfortable to ride in. They took a room at an inn for the night, stabling the horses for a good rest. As day faded to night, the nourishing rain was joined by wind and hail so violent, it was likely manifested from Illiah's nightmares.

At the late hour, the common room of the inn was almost empty. A warm fire burned in a long, low hearth. The rain lashed at the windows, more like claws and clicking teeth than weather. Illiah was thankful to be indoors.

A late supper had been prepared. The cook had been ready to seek his bed, but Illiah had asked nicely and the landlord assured him kindly that for the lost prince, nothing would be too much trouble.

Kaile and Illiah were eating. Tarran, who had been seeing to the horses, tumbled in the door with a blast of cold, wet air. Another figure loomed behind Tarran, tall, obscure as the night, peering warily about the room from under a glistening wet hood.

Illiah, in a tired moment, imagined the man was the storm come alive, his cloak a dripping cloud, his footsteps intent as thunder as he stepped into the inn. The man spotted Illiah and closed the distance between them, pulling his soggy hood back, dissolving Illiah's fanciful ideas.

"Tarek, what for the love of little green apples are you doing here?" Kaile said.

Illiah observed Tarek's blanched expression, the manner of his dress, his boots covered in a layer of mud. Something about him spoke of trouble. Illiah's heart was pounding before Tarek opened his mouth.

Tarek ignored Kaile and knelt beside Illiah with an eerie calm.

"This is good tidings that I found you, my lord. It's Eva. They took her," Tarek said. Despite his calm, he gripped Illiah's chair with white knuckles.

"What? Who took her? Is she okay?" Illiah asked as levelly as he could. The niggling unease in his gut asserted itself, demanding attention.

"Serac took her. They accused her of adultery, of having relations with you. Caeris broke their engagement and sent her to the Temple."

Serac was a dead man.

Illiah's hand gripped his sword instinctively. He wanted to break something. He wanted to run into the night, not stopping until he stood before the Temple. He would break apart the Temple piece by piece until he found her. Somehow his body stayed where it was, frozen by rage.

"My lord?" Tarek asked when Illiah said nothing. "I know you care for her. You must help her. Serac will rape her if he hasn't already, and I don't know what else. He is a monster." Tarek's voice broke, just a little.

"I was riding to Caer Andri to declare my intentions for her. I am too late," Illiah said in a whisper as he finally found his voice.

"Where are you going?" Kaile demanded as Illiah stood up.

"Going. Now."

"You can't - Penn is too tired, we rode hard all day. Think about it, Illiah. We can make better time if we rest tonight, leave early tomorrow," Kaile told him sternly. Illiah was shaking his head.

"Illiah, Eva was taken five days ago. Whatever Serac's intentions for her, I am sure he has already acted on them," Tarek said through gritted teeth. Tarek's red-rimmed eyes were bright with tears.

"Tarek, where is Mahone?"

Tarek looked away, hiding his face. A quiet, strangled noise escaped his lips.

"He's dead." His voice was ... broken. "Serac had him butchered. Serac knew about us. I don't know how, but he did. He came after me too. I just barely got away in time. I knew I had to find you - for Eva's sake. Mahone would have wanted it. He loved her, as do I."

Illiah put his hand on Tarek's shoulder in what he hoped was a comforting gesture. "Thank you, Tarek. I will get her back, and I will make Serac pay, if I can."

"I will come with you," Tarek told him. "You have my sword."

"No, Tarek. I can't let you do that. If you go back, you will be killed, or worse. I will not have that." Illiah let his command slip into his voice. Tarek looked angry, defiant. "Trust me when I say revenge doesn't bring justice, I know. My little brother was taken, tortured. He was only seventeen. When I found his killer, I got to look into the monster's eyes as I cut his throat. I watched his lifeblood drain at my feet. It made me sick, not satisfied. There is nothing in this world that can make what happened to my brother better. Nothing. There is no blood spilled that will make Mahone's death easier." The words choked in Illiah's throat. Mahone had been a good man, and for Tarek ... his love, his life.

Silence. Cold grief filled the silence and made it heavy and oppressive.

Illiah's heart ached. His mind raced. Distance was his enemy. Time, his betrayer.

"Find her. Marry her. Make her happy," Tarek said, getting up slowly.

Illiah nodded, his lips set in a thin line. "Go back to the Keep. You will be safe there."

Tarek didn't reply right away. "Maybe. Maybe not."

"Stay here tonight, at least," Kaile suggested. Tarek looked dead on his feet. "Tarran, take Tarek upstairs. Give him my bed." Tarran nodded wordlessly.

Illiah took another swig of his drink. The room was too full of people who knew too much grief. Even young Tarran. A boy. A little boy who was an instrument of death.

☾

Illiah slept poorly if he slept at all. He lay on the warm ground beside the fire. He was used to a hard, unrelenting bed. It was the anxious knots in his stomach that kept sleep at bay.

His heart cried out for Eva. His mind echoed with promises. He vowed to find her, mend what hurts he could. Once he found her, he would keep her safe. He would do everything in his power not to fail her again.

Tarek had also warned them of the king's failing health. Illiah felt another pang in his broken heart at the impending loss. He didn't know the king well, but he was his father, his blood. He had feebly hoped for at least a few seasons to know the man who had fathered him.

In the morning, they parted ways. Tarek rode off in the direction of the Keep and they continued toward Caer Andri. Illiah didn't know if he would see Tarek again. Tarek would not say what his final destination was.

The landscape was ever changing, but every inn, every farm they passed, did not pass by fast enough. Despite Kaile's assurances, their journey was tortuously slow.

Five long days later the walls of Caer Andri loomed before them in the morning sun, yet Illiah did not feel relief. He was only more apprehensive and desperate. Desperation was a dangerous entity.

The king's flag still flew from the palace tower, which meant he was still alive. One small victory.

Illiah turned to Kaile. "Go to the palace and find Clarette. I want to speak to her. She may know more of what transpired. Tarran," Illiah turned to his ward, "you go in disguise and find out what you can. We will meet at noon at the tavern on the edge of the city. You know the one."

Tarran nodded, flashing a ready grin. Tarran's street-rat sense was an advantage - he had an uncanny ability to weasel out information, and the boy was a genius at disguise.

"You don't think it best to talk to Caeris?" Kaile asked once more. They had been over the plan the night before as well.

"No. I think if Serac knows my true purpose, he will use all his influence against me." Illiah did not trust Serac an inch. And Illiah did not know Caeris's mind. Caeris might be too angry with him to listen to what he had to say, preferring to listen to his counselor instead.

"Okay, if you're sure. I will see you at noon."

The three disbanded. Tarran disappeared into the city on foot, Kaile rode to the palace, and Illiah made for the tavern.

The morning was fair, but Illiah kept to the gray alleys, his hood covering his face. He didn't want to announce his presence in the city.

The tavern was not the most respectable establishment. Its reputation, if it had one, did not entice courtiers. Tarran trusted the owner, so Illiah chose to trust him as well. Being early in the day, it was more than likely empty. A good place for secrets.

The rear of the tavern joined the nearly abandoned alley. The windows of the neighboring buildings were filthy. The grime of neglect was Illiah's disguise. Illiah tethered Penn along with Tarran's sweet-tempered mare to a post. The horses were tired - not even the stallion would complain of the shadowy corridor and hard cobbles under his feet.

Illiah opened the door and stepped into the dim room. The ceiling was low, black from decades of soot from the large, leaky fireplace dominating one corner. The room smelled the way it looked: smoky, slightly damp, like an overabundance of ale and poor decisions. The room was deserted but for the tables littering the room. A bell had been struck as the door opened, alerting the owner to Illiah's presence.

An old man came into the room. He had a wiry, lined face, and tight, pointy eyes. He had clearly been at work in the kitchen, his apron and beard white with flour.

"What can I get for you this time o' the day?" the man asked, his voice as grizzled as his appearance.

Illiah pulled back his hood and took a seat at the bar. Predictably, the man's expression changed as he recognized him.

"My lord, an honor! We have fine wines. Ale from the East. What would you like? Though it be early for such things. I have fresh bread baking if you have a mind to wait."

"Thank you. My business in the city is not yet known to my brother. I would like a quiet place to wait for a while."

"Aye." The man had a twinkle in his eye. Unfortunately, it did not improve his appearance. "No better place for some 'quiet' than old Alasker's Brewery."

"Thank you. Some bread would be welcome."

"Aye." The man disappeared into the kitchen, leaving Illiah alone with his thoughts and misgivings.

It took considerable strength of will to take a deep breath, pick a table at the back of the tavern, and wait for the fresh bread that was promised.

Illiah could feel the snake that was his terror, lurking and slithering inside him, trying to swallow all coherent thought. He needed Eva in his arms, her soft hair against his lips. If Serac touched her, he was as good as dead.

But he did have a plan. He wasn't sure it would work - he needed to hear what Tarran and Kaile had to say first. Battles were won strategically. The trick was to silence the screaming anger in his heart and let logic take over.

His body did not want to sit. Waiting was its own form of torture. Illiah had been on the cusp of battle many times, waiting for the perfect moment to strike, sitting on the edge of a knife, going over plans until doubt threatened sanity. Once the flood started, it was easier. Doubt was silenced by action and reaction. Survival relied on instinct over thought. Yes, that was easier.

The man came back with steaming bread and a variety of cheeses. The fine selection was surprising for the simple establishment. Illiah ate what was brought to him but didn't recall the taste. The tavern owner asked him how it was and he must have said something, for the man left smiling, appeased.

The sun moved shadows across the room. The dust settled after every subtle movement Illiah made. He breathed in and forced himself to exhale.

Finally, the bells tinkled. A bright beam of sunlight entered with Kaile. Illiah squinted. He had been inside the dim room too long.

"And?" Illiah asked at once.

"Clarette wouldn't come back with me, but she told me what she knew," Kaile began, taking a seat opposite him. Kaile's voice was hushed, even though they were alone. "She told me the morning after they arrived, without her knowledge, Eva was sent to meet with Caeris. Serac and Caeris convicted her of treason, claiming she had an affair with you. She apparently admitted it, the betrothal was broken, and she was sent to the Temple."

"What else? How did they know?" Illiah wished Clarette would have come herself. The woman had many insights into court machinations. He would have appreciated her thoughts.

"Clarette said Serac claimed the Goddess told him. She didn't believe that, but she thought perhaps there had been one of Caeris's guards from the Keep."

Not that he cared at the moment. He had to get Eva. "So Clarette thinks she is still in the Temple?"

"She does."

Illiah nodded, thinking. He had thought Eva would either be there or in Serac's house. He wasn't sure which was worse. Illiah had only seen the surface of the Goddess's hive, but he had no doubt inside was infested with Serac's people, a suitable prison. Eva would be somewhere secure, yet within Serac's easy reach. She was clever - if she saw a way to escape, she would try.

"Clarette told me she blames Serac for the whole thing. She said the man is conniving and has had his eye on Eva ever since she first came to court. She told me Serac and Eva were betrothed as babes, an agreement made by Eva's father and the king to appease Princess Fara."

"What?"

Kaile nodded. "No one knew of it, not even Eva. Clarette thought all knowledge of the betrothal died with Fara, that Serac knew nothing of it. She thinks differently now. She told me she believes Serac knew all along, that his mother must have told him before she died. Serac must have felt slighted, but bade his time. He was only waiting for an excuse."

The news was deeply unsettling. Illiah struggled to find calm. If he had given in to anger and hate when the invaders came, like so many wanted, they would have all died. Instead, he convinced his men to wait, to rely on tactics, to have patience. Now he was eating his own words and they tasted like bile.

"Tarran's not back yet?"

Illiah shook his head. He started pacing again.

"Do we go ahead with the plan?" Kaile asked. He too was starting to fidget.

"Maybe."

Neither of the men noticed Tarran until the boy was standing in front of them. He had not come through the front door. Illiah didn't know what corner the boy materialized from. Tarran grinned when Illiah pulled off the boy's tattered hood to reveal his ward beneath.

"Scoundrel," Illiah muttered. "What have you learned?"

"She is at the Temple. The women say she is a bother. Serac is at his house. He limps like he is injured."

What could that mean? Did Eva manage to hurt him before he could assault her? Or after. He wouldn't think of during. He had to stay rational.

"There are more guards at the Temple than before, that's for certain," Tarran told them. "They look meaner than the regular lot. They have a bad look in their eyes. Raygl is there. I never liked him, not one bit."

Illiah agreed that Raygl, one of his brother's men, was a mean sort. Illiah would never have hired him. At the Keep, Illiah had kept a close eye on him.

It was only him and Kaile. He would never ask Tarran to fight. He would not put the youngster at risk. He and Kaile were strong, good fighters, but if it came to a fight, he didn't want to be so far outnumbered. Luckily the plan turning around in his mind didn't rely on strength of arms. It merely risked incurring the wrath of his brother, the ruling prince.

EVA

EVA LAY ON THE BED staring up at the ceiling. She was fortunate the ceiling was paneled wood; the knots swirled and twisted, so her imagination became her distraction. She could pretend queer little faces were looking down on her. She could see landscapes, hills, all sorts of things - she had nothing else to do.

The window did not open. The air was stale. Eva could not seek the *simul rami* to find the visions her heart desired. The window was too high to look out, and she could not reach the ledge. The walls were gray plaster.

She turned over onto her side. Her face hurt. The bruises were amassing bruises. Her tongue got the better of her, and a guard was always ready to strike his hand across her cheek. Serac added to her bruises with his own hand, but she hadn't seen him for several days.

The last time Serac had visited, he had grabbed her, wrapping his arm around her torso, grabbing at her breasts, whispering vile promises in her ear. She had wrenched free, making him move in a way that compromised his barely healed injury. Idiot. His breeches had been stained with his own blood. He had hobbled from the room. She laughed to his back as he left. Then a guard came and she suffered blows for her insolence.

She touched her face gingerly. At least nothing seemed to be broken. Her teeth were fine. It was just bruising. Apparently, they wanted to maintain her beauty.

Eva felt a slight pang of pity for the acolytes in charge of that. They had been trying to turn her hair a beautiful black in the image of the Goddess, but, for whatever reason, no method they used, no dye they could obtain proved capable of changing the color of her hair. It remained stubbornly pale. Some of the sheen was gone, but it was anything but black. The girls looked anxious every time they tried a new technique. Eva guessed Serac, or the Goddess herself, was angry with their failure.

After the last failed attempt, Deotha was not seen for two days. Eva overheard the girls whispering that Serac had her punished. Eva could only guess how. She hoped Serac had an infection from all his antics. She hoped it would spread to his blood and poison him with a slow, painful death.

They brought her breakfast, if it could be called that. She ate it. Later the young girl would come and take the empty tray away. Never a word spoken.

Eva, who enjoyed solitude, was surprised at how much she missed having someone to talk to. She added loneliness to her list of despairs. She had long since given up tears.

The ache in her heart, the emptiness in her gut, remained, occasionally dulled by fear. Her heart pounded and tripped when she heard booted footsteps in the hall, fearing it was Serac come to finish what he had attempted to start. It would happen. When he visited, anger made his eyes flash with excitement and lust, his body ready.

Every day was the same routine. Just before the midday meal, Eva expected the girls to come and take her for her cold bath. She was sure they meant to bathe her until she caught an ague from the cold.

This time, for once, she was told to scrub herself, a small triumph she could not claim. When she got out, they gave her a towel and a dress to wear. A proper dress, not an acolyte's shift, and even new small clothes. She wondered about the change of attire.

"What, no attempt to dye my hair today? Did you run out of options?" Eva remarked dryly.

They did not reply. Not that Eva expected them to.

The woolen fabric was comforting against her skin. The sleeves were long and came down past her wrists, covering her bruises. For the first time since her arrival in her prison, she was almost warm. They even gave her a pair of leather slippers and stockings for her cold feet. They led her back to her room where Deotha was waiting patiently.

"Prince Caeris is here. He wishes to see you," Deotha said. There was no outward sign of injury, but Eva could tell from Deotha's downcast eyes and slumped shoulders something bothered the woman.

Eva reached out and grabbed the woman's arm, holding fast, locking her eyes with Deotha's. Deotha was shocked and didn't pull away, didn't try to move. Eva used the physical contact to feel with her magic, through the woman's body, searching for injuries. Deep down, violent lacerations brimmed with infection. Every step Deotha took must be agony.

"Do you still feel gifted by the Goddess?" Eva asked. Deotha held her gaze, but her eyes were bright and wet. Eva used her healing magic, watching as the woman felt it course through her body. The magic was painful, but it was only an instant, a breath perhaps, and then the woman's pain would be soothed. Eva didn't heal her completely. She didn't want to compromise her own strength. Deotha had not earned that right. But the infection would be gone, and she would heal much quicker.

"What did you do?" Deotha whispered, touching her navel.

Eva didn't answer.

"Come with me," Deotha said unsteadily. "The prince is waiting." Two guards stepped up to flank them as they walked.

She was led to a beautiful room opening onto the garden. A small statue in respect to the Goddess leered at Eva from a small table. Beyond it, past the garden, Eva could see the walls that marked the edge of the Temple grounds. Her mind immediately thought of escape.

Caeris was already there, kneeling with his back to them, gazing out at the statue serenely. Eva wanted to scream at him.

He turned. His gaze raked over her bruised face. His eyes flashed. Her gaze faltered, and she looked at the floor. He was still angry then. What reason could he possibly have to see her?

"The king is dying. His last wish is to see you," Caeris said in his usual haughty manner, standing up tall. Eva's hopes flared. Perhaps she could plead with the king. Rhais would listen to her, wouldn't he? Or was he beyond such things, so close to death? It didn't matter. To say goodbye, to hold his hand one last time, was a gift.

"Please, please, let me see him," Eva said, discarding her pride.

Caeris nodded hesitantly. "Come with me. She will be brought back in one hour," Caeris told the guards. The women looked uneasy, but he was the prince. They couldn't do anything. Serac was nowhere to be seen. Likely abed with his wounds. It was a satisfying thought.

Caeris gestured for her to prelude him out into the garden, down the path to the gate. Eva shook her head to clear her thoughts. Days spent in the little room had left her feeling slightly odd in the head. The sun on her body felt good, nourishing, but it also made her dizzy.

Eva wanted to run. Caeris at her back inspired her like a hawk inspires a rabbit. Perhaps she could be fast enough to get away from him. She couldn't see any of his guards around, which was odd. Caeris was not even an arm's reach behind her. If she ran, he would surely catch her, and she would lose her chance to see the king.

A shadow passed over her as she walked beneath the arching gate. She was free of the Temple grounds. The longing for flight intensified. Her feet moved faster. Caeris came up behind her, walking briskly to match her pace. Her head felt light. She wavered slightly.

"This way," Caeris said, leading her across the street toward an alley.

Her ears pulsed. They were not going to the palace. What did Serac have planned for her now? Her footsteps became hesitant. She almost tripped. Caeris grabbed her arm, his grip painful against her bruised flesh. He ignored her cry of pain and propelled her forward into the shadowy road between the two buildings.

A horse appeared that was impossibly tall and impossibly black. Eva must be dreaming. Caeris ordered her to mount up. She didn't. She was trying to understand why she needed to get on the horse. Her head was a fractured pot, her senses slipping through the cracks. Her arms were weak and she couldn't - wouldn't - pull herself up into the saddle.

Caeris shoved her up, and the man riding the horse pulled her behind him on the saddle. He was rough, and his grasp put pressure on her tender bruises again. She yelped a little before biting her lip to stop another cry. She looked at Caeris for an explanation, but he looked distracted, worried even.

She heard shouts. Caeris hissed something Eva couldn't comprehend. The horse spurred forward, and Eva had to grab the rider's belt to keep from falling. It was a long way to the ground.

"Come on, Eva," the rider said. Eva recognized the voice and took a closer look at the rider she now clung to.

"Kaile," she breathed. She spun around, nearly falling off the horse again. Illiah's name almost made it to her lips. Illiah's face was a mask; a monster lurked behind his eyes.

"GO!" Illiah commanded. Kaile took off down the street. His horse's hooves clattered loudly on the cobbles. Illiah was lost from sight almost instantly. She had been stupid. Really stupid. Blind. What other tall black horses were there other than Kaile's and Illiah's? He had come for her, against all odds, he had come.

"We have to get out of the city," Kaile said to her as they rode. Eva clung to his back, hoping she wouldn't fall off. Her captivity made her weak. Her back ached almost immediately, but the tide of relief was immense. Coherent thought was still a great effort. She gripped Kaile's belt tighter.

"Where are we going?" Eva asked Kaile as the streets of the city retreated behind them, leaving them surrounded by farmland.

"To a safe place where we will wait until Illiah comes back. He has other business to attend to. Should only be a few hours," Kaile told her. Eva nodded, not that Kaile could see it. Kaile was quiet, keeping his attention on the horse, the road, and their surroundings. Eva was tired. She leaned against his shoulder. He didn't seem to mind.

After an hour or so of riding, although Eva couldn't really keep time, they came to a stop on top of a hill overlooking Caer Andri. Her back ached, her legs ached, her mouth was parched. She was further relieved to learn it was the place where they planned to wait for Illiah.

She sunk into the grass. Kaile handed her the canteen before gathering some things to start a fire.

"Thank you, Kaile." Eva had so many questions for him that she didn't know where to begin. Instead, she looked out to Caer Andri. She could see the palace clearly. Suddenly the realization of what she was seeing hit her like a blow to the gut: the king's flag was down. His standard, a golden eagle on a plain of green was replaced with a black flag. The flag of death. Eva choked on her water.

"Kaile, the king!"

Kaile nodded sadly. "Yes, he passed just this morning, to hear tell."

Tears filled Eva's eyes and fell like rain onto her lap. She wiped them away. She had no strength left to hold them back. Rhais, her beloved king, was gone.

"How did Illiah know to come?" Eva asked Kaile a while later. Kaile made a little fire and fed Eva a meager lunch. After days of dry bread and goat milk, the soft bread, rich butter, and cheese were glorious.

"Tarek met us on the road and told us what happened."

Sorrow and relief waged war inside her.

"Was he okay? He wasn't hurt?"

"No. He was not hurt. But Mahone is dead," Kaile told her softly.

Eva nodded without meeting Kaile's eyes. Yes, she knew that. Eva closed her eyes and put her forehead on her knees. If she hadn't chosen Illiah, Mahone would still be alive and Tarek would be with his lover. The fact was undeniable and unforgivable.

"Are you going to take me back to the Keep?" Eva asked, wondering if it would bring her happiness.

Kaile flashed her a grin. "Yup. Illiah means to marry you. It is the only way to keep you out of trouble, it seems," Kaile told her with a wink.

Did that mean Illiah loved her? Or was this one of his brilliant solutions to overcome his guilt? She wished she knew.

All her thoughts were sad and heavy and her heart was wrung and limp. She was so tired. In the back of her mind she thought of the prophecy and her one day child. Suddenly relief was like a drug, lulling her to sleep. Fear had kept her mind and body strained. She had slept fitfully at the Temple. She curled up in the grass, warmed by the fire and the sun, and fell asleep almost as soon as her head lay upon her hand.

There were tears on the edge of her mind. Her dreams were sad.

CHAPTER 35

ILLIAH

TIME WAS A SLIPPERY EEL. And Illiah did not possess a trap to catch it or slow it. He did not have the chance to tell Eva what was in his heart, and he wanted to more than anything. He had to cling to the illusion that he was Caeris. He couldn't kiss or touch her, but his heart didn't waste a moment reminding him of how much he needed her.

Eva had believed he was Caeris. It worried him more than anything else to see her senses dulled, her mind muffled. He had never seen such vivid fear in her eyes before. It reminded him of when he found Tarran. He hated that fear. He would do anything to banish it.

Then finally, Eva's face shone with realization, her tongue silenced by surprise. Then they were gone, urged out of the city at his own insistence in case Serac's guards decided to wage war.

Eva's face had been bruised and swollen. It made him furious. Any other injuries he could see no sign of.

He forced himself to turn back toward the heart of the city. He had two more errands to make before he could meet up with Kaile and his beloved. At least she was safe now.

He was so tired of death. Of saying goodbye. He had learned an hour ago of his father's passing. And now he had to confront his brother, whose grief was a raw wound he was about to throw salt in.

The news of the king's death had not yet spread to the city. Soon the king's flag would be replaced with the black flag of mourning that marked the passing a king. Soon the streets would be lined with the grieving.

As he waited in the prince's solar in the Temple, one of the acolytes told him Serac was ill and abed, under his physician's orders. When he asked what had befallen the lord, the young girl went silent. Even under the guise of Prince Caeris, she wouldn't tell him. It was an uneasy reminder neither Illiah nor Caeris knew the inner workings of the Goddess and her Temple Master.

Illiah found a secluded alley and shed his princely surcoat and his shining leather boots. Instead, he dressed in something nondescript that transformed him into a nobody. His long, rough-spun cloak was gray and hid the longsword and dagger at his belt. He pulled the hood over his head and made his way unobtrusively through the city. He threw intention into his dagger, and it helped him blend into the shadows. No one would mark his passing.

Serac's house was tall. He had his own house guards: mean ones, as Tarran had pointed out. Illiah gained access through the back alley, leveling a guard silently with a trick his mentor had taught him. Two hands, two specific pressure points in the neck, then a little twist - well, actually, a big twist. The resulting crack was sickeningly satisfying. Illiah imagined Serac's handsome neck beneath his hands. He had told Tarek revenge did not bring solace - he hadn't been completely honest.

Inside, the house was dark. The ceilings were tall, the windows covered. It was cold. Empty. The last battlefield Illiah had traversed had been cold too, but mucky from gore and dirt and blood. He had fought monstrous invaders; now he hunted his own kin.

Illiah crept through the house, ears strained, dagger in his hand. Its magic pulsed, warm and alive in his hand, anticipating blood. The weapon loved to work.

A woman came out of one of the rooms carrying a bowl filled with bloody rags. She didn't see Illiah crouched in the corner. He had no desire to dispatch the girl as he had the guard. He waited until she was gone, and then slipped into the room she had vacated.

The room was warmer than the rest of the house. It was lit by candles and the fire, the windows shrouded in thick cloth. Serac was sitting before the fire on a couch. He had not heard Illiah open the door. Illiah closed it behind him and locked it.

Serac sat gazing into the fire, slumped, shirtless, his abdomen wrapped in freshly changed bandages. He saw Illiah and jolted, clearly a painful reaction. His eyes narrowed in fear or anger or pain, Illiah could not tell which.

"You." Serac's voice was venom.

"Serac."

"I should have known to expect you."

Illiah stood before Serac, his dagger held openly. Serac looked at the dagger, his face stained with jealousy. He knew what it was, Illiah was sure of it.

"You can't kill me," Serac said.

"Oh?"

It was not mercy that stayed Illiah's hand. He was tired of mercy. He wanted to cut off Serac's cock and force it down his throat. He wanted to watch him bleed out from several long wounds as the dagger sang in his hands. It was Serac's next words that rankled his sanity.

"If I die, Caeris will know it was you. He loves me like a brother. And you? You are just an upstart. A peasant. You were not there to support him when he was forced to shoulder the responsibilities of a king. You were not there when his father fell ill. He knows you hate me, that you are jealous of my influence, my prestige."

"He will not know."

"Oh, he will. And he will know Eva was part of it. You will both be hunted and executed for treason. You will never be safe. Your friends? Dead. Your family? Dead. Your allies? Dead. Dead. Dead."

"You lie. You do not have that power, especially from the grave."

"You think to use the dagger to influence me, or Caeris? You don't know what it is, do you? I don't know why the Goddess thinks you are such a threat. You are just a lucky fool who happened to come across an enchanted dagger."

Serac's insight into Illiah's mind was a bitter, swift poison.

"How did you know about the dagger?" Illiah asked.

"The Goddess told me. She wants you dead, you know. How you survived this long with a target on your back is beyond me."

"Luck, I guess," Illiah hissed.

Serac raised a mocking brow at him. "Well, are you going to kill me and send your lady-love to the executioner? And your serving boy? Your foster brother? They will all die if you kill me." Then he shrugged. "It is your choice."

Illiah's heart pounded. Doubt eclipsed his need for vengeance. His past victories had made him bold, confident. He saw the world from the perspective of a man who held an enchanted dagger. In his mind, he was unstoppable, untouchable. He had been wrong. He had been a fool. He could not risk his loved ones for his own vanity. Serac was right. Damn him, he was right. But still, the dagger wanted blood.

Illiah pounced on his quarry, his knee pressed against Serac's injury, his arm across Serac's chest making Serac immobile. Serac gasped, his eyes bulging in fear. Illiah used his dagger to carve three long lines into Serac's skin, just below his ribs. He did it slowly. One for Mila, one for Eva, and one for good measure. Serac flinched and wriggled, attempting escape, but Illiah used all his weight against him, and he had the dagger. The dagger hummed, hot in his hands, hot as thick, fresh blood. Satisfied with his artistry, Illiah stepped back. Serac slumped over, his eyes rolled back into his head, passed out from the pain. Coward.

Illiah cleaned his dagger and hid it back in its sheath.

CHAPTER 36

ILLIAH

THE CITY HAD CHANGED. Illiah heard it in passing conversations as he walked back to the alley where Penn was waiting, tethered patiently. A soulful lament carried across the square - faint, not quite disguised by the clucking of huddled gossipers already clothed in the black of mourning. Illiah pushed his pace harder.

He attired himself once more like a prince; his sword he wore openly. He did not expect a challenge as he rode Penn through the city (which was remarkably faster than on foot) and there was none. The people watched him pass. Some called out to him. He met their eyes with a nod here and there in acknowledgment, but he did not slow down.

Caeris would be with their father, of that Illiah had no doubt.

Two guards stood at attention outside the door to the dead king's chambers. They nodded gravely, opening the door for him.

The king's room was dim. Caeris sat next to the bed, his head bowed, a boy-like presence in the empty room. The body of his father lay on the bed where he had spent much of his remaining years. Rhais looked asleep, propped up by the pillows, a single white rose placed upon his chest.

"Caeris," Illiah whispered into the grief-filled room. Caeris looked up slowly, as if coming up from a deep memory. Illiah had no desire to disturb his brother's mourning, but what he had to say could not wait.

"Illiah," Caeris said, rising, a trace of a smile on his lips. He took several tired steps across the room to greet Illiah, pulling him into an embrace. He had not lost his brother's affection - yet.

"How did you know to come? The messengers left not an hour ago to carry the news throughout the realm," Caeris said, but his eyes narrowed as he looked Illiah over. "I thought we agreed you would keep the beard so we wouldn't confuse the subjects?" A ghost of a smile played on his lips, though there was no humor in his eyes.

Illiah took a deep breath. He glanced at the body of their father, wishing he could just grieve alongside his brother. If he had listened to his heart months ago, he could have prevented so much grief.

"I didn't come here because of Father. I didn't even know he was so close to death," Illiah admitted. "I came here for another reason. I came here to apologize."

Caeris nodded, as if expecting it. "Think nothing of it, brother. Eva's deviation was not your fault. If our places had been reversed, I can't say I wouldn't have done the same if she had come to my chambers at night."

Illiah's gut tightened. He knew Caeris had never loved Eva, but he hadn't known his brother thought her desirable. He didn't like it. It was irritating how Caeris laid the guilt entirely on Eva, as if Illiah had not been a willing participant. And how did Caeris know the specifics of that night?

"Did you love her?" Illiah heard himself ask.

Caeris shook his head. "No. She and I never really got along well. She is beautiful, though."

"I should have come sooner. I should have come right away. I wanted to tell you that I love Eva. I intend to marry her," Illiah said, watching his brother's face closely. "I didn't know you would find out about that night. I didn't think she would come to any retribution."

"You love her?" Caeris asked, his voice incredulous. Illiah swallowed his annoyance. His brother was now king. If Illiah were smart, he would keep his mouth shut. At least some of the time.

"I do. We planned to speak to you," Illiah lied smoothly.

Caeris looked thoughtful, and then turned to his dead father.

"Father would have been pleased. He loved Lord Finnan like a brother. He loved Eva like a daughter. I would be pleased to grant you her hand in marriage."

Illiah had not expected the force of his relief. It was a gust of warm summer wind. Not that he needed his brother's permission, but he was already short on allies.

"You need not worry about your reputation. Eva's dalliance was not made public. Only Clarette knows the truth. I told the court that the engagement was off because she wished to join the Temple and serve the Goddess," Caeris said with amusement. He had known of Eva's aversion to the Goddess. He had wanted to punish her.

"That was kind of you," Illiah forced the words out. He cared nothing for his reputation, but at least Caeris had not slandered and humiliated Eva. He only sent her to the Temple in the hands of a rapist. Again, Illiah held his tongue with great effort.

"I will send a guard to the Temple to request that Serac bring her back to the palace. Lord Serac hasn't been feeling well of late, but I will need him here to help prepare for Father's wake."

"There is no need for that," Illiah said curtly.

Caeris gave him a questioning look, which turned accusative. "You impersonated me at the Temple. That is why you shaved your beard." Caeris looked ready to spit fire. Is that what Illiah looked like when he was angry?

"I heard Eva was in the Temple. I know she is terrified of the place. How could I walk right by and not retrieve her? I knew they would obey you without question."

"Just don't do it again." It was the command of the king and Illiah nodded, trying to look humbled.

With that unpleasant business aside, Illiah could sit beside his father, which wasn't any more pleasant. The dead man before him had been a stranger. He had some pleasant, short memories with him, and now he was gone.

The old man's face was lined and sunken, his mouth no longer turned up with pain, as it had been last time Illiah had seen him. King Rhais was at peace. Illiah took the dead man's hand in his. It was cold, but not yet fully stiff. The fingers were long and shaped like his own. Illiah had sat next to many dead bodies, some whom he loved better than the king. He had thought, once, that it would get easier with practice. It didn't.

Caeris returned to his seat on the opposite side of the bed, taking the other hand of the king.

Caeris talked. He told stories of their father, of his childhood. He talked and talked until his throat was hoarse and tears fell from his face, landing lightly upon the dead. Illiah was not strong enough that tears did not mark his cheeks. He appreciated his brother's candor. It was unlike the Caeris he knew. Grief had softened his brother, at least for the moment.

The stories Caeris told painted a picture of a kind, wise man who loved his son, his late queen, and his realm intensely. A good father, a good king.

Caeris fell silent. They sat absorbed in their own thoughts. The air shifted, as if a long-held breath had been released, the end of a lamenting sigh. The hairs on Illiah's arms rose, but it was not an unpleasant sensation.

"I am glad you are here, Illiah," Caeris said at length. "You are my family, my brother. I am glad you are here," he repeated.

Illiah nodded, standing up. His legs were stiff. He put a hand on Caeris's shoulder as he turned to leave.

"I will see you and Eva at dinner. I will announce your intention. It will be good, I think, to have a wedding, even if it is not mine. The people will be sad. Perhaps it will bring them joy."

"Thank you, Caeris," Illiah said. It was a kind thought.

CHAPTER 37

EVA

THE SOUND OF TALKING MEN roused Eva from her dreams. Among the bad dreams, one had been almost good. In the dream, Caeris and Illiah talked about her. Illiah asked for Eva's hand in marriage. The king was there, watching over his two sons, but he was cold, pale, eternally still.

Eva woke with Rhais's voice in her head, the faintest of whispers, *my daughter.* She heard it as a sigh. A breeze caressed her face.

The men's voices became loud and real as Eva moved from the space between her dreams and wakefulness.

She opened her eyes. The sun was getting low. Two figures stood on the edge of the clearing, their identical brown cloaks tinged red by the low sun. Kaile and Illiah.

Illiah's face looked more like Caeris without his beard, but she knew him as him, beard or no beard. Fear had clouded her perception; she should have known him immediately at the Temple.

He sensed her gaze and looked over at her, his eyes calm, his expression unreadable.

"Go on ahead, Kaile. We'll catch up," Illiah said, not taking his eyes off Eva's. Kaile nodded, mounting Helti, riding off with a parting wink in Eva's direction.

Eva sat straight, pushing herself up on shaking arms. Her heartbeat was that of a grounded bird.

"You came for me," she said, her voice thick.

"Too late."

"Far too late."

Illiah said nothing.

"Mahone is dead," Eva said, rising to her feet. "I watched Serac butcher him." She didn't know what else to say. Anger was easy, unreasonable as it was, even cruel.

"I know," he said softly. Too softly.

"Illiah, what have I done?"

"Eva!" His voice was edged. Eva preferred his anger to his pity. She didn't deserve pity. "You are not at fault here."

"That is not how it feels."

"Eva -"

"You are only marrying me out of guilt." Why couldn't he stop her from talking? She was going to ruin everything. Her words were dipped in poison.

"What are you talking about?"

"Kaile said it was the only way to keep me safe. I know you, Illiah. You protect people. You love being a hero."

"You say it like it's a bad thing."

"Sometimes it can be. People come to rely on you, and then you are not there."

"Don't. Please."

"If you loved me, you would not have let me go that night. You would never have sent me away."

Eva couldn't look at him. She knew her words would cut him, hurt him. She didn't want to acknowledge her own cruelty. "I don't want to be your wife." The words slipped out in her guilt-ridden anger.

Silence.

"I-I want you to love me. Just that." Eva pushed the words into the gaping silence between them. They were vulnerable words, and her tears came with them, and her hopes and her dreams.

"Eva, I do love you." Illiah's arms wrapped around her, strong and perfect. Whole. Real joy trickled around the dead, grief-filled veins of her heart.

He stepped back from her. In his hand was his strange dagger. His eyes were desolate, not exactly empty, but lost and yearning.

"This is no ordinary dagger," he sounded defeated.

Eva took the weapon in her hand. The dagger was light, smooth, warm. Alive. She could sense the *simul rami* running through it. Her stomach dropped. The vercuri. She had sensed it all along but not recognized it. She had been too distracted by her attraction to its master. Eva would bet her life Tayeh knew Illiah had the vercuri.

"Illiah, I think this is why the creature in the forest was after you," she said after a deep breath.

Illiah didn't look exactly comfortable with the idea, but he didn't look shocked either.

"What does it do?" she asked.

"It forces my will, my desires onto others. It gives me strength and stealth. It made me a hero." The last word was mud in his mouth.

"I can feel its magic," Eva said smiling up at Illiah. He was not smiling. Her smile fell, dying a small death.

"Don't you see, Eva?" Illiah stated. "I was sure you had been influenced by the dagger, by me - not intentionally. I thought you didn't love me, not really. I see now that I may have been wrong and it kills me. What happened to you happened because of this - tool - because of my ignorance. And because I love you, desperately."

"You allowed me into your bed believing I didn't really love you?" Eva continued. "That I was giving myself to you because of some magical dagger?"

"Please, forgive my weakness."

Eva fingered the dagger. It looked like it was made of stone, but it had grains and lines like wood. Cendari wood. Like her pendant. A fallen cendari branch carved into the nine vercuri …

"Eva, this dagger influenced my little brother," Illiah continued, his voice so full of guilt Eva opened her mouth to protest. "Wait. Listen. During the war, I would lie awake at night, holding the dagger, wishing some brave soul would step forward and volunteer to sneak into enemy territory - basically a suicide mission. I was desperate for information, but I could not bring myself to send a man to his death. Then one morning, Aralis was gone. I learned he had done just that, left to spy on the enemy … The dagger is the reason Aralis is dead." Illiah's voice caught. "He was not a reckless boy. He would never have left on his own accord."

"Illiah," Eva wrapped one hand around his. His fingers laced with hers like she was his lifeline. "You never knew your brother's mind. Maybe he left so you wouldn't go yourself - I am sure you considered it."

"I did." The weight of the world pulled Illiah's eyes away from hers.

"After that, why didn't you get rid of the dagger?" she asked.

"I tired to destroy it, but I couldn't. It doesn't burn. It's impervious to steel or force. And I couldn't abandon it - if someone else found it …"

Eva pulled him close. His arms came around her, tight, full of need. The vercuri fell to the ground between them. "The dagger did not make you a hero," Eva told him. "Your heart did - does."

"Eva," Illiah said, "I was afraid. I need you, and it is terrifying. I want you. I love you. The wife thing is just formality." Eva heard a smile in his voice and pressed her face against his chest, drying her tears on his shirt.

"I love you too," Eva said after a moment. "And I'm sorry for being … difficult. You really don't deserve it."

"Are you sure about that?" Illiah asked with a hint of his roguish nature. He kissed her mouth firmly. Eva melted, her senses momentarily jumbled. Home. Illiah felt like home. Smelled like home. Tasted like home. A home that, until now, she had never known but that she had been homesick for, for a long, long time. Illiah pulled back from her once more, his eyes serious.

"Are you okay?" he asked, brushing a lock of hair from her bruised face. "Did Serac - did he hurt you?"

Eva's smile widened. The simplest touch of Illiah's finger was precious to her. She leaned into his hand. "Not really. He tried, but I had my knife in my boot, and I stabbed him right there." She pointed to the tender spot just below Illiah's navel. Illiah grinned at her.

"Remind me to search you, always." Illiah gave a little laugh. His thoughts turned, and he stiffened. "I went to kill Serac, but I couldn't. He threatened me. Us. Our future. I cannot risk losing you. But I don't know how I can live knowing he beat us."

"He did not beat us. He will never beat us. His day will come, somehow. Perhaps he was not yours to kill."

They stood silent, together. The wind rustled the grass. The little fire crackled, gnawing at a pinecone. The smoke blew into Eva's nose. It smelled sweet and comforting.

"Can you use the dagger to influence Serac?" Eva asked her lover. She liked thinking of Illiah as her lover.

"I might be able to. I do plan to try. But he knows about it, what it does. The same way he knew about us. Crea told him about it."

"He is no ordinary man. He has Crea's blood in his veins - at least that is what he told me. Which means you do too."

Illiah groaned. Eva agreed it was not a pleasant thought.

Illiah moved, reaching into his pocket for something, and held it out for her. Eva clutched her pendant without hesitation.

"I thought I had lost that. Wherever did you find it?"

Illiah looked sheepish. "I found it in the stables after you left. It was then that I knew I had to get you back."

Goose prickles tickled Eva's skin, making her shiver. She felt something bigger and wiser than herself. She looped the pendant over her neck and the little leaf nestled between her breasts. Illiah watched her, his eyes lingering.

"Illiah …" Eva began, then faltered.

"What is it?"

"Something is coming. Something dangerous and beyond our understanding. I think it has to do with magic," Eva said.

"I can not deny that I have felt it … that day in the forest …"

"Yes … The Guardians told me if Caeris and I have a son, that boy would be destined to fulfill a prophecy. A child of two thrones who will bring balance and peace to the realms."

"Two thrones?'

"My mother was royalty," Eva reminded him.

"Right - the hair," Illiah said, pulling a strand of her hair through his fingers.

"This is serious, Illiah!" Eva told him, swatting his hand. "A son of ours would also fulfill that prophecy,"

Illiah caught her hand and wrapped his arms around her again. "Don't worry, Eva. Any child of ours would be just that - ours. No prophecy can change that."

Eva closed her eyes against his chest and listened to his steady heartbeat.

"So, being your wife, does it mean I have to give you back Sasha?" Eva asked.

"Yes. Absolutely. That was completely out of guilt," Illiah assured her, making her laugh in disbelief. "There are many ways you have to appease me as your husband." His eyes were nothing but mischievous.

"Right," Eva murmured sarcastically through lips pressed firmly against those of her lord.

A long, sunlit moment later, Illiah spoke. "This pains me more than you will ever know, but we really must get back. King Caeris is planning a grand announcement in our honor this evening at dinner, one hour from now." Illiah announced it as if he had just remembered. He held Eva at arm's length, his hand lightly touching her bruised cheek. His green eyes were clear, almost peaceful. "And you look like you were tumbling about in the grass with some random by-blow, so we best get you back to the palace, clean you up a bit." The humor was the Illiah Eva knew so well. He was grinning at her, and she at him, although she couldn't help but smack his shoulder playfully anyhow. He kissed her again.

"I like this," he decided.

"Come on, 'random by-blow,' let's go. We really must be short for time if you are insisting we get going," she said, taking his hand. She could throw around veiled insults too. Illiah laughed.

Illiah picked up the vercuri, sliding it into his boot before mounting up on Penn, gesturing for Eva to sit in front of him. She barely fit with all her skirts. Illiah's arm came around her, holding her close, his other hand guiding the horse. Eva wondered how such a simple thing could feel so right, so comforting.

As they rode, Illiah told Eva how he met Tarek on the road, which Eva had already heard from Kaile. In turn, Eva told Illiah of her capture and Mahone's death. Illiah gave her a little squeeze, his chin resting momentarily on her shoulder.

"That was not our fault, Eva," Illiah whispered in her ear. "Mahone was proud to die for you, I know he was. Serac would have found a way to get you, one way or another. He is dangerous, and he is used to getting what he wants. Mahone would have always stood in the way. It was his job, and he did it willingly." Illiah's voice broke. "Kaile told me once that I should not spend my lifetime thinking about the pain and guilt of the past. He is right. I think - I think it would poison the love we have found in each other. Mahone would never have wanted that. We both need to forgive ourselves, and live life well. That is the best way to honor the fallen."

Illiah's arm tightened around Eva as her body heaved with silent sobs. But this time, her tears were not all for the dead. Happiness settled in her heart. Her soul had found its way home.

EVA

THE ACRID SMELL OF DEATH filled the air. The fire burned hotter than any other. Those gathered pressed against the edges of the square in a vain attempt to escape its heat.

The timber had been dry, drenched with oil. The fire caught and spread quickly. The flames stretched up into the black night sky, calling to the stars above, its kin. Beyond the fire was nothing. The darkness of the night swallowed every building. Every torch and lantern was extinguished next to the funeral pyre of the king.

Illiah's face was bathed in the reflection of the flames, his profile identical to his brother who stood beside him. His eyes were black and shadowed with memories. He had seen death many times. He had seen countless bodies, enemies and friends, consumed by the fire after the battle. Only Eva could see the pain his memories caused him. She had her own relationship with death and fire, but tonight she would not allow it to influence her. She gripped Illiah's hand, turning her attention back to the fire.

The body of the old king was invisible now under the flames. The flames were eager, alive, calling to Eva's *sanarii* magic, promising visions. The *simul rami* pulsed through the flames and Eva couldn't help but reach for it. She steadied herself against Illiah, knowing no one would notice if she fell into a trance.

The vision that came to her from the devouring flames was unexpected. Eva was beginning to learn that what she saw would seem random, but someday she would know the reason for it, or so she hoped. So it had been with her visions of Illiah. She knew now he was part of her, part of her soul.

The fire and night dissolved into a daylit place. The sun was bright, a contrast to the night her consciousness suddenly left. She was shown mountains, tall and imposing. A tall peak dominated the horizon, a huge, tooth like mountain of rock, spiraling up to kiss the blue sky. At the mountain's roots was a great river, wide and slow. Its silty water was gray and heavy with spring rains. A great city stood along its bank.

At the foot of the city was a port. Countless ships docked along the river, bobbing in the water as the current worried them in their berths. Boats small and swift for fishing, large barges for hauling ore. People worked among and on the myriad of ships, and also Kitarrans, tall and lean, fierce and proud, fur glistening in the sun, tails outstretched.

The city rose from the river against the mountain, like a child hiding against the folds of its mother's skirts. At the top of the cascading city was a palace built of white stone, nestled against the green forest of the mountain side. The palace reflected the sun like a flake of gold in the sand. The flags upon its battlements were black in mourning. Had their queen died as well? Or perhaps her consort. Eva couldn't remember if the queen had a husband.

The vision shifted. Eva was inside the palace. A Kitarran woman stood by the window with her eyes closed, letting the sun warm her face. Her fur was gray, or rather silver. A great sadness hung over her, yet she cried no tears. Eva wondered if Kitarrans could not cry, or was it only the status of the Kitarran that forbade the weakness of tears, for surely, she was royalty. It was writ in her bearing, in the stubborn pride etched on her face.

A voice roused the Kitarran woman. Her eyes flashed open, a pale, piercing green.

"My queen!" The voice shook in urgency.

The queen turned slowly.

"What is it?" Her voice was tired, as if there was no news that could bring her from her despair.

"He lives, the babe - the boy lives!"

Like the dead awakened, the change that came over the queen was the impossible made real. Her eyes became wide, full of hope. She crossed the space between her and the messenger in one swift movement, gripping the other Kitarran by the forearms. Her long fingers ended in delicate but sharp claws, digging into the muscles of the messenger.

"Where is he? Where is my son?" she said in a fierce whisper. The messenger showed no sign of discomfort as he stood, taller than her, but somehow diminished next to the fierce presence of this queen.

"I-I don't know."

"Find him, by the Spirits of the Trees, by the Allmakers of the Forest, find him!" Her voice was tremulous with hope and a terrible fear.

The uncomfortable heat of the fire and the lingering smells of the funereal pyre enveloped Eva once more. Despite the heat, Eva shivered. The vision was gone. The daylight, the spring sunshine, was replaced by the blackness of the moonless night.

Eva sighed, holding the vision in her mind. With her limited knowledge of Kitarra, she could only speculate how the vision of a faroff queen could possibly relate to her. It was unclear what had happened, except there had been death. And life. She remembered her friend Emri, from when the Kitarrans visited Caer Andri. The vivacious young warrior who wed the prince, the queen's son. Was there only one prince of Kitarra? Eva could not recall. Tayeh had told her many tales over the years, but the everyday business of Kitarra was a mystery to her. She had never heard from Emri since that summer. Kitarra was so very far away.

Apparently, Eva was not good at vigils. She suppressed her urge to fidget, but her feet began to ache. She caught herself wiggling, earning a look of reproach from the young king who stood just beyond Illiah.

"Is it okay if I go?" Eva whispered in Illiah's ear. Others had already retreated into the night. Only the dead king's sons were required by the Goddess to stand vigil until daybreak. At the first lightening of the sky on the third day after the body's death was when the spirit was said to leave. The flames were intended to speed that divine spark to where it was that spirits go.

Illiah gave her a brief kiss in answer. She dropped his hand, pulling her cloak about her. Stepping away from the fire was like being swallowed by the night.

Darys helped her mount up onto Sasha's tall back before settling onto his own horse. They rode together back to the palace, a short journey usually made on foot, but Illiah was loath to be vulnerable on the streets.

Darys saw her to her room and left her. A guard stood at her door, a man she didn't know very well, but he had spent the winter at the Keep. Illiah trusted him completely, so Eva did too. He gave her a respectful bow and closed the door behind her.

Eva lay in bed. Sleep was elusive despite her fatigue. Her mind kept turning over and over with thoughts of the future. She found herself thinking of her and Illiah's children, should they be blessed to have them. She realized if Caeris did not wed soon and father a legitimate heir, if she and Illiah were to have a son, their son would be heir to Jullayah.

She imagined their children running around the Keep, a daughter with streaming white hair and green eyes, running to her father in the council room, sneaking off into the forest with her friends. Such thoughts made Eva smile, but also made her fearful. To be a mother would be a task indeed. She fell asleep and dreamed fitfully of chasing children around the Keep - and losing them in the dark passageways and many rooms.

(

Eva's heart swelled at the sight of her home. Their home.

A black ball of feathers collided into her, squawking and clinging to Eva's shoulder. Illiah laughed so hard, Penn decided he needed to jump. Eva soothed her raven friend, promising him that she was never leaving him again. Calypso chirped and nipped her ear before taking off once more. He really was too big to sit comfortably on her shoulder.

The Keep gleamed silver in the summer sun that sparkled off the glazed windows. The tall trees of the Great Forest swayed above in the warm breeze, echoing the movement of the lord's flag, which had been raised when the scout brought the message of their imminent arrival.

Men and women worked in the pasture, raising fences, tending to animals. They paused and bowed as their lord and lady passed. Illiah grinned and waved back.

The industrious work in the courtyard came to a halt as they rode in. Everyone set down their tasks to welcome them, a small crowd full of familiar faces.

Illiah and Eva dismounted quickly, and Tarran took their horses' reins so they could greet their people. Mila swept Eva into a quick embrace.

"You heard the news?" Eva asked.

"Of course we did! My lady," Mila exclaimed.

Many excited congratulations ensued. Scrub announced a grand feast for the next day, begging their pardon, he really needed an extra day to prepare as this one would be a night to remember. Eva's new family embraced her. Lindin and Freya grinned their approval of their brother's choice. Family. They welcomed her as family. Illiah couldn't stop smiling.

Once all had wished them well and welcomed them home, Mila pulled Eva aside, her face sad.

"Tarek is waiting for you in the council room. I managed to talk him into staying, at least until you came back."

Eva's heart tightened in anticipation of another farewell, which warred with the relief she felt at Mila's words. She had been afraid Tarek would leave without saying goodbye, as Illiah had feared. Eva went to the council room immediately.

Tarek was not in the council room, but the door to the garden was open. Eva knew it was where he waited. The little garden was bathed in green shadow. The ferns were lush, the moss a cascade across almost every stone. Tarek was almost invisible against the green in his bland traveling clothes. He looked up at she entered, his face haggard, his hair lank, but he smiled at her.

"Tarek," Eva whispered. She wished she could find the right words for him, to speak of the sorrow of her heart, the guilt she felt, the relief to see him alive. But no words were necessary. Tarek engulfed her in his arms and Eva drew him close. She could feel his pain through the tremors as his arms gripped her.

"Oh, Tarek, I am so sorry," Eva sobbed, her grief suddenly anew. She couldn't help herself.

"Shh. It's not your fault. He was proud to die for you, as I would have been should the place have been mine. It was our duty. I just miss him so much," he added, taking a deep breath. He stood back, assessing her. "Are you okay? Are you hurt? When I heard Serac had taken you-" His voice was a low growl.

"I am fine. Serac didn't touch me. I stabbed him with my knife."

Tarek's brows rose in amusement, but the humor was almost instantly replaced by lines of grief.

"Wasn't a long-enough knife, though. He was still alive last time I checked," Eva added. Tarek looped his arm over her shoulder, and they sat down on the bench together, side by side.

"Mila said you are leaving. Leaving where?"

Tarek took a deep breath. "I am going north. To the Midlands."

"Tarek, no! You can't."

"I can't stay in Jullayah. Serac will make sure every town knows my face and name. Every step I take I will be looking over my shoulder. There is nothing for me here."

"But the Midlands? You know nothing of that place."

"Regardless, that is where I am headed." His voice was that of a lost child, steeped in sadness. Eva had been that child once.

Eva frowned, wishing some wisdom would come to her to help convince him otherwise, but none did.

"I wish I could change your mind," she said instead.

Tarek shook his head sadly.

"I can't stay here," he said, looking around as if the walls, even the cracks of the stone held ghosts none but he could see. "I can't ... Already I have stayed too long. My heart yearns to flee this place, and the memories in every corridor, every tower. I know that makes me a coward. I only came back because I needed to make sure you were safe, and loved, and that you befell no harm."

Eva sighed deeply. Tarek echoed it with a slow exhale.

"I will miss you," Eva said quietly, her voice unsteady.

"And I you, Eva."

☾

Tarran was successfully inconspicuous. Eva would have been content to go alone into the fall forest, but Tarran insisted - to the point of begging - on trailing her. He claimed he needed to work on his shadowing, but Eva was pretty sure he was an expert already. She could not see or sense him anywhere. The boy had uncanny skills.

The fall leaves were deep in their transition to winter. A sneeze could lift them from their tenuous clutch upon the branches. Eva wanted to enjoy them before they fell. She wouldn't be gone long; Illiah asked for her help assessing the latest bunch of recruits. She promised him it would be just a quick ride. Calypso joined her, darting from one tree to another. Every so often a drum-like trill would echo down to her.

The golden birches gave way to the tall evergreen trees of the Great Forest where once, an age ago, the road led toward Allati. The gate still stood, made of trees and magic and cowardice.

She paused to look into the gate: the chink of the cliff where only shadows grew, and sunlight could not penetrate, where she had said farewell to Tarek some weeks earlier.

Sasha stamped his foot and tossed his head, signaling his unease. Eva ignored his misgivings and dismounted, letting his reins drop to the ground. The horse would not move from his spot. He was well trained. Calypso's glossy feathers glinted as he glided through the trees and into the looming crevice, lost in the blackness.

A shadow within the shadows caught Eva's eye. It was not the raven. Something akin to the *simul rami* tickled her senses, urging her to follow Calypso. The narrow walls of the cliff rose on either side of her, dim light surrounding her. The air changed. The path was steep, but soon enough Eva emerged into the Great Forest proper. The familiar landscape of huge trees and moss floors embraced her.

The strange shadow was a creature, almost like a mouse, but bigger. It darted into the giant twisting roots of a tree for reassurance before turning its bright eyes on Eva. More creatures appeared, from behind trees and ferns, gathering around her.

They were tentative at first, staying close to the roots of the trees, out of the sunlight. They watched Eva with strange eyes, eyes dark as night, eyes livid as an eagle, eyes faint and mysterious like a snake. Eva could sense the magic in them. She could see the magic in the shift of their form, the changing of foot to claw to root. But it was not alarming. Unlike the wanderer, this magic felt right - if not altogether safe.

Eva gazed from strange face to strange face. For the first time in the Great Forest, she felt unnerved, vulnerable. The creatures watched her with great interest. Their magic called to hers like a long-lost sister.

They crept slowly toward her. Eva could not count them. Pressed close together as they were, she could hardly make out one from the other. Their strange flickering expressions were unreadable and not wholly safe. A fluttering of warning and danger rippled through her. She wanted to run, but couldn't. Magic called to magic and held her rooted.

A white form suddenly came from nowhere, or everywhere. Lula-nan bounded in a fox but stood up tall as a woman. She appeared to grow both in size and stature, gazing around the circle of encroaching creatures. She hissed low in her throat, a command and warning. They slunk back into the green shadows, back into the trees and the moss. The connection vanished. Eva was alone with the Guardian.

Lula regarded her with a wondrous expression. Before Eva could ask for an explanation, Tayeh dissolved from sunlight.

"What just happened?" Eva asked them.

"Magic. They sense the strong presence of magic," Lula whispered.

"My magic?" Eva asked, wondering what could have possibly changed. Magic had always been in her blood. Why would the creatures choose that moment to acknowledge it?

"Yours-"

"And his," Tayeh finished, cutting Lula's words with his. His hand hovered above Eva's navel, his eyes full of a strange light. Tayeh nodded, a slow smile spreading across his features, his sharp canine teeth showing. "Your son."

A strong emotion swallowed Eva's tongue. Not joy - joy was loud and fleeting. This was perilous, precious, everlasting. A moment could change everything. A second. A word. This moment changed her life. Her heart was no longer beating for herself, but for her child. Her son. The child of the prophecy.

"Go tell your man," Lula suggested, her fox eyes dancing.

"Now what, Kitarran?" Lulanan asked her companion. "Your plan worked after all. The two are together. The boy will be born. The child of Kitarra. He fits your precious prophecy, does he not?"

Tayeh nodded as he took a deep breath. His heart, old as it was, was infused with hope, pride, and excitement, but also a terrible sadness.

"Now? Nothing. Soon? We must break her heart." His voice was a pained whisper. "For through her pain, her sacrifice, another could be saved. Another whom Kitarra needs almost as much as it needs the child."

PART TWO

TAYEH'S PROPHECY

~ FIVE YEARS LATER ~

CHAPTER 38

ILLIAH

ILLIAH PROWLED the high battlements of the Keep like a caged beast. Below him, above him, around him was a blanketing mist. Every breath was thick and moist. What he was hoping to see through the mist, he couldn't tell. The dawn had called to him, and he had no answer for it.

The damp made Illiah shiver. Perhaps it was the dreary weather that caused his unease, or the list of tasks in his mind that ebbed and flowed but never fully dissolved. Whatever the reason, Illiah could not sleep. He knew better than to disregard such feelings. They were instinctual and had served him well on many occasions.

Misty mornings fell heavily and often enough around the Keep in late fall. The dense air made signals hard to see or hear. The guard tower was all but invisible. If he were to plan an attack against the Keep, it would be on a morning such as this.

He shook his head to dispel his paranoid thoughts. No one would storm the Keep. They were not at war. He had enemies, but none so bold as to attack his fortress.

The weather was foul, but he admitted, ruefully, the unease likely stemmed from the argument with Eva the night before. Eva, his dear wife, the mother of his son, the one person who could somehow disrupt all thought and reason. The one person he loved like no other, who could infuriate him like no other and hurt him to his core like no other.

Rhyl had been asleep. Illiah had just recently returned from Caer Andri, so he and Eva should have been making love, making up for lost time. He had missed her. She had missed him. They hated being apart.

Instead, they had argued and gone to sleep in fitful silence.

When he left to feed his restless thoughts, Eva had been sleeping, her pale hair surrounding her face like a halo in the dim light of their chambers, her bare shoulders peeking out under the heavy feather blanket. He had longed to touch her, to wake her, to make it right. He wanted desperately to fix the troubled look in her eyes. But he didn't know how.

It wasn't that she was mad at him, nor he at her. Not really. It was just hard. Eva yearned for another child. She wanted Rhyl to have a sibling, a little brother or sister. She had grown up alone. She saw how close Illiah was with his foster siblings and knew the joy of a large family. Rhyl was four years old, almost five. Eva despaired of getting pregnant again. She claimed it shouldn't take so long. Will's wife already had three wee ones. Talamir and Freya were expecting - again. Babies abounded at the Keep.

Illiah was at a loss as how to help Eva. The desire for another child didn't consume him the way it did her. He had no maternal instinct that called to him.

Eva blamed him for being away too much. It was the fuel that sparked the argument, ignited the hurt. Illiah did not want to be gone from the Keep, but he was needed in Caer Andri as well. And he couldn't bring Eva and Rhyl with him.

Eva refused to go to Caer Andri, and Illiah agreed with her decision. When Serac saw Rhyl for the first time as a babe, his slithery gaze had been full of wanting. Rhyl showed no indication he had inherited Eva's magic as well as her features, but Eva remained certain he had.

Serac made Illiah's sword arm itch. Time had not been his ally in his war against his cousin. His influence was thin with the Temple master. The dagger did not obviously affect Serac. Or Caeris. Illiah had no leverage with his twin brother. Eva speculated their shared blood had something to do with the dagger's ineffectiveness. No, he wouldn't - couldn't - take Eva and Rhyl to Caer Andri. They were safer at the Keep.

Illiah sighed deeply, breathing in the moist, mossy air that still held no answers for him. He pulled his cloak about his neck and retreated into the Keep.

His eyes acclimated to the dim light quickly. He knew the Keep intimately. The dark, twisting passageways held no challenge for him. He opened the door to his chamber quietly, not wishing to wake his family if they were still sleeping.

Eva was no longer in bed. Voices echoed from the bathing room. By the sound of Rhyl's little voice, he was already bouncing around his mother with his exuberant energy.

Rhyl bounded out of the bathing room and clambered loudly over to Illiah, wrapping his small arms around Illiah's leg, laughing as he sat on Illiah's foot. The familiar feelings of love and pride filled Illiah as he beheld his young son.

Illiah pried Rhyl off his foot, grabbing him playfully. Rhyl squirmed and squealed, trying with gleeful desperation to get out of his father's grasp. Illiah launched him onto the big, cushioned bed. Rhyl's peals and shrieks of laughter echoed through the room while Illiah tickled him mercilessly.

"Mummy said I get to go with you today," the boy said when Illiah finally let him breathe. Rhyl's words sometimes still slurred and muddled together, but his speech was getting more and more grown-up every day.

"Really? Mummy said that?" Illiah said, glancing at his wife cautiously as she came out of the bathing room.

Eva regarded him solemnly. There would be no smiles from her this morning, especially not for him. At least she came and sat next to him on the bed, a conciliating gesture. He took a deep breath. He could not be angry with her. She was just tired and upset. She needed space.

"Can we practice bow and arrows?" Rhyl asked at his most charming, his head tilted, his large eyes devouring their favorite prey: his father's resolve. Rhyl's charm was compounding - a hint of smile turned Eva's lips. Illiah nodded. "Of course, we can."

"Thank you, Illiah," Eva said.

"Don't get lost in the mist," Illiah teased, satisfied as her smile widened and reached her eyes.

"Oh, it will lift quickly from the Great Forest. It'll leave behind little drops of water and the Forest will be beautiful," Eva told him with more softness in her voice. "I'll be back after lunch." She gave

Rhyl a kiss and brushed her lips briefly against Illiah's, washing away the last residue of tension between them. She grabbed her cloak from the hook and was out the door with a last wave and a sad smile.

Usually, Rhyl trailing him around the Keep was a surefire way to accomplish nothing. But there were times when Illiah could sacrifice his time with his men for his son. He welcomed those days. And as the lad grew, it would be easier to incorporate more time with Rhyl into his day. He planned to teach him everything he knew, though Rhyl claimed to know it all already.

After a quick breakfast in the kitchen, Illiah bundled Rhyl up and took him out to the practice yard where the men and a fresh group of trainees were working.

Rhyl never ceased to be amazed, eyes wide, as he watched the young men. One group was working with broadswords in well-fashioned lines, moving through their morning routines. Most were adorned with grim expressions as the task challenged them. Another group shot arrows at targets. A smaller, third group was talking softly to Kaile, the recruits Illiah had selected for specialized training.

"Good morning, my lord," Irri said with a respectful nod. "And you, my young lord," he said, bowing to Rhyl who squirmed under the recognition.

After Illiah wed Eva and his list of enemies grew, he recruited some men to form his own personal guard. They were boys really, orphans and street kids of Caer Andri. Illiah had offered them a life beyond the streets and had earned their loyalty in return. Irri was one of Illiah's first street boys to come to the Keep. He was growing into a fine man and was one of Illiah's most loyal men-at-arms.

"Good morning, Irri," Illiah said. "Just the man I was looking for. The morning's mist is lingering, making me uneasy. I need you to send some more guards to the outer posts and place three more guards on the turrets."

Irri nodded, his gray eyes glinting. "Why are you uneasy, my lord?" Illiah's men were bolder than some. Illiah respected their curiosity, as long as they were impeccable at following orders, or had an excellent reason not to.

"I don't know. It's just a feeling. I have learned not to underestimate such gut feelings. It's likely nothing, but it's good practice for the men anyhow."

With another nod, Irri went about his task.

Illiah took Rhyl's hand as they went about his morning rounds, checking on the progress of the men - and women.

Kota was hard at work in the smithy, her apprentice quietly obedient. Illiah didn't begrudge him the task. But the young man seemed to manage Kota's volatile nature well. Not many could.

Mila was heading to the laundry room on some errand or other, but she stopped to say good morning. She grinned as Rhyl told her about how he was going to shoot bows and arrows like a warrior. Someone called her name, and she had to hurry off, a typical morning of industrious activity.

There was now a collection of child-sized bows and arrows in the armory. The children of the Keep were getting old enough to learn to use them. Rhyl selected one and a quiver of arrows, carrying them on his shoulder as if they were the heaviest of responsibilities.

Illiah marveled at the pleasure his son took from such a simple thing as shooting a bow with the help of his father. He was humbled by it, wishing once again that he could spend more time at the Keep.

They set up far beyond the main practice yard where there was a small target made from an old hay bale.

Rhyl carefully selected his arrow. With great concentration he skillfully nocked it in place. He drew back with a questioning glance up at his father. Illiah told him his form was great. Rhyl grinned, making the arrow slip from the nock. Rhyl grumbled as he started over. Illiah stopped himself from helping, not that Rhyl would have let him. Rhyl wanted the accomplishment to be his own.

The arrow made it to the target and stuck firm. Rhyl was triumphant under Illiah's praise. Rhyl shot another arrow, and another, each making their way steadily closer to the center of the target.

After about an hour of archery - a record for his son's short attention span, they were about to turn to a different activity when Irri reappeared out of the mist looking flushed, followed by a handful of grim-faced guards.

"My lord!" he said breathlessly. "We went to the outpost, and the guards on duty have been drugged. They were all asleep at their posts. We could not wake them. Something foul is afoot."

A dozen notions flitted through Illiah's head. He thought foremost of Caeris, on his way at that moment from Caer Andri to the Keep. Perhaps it could be some plot against the king, who was not loved by all these days. It was unlikely; Caeris was still several days to a full week away.

"Take Rhyl into the Keep and place him with Tarran or Murryn," Illiah instructed young Irri. He wished he could do it himself, but he was the lord. It was his duty to lead his people, to oversee his men.

Illiah gave his son a kiss and promised to see him in a bit.

"What about Mummy?" Rhyl asked his father as he circled his arms around Irri's neck.

"Mummy is in the Forest. Don't worry about her," Illiah answered with a smile.

Rhyl nodded, as if that was the safest place for his mother to be, which was probably the truth.

Illiah barked orders at his men, but a great blast muffled his voice. The great horn of the Keep rang out, a sound Illiah had only heard once, and only because the recruits insisted on testing it after they had been ordered to clean out the neglected, massive horn. The sound vibrated the stone, moving up Illiah's legs into his rib cage, rattling his already elevated nerves. The sound meant danger. Illiah yelled for everyone to fall back to the inner Keep.

He ran through the stables, darting through a side entrance into the courtyard. The portcullis was still raised. It should have fallen with the sound of the horn.

The danger was already within the walls of the Keep. The court-yard was deathly still. The horn had been in vain. The mist had con-cealed them until it was too late. The guards had been drugged so there would be no warning.

They stood in loose formation in the courtyard, some just beyond the gate, melting into the mist. Kitarrans. Silent, tall, a small army of strange warriors. No one moved. No one spoke.

The Kitarran warriors' feral expressions immobilized Illiah's men, himself included. Their strange eyes, their lips parted in warning, showing pointed, lethal teeth. Their hands grasped weapons no human had the strength to wield. Their fingers ended in claws. Their bodies were covered with fur and protected by armor.

Illiah's men had fought monsters before. It was not a lack of courage that stayed their weapons. Three Kitarrans stood before the others. Each held a woman captive, knives pointed at three delicate throats. One was Freya, Illiah's sweet sister. The others were beloved wives of his men. He swallowed hard.

He stepped forward through the immobile sea of bystanders. He had no choice but to slip his sword back into its scabbard and open his palms as a sign of submission. His men stirred. Talamir gave a loud shout in outrage. Illiah held a hand high for silence.

"What is this? What do you want?" Illiah asked into the charged silence, coming to a halt before the Kitarrans. Freya's eyes pleaded with him. His sister was with child, due in the coming spring.

A Kitarran stepped forward. He was taller than the others, his shoulders broad and well muscled, his red fur the color of fall leaves. His gray-green eyes were steely. He held a strange weapon in his hand, longer than a sword, with two lethal blades, held adeptly in the middle. Illiah had seen its kind before. In the hands of the Kitarran Guardian.

This Kitarran was not a spirit. He was flesh and blood and on a mission. Illiah's archers, poised and ready on the wall, would have a hard time penetrating his leather armor with their arrows. Each Kitarran was dressed in thick armor, each with a heart-stopping weapon in their hands.

"Are you Lord Illiah?" the Kitarran asked in a deep, accented voice.

"I am."

"My terms may sound strange to you, but I warn you, if you do not comply, these women will feel cold iron upon their throats, and their lifeblood will pour upon your stones." The Kitarran's deep voice vibrated across the courtyard. "My name is Deecon, son of Aroon, Keeper of the Long Isles. We are here for you, Lord Illiah, and your son. If you and your son come with us, these women will go free, and no one will be harmed. You have my word," he added in a more gracious voice.

For a moment, all Illiah could hear was the pounding of his blood in his ears. They wanted Rhyl. He would gladly trade himself for the life of the women. It was his duty, his honor - but his young son?

The Kitarran leader named Deecon must have sensed Illiah's internal battle. He turned to his men and commanded them to search the Keep for the boy.

"Call off your archers, Lord Illiah. You cannot win this. If you try to fight us, your people will die, and it will be on your soul." Deecon spoke the truth. Illiah yearned to fight, but in the end, the blood soaking the stones would not be Kitarran.

Illiah signaled for the archers to stand down. They obeyed, reluctantly. More Kitarrans poured into the courtyard of the Keep. Illiah lost count at fifty. Human Kitarrans were with them, carrying human-sized weapons no less fierce than those of their cat-like counterparts.

The Kitarrans took every weapon from Illiah's men, placing them in a pile in the open space between the hostages and the mob of Illiah's people. They took Illiah's sword and his dagger. His vercuri was handed to the man named Deecon, who looked at it shrewdly before pocketing it.

Illiah dared to hope they wouldn't find Rhyl, that Murryn had hidden him, or escaped. But Illiah's hope was tainted; without Rhyl, the women would die under the Kitarran's blades in a cruel game of balance.

Illiah held the Kitarran's eyes tightly. What kind of man steals a child? Illiah asked the women if they were okay. Freya whimpered, her eyes panicky. Illiah's hands were fists at his sides.

The Kitarrans returned with Murryn and Rhyl at the head of a small procession. Murryn was pale and caught Illiah's gaze, her eyes wide and beseeching. She wasn't afraid. She would fight them all, Illiah knew. He gave his head a subtle shake to tell the girl to stand down. Tricks would not save them.

Rhyl let go of Murryn's hand and ran across the cobblestones. Illiah swept him into a protective embrace. He was so small, so fragile. Rhyl was unafraid, looking at the Kitarrans with interest. Rhyl had met Tayeh several times in the Great Forest with Eva. The fierce face, the claws, and long, lithe tails would not be alien to him.

Betrayal was more potent than the strongest fire wine.

The Kitarran leader came over to him and Rhyl, his eyes full of wonder and something Illiah couldn't quite put his finger on. Respect, perhaps. The Kitarran's curious expression was at odds with the grim errand.

"The women will come with us. If you follow, we will kill them. If we see one man following, we will kill them." Deecon called out to Illiah's people in his accented voice. "If you do as I say, we will release the women unharmed."

To Illiah, Deecon said, "Come with me."

Deecon led Illiah and Rhyl to a horse, saddled and waiting nearby. Illiah turned and raked the Keep with one last desperate look. His people stood silent, their eyes full of murderous intent. Then Illiah's street boys began jostling through the crowd, shouting, desperation making them bold.

"Stop!" Illiah bellowed. His voice echoed across the courtyard, bouncing down from the craggy cliffs. "I will not see you cut down needlessly before me! I will not let these women die. I will not let these children see their mothers murdered," Illiah said, thinking of Oryn who watched his mother held by a particularly nasty-looking Kitarran. Already the knives were driven closer to skin as the crowd reacted to Illiah and Rhyl's captivity.

"My son and I go gladly knowing that you, our people, will be safe." He paused to let his heartfelt words penetrate. "I order you to stand down, to let us go. I -" Then his voice broke, his words choked by threatening tears he would not let fall. His eyes found Mila's in the crowd. She knew what Illiah wanted to say. She could read his heart in his eyes and would keep it as a message for his wife, for his dear one. His love, who was somewhere watching the sun rise above the murk, watching the beauty of the place she loved more than any other, never imagining what she would come home to.

Deecon gripped Illiah's arm hard, pulling him into action. The Kitarran's desire for haste made his face an ominous mask once more.

Illiah forced his feet to move toward the horse. His sister's scream made him mount up. He saw a small smear of red on her neck where the blade had nicked her in warning. He heard Talamir's cry of frustration, unable to come to the aid of his beloved or his lord. Illiah settled Rhyl before him. The boy was silent. It was eerie for such a young child.

Deecon took hold of the horse's lead. Within moments they were enveloped in the mist, running through the forest. Illiah gripped Rhyl tightly to his chest. He had never dreamed the Kitarrans could be so fast. Deecon ran as fast as the horses, easily keeping pace. The rest of the Kitarrans were close, a surge of alien warriors, running, leaping, faster than any wild creature. Their long, powerful legs and balancing tails made them as agile as any horse. Only the human Kitarrans rode horses. The cat-like race had no need for them.

The Kitarrans followed no path. Too soon, Illiah was surrounded by strange woods. He clutched his son tighter for fear Rhyl might fall. For comfort. The forest and mist sped by.

CHAPTER 39

EVA

THE QUIET WAS ABSOLUTE. But it was always quiet in the Great Forest. Eva tried to shake the unease that clung to her like the mist clung to the trees. The sunlight filtered through the boughs of the trees, the drips sparkling and flashing like ripples in the air.

She reached the glade, but the feeling only intensified.

The glade was empty. Eva stepped into the sunlight and circled the tall mossy stone. There was no sign of Tayeh or Lulanan.

She felt a taint. Something was wrong. But Eva could see nothing to cause alarm. There was no sign of Forest creatures, common or uncommon, ordinary or magical, good or evil. No wanderers had been seen for five years.

Five years had made Eva's life was unrecognizable. But in a wonderful way. Her life was filled with endless tasks and responsibilities, which she welcomed and enjoyed, but it left her little time for the Guardians. Her husband, her son, her Keep, came first.

Tayeh had smiled and assured her that was how it was meant to be. He told her that when she had time, she could still come to the glade and he or Lula would always be there for her.

For the first time, they were not.

Years and years she had been coming to the glade to seek their counsel. They had never once been absent. Confusion, rather than worry, furrowed her brows.

She sat in the sun and soaked up the quiet of the place and waited.

She yearned for quiet sometimes. Well, actually quite often. The Keep was busy. So different from the quiet place she had known for so long. The Keep was full - men from Caer Andri, Illiah's men and their families, Illiah's street boys. She loved most of them dearly. They were her friends, her family. Still, some days, she yearned for simple peace and quiet. It was doubly hard to find with Rhyl running circles around her all day long. She loved her son. She would do anything for him, but sometimes she needed to be alone, to breathe.

She sighed heavily. She wanted to be alone, but she also wanted another child. She was fully aware of the contradiction. She yearned for the excitement of its little kicks, the stretching of her body to accommodate another little miracle. More so, she wanted Rhyl to have a sibling. Four years was long enough. She should have conceived again. She feared she would not have another child.

The yearning for another baby was strong, yet she chided herself. She shouldn't be greedy. She had an amazing, healthy boy. His birth had been hard, but not as hard as some. She reminded herself to rejoice in what she had. She did, and yet ...

Where were her mentors? It was so strange. She wanted to call out to them, but she found herself tongue-tied. Yelling out to a Guardian, as one would a dog, did not seem respectful.

Eva grinned in relief to finally see the white form of the fox trotting through the green shadows between the trees. But she still couldn't see Tayeh.

Lula as a fox had none of her usual buoyancy. She came and sat in the sunlight, then suddenly, in a heartbeat, she was a woman.

"Lula!" Eva greeted the Guardian, trying to ignore the sad look on the fox-woman's beautiful face. "Where were you? Where is Tayeh?"

"Eva," Lula began, taking a step closer. Her movements were wary, as if Eva were the wild creature, not she.

"What?" Eva felt inexplicably uncomfortable. The Guardian's eyes were full of regret, remorse.

"You should go home."

"What has happened? Where is Tayeh?"

"Tayeh went home."

"I don't understand."

"You will. Go home." The Guardian's voice lost some of its kindness. It was almost a command.

Eva's feet echoed the panic creeping into her mind. She turned and fled the glade, running through the Forest. She swerved fallen logs and branches, nearly tumbling down the steep steps in her haste. She burst into the little garden expecting to see something, but it was empty.

A din rose from the courtyard far below: the stern shouts of men, the clanking of weapons, boots and horse hooves clashing against the cobbles. Through the slit of a window, Eva glimpsed the hive of activity. A large group of armed guards was amassing. Perhaps her ambitious husband was staging a mock ambush. But usually Illiah planned his sorties with her help and not on such short notice.

Eva burst into the council room. Illiah's men stood around the large table, maps littering the table. Their talk instantly dissolved when they saw her.

"Where is Illiah?" Kaile, Lindin, Tarran, Talamir, Will - they were all there. Where was her lord? "Where is Illiah?" she repeated, her voice harsh and demanding in her worry.

Tarran's pale face highlighted the livid anger in his eyes. He came over and took her hand in his. "He is gone. They took him," he whispered.

"Who?" Somehow, in her heart, Eva already knew.

"Kitarrans." Hate made Tarran's voice thick.

Eva's knees threatened to slide beneath her. But she had trained as a warrior. She didn't fall. She caught herself, with Tarran's help.

"There's more."

"Tell me."

Tarran choked on his words, biting his lip, drawing blood. "They took Rhyl too. They took your son."

The room collapsed around her. Somehow, she was still standing, but she couldn't move. Her feet were roots entombed in ice. The cold slid down her spine, severing her heart in two. Her fingertips tingled with her hate, reminding her that she was still alive.

Her mind screamed Tayeh's name.

Kaile led the group that went after the Kitarrans. Eva intended to go with them. She was in the stables, saddling Sasha. What if they couldn't get to them in time? What if the Kitarrans harmed Rhyl or

Illiah? what if ... No matter how hard she applied herself, she could not calm her mind. She could not calm her breathing.

Panic threatened to overwhelm her. The pieces of her sanity were slipping. She could feel her shattered heart lose its shape bit by bit, thought by thought. Behind it all was a little girl calling a name over and over again. Tayeh. Tayeh!

The saddle buckle refused to latch under her fingers. Eva cursed, earning her the attention of her brother-in-law. Kaile came over to her. His face held no kindness, no pity. The men hadn't said a word when she told them she was coming. They didn't question her capabilities or her motives. But now Kaile placed his hand over her trembling one.

"Did you look?"

With difficulty, Eva answered, "I couldn't see them. Something is blocking me. My magic shows me nothing."

"Stay," he said. It was a captain ordering one of his soldiers down, not the suggestion of a loved one.

Eva cursed again. She was in bad shape. She would hinder them more than she would help. Kaile's men were seasoned warriors. A mother was not dissimilar to a warrior, but she had just lost two parts of her soul.

She nodded, pulling the saddle off Sasha's back, her eyesight blurry, her throat tight. Kaile left. He didn't offer consolations or promises. She did not want him to.

Eva locked herself in her chambers.

She must be strong. She must not give up hope. She must remember that Illiah's men were the best there were. They would catch up to the Kitarrans. They would get her family back. She must have faith in them.

Somewhere, deep and almost hidden in her mind, was the question: what human could stand against the will of a Guardian?

☾

Night had settled over the Keep before any word came. The Keep stood on the edge of a knife, waiting, hoping. Eva kept to her rooms.

The captive women had been found, shaken but unharmed. Eva could not look at Etty with her young sons, settled on her lap for a hug. She could not stay in the great hall where next to hers, Illiah's chair sat empty. She could not bear it.

Her chambers were little better. They were the heart of her existence with Illiah and Rhyl. At least alone, she didn't have to be strong. She could weep and scream and wail.

Someone left food for her, then some tea. She wouldn't let anyone stay. She had them put the food on the table and forced them to leave.

Some indeterminable amount of time later, a loud knock came at the door. Eva jumped from her reverie and opened the door, her hands shaking with anticipation.

Caeris stood in the hall. Eva would have been surprised to see him if she hadn't been consumed with her own concerns. The king had not been expected for another week at least.

Over the years, she had become immune to his eerie likeness to her husband. She had known Illiah intimately for long enough to see the many subtle differences between the twins. Caeris looked nothing like Illiah to her now.

"Eva," Caeris said in a heavy voice, stepping into the room. She let him. He was the king, and he had news. She could tell by his manner.

"Tell me, Caeris," Eva commanded the king.

"We met Kaile's host in the forest. He told us what happened. We went with him, adding our numbers to his. We caught up to the Kitarrans just before the Great River. It was too late. Too late to save them, Eva," Caeris told her, his voice like ash.

"Where are they?" Eva heard herself ask.

Caeris hesitated, taking a deep, shuddering breath. "Dead. Burned."

Caeris dropped something black and sooty into her hand. Rhyl's pendant. Her pendant. The gift from Tayeh, the leaf carved from a cendari branch. Rhyl had been wearing it. She pressed it in her hand and the edges crumbled, the stem snapped. It would never sit upon a chain again. "The bodies were not quite burned. We got there in time to stop the flames. There was no mistaking their identities."

Something was crushing her chest. She couldn't breathe. An invisible force was pulling her down. She fell hard onto her knees. The pain was almost desirable under the pressure of her chaotic emotions. Her eyes couldn't focus. She felt as though someone were pouring water over her face, drowning her slowly. She heard someone screaming. She could feel fire in her throat. She was being tortured. Water and fire, love and pain, consuming her.

CHAPTER 40

COTOCH

THEY WERE NOT KITARRAN WARRIORS, but they were his warriors.

If Kitarra had been the Kitarra of old, brimming with fighters of unmatched strength and skill, taller and faster than any human, Cotoch would think himself a fool. His army was nothing compared to the legendary protectors of old Kitarra.

Luckily, he was not a fool.

That Kitarra was long dead. The Peace Guards were spread thinly across the realm. His one thousand men would be more than enough.

The men rippled out across the flat practice field like the well-ordered force they were. Creating his army had been no small task. But it was done and Cotoch was pleased. Proud. His men had worked hard. They would be rewarded.

"They are beautiful, aren't they?"

Cotoch turned to see a vision in purples and reds beside him. Sandra looked every inch the merchant's daughter. She loved her finery. Her things. The wind tried to whip the pearls from her hair.

"They are. I am quite enamored."

His wife loved her possessions. Dresses, jewels, art, men. One of her things was before them. One of Cotoch's captains, a young, ardent man with a handsome face and bright hair.

"You were with your whore again last night. I feel like you are trying to replace me," Sandra said in an icy breath. Cotoch held her eyes with his, cocking his head in admission, and amusement. Sandra was a patch of invisible ice. He was never sure when he was going to slip and crack his head. Some days she couldn't care less about his mistresses, but then, some days, she was lightning in a drought.

"As were you," he reminded her.

Sandra smiled for an instant. Then her face was stony. "I'm pregnant."

"No, my love, you are not."

Sandra's face flushed with anger. His wife was barren. She had never quickened, not once, not even suffered a miscarriage. He knew her lie. Her inability to have his child was ever festering away at her sanity. Not that she had been entirely sane to begin with.

"What if your whore gets pregnant? I can't stand the thought of your natural children."

Sandra couldn't stand a lot of things. Cotoch wasn't going to get rid of every mistress she complained about.

"My flower, someday we will have a son. You know this." Just not of your body. He didn't say it out loud. There were only so many storms he was willing to navigate at one time with his lovely wife.

Sandra simpered, fidgeting with the hem of her elaborate cuff.

"And in the meantime, we can have our fun. Together. Apart. You know I could never replace you."

Sandra smiled under her lashes at him. She was beautiful and desirable when she wasn't irritating. Yet sometimes Cotoch pictured bright, starlit hair and another face entirely when they made love.

He had not forgotten Eva. He would never forget her. She was a promise. A reward for patience and perseverance. Crea had failed to keep Eva and had failed to kill Illiah. Cotoch was losing faith in the Guardian's determination. But the army he had built was proof he didn't need the spirit woman.

His sight of Eva had been foggy at best. He tried to clear it, taking so much *varing* he should have seen across the world and a thousand years. Something - or someone - was protecting Eva. He had glimpses of her and Illiah and their son Rhyl - it was not clear if he was the child the vision spoke of. The boy looked ordinary to a fault, although he did share his mother's features.

Eva was still beautiful, still alluring. Motherhood had only made her more desirable. Time had only given her qualities strength and potency. His rare glimpses were hard won and more tantalizing for it. But there was never enough information to base any sort of action upon. Frustrating.

He had continued with his planning. And now his army stretched out before him. Soon. Soon it would begin.

"What does Imal say?"

"Imal is ready. When I tell him, he will send his men."

"It's a long journey across the ocean."

"His captains know the way, do not fear."

Sandra straightened and preened thinking of it. His wife was as much of a monger as he was. They both craved power. They were well suited that way. If only she could have a son. Not that a child of hers was the son he really wanted. He wanted a son who would someday rise to be his legacy, his pride. Sandra was merely a merchant's daughter with no magic in her blood. None at all.

"What about her? What does she say?" Sandra asked.

"Crea? She seethes. In Jullayah, her plans have not been going her way. But I don't know what she was expecting. She is a spirit. She can not affect us mortals - much."

"I always thought the Guardians were more powerful," Sandra mused, linking her arm in his. "But really, Crea seems a bit pathetic."

Cotoch wasn't sure pathetic was the right word. Addled, maybe. Yes, Crea couldn't smite down her enemies or use magic for her gains, but she had her pawns. She had influence. When a spirit appeared from thin air inside your locked chamber, it inspired a certain amount of awe. It made one believe in the impossible made possible. And Crea was immortal. She had time on her side.

"Why does she hate Kitarra so much, anyway?" Sandra asked.

"Something about trees and the Allmakers. If Kitarra dies, they die. She wants revenge," Cotoch told his wife. Crea hated Kitarra and the Allmakers, but she had never told him exactly what they had done to her. But then he had never asked - because he really didn't care. He had no pity for the spirit woman.

"I hate waiting." Sandra sighed, leaning her head against his shoulder.

"Me too. But patience is a necessary evil, my sweets."

"I am going down to see Okil," she announced, walking with a sway in her step as she went to visit her latest acquisition.

Cotoch watched her with amusement. He wondered if he should feel jealous. Or possessive. No, those words did not apply to his relationship with his wife. He had spent those emotions elsewhere, on another woman.

Yes, patience was a necessary evil.

CHAPTER 41

ILLIAH

AS THE DAY WANED, Deecon, the leader of the Kitarrans, called a halt. Illiah was told to dismount. He obeyed, pulling Rhyl with him carefully. His boy had fallen asleep when their pace slowed and the horse's gait became less jostling.

Illiah cradled his son to his chest and gave his captor a murderous glare before taking in their location.

They were still in the forest, but the air smelled tangy, like the river. Only a handful of Kitarrans surrounded him and his son; the others were nowhere to be seen. Illiah had not noticed them disband.

Deecon handed him a canteen of water and some food. Illiah took it wordlessly. He was weary. His heart was an anvil. Rhyl woke and squirmed from his arms onto the ground. Illiah asked if he was hungry.

"Mummy?" Rhyl asked hopefully. Illiah could only shake his head. He had no words. Rhyl took some bread and cheese, nibbling on it like a mouse, watching the Kitarrans silently.

The Kitarrans were on high alert. They stood still and silent as they watched the forest around them. Their large, pointed ears shifted slightly as they studied the noises on the air. Illiah wondered if they had superior hearing in addition to their other obviously superior advantages. Their intensity made Illiah nervous. Or more nervous. He had yet to decipher why exactly they wanted him and his young son. They weren't going to let them starve, which was encouraging.

The Kitarrans jerked to animation as a strange call, not unlike a raven, reached them. Deecon cupped his hands together and put them to his mouth, using them as an instrument to create an echo of the noise. Hardly a score of minutes later, the other group of Kitarrans came through the forest, the humans on horseback.

"Deecon," a human, the leader of the newly arrived group, said in a hushed voice. Illiah strained his ears to overhear. He could make out a few words. "King - arrive -sooner than planned- plan B." It was not much to go on. Deecon looked worried yet determined as the two leaders, Kitarran and human, turned their attention to their captives. Deecon produced a bag and gave it to Illiah.

"You need to take off your clothes, and the child's. Put these on," he insisted not unkindly. "I also need the boy's pendant."

Illiah stared up at the Kitarran. Rhyl's pendant had been Eva's. She had gifted it in love to her son. Rhyl shook his head as Illiah asked him for it, raising his voice an octave, the start of a tantrum. Illiah hushed Rhyl as best he could. He didn't want the Kitarrans to have a reason to get angry, but his son could be a loud, stubborn boy when he wanted to be.

"Noooo," Rhyl said, clutching the necklace. The human Kitarran looked displeased, but Illiah was surprised to see that Deecon had an amused, apologetic smile on his face. The huge warrior knelt at Rhyl's level, his strange cat eyes even with the little boy's. Rhyl quieted under the steady gaze.

"Please, Rhyl, I need it very badly. Here." The great warrior pulled out a little wooden token from his pocket. It was in the shape of a little dog, carved with great skill. The detail on the tiny piece was exquisite. "How about we trade?"

Rhyl looked unsure. He loved his mother's trinket, but the little wooden dog clearly piqued his interest. Rhyl squirmed for a minute, then relinquished his beloved possession, but not without tears. He was tired, weary both physically and emotionally. He was charmed by the little dog and clutched it in his hands, but he still cried. Rhyl turned to his father and buried into his neck with loud, angry sobs.

Illiah changed his clothes, difficult with Rhyl clinging to him like a squirrel to a branch. The new clothes were of good quality and a soft weave, the same camouflaging colors as the rest of the Kitarrans. They gave him a new traveling cloak made of thick, heavy wool. Rhyl was given a matching child-sized one. Illiah's attempt to reason with Rhyl failed dramatically. Rhyl refused to undress. Illiah glared at Deecon as he changed his son, who was protesting loudly.

When it was done, Illiah was vibrating with silent anger as he held his son close. Rhyl was finally silent, but miserable.

A new horse was brought from somewhere. Rhyl and Illiah were quickly mounted up and running once more through the forest with Deecon at the lead, Kitarrans all around. Rhyl clung to his father.

The human Kitarrans had gone in a different direction with their clothes. Illiah had an evil feeling in his gut.

The sun set and twilight descended upon the forest. Still they rode on.

Rhyl started to whine, a small piteous sound that made Illiah's heart ache. The boy was hungry, scared, and undoubtedly tired. Illiah pushed his horse faster to catch up to Deecon. Immediately the others pressed in against him, thinking he was going to bolt.

"Deecon!" Illiah shouted at their leader. "You must stop. Rhyl is tired and hungry. He is just a child. This is too much for him."

Deecon stopped and regarded Illiah and his boy. "We will stop for some food."

"Sir," one of Deecon's men hissed, "We must press on."

"The child, Anru. The child needs to eat and rest." Deecon's tone left no room for argument. Illiah reassessed his perceptions of the Kitarrans. Deecon seemed greatly concerned for Rhyl's welfare.

They stopped right there and then. Deecon gave Illiah some food to share with Rhyl. He also gave Rhyl a soft, warm blanket that Rhyl settled into immediately, still clutching the little dog. Rhyl was so tired he didn't want to eat, but after some coaxing, Illiah got his son to eat enough to fill his stomach for a little while.

Illiah wrapped his son tightly in the blanket, the same tight swaddling he and Eva had used many nights when Rhyl was a babe. Rhyl was not a boy to give in to sleep easily, but he closed his eyes and was asleep almost instantly. His son was so precious and vulnerable. He held Rhyl tight, his anger moving like a wildfire within him.

Deecon ordered them to get ready to move on. Illiah was loath to release his sleeping son, but he couldn't hold him and mount up onto the horse at the same time. Deecon held the boy, a little awkwardly, as Illiah stepped up into the saddle. Illiah never took his eyes off the Kitarran. Deecon handed his precious bundle with care up to Illiah, and Illiah settled Rhyl in front of him on the horse.

Within the hour, they came to the edge of a river. The Great River, Illiah realized with a sinking feeling, that ran along the border of Jullayah and the Midlands.

After a quick pause and a quicker assessment, Deecon led them south. They kept as close to the river as they could easily travel.

Twilight deepened. The daylight was almost extinguished.

Deecon became intensely still. Another raven-like call pierced the air, lilting above the frog song that had filled the approaching night air. A flicker of relief settled across Deecon's features, and he called back. Somewhere ahead a lantern was lit, and they made toward it.

Boats. Illiah was unsurprised.

Three boats were moored, bobbing against the uneven bank. Deecon greeted the man waiting with a smile. There was hushed talk, but it was a relieved talk, their manner easy and almost jovial. Whatever they spoke of, it bode ill for Illiah and Rhyl. Behind him, the black, pathless forest was despondent. Rescue would not be coming.

Illiah was told to dismount. He clutched his sleeping boy tightly, overwhelmed with a sudden fear the Kitarrans would take Rhyl and leave him stranded on the riverbank, helplessly watching the boats float off into the darkness. It was becoming clear that the Kitarrans wanted Rhyl, not him. Not the War Commander of Jullayah, but his son, the current heir to the throne. If they took Rhyl, they would have to take him as well. He would not allow anything else.

Deecon made his orders clear without raising his voice; the water would carry their sounds farther than was safe. Illiah thought about calling out, but he didn't want the Kitarrans to have a reason to steal his son from his arms and leave him alone on the shore, or worse.

The boats were ready. Illiah was told to get on board the largest of the three. His horse was unsaddled and released into the wild woods behind them.

Illiah had little experience with boats. He had burned the invaders' boats upon the southern sea shore. Those vessels had been a similar size, but not so finely crafted. He caught a brief glance at the workmanship as he was ushered inside the small cabin.

"You will stay here until we clear the river," Deecon ordered. "Not that the Jullayans will come after us. We travel by night and King Caeris does not possess boats that would match ours for speed."

He was right about that.

"You should know," Deecon added in a tired voice as he stood in the doorway, "that they think you are dead. We fooled them - your clothes, your items - we used them to create an illusion to make your men think you are dead. We don't want them following us. It was not what I wanted, and I am sorry."

The burning emotions of Illiah's heart were doused, forming a shapeless sludge of ash.

"Why? Are you trying to start a war?" Illiah heard himself ask in a voice cold as iron on a midwinter night.

Deecon didn't say anything. He gave Illiah a parting look that was both sad and triumphant. The boat moved, beginning its journey down the river.

Rhyl was still sleeping, nestled into one of the several bunks in the small cabin. Illiah lay down beside him and held him close. He closed his eyes tight against his waking nightmare.

Soon, or perhaps already, Eva would hear the news that would tear her apart, down to her fragile soul - her son and husband were dead. Would she believe it? Would Eva know in her heart that they were still alive? Would the magic that coursed through her veins tell her the truth? Illiah was sure she would know; she had her visions, after all. But what difference did that really make? Eva's heart would surely break. Illiah's had already.

EVA

SOMETIMES EVA SURFACED. Cool hands touched her forehead. A woman's soft voice spoke quietly in her ear. Cold liquid slid down her burning throat. But the maelstrom of abandonment and loss took only a moment, a heartbeat to consume her, pulling her back into its sightless depths.

This sequence repeated more times than she could count.

The Forest opened into a meadow of grass. The grass surrounded a pool, round and completely isolated from stream or brook. The water of the pool was black, still. Not a ripple marred the perfect reflection of a thousand stars. The pool was the night sky and held all the mysteries of time within its depths. The stars shone with tantalizing answers never to be spoken. Whispers stirred the grass. Warm wind caressed Eva's face. The water was night, but the sky above was as bright as forget-me-nots.

A bird landed beside the pool. Its wide, black wings swept back the grass with the force of its landing, but not a ripple did they make. With an eye the color of the sky, it looked into the water. The raven looked lost, but not as lost as Eva was.

"Calypso," Eva said as she sat upright in her bed.

The dream dissolved as her eyes focused on the light of her room, seeking out the windows where the sun poured in. Her body, her throat, ached. She felt like a wooden stake was buried in her chest, twisting and twisting, deeper and deeper, only she didn't die, even if she wished it.

She blinked back tears. Logic struggled against her emotions. Questions plagued her broken consciousness. What Caeris told her just didn't make sense.

Confusion urged her to take in her surroundings. Tarran was at her side, his eyes red, swollen. Something lurked beneath the surface of his expression. Anger so deep, so rooted in grief, it created something that gave her pause. She was suddenly afraid for her young friend.

"Tarran," Eva breathed, her voice rough. It was physically painful to speak. "Fetch my robe."

The young man complied. He helped her put it around her nightdress. She was weak.

"How long has it been?"

"Four days." Tarran's voice was little better than hers.

Eva nodded, feeling a remorseful pang added to the others. She despised her weakness, for losing herself to grief when too many questions were left unanswered.

She made her way to the fire, almost collapsing on her knees, she was so weak. She stirred the sleeping embers until they blazed. She reached for the *simul rami*, for Rhyl and Illiah, and the murdering Kitarrans. All she saw was the pool from her dream, pricked with stars and luminous as the night. She searched deeper, but could not find another vision. The fire blazed with life, its flames reaching out for her. Eva recoiled, her heart pounding.

"Why did they do it, Tarran? Was any reason given?" she asked, turning to the young man.

"We captured one of their scouts. He won't talk." The ugly beast in Tarran's eyes asserted itself.

"Is he still alive? I want to see him," Eva said, getting up.

Tarran nodded. He didn't look happy about it. "I will take you to him."

"Is Caeris still here?"

Another nod.

"Caeris is staying on for a while. Then he will return to Caer Andri. He appointed Kaile as War Commander," Tarran told her.

Eva didn't bother dressing. Her robe was warm enough. She put on her boots, slipped her knife inside, and followed Tarran.

He led her down, past the great hall, past the curious looks of her people. Eva didn't acknowledge them. She couldn't spare them a thought. Perhaps it was cruel, but she loathed their pity.

Tarran led her beyond the cellars, beneath the Keep, to a series of dusty, despicable rooms that had sat unused since before Eva's father's time. Once they had been prison cells; it seemed the time had come to utilize them once more.

The temperature dropped the lower they went. Daylight had never seen the depths. It was another world, an unsettling one, one Eva had never had the courage to explore as a child. The stale air smelled of excrement and damp.

Tarran grabbed a torch and led Eva into one of the cells. The torch light forced its way into the small, square room, highlighting the figure of a lanky Kitarran.

The prisoner was shackled hand and foot to the wall, making it impossible for him to sit, though it was clear he could hardly stand. It must be excruciating for him. His fur was matted. Wet blood glinted in the torchlight. He didn't move. He didn't appear alive. Despite her anger and hatred, Eva's heart swelled with pity.

Eva took the torch from Tarran and moved closer. The Kitarran sensed the light and moved his head slowly, opening his eyes. One eye, actually. The other was closed shut under a swollen mass. Blood dripped from his nose, his mouth, bright red against gray.

"Why did they kill them?" Eva wondered if she would get an answer.

The Kitarran focused on her.

"The lady." His voice was almost nonexistent.

"Do you want a war?"

"Even if … I tell … no one will … believe." His voice was accented.

"Are they really dead?" Eva thought something flickered in his expression. She could have imagined it. Tarran stiffened.

The Kitarran said nothing.

"Tell her, beast," Tarran hissed.

"I still not … afraid of you … child," the Kitarran said, his mouth jerking in what might have been an attempt to smile showing a jagged, broken canine tooth. Others were missing completely. Eva could tell it was hard for him to speak. His body vibrated with pain.

"You did this to him?" Eva asked Tarran, her gut churning.

Tarran didn't reply. His look of disgust and loathing toward the Kitarran said enough.

"Leave us," Eva ordered Tarran. He looked startled at her request, but he obeyed. Tarran sulked into the darkness like he belonged to it.

"You know who I am," Eva said once they were alone. The Kitarran nodded. "Why? I must know."

"Your son … alive."

"Rhyl is alive? And Illiah?" Hope stretched its wings; Eva quickly clipped its feathers. Hope was too perilous.

"Both … Ruse," the Kitarran managed. His chin sagged against his chest once more.

Eva closed her eyes. The wings in her heart fluttered, stretching to brush against the singed hole of her grief, searching for freedom.

"Why did your people take them?"

"Kitarra needs … child."

Eva heart dropped into her feet. The prophecy. But how could Tayeh take her son away from her?

"What is your name?" Eva whispered.

"Dar-ish." Between the garbled speech and his strong accent, he was hard to understand. She repeated it back to him, and he managed a nod.

"Darish, if I get you out of here, will you take me with you back to Kitarra?" Eva asked ever so quietly. The Kitarran raised his head to regard her with his one good eye.

"Yes, Muhala … I would."

"Do I have your word? Swear on the blood of your mother."

"Yes." His head hung once more, his strength gone. Eva cupped his jaw lightly with her palm. She closed her eyes and used her magic to see what lay behind the bruising and swelling, and the blood-caked fur. There were multiple fractures: his head, his nose, one of his collarbones. More bruised flesh than she could enumerate. She couldn't ease all his pain. She couldn't heal all his hurts. It would leave her too weak. She would do what she could and manage the rest later.

"I don't know what the king has planned for you, but I will try to come tonight. I don't think I can get you out without the cover of night."

"My thanks …. my lady."

Eva gave him a last parting look and moved out of the cell. Tarran was waiting for her in the corridor, his pale face stark against the perpetual dark. His eyes absorbed the blackness, and Eva felt another sharp pang of worry for her husband's ward. It seemed cruel not to tell Tarran that Illiah was alive. Illiah was everything to him.

Before, she would not have hesitated to bring Tarran with her. But now Eva wasn't sure she could trust him. What Tarran did to the Kitarran was cruel, heartless. The Tarran she thought she knew, the Tarran she had watched grow from boy to young man, would never have acted with such cruelty out of anger. He would never have displayed such hatred.

"What does Caeris plan to do with the prisoner?" Eva asked.

Tarran shrugged. "Keep him around for a few days, wait to see if his current situation will encourage him to talk. Then put him to the sword."

Eva nodded. It was as she expected. She would leave that night; Caeris was not a patient man.

☾

A great clatter echoed from the courtyard loud enough to distract Eva from her planning and packing.

The noise rose and came in her open window: the angry, accusatory shouts of men, the clatter of boots on the cobbles. She looked out to the yard far below her to see a crowd gathering, shuffling across the yard. A terrible feeling spun sticky webs of fear in her gut. She abandoned her tasks and ran down the steps, skipping them in twos and threes.

She exploded into the courtyard. The crowd parted for her without a word. The silence grew as the people took in her urgent manner, regarding her like a wild creature.

The prisoner was next to Caeris, on his knees, his head almost level with the ground. The pose of a conquered warrior, too sick, too hurt to find an ounce of strength to confront his enemies.

"Caeris, stop." Eva didn't yell or raise her voice. All were listening, watching her warily.

"This man was party to the death of your husband and son," Caeris answered, his voice loud and clear, carrying across the cool expanse.

"Don't kill him," Eva said.

The king's eyes widened. "This man deserves to die."

"No," Eva said, her voice louder with desperation. She moved to stand between Caeris and the prisoner. "You can't - what if - what if they are still alive? What if they planned this? What if this Kitarran can lead us to them?"

Caeris regarded her with a sad expression. He took a deep breath and placed his hand gently on Eva's chin, looking directly into her eyes. It was a kind, almost intimate gesture. "Eva, you did not see what I saw. You must not live in this lie. They are dead. And this man will not talk. He deserves death."

Eva wanted to tell him he was wrong, that they were alive, but her tongue was thick in her mouth. Doubt seeped into her resolve. Caeris was right - she hadn't seen the bodies laid to rest while she had been lost in turmoil. What if the Kitarran had lied to her? Perhaps all Kitarrans were liars and betrayers.

Caeris put his arm around her shoulder and moved her away from the prisoner, keeping her at his side. It happened so quickly. Caeris handed his sword to Tarran. The boy stepped up and brought the sword down upon the Kitarran's exposed neck. With one swing, the head was severed. The body slouched, blood pooled red upon the stones. Some splashed upon Eva's skirts. Tarran was an efficient executioner.

Tarran straightened. Eva didn't miss the exchange between the king and the young man. Caeris's slight nod of acclamation. Eva looked from Tarran's hollow gaze to Murryn. The young woman only had eyes for Tarran. The two had recently embarked on a relationship that was more than the friendship they had previously shared. Murryn looked at her lover with a haunted worry that echoed Eva's.

Eva searched the circle of those assembled. Some looked pleased with the execution, some looked sickened, and some wore masks Eva could not disassemble. Irri stalked away. Eva couldn't read his body language.

Eva turned from them all and went back into solitude.

CHAPTER 42

EVA

BOATS ON THE OPEN OCEAN. Eva could smell the brine, hear the sea birds. She could see a small figure standing close to the edge of the boat, his bright hair reflecting the wintry sun, the wind tussling it every which way. Illiah hovered, ready to prevent Rhyl from falling into the churning, foamy water, just in case Rhyl forgot the dangers of the water below.

Eva could almost feel the rocking motion beneath her feet. She had to remind herself she was precariously perched on the edge of a cliff. The wind caressed the sails of the ship before returning Eva to her body.

Her family was alive. Safe.

She breathed deeply, cherishing every vision she saw of them. She had no doubt in her heart the visions were real, not some figment of her deepest desire. Her husband and son were alive - the dead Kitar-ran had spoken truth.

But she couldn't tell a soul. Her friends and family watched her, waiting for her to show some sign of madness, to claim once more that her family was still alive. In secret, she began her preparations. She was going to Kitarra.

Eva shivered. Her heart fluttered with warmth from the vision, but winter was persistent. Even the visions were not enough to keep the chill from her exposed skin.

Winter complicated things.

The snows had begun to fall, already lying thick upon the ground. It was not even past the solstice. There was talk of a hard winter. To travel in such weather, alone, in an unknown land, would be suicide.

She hated it, but she had to wait, at least until the weather cleared. Perhaps, a small voice in her mind admitted, even until spring. It was infuriating, frustrating. She cursed the weather.

Confined and prohibited, she spent several hours every day exercising her skills with her sword. She had lapsed from constant practice since Rhyl was born, being too exhausted or too busy to give it much of her time. Now once more she trained as a warrior. She would need every instinct she possessed, all her strength and skill to get to Kitarra. The journey would be dangerous, nearly impossible.

Eva looked down to the forest below her. The Great Forest at her back was silent, brooding, like her thoughts. She stood on the cliff's edge, arms spread, wishing she was a raven or an eagle so she could take flight and make the long journey with the wind and clouds.

Calypso was making daring aerial displays in the currents, clearly enjoying the cold air more than she. She had missed him. Where he had been over the past year, she did not know. She wondered if he were a true creature of the Forest and half expected one day he would come before her as a young man. He had not been around that day. His loud voice had not warned them of danger.

Eva stepped away from the wind along the exposed cliff to head back to the Keep. The Great Forest was covered in a generous layer of snow. The bark of the trees contrasted against the endless blanket of white. Something else stood out with equal clarity. Eva's heart skipped a beat. Fear froze her to the rocks.

A tall man stood immobile under the trees, his face bearded and hooded. The colour of his clothes made him meld with the Forest. He was watching Eva with steady gray eyes that glinted from beneath his hood dusted with snow.

Eva didn't know what to do. Was he real or a figment of her imagination or one of the magic creatures of the Great Forest in a human-like guise? The creatures of the Forest either took the form of wild animals, or as humans wore nothing at all. This man was dressed for the cold.

The man moved slowly toward her. Perhaps she should run, escape. But something familiar about him thawed her fear. Perhaps he was a concoction of her troubled memories and her wounded heart.

Regardless, Eva closed the distance between them, taking his gloved hand in hers. He was solid. Eva could feel his fingers underneath the thick leather. He gave her a ghost of a smile, his scarred lip turning at the corner.

"Tarek," Eva breathed, her voice loud in the hushed Forest.

"My lady."

"You are real."

Tarek nodded, his smile widening, his eyes crinkling. "As are you."

"What are you doing here?"

Tarek shook his head slowly. "It is a long story."

"It's freezing. Let's go inside. You must have traveled a long way."

"I am not here for long. I don't want to speak to anyone but you. No one needs to know I am here."

Eva nodded. The Keep was full of king's guards; some would remember him from before. With Illiah gone, she did not trust their loyalty. "You will find things much changed around here," Eva told him sadly. He nodded as if he understood. "I will sneak you into my room. No one will find you there."

"Thank you. I am cold, despite my layers," he added ruefully.

She studied him as they walked. Tarek looked older, wiser. His beard obscured most of his face, but his clear eyes were filled with concern. The last time she had seen him, five years ago, he had been broken and lost. She thought he had wandered off into the wilderness to disappear from her life, from Jullayah, forever.

She had been wrong. He was back. He was whole. He looked - good, she decided. The worried looks he passed her way told her he didn't find her under the same circumstances.

"How did you know to find me here?" Eva asked.

"Last time I was in this Forest, I met a friend of yours. She helped me before. She helped me this time as well."

Eva looked around the empty Forest for Lulanan. She had not seen the fox-woman since that day her heart had shattered. If the Guardian was watching, she was not to be seen by human eyes.

"Wait here while I make sure no one is around," Eva told Tarek as she slipped inside the hidden door. The garden was empty, covered in snow. She could see her crisscross of tracks that were designed to hide any trail to the hidden door. She had never shared her secret with anyone but Illiah and Rhyl. The council room was empty too.

Tarek came at her call, sneaking through the door into the walled garden. His brows rose. It was clearly not where he expected to arrive. Eva never told him the full details of her secret. He said nothing, knowing the need for secrecy and silence.

The hall was empty, so it was easy to sneak Tarek into her chambers. Once inside, she bolted the door. They would not be disturbed.

First and fore-most, Tarek knelt before the fire, tossing on more wood. He took off his gloves, his hood, his cloak. Eva helped him hang his wet clothes before the fire. As he did, he looked around at her room, taking stock. His eyes flitted from Illiah's sword on the mantel to Rhyl's toys piled unused in a corner to her son's little cloak hanging from the peg to the little room where a snug, cozy child-sized bed sat gathering dust.

Eva turned away. She couldn't look at the objects. She drew her arms around herself to contain the pieces that threatened to break apart.

"I saw them," Tarek said softly, taking a seat. He looked exhausted. "That's why I came back. I had to know. I had to know if you were okay."

"Tell me," Eva said, sitting across from him. She should find him some food, some warm drink, but she needed to hear what he had to say first.

"We were in Fishtown, a large, independent settlement along the sea. We were working on the docks for the day. I saw the Kitarran boat - we all saw it. Not a common sight, not altogether unheard of either. But still, they beg your attention, the Kitarrans. And the Midlanders' vessels are rafts compared to the Kitarran ships. Among the Kitarrans were humans, common enough. Kitarra is home to many humans. We were there a year ago, for a season. One man stood out - to me, anyway. I knew Illiah instantly. He stood watching the activity on the docks with interest, a guard at either shoulder. Next to him was a young child with hair the color of starlight and your eyes." Tarek's eyes were wide as he recalled the memory. "I couldn't believe it. It was so startling, yet I knew - I knew it was your child. But why? I watched them for some time. It was clear to me that Illiah was not there by choice. He never saw me. Then they set sail. They had stopped for supplies, I suppose."

A tear slipped down her cheek. Eva rubbed it away.

"Why? What happened?" Tarek asked her, leaning across the table, taking her hands in his.

"When I was a young girl, just after my parents died," she began, "I found the door into the Great Forest. There I found Tayeh, the Guardian of Kitarra, and Lula, Guardian of the Great Forest. They were waiting for me. They taught me how to use the magic in my blood. They were kind, loving. But what they wanted was my son, and his - Illiah's. They told me I was special, that my son was destined to fulfill a prophecy.

"The Guardians are gone now. They left me the day they took my family. They betrayed me. They used me to get what they wanted, my son, and then they took him. They made me believe that Illiah and Rhyl were dead. They left me behind and I don't know why." Eva took a deep, shuddering breath before telling Tarek the rest.

"That must have been hard for you, to think that they were dead," Tarek mused once she fell silent, squeezing her hand.

"I died that day," she told him. "When you saw them, did they look well? When was that?"

"That was two weeks ago. I went straight from there to here. They did look well. They did not look misused. Your son looked content enough, talking to a big Kitarran warrior, a fearless child." Tarek added with a smile.

"In some ways," Eva admitted. "But he is still so little. He needs me." Eva took another deep breath to swallow the sobs threatening to halt her speech. "Enough of this for now. I am going to the kitchens to get some food. You must be famished."

Tarek gave her a sad smile, nodding ruefully.

Eva spent most of her days in her room. Scrub was accustomed to her taking baskets of food to save her the trip later on. He had given up entreaties to join the rest of the Keep and long ceased teasing her for hoarding like a squirrel. Tarek looked like a greedy raven as she returned with the heaping basket.

"So who is this 'we' you spoke of?" Eva asked as Tarek ate like he hadn't seen food in a year. He did pause to swallow and answer her question.

"My crew. I joined a band of mercenaries. We travel, throughout the Midlands mostly, hired for protection or what-have-you. There are seven of us. We do well enough." He spoke with contentment.

"You sound happy."

"Aye. I am. Mahone would be pleased. He was always concerned for my happiness." Tarek's voice held emotion, but not the raw grief Eva remembered. "When can you be ready to leave?" he asked before Eva could formulate the question in her mind. "I know you are going to ask me."

Eva grinned. "I can be ready now if you like."

"Tomorrow should be soon enough. My bones like the warmth. There will be none of that where we are going. Not for a while anyway."

"Tomorrow, then. It would be easier to get the horses without being seen if we leave at night."

"Horses?"

"Doesn't it make sense to take the horses, follow the old road that I showed you years ago? We can go much faster by horseback, even through this snow."

"Makes sense. Fine. We leave tomorrow, after dark."

There would only be two guards, three at most, on watch in the dead of night. They would be looking south, east, and west from the battlements. Another would be in the high guard tower. Their attention would be drawn away from the Keep, not within it. The hallways and staircases would be empty. People of the Keep would be abed, the recruits had their curfew.

Tarek helped Eva prepare. Their need for haste meant she packed light, but there were some things she would not leave behind. She packed Rhyl's favorite toy and Illiah's cherished weapon. She vowed she would see those things returned to her beloveds.

There were no goodbyes spoken to her family and friends. She regretted the necessity of it greatly. If her friends knew her plans, they would stop her any way they could, telling her she was addled in the head. She would leave clothed in secrecy, or not at all.

Tarran was at the forefront of her mind. His heart was bleeding badly. The young man who had executed the prisoner with brutal coldness was not Tarran's true self. She wrote him a note that held the truth and then slipped it under his door as she passed by. She hoped the truth would give him solace and force the monster back from his eyes. If he believed her.

They made a quick stop in the stockrooms, packing as much smoked meat and dried rations as they could fit into their packs. The certainty of long, cold days before them was absolute.

They didn't speak as they made their way through the Keep's maze-like corridors. They crossed the cobbled yard to the stables as lightly as their heavy winter boots allowed. The gray weave of their cloaks hid them. There was no moon to cast even the weakest of shadows. The horses seemed to sense the need for quiet. They didn't even neigh in welcome, merely regarded them with brown liquid eyes as they were saddled.

Dark nooks and abstract shadows were the Keep's bedfellows, but crossing the bright, snow-covered fields to the forest was another matter. Even without a moon, any ripple of movement would alert the guards.

They kept to the deepest shadows, the little hillocks and ravines. The cold climbed into Eva's nose. Every exhale was a cloud in the night air. Every hoof fall on the frozen snow was like a bell in her ears. Finally, they reached the thick forest beyond the pastures. No alarm had been raised. Not even a sigh escaped the sleeping fortress.

Eva exhaled slowly, turning to look at the Keep through the black skeletal trees. The snow outlined the fortress. The faint glow of torches added depth to the darkness. Eva wondered if she would ever again sit in the mossy courtyard on a sunny morning or feel the cool stone under her fingers or look up at the treetops while floating in the hot pools.

Eva turned her back to the Keep.

The horses made tracks across the snow. They could hope for fresh snow to fall, covering any sign of their direction, but it was a faint hope. The clouds above were light; the brightest stars tried to peek through here and there. Eva hoped to make speed and distance their allies. Once in the Great Forest, their trackers would be leery about following.

Without the moon, the snow was gray, and the forest shadows taunted the mind with lurking dangers. The horses seemed unperturbed. Eva trusted the intelligent animals would find their footing. She knew the way well enough to guide them.

Even with the night slowing their progress, they were soon at the place where the two realms met: Jullayah, a place of men, and the Great Forest, a place as old as the earth and steeped with magic.

The vertical fissure that broke the jagged cliff face loomed before them like a great mouth. The gate. The hungry shadows were thick, endless. The Great Forest was about to swallow them up.

"It's not too far, several hundred yards, then it opens up into the Forest," Tarek reminded her, sensing her hesitation. He pushed Penn ahead, taking the lead. The charger snorted at the challenge. The darkness swallowed them, but not for long. They came out of the narrow canyon into the Forest, which was bright in contrast, almost like dawn light.

They rode through the long night. Daylight came slowly, seeping timidly through the trees. Still they pushed their weary horses farther. When they could, they cantered, making as much distance as they could. The ancient path resembled an old road in places, mostly straight, carving a line through the giant trees. Everything was covered in snow. Several times they had to backtrack to regain the trail.

When the sun reached its low winter zenith, they came to a stop, resting beneath one of the giant trees. The ground was bare. Snow could not penetrate the dense evergreen branches. They sat in reasonable comfort and shared a meal.

Eva's back ached, and her legs were sore. She was unaccustomed to hard riding. She leaned against the tree, resting comfortably in a giant root well. Her eyes were heavy. Tarek suggested she take a rest. They could afford a brief stop. Eva nodded, grateful to hear it, grateful for her friend who was helping her on the difficult journey. She was so tired of being alone.

Eva woke and looked for Tarek. He was gone. She didn't see the horses. She noticed her pack was gone. Everything was gone. There were no tracks. No sign of Tarek. Eva leaped to her feet, running out into the snow, into the open Forest.

Silence greeted her. The Forest was empty but for the white carpet of snow and huge trees. Her calls died as soon as they left her lips, cushioned by the snow.

All she could hear was the pounding of her heart.

Had Tarek betrayed her? Or was he the product of her sick mind finally gone mad? Maybe he was a vessel sent from Tayeh to torment her. To bring her into the Forest to die. She would never get back to the Keep on foot before nightfall. She would perish from the cold without her supplies.

"Tayeh." A desperate growl rose in her throat.

"Tayeh can't hear you." A strange voice carried across the snow behind her.

Eva whipped around to see a man standing in the snow. He was naked, save for his long, tangled hair. His hair was white as the snow, but he was young. He wore no beard, his body lean. His eyes were clear, the color of fresh spring leaves. He was strangely beautiful, but wild. Eva's spine stiffened in preparation to flee, but she was prey caught in a predator's gaze. The hair on her neck stood on end.

Her hand reached for her sword. It was gone. Eva swore it had been clipped to her belt when she lay down to rest.

The naked man sauntered - or stalked - over to her. The way he moved reminded her of a cat, the articulation of movement, the level gaze as it keeps check on its prey before the strike.

Eva didn't move. He was a creature of the Forest whose blood ran thick with raw magic. A dangerous, fickle creature. Lula had warned her of them, though promised that they would not hurt her.

"Where is Lulanan?" Eva asked the predator with the body of a man.

"Here and there and everywhere," he answered.

He came to a stop before her, studying her, as if wrought with some kind of mysterious indecision. As he stood watching her, more Forest Folk appeared. Some were animals still - a stag, a doe, a little song bird, an otter. Others changed into human-like guises, though the wildness still clung to them. A woman with a round face like an owl. A boy with a shock of curling, coal-black hair. For a moment, Eva saw nothing beyond the sadness in his beautiful, piercing blue eyes. A farewell. They all possessed a sameness, yet were starkly individual. Some approached her timidly, some with avid curiosity. The otter circled her ankles no fewer than three times.

Finally, the predator-man, who had never once taken his gaze from her, nodded. Those gathered became still, watching her.

The man demanded her attention with his closeness. Eva could feel the heat radiating from his bare skin. He pulled at her cloak fastener with his hand, pushed her shirt aside, and placed his palm upon her chest, skin to skin.

His forceful proximity was unnerving, but the heat of his hand was almost comforting in the cool winter air. The comforting heat changed almost instantly, his hand felt like fire, branding her skin. Piercing, invisible flames spread from her chest, licking toward her fingers, all the way down to her toes. Invisible chains held her immobile. She wanted to scream. Her lips wouldn't move. Her tongue could not shape the sounds.

The man blinked. His gaze faltered. Another came and placed a hand upon his, and the fire continued. Then another and another until Eva was sure she was ashes beneath the mass of ethereal people. The pain became everything. She couldn't see. She couldn't hear. In her ears was only a raging inferno.

Cold washed over her. Instantly, the pain was gone.

She struggled to move, to open her eyes. Her body was still frozen. She was sitting. Her back rested against something solid. She moved her feet one by one, then her hands. She opened her eyes, blinking hard.

Her head was resting against the tree. Beyond, the snow accumulated in drifts, falling steadily outside the shelter of the tree well. Tarek was sharpening one of his daggers on his small whetstone. The horses stood beyond him, still and silent, watching the snow fall. The day was still bright.

"What's wrong?" Tarek asked, noticing that she was awake, sensing her agitation.

Eva shook her head, trying to clear her thoughts. She clutched her chest where the magic had branded her. A dream. It must have been a dream. But it had felt real, as real as she felt sitting across from her old bodyguard - whom she was relieved to see had not abandoned her in some trickery.

She pulled back her cloak, her shirt, to expose her chest. She jerked in alarm to see a red mark, the skin tender.

"What is that?"

"Did you leave me alone while I was sleeping?"

"No. I have been right here the whole time. You have only been sleeping a little while, not even an hour."

"They did something to me while I was sleeping. It was a dream, only it wasn't a dream."

"Who?"

"The people of the Forest."

Tarek's eyes widened with fear. "Maybe we should press on."

"I think that would be best."

The snow began to fall while Eva's sleep had been hijacked by the magical creatures, covering their tracks within minutes. A search party would be unable to track them, even if they did brave the Great Forest.

The knowledge wasn't comforting. They both wanted to get out of the Forest as soon as possible. Eva had no desire to find herself under the influence of the creatures once more, awake or asleep. There was no sign of Lulanan, who could offer them safe passage.

They traveled, taking short breaks when necessary, until exhaustion and cold and failing light forced them to stop.

Tarek made a small fire from some dry, dead branches, and cones. It wasn't a big fire, but the tiny flames were warm and comforting.

Almost as soon as the flames took hold, Eva felt the *simul rami* pulsing through the element. The vision she saw was clear and captivating, like colors suddenly lit by a cool winter sun.

It was the Keep, the great hall. There was no music, no laughter.

Lindin stood at the head of the long table. He raised his glass.

"To Eva. Wherever she may be, may she find solace and peace," he said. Everyone drank. They were mourning her, she realized with a pang of guilt. Mila was crying openly. Murryn heaved a great sob into Tarran's shoulder, his arm around her. As the vision faded, Tarran's eyes hardened with determination.

The vision of Eva's friends, her family, the only real home she had ever known, was gone. Other visions lingered within her grasp. She pulled back. The *simul rami* was potent in its clarity. Part of her yearned to delve into those visions, immerse herself in the great river that was the *simul rami*. But another part warned that if she did, she might never weave her way out again.

Tearing away from the *simul rami*, forcing her consciousness back into her own body, was almost painful. Cold air caught in her lungs, threatening to make her cough. Tarek watched her, a question in his eyes that he didn't voice.

"Do we need to take turns on watch?" Tarek mused.

Eva shook her head. "Whatever threats we face in this Forest, it seems that sleep is no barrier. Let's both get some rest - and hope we wake."

The Great Forest, once so familiar to her, had become like a wild animal, controlled by its instincts. Eva was a fool to believe it could be tamed.

EVA

DESPITE EVA'S APPREHENSION about being accosted by the unnerving man as soon as she closed her eyes, no strange dreams interrupted her sleep. Tarek reported nothing amiss in his dreams either.

They saddled the horses and moved on as the Forest turned the cool colors of a winter dawn. It had stopped snowing, but a cold, biting wind swirled the new fallen-snow, giving the illusion that it still fell from the heavens. The snow stung their faces, making it hard to keep a good eye on their surroundings. They had to be doubly careful not to lose the road.

Visions hovered on the icy wind, taunting Eva with perplexing, enigmatic snippets of stories untold. With effort, she pushed them away and concentrated on the obscure, snow-laden path ahead.

Her magic was potent. Something had changed. Eva suspected her increased abilities and the Forest Folk's invisible fire was connected.

The days went on. The cold did not relent.

Eva and Tarek dismounted and walked just to move warm blood through their extremities, to keep their toes from freezing and turning numb. When they could, they built a fire from any bits of dry timber they could find. Their supplies began to run low. Tarek thought perhaps two or three days more and they would be out of the Forest. Any more and they would run out of food. Hunting was almost out of the question in the current conditions, and Eva didn't want to take down an animal in the Forest.

As the days, and cold, wore on, it was easy to forget about the wild, ethereal creatures. It was easy to forget her worry and grief as Eva became numb and frozen. The cold was all encompassing. It crept into every thought, every movement. Eva just wanted to be warm. She just wanted to remember being warm. She wanted to get out of the snow, sit in front of a blazing fire, hot tea or mulled wine slipping down her throat and warming her innards.

Tarek promised her such things. He told her once they were at his camp, things would be better. Things would get even better when they arrived at the small village of Stonyhill, where his company had secured lodging and employment for the winter. There they had warm rooms, warm water for bathing, good food, other simple comforts. Eva's frigid body agreed his plan was an excellent one, but her heart wanted to get to Kitarra.

"Eva!" Tarek called from some ways ahead. Eva pushed Sasha into a canter to catch up. She had lagged behind trying to remember what warm, fresh bread tasted like.

Tarek's voice held a note of relief. Eva could barely entertain the thought that they were almost out of the Forest. She didn't want to feel the keen pain of disappointment.

Tarek came into view quickly, standing at the top of a hill that led down through the rocks. The trail wound down through another small, rocky fissure, much like the one on the border of Jullayah they had left seven days ago.

"We are almost there. Just beyond here is my camp. They are waiting for me." Tarek grinned.

Eva grinned back. Her excitement succumbed to caution as something moved, low on the ground, almost invisible in the white snow. A fox, its fur purest white, its eyes bright amber.

"Lulanan," Eva whispered. The fox became a woman, and Lula walked gracefully over the snow, her bare feet leaving no tracks.

"Evangeline."

Eva dismounted to face the Guardian. Lula's pretty mouth was a thin line, her eyes sad. She put her hand over Eva's heart as the other creatures had done, but there was no fire, no warmth, not even a flicker. The Guardian was a spirit, not tangible beings like the Forest Folk.

"My people have infused your blood with their magic. It will not last forever, but it will help you get to Kitarra. It will enable you to see further, clearer." Lula glanced behind her. A mountain cat stood upon a hillock, full of self-assurance. The cat's fur was white with light gray spots. Its green eyes were the same as the predator man, the same fierce grace. It could be no other. Eva inclined her head in thanks. He gave no recognition, but the tip of his tail flicked.

"You must get to your son, Eva," Lula said, turning back to her. "He needs you. His path is a hard one. His task will tax him greatly. And Illiah will need you." Her sad words stirred Eva's anger and fear. Eva clenched her fists, hating the one who had caused it.

"Why did Tayeh cast me aside, then, if I am so needed?"

"Perhaps there is some piece to the puzzle I cannot see, some ripple that needs to stretch and reach some distant shore. I don't know Tayeh's mind, I never did. Perhaps even Tayeh does not know." With that said, Lula was once more a fox. She touched her black nose to Eva's hand for the briefest instant. It almost felt wet. Then she bounded off, disappearing in the white.

"Let's go," Eva begged, turning to Tarek. Tarek nodded, a smile of anticipation returning to dance upon his lips.

They passed through the narrow canyon and emerged into the bright light beyond.

They entered a whole new world. The pale sky was bright, stretching for miles, unhindered by tall trees and branches. A faint layer of cloud covered the blue, coming to rest upon the tall mountains to the north and east. The thin light cast queer shadows on the faded hills to the northwest. In the distance, the sun broke through and shimmered across a small, rippling river winding toward the western hills. The hills were lazy, dotted by a few trees. The wind shook the snow from the grass and moved it with the wind, where it settled mostly in drifts.

Eva took a deep breath. As she exhaled, her consciousness went with the breeze. She was like a bird, swooping and weaving over the landscape, over the river, the odd clumped trees, crooked and bent from the wind.

As the wind, Eva saw something out of place in the open, snow-ribbed landscape: smoke from a small camp, rising with the breeze. Two canvas tents sheltered in a hill nook not far from a crook in the river. She could make out several figures but couldn't tell if they were men or women, travelers or warriors. They kept close to the fire, out of the cold wind. There were horses tethered just beyond the camp by a wagon.

Eva staggered in the saddle coming back to herself, holding fast to the reins. She shook her head, breathing fast. It had been exhilarating.

"Is that where we are headed?" Eva pointed in the direction she had seen the camp. Tarek nodded. "I saw them."

"That could be a useful skill, Eva, to see the road ahead. The Midlands are a dangerous place. No king, no rules except those of the sword. To look ahead for ambush or other dangers would be a great asset. Come, let's go."

He pushed Penn forward at a canter. Eva followed, enjoying the freedom of the open countryside. The horses excelled over the grassy hills. Penn tossed his head in pleasure. The stallion loved a good run.

Soon, they both saw the smoke rising in the distance. A lone figure ran toward them.

Tarek pushed Penn harder, then stopped short of the other man, sliding off Penn's tall back. The other man, who was slighter than Tarek, shorter, thinner of build, grinned widely, his handsome face turned toward Tarek's. They embraced, kissing like young, foolish lovers. The happiness of her friend was both blessing and curse. Eva put her fingers on her lips, remembering the sensation of love-sick kisses.

She slowed Sasha to a walk to allow the two lovers a moment. She dismounted so she wouldn't loom over the pair.

Tarek's lover had already broken free of his embrace to regard her and the horses. He had an amiable face. His curling red-brown hair looked like it was trying desperately to escape from his head to be one with the wind. At first Eva thought him young, but as he smiled his eyes were rimmed with wrinkles that were part age, part character.

"This is Eva. Eva, this is Elish, my partner."

"Wonderful to meet you, Eva," Elish said. "Tarek told me about you. I am glad that he found you safe - he was so worried." His eyes were curious. Eva could tell he was taking stock of her appearance, his eyes lingering on the strands of pale hair the wind coaxed out from under her cap and hood.

"It's good to meet you as well," Eva replied.

"Come, let's get to camp, out of this wind, before the fire," Elish suggested, pulling his hood over his head once more. "Macyna and Siracus took down a deer yesterday. There is plenty of hot stew! You can tell us the tale of the Dark Wood."

Eva sunk with relief before the large camp fire. The heat was luxurious on her exposed face. She pulled off her gloves so her fingers could share the experience. Elish gave her a bowl of hot stew in an earthen bowl. Steam filled her nostrils. She had never smelled anything so good.

Tarek's six companions were a mixed bag. They called themselves the Iron Wolves and hired out under that name. Tarek told her they were renowned throughout the Midlands for their skill and dependability, a rare combination apparently.

Elish was friendly and welcoming, as were Boe and Yuri. Hector was solemn, his face unreadable. Siracus and Macyna were brother and sister. Siracus was welcoming; Macyna had a pinched expression when Eva was introduced. The only woman in a group of men. Macyna looked like she preferred it that way.

They were clearly all warriors. Their worn, leather armor was etched with wolfish designs, crude compared to the guards of Jullayah, but armor did not the fighter make. Hector was honing his blade with an edge profile to slice bone. He was a big, well-muscled man. He wouldn't need a sharp blade to extract death from his opponents.

The company wanted her tale, and Tarek's, but the horses needed attention. They were cold and hungry too. After seeing to their comfort, Eva took her gear to a corner of the large tent where Tarek said she could sleep. Inside was warmer than out. And it was dry. Eva fought the strong desire to curl up right then, but Elish had promised a hot brew.

"I knew I was hauling around this bottle for a good reason," Elish said as he poured each their own cup of mulled wine. Eva let the hot, fiery liquid drip slowly down her throat. It made her dizzy, but she hardly cared.

"So, tell us the tale!" Boe asked.

"Well, I told you of the ship I saw at Fishtown," Tarek began. There were nods around the circle. "I told you the man was someone I knew from Jullayah, a trusted friend. Eva is his wife. The child I saw was theirs. They were kidnapped from Jullayah by Kitarrans."

"What do the Kitarrans want with them?" Yuri asked Eva.

"I don't know," Eva replied quietly. "It doesn't matter. I must get to them. They are my family. My life is nothing if I am not with them. I am going to Kitarra."

"How are you going to do that?" Macyna asked in a voice that matched her expression. "Kitarra is a long way from here. The land between is filled with dangerous people. And you are, what, some strange breed of noblewoman?"

Eva regarded her levelly. "I have skills to assist my journey."

"Aye. Aye, you do," Hector said. "You are royal Allati. You have the sight - magic runs in your veins." His eyes were slits in his grizzled face.

Silence followed his bold statement. Eva wished he had not spoken of it, that she could keep her magic secret, even if her errand was not. She did not know what to say to dissuade their curious stares. Her silence was an admission.

"It is true. There is magic in my blood," Eva admitted finally.

"Keep well away from Allati. They would pay a blood price for you," Hector huffed.

"Hector hails from Allati," Elish explained. "Not too fond of his own people, not after they exiled him for sleeping with a nobleman's wife."

Hector narrowed his eyes at Elish briefly, then shrugged and turned to Eva. "It was worth it. Some women are." Hector's face remained stoic. Eva must have imagined the wink turned her direction.

"What kind of magic can you work?" Yuri asked. The question echoed in the eyes of all the companions, except perhaps Hector. Hector's eyes were full of knowing.

"I can see across great distances using the elements. I can see visions of the past," Eva told them. Yuri looked crestfallen, as if expecting her to be able to set things aflame or kill with a look or incantation. If only.

"Can you see into the merchant quarters of Fishtown?" Boe asked eagerly. Siracus slapped the back of his head.

"We are not thieves."

"Yeah, but could you?" Boe asked again, dodging a second blow with practiced ease.

"I don't know," Eva replied. She didn't mention her other gift. She gave Tarek a look under her lashes to see a faint nod of approval from his shadowed face.

"Tell us about the Dark Wood?" Boe asked eagerly. "What of the creatures there?"

"It was cold. The trail was hard to follow," Tarek told him in a patient voice. "There were no creatures that we could see." He lied easily to the young man.

Boe looked disappointed. "They say the creatures there turn into beautiful women. Naked, beautiful women."

"Why don't you go see for yourself, Boe?" Macyna teased. "I know you are desperate, but the cold would freeze off your member before you could find somewhere warm to put it."

Boe blushed. Even in the firelight it was obvious. Eva pitied him a little.

"Has there been any news from Stonyhill?" Tarek asked.

"Yes." Elish pointed to Siracus. "Sira and Mac took down the deer on their way back. Felis is waiting for us, like last winter. He will give us room and board in exchange for protection and help around the village. We leave tomorrow morning, so best get some rest." The look he gave Tarek under his long lashes implied the two lovers had other plans.

Eva slipped into her corner of the tent. Yuri kindly gave her some extra furs. The tent was big, with heavy canvas hanging from the supports to create distinct rooms. She shared her small corner with crates of food stuff and horse fodder. She didn't mind. The oats were a welcome, familiar smell. She had a candle to light her space so she could sort out her clothes and her pack.

She lay down listening to the others settle around the tent. The noises were comforting. The canvas curtains granted some privacy. Tarek and Elish had their own tent. Macyna had her own curtained area. The other men slept in a room together. Eva was glad she didn't have to share with Macyna. The other woman seemed disapproving and sour, bitter for one so young.

The bed Eva made for herself was luxurious compared to the cold Forest. The furs were dry, welcoming, and soft against her cheek. The wind whipped around the outside of the tent, lulling Eva to sleep with its unobtrusive noise.

CHAPTER 44

ILLIAH

COLD, numbing, *fucking* wind.

Illiah had lost count of the days the Kitarran ship had been following the cliffs. Cliffs so malicious any ship that so much as glanced at them would be thrashed to pieces. The cliffs towered sharp and cruel above the ocean, giving birth to a spiteful, chaotic wind. The wind was its own entity. Like a plague. Or an army. The ship's sails cut through it relentlessly, as if they commanded the wind and not the other way around.

Also, the waves. Rough and monstrous, they inspired white knuckles and stern footing. But the Kitarrans did not worry. Their ships were tough and their sailors tougher. Illiah had no experience sailing, but he could see their competence and was glad for it.

All three Kitarran boats had handled the Great River of Jullayah with speed and delicacy, pulling Illiah from his homeland at an alarming rate. They handled the ocean nearly as neatly, even with the coarser waves and the salt spray caressing the tough sails.

The cabin below was large enough for the crew to wait out the worst of the weather away from the damaging elements. Illiah spent a fair share of the voyage below deck. Sometimes because of his son. The deck above could be slippery and was often dangerous for his young boy. More often, he was abed sick from the rocking motion of the boat on the waves. At least he was fairly certain it was from the boat. Sometimes, in moments of weakness, he thought of Eva and his stomach churned in a fair imitation of his emotions.

Rhyl seemed to handle the journey better than his father. Illiah had finally gotten over the worse of his seasickness. His stomach still roiled after several hours of rough water, but at least he could hold his food down. He no longer felt like death personified.

The first days on the ocean had been rough. The Kitarrans took pity on him and made him broths and tea. They did not complain when he couldn't make it to the edge of the rail before expelling the contents of his stomach on the deck. They cleaned up after him without a word. They watched over Rhyl when he was too exhausted to care for his son. Illiah detested the weakness of his body.

At least the Kitarrans had his son's safety foremost in their mind. And they were kind. Rhyl thought his captors to be the best of friends. If Illiah wasn't careful, he was going to think the same too.

Then the weather turned cold and wet, forcing him below where the rocking motion was doubled by the loss of the horizon, making him sick all over again.

Also, winter. From the talk of the Kitarrans, they were making all haste to Kitarra before the worst of the late autumn and winter storms hit. So far there had been no snow, but the cold was piercing, and mixed with the sea spray, it was downright unpleasant. Illiah didn't want to think about when the temperature dropped and the deck held a slick of ice.

Thankfully, he was not expected to help with the complicated dance of ropes, knots, and balance that was sailing. When he was cold and miserable, he could go below where a little brazier warmed the small space. The sailors had no such option; they were slaves to the wind.

The elements were awful. Inhospitable. But Illiah chafed below deck. He stood on deck and watched the sailors at work, Kitarrans and humans alike. Sailing in rough weather required constant attention to the sails, rigging, and navigation. Deecon, of course, was the captain.

Deecon stood poised on the command deck, his tail stretched out for balance, his ears back against the onslaught of wind and wet. When weather was rough, only he steered the ship. He moved with the ship like Illiah moved with his blade, as one.

Illiah tugged his cloak tighter around his throat and took several hops to stand beside the captain. Deecon shifted his gaze for an instant to see who had joined him, keeping his arms locked on the wheel lest it pull from his grasp, sending the ship off its delicate course.

"Is Rhyl below?" Deecon asked in a sharp voice that just barely cut through the wind.

"Of course," Illiah replied patiently, gritting his teeth. The Kitarrans seemed to think he was barely capable as a father - as if he would bring a young child onto the deck in such conditions. The Kitarrans treated his son like a revered prince. The child of a prophecy Illiah knew little about. He had asked, many times. Apparently, it wasn't up to them to explain. Kitarrans were stubborn, he had learned. He and Rhyl fit right in.

Deecon finally lost his temper the last time Illiah had petitioned for answers. Which was a first. The Kitarran was as patient as an ancient oak. At Illiah's persistent questioning, Deecon lost his calm and slammed his fist into the rail with enough force to splinter it. At least it had not been Illiah's face.

In his month sailing with the Kitarrans, he had learned they were a patient, steady race. They were not rash or given to unpleasant vices. He had tried desperately to find fault in their countenance. He had tried to hate them. Really, he had.

The only thing he hated about them was that they had kidnapped him and his son. It was unforgivable, but they were kind kidnappers. The humans with them seemed to take on the Kitarran qualities. They were a reasonable lot; there hadn't been a single dispute among the crewmen, despite the cramped and often miserable conditions on the boat. It was enough to make one suspicious, but in the end, it was just good leadership and character.

Illiah found it hard to stay angry when he watched how they entertained Rhyl endlessly on what would be a long, boring voyage for a small child confined mostly to the cabin. They played games with him. They were silly, trying to make him laugh, often succeeding.

Sometimes Rhyl would sink into silent and moody fits, and nothing would raise the boy's spirits. In response, a silent, despondent guilt fell over the ship. Illiah knew the Kitarrans felt the weight of what they had done by taking a boy away from his mother and his home, and they felt ashamed by it.

Illiah could barely recall the acidic fear of their first week surrounded by the feral-looking Kitarrans. Illiah's growing respect for the Kitarrans slowly washed away his fear until only undissolved anger remained. He could control his anger. Fear was harder, much harder, especially when it was all for his son. Illiah had been afraid he wouldn't be able to protect Rhyl if the Kitarrans hurt him.

But the Kitarrans were devoted to his son - they came to Rhyl's beck and call. They would not hurt him. Illiah was almost certain the Kitarrans would give their lives for his son. It was an immense relief. Illiah cursed his past self for not investigating the prophecy more - what had he been thinking? He should have known his son, marked for greatness by the Guardians, would not be allowed to live a quiet life in the Keep. But he had hoped Rhyl would have the chance to grow into a man before destiny came calling. Illiah had hoped for time to prepare him - if that were even possible.

"Tomorrow we should enter the river delta. The waters will be smoother, the wind less bitter," Deecon told him.

"From there, how far is it to Kilev?" Illiah asked.

"Not far. A day or two at the most."

Two more days and Illiah would feel dry land under his boots. But then what? Illiah knew they were headed to see the queen and he hoped he would finally get answers. The nagging fear asserted itself once more. Illiah's greatest fear, beyond the safekeeping of Rhyl, was that they would separate them. Beyond Rhyl's smiles and enthusiasm, there was a great hurt caused by his separation from his mother. Rhyl's sudden silences, his flashes of temper or tears, common to a four-year-old, were different. Illiah knew his son.

Illiah couldn't speak of Eva. Rhyl's questions about his mother, his pleas, fell on deaf ears. Nothing Illiah could say would make it better. All he could do was hold his son tight and comfort him as best he could.

The next morning it was evident that they had entered the river delta. Below in the cabin Illiah no longer had to concentrate to stand upright. He wasn't woken by a violent lurch of waves. His stomach was not trying to escape through his throat.

Illiah slipped carefully from beside his son. He resettled the blankets tightly around the little boy to ward off any chill. He threw his heavy cloak around his shoulders and went up, squinting against the daylight.

The sun peered out from between two fluffy white clouds, just glinting over the edge of the mountains far to the east. More clouds were on the horizon, but the wind had died down considerably. It still fluttered in the sails, but it did not choke one's breath or try to rip the sails from their masts.

Seabirds filled the air with their raucous calls, swooping close to the boat, looking for morsels. Illiah had emerged just as they passed a lively seaport, the docks laden with boats and people despite the early hour, or perhaps because of it. Beyond the apparent jumble of piers, boats, and people rose a town along the banks, above the high-water mark. Smoke rose from innumerable buildings. People on the pier stopped their work to gaze at the passing ship. Many took a moment to wave or whistle in greeting, their gestures returned by the crew. The Kitarrans were irritatingly genial.

The water turned brackish and murky. More and more and yet more mountains rose from the mainland before them, to the east, to the west, to the north. Kitarra, it seemed, was a land of mountains, most dusted with the first snow of winter.

The town quickly gave way to forest and wetlands. The river was wide where it met the sea, but the channel for boats was not. Deecon was at the helm, navigating through the invisible safe-track, carefully heeding the other ships journeying up and down the river.

"There - you can see Kitarra Peak. At its base is Kilev, our destination, the great city of Kitarra." Jona pointed out the spire-shaped mountain rising distinctly before the more distant peaks. "Not long now," the sailor added with a grin.

Illiah wasn't the only one looking forward to solid ground beneath his feet. No doubt Jona had a family waiting for him back home, a wife, children of his own. He had that look about him, like the kind of man who would want a home to come back to. Illiah wasn't about to ask him. He had no desire to hear of another man's comforts.

"Daddy!" Rhyl said, coming over to him, grasping his hand tightly, following his gaze up the river. "Where are we?"

"We are on the river," Illiah told him. "Soon we will be at our new home."

"Will Mummy be there?"

"No," Illiah told him resolutely.

"Look, Rhyl, you see that black lumpy thing in the water over there?" Jona said, pointing. "That is a seal looking for fish!"

"A seal?" Rhyl strained to look. "Oh yes! I see it." He flashed a toothy grin at Jona, then at his father. The black head of the animal vanished without a ripple into the murky river. "Oh, it's gone."

"Keep your eyes out for more, and otters too."

"Come Rhyl, let's go see if Sergil has some breakfast ready," Illiah suggested.

As the day waned, the momentum of the ship seemed to echo the enthusiasm of the men, eager for their homes and warm beds. The ship sailed upriver with the efficiency of a horse over land. The river grew narrower, but the channel for boats grew wider, and their course demanded less precision. Deecon gave the wheel over to his first mate and began preparations for landing.

Even above the delta, the river was far from small. It was broad, with a strong, deceptive current. Only a brave fool would attempt to swim across it.

They passed many vessels. Some slow, large and low in the water, carrying crates of goods being conveyed up and down the river towns. Others were small and swift, some with two or three men aboard, their fishing poles out. Always a friendly wave or nod of the head. Illiah found himself waving back.

"Keep your eyes out for the gentle river giants," Deecon told Rhyl, coming up beside where Illiah stood with Rhyl, gazing out at the passing landscape.

"Giants?" Rhyl echoed in awe.

"Yes. Sacred fish live in these waters. We call them the acipenae. They feed on dead fish, roe, stuff lying around. They are not predators, but they are smart. They live forever and can grow almost as long as our boat," Deecon said with a smile.

"As long as the boat?"

Deecon nodded. "They love to jump high out of the water."

Rhyl's gaze, which had been discerning the length of the boat, shot like an arrow back to the river, as if he had already missed the spectacle.

"It's getting late in the season for fishing, but perhaps next summer

I shall take you out on the river and teach you how to catch a giant," Deecon told the boy. Rhyl's face was so full of child-like exaggeration, wide eyes and gaping mouth, that the large Kitarran gave a great huff of amusement. Rhyl bounced from one foot to the other. Illiah couldn't help but smile too. Rhyl's excitement was infectious.

The looming Kitarra Peak had grown closer all morning, giving the illusion it was coming to them, and not the other way around. The great tooth of rock and cliff dominated the sky. The highest crags were brushed with fresh snow, making it gleam in the sunlight.

The river turned in a great, lazy arc. When they broached the bend, the view opened before them, exposing the foot of the peak and the city of Kilev.

The great Kitarran city nestled at the foot of the mountain. Docks lined the shore, and boats lined the docks. The city spread and spiraled up the mountain, clinging like lichen to a tree trunk. Perched like a falcon at the top of the city was a white fortress. Three golden flags moved lazily in the winter breeze atop three white towers.

The queen's fortress stood above the rest, its back to the mountain, and the wild forest beyond. It reminded Illiah strongly of the Keep, on a much grander and larger scale. Eva had mentioned something about the Keep's mysterious history and how she thought it had been built by Kitarrans long, long ago. A piercing pain in Illiah's chest accompanied the memory, and he hurriedly dismissed Eva from his thoughts. The pain lessened. Or at least he could ignore it better.

They sailed past the city docks until they were below the fortress. The dock they approached was practically deserted compared to the bustling city wharfs, only a group of guards standing in formation. Their fine leather armor was dyed golden. Russet cloaks hung from their shoulders, rippling in the breeze. Each carried a helm under one arm and a staff in the other, atop which swayed the flag of Kitarra: a bald tree on a field of gold, surrounded by a wreath of white leaves.

With the sails trimmed, the boat slowed. Deecon shouted orders and ropes were thrown to the dock.

Several of the golden-garbed guards abandoned their picturesque post to retrieve the ropes. The boat was pulled against the wooden dock, securing it to the land. Illiah's hands tightened on Rhyl's shoulders as the boat jostled slightly when wood collided gently with wood.

"This way, my lord," Deecon said, gesturing for Illiah to precede him down the gangplank effectively secured by the waiting guards. Deecon always called Illiah by his title. Illiah liked to think it was out of respect.

Rhyl squeezed his father's hand tighter as they walked ashore.

The guards stood at attention as they passed. Only two of the nine or so guards were Kitarran, with their creature-like, furred faces, clawed hands, and long, tufted tails. The rest were human. In fact, from Illiah's short observation of this new land, humans well outnumbered Kitarrans.

"The queen will be anxious to meet both of you," Deecon told them as they walked. "But she will understand your need to rest. We have been on that boat for a long time."

The gaze of the guards followed Rhyl, oblivious to their curiosity, his green-blue eyes fixed on the towering fortress rising above the trees.

A winding cobblestone road led upward through the trees to the fortress. They were expected to walk. Illiah didn't mind. After so long on the water, it was satisfying to feel solid earth beneath his boots.

The guards fell into step behind them, a parade of sorts. Illiah doubted they meant to keep him from escaping - where would he go? The land was alien to him. The river was the only path he knew, and he wouldn't risk his son's life on his ignorance of boats. With the Kitarrans' devotion to Rhyl, an honor guard made more sense.

The gates of the fortress were open and welcoming. They arrived in a place where the city met the fortress and citizens meandered here and there, some businesslike and brisk, some languishing, strolling out into the city. As they passed, most people halted and stared; some pointed and whispered.

Once inside the fortress gates, Illiah reassessed his opinion of the place. It was less like a fortress and more like a palace or villa. The stonework was beautiful and ornate. Winding stairs led up to the many levels, tall arching ceilings, carved lintels and statues. Gardens filled with late-season flowers had not yet felt the icy breath of winter, the bright colors contrasting against the gray-and-white stone walls. Illiah knew he should be impressed, but he didn't really care.

Illiah expected the inner corridors to reflect the exterior, and he was not disappointed. Statues and tapestries lined the walls; lush carpets softened the sounds echoing in the cool stone walls. They crossed a spacious courtyard filled with towering trees. People mingled, clothed in furs to keep the chill away. Brightly colored leaves fell from the large trees, littering the ground.

They came to a set of ornate doors. Two guards stood at attention on either side, barring public entry. The guards, all human, bowed their heads in unison to Deecon before opening the doors for them. The honor guard remained outside. Just Deecon, Illiah and Rhyl entered.

Inside was a warm and welcoming receiving room. Tall glazed windows looked out to the city below. There were couches for lounging and tables laden with delicate arrangements, but the room was empty except for a young human woman who had obviously been expecting them.

"Deecon! The queen is overjoyed that you are back." A slow smile spread over the young woman's face. She looked at Illiah with deep-brown eyes. She turned to Rhyl and her smile broadened, lighting up her pretty face. "Welcome! A room has been prepared for you. You must be exhausted, and have many questions." Her voice was warm.

Illiah's brow rose in response. Of course he had questions.

She wilted a little. "I know. Questions is an understatement, but the queen will do her best to explain. My name is Selene. I am Queen Arrah's handmaiden. She has given me the task of making sure you and your son are comfortable here in Kilev," Selene said with a slight curtsy. She was a delicate woman, with slender arms and a womanly figure. Everything about her screamed feminine youth and beauty. "Come, I will show you to your rooms. Deecon, the queen awaits you in the morning room."

"I will see you soon." And then Deecon left with a light bow toward the queen's woman and another for Illiah and Rhyl.

Illiah said nothing. Rhyl had slipped into silence as the new surroundings muted his courage.

Selene led them wordlessly down another hall to the chamber she announced was theirs. It was a large room with lavish furnishings and linens. The bed was proportionally large and comfortable, heaped with plush furs to ensure the winter chill was a passing thought. Tapestries depicting mountains, forests, and little creeks lined the walls. A large hearth blazed with a cozy fire. A long table held several baskets of fresh food, and a crock steamed with some hot drink. More tall, glazed windows faced south overlooking a terrace and the city stretching out below. The curving river hugged the low folds of the land, dissolving into the horizon.

"Here is Rhyl's room." Selene gestured to a door leading off the main room. Rhyl's room had a child-sized version of the grand bed, more furs and lush carpets complete with wooden toys, a small practice sword, and anything else a little boy might like to play with. Rhyl would soon be the most spoiled child in the three realms.

"This leads to the bathing rooms, the pools, and the royal gardens." Selene led them through yet another door. Beyond was a covered, open-air room that contained privies, protected from prying eyes by a generous screen. The screens opened into a large courtyard. Steam rose in the air, and Illiah knew Eva had been right: Kitarrans had built the Keep.

The pools before him were almost identical to the ones at the Keep. The green-blue water was partially obscured by drifting clouds of steam, filling the air with the familiar pungent smell of minerals. The three large pools were larger than the ones at the Keep, curved to match the round courtyard.

In the center of the courtyard on an island made from the pools stood a tall, arching tree. Its trunk was wide, the gray bark smooth. Its roots twisted, some holding tight to the rocks, some dipping into the pools like gnarled fingers. The thick branches reached out into the courtyard, overhanging parts of the pools. Where all other trees were mostly bare from the end of the season, this tree still wore golden-green leaves that rustled in the silent courtyard. It was the kind of tree Eva would fall in love with.

The royal garden backed onto the forest full of ferns, moss, and little pathways leading into the sparse undergrowth. Beyond the forest, above the palace, loomed the peak. The failing sun cast orange shadows on the crags. It was menacing and beautiful.

The garden was silent. Empty. Other doors led into the palace from all angles of the courtyard. Where were all the people?

"I will return later," Selene said with another curtsy. "Rest, eat, sleep, bathe. If you need something, just call. There are always guards on duty. They are instructed to help you in any way they can, or they will fetch me."

Illiah had nothing to say. The woman left, walking briskly across the courtyard, disappearing through a door opposite.

Illiah was alone with his son for the first time since becoming captives. He breathed out a sigh, leading Rhyl back inside, away from the cold, damp air.

Rhyl was interested in his room, the toys, the little sword, the soft feather bed. Illiah inspected the storage chest filled with finely crafted clothes for both him and Rhyl. He selected some and enticed Rhyl to come for a bath.

After a quick snack, they swam. Illiah gave his son a good scrubbing. It was just like the Keep - the water was hot and constantly circulating. The murk created from their travels left quickly. Rhyl was a good swimmer and enjoyed splashing in the water like an otter. A game of chase ensued, and Illiah had Rhyl in shrieks of laughter that echoed off the silent stone.

Someone was watching them. A small, discreet, creeping shadow hid behind the leafless briar growing around a nearby stone pillar. Illiah had spotted the shadow from the corner of his eye as soon as they entered the pool. A Kitarran child. He pretended ignorance. He had some experience with shy children. Some were best ignored until they could decide if you were friend or foe; some warmed with a friendly smile. He didn't know which method would work on this strange child.

The child caught his eye, and Illiah took a chance.

"Hello there," Illiah said in what he hoped was a neutral, friendly tone. Rhyl turned to see the young Kitarran step out from his hiding spot, slowly, cautiously. His son didn't say anything. Rhyl could be shy as well, and he had never seen a Kitarran child before. "What is your name? My name is Illiah. This is Rhyl."

The Kitarran took another step closer. The child was tall and thin, with long legs and arms. Stick thin, really. His tail was a fuzzy whip.

Illiah wondered if they fed him enough. Illiah thought maybe he was a boy. It was hard to tell - he wasn't familiar enough with the Kitarrans to know for sure.

The Kitarran had beautiful tawny-brown fur - it was a boy, Illiah decided, even if he couldn't decide what made the distinction. The boy's hands and ears faded gradually to a darker shade, almost black. His eyes were captivating, round, and luminous, the color of the sky on a clear fall day. He stood still as a statue; not even his tail twitched. He wasn't staring at Illiah - he was staring at Rhyl. Rhyl stared back. Illiah wondered what passed between the two children.

Suddenly, the Kitarran relaxed and his mouth pulled into a thin smile. He crept forward to the edge of the pool.

"Talo. My name is Talo," he said, crouching down close to Rhyl and Illiah's level.

"How old are you?" Rhyl asked.

"I'm almost six. How old are you?"

"I am four, but soon I will be five," Rhyl answered proudly as if it were a competition.

"I was supposed to stay away," Talo admitted remorsefully. "But I didn't want to. I wanted to see you."

"Will your parents be angry?" Illiah asked him.

The boy looked down at his furry feet. His little toes ended in tiny claws, a miniature version of the fierce Kitarran warriors. "My parents are dead."

Illiah wanted to smack himself. Poor child. "I'm sorry," he said. What else did you say to an orphaned child? He wished he knew the right words.

"Muhala will be cross, but only for a little while," Talo said with a ghost of a smile.

"Muhala?" Illiah asked.

"The mother of my father," Talo replied. Talo gave him a lingering look. Then with a dash of fur, he was gone, skipping over the stones and gardens, back through one of the other doors leading out of the courtyard.

Rhyl gave a huge yawn, indifferent to the other boy's sudden departure.

Illiah reluctantly stepped out of the water and threw a huge towel about his person before scooping out Rhyl and doing the same. He carried his son back to their room; the stones were cold underfoot.

In their room, the fire was dying. Illiah banked it, keeping the room warm against the chilly air that followed them inside.

Dressing in their new clothes felt strange and welcoming after so many days on the boat. Rhyl snacked on cheese and late-season fruit, and then asked to go to bed. The boy must be truly exhausted - Rhyl never asked to go to bed. Sleep was Rhyl's greatest adversary.

Illiah tucked him into the little feather bed, wondering if his son would be all right sleeping alone, even though he wasn't far away. He would leave the door open and a lantern burning. He wondered if he would be the one unable to sleep without his son next to him.

"Mummy?" Rhyl asked hopefully. Illiah shook his head, the familiar weariness of grief crushing him. Rhyl stuck his thumb in his mouth, turned over, and went to sleep.

Illiah sat before the fire. He was tired, weary beyond belief, but not the kind of weariness easily cured by a good sleep in a soft bed. The pale winter sun had set; twilight would be fleeting. A knock came at the door, a welcome distraction from his darkening thoughts.

Illiah opened the door. A Kitarran woman stood in the flickering light from the many elaborate lanterns decorating the halls. She was tall, nearly as tall as he was. She was thin, with narrow shoulders and delicate arms and legs. Her face was tilted up, her back straight. Her posture screamed status and power despite the fragility of her figure. Her head and shoulders were adorned with fine chains dotted with tiny gems that danced in the low light. Illiah thought he had grown used to the strange eyes of the Kitarrans, but this woman penetrated him with a gaze so deep the hairs on his arms rose. Her gray-green eyes were sharp; the cat-like pupils dilated in the dim light, round pools of immeasurable depth.

"May I come in?" she asked in a deep voice. Illiah stepped aside and gestured for her to enter. She dipped her head in thanks, the chains tinkling as she moved.

"I am Arrah, Queen of Kitarra, mother of my people. I owe you much, my lord."

"Yes. You do," Illiah said after a moment. His voice was quiet, his anger close, but he was not one to lose his temper. Arrah looked at her hands. She held something wrapped in a fine piece of fabric. She met him with her clear gaze once more.

"What I did, I did for my people. You can understand the need for a leader to make difficult sacrifices. Unfortunately it is your sacrifice my people need, and his." Arrah gestured to the doorway of Rhyl's room where the boy lay sleeping.

"He is just a child!" Illiah said through his anger.

Arrah looked into the fire, her face desolate. Illiah's anger slipped a little.

"My people are dying. My sons are dead. My daughters are gone. All that remains of my family is my grandson, a little boy filled with sadness." The shadows lingering in the corners of the room seemed to stretch and grow around her. Illiah sensed a deep well of pain under her calm countenance. "Kitarrans do not have children easily. It is hard to conceive, even harder to carry a babe to term. My granddaughter died before her first breath. My grandson's mother died giving birth to him." Arrah paused, her face hardened. "His father, my son, died soon after."

"You think Rhyl will be a great healer and save these stillborn babes and their mothers?"

"Your son will be a healer like his mother. He will be a leader of men like his father. He will inspire hope where there is little. There is a prophecy that speaks of a darkness, hailed by the death of babes unborn. An evil that can only be lifted by a starlit child of two races, of two thrones, touched by the Guardians. That time is upon us. It gathers in the broken hearts of our families. It reaches with cold fingers through the forest and into the trees. But it is not just heartbreak and death. There is something else. The Allmakers feel it. The trees feel it. Without your son, all could be lost." Her voice trailed into the unknown of which she spoke.

Grief lodged hard and calculated in Illiah's throat. His tongue would not form words. Tayeh had planned this. He had used Eva and Illiah to conceive this child, when all along he intended for Rhyl to be brought to Kitarra. Allmakers be damned.

"But why now? Why not wait? Why rip my family apart?"

"Your son will be safe here, Illiah. I have spies in Jullayah. I know your enemies; they are cunning and ruthless. How long would you be able to keep him safe? How long would you manage before your allegiance was ripped in two, forcing you to choose between your family and your king? You are no worshipper of the Black Goddess. Here, you are untouchable. Here, your son will grow and learn alongside the prince. He will have freedom, knowledge, anything he desires. My people love him already. No harm will come to him, this I can promise."

"And my wife? What happens to her?" Illiah's eyes were burning, his cheeks wet despite his desperate desire to control his emotions. "My enemies are hers as well. She can only protect herself for so long. And she thinks that I - that we - are dead!" Illiah started pacing, his chest boiling. He wanted to yell and scream and weep, but his son slept soundly and peacefully in the next room, and war had taught him to control his grief. Once, he had been a hero, though Eva would tell him even heroes were allowed to weep. A sob escaped with the thought.

"Your wife has magic in her blood. She will know the truth," the queen assured him.

"Why didn't you bring her too? We need her."

Arrah closed her eyes and breathed deeply. "I regret it deeply. The pain I have caused you and your son is terrible, unforgivable, but I was instructed that only you and Rhyl could come. I questioned it, I did, but he was adamant."

"Who?"

"The Guardian of my people - Tayeh."

Illiah snorted in disdain.

"I am truly sorry, my lord. I see that you love her deeply," Arrah said in a soft voice.

The chains on Arrah's head tinkled as she took several steps and placed her silken bundle on the table. She folded back the cloth to reveal Illiah's confiscated dagger.

"Do you know what this is?"

"It is an enchanted dagger." Illiah's voice was tight.

"Yes, I guess you could call it that," Arrah said. "It is a vercuri, an object carved over an age ago from fallen cendari branch. There are many tales around the vercuri. The branch was carved into a spear first, which was then carved up into the vercuri, many of which are missing."

Eva had told him the tale of the vercuri long ago, but Illiah wasn't sure what it had to do with him or Rhyl or anything. Again he cursed himself for not searching out answers.

Arrah took something small from her pocket. Eva's pendant. She placed it on top of the dagger. Illiah felt dizzy, like his world had shifted. He blinked. The pendant was gone. There was a small raised leaf on the dagger, a design where there had been none. The two objects fused together and became one.

"Why did you show me this?" Illiah asked.

The queen looked sad.

"Because it is the beginning. And you are part of the end." Then she straightened her back, her chin raised. She gave Illiah a tight approving nod before sweeping out of the room.

The next day, they gave Illiah a sword.

CHAPTER 45

ILLIAH

THE SWORD was not merely symbolic, it was a well-crafted implement of death. The steel was strong, the edge sharp. Once, it had belonged to a prince. But it was not a latha. And it was not a vercuri.

The queen made it clear that Illiah was not a prisoner, not really, nor was he merely an honored guest. He was treated as a member of the royal family. He was free to go wherever he wanted, do whatever he wanted.

The queen did not fear his rebellion. She was not afraid he would whisk his son away and try to navigate the Kitarran lands. The queen knew he was a reasonable, clever man who would never endanger his son. And she was right.

Kitarra was a land of mountains and rivers; traversing it alone with a young child would be impossible. Even with the good grace of the queen, it would be nigh on impossible.

And then there were the Midlands filled with bandits and tyrannical exiles.

And Allati would be just as dangerous. The queen explained how Rhyl was tied to the royal bloodline of Allati, unmistakably marked by the unusual color of his hair. In Allati, Rhyl would be given titles and wives and raised to be a selfish, cruel Allati lord. Illiah preferred the Kitarrans. He was suspicious of a man with more than one wife.

Deecon left two days after their arrival. Illiah was surprised, but Deecon was the Keeper of the Long Isles. It made sense he would return to his duties and home, his mission for the queen completed. The old warrior's constant presence over the last few months made his absence felt. Illiah could almost call his captor a friend. Perhaps the sea voyage had addled his wits as well as his stomach.

Rhyl spent his time with the queen's handmaiden, Selene, and the queen's grandchild, the curious, young Talo. Rhyl seemed to like Selene, and he doted on Talo. The two boys formed a fast friendship and were rarely apart.

They enjoyed lessons with an old graybeard of a Kitarran named Mehmet. Illiah sat in on their lessons at first, which weren't really lessons at all, not in the traditional sense of the word. Mehmet was an endearing personality with endless knowledge on just about everything. He answered the boys' questions with questions, and Illiah smiled to see the two children thinking hard together. The boys rarely sat still, but they did for the old man, evidence of their great affection for him. There were many ways to learn; Illiah approved of the old warrior's technique.

It was tradition, Illiah was told, for every young Kitarran to learn to wield a sword, a bow, to learn how to move like a fighter. Mehmet was too old for such lessons. He complained of his aching bones, especially during the coldest winter days, which he spent before the fire. The queen appointed a young Kitarran named Aisha to teach the boys their first lessons as warriors. Aisha was a cousin (of sorts) to Talo. His father was an obscure relative of Arrah, though Illiah could not recall how.

Illiah looked over the rakish young Kitarran skeptically. Aisha was very young, hardly fifteen.

"My lord," Aisha addressed Illiah in a rather small voice. "I would be honored if you would spar with me so I could prove my worth as an instructor for your son."

Illiah smiled a little, knowing full well that was only part of the boy's motive. The eagerness in the young Kitarran's eyes reminded Illiah of himself as a youth. He had been that boy once, determined to push his limits, to absorb every possible sliver of knowledge. At that age, Illiah had lived for his sword, for his strength and skill. Then Eelan gave him the vercuri, making him unstoppable.

"I would like that," Illiah told Aisha. The boy's face stretched into a weedy grin. "But no lathas."

"No. That would not be fair," Aisha said, then looked at his feet, ashamed perhaps that he spoke too arrogantly. "When would suit you, my lord?"

"Call me Illiah. And now, in the garden."

Aisha's grin widened. Illiah would not have thought it possible.

Aisha insisted they dress in leather armor and greaves so they could spar with real blades. Illiah didn't feel inclined to disregard the cautionary practicality. Selene helped him lace into a borrowed cuirass and greaves.

They had a small audience. Talo and Rhyl crooned with excitement. Mehmet settled on a bench to watch the bout. A servant brought a blanket for his shoulders and a cushion for his rump. Selene sat beside him, her hands folded in her lap.

Illiah stood across from Aisha, his sword drawn.

"Ready?" Illiah asked his opponent.

Aisha nodded. The grin was gone, his face fixed with intent.

Illiah no longer had his dagger to enchant his movements with additional speed and strength. And Aisha was fast. Illiah struggled to anticipate the Kitarran's movements. The boy was clever with his technique. Aisha's style was different from any Illiah had seen or known or fought, a realization that went both ways. Aisha's furry brows were tight with concentration.

Aisha's sword tip glanced heavily against Illiah's wrist. The leather protected his flesh from the cutting edge, but the force made him skip a breath. But he didn't let it slow him. Aisha's aim was to force Illiah to create holes in his technique, within which Aisha planned to strike. Illiah twisted away, feinting. Aisha followed. Illiah backtracked, not without effort, knowing Aisha would not expect it. As he did, he pushed his blade toward Aisha's neck. Illiah felt a surge of pleasure that even without the vercuri, he was still fast. Even with an untested sword, his reach was exact.

For years, Illiah had let himself believe the magic of the vercuri was his only asset. But that had been foolish. He had been an expert before Eelan had gifted him with the enchanted dagger. He had just forgotten it under a fog of guilt and grief. Maybe he owed Arrah his thanks for taking it from him.

Mehmet whistled loud and sharp, calling the end to the match.

"Illiah's favor."

If the fight had been to the death, Aisha would be bleeding out from a diagonal wound to the neck.

Aisha's grin returned as he bowed graciously to Illiah.

"I am honored to have been defeated by a master," Aisha said.

Illiah raised one brow at him. "Your manners are very pretty, but you will best me next time. If you were fighting with a latha, you would have bested me easily. You are exceptional, Aisha." And Illiah meant it.

"Thank you, my lord."

It was not long before the boys worshipped Aisha. Mainly because aside from the technical exercises they learned, he played games with them. The boys loved games. The more rough and raucous the better. Sometimes Aisha was more big brother than teacher.

Content leaving his son with Mehmet or Aisha or Selene, Illiah was left to search out his own distractions.

He wandered the city, observing the people, the order of things in Kilev. The docks were the heart of the city, the river its lifeblood. Boats continually came and went, unloading and loading riches from the sea downriver, or food, or building materials, or livestock. The people of Kitarra used the river like a road, going up or downriver to traverse their land.

The dockside market was an eclectic assortment of people and things. If Kitarra were a tapestry, it would use every conceivable color and texture and pattern. Fishy smells mingled with the silty smells of the river, though not altogether unpleasant. Dozens of different kinds of fish, crabs, and other small creatures of the sea were brought upriver almost daily. Illiah never imagined there could be so many varieties; Jullyah's seas were barren in comparison.

Besides fish and more fish, the different guilds of Kitarra were represented at the market. Weavers and artisans, metalsmiths, and gemsmiths, for Kitarra was a land rich in earthly attributes. The swords for sale outmatched many, even Kota's creations from Jullayah - such was the high quality of their mined steel and skill.

There were weavers from the highlands, the lowlands, the isles, selling their prized sheeplike creatures, the alra. They each had their own wools and method of dying and seemed constantly engaged in tense competition. One man spied Illiah's fine cloak, bragging he had shorn the alra himself. An odd but amusing bunch - maybe they spent too much time in the mountains.

Beyond the docks, the city rose slowly up the mountain. The city's heart was the Queen's Keep; the paved streets were its veins. Lanterns were lit at dusk, hanging from tall posts, illuminating the city with a gentle glow. The streets were clean. The sewage system was well engineered and practical. Wells were plentiful, bringing fresh water from deep within the earth. Public and private bathhouses dotted the city, utilizing the hot mineral water piped down from the mountains.

The Peace Guards patrolled the city: Kitarrans and humans working for the people, keeping the peace and helping with minor disputes. Only when they could not solve a conflict would it be brought before the queen and her high council.

It was impossible to mistake a Peace Guard. They wore golden plumes atop their helmets and a cendari flower sewn upon their left shoulder. They seemed well respected by the citizens, peasant and courtier alike. Illiah watched as they settled disputes as patient negotiators. He respected their technique. It took a certain kind of person to attain patience and calm when dealing with irate and often unreasonable people.

The Peace Guards trained within the palace walls. After five years of training, only those with the correct temperament, honed by their training, were selected. They were then sent throughout Kitarra to uphold the queen's laws. A special few were selected as members of the Queen's Guard, who stayed mostly in the palace, close to the queen. A Queen's Guard was the highest contingent within the Peace Guards, only outranked by the First Defender of Kitarra.

Illiah was surprised to meet the man who held the title, for his temperament was lacking, and Illiah immediately found him irritating.

Illiah had the permission of the queen to do whatever he liked (within reason) and to speak to whomever he wished (manners considered). So far he had found the people of Kitarra helpful and kind, often initiating conversation with him instead of the other way around. Everyone seemed to know who he was and greeted him as Lord Illiah.

The one exception was Scytt, the Queen's First Defender, leader of the Peace Guard and the Queen's Guard. Illiah learned Deecon had held the position for a time after the death of Princess Emri, but he had since retired, becoming Keeper of the Long Isles. The position of First Defender was currently held by a human named Scytt.

Bored of the docks, at least for the moment, Illiah wandered into the designated section of the Queen's Keep that held practice yards and barracks for the guards in training. He knew their training included many skills: negotiation and politics, but also how to defend themselves and others, to be warriors. The novitiates were taught the sword, the bow, and the staff, which was generally favored by the guards. And eventually the latha, the double-bladed, mechanized weapon he had seen on the Kitarrans who had taken him from Jullayah. If they proved themselves worthy, it was a requirement for a Queen's Guard to carry a latha.

The weapon intrigued Illiah. It was unlike any he had ever seen or imagined. When rested it was folded upon itself. One needed to learn how to extract it quickly from its sheath and engage the mechanism that unfolded the blades and snapped them tight and strong. Then it was also a matter of using the double blades effectively. Illiah expected it would be extremely effective when wielded by a master. And he expected a novice would lose an ear or nose.

The green recruits were lined up loosely, each holding a long wooden staff, waiting. They chatted quietly, falling silent when Illiah meandered into the gravel yard.

"Where is your captain?" Illiah asked casually, squinting against the cold winter sun. The young recruits were dressed thinly, ready for exertion. Some jumped up and down or rubbed their hands to stay warm.

"He is late, m'lord," one man said, the only Kitarran in the group.

"He is always late," came a barely distinguishable grumble. Someone shushed the speaker, who sounded female. Illiah peered around the men and sure enough, at the back was a young woman, staff in hand. She couldn't have been older than fourteen. Illiah recalled the women of Kitarra could train along with the men, if they desired. There were several in the Peace Guard and one in the Queen's Guard. This girl could easily pass for a boy - she was lanky, with short-cropped hair. Only the soft lines of her face, the feminine look to her eyes, gave her gender away.

"Would you like to see our progress, my lord?" another asked hopefully, a glimmer of pride in his eyes Illiah didn't want to extinguish. Illiah nodded, backing off from the group as they separated into a well-formed line.

Illiah had gone over his technique with Eva, who had been trained mostly by Tayeh himself, and they both came to the conclusion that old Eelan must have been trained in Kitarra. So the technique used by the trainees was not new to him, just the weapon. Illiah could see the value of the staff: it was less lethal than a sword, and its length was greater. Because it didn't fit in one's hand like a weathered sword handle, it forced its wielder to concentrate harder. Illiah knew challenge could make or break a warrior.

The young men - and woman - finished their routine.

"What is your name?" Illiah asked one young man with red hair and a nervous complexion.

"Kunit, m'lord."

"Straighten your back a little more, don't lock your knees, keep your weight balanced on both legs." Kunit nodded. Illiah gave them all some pointers, basic technique really, as they were still so green. The girl he saved for last.

"Don't lock your elbows," was all he said to her. She gave a tight nod, looking down at her feet. "You all did well, don't doubt it."

"And how does a foreigner know what makes a Kitarran warrior?" a derisive voice said from behind. Illiah turned to see Scytt, the First Defender, walking across the yard, his helm tucked under an arm. The older man's eyes were hallowed. The faint, sour smell of strong spirits accompanied him. Illiah guessed Scytt was only several years his senior. He had just a flicker of silver in his wheat-colored hair.

"They wanted to show me their growing skills with a staff. They are learning quickly," Illiah told him cordially.

"We only accept the best for training. They must be able to prove themselves before they are accepted. Even then there is no promise they will graduate to be Peace Guards." Scytt turned his critical eye to the young recruits standing at hisana before him. They quailed under his look like scared children.

Illiah turned on his heel, moving out of their way without a word. But he didn't leave; he wanted to watch the captain in action. He leaned against the far wall, beneath the stone overhang that tamed the wind, observing.

The captain's irritation was somehow satisfying. And under the queen's orders, Scytt couldn't say a thing.

Scytt began the lesson by demonstrating. He was quite good. Strong, adept, fast, maybe too fast for beginners. Most of the students' brows were pursed in concentration, trying to follow the demonstration with little pause and no explanation. It looked like an exceedingly difficult way to learn.

"Do you have a spare staff?" Illiah asked when Scytt called a short break. "I wish to join the lesson. I have no experience using a staff." Scytt glowered at him, but one of the students tossed him a spare. Illiah caught it easily. It felt good in his hand. The wood was smooth and hard, almost slippery, like it had a mind of its own. The stirrings of excitement at learning something new made his fingers itch with anticipation. He joined the ranks as Scytt began the next demonstration.

It was more challenging than it looked, which was to say, it was very difficult. At first, Illiah was sure he was going to drop the staff. It tried to slip from his hand, eager to be rid of him. But he recovered, telling it who was boss. It was about balance, just like swordplay, and finding the unity between staff and body and working the muscles, fusing the staff to his arms. At the end of the series, Illiah was out of breath. His arms protested silently, but with fervor. He cursed himself for being out of shape.

"You are a distraction," Scytt told him sharply, interrupting Illiah's self-assessment. "Liffen almost knocked out Heri's teeth - yes, I saw that - he was too busy watching you from the corner of his eye." Scytt slapped Liffen on the hand with the tip of his staff. A red welt appeared on the boy's skin. Liffen ignored the pain, but looked guilty. "One-hour break, find some lunch," Scytt told his students, striding off into the fortress.

"You are quite good for someone who has never used a staff before," Liffen murmured, once his captain was out of earshot.

Illiah grinned. "Thanks. But Scytt is right, and I don't want to be a distraction. You should go in before you catch a chill." Illiah tossed the staff back to the young man named Finnis. Illiah turned to go.

"Wait - m'lord- please, I heard you were a great warrior," the young woman, Diea, asked haltingly. "Is it true?" The others waited for his reply.

"A great warrior?" Illiah repeated, amused and humbled by the title. Some considered him a hero, but he had had help. "What exactly does it take to be a great warrior?"

"Unbeatable skills with the blade."

"Fearless."

"Clever."

"Honorable," Diea said.

Illiah nodded, agreeing. "A great warrior is someone who protects their people, who stands up for those below them. And a great warrior does not live long against his enemies unless he is cunning with a blade. I survived a war, so I guess that means something. I led my people to victory, so I guess that means something too," he told them. "Kitarra is a land of great warriors. What does that make me now?"

"There are not many left."

"Deecon has gone back to the Isles."

"The prince was a great warrior. So was Princess Emri, but they are dead," Liffen said sadly.

"Aisha will be a great warrior someday," Diea mentioned.

"Aye, but he is barely older than you," Kunit remarked. Diea stuck her tongue out at him and then glanced at Illiah to see if he had caught her act of immaturity.

"What about your captain?" Illiah asked, pretending he hadn't seen it.

His question was followed by a rueful silence.

"Perhaps he was once, but not anymore," the Kitarran, Sev, admitted.

"He drinks too much," Diea muttered.

"Don't let him hear you say that," Liffen stated.

Their remarks convinced Illiah that they didn't have much respect for their captain. Not a good sign.

"Will you join us for lunch, my lord?" Liffen was bold enough to ask.

Illiah shook his head. "I will be joining my son for lunch, but thank you for the offer. Perhaps another time." He gave them a bow and took his leave.

Illiah took his meals with Talo and Rhyl, often joined by Mehmet, Aisha, Selene, the queen herself, or all of them. Lunch was served in his chambers, which was where he went, his growling stomach leading him.

He was glad of his warm chamber after the cold of the practice yard. Pale winter light filtered through the glass windows. Rhyl and Talo were working in a patch of sunlight on the floor making something with blocks of wood, a tower of some sort. Neither looked up as he entered. They were too absorbed in their project.

Illiah stood before the lively fire, warming his frigid hands.

"Were you out in this cold, my lord?" Selene asked, her voice full of concern. She was reading a book on the couch while the boys played.

"Aye, I was watching the new trainees for the Peace Guard," he told her. "Rhyl, are you going to come have something to eat? Talo?" he asked the boys, noticing the table of uneaten food.

"Soon."

"Soon," Talo echoed.

"Okay, a couple more minutes, then you need to eat something," Illiah told the boys. Rhyl's good nature was linked to the amount of food in his tummy. There was cooked fish and fresh bread, baked roots, and some dried fruit and cheese. Illiah's stomach rumbled. He sat down at the table, though he barely filled his plate.

There was a knock on the door. Illiah nodded, permitting Selene to open it. It was Queen Arrah. She didn't always join them, but when she did, Illiah was surprised to find her company companionable and entertaining. Her presence would always remind him of the deep lingering pain in his gut, but he was beginning to accept she was a caring, clever woman who ran her realm capably. He couldn't help but respect her for it. Plus she loved her grandson with a fierce pride, and now Rhyl too.

She greeted the boys and asked what they were working on. They explained gravely that it was a castle. There was an elaborate story involved, with two protagonists, one of whom had turned evil. There was some indecision as to how the story ended. Arrah smiled and praised their work and creativity before coming to sit opposite Illiah at the well-laid table.

"Did you know your captain is a drunk? Your noble, First Defender of Kitarra," Illiah said by way of a greeting. He took advantage of the queen's guilt over his circumstance - he got away with plain speaking around her when others did not. Illiah was beginning to suspect she didn't mind, even welcomed his blunt honesty. She raised a finely furred, indiscernible brow at him.

Arrah gave an aggrieved sigh. "Yes, I am aware. Why, do you want his job?" she chided him.

"No, I do not," Illiah told her, not sure if it was the truth.

"Scytt has his problems, but so far it has not affected his work, nor his students. The Guard runs smoothly enough. Deecon was the captain before him, but his home, his heart, is in Pinnae, in the Isles."

"Talo was in our room again last night." Illiah changed the subject, keeping his voice low so Talo wouldn't hear. Talo was a sensitive child, and Illiah didn't want him to feel ashamed of his odd behavior.

"How many nights is that now?" Arrah's lips pressed into a thin line as she glanced at her grandson.

"Seven - in a row."

"I'll speak with him again, but the boy is headstrong," Arrah said.

"Perhaps you should just move his bed in with Rhyl. I don't mind. Rhyl doesn't mind. In fact, I think he sleeps better with Talo there. He has only woken from nightmares once since Talo has been sneaking in."

"If you are sure."

"I think it would be best. They are both lonely," Illiah said, looking at the boys. "Boys, come eat," he encouraged them in a voice that penetrated their deep play. They reluctantly put down their blocks and sauntered over to the table.

"You make sure your boy eats, but you hardly eat yourself. Eat, young man," the queen clucked at him.

Illiah had little appetite. The queen's scolding wouldn't change that.

"Selene, did you get something to eat, dear?"

"I did, your grace," Selene answered with a smile for the maternal matriarch.

Arrah turned to her grandson. "Talo, how would like to share a room with Rhyl?"

Talo turned his wide blue eyes on her and gave a small nod. Rhyl grinned and bounced in anticipation. He clearly thought it was a marvelous idea.

"You two can help Selene move Talo's things after you eat," Arrah told the boys, who suddenly fell on their food like ravenous pigs. Illiah shook his head in amusement.

"Scytt came to tell me you were disrupting his training session," the queen told Illiah with amusement.

"Did he? He must have come straight to you, then. I was just there before I came in. I merely asked to join in. I have never trained with a staff. Did he say what kind of distraction I caused?" Illiah asked, curious as to what the ill-tempered man had to say about him.

"No. If you want to join the practices, go ahead. Ignore Scytt. He's all grown up. He can handle it."

"Thanks."

Arrah laughed softly. "I know you warriors: not happy unless there's a weapon in your hand. My son was like that too. Although he abhorred violence, he loved to practice. I think it was the movement and concentration that evoked him, not the actual fighting. Talo's mother was also a great warrior, better perhaps than Arrain was." Arrah looked into some far-off memory. When her eyes flitted back to Illiah's, they were filled with sadness.

CHAPTER 46

EVA

THE COUNTRYSIDE Eva traversed with the Iron Wolves looked docile, but Tarek assured her it was not. The Midlands were mostly empty. A land of rolling grassy hills, wild groups of pine trees, here and there rocky outcrops. The people clung to each other and formed little colonies, each enclosed and each governed within. Nomads prowled the space between the settlements, often ready to ambush and kill a traveler for their horse. Or their shoes.

The wind grew colder every day, every hour. The snow fell softly, not accumulating into much of anything, luckily.

After her sojourn through the Great Forest and days of numbing cold and blinding snow, Eva was forced to accept staying the winter at Stonyhill was not just wise, it was necessary. Traveling to Kitarra in the depths of winter would surely make her chances of getting there slim to nonexistent.

The small company forged a line through the rugged landscape following an old track that could almost be called a road. At the head was Elish, their leader. Eva understood why Tarek loved him. He was wiry and hardened, his decisions decisive and smart, but he was also kind and quick to smile. He rode straight as the sword at his back, his eyes sharp as a falcon's.

Behind Elish rode Siracus and Macyna, the siblings. Eva wondered if they were twins, but declined to ask. They were a prickly pair. They had not warmed to the idea of having a new addition to their group, even if Eva's presence was temporary. Eva heard Macyna's slanderous mutterings and chose to ignore them. The siblings were the newest members of the Iron Wolves, Tarek informed Eva. They had only been with them two years. Elish trusted them, so Eva tried to hold back her misgivings.

Boe drove the wagon loaded with gear and supplies. The mule pulling it pressed his ears back with a temper, reminding Eva of Macyna. Boe was young and patient - the mule seemed to like him, and only he could handle the beast.

Hector rode in line with Eva, silent, observant. Eva didn't mind the old man's companionship. They both rode with their thoughts for company.

Yuri took up the rear with Tarek, who was back on his old charger. Penn didn't mind being demoted to pack horse.

"How did you know I have the sight?" Eva asked Hector as they rode, breaking the silence for the first time.

Hector turned an eye to her, his grizzled brow dusted with gray hairs. His nose was wide, his jaw thick, but Eva thought in youth he would have charmed the fine Allati ladies as Elish had disclosed.

"I left Allati for more than one reason," he told her firstly. "I was a street boy, the lowest form of Allati. A boy whose father had too many wives and too many sons, so I was given to the streets to be raised by judgment and garbage scraps." He gave Eva a feral grin. "Don't look so horrified. Since I was on the streets, it took a long time for them to find me. I was ten when the Shadow Guard came for me."

"The what?"

"A Shadow Guard is part of an ancient order of warriors, created by the Guardian of Allati himself. They are born with the ability to see magic in others. Once, the Shadows Guard all but ruled the realm, training magi, seeking those of royal blood to be healers and seers, seeking those to be trained up as the next generation of Shadow Guards, to keep the old rites alive, to do the will of Attin. The Shadow Guards were revered and respected. Now there is a handful left, a pitiful scrap of an ancient time. They keep mostly to themselves in the Wanderling Mountains. To become a Shadow Guard, one must sacrifice every part of his life. He must cast aside his dreams, his loves, his everything. Training is brutal, taxing - initiates often die as fledglings. The demands are high, the rites of passage haunting." His voice trailed into silence, their conversation almost forgotten. Then he turned to her, his eyes bright once more.

"You were a Shadow Guard?"

"I was taken to the Mountains. Once they find you, there is no choice. I was already ten, old for an initiate. Usually, initiates are brought into the order barely more than babes. But the years have worn the order down like an old stone. Their power has faded, their grip has weakened. It is a cruel calling, a cruel education - I will spare you the details - I ran away, a harder task than you might imagine. I evaded their clutches for a long time. The incident with Lady Carin and her husband brought me to their attention anew, so I was forced to flee Allati and come to the Midlands."

"Why is the order so cruel?"

Hector shrugged. "Not sure. One man's cruelty is another man's justice, or duty. Your mother was royal Allati?" he asked changing the subject.

"Yes, I suppose. She ran away from Allati. I don't know why. I never got the chance to ask her. She died when I was seven."

"Ah. And you haven't looked into her past?"

Eva shook her head. She never had, never wanted to. Her mother's pain and anguish had forced her to flee across a merciless land into the Great Forest. The past was done, set in stone. Whatever demons her mother had faced and fled, Eva had never felt the desire to share them. And now she had her own grief, her own journey.

"You ride like a warrior. Macyna is jealous," Hector told her, changing the subject.

"She called me a waif. Not to my face, but I heard her say it. And another word I will not say," Eva said, trying to ignore the feeling of indignation the slight caused.

Hector laughed. "You do have a slightness to you, but that doesn't mean you aren't tough as sliver grass. I reckon she will get over it. She is not always so persnickety."

Eva snorted and pushed the other woman from her thoughts. The wind had picked up again, and Eva rewrapped her scarf around her neck and pulled her hood lower.

The Midlands were not as cold as the Great Forest, where the dense trees and the dampness of the air gave birth to the chill and cultivated it. With the wide expanse of sky, the cold had no purchase, nothing to cling to. It was cast about the hills and warmed by the winter sun. But it was still cold, just of a different sort. Eva thought of Stonyhill eagerly. Tarek explained how the Midlands were a cruel place and there were those who were willing to pay to have a safe, warm place to wait out the winter months. Stonyhill was that place.

The Iron Wolves were fortunate; they could stay in exchange for their service as protectors and guards, to keep the peaceful residents of Stonyhill safe. Other gangs roamed the wild, lawless lands, preying on the weak, taking whatever they wanted. Winter made resources scarce, making the gangs bold out of desperation. But no gang would dare attack Stonyhill when the Iron Wolves guarded it.

Five days of travel brought a gradual change in the landscape. The grasslands disappeared, leaving rocky ground and pine trees to dominate the rising hills. The hills grew taller and sharper. The rugged road grew narrower, forcing them into ravines and valleys.

Eva used her magic to sail with the wind, keeping a lookout for ambushes along the treacherous route. Even in winter those brave or desperate would plant an ambush. The Iron Wolves could not travel without wariness.

"There is something ahead," Eva told Tarek as they broke camp. "The road goes down a long slope, then round a bend, then through two pier-like rocks." She tried making the shape with her hands. "I saw a group of travelers there. They have a fire. They might just be resting."

Tarek relayed her information to Elish and the rest of the Wolves. They prepared for an ambush, assuming the worst, and pressed on.

By noon, they were approaching the place. Eva took another look and could see that the men were still there, hugging the rocks as if they wished to remain hidden. If it wasn't for the gleaming blades held ready in their hands, Eva would assume they were frightened, trying to remain obscure.

She told Tarek, and the Iron Wolves prepared for combat. Eva unsheathed her own blade and rode forward slowly, following the others.

Tarek and Elish took the lead, the others trailing them. Macyna pushed her way in front of Eva, forcing Eva into the rear. Eva didn't mind. She was not in the mood for killing. Besides, the Wolves were seasoned warriors.

Five men were waiting. Eva was fairly certain there were no more. The ambushers were outnumbered. Surprise had been their only leverage, and that was gone. The melee would be short-lived.

Perhaps the men in hiding spotted the naked, ready blades of the Wolves or the wolf emblem sewn upon their cloaks. As the Wolves approached the place, not a figure stirred. They rode closer, and still no voice of challenge rang out.

"Come out!" Elish cried, sitting confidently astride his horse. His wild curling hair tousled by the wind contrasted against the sharp features of his face. His congenial features turned hard and cold, the face of a mercenary leader. "Cowards," Elish muttered. "We know you are there."

The so-called cowards still didn't come out. Their cowardice was the only thing that would preserve their skin and they knew it. There came no cry, no sign of life from the crags above. Perhaps they had fled.

Elish nodded to the others, and they dismounted, swords ready. Elish, Tarek, and Eva stayed behind. The others scrambled with surprising speed and agility up the half-snow-covered scree slope.

Grunts and cries came from beyond the crags. One bandit was hurled down the slope, rolling to a stop at the feet of Tarek's horse. He slowly came to his knees, defeated and hurt. He was soon joined by three more escorted at the tip of Macyna's sharp blade and Boe's long knife. One man held his bleeding gut and staggered more than he walked. Hector came down behind them, his sword dripping red upon the snow.

The four captives were pushed into a line, not unlike sheep, their faces a mix of blank acceptance and terror.

"Who is your leader?" Elish asked.

"He's dead," one man answered, spitting blood into the snow, his lips red. Macyna nodded. The fifth man they left behind.

Elish dismounted and pulled out his sword. He walked down the line of men, assessing each of them briefly. The second time he walked down the line, he slit their throats, one by one.

Eva jerked her head from the scene as the blood gushed from the first fatal wound. She heard the thumps as the bodies hit the ground.

The wordless men died as their lifeblood drained from them. Elish spared only one man, the youngest and fittest, who looked on with horror at the wet, hot blood saturating the snow.

"You will go forth and let others know that the Iron Wolves are at Stonyhill," Elish told the young man whose ears were likely deaf with terror. "Now scat, before I change my mind." The man took off down the road they had just traveled. He would not get far without food or mount or shelter.

"The Midlands are a place of swift and harsh justice, my lady," Tarek said softly, sidling his horse close to Sasha. Eva merely nodded, her mind on the path ahead.

Stonyhill was more of a valley than a hill. The crags and scree slopes were left behind; the slopes meandering down to meet a little weaving river were slow and kind. The sharp, twisting pines gave way to tenderer trees whose leafless, skeletal branches stood out against the graceful curves of the snow. Stonyhill was surrounded by what could have been cultivated pastures, but gripped with winter and white with snow, Eva couldn't tell for sure. She thought she could make out fences and shelters for animals.

The settlement itself was a cluster of gray buildings, smoke rising from a dozen chimneys, built just past the high-water mark of the little rocky river.

As they approached, Eva could make out the buildings with more clarity. They were made of stone and thatch and built with more finesse than she would have expected for such an outlandish place. The stonework was precise and elegant. Many of the windows were even glazed, frosted by the cold, while others were shuttered tightly. They passed a cluster of large buildings that could only be barns. The aroma of animals was in the air as they passed. Several large, luminous eyes looked out from the shadowy depths. A few villagers moved about, dressed in heavy furs and leathers, their faces obscured by oppressive hoods or caps.

All Eva could think of was a solid roof over her head. Thick walls to keep out the prying wind. A bath. She wasn't sure what kind of accommodations the Iron Wolves received in exchange for their services, but to hear Boe and Siracus talk, it was far better than the canvas tent.

The building they stopped before appeared to be the oldest of the lot, with heavy, aged wooden beams, the carved wood door stained with age. A man opened the door and peered at them through the snow, wearing a wide grin framed by a short, well-trimmed beard.

"Well met, my friends!" the man said stepping out into the snow, shivering. He lacked the heavy furs and leathers that made the cold tolerable. His voice was coloured by an accent Eva was beginning to mark as Allati. He fixed them each with his welcoming gaze. His gaze fell on Eva last of all. "And who is this? I had not heard there was a new member of the elitist group that is the Iron Wolves," he said with a touch of humor.

"This is Eva," Tarek told him with no humor. "A friend."

"Well, then, she is a friend of mine as well," the man said in a way that left Eva with no doubt of his sincerity. "I am Felis, my lady," he said with a bow. "Keeper of Stonyhill."

"I am no lady, but I thank you," Eva told him. The man's grin widened.

"You lie, but that is for another conversation. Come, friends! Come out of the cold." He gestured for them to precede him.

"Come, Eva, let's see to the horses," Tarek said, taking the reins of the other animals. Eva had been assigned the duty of caring for the horses. She hadn't minded in the slightest. Each of the Iron Wolves had their tasks, and she insisted on pulling her own weight. Boe was in charge of the wagon and goods and the cantankerous mule. He took them round the back of the building, presumably to unload.

Tarek led Eva to a big barn with many ample stalls. The hay loft smelled of good, dry hay. They rubbed the horses down and fed them good oats and a generous helping of hay before seeking out their own comforts.

Felis's house was warm. Eva inhaled deeply as she stepped inside. The warm air filling her lungs was a welcome change from winter's chill. She could smell homey cooking from a kitchen close at hand.

The large room they entered reminded her of a tavern. The low ceiling was dark from the soot of the fireplace. The stone floor was covered with clean rushes to keep away the cold. There were many tables and chairs, some of which were taken. Hooks lined the wall laden with cloaks and jackets. Eva unfastened her fur-lined cloak and hung it up, stuffing her gloves into the pockets. Tarek did the same, letting out a long, contented sigh. Eva's nose told her the kitchen was through the big door to her right.

Felis came through from the kitchen carrying a tray of steaming bowls and sliced bread. The smell of the fresh bread made Eva's mouth water. An older woman followed Felis with a steaming pitcher and mugs. Felis spied them and grinned.

"Come, sit, eat!" He ushered them to a table by the fire where Elish sat with his legs up, boots off, toes warming before the fire. Tarek sat down beside his lover, putting his hand on Elish's knee. Elish smiled at him with shared contentment.

Eva sank into a chair of her own, taking a slice of bread with her. She cherished each mouthful. The heat of the fire washed over her, but she kept her eyes away from the flames. There were faces there, stories waiting to be shared. Later, Eva told herself. Later she would look, later she would seek them out.

Felis sent the empty tray back with the cook and took the chair opposite Eva, studying her intently.

"You don't have the look of a warrior," Felis announced after a while. "Not like Macyna, for instance. That woman exudes aggression." Felis gave a fond laugh.

Eva raised a brow in his direction but said nothing.

"You have the look and bearing of a lady. Those we don't often see around here."

"I thank you for the compliment, but like I said, I am no lady."

"Fine, you are no lady," he conceded. "But you are beautiful, and you grace my humble home with your presence," Felis said with a sweep of his hand.

Eva studied Felis closer, trying to ferret out the reason for his flattery. He was a handsome man, with his brown eyes and hair. He had a face meant for grinning and knew it. He was not as tall as Tarek or Illiah, but he was well built, lean but not skinny. She guessed his age by the lines in his face to be somewhat older than herself, though there was not a touch of gray about his hair nor beard. His talk was generous and bold, though she couldn't detect any undertones that would suggest that he was trying to seduce her.

"You are making her uncomfortable, Felis," Elish told their host with a chiding smile.

"I merely complement her fair features!" Felis said, feigning outrage.

"I would rather you compliment me on my skill with a blade, or my devotion to my horses. Beauty is a passing, useless thing," Eva remarked.

Felis turned back to her and raised his brow, a smile flashing across his features once more. "Aye, I hope I get the opportunity."

Someone called Felis's name from the kitchen, and he bounded off with the energy of a pup.

Eva ate her meal in silence. Elish and Tarek talked softly to each other about duties and watch schedules. The room was mostly quiet, except for low murmurs and the irregular snapping of the fire. The combination of a full belly and a warm body lulled Eva to sleep.

Something touched her arm, waking her abruptly.

"You will be wanting your room, and a hot bath, no?" Felis asked her, his eyes apologetic.

"That would be a mercy," Eva told him, slowly standing up.

"Your comrade Boe has already brought in your things," Felis said, leading her up the narrow stairs that receded into the back corner of the room. Felis held a lantern. Outside was already darkening with night. The winter days were short.

The stairs ended at a long hallway with many doors leading off it. Felis didn't stop until they were at the far end. He opened the very last door on the right into a room he said was hers. The only light was from the small fireplace where a fire was already burning, a pile of chopped wood beside it. Not even a whisper of icy wind came through the shuttered window. The bed was larger than she had expected, with several heavy woolen blankets. There was a small brass tub in one corner filled with steaming hot water.

"A private room for the lady," Felis said with a teasing grin.

"Thank you, Felis. You are very kind," Eva said, taking the lantern he handed her. "Don't you need this?"

"It is my house. I know all its curves and tricks, like any good lover. Good night, my lady," he said, bowing his way into the darkness.

Eva latched the door behind him, sending the lock home, thankful that there was a lock. Not that she didn't trust Felis - she did, surprisingly. She just liked the feeling of being secluded in her own space.

Her bag was on the floor, as was Illiah's sword. She picked up the weapon and drew the blade from the sheath, inspecting it for any signs of neglect. The blade was bright and sharp, just as her husband had left it. It was heavy in her hands, as it always was. She leaned the pummel against her forehead and breathed in the smell of the weapon, the faint smell of leather and sweat from the handle, the cold, sharp tang of the metal.

She closed her eyes and imagined Illiah was in the room with her, taking the sword from her hands, wrapping his fingers around the handle as the sword became an extension of his body. Eva loved to watch him. When Illiah moved with his sword, he was a thing of beauty. Like a bird using the air, catching the currents, manipulating the wind. As a bird is born to use the air, Illiah was born to use a sword. Except the air was pure, elemental, life-giving, bringing rain to the parched earth, carrying a warm summer breeze. A sword was devised by man, a bringer of death and blood and grief and turmoil. Such was Illiah's destiny. Eva knew, of all people, he was strong enough to carry the burden of such a calling.

Eva slid the sword back into the sheath, her eyes half-blinded by tears, her throat burning. She almost dropped it. Her hands shook.

She piled more wood on the fire, and the coals became licking flames, fanning her face with the hot air. Finally she indulged her heart's desire and looked into the potent power of the fire element.

Visions lingered on the edge of the *simul rami*. It took a moment to sift through them to find the one she wanted. The potency of her visions was both a blessing and a curse. Finding what she sought was like sifting through sand to find gold. But she found them, fast asleep, nestled on a large bed filled with soft blankets and pillows in a room fit for a king.

Illiah lay with Rhyl tucked close beside him, his eyes closed fast, his jaw clenched in the throes of some bad dream. In contrast, her son slept with a serene expression. He looked so young in his sleep, like a babe. On the other side of Illiah was another sleeping form, a tawny, furry form of a Kitarran boy. He slept soundly with one of Illiah's hands clasped in his. Illiah looked like he had his hands full with his son and another boy who seemed to have adopted him. Eva wondered who the child was.

The short days passed slowly, the long nights even more so.

Eva watched the mountains. They were a promise - beyond them lay Kitarra.

Eventually, there came days when spring seemed more than a passing thought. The sun would come out, the snow would start to melt, making muddy rivers on the road, pouring off the roofs in little waterfalls. The mountains shook off their white dust.

Then another day would bring blustery wind and gusts so cold, they would pierce the chest, halting one's breath. The snow would fall once more, and the wind would toss it around, molding it into more drifts, pushing its way through cracks, leaving fine white dust behind. The mountains became obscured for days behind thick gray clouds.

"Do you read, Eva?" Felis asked her on one such morning as she stepped in from outside, a blast of cold, snowy air chasing her. She quickly closed the heavy door, shaking the snow off her cloak before answering. The barns had been cold, but a morning of shoveling manure from the stalls had warmed her enough to keep her hands and toes from going numb. She did her best to kick the muck off her boots so as not to dirty Felis's floor.

"I do," she told Felis with a nod as she put on another pair of thick woolen socks.

"Ah, I thought as much. I have a good collection. Many stories from Allati you might enjoy," he offered. Felis had probed her about her heritage on more than one occasion, but she was reluctant to talk about it.

"Thank you. I would love to look if you don't mind."

"Not at all." Felis led her behind the kitchens to his personal chambers. He had a comfortable sitting room and beyond, a cozy bedchamber. From the gossip that flew around Stonyhill, Felis and Macyna were known to be lovers, which explained why Macyna's attitude toward Eva had become bitterer since their arrival at Stony-hill. She seemed to resent any attention Felis expressed toward Eva, even though Felis gave his attention freely and graciously to anyone and everyone. He loved people; Macyna's jealousy was unfounded.

Felis's private sitting room had a large bookshelf filled with many leather-bound volumes. Eva searched through them, feeling her love of the written word ignite her curiosity.

"Where did you get all these?" she asked Felis, who was sorting through his collection, offering her suggestions.

"Oh, here and there. People know I like to read. In winter, when we all congregate under my roof, they bring me books they have traded for, or come across," Felis explained, handing her a book about horse mastery. Eva read several lines and decided it wasn't worth her time. She handed it back to Felis who shrugged and placed it back on the shelf.

Felis handed her another book, his eyes glinting mischievously. She read the title and shot him an amused look. *How to Obtain Ten Wives by Your Third Decade.* Eva almost laughed.

Felis sighed as he handed her a book with an even more outrageous theme. Eva didn't even open it, but tossed it playfully back at him. Felis laughed and put it back on the shelf.

"Who gave you that one? Macyna?" Eva teased, unable to stop herself. Felis gave a bark of laughter in response. "Why did you come to the Midlands, Felis?" Eva asked, suddenly curious.

Felis gave her a sad smile. He was always smiling, even when it was obviously an unpleasant topic. "When I was young, I fell in love with a girl. I was fifteen. She was fourteen, young, but old enough to wed," Felis told her, his voice light. "I approached her father on the matter. I thought he was willing to see us wed. I had enough money to pay her bride-price."

"Bride-price?"

"Yes. In Allati you can buy a woman to be your wife from her father. The status of the woman's family generally decides the price, or perhaps her attributes. Some women are more expensive than others," Felis said with a touch of uncharacteristic bitterness. "Anyway, I was telling a story," he chided. "So, I thought he would accept my offer, which was a good offer for a man with so many daughters and very little status, but one morning I woke as three large men grabbed me, pulling me out of bed. They threw me out of my own house I had inherited from my father and told me to leave Allati and never come back. Of course, I didn't listen. I went to Iana's father. He told me that Iana was to marry the village precept, an old fat man with twenty wives and lots of money. I couldn't believe it. I was angry and hurt, and fearful for Iana. The precept was not known to be a kind man. They often aren't."

"What is a precept?"

Felis gave her a searching look for a moment. "A precept is a judge. There is one in most of the large Allati villages. They uphold the king's law, proclaim punishments, etc. Anyway ..." He glowered at Eva for interrupting his tale. Felis didn't glower well. He looked like a kitten trying to intimidate a bear. "I was not allowed to see Iana. The three large men were joined by three more, and they escorted me to the border of Allati and told me that if I came back, they would kill me, and Iana. My heart broke, but I left. I wandered the Midlands, eventually coming here to Stonyhill. I worked hard and the master of Stonyhill, who had no child of his own, took me in. When he died, he left it to me to tend the valley and its people."

"What happened to Iana? Did you ever find out?"

Felis nodded sadly. "She died in childbirth several years later. A traveler friend from Allati brought me the news."

Eva turned back to the books. Her heart would hurt for his loss, but it had no room for someone else's pain.

"You are Allati, yet you know little of Allati ways. Why is that?" Felis asked. He deserved her honesty; he was a friend, after all.

"I am half Allati. My father was Jullayan. I grew up there."

"Your mother was like you?" He gestured to the shade of her hair.

"She was. I don't know why she ran away from Allati, but she made her way to Jullayah and fell in love with my father. They both died when I was seven, in a fire."

"Allati men can be cruel to their women. Not always, but in Allati, what a man does with his wife is his business only," Felis told her with a clenched jaw. "Perhaps your mother ran away from a cruel man. What are you running away from?"

Eva smiled a little at his concern, a tired smile that came nowhere close to her eyes or her heart.

"I am not running away from anything. I am going to Kitarra."

Felis's kind eyes glinted with trepidation. "Kitarra? That is a long and dangerous road, my lady."

"I know."

"Why Kitarra?"

Eva turned away, biting her lip.

"My lady," Felis breathed. "Do you know what they will do to you if they find you? The Allati, I mean. Royal blood runs through your veins. They will wed you against your will to the most eligible man. You will be a prisoner for the rest of your life. They will pay a hefty price for you - any vagabond who knows even half a thing about Allati would see you as a prize beyond compare. A lone woman of royal blood? A great treasure indeed."

The growing unease of her upcoming journey was a lump in Eva's throat. She was not surprised by what Felis told her. She was more surprised by his concern.

"I must go."

"Why? Stay here, with me. I will keep you safe." Felis moved close to her, tracing her cheek with a warm finger. A sweet, intimate gesture. She didn't back away. She liked Felis. His desire to comfort and protect her was like a warm blanket thawing her heart just a little.

"I can't, Felis. My heart is in Kitarra. My husband was kidnapped and taken there," she said in a quiet voice.

Felis furrowed his brows. "Your husband was taken by the Kitarrans? What kind of strange tale is that?"

"Not a tale for telling."

"All right." Felis gave her another one of his searching looks. "I understand. Love is a powerful thing. It drives us to do things against our better judgment." There was a sharpness to his voice, like disappointment. His offer had been real. His desire to keep her safe was born of his sincere fondness for her.

"Perhaps this would be more to your liking," he said, taking down a hefty scroll from a high shelf. He unrolled the thick paper to reveal a map, roughly drawn and old, the parchment flaking and aged. There were several maps curled within each other.

"Is this the Midlands?" she asked eagerly.

Felis nodded. "Yes. And no. This is a collection of maps. Some are more accurate than others. They outline the Midlands, the borders of the three realms, the notorious Tarm. This one," he pulled out a smaller, worn map, "once belonged to an infamous raider. He lists all the best ambush points and the Xs mark all the towns and farms he liberated," Felis said with grim humor. "Elish killed him a couple years ago and brought me his map, knowing my fondness for collecting such things."

"Thank you, Felis. Really, this is wonderful," Eva told him. "And thank you for your offer. You are a good man." Eva put her hand on his cheek, his beard rough against her cool skin. He gave her one of his charming smiles. The look in his eyes would have melted many a girl's fragile heart, but Eva's heart was already ashes.

The next morning, Macyna looked smug as she came down to breakfast. Eva sipped tea and looked over the maps Felis had loaned her. She met the other woman's eyes over the rim of her cup and knew that Macyna had shared Felis's bed.

Jealousy roiled in Eva's gut. Well, not precisely jealousy, but its close cousin. She didn't want Felis for herself, but part of her yearned for the comfort of a man's strong embrace, to feel loved and safe. In her mind, Eva briefly went over the idea of having Felis as a lover. The comfort she would find with him would be short-lived. His affection would melt her heart and mend it with thin, tenuous thread, but in the end, it would tear, wounding her deeper. When she found Illiah, it would break them both to know she had been with another man. She would die a thousand lonely deaths before she would be the cause of that pain.

Felis came into the common room a while later, uncharacteristically serious. He singled out Elish, honing his blade by the fire.

"Elish, a message came from Greengrove. They need help." Felis was followed by a young boy who had cheeks red as apples from the cold. Despite the rosiness, his face was haunted. "The snows are melting more than we thought, enough to open the pass. Someone decided to take advantage of it."

Elish was up, pushing his curly hair out of his eyes, sliding his sword into the sheath at his belt. "I will get Tarek and Yuri. We will leave right away. Where is Boe?" he asked Macyna.

"He is still on watch with Siricus," she told her leader.

"We will take Hector, then. Go wake him up," Elish ordered Macyna.

Several minutes later, dressed for a long ride, Tarek knelt beside Eva's chair.

"We are going to Greengrove, a day's ride from here. The boy was woken by his mother in the night, put on a horse, and told to head to Stonyhill. He says there were bandits in the valley. He was sent here to get help."

"You want me to look?" Eva asked, eager to help. Tarek nodded.

"It would be a great help to know what we are riding into."

Eva nodded again.

What a difference one day could make. The day before had felt like midwinter, but the morning sun had dawned bright and held the warmth of spring in its gaze. The snow would take some days to fully melt, but Eva hoped the days of endless drifts and biting winds were behind them. She put on her cloak and her thick boots; they were still a necessity. The distant mountains called to her.

Tarek followed her to the edge of the little village where the wind was free to gather speed across the land and twist, rise, and dip over the air currents of the river. Eva joined it effortlessly.

Greengrove was northeast. She wove through trees and hills, following a fork in the river as Tarek had told her.

It was not far as the wind flows. Greengrove was a little farm nestled in a sheltered nook of the northern hills. Smoke rose from a large fire burning in the yard. At first, Eva could see little amiss. She focused on the fire; the element called to her.

What she thought were blackened sticks were not. She saw an arm. A leg. Fire was ever adept at cleaning the dead.

She pushed herself to the window of the house and could hear the voices of men. She searched for any clue that might tell her whether the bodies burning were those of raiders or the farmers.

A young girl came out, not much older than the boy. Their features were similar, likely the boy's sister. She carried a basket, walking across the snow to the barn on some errand. Her face was red, her eyes swollen with tears. She tried not to look at the fire, but she couldn't help herself. Her small face glanced toward the smoke and Eva knew that the girl's loved ones were in that fire.

For a moment, Eva was the girl and felt her pain and her grief and her misery. The longing was worst of all.

Rejoining her body was always a strange sensation, as though she jumped from a great height and landed on a hard, unyielding surface. The shock moved from her toes up to her ears. She shook her head to dispel the feeling and turned to Tarek.

"It doesn't look good. I couldn't tell how many men, but some of the farmers are dead. I couldn't see anyone on watch. Perhaps they didn't know a boy escaped."

Tarek nodded grimly. "Thank you."

He walked with her back to Felis's house.

"We will be gone a few days."

"Be safe," Eva told him with a cluck, earning a rakish grin.

"Of course, my lady," Tarek said with a bow. Then he swept her into a hug, engulfing her with his long arms briefly before releasing her.

Eva turned to go inside. Felis watched her thoughtfully.

"How did you ever meet the big man, anyhow?" Felis asked her as she passed him to go inside.

"I thought you knew? He was my bodyguard," Eva told him, knowing it would intrigue and irritate him.

"So, you are a lady!?" Felis said with a laugh.

Eva sat in the bath, thinking of Rhyl and how he cried almost every time she would wash his hair, how he hated getting water in his eyes. How such a simple task was turned into a great debacle because he refused to close his eyes at her suggestion. The boy could swim like an otter in the hot pools of the Keep, but as soon as his mother washed him, it was torture. Her son was such a stubborn child. She loved him for it. Soon. Soon she would leave Stonyhill. Soon, she would find him.

When Tarek returned, she planned to talk to him about the next stage of her journey.

The weather continued to warm. The roads and paths were mud. The roof of Felis's house was bare. Eva could feel the stirring in the air that meant the season was losing its grip upon the land. The mountains called to her.

Felis's house was full of comforts; Eva was loath to leave them. The road to Kitarra would be cold and wet, even with the changing season. She despaired at leaving. Yet she yearned to feel the distance between herself and her family diminish.

The bath was hot. Steam filled the room. Her fire was dying, and the room had cooled. She heard voices and assumed they were coming from the hall, but they grew louder, and she could hear no footfalls. Her consciousness penetrated the steam, and she saw the vision her ears perceived.

Macyna was the speaker. Eva thought she was eavesdropping and nearly balked from the vision. But then she heard her name and her interest piqued.

"Tomorrow," Macyna was saying. Boe and Siracus leaned across the table to hear her quiet words. "Tarek could be here in as little as two days. If we don't leave tomorrow, we won't outrun him."

"If Tarek catches us, he will kill us," Boe said a little too loudly. Macyna gave him a shushing glare.

"*If* he catches us. It's worth the risk. Once we get Eva to Allati, they will pay us more than you can imagine. We could do anything with that money - anything," Macyna told Boe. Boe's eyes shone bright and eager. Siracus grinned in anticipation. "Eva locks her door at night. Boe, you will need to pick the lock." The young man nodded.

Macyna outlined the rest of the plan, how they would abduct her that night as Felis lay abed with Macyna. Macyna was sure their host would object - best to keep him distracted. She would meet up with them at Fool's Gorge.

The vision dissolved, leaving Eva with her pounding heart, sitting in a tub of lukewarm water. She clambered out of her bath, dressed quickly, and began stuffing things into her travel sack. Her hands shook, her ears poised to the hall beyond.

Once, she heard footsteps and unsheathed her blade, ready for the attack. But they passed, and she continued to pack. It didn't take long.

The kitchen was blessedly empty. The cook had gone to bed already. Eva took some fresh bread and preserves, as much as she could carry, and filled her canteen from the pump. She passed Felis's door and heard voices beyond it. His and Macyna's, she didn't doubt. She passed by quickly, regretting she could not say farewell to Felis, who had become her friend. She was furious with Macyna for being a deceitful whore.

It was a good night for quick escapes, with only a thin and ambiguous sickle moon. Any minute Siracus and Boe would be in her chamber and realize she was gone.

In the barn, Eva was forced to light a lantern to find her tack and saddle the horses. The barn was far enough from the main buildings that it would be unlikely anyone would notice the light. Boe and Siracus were supposed to be on watch, and she knew that they were not.

Sasha and Penn were munching hay and greeted her eagerly. Eva saddled Penn swiftly, loading her belongings onto Sasha. If it came to a fight, she would rather be riding the war charger who knew how to use his hooves and his teeth.

Breaking out into the night, Eva was thankful there was little snow, but the mud would show her tracks. She needed to reach firmer ground. Even then, they might be able to track her. She must rely on the superior speed of her mounts. Her horses could outrun the other beasts easily, but she was still at a disadvantage being unfamiliar with the land.

She cantered into the night for as long as she could, ever thankful her horses had excellent footing. She went until the horses needed rest, they were not accustomed to long runs at night.

Eva used the wind when she could, though it was dark and difficult. She followed her own trail to find Siracus and Boe riding behind her. They weren't making much headway. Around midnight they gave up and turned back. Eva sighed with relief and continued on. What they would tell Tarek and Elish was beyond her comprehension.

Eva turned her attention to the road ahead. She would have to be careful, and watchful. She was alone in a land with no rules and no honor. That had been proven to her.

CHAPTER 47

ILLIAH

WINTER CAME TO KITARRA and Illiah was thankful he was not on a boat. Snow covered the streets, the palace, the trees. The clouds exhaled little white flakes into the long, dark nights. The Kitarrans did not despair of the season, they celebrated the winter solstice with a night of festivities referred to as the Dark Night. The Dark Night was an ominous name for a night that was anything but dark. The night of celebration was to dispel the bitterness of winter, the bleak, endless feeling when the sun is pale and the days are short.

The doors of Kilev were thrown open. Drinks and food were served to raise the spirit and warm the body. A great spirit of charity and gratitude came over the city from the Queen's Keep to the artisans' shops to the brothels. Huge fires were lit all over the city to warm the people of Kilev as they moved from one place to another. The night sky was bright from the bonfires, the warm glow reflected off the snow. All night long the people of the city made music, played games, made love, and told stories of summer with laughter and theatrics. Lanterns were lit and hung from every window - small, large, elaborate, and simple. The city took on the appearance of some forgotten fairyland.

The queen invited Illiah to her evening of festivities. It was a tradition that every year the queen hosted a grand production, a play featuring one of the famous Kitarran legends set to music.

Illiah watched for some time with the boys. The queen's musicians were mesmerizing in their skill. Their voices were perfection. The story was of a young Kitarran woman who traveled to the Great Forest to seek the Allmakers and learn the secrets of a forbidden scroll, a story of magic. Illiah knew something of magic and deemed the story to be pure fantasy, but it was still enjoyable.

The boys enjoyed the music and the theatrics immensely, for a time. But then they began to yawn and begged to leave the grand hall for their quiet chamber, their short attentions exhausted. Illiah put them to bed long before the midnight chimes. He never found out what happened after the girl found the magic scroll.

The boys were sleeping when a soft rap came at his door.

"Aisha."

"Illiah." The Kitarran's eyes were pure youthful deviance. Selene stood patiently behind him. "Come out with me. To the city. You have never seen a city like Kilev on the Dark Night, I promise you."

Illiah opened his mouth.

"Selene offered to stay in case the boys wake," Aisha said before Illiah could protest. Clearly Illiah was outmaneuvered.

The city was bright and beautiful, just as Aisha promised. They met up with several of the young Kitarran's friends and toured the city together, moving from one bonfire to another, from one bright doorway to the next. Aisha's exuberance was contagious.

Each way Illiah turned there was more food to taste, and more drinks appeared whenever one felt the slightest thirst. Illiah sampled more kinds of ale than he knew existed in all the city. Honeyed ale. Mulled ale. Ale brewed by Aisha's aunt. Ale brewed by a shepherd in the northern mountains using gruit from herbs only found on the slopes of one mountain - and quite possibly the spit of an alra in season.

And then there was Kitarran polii. A doughy, dumpling-like, berry-filled bit of goodness served with a sauce made of caramelized butter and cream served by little old ladies who rolled the dough and folded dumplings all night long.

Aisha watched with great expectation as Illiah took his first bite. The polii was soft and warm in his mouth, savory and sweet, the berries hot. He had never tasted anything like it. It was rich and very good. He grinned, his mouth full, and assured Aisha it was as delicious as promised. Aisha told him it was only served the one night of the year. Illiah could see why; it was labor intensive and made of almost pure cream and finely sifted flour. The Kitarrans would be a portly race indeed if they dined on polii all year round.

The Dark Night was enjoyable, almost fun, but the rise in Illiah's spirit was quickly diminished, even with the sweet Kitarran music and the delicious food. The shadows called to him more than the open doorways and bonfires. The drinks and food warmed his throat but not his heart.

As the night wore on, their small company dwindled down to two as Aisha's human friends were whisked away, lost to the desires of their bodies and their hearts. Illiah suddenly felt aged as he watched the lovers, more than half drunk, dissolve into shadowed nooks and doorways in their carnal trysts.

Aisha pretended to ignore the way it hurt him as he was left alone. The young man had no special partner that Illiah knew of. Aisha's eyes were full of yearning and romantic wishing. He was a young man after all, new to manhood, easily influenced by the desires of his body. The Kitarran race were a fiercely loyal people, taking but one partner for their whole life. A lonely life that could be. Illiah knew the joy of having one woman. But that joy also brought pain, a stark and lonely pain that would be with him always. But he would never resent the choice of his heart.

Aisha drank too much, forcing Illiah to steer the young man home to the Queen's Keep. It was amusing, and Illiah wondered if the poor boy would have a headache the next morning. Likely not - Kitarrans seemed impervious to many ailments. Illiah was sure the boy would be back on his feet come the pale winter morning.

With Aisha safely tucked away in his own bed, Illiah returned to his chamber to find Selene asleep on his bed, an open book in her hand. He touched her shoulder softly, and she stirred, mumbling an apology Illiah refused to hear. He ushered her to her own bed, thanking her loyal duty to his sons. If she heard the unintentional plural, she made no sign of it.

He peeked in at his boys before seeking his bed. Illiah hoped their dreams on the longest night were as magical as the queen's production. Next year he would have to steal them out into the city to taste polii.

The days lengthened. The season changed yet again. The sun crept into Illiah's room before Rhyl and Talo woke. The pale dawn brought the loud but pleasant calls of a dozen birds. They flitted from the forest nearby to the royal gardens in their courtship.

Illiah lay listening, waiting for the boys to wake. He was glad the children had not crept into his bed. His shaking would have startled them. He wasn't sure if he had uttered the cry on his lips or merely dreamed it. Either way, he didn't want his son or Talo to sense his agitation.

After the war, he had accepted his sleep would forever be haunted by nightmares. Almost every night he had dreamed of the dead, and the tortured, and the wounded. He had managed as best he could.

Then he found the love of his soul and married Eva. The night terrors subsided. With the comfort of his wife's kindness, her body, her love, the war was a far-off memory. So were those he had lost - his brother, his friends. He grieved them deeply, but with effort, he found peace in his new life, with his new family.

Now, once again, his nights were plagued by night terrors. But the recurring dream haunting him was starkly different from the old nightmares of war.

In his dream, he was in the Great Forest, surrounded by the dense quiet of the place, the oppressive sense of otherness. More unsettling was the wooden box set upon the moss - a strange thing even for a strange forest.

The box was large enough to hold several barrels of wine. Illiah searched but did not find a lock or latch or hinge. Someone was inside. The heart can often perceive what the eyes cannot, and Illiah knew Eva was in the box.

He heard her plea, plaintive at first, but before long it was a desperate wail. Her nails clawed against the wood. She lunged herself against the sides like a trapped wild thing, desperate to get out, screaming. He knew his wife's voice. He would never forget it. But it occurred to him that he had never heard her scream like she did in the dream. The scream froze his blood.

In his dream, he tried desperately to open the box but couldn't. He had no tool to break the wood. The wood would not even groan against his brute force. Eva couldn't hear or understand his frantic reassurances.

Illiah woke with a cry on his lips, her screams and his pounding heart in his ears. His hands shook as he ran his fingers through his hair. He had the same dream often. Sometimes Eva screamed. Sometimes she was silent as if the box were empty. He knew it was a silence born of hopelessness.

What his dreams meant, he had no desire to speculate. Not if he wanted to retain his sanity.

The spring birdsong sounded sweet. He wished the simple beauty of their songs could penetrate the cold sweat on his brow and dissolve the knot of fear in his stomach, the loneliness in his gut. He couldn't let himself think of her. The memories were too sweet, too painful.

Anger and helplessness made him restless. He tossed back the heavy feather blankets and dressed simply. He pulled out his staff and worked on his routine. The captain still hated him, but Illiah worked hard to ignore Scytt. He didn't need to like the man to learn from his lessons.

The staff was merely a learning tool to teach the dexterity and strength needed to wield a latha. Not everyone could master the skill, but Illiah was determined to. It gave him something to work toward, something to kidnap his mind.

Deecon had carried a latha. The double blade was heavy, made from a rare metal, smithed by a master. There were not many in the queen's armory. Most had fallen into disuse, their metal tarnished and dull, the mechanisms faulty. Talo had a small, dainty one that had belonged to his mother. It was set aside in velvet for a time when the boy could learn to wield it. Talo's father had held one too, but it had been lost when Prince Arrain died, sunk to the murky depths of the river with the grieving prince. Illiah's gut still wrenched thinking of how Prince Arrain leaped from the cliffs the day Talo was born.

Illiah's practice had always been a respite for his mind. As he forced his muscles into subversion, his nerves calmed, and his hands stopped shaking. His chest felt less constricted.

The boys were still asleep. Illiah peeked into their room. Talo was lying curled up on himself, and Rhyl lay with his feet on his pillow where his head should have been. No wonder he fell off the bed sometimes. Illiah left them to their slumber and went to the pools to bathe.

Servants were bathing in the far pool; Illiah couldn't make out who they were. He thought it gracious and generous that the queen allowed her trusted house staff the luxury of exploiting the grand pools. She treated her servants almost like family. Illiah didn't mind; there were enough pools for everyone. Besides, Kitarrans were not prude. They had no qualms about nudity. Illiah had adjusted accordingly. He shed his clothes and slipped into the steaming water.

The geography of Kitarra, he had learned, was built around naturally occurring hot springs. When the Kitarrans found one, they built a city or town around it, even as far south as Jullayah. The Keep, Arrah informed him, had been an outpost almost an age ago, before humans had come to this land, before the three realms were established, when Kitarra had been the only realm.

Illiah could understand the Kitarran's enthusiasm for the hot baths. It felt good to be clean and warm, and the Kitarrans were zealots when it came to cleanliness. There were public baths within the city, but the water was not quite as hot, as it was piped down from the source in the mountains above the fortress.

"Good morning, my lord," came a soft voice. A figure appeared through the morning mist clothed in a robe of deep red. "You are up early," Selene commented.

"As are you."

Selene smiled sweetly as she undid the tie in her robe and let it slip to the ground. Illiah turned his gaze from her naked body. He was not about to stare rudely. He heard her slip into the water not far from him. Nudity was commonplace. Illiah had seen her naked before, bathing with the boys. It didn't bother him, not really. She kept a polite distance from him and made no show of her body. There was no play for his attention. But still, Illiah would have preferred she choose a different pool.

"I am usually up early. Lots to do," Selene replied, undoing the tie on her bag of soap.

Illiah didn't want to watch her bathe, so he took his own soap and washed.

"The queen received word yesterday that Innis is in the city. He has a gift for the boys that will be presented after breakfast," Selene told Illiah.

"Who is Innis?"

"He is the keeper of the uandian. The uandian," she continued, knowing that Illiah didn't know what she was referring to, "are dogs, special dogs, bred for their loyalty, intelligence, and instincts to protect. An uandian will be a companion for life. They live longer than an average mutt. Some say they are descended from a spirit animal."

"Dogs? He is giving the boys dogs?"

"Puppies, yes."

"Puppies?"

Selene grinned at his disparaged expression. "They are not like normal dogs. You will see."

Illiah had never owned a dog. He had no experience training them, only horses. Dogs were not horses.

"It's tradition for those of royal blood to have at least one uandian. The queen has two - you have seen them."

The queen's dogs were well trained, but they were big. Bigger than any dog Illiah had seen, and wild looking.

"Do you not like dogs, my lord?" Selene asked, a glint of amusement in her eye.

Illiah ignored the chide and submerged to rinse the rest of the soap from his body before pulling himself out of the pool. He caught Selene watching him as he pulled on his robe, covering his nakedness. She gave him a faint smile that could have meant something, or nothing. Illiah chose to ignore it.

The boys were awake and already in full swing, playing some sort of physical game that involved hiding under their blankets and jumping on each other. The kind of game that usually led to injury and tears. They saw Illiah and immediately complained of their hunger. Illiah told them the queen had something special for them that day, so they best get dressed and cleaned up doubly quick and proper. It didn't really work; the boys were too distractible to be properly bribed.

Selene arrived with breakfast and announced that as soon as they were ready, the queen would receive them. The boys sat quietly, more or less, and ate, more or less. Afterward, Illiah managed to wrangle them into presentable clothes, and they were ready to see the queen.

The presentation of the uandian was more of an affair than Illiah had imagined. Half of the queen's court was in attendance, dining on a fine breakfast, and the entire high council.

Once, at the queen's insistence, Illiah had sat through one boring dinner party, trying to keep his son and Talo from acting like monkeys. It had turned into an epic task. He refused to attend any more, to put himself or the children through such boredom. If Arrah's people wished to see Rhyl, she must make it an event a child would enjoy. The queen acquiesced.

As Illiah entered the queen's tertiary atrium, the one Arrah preferred for morning avocations, his heart sunk. He imagined the event was going to turn into a spectacle during which his son would be expected to act with the patience and attitude of a mature lord. To expect such behavior from any four-year-old was an unkindness. And he was grossly underarmed for the task.

"Good morning, Lord Illiah, Prince Rhyl, Prince Talo," Arrah said warmly, floating across the room to them. She was wearing a gown of deep gold, an elaborate gold leaf brooch clasped to her shoulder. More delicate chains adorned her head than usual, an indicator to Illiah, who was becoming quite familiar with the queen, that she was dressed to impress. He had a fleeting thought that he should have put more effort into his appearance, and that of his son, but dismissed it quickly. He had no need to impress these people.

"Good morning, Mua," the boys said, turning their bright smiles to the queen.

"I have a surprise for you," she said, taking one boy in each hand. The crowd of delighted courtiers parted to reveal a large wooden box. The boys were hesitant, wondering what could be in the box. Illiah moved so he could see his sons' reactions.

Rhyl had to stand on the tip of his toes to see over the edge of the box. He was rewarded by a wet nose in his face as one of the uandian pups greeted him eagerly. Rhyl laughed, a delightful, tinkling sound that put a smile on the face of almost every courtier gathered. Talo reached his hand over the edge to pet the other pup.

Illiah smiled. They were sweet animals. The boys were enchanted. One was stone gray and the other was black as night. They were big for young pups, their huge paws an indicator that they would indeed be similar in size to the queen's two faithful guardian canines. They had light-brown eyes full of intelligence, long pointed muzzles and ears. They reminded Illiah more of wolves than hounds. Their bottle-brush tails wagged furiously.

A man, who must be Innis, stepped forward and lifted the two pups out of the box and let them sniff around. The gray pup came to sit at Rhyl's feet almost immediately, looking at him with a sudden devotion that impressed Illiah. Selene was right - these were not common dogs. The black dog nipped Talo's hand and lay at his feet, resting his head on his paws. Talo bent to stroke the animal's smooth head, his face transformed with awe. Rhyl giggled softly.

The crowd around the two boys looked equally transformed, beaming at the two young princes.

"The black pup's name is Cracuos. The gray one is Pudiam," Innis told the boys in a warm voice.

"Pudding!" Rhyl announced, interpreting the name his own way. He laughed loudly as the dog yipped in agreement.

"Pudding," Talo echoed with a happy laugh. "This one will be Crackers."

Illiah looked at the queen to see what she thought. She met his eyes with arched brows. Illiah grinned. Perhaps they gave the boys too much freedom, but they looked enchanted. He wasn't about to stop them. They were their dogs, after all.

The boys lay on the floor playing with their pups. Illiah pulled Innis aside.

"So, who will be training them?" he asked.

"Oh, they are already trained, my lord," Innis replied. "Uandians learn very quickly," he said proudly. "The bonding has occurred. The dogs will listen to the boys very well. But perhaps the boys will need some training?"

Illiah laughed softly. "Probably more than the dogs. All right, my thanks."

"It is tradition. The princes and princesses of Kitarra have always had these guardians at their side. It is a pleasure to see it."

It was a pleasure, Illiah realized, to see his son with such pure joy on his face. He treasured it greatly.

"My Lord Illiah," Arrah said, catching his attention. "I have a surprise for you as well."

Selene came into the room carrying a third pup. This one was gray but so light, it was almost white. It looked huge in the arms of the young woman. Its ears were back, its tail between its legs. It looked anxious compared to the happy, confident pups on the floor with the boys.

"If you want her, she is yours," the queen offered. "You are a prince, after all."

Illiah touched the dog on the ears. Her fur was soft, softer than any he had touched before. The puppy whined. Selene put her down, and she cowered against Illiah's legs, looking up at him with wide, trusting eyes. Illiah had never had a dog before, had never wanted a dog before. The look the animal gave him made his heart shift, and he admitted it would be hard to let the dog go.

"What is her name?" he asked Innis.

"Armeria."

Illiah nodded. "Thank you, your grace. I will keep her." He stood and bowed to the queen who smiled with genuine pleasure.

☾

The docks were busy. The river was starting to rise with the spring thaw, but (as Illiah was told) for all the snow, it had been a mild winter. The river was not expected to become unmanageable.

Illiah liked to walk the docks. He found the diversity intriguing and had half a mind to get on a boat and travel Kitarra to see the different cities. The isles to the west, where the ocean was blue and green and the beaches white, or the mountains to the north where they mined fine gems and metals. He was curious of the farmlands and orchards across the river and how they compared to the south of Jullayah where he grew up.

Not that he could just leave and appease his curiosity; he couldn't leave Rhyl. His heart would ache too much for that.

Armeria followed his every step. She was getting big and lanky, as were the boys' dogs. Illiah enjoyed his new companion. She was smart and followed his every command. She had excellent intuition and bossed Crackers and Pudding around relentlessly. Sometimes at night, his bed was filled with two boys and three dogs. Luckily, it was a big bed.

"Good morning, my lord," one boat master said as Illiah passed. Illiah saw him often, a burly Kitarran with gray, faintly mottled fur and tawny eyes.

"Good morning, captain," Illiah replied. "Good weather for fishing?"

"Aye. You should come out sometime," he said, leaning against the edge of his boat. He had been unpacking crates of small fish, but he paused in his work to squint at Illiah.

Illiah smiled. "I haven't been fishing since I was a boy, and never in such a big river."

The Kittaran chuckled. "Not in the river. We go out just beyond the delta, where the water is salty. There are some big ones out there this time of year. Nothing like fighting one of them to quench what ails you. Excellent eating as well."

Illiah grinned at the fisherman's enthusiasm. Illiah was always looking for a distraction. Scytt had been getting on his nerves more than not of late. He had taken a break from practicing with the young recruits. He enjoyed working with his young mare, an energetic young horse, but even after taking her through her paces, he needed something to keep his mind occupied.

"Truly?" Illiah asked.

"Aye! My kinadra and I would be honored to have you on our ship!"

Illiah knew the old Kitarran word for wife.

"What's this you are saying about me?" a feminine voice piped up. She was carrying a sack of something on her back as she sauntered down the docks to the boat. She was thin and short for a Kitarran, about the same height as Eva, Illiah figured. She had brown fur with lighter stripes and light eyes, not unlike her husband's. She wore the long, loose pants some Kitarran women favored over a skirt. Her long tail hovered just above the ground.

"I was inviting Lord Illiah here to join us on the hunt for strikers. This is my woman, Bellah."

"Pleased to meet you," Illiah replied with a little bow.

"Oh, and I'm Turk," the captain added.

"Turk, I would love to come fishing with you. When is a good time?"

"Meet us tomorrow, first light," Turk replied.

Illiah nodded. "First light."

That next evening, they dined on roasted striker fish. Illiah managed to catch one that was as long as his arm and as thick as his torso. Turk was right - it was exhilarating to catch and fight the fish. The satisfaction of pulling it into the boat sparked something primal, and Illiah yearned to repeat the experience. Illiah invited them to dine with him and instructed the palace cook to prepare the fish.

Turk and Bellah were delighted to meet Rhyl and Talo. The queen was not there that evening, for which Bellah expressed great relief. To be in the palace was enough, she told Illiah. She would be far too intimidated to dine with the queen.

Illiah had learned, along with how to tie tricky fishing knots, Turk had trained as a Peace Guard before abandoning the Guard to take up fishing. Fishing was in Turk's blood, the profession of his father and grandfather and great-grandfather and so on. He told Illiah with a laugh that only a foolish man denies his heritage. The sea always claims its own, Turk said.

But Turk could not resist bringing his own latha to show Illiah. He still kept it, even if he didn't use it. Illiah asked Turk to give him a demonstration, and he did, only because Talo and Rhyl begged. Turk couldn't resist the boys' compounding charms.

"Teach me," Illiah said after Turk was through with his demonstration. The Kitarran was out of practice, he complained over his rough transitions, but it was still evident he was skilled with the difficult weapon.

Turk's brows rose, mostly out of amusement. He pretended to ponder the proposition.

"I will teach you the latha - if you come fishing with me. I can always use more poles in the water."

"Done!" Illiah said with a laugh, shaking the Kitarran's furry hand.

"Can we come fishing too?" Rhyl asked his father.

"Ask the captain," Illiah suggested.

"Of course, you can, lads," Turk answered with a grin. "The more, the merrier."

CHAPTER 48

EVA

EVA WAS AN EXILE in a land made for exiles. The Midlands was a lonely, barren place, a fitting place for lost souls.

The wounds of her aching heart bled bitterness from her betrayal. That Tarek's people would succumb to greed was one thing; that they would betray one of their own was unforgivable.

Eva had tried to find a vision of Tarek in the fire, but all she saw in the *simul rami* were images too many to pick out. It was like trying to see a drop of rain in a torrential river. So, she used the wind. She saw Tarek in Stonyhill, going about his chores grim-faced. She could not tell what he was thinking. She had no way to know what he believed about her abrupt departure.

When she returned to her body, more time had passed than she realized. She used the wind once more to scan her surroundings. She jolted in panic when she noticed three armed travelers coming up behind her. She narrowly managed to find shelter in a small copse of trees before they crested the hill behind her.

With difficulty, Eva forced Tarek from her mind. She needed to be constantly alert and watchful. Her life depended on it.

The landscape changed and melted past, as did the days. Gone was the rocky valley of Stonyhill with its little river and quaint pastures. Gone were the treacherous scree slopes and rocky ridges that canvassed much of the Midlands. The pines lingered, along with other trees unfamiliar to Eva, leafless structures stark against the empty landscape, their leaves hidden, the leaf buds tight. The snow was gone, but the wind was still cold, and some nights Eva wondered if she would wake to a thin layer of spring snow upon her camp.

Eva's lonely track lead her ever northwestward. Not that she was alone, not really. There were other travelers, here and there, traversing the rough, poorly trodden roads. She saw them camping in the wild, a guard always posted. The Midlanders were a suspicious lot, hardened and greedy, driven by survival. Morality was not a luxury to be afforded. Kindness was a weakness.

Straying too close to the travelers was to court a dire fate. She kept her distance and kept her nightly fires small, making camp in hidden places.

Her sight was long and clear. Like an eagle, she followed the wind and surveyed the lands around her, seeking out any danger, finding nooks and crannies in the landscape, sheltered places to hide.

There were days when the weather was almost warm. The thaw of spring became more potent, more real. Creeks ran in a rush. Birdsong pierced the cold morning air. With the slight change of season, more people wandered the land. More and more Eva was forced to find new, hidden routes that would take her around the other wanderers. She would trust no one.

Traversing the Midlands through constant detours was agonizingly slow. To leave passable roads for rougher, more secluded country was frustrating, but she was thankful for Felis's old maps. The old raider's maps had proved invaluable, showing her routes and trails not obvious even with her heightened sight. She did not feel guilty about the theft.

As Eva gradually approached the land labeled the Tarm on the maps, the trickier it became to stay hidden. The trees thinned around her as the land flattened into a long, wide valley. Grasslands stretched almost as far as she could see. To the south was a jagged line of hills. According to the map, beyond the hills the land gave way to great rocky cliffs, plummeting hundreds of feet to the sea.

To the north, the hills rose into higher mountains, their craggy heads still covered in fresh snow, the sides steep and rocky. These would be impossible to cross with the horses, even on foot it would be treacherous, and the snows and storms at such a height were surely just as dire.

Eva decided to keep close to the hills at the north end of the valley plain with the mountains rising at her shoulder. If needed, she could hide in the woods covering the hillocks before the rise grew steep and rocky and inhospitable.

The plain valley was open, both advantage and disadvantage. Eva could see for miles and miles with her magic. She hoped to pass unseen.

On her map was a winding track marked through the mountain crags and valleys, but it went to Allati, not Kitarra. She would take nomads and wild men on the grassy Tarm over Allati any day.

The broad valley of the Tarm stretched on and on. For days the landscape hadn't changed, except for little ponds here or there, or a gentle rise or fall of the land. The road was a ribbon winding through endless grass constantly before her.

Eva could scarcely recall when the wind did not pull at her clothes and hair, or torment her meager canvas shelter. She doubted she would sleep at night without its temperamental company. For a camp, she chose a sheltered nook against the hillside, surrounded by a scattering of short, leafless trees. The wind still presided, but she liked to think it was tamed slightly by the hillock.

Her fire whipped about but managed to cling to the dry branches she had gathered. Some of its heat found her cold fingers before the wind tore it away, along with the smoke. The wind was a mixed blessing.

Her food stores were running low. She had spent the day before hunting instead of traveling. The Tarm was full of birds, and Eva shot down a decent-sized goose, even with the wind's perpetual challenge. There wasn't much meat on its bones, but it was better than starvation. If she managed to bring down a couple more birds, combined with the last of her preserves, she figured she might make her rations last. The horses ate the dry winter grass that was everywhere on the Tarm. At least her horses would not starve. According to Felis's map, Kitarra was not too much farther - she should manage.

Even with Kitarra within her sights, Eva felt no sense of excitement or relief, only a growing apprehension the closer she drew toward its borders. She studied Felis' map, hoping for an answer to her unease.

Between her and Kitarra lay a settlement called Mahlas, run by a dangerous, greedy, self-serving man. Tarek had spoken of him with disdain and caution. The Iron Wolves were not welcome in Mahlas. Eva had not bothered to ask why. Now she wished she had. The dead raider's map had a scrawling side note saying the town was well guarded, impervious to looters.

Eva would use her magic to skirt around the town. It would be difficult, but she could see no other option. The map showed that soon she would come to a crossroads, one road going northeast, winding through the jagged mountains to Allati, another the road she would leave behind that led to the Midlands, and the last road northwest to the settlement called Mahlas, and beyond to Kitarra.

Over the past few days, she had seen several bands of men heading east, looking armed and dangerous. The road was busier than she had expected.

One day to hunt was enough. She didn't like to linger in one place too long. Her feet itched. The road, dangerous as it was, called to her. Kitarra called to her. The hazy purple smudge in the distance was the mountains, and she yearned to be at their feet.

With her human eyes she could see a long distance. The expanse was great, but others had that advantage as well. A figure such as herself with two horses would be a beacon. But with her magic, she could *see*.

Before leaving her secluded camp, she used her sight, but there was nothing - no sign of life beyond the birds and the occasional deer, nothing but the wind and grass and scrubby trees and bush. The space between her and the crossroads was clear. She packed up her camp quickly.

After a time, Eva reined in Penn, looking over the endless sea of grass. The road had climbed slowly, bringing her to the top of a low hill. Before her lay the crossroads.

There were no people. From her vantage point, the land was empty and desolate. She felt like a ghost riding through a timeless, never-ending landscape. It appeared utterly deserted, but she had to be sure.

She lifted herself beyond her body into the wind and felt the familiar weightlessness as she cascaded across the grass, lifting higher and higher until the road was thin, far below. Her gut wrenched in fear, even though her consciousness had temporarily abandoned her body. There were people ahead. And they were making good speed down the road toward her. Her meager human eyes had deceived her.

The men - perhaps twenty - were traveling with haste and purpose, mounted on horseback. They were chasing something, someone: a Kitarran man, running at great speed down the road. He was some ways ahead of his pursuers, his long legs working hard, his long tail lithe and balanced behind him. He was fast, at first. Eva could hardly believe how fast. But he slowed and faltered, stumbling. He fell heavily into the dirt.

Eva knew she should retreat, hide, and find shelter, but the scene captured her, chaining her to the Kitarran's plight.

It took a moment for the Kitarran to pick himself up. His legs shook under him. He wavered and lurched forward once more, his white-gray fur splotched by mud. An easy target in the land of brown and grays.

Perhaps he would have outrun the men, but he stumbled again. Clearly, he could not keep up his lightning pace. The humans were gaining on him. Their triumphant shouts echoed in Eva's vision. They urged their horses faster, sensing victory, the weakness of their quarry giving them strength.

They caught up to the Kitarran at the crossroads. He stood tall, turning to face them, ears pressed back, lips curved exposing feral teeth. He looked fierce but his breathing was labored. His hands shook as he drew his latha, preparing for engagement.

The men were not afraid. They knew he was weak. It was hardly a fair fight. The men attacked. The Kitarran fell. He managed to take one man with him with a blow to the gut. The grass was stained with Kitarran blood nevertheless.

Then the men left, leaving the bodies where they lay for the buzzards and ravens. Why the men craved the Kitarran's blood, Eva's sight could not tell her. It was cruel and merciless. Perhaps the Kitarran was a criminal, doomed to his fate by his own acts of cruelty.

Eva's hands were cold and bloodless on Penn's reins. She shook her fingers to get her blood moving, hardening herself. She needed to hide. The men had continued on the road toward her. She needed to disappear into the landscape before they arrived.

There was a creek to the south, sheltered by the same low, scrubby trees that had hidden her numerous times before. It was the best place she could find. Thankfully, the ground was hard, so the horses left no tracks for the men to follow unless they were looking for them.

She waited in the trees and watched with the wind as the men passed, continuing southeast on whatever errand hastened their travel.

Eva resolved to stay in the thicket until daybreak. She dared not light a fire. The men were still too close. The risk was too great. They might smell her smoke and assuage their curiosity.

It would be a cold night. There was no sun; a high blanket of clouds kept its warmth away. The air smelled tangy with snow.

In the morning, the road lay before her like a bad dream. Death and cruelty waited at the crossroads. Wasted life. She couldn't help imagining the hope the Kitarran must have carried with him as he ran. How he tried with all his strength to escape the men, hoping he could be fast enough.

He hadn't.

He had been cut down and now lay rotting.

She wondered again what the Kitarran had done to deserve such a death, or was it just the nature of the men who chased him, to kill and maim as a matter of course? To kill or be killed.

There were no buzzards, no ravens. The birds of war had not yet found the dead men. The air was too cold. The bodies did not stink of death enough to invite the grizzly feast. But they would come. The horses smelled it as they neared. Penn snorted and stamped; Sasha's nostrils flared.

The human lay on his back where he had fallen, his eyes pinched and glazed over in death. He had a wound in his gut, another on his neck. It was hard to tell which had brought his end.

Eva dismounted. She felt compelled to see the Kitarran's face.

He was on his back. His clothing was a black, bloody mess, his fur matted with blood and mud. His face was untouched. He was big, long. Eva imagined he was taller than Tayeh in life. His fur, where it was not obscured by dirt or blood, was beautiful, so light gray it was almost white, with dark spots and stripes. His fur was not silvered by age. He looked young, a man in his prime.

His eyes were closed, his expression drawn. He died in pain. Eva felt a pang of pity. Pity - and anger. Maybe he deserved to die. Maybe he was a criminal, a betrayer. Maybe all Kitarrans were immoral.

The Kitarran's mouth was slightly open, just a hint of bright red blood at the corner. The blood was wet and shiny. It should be dry and cracked. Eva removed her glove, placing her bare hand over his mouth. She felt the heat of his body, the slight push of warm air on her cold fingers.

He was still alive.

How, she could scarcely guess. His wounds were dire. He had been lying on the cold ground overnight. Eva could only imagine the foul humors spreading through his body. His death would be slow and painful yet, and soon the birds would come. She felt his pulse. It was slow, and weak, but determined.

Pity broke the anger in her heart a little. No one deserved that kind of death, not even a Kitarran.

She drew her long, sharp dagger. One quick, deep slice to his neck would spill the last of his lifeblood, letting him die almost instantly, before the birds came to pick him apart. It was the merciful thing to do.

The steel was bright, thirsty. Eva moved it closer to his neck, the blade resting against his furry skin. She could see the rise and fall of his uneven breath. She could feel it against the blade. She would have to use a lot of force to sever the large artery in his neck.

Her hands shook. The blade wobbled. Her chest was on fire. She took a deep breath, not realizing she had been holding it. The knife edge was sharp, an invaluable tool along the road. It had carved meat for stews, sliced bread and tubers, and now she would use it to end the misery of a lost soul.

Nothing happened.

Eva's hands did not move. The blade did not slice through the last threads of the Kitarran's life. Killing him was logical, but her hands still shook, protesting. Logic was for other people; Eva was a *sanarii*.

Eva cursed. She put the blade away, resolved to the decision in her heart.

The Kitarran was big. Moving him would be challenging. She needed to get him back to the thicket quickly to avoid any more travelers or brigands. She put her hand upon his brow and let some of her healing magic seep into him. It would be no good if he died after her efforts. She would not allow it.

Satisfied that he would keep a little longer, she unrolled her canvas tent and laid it on the ground next to the dying man. She cut his bulbous pack from his shoulders. She would bring it with her.

As for the Kitarran himself, it took all her strength, but she managed to get him onto the canvas. First his shoulders, then his legs and rump. He was heavy, but not as heavy as she expected for his size. His tail was dirty but unharmed. She tucked it next to him. Eva wrapped him up like a package and tied the rope to the canvas, pulling him along behind the horses like a sled. It was a bumpy ride, but there was no other way.

Eva had some difficulty picking a trail to the thicket that would not show the strange track her parcel made along the ground. There were more bumps and rocks, but Eva would not risk discovery. At least the man was unconscious.

The thicket was deep and tangling. Eva went farther in than the day before, following the winding creek bed. Finding a path through the tight trees that allowed her horses and her awkward passenger was trying. Some backtracking was required. She was pleased and relieved when the trees opened into a grassy clearing beneath some arching, leafless willows. The spot was right beside the creek. She couldn't have begged for a better place.

Before seeing to her patient, she left the clearing behind and used her magic to make sure she had not been followed, but there was no one for miles and miles.

She unwrapped the Kitarran and checked to see if he was still breathing. Fresh blood seeped from his wounds. The bumps had not been kind. She would need to sew him up quickly, but first she needed a fire and hot water.

She didn't have to wander far to find sticks that would burn. The creek widened into a good-sized pool. She spied fish darting under the logs. Some were a decent size to eat, if she could catch them.

While the water boiled in her camp pot, she took her knife and cut the Kitarran's clothes from his body, revealing the nasty patchwork of deep punctures and gashes the brigands had made in the Kitarran's gray skin. She discarded the dirty clothing. Anything that wasn't too badly damaged she sliced into strips and put into the pot of boiling water.

She cleaned his wounds with both cloth and magic. She couldn't heal him completely, not even close. She was already exhausted from the effort of moving him. He was too close to death. She could only give him the strength he needed to stay alive, at least for now.

She stitched until her fingers were stiff and aching. She made compresses with herbs from her healer's bag. When she was done, the light of the day was leaving, and her fingers were numb, her arms heavy. Her back ached from leaning over her patient. She nibbled a bit of smoked meat and went to sleep beside her fire.

The Kitarran did not look better in the light of morning.

Eva frowned as she lifted his bandages to see fresh blood, but the wounds did not smell rank. At least there was no infection - yet. Eva poured a little water gently into his mouth. He seemed to swallow a few drops. She needed to hunt, to find food. Proper nourishment would be essential to the man's recovery, and a good bone broth would be useful.

She took her bow and went out on foot, scanning the open, wild lands from the air for both humans and prey. A reedy pond was not far away, a small hub for ducks and geese. Eva approached cautiously and was rewarded for her patience and stealth as she took down another big goose close to the shore.

She set some of the meat to roast and made a broth before turning back to the Kitarran. She would have felt better if she could see some sign from him, some stirring or groaning. His absolute still-ness unnerved her. She cupped his big, furry head with her hands and closed her eyes, searching his body.

His head was fine. She had been worried it had been damaged beyond repair. But no, it was better than the rest of his bruised and beaten body. Heartened, she continued, easing what pain and damage she could without giving too much of herself. His body was hurting badly, fighting to survive.

Something else tainted his blood. More than just his pain and her magic. Culla. She would never forget the feeling of its all-consuming fire against the arsenal of her magic. The drug pushed her away, wrapping around the fiber of his being as if shouting "Mine, mine, mine!" Eva recoiled, furious, but there was nothing she could do. She was already committed to helping the Kitarran. If the culla killed him in the end, it would be a bitter disappointment.

She fed him broth. He swallowed a little. There was still no sign of him stirring.

Eva went through his pack and found extra clothes, some food, a blanket. There was a little pouch filled with tiny glass vials, each filled with a minuscule amount of sweet-smelling herb ground into a harmless-looking gray powder. She guessed it was the culla. She had never seen it before, but she knew what form it took from Mila's description. She put it aside with great distaste. The clothes she returned to the pack.

She cleaned the Kitarran's body, washing his matted fur, and tucked the extra blanket around him like she would a little child.

The goose cooked, the horses munched on the grass. The wind rustled the treetops but did not break into the thicket. Eva lay and watched the bare branches sway in the wind and felt the quiet of the place seep into her bones. She wondered what kind of man the Kitarran was and why he was running through the Tarm.

She sat, focusing her attention on the fire, listening as it crackled, devouring the wood. The *simul rami* was close. She leaned into the magic and sought the Kitarran, hoping for a vision of his past. Just like when she had sought out Tarek and the Iron Wolves, she could not sort through the avalanche of images. The *simul rami* was too strong. Frustrated, she slipped back into her body. She had almost always been able to find visions of Rhyl and Illiah in the *simul rami*, but she wondered if that was because they were part of her, tied to her by the heartstrings of her soul. More and more, Eva wondered if the *simul rami* were alive, sentient. It felt like it was keeping secrets from her.

Sanarii of old had tools made of gold or other elemental ores to help them use the *simul rami*. Eva had nothing. The gold bowl had disappeared with Tayeh, and for all she knew, he had never wanted her to learn how to be a proper *sanarii*.

Eva had once put her trust in Tayeh, but he had betrayed her. She had put her trust in love, in hope, in magic, but they were too precious and fragile. It was time to trust herself, to trust her gut, her instincts. So far they whispered that she was on the right path. Saving this man felt right.

COTOCH

"WELL, COTOCH?" Crea said, startling him.

Cotoch had just sat down, a glass of wine in hand - Kitarran wine - a fire blazing comfortably before him, the cold damp night locked away behind his shuttered windows. Now, he took a towel and dabbed the wine that had spilled on his tunic, biting his tongue against the rude words he wanted to throw at the spirit woman.

"I hope I am not interrupting?" Crea asked but looked unapologetic.

"Of course not," Cotoch growled.

"The Kitarrans have kidnapped Prince Illiah and his son," Crea said. Her great black wings twitched.

"I thought you planned to have them killed?" Cotoch asked, thinking back to the last conversation he had shared with the Guardian of Jullayah. It had been some time ago, almost a year.

"Illiah is smart and surrounded by his loyal men. It has been a harder task than I imagined. And now it is too late! The Kitarrans have him - and the child. Damn Tayeh and his *velidar* whore!"

"I told you the Kitarrans wanted the child," Cotoch said.

Crea glared at him. "It would seem you were right."

"What about his wife?" Cotoch hoped Crea could not hear the longing in his voice.

"The Allati girl? She ran away. Probably dead in a ditch somewhere."

Cotoch felt his heart sink at the thought. "Why are you here, Crea?" Cotoch asked, pouring himself another glass of wine. "To acknowledge that I was right all along? That does not sound like you."

"I want to destroy Kitarra," Crea said smiling. "Time to contact your cousin."

Cotoch opened his mouth to reply, but a loud knock on his door stole his breath. The knock was followed by another, then another.

Crea glared at Cotoch, then the door, then gave him a fixed look that demanded his complacency, and then disappeared.

"Who is it?" Cotoch asked.

"Okil, sir."

"Come in," Cotoch said, looking longingly at his wine. "What is it?"

"It's Stone, sir. He killed the Colossal."

"Fuck me," Cotoch huffed, putting his wine aside.

☾

The prisoner quailed under his anger. Cotoch couldn't see it in the dark. But he was intimate with the concept of fear and despair. The crypts were full of shadows to hide in, corridors and tunnels and cracks. But they led nowhere. Escape was a forgotten concept, like the sun. Or hope. Eaten by stone and rot. The prisoner had been in the crypts a long, long time.

Cotoch's arms were painted with blood to his elbows. He could not see it, but his mind knew the color. The bright red. The color of power. Of magic.

Normally, he conducted the abhorrent business without the mess. But he was pissed. Furious. The *varing* slipped and spilled around him, clumsily harvested, but it would keep him a little longer. It would give him strength for his task.

In his rage, Cotoch almost forgot to wash before climbing back up to the day above. He wondered, with a moment of amusement tinged with horror, what his house staff would say if he arrived covered in blood, his eyes pulsing with *varing*. They would call him a monster. Men do not follow monsters. Not willingly. And Cotoch knew it was easier to have willing followers than to coerce them.

He scrubbed off the sticky, itchy mess. He redressed in clothes free from blood. He checked himself thoroughly in the mirror.

The Colossal was dead. The man had been useful, if a little bit of a brute. Quite a lot of a brute, actually. Sandra had detested him. At least she would be happy.

Stone was gone. Cotoch was not sure what enraged him more, that Stone would kill his man, or that Stone would run away from Cotoch's wrath. Stone, his loyal cat-man. His warrior. Cotoch thought he had secured the man from such weakness of character with the culla. If Stone did not come back soon, he would slip into withdrawal and most likely die.

Cotoch felt another ripple of anger. He did not like to lose his weapons. And Stone was one of his best. He had men out searching, but they had not found him. Stupid, unpredictable, childish Kitarran.

A marauding band of brigands had been spotted in the Tarm. Cotoch had to deal with them as well. He could not allow thieves on his land. His people looked to him to protect them from the ilk of the Midlands. It was why they loved and followed him.

Stone's murderous fit and disappearance couldn't have come at a worse time. Cotoch had his pieces on the board and was about to move them into place. He needed all his force behind him. He didn't have time to babysit a high, unstable, rogue Kitarran. He thought about sending Stone to the crypts, but who was he kidding? He could never take the Kitarran alone. Even high, Stone was uncanny.

Well, he would just have to wait for his men to return. Dwelling on the inevitable was as useful as a woman with a sword.

He had a message to send.

Cotoch's fingers itched. There was still blood under his fingernails. He would deal with that later.

The water in his gold basin shimmered and gave a serpentine ripple. A familiar face appeared; his black hair was slightly streaked with gray, his eyes no less volatile, no less heightened by the *varing*.

"Imal, cousin," Cotoch said.

"Yes?"

"It is time."

Imal's mouth stretched into a smile better suited to a dragon, or perhaps a very big and very poisonous snake.

CHAPTER 50

STONE

AN ACHE. No, not an ache. An ache was something to be borne and endured with mild discomfort. This was a throbbing, droning, pinching sort of pain that laced up Stone's arms, his spine, into his head and split his ears like a cleaver. And there was thirst, unquenchable thirst that made his tongue raw and swollen.

It was excruciating.

Still, Stone thought dying would feel worse. Or better. It must be true what the mother-wives say. Kitarrans must be descended from cats. How else would he have so many lives? He had died twice already.

His eyes were closed. He couldn't open them. His body wouldn't obey his commands. His strength had deserted him like a coward before a brute. He gave up. His arms felt like part of the earth itself, riddled with pain as the earth is riddled with roots.

Why couldn't he just die?

Oh, right. She wouldn't let him.

Her lovely face swam before him in a half-remembered dream. She was smiling sadly, shaking her head patiently in that way she always did when he was acting like an idiot. It was a mark of how much he had changed that he hated her for it.

When the rogues caught up with him, he knew he was sluggish and outnumbered. He thought then that dying might be peaceful, even wonderful. But when his vision went black, and he felt the painful crunch of his head hitting the ground, the terror had been so fierce, even to remember that last moment of consciousness made his heart race and his breath catch.

His truth was his cowardice. His fear of what awaited him beyond the veil of blood and flesh terrified him more than anything in life could.

Maybe it had been Cotoch's men who ran him down, sent to punish him for his offense. Probably not. Cotoch was ambitious, and dangerous; Stone had done enough to earn his employer's disfavor lately, but cut down mercilessly in the bleak wilderness was not Cotoch's style. The self-proclaimed lord had some honor. Or principle. The two were not quite the same.

Honor.

Stone's mind recoiled from the concept. He had cast honor away a lifetime ago and despised himself for it.

He needed a distraction. He tried to open his eyes once more and failed. He tried his arms again. His body must be in rejuvenation. He had experienced the state of almost unconsciousness the first time he had felt death's grip and its slow, painful release. Again, he wouldn't allow himself to dwell on that time, that other life.

He groaned involuntarily as a spasm of pain ran up his arm for his efforts.

He was not alone. A cool, wet rag was placed on his lips, and cool, delicious water trickled onto his tongue, followed by warm broth. His alarm was almost forgotten as instinct took over and all he could think about was the nourishment his body craved.

"More?" a voice asked. It was a light voice, yet slightly hoarse. A woman. Probably alone, judging by the unused quality to her voice. He didn't make a sound but whatever sign he gave was interpreted correctly. A cup this time, held to his lips. His head was propped up, so the liquid spilled mostly into his waiting mouth. Gentle hands placed his head carefully back down, wiping away any mess from his clumsy lips.

Curiosity was apparently stronger than self-preservation because the mysteriousness of his situation gave him the strength to open his eyes. Slowly, the blurred vision came into focus, and he took in his surroundings.

It was a small camp, of sorts, hidden away in the thick brush that grew up in patches all over the Tarm. Willow trees arched above his head, the faint sounds of a trickling creek and horses were off to his right. To his left, he could see her, just barely. The woman.

She sat with her knees under her elbows, watching him, her expression calm - too calm. It was the same expression he practiced daily until it was his only expression. The look of someone who holds tightly guarded secrets. Yet it wasn't the only strange thing about the woman. She was of royal Allati blood. Her long, silver-gold hair was dirty from travel, but the long braid draped over her shoulder was an unmistakable sign of her heritage. Strange. Allati women never traveled alone. A treasure such as her would never be allowed to leave the house of her husband, much less the borders of Allati.

"Don't try to talk," she told him in a stern voice. Not that he could. His throat burned. He couldn't move his tongue to bend around any comprehensible sounds. "You have been asleep for three days since I found you, and you were lying in a field for a day and night before that." She bent over him, rummaging around his body. He couldn't tell what she was doing. Adjusting bandages, he supposed.

Before he had blacked out and hit the ground, he remembered a lot of blood - unfortunately most of it his own. Twenty men armed with sicaras used him to test the sharpness of their blades. Again, he wondered how he was alive.

Yes, it was true Kitarrans' skin knits together almost before the eye. But Stone remembered blood, a lot of blood. A body can't heal without keeping at least some within the flesh. Too much thinking. His head hurt.

"You should close your eyes and rest," the woman said.

He didn't, though. He kept studying her. This slight scrap of a human woman who had somehow saved his life.

Whatever else he had done in his life, he could not ignore the fact that now he was bound to her. Bound to repay the debt. It was a sacred Kitarran writ that not even he had the will to break. The strange woman faded from his sight as his world went blurry once more, then dark.

His last coherent thought was a curse.

☾

When Stone woke again, his eyes flew open immediately. He attempted to force his body into a sitting position. He could move his arms and legs, and turn his head with minimal pain. Progress.

"Stop!" came the woman's worried voice. "You'll pull a stitch, or ten - you have a lot of them." The woman was beside him, her hands on his arms, trying to coax him down. She was a little thing, really. And young, barely older than twenty. Her accent was odd. He couldn't quite place it, but his head was still clouded by pain, and other things.

"I'm okay. I'm okay," he said gruffly, shoving her off, gently enough. Finally, he sat. The girl glowered at him, clearly unhappy with his insubordination.

"Let me check." Without waiting for his permission, she undid a bandage on his stomach to make sure all was fine. Stone wanted to laugh at her expression. Clearly, she didn't know very much about Kitarrans. She pulled off some of the other bandages, leaving his wounds exposed. They could both see her stitches were now in vain. His flesh had mended nicely, leaving tender pink scars instead of torn skin.

"Kitarrans heal much faster than humans."

"I see." But she had backed away from him, suddenly wary.

"I am in your debt, milady," he said in what he hoped was a trust-worthy manner. "I owe you my life, and for that, I am pledged by the Allmakers to be your amourii. In other words, your protector, your servant, for as long as I can."

Her eyes had gone round and then narrowed in distrust. Her fingers fiddled with an invisible necklace absently as she pondered this. She didn't trust him, that was obvious. How could he blame her, really? A lone Kitarran, far from Kitarra, found in a bloody pool, possibly of his own making. If she had any sense, she would have marked him a traitor and a thief immediately. And she seemed intelligent, if a little naive. He wondered why she bothered with him at all.

"Okay, then," she said matter-of-factly. "As it turns out, I am in need of someone like you. I am bound for Kitarra. I need to see the queen."

Excellent. Better and better. It would have been so much easier just to die.

"You wish I had let you die?" she said, reading his thoughts. "Because I came very close to slitting your throat to ease your pass-ing. But I couldn't. I am a healer, not a butcher," she added quietly.

"There are worse things than death."

"Agreed," she said, her face masked with that eerie calm.

"My name is Stone," he said, testing his muscles, flexing his wrists, already wishing his hand held a knife or a latha. He felt naked without his weapons.

"Mine is Eva."

"Eva." He rolled the name on his lips, testing it. "A royal Allati with a southern accent. Traveling alone." He knew he had heard the accent before. Cotoch had many Jullayans in his employ.

"I'm only half Allati. My father was from Jullayah."

"You don't look it."

"You don't look like any Kitarran I've ever met either."

Stone knew what she meant. He was tall surely, but his fur had silvered in a strange pattern that even he had never seen. As if his body was also trying to forget his past. He had heard of a Kitarran's markings changing as they age, fading to a lighter shade, or a bit more spots around the feet and face, but nothing like his. And it wasn't age. He was only in his third decade. He was almost to the point of being self-conscious of his silver fur with its striking black stripes and patterns. As a youngster, it would have made him feel handsome. Now it was a sign he was not the man he once was.

Wait - how many Kitarrans could a half-blooded girl meet in Jullayah?

"Your weapons should still be in the field where I found you," Eva said. "Unless your attackers picked them up. Otherwise this piece of road has been pretty quiet."

"How far are we from the road?"

"Not very. You are too heavy. But far enough."

It was no small feat that she had moved him at all. Sure, Kitarrans are light for their size, but still, the girl was small.

"How long do you think it will take to travel to Kitarra?" she asked in a businesslike manner, handing him a bowl of what appeared to be stew. He sniffed it apprehensively.

"A few weeks maybe," he said, taking a bite.

Her lips formed a thin line. She was biting her cheek.

"Milady, it's rough country here. They call this land the Tarm. It means between in the old tongue," he told her. "There are no laws, no rules, no retribution. Well at least not of the formal sort," he added sourly. "No Guardians to step in and assert their mystical powers," he said sarcastically, taking another bite of the stew. It really wasn't bad for a camp meal. The meat was fresh. The girl must be an accomplished hunter. Of course she was; she had traveled all the way from Jullayah.

"Yes, I was warned about this place. Another reason I saved you. I thought perhaps you would help me. Guess I was right." There was a note of smugness in her voice.

"Don't let it get to your head," he remarked. He could see a faint smile tug at her lips, but her eyes were sad.

"Get some rest. I want to move as soon as we can." She stood in a smooth liquid motion. She wore a sword at her hip. A dagger handle peeked out from the top of her boot. She was dressed like a man, not quite hiding her feminine curves. Her boots were of fine leather, if travel worn and stained. Her cloak was of fine wool, a good, tight weave. This woman either had money or else was a very good thief.

He watched her leave the thicket enclosing the small camp to tend to the horses beyond. More than one, perhaps two. He couldn't see them, but he could hear them shuffling, smell their familiar horsey smell.

It felt good to fill his rumbling stomach. It made him tired, but his thoughts were restless. He would have to tell her about Cotoch. To travel through the Tarm would be impossible if he didn't sort that one out.

Cotoch had spies and watchers everywhere, working tirelessly to keep the humble town of Mahlas safe. Regardless, plenty of bandits and thugs plied their trade on the Tarm. Out on the plain, any travelers would be ripe for picking, like apples in autumn.

Four days. He had been out four days. How far could those bandits have gone? If they were Cotoch's men sent to punish him, he didn't feel optimistic about their chances of passing through the Tarm. Still, if the girl were wealthy, perhaps Cotoch's greed would outweigh his irritation that Stone had killed his brute.

A drunken bout, led by a drunken bet, Stone had been high and rightfully stupid. He had still won, though, making his ego soar ever so slightly. Cotoch would be furious at the loss of one of his most feared enforcers. Stone had made the only logical choice his affected mind could and ran into the frigid wilderness like the coward he really was. Look where it had gotten him.

His hands shook as he put the empty bowl down. His clothes were gone. That could be interesting. He hoped his pack was not rotting in the field. However, clothes were not his primary concern. A familiar feeling of rising panic caused him to search around the small camp for his things with an eagerness bordering on manic.

The sudden movement made him dizzy. His body was weak. He closed his eyes tight against the feeling, the pain in his head. He took deep breaths to steady himself against the vertigo and anxiety. His body still hurt, but there was something else, something missing. The usual thirst, which had nothing to do with water, was gone from his flesh. The feeling of constant need had been replaced with - what was he feeling - relief? Could he truly be rid of the culla? Was it possible? He guessed four days was enough to fall into deadly withdrawal and come out the other side.

His dependence on the drug had created a state of comforting obliqueness. Without it, he faced everything he was running from. Already memories forced into subversion rose real and painful. It took all his strength to ignore them and fight his way into the present, forgetting the past, dismissing it.

Well. Stone was no longer a slave to the drug. Instead, he was an honor slave to an Allati girl who only wanted one thing: to get to Kilev. The last place on earth he would have chosen to go. He could see the determination in her eyes as she spoke of her quest. There would be no swaying her. But first, they had to get through the Tarm.

Stone shivered. Kitarrans were rarely affected by the elements; being covered in fur helped. But this was different. He couldn't stop. He wrapped the small blanket around his shoulders and tried to get closer to the fire, but he was too weak.

The girl came back and tossed him a bundle. His extra clothes, his dagger in its sheath, his belt. She must have collected them from his pack after all. He looked through the pockets with unsteady hands before dressing. Was it need or fear that fluttered in his chest as he looked for his culla? He didn't know. The warming, brazening effect of the drug had wrapped around him like a promise. It had advantages. Like numbing emotions, blocking memories.

"Looking for this?" the girl asked. She held up his small leather satchel containing the dose vials. Her expression was a storm waiting to break. Without an answer, she smashed them against a rock by the fire. Stone heard the crunch of breaking glass. She fed the remains to the fire. The aroma of the dried herb filled the air for a second, and then it was gone. Stone watched it turn to ash. Relief. Yes, it was relief.

"Who gave it to you?" she asked, her eyes glinting dangerously.

"A man named Cotoch." He wasn't about to lie to her, not with that look she had. Not if he could scrap together enough of his pitiful honor for the plain truth. "I took it willingly." The point seemed important.

"Why would anyone make themselves a slave?"

"I wanted what only it - he - could give me."

"No more," she said. It was a command, one that he must obey. She was his master - mistress? - now, after all. "You are lucky it didn't kill you."

"It should have," Stone replied.

Eva added more wood, making the fire blaze hungrily. The warmth reached Stone, but he still shivered slightly.

Eva busied herself with the small pot, making another hot meal. The rush of gratitude Stone felt toward her surprised him. He kept upright long enough to eat the second stew she made. After, he lay back down, hoping when he rose again, he would be stronger.

He gazed across the flickering fire at the girl. Her eyes were sad, ringed with deep circles he had not noticed. Her skin was pale. She was exhausted.

Before he could say anything, she lay down next to the fire, atop her leather cloak, a blanket pulled over her. She met his eyes before closing hers. She was asleep instantly, her breath settling into the routine of a dreamless sleep.

Stone gazed up at the trees, hoping there was no one traveling nearby. They would be an easy target - him too weak, her too exhausted to stand watch, the night too cold to sleep without a fire.

CHAPTER 51

STONE

STONE EXPERIMENTED with sitting. It was a vast improvement. He ventured to stand and found his legs relatively stable, but he was a little out of breath. He managed to stir the fire and put on more wood.

The day dawned bright enough, but there was a hint of rain in the air, or perhaps snow. Snow, though rarely seen on the Tarm, was not unheard of. Spring often began with the coldest storms.

The girl was still asleep, curled around herself, her hands under her face. She looked like a child. Or a heroine from an old tale. She didn't stir when he started moving about. He went off to urinate.

Walking was stiff work after lying on the hard ground for four days. Even his tail felt heavy. He could hardly keep it from dragging. The horses shuffled uneasily when they smelled him. He put his hand up to the big black one. It sniffed him, then seemed more at ease, if a little indignant. They were big horses. Stone hadn't seen the like of them before. Usually Kitarrans didn't ride horses, being swift of foot. Horses were generally too small to take a Kitarran any distance, but Stone figured these two would.

The creek was nearby. He filled the pot with water and went back to camp, placing it on the fire to heat. He looked around for any food stuffs: a bit of cooked meat, some wild tubers. That was it. Stone could hunt, the girl could hunt. They were not without resources.

He made a stew of sorts from what he had found and watched the girl sleep. He wondered how much sleep she had gotten the last few days and guessed it had not been much. What would he have done if he had a strange, potentially dangerous albeit injured Kitarran sleeping in his camp? He would have stayed awake and kept watch until he knew it was safe. Poor girl.

Once he was reasonably pleased with his stew, he sat down heavily and let it, well, stew. He regarded the sleeping girl again. She almost looked peaceful, but for the lines and shadows under her eyes, the signs of grief, or perhaps fear. Her clothing was well worn, but under the grime he could see the delicate stitching around her sleeves, the pretty etched leather on her boots, only noticeable because Stone was looking for it. He wondered again at her heritage. She had told him she was part royal Allati. She spoke with a Jullayan accent and said she hailed from those parts.

Perhaps it was a guise, the accent donned to hide her identity. But nothing could hide her distinctive hair. The Allati watched over their women like dragons over their treasure - she wouldn't have escaped easily. And there were better ways to get to Kitarra from Allati than through the Tarm.

No, she must be from Jullayah as she said, and he had sensed no lie in her words.

In another life, he had known more about Jullayah than he did presently. He vaguely remembered an Allati girl was to wed the prince of Jullayah, but he doubted it could be the same girl. The prince would not discard a bride like her so easily, and that had been many years ago. That princess would be older and likely have children of her own. What mother would leave her children? It could not be the same woman ... unless ... Stone shook his head to dispel such quandaries. That life was forgotten. He wanted to keep it that way.

Whatever her origins, she was in the Tarm, wanting to get to the capital of Kitarra, Kilev, the queen's city. He was her amourii. She was his, as surely as he was now hers. He would protect her as best he could.

It surprised him how easily the task sat upon his shoulders. He would rather be pierced by cold iron (or hot) than head back to Kilev, but at the same time, it felt good to watch over someone, to have a purpose. He already felt possessive over her. She looked helpless and vulnerable, especially asleep. And this was a wild, rugged country that could very well rip her apart.

Yes. For the first time in a long time, Stone felt good. His wounds were still sore and his muscles stiff from disuse, but, perhaps because the culla did not consume him, his spirits felt lighter. He would still have to face Cotoch. There was no way around that. No one traveled the Tarm for long without paying homage to the self-named lord - not if they wanted to live.

Stone had seen a longsword attached to one of the saddles. Not the girl's weapon, obviously. Hers was smaller. (An Allati with a sword of her own?) This was a man's weapon requiring a strength he doubted such a slight person could produce. It would be as useful to her as nipples on a breastplate. She could have been traveling with someone. If her partner had been killed, it would explain the grief in her eyes, the extra horse. The sword, even from his quick review, looked well forged, the sheath an exquisite work of leather, worth a small fortune.

The wind penetrated the thicket, worming its way through the dense branches. If it wasn't snowing by sundown, he would be pleasantly surprised. His fur was thick and seldom did such a wind bother him, but the girl was fragile, despite her warm layers. He piled more wood on the fire, taking care not to bump the pot of precious food. The fire blazed to life amiably.

Waiting was not one of his strengths. Stone stood and began flexing his protesting muscles, running through his morning routine. He pressed on, ignoring the twinges of pain, if somewhat slower than usual. He didn't have Mistura, his latha, but he could imagine it in his hands as he moved through his paces. He hoped he would be reunited with his weapon once they went back to the crossroads. He doubted the bandits would have taken it. Mistura was heavy and big, more than most men could handle. It was not a pretty weapon. It was not valuable. To smelt down the rare Kitarran steel was beyond the skill of most blacksmiths.

His muscles told him when they had had enough. His stomach pinched uncomfortably. His bandages were spotted with fresh red blood. The thin, pinks scars were tenuous; they must have torn a little. Eva would be displeased.

It must be almost midday and yet she was still asleep. They needed provisions, and it would take two days to reach Mahlas, but he couldn't bring himself to rouse her. Instead, he took her small bow and went out to hunt. He would stay close, to make sure no harm came to her.

The horses had eaten every speck of wispy grass where they were tethered. Stone moved them to a new area, just next to where they had been. They set about the new grass eagerly. Even under the thick wood, there was ample grass, dry as it was. The Tarm was full of grass. Tall grass, short grass, soft grass, cutting grass. In places it grew up to his waist in the warm months. It hid rabbit and grouse, or geese and ducks in the marshes. A deer would be a bit of a task, if he could find one.

He stepped out of the wood and looked around. The wind was wild away from the shelter of the dense trees, freezing his lungs, pulling the warmth from his body. The sky was gray and heavy, but no snow yet. He got his bearings quickly. They were closer to the road than he would have liked. He couldn't discern any smoke from their camp. The wind dissipated it, making it invisible. Even so, he would stay close and hope there was game close by.

It didn't take long before he took down two ducks. The birds were basically skin and bones, but it was something. Once the birds were cooked, in this cold, the meat would last until they reached Cotoch. He found a small plant of bojar, which would make a nice reviving tea. Satisfied with his spoils, Stone returned to the thicket.

He sat in front the fire, enjoying its warmth, even if his fur kept it from being a necessity. He had already dressed the birds, but they needed plucking. He set to his task, listening to the wind and the even breathing of the girl as she slept.

The girl woke slowly. She must have truly been deep in sleep. She groaned and stretched and slowly sat, wrapping her blankets around her shoulders. She looked into his eyes for a moment, as if studying him with great intent. He couldn't read her expression.

"I can't believe my neck has the audacity to be cricked after so many nights on the hard ground," she complained. She yawned. Circles still hallowed her eyes, but not as dark as Stone remembered.

"You must be hungry. You have been asleep for a long time."

Stone poured her some stew from the pot and placed it into her grateful hands.

"Thank you," she said, smelling the hot meal.

"There is tea as well." He gestured to the other pot.

She raised an appraising eyebrow at him, which devolved into concern. "You went out hunting?"

"I didn't go far."

She narrowed her eyes at him and mumbled about having a look at his wounds once she had eaten. Stone helped himself to some stew after she had her fill. It settled in his stomach like a pound of lard. He was still not long from his sickbed. His stomach was weak like the rest of him.

"Here." Stone handed Eva a cup of steaming tea. She inhaled deeply and smiled a little.

"What's in it?"

"Mint and bojar, for clarity."

"Bojar? I have never heard of it."

Stone shrugged. "I don't know the plant's range. It might not grow in Jullayah, but in Kitarra and the Tarm, it is plentiful enough. Best picked in summer, though, as it was, I plucked it bare."

"If you find more, show me. Herb lore has always interested me," Eva said before settling in with her tea. She looked more relaxed. There was no hint of suspicion or wariness in her expression. It seemed that she had decided to trust him.

Once she finished her meal, she turned a determined eye on him, subjecting his injuries to an inspection. She tsked him for over-stretching his newly healed body.

"This one was bleeding. I warned you not to do too much." She quickly took off the old bandage. He opened his mouth, about to say something in his defense, and closed it again, deciding it wasn't worth arguing over.

Eva bandaged his wounds that had opened. She used his torn clothes, boiled clean and ripped into suitable strips. She took herbs from her bag and made a compress before wrapping him back up. She was quick and able. Stone was impressed. Obviously, she had skill with healing.

A thought sprung into his mind he could not dismiss - and he was exceptional when it came to dismissing things.

"You are a *sanarii*." The old word spilled off his tongue, loosened by his certainty.

She looked up at him with her blue-green eyes. Her eyes reminded Stone of summertime, warm blue skies and cool moss forests.

"Yes. I am." She turned her summertime eyes away from him, looking out, looking back into some memory or sad thought. He hadn't heard of any Allati magi in recent times. He had never heard of a woman *sanarii*. The Allati probably considered it a waste to teach a woman to harness the magic in her blood. The Allati valued their women as breeders, to warm their beds and satisfy their masculine urges. Humans were often a callous breed.

"We need to move on," Stone told her, pushing the quandaries from his mind. Food, escaping brigands, reaching Mahlas - all more important than discussing an ancient Allati culture. "We need food. These ducks won't last long."

"Can we buy provisions from Cotoch's town? Or should we skirt around it?"

Stone grimaced but nodded. "There is no skirting around Mahlas. The hills are patrolled. We will go to the city and bargain with its lord for safe passage. We can get food there. Do you have any money?" Stone asked hopefully.

She studied him before pulling a little pouch from a deep, hidden pocket. She poured a varied selection of perfectly cut gems into the palm of her hand. Emerald, sapphire, a large ruby the size of her thumbnail - a small fortune in gems. Stone didn't ask her where they came from, but he smiled at her.

"Cotoch will enjoy these. His wife Sandra loves sapphires. We will offer him those. I thought maybe you would have to sell your sword or a horse or something."

"Is it enough?"

Stone gave her a hesitant look. "Cotoch, the man who calls himself Lord of the Tarm, takes a tithe from those who wish to pass his land. Either you go to his home and pay him, or he takes it, along with your life. The sapphires should be enough. He is not unreasonable, just ambitious."

Eva crossed her arms tightly over her chest, her eyes cool and pointy.

"Cotoch gave you the culla," she said in an icy voice. She had a deep disgust for the drug, that was clear. He could hardly blame her. It was a despicable thing. A cruel way to keep people in line, but then the Midlands and the Tarm were cruel lands. Cotoch did his best to manage Mahlas and its inhabitants, etching out a place for the lost, who had nowhere else to go. "What did you do for him in return?"

Stone shrugged non-committally. "Intimidation, mostly." He would say no more. She would despise him if she knew. He despised himself enough for the both of them. He had done whatever Cotoch wished and hated himself for it. He would not speak of it to anyone, oath be damned.

The look - no - the glare she penetrated him with left him with no illusions of her feelings on the subject. Stone felt like a child under her righteous look and gave an uncomfortable bark of laughter.

"I vow I will not touch it again," he said with mock fear, placing his hand upon his heart, bowing his head in respect of her authority. He meant every word. He hoped she could read the sincerity behind his facetiousness. He had never been good at being serious. His heart and tongue were never in harmony.

"Good. Tell me of this Cotoch." The apprehension in her eyes made her look less like a sorceress and more like a young, vulnerable girl.

"Short version: Cotoch's father built Mahlas and gave exiles a home. Cotoch wed a Kitarran merchant's daughter. They have no children. He is smart. The Allati do not like him. But his people worship him. People trickle to Mahlas from Allati, and Kitarra, even Jullayah. It takes a lot to banish someone from Kitarra. You will not find many compassionate souls anywhere on the Tarm." She did not ask why he was banished.

"Cotoch suffers from a particularly irritating form of narcissism. He believes he is more than a bastard son of an exile. When we arrive, I expect Cotoch will welcome us into his house, feed us, entertain us like old friends. But if we don't pay his price, we will not leave Mahlas."

"I heard he was dangerous."

"Yes. He is. The Tarm is a harsh place. But unless you wish to risk the mountain passes or traveling through Allati, this is the only way to Kitarra. Allati would not be safe for you, and the mountains would be certain death. Even in summer, they are treacherous and unpredictable," Stone told her. It was a grim fact. She looked unsurprised to hear it. "Two days should see us to Mahlas"

"Two days," Eva repeated. "We should leave tonight. If we pack up now, we can make it to the crossroads and make shelter in the strand of trees beyond for the night. It's not ideal, but better than nothing. And you can find your weapon before the snow buries it, if it falls."

"Do you see visions, as well as heal?" Stone asked, thinking of the skills accredited to Allati magi. Not that he was an expert. Anymore.

"I do," she admitted in a quiet voice.

Stone took a moment to appreciate the treasure he had come across. This girl was a rare creature indeed, far rarer than the stones she carried in her purse. He thought of the Allati, the riches they would pay to have her in their grasp. They would wed her to their princes for the children she would bear them.

It turned his stomach thinking of it. She was no Allati wife. There was no calm acceptance in any inch of her body. She was a little thing, but she was tough and determined. Stone knew her type. A woman not to be underestimated.

"Onward and upward, I hope," Stone murmured, getting up. His muscles protested, his barely healed wounds pinched, but he hid it well. He didn't want to raise Eva's concern. He could handle the discomfort. It was relatively nothing.

Together they packed up her meager supplies and saddled the horses. Stone earned a look of approval as she surveyed his skills with the horse, making him smile.

"I have skills, milady," he assured her in an amused voice.

"I can see that," she retorted. "Here, take this."

She handed him the longsword he had seen belted to her saddle. He took it gingerly, with respect. He pulled the sword from the sheath to regard the blade. It was bright. It hurt his eyes. The steel was of exceptional quality, smithed with great care and skill.

"You need a weapon, but I will ask for it back someday," she added.

Stone bowed to her in thanks. "I will keep it well, until that day," he vowed.

"I did not know Kitarrans knew much about horses," Eva mused.

Stone shrugged in response.

"Can you ride?"

"If your horse will take me," Stone said, stroking the nose of the big stallion. Penn was the name Eva had for the black horse. A complacent enough creature, though his black eyes were intelligent and full of spirit and personality. Stone liked animals. It would be a pleasure to ride the magnificent beast.

"He likes you."

Stone had ridden before and knew the commands of the horsemaster. With Eva's guidance, it came back to him quickly. Penn did not need a heavy hand; he barely needed a hand at all. He could read his rider's seat. Stone was agile and well coordinated, an essential instinct for any warrior. It was not long before he rode in harmony with the big black.

Eva cast her healer's eye upon him from time to time, no doubt watching for some sign of weakness and strain, ready to berate him and cover him with compresses. It was endearing, but Stone would not show weakness, not even to her.

It was eerie watching Eva pause, bringing her gelding to a halt. She sat still, like a statue in the saddle. Her hands clasped the reins lightly, her back straight. But her eyes were lost. They were open to the sky and Stone knew she was gone, wherever it was that she went. With the wind, she said. He could almost feel the vibration of her magic as he waited.

Stone sighed, jealous. To fly with the wind, to be free of the confines of his body. To be something other. He would give many a vow for the chance.

She was not gone long. She stirred and blinked and turned to him, her eyes earthbound and hers once more.

"There is nothing. We should have the road to ourselves for some time," Eva reported. "Except for the crows and vultures at the crossroads."

Stone didn't want to think about the crossroads.

It had been four days since Eva had found him. The scene at the crossroads was as she had left it. No rain had removed the signs of violence from the grass. No snow had covered it. The birds took flight as they approached. The air was cold. Stone could not smell the stench of rotting flesh and was thankful.

He dismounted and looked for Mistura. All he found was dried blood, the body of the man he had killed, and the unfulfilled promise of his own death.

"Mistura's not here," he said at last.

"Your weapon has a name?"

"Yes, it has a name. And it is gone."

"I guess you will have to keep the sword awhile longer."

Stone was not ready to give up. He searched again. His blade had been with him always; it was part of him. Disappointment was uncomfortable for him. Maybe it was better that it was gone. The less of his old life to remind him of his opprobrium, the better. The little story he told himself did not lessen the feeling of loss.

"Let's move on. Find shelter before night falls," Eva told him, nudging her horse forward.

Stone followed her reluctantly, climbing up onto Penn's back.

They made it to the strand of trees just as the last light marked the end of another wintry-spring day. They quickly gathered wood, though most of it was wet. Stone did not relish the idea of a cold night with no fire. Eva was too fragile for such cold. It was Stone's duty to keep her safe, and that meant they needed a fire.

The wood was wet, but Stone coaxed a fire to life and the wood was forced to give up its warmth. Stone made another stew with the duck along with some tubers he had found while gathering the wood. Eva was interested in the edible plant. He decided to start pointing them out to her when they rode on.

They talked about plants as they waited for their meal and compared the different species from her realm of Jullayah and what could be found on the Tarm. He was reluctant to speak of Kitarra. Thankfully, the girl didn't pry for information about the land that had once been his home.

"What is it?" Stone asked, noticing her expression was suddenly cold and calm.

She shook her head and looked away. "Nothing. I'm starving. Is the stew ready?"

Stone stirred the haggard meal and nodded. He came around and sat beside her so they could both eat out of the pot. It was not a great meal, but after their stomachs were warm and full, Eva was fighting her fatigue.

"I'll take the first watch. This close to the road, if someone comes, they will see the fire," Stone told her.

"We should put it out," Eva muttered unhappily. "Better to be cold than dead."

"It's going to get colder."

"Are you so anxious to relive the ambush from four days ago?"

"Fine. We'll douse it. But lie here next to me. It'll be warmer."

She didn't argue. She arranged her blankets and settled into them. Stone sat close, curled around her slightly, protecting her as best he could from the unyielding wind. She tucked her face into her blankets and pressed close to him.

Strange. She was more or less a stranger, and a human, but sitting close to her was - good. Right. He listened to the night, to the steady, reassuring rhythm of his heart. He breathed in the cold night air and felt a peace settle about him. His memories stirred but did not ravage his heart.

CHAPTER 52

EVA

JUST PAST MIDDAY, the wind nudged Eva like a cough tickling the throat. She reached out to the *simul rami* to appease the odd sense.

The wind showed her a troop of men on the road, riding toward them in tight, disciplined formation, obviously not the same rabble of men who left Stone for dead, though these men looked equally dangerous. She hoped Stone's relationship with the Lord of the Tarm would prove to be an asset. She hoped her trust in him was not unfounded.

"There are men on the road ahead," Eva told Stone once her consciousness returned to her body.

Stone squinted at the road on the horizon.

"I see nothing, and I am Kitarran. We have keen eyes compared to a human, but I will trust your *sanarii* magic. How many men?"

"Twenty at least. They look formidable. They are mounted."

"Are they dressed in black?"

Eva nodded.

Stone lips twisted. "Cotoch's men. How long do you think?"

"An hour, maybe."

"Well, I probably know their captain. Hopefully, it will be Rory. But whoever is in command, they will no doubt escort us back to Cotoch. Perhaps, if we ask nicely, they will even have a warm meal to share with us." Despite the chance for a hearty meal, Stone didn't look particularly elated about sharing camp with the armed men.

A large group of men - fighting men. Without Stone, Eva might have been at their mercy. Trust was a fragile commodity.

Stone had an uncanny sense to pick up her thoughts. "Don't worry. I won't let them hurt you." He gave her a feral grin. The look in his yellow eyes was enough to quail even her bravery, and she was starting to consider him a friend. The fierce look heartened her. Stone was not Tayeh. He was not driven by some divine cause. He was bound to her; she was his master.

Stone slowed Penn to an easy lope to match Sasha. Stone pointed out plants to her, naming them and listing their usefulness to a forager or healer. He was trying to distract her. Was she so timid and innocent that this group of men scared her so? She didn't like the answer, so she allowed Stone's diversion.

"What are you doing?"

"See that plant, the one with narrow, silver, needle-like leaves?" Stone said as he leaned way over, one foot completely out of the stirrup, his tail out for balance, ears back in concentration. "Almost - got - it."

And he almost did, until Penn skittered and danced sideways. With an elaborate slithering motion, Stone was back in the saddle proper, but he was laughing so hard at his own folly Penn pressed his ears back and snorted.

Eva shook her head, but she was grinning. Stone was an interesting creature, fierce, but also given to fits of odd humor.

"Do not let Cotoch's men know you are a *sanarii*," Stone suggested after a lull in their conversation, the laughter forgotten. "There is no hiding that you are of royal Allati blood, but it would be even more dangerous to spread the rumor that there is a female *sanarii* wandering the Tarm."

"You are one of a handful of people still alive who know. I have always kept my magic hidden," she told him quietly, trying to keep the acid out of her tone.

He looked ahead and pondered as they rode side by side. "You are in more danger than you know," he said after a decided moment. "If you should have a son with the same gifts as yourself, he would be considered an Allati prince by right. The factions of Allati would fight tooth and nail to get you, to get your sons - and your daughters would be valued for their ability to create more sons." Something flickered across his face as he spoke: realization, understanding. A mask slipped over his expression, and his face became unreadable. He looked away.

Eva was glad he looked elsewhere. Grief pulled at her mouth, and her lip wobbled. She would not think of Rhyl.

Now. There was only now.

When she could trust her voice, she asked, "How do you know so much about Allati?"

"I have spent over five years working with Cotoch. His lands border Allati. The Allati do not like the self-proclaimed lord. They do not like his army. I have been into Allati many times to help him negotiate." His voice was heavy on the last word. Eva wondered again what his job for Cotoch had entailed. She wasn't sure she really wanted to be enlightened.

"What exactly would the Allati do with me?" Eva asked, curious if his education on Allati ways paralleled Felis's.

"They would marry you off to the highest bidder and beget a son or two or three with you. You would spend the rest of your life with a baby in your belly. You might be traded to another man, separated from your children to bear more for another man. The Allati can be careless with their women." There was a clear note of distaste.

"The Allati must have some protocol? I am hardly a young maiden, surely their royal wives are expected to be young and virtuous."

Stone flashed her a grin, his eyes full of humor. "I am sure they would make an exception in your case, being a *sanarii* and all."

Eva felt her face flush, wishing she could punch him for his teasing.

"C'mon, you walked right into that one," he said, still smiling.

In less than an hour, they saw blurry dots on the distant road. Cotoch's patrol. Stone drew up straighter in the saddle. His poise reminded Eva of a brewing storm.

They halted, waiting for the approaching troop. Small flakes of snow fell from the gray clouds.

The men rode double file with the captain in front. He put his hand to call a halt as they drew up.

"Captain Easra. Stay close. He is a nasty piece of work," Stone muttered for Eva's ears only. He nudged Penn forward to meet the captain who hailed him.

"Stone. Greetings. We were out looking for you. The lord expected you back some time ago," the captain drawled, his gaze drifting to Eva where she sat silently, cloaked and hooded on Sasha. "Who is this?"

"No one to concern you, Easra." There was no softness in Stone's voice. "A wayfarer. Her business is with your lord."

"Interesting." Easra turned his horse toward Eva. "My lady, we will be happy to escort you and Stone back to the village and our lord. The weather is far from fine. We offer you our hospitality, lacking as it may be."

Eva said nothing, letting them interpret her silence as they would. She pushed Sasha forward. The captain's words were an invitation, but there was only one answer to it. Easra's eyes said it all - come with us, or suffer at our hands.

Stone kept close to her as they rode. His body was relaxed, his seat in the saddle easy, but Eva knew it was a ruse. His back was aching. His eyes were weary from pain. It was obvious to her healer's eye.

The men kept their distance from Stone, glancing at him under their hoods. The captain was all arrogance, but even he had fear behind his eyes. Stone had a reputation. The men's body language hinted at fear and reverence both.

They made camp openly beside the road as the sky darkened. No one would dare attack such a large contingent of well-armed men.

Easra chose the location for its proximity to a small lake, hidden by the grass. A spring came out of the earth, feeding the pond. The water was clear and clean.

The snow came down with more urgency, frosting the ground.

The men made a large fire and cooked some crudely skewered meat. The warmth of the generous blaze penetrated Eva's woolen clothes and felt wonderful.

Stone shadowed her every move. The men made her nervous with their curious glances. Some were brave enough to make a smart remark or two before Stone turned his tongue-silencing yellow eyes upon them. Eva was grateful for his presence.

Stone sat close enough for Eva to feel the warmth of him, the softness of his fur, damp as it was with the falling snow. She put her hand on his arm and drew out some of his pain. She sought his sore muscles, his scars that were still new and raw, especially deep underneath where his vitals had been punctured. She could help him a little. His Kitarran blood would do the rest.

Stone said nothing, but Eva could feel the moment when his breath came easier. His fingers released their tension, one by one. He watched the men. He watched Easra.

"Where are you from?" Easra asked her, handing her a cup of something hot. "Lonely place for a woman, the Tarm."

Eva did not answer.

"Leave her alone, Easra."

"Just being friendly."

"Right. Is that what the women tell you? I heard you tried to take Yeri without her permission."

The man's boiling eyes were admission enough.

"You didn't know Yeri was one of Cotoch's mistresses, did you? I can't believe he didn't exile you for it. Imagine if you had fucked her? You would be gone, like the rest of Mahlas's filth."

"Shut your mouth." Easra stood and stalked off into his tent. Stone watched him leave, his eyes like a hawk's singling out a mouse.

Eva wrapped her cloak and blanket tight around her, settling beside the fire where it was warm, if still damp. Stone settled close behind her, their bodies touching. She fell into a dreamless sleep.

Mahlas, Cotoch's town, was a sprawling affair. The buildings were old but well built. Though not large, they were practical structures that obviously withstood the perpetual wind and other harsh elements of the valley plain.

The town was built beside a lake and against the foothills of the mountains, which had become more steep and rocky. A thick forest of conifers covered the foothills, the tight boughs of the trees contrasted by the late winter snow. There were pastures and fields, some white with a fine dusting of spring snow, waiting for warmer days and crops, some brown and muddied as steers and cows loped mindlessly along. All the dwellings were surrounded by a tall stone wall accessible only through a tall, ominous gate and a raised portcullis. Eva felt like a cow herself, shepherded under the tall arch into Mahlas, but there was no choice on the matter. Stone continued to appear unconcerned.

Inside the wall, people milled about, women carrying baskets of goods down muddy streets, men pulling wagons or horses. The sounds of hammering metal were loud as they passed a smithy. The town looked perfectly ordinary and orderly.

The mud gave way to cobbles. The narrow street gave way to a large square. There, shops, a bakery, a butcher, a clothier. Deserted tents lined the square; perhaps there was a market when the weather was fair. Mahlas was more civilized than Eva expected.

There was no mistaking Cotoch's own dwelling. His house was the largest building and had a certain grandness about it. Eva wondered how long it had stood and what it had been before the self-proclaimed lord had claimed it for his own. It looked older than the town, certainly older than its owner. A temple, perhaps? There were carvings around the generous front door that spoke of deities, reminding Eva of something she had seen at the Keep.

A servant girl greeted them at the door where Easra left them. Several more servants came from the house behind her to take the horses to the stable. Eva was hesitant to let them go, but Stone assured her the animals would be well looked after.

She followed her big Kitarran into the house he seemed familiar with. The servant told Stone his room was ready for him, as always, and a room would be made ready for his companion. Stone assured the servant they would be sharing his chamber. Eva didn't argue.

How was it she had come to trust this Kitarran so completely? She accepted his judgment, accepted that he knew what was best for her, at least at present. She trusted him to keep her safe, as he had vowed. His words had been stalwart, but they were just words - Eva knew actions spoke louder than promises.

Stone had worked for this man Cotoch willingly. An ambitious, self-serving man who had no qualms using a dangerous, life-destroying drug, with a reputation of fear and harsh retribution. How could Stone's morals allow him to do Cotoch's bidding and then swear a vow of honor to protect her? Eva tossed her useless thoughts aside. She had already accepted that trusting Stone was the right choice.

Stone's room was large, the furniture of reasonable quality and craftsmanship, though somewhat lacking in character. It held nothing personal. Only a bed, a couch, a chest - that was all. A servant was busy making a fire, watching warily behind her as Stone prowled into the room. He opened the window coverings and looked out onto the village.

"Lord Cotoch will see you at dinner. He is eager to talk with you and your guest," the girl told Stone in a voice that barely quavered. Stone gave her a curt nod. He remained stoic and scrutinizing until they were alone.

He dropped his gear onto the floor with a plunk and took one long stride across the room to open an adjoining to reveal a private bath and privy, telling Eva to help herself to the bath. The look of relief must have shown on Eva's face for Stone's stoic expression dissolved as he rolled his eyes and grinned.

The bath was already filled and steaming hot. Eva closed the door behind her and stripped out of her travel-stained clothes, settling into the hot water. Her skin burned from the heat, but she didn't care.

Stone came in without so much as a by-your-leave, picked her dirty clothes from the floor, and went back out again before she could think of anything to say. Protector and servant - somehow the latter did not dilute the former.

The soap smelled of wild roses, reminding her of summers past. She scrubbed herself clean, trying hard to get the grit out from under her nails. She washed and rinsed her hair, wondering if she would ever get the tangles out of it. She had half a mind to cut it short, but wasn't sure that would really solve her problem, unless she cut it ruthlessly short like a man's. She imagined the look on Illiah's face if he saw her with hair like a boy. Her husband loved her hair; even after so long apart, she was sure he would have a few words to say about it. She sighed. The desire to please her husband was strong, even with so much distance between them. He would pay dearly for such homage, if he ever got the chance.

The water was cold before she got out.

Stone was sitting on the floor by the fireplace, rubbing down his borrowed sword in the exact manner Illiah used. The resemblance was uncanny. Except for the fact that Stone was seven feet tall if he was an inch, had yellow eyes, spotted fur, and his fingers ended in perfectly curved claws - not to mention the long tail that curled around him ending with a tuft any house cat would be jealous of. It twitched now and then, at odds with Stone's calm demeanor.

Stone gestured to the bed where he had emptied the contents of her bag, arranging her last clean clothes in a neat pile - her serviceable tunic and leggings of soft wool. They were finer than her travel clothes, and she had worn them often at Stonyhill. The tunic had been a gift from Mila, who had some skill with needle and thread when she had time to apply herself. The edges were embroidered with the forest in mind. A little bird here, a leaf there.

Eva ran her finger down the edge, thinking of her dear friend. She had been a different person then, with friends for silly talk, for laughter, for confidences. Now her only friend was an exiled warrior with a dubious past and a gift for intimidation. She almost smiled at the juxtaposition.

Another batch of servant girls came in with more hot water in steaming buckets, preparing Stone's bath. Eva wrapped her towel more securely and started working on her hair. She had no desire to dress in front of the Kitarran or the servants.

Once the servants had accomplished their chore, Stone left Eva on her own, telling her to lock the door and not to open it under any circumstances.

She pulled on her clean small clothes, her clean undershirt, and leggings. The tunic went over top, and she tied her belt around her waist, her sword hanging at her hip. She finally managed to tame the last of her tangled hair and braided it down her back. She looked in the polished mirror and could see that her hair was already coming out from her braid, clean and sleek as it was.

Stone was done quickly, his fur tousled and wet, clean and bright. The contrast in his markings was striking as his spots smoothed into stripes and back into spots. He looked remarkable.

He dressed quickly without modesty. Kitarra must be a land where nudity was nothing more than a natural state, the fur alluding to the lack of vulnerability when unclothed.

"Do you have the jewels?" Stone asked. She nodded, fingering the pouch at her belt. "Can I see them again?"

She handed him the bag that carried the wealth of safe passage. Stone dumped some of the stones into his hand, sifting through them. He put some back in the bag.

"We should hide these. I don't want him to get greedy. And believe me, he would. Offer him the blue sapphires. He will ask for more but don't give him all of them. He won't really expect it." Stone took the other gems and placed them in another small pouch. He opened a small plank in the floor that should have been nailed down. Underneath was a hole meant for hidden things. He placed the pouch inside. Eva could see some bottles and several knives.

"What else is in there?"

"No culla, if that's what you are wondering."

"Don't lie to me." She did believe him, but a reminder never hurt.

"I won't take the culla again. I gave my word."

Some men's words were worth less than others. She would watch him.

"Ready?" Stone asked her.

Eva nodded. She was fidgeting, a telltale sign she was uneasy. She put her hands at her sides.

A servant waited for them. They were taken down a long, cold hallway shrouded by stone to a small hall. There was one long table, neatly laid with winter greenery, candles, several wine bottles, and three glasses made of clear, even glass. The walls were lined with sconces, candles burning brightly, filling the room with the scent of beeswax. The hearth was large, and the fire burned steadily, making the room warm and comfortable. There were glazed windows, but already the daylight was fading. Soon they would reflect only the candles.

The kitchen could not have been far. Eva could smell roast and vegetables, bread and fruity smells. She glanced at Stone; hunger reflected in his eyes. They were both tired of camp stew. He poured them each a glass of wine as they waited for their host's arrival.

Eva's boots clicked against the stone as she paced before the fire, wishing Cotoch would come. Mostly so they could eat - she was starving. The wine hit her empty stomach hard. She had never been good at keeping her spirits. She didn't want to lose her edge, if she had one.

"Ah, my favorite warrior has finally come home." A warm voice filled the room. Stone and Eva turned to face the lord who had finally decided to grace them with his presence. He walked purposefully across the room to greet them - first Stone, who offered him nothing in homage but an icy stare. Cotoch looked nonplussed. Then he turned his gaze and smile to Eva.

Something euphoric flickered in his eyes, a glint, a grin. The moment was lost. He gave her a little bow. Eva felt dizzy. Damn wine.

"My lady, I welcome you to my home," Cotoch said. Eva inclined her head to him. He was not a tall man, especially standing beside the lofty Kitarran, but he was thickly muscled and seemed to carry himself with an air of authority. His hair was black and long, tied neatly at the nape of his neck. His face was shaved; dimples showed in his cheeks as he smiled. His dark-brown eyes were laughing, yet shrewd. A handsome man in some respects. "I heard you brought a stray in with you, an Allati, the men are saying." He didn't take his eyes from Eva. He was assessing her from her crown of silver-gold hair to the way her boots outlined her finely shaped legs. Eva met his gaze evenly. She didn't want to submit to this man. She would not play the shy maid.

"This is Eva. She is my amourii," Stone told Cotoch.

"Really?" Cotoch's voice was all drama but gave no hint of his real emotion. "This sounds like a tale indeed! I am desperate to hear it. Sit, tell me as we eat."

They sat at the long table, the three of them. It seemed no more were joining them. Stone had talked of Cotoch's wife, but if she was going to make an appearance, it was not for dinner. Five servants came in with five dishes, each portion generous and delectable. There was roast, which Eva eyed hungrily. The servants served as Stone talked.

"I ran after the fight with the Colossal. I knew you would be angry and I was not in my right mind. I didn't mean to kill him." Stone cringed.

"You were high," Cotoch stated with amusement.

"Yeah, I guess I was," Stone said quietly, glancing at Eva under his furry brows. "A group of men found me, and I ran. I didn't know if they were your men or rambling brigands. By then I was in withdrawal. I couldn't take my dose with them chasing me. I could barely keep my feet straight on the road, much less fight. At the crossroads, I was overtaken. There were too many of them, and they had sicaras - I hate sicaras. As much as it pains me to admit, they cut me down efficiently and left me for dead. Eva found me and took pity on me. She dragged me to safety where I was able to heal."

"I had heard tales about Kitarran amourii, and my path leads to Kitarra, so it was advantageous for me to save him," Eva added, lying smoothly.

"Yes, advantageous indeed," Cotoch said, taking a sip of his wine. "As it happens, Stone, I am happy to see you alive. My men found the party that ambushed you. They are dead now. A band of rogues from the Midlands, the usual filth. And I have forgiven you the death of Colossal. He was getting tiresome. Kept raping all those poor girls. Sandra was ready to have his head."

Stone nodded. "Did you find my blade with the rogues?"

"No," Cotoch replied. "Not to my knowledge."

Stone scowled to hear it.

"Well, that was an interesting, albeit short tale. My Lady Eva, let me tell you a tale of my own, of when I first met this Kitarran and how he came into my service." Cotoch's mouth sharpened, but when he continued, it was that of an amiable storyteller. "It was five years ago, late spring. A group of my men were out scouting, I was with them, as sometimes I like to go out and survey my territory. We came across this Kitarran. He was thin, fur tousled like a drowned cat." Cotoch spoke with fond remembrance, but Eva could see none of it reflected in Stone's silent, brooding gaze. "He was armed to the teeth. There were ten of us, but he looked so formidable, no one dared approach him. It is strange for a Kitarran to be so far from Kitrarra, alone - almost unheard of. Some of my more imaginative men thought he was the great Tayeh, Guardian of Kitarra, here to slay us for our wrongdoing. Of course, that was nonsense. So, I rode up to him, sword sheathed, to see what he was about. He could have killed me and my men easily. I have seen it done. There is no match for a Kitarran warrior, in his right mind. But I went up to him and spoke plainly. I offered him a room, a job, and something to take the pain and suffering away, for it was plain to me that this was a Kitarran who had suffered and bled from many wounds to the heart and body. I still do not know his story, but it was clear he would not go back to Kitarra.

"And now here he is, ensnared in his own honor, bound to face his demons." He pulled something from a hidden pocket, a little velvet pouch. He swung it from his finger, watching Stone.

Stone became still as a hare knowing any movement would be its last.

Eva watched Stone too, knowing what was in the pouch, knowing what Cotoch was offering her amourii. Stone shook his head. Cotoch put the pouch of culla powder away.

Eva favored Cotoch with a cold smile. It was over. Stone was hers. Stone would go where she told him. Stone owed her that. The Kitarrans owed her that. She would make him pay for it even if it was like a canker to his heart. His people had wounded her beyond recompose.

"Stone is mine. You never owned him like I do. He has no choice but to follow me. You may consider his services rendered," Eva told Cotoch simply, her head held high. She was a princess, after all, and Cotoch was nothing but a lord who bought power with drugs and fear.

Cotoch inclined his head to her, accepting his defeat. Then he shrugged as if it was a trivial matter after all.

"So, tell me, my lady, why would you, an Allati with a Jullayan accent, be traveling to Kitarra?" Cotoch asked politely. "A lonely place for a lady like you, full of warriors and scholars, mountains and cold winters."

"What better place for a woman?" Eva countered, glad for the change of subject. She had known this question would come; she had prepared an answer. "My mother fled Allati to Jullayah where she wed my father. She died when I was young. The man my father chose for me was old, a cruel man with no fondness for women. He needed an heir, that was all. I didn't want him. My father insisted, threatened me, so I left. He gave me no choice. I took my father's best horses, his sword, and left during the night. They tried to track me down, but after I crossed the river, there was no way for them to find me.

"Kitarra is ruled by a woman. Surely she will take me in and let me live my life in peace. I am able and smart, well schooled, an asset to any household. I have always longed for adventure, so here I am." She gave him her best smile. Her aunt had taught her a little charm helped distract a man from the fact that he was being lied to.

"Ah, yes," Cotoch said sympathetically, turning his liquid brown eyes on her. They were beautiful eyes. Deep, like the earth. "Tell me what you have to pay for such an adventure? Surely a woman with your ambition would have resources."

Eva had the feeling that there were two correct answers to the question, but one was unthinkable, so she pulled out the pouch around her neck. She looked at him under her lashes as she pulled out a blue sapphire, then another, until there were five little jewels on her palm. She placed them before him.

He picked one up, scrutinizing it, holding it against the candlelight. Blue flecks of light danced around the room. "Beautiful," he exclaimed. "How did you know sapphire was one of Sandra's favorite gems?"

"Sandra is Cotoch's wife," Stone said.

"She told me to tell you she is indisposed this evening. She and Stone do not always get along. She does tire of your sarcasm, Stone," Cotoch said with a smile toward Stone.

"I thought it was because she couldn't seduce me, being a different species and all," Stone quipped boldly. The comment slid off Cotoch like oil.

He turned back to Eva, rolling the sapphire between two long fingers. "What other gems have you got in your purse?"

☾

Had she pulled out the rest of her gems? She had. She did. Why?

She remembered Cotoch sidle beside her, picking through the stones she hadn't planned to show him.

Cotoch's hand covered hers. She didn't mind. His fingers were warm, his touch meant as a kindness.

The room became hazy. His touch became distorted. Everything tilted.

Stone was gone. Not just gone, he left.

Eva started dreaming. A good dream. There was laughter. A man put his arm around her waist, and she leaned into him. The comfort of his hands as they slid up her ribs, her neck, was intoxicating. Only Illiah touched her with such intimacy. Oh, how she had missed him.

He unlaced her tunic, brushing his fingers against her bare skin. His fingers worked to expose her breasts, her thighs. Her leggings were pulled down. Why was he in such a hurry? Surely after so much time apart, his need for her was forcible, but he had always been a considerate lover. Why didn't he slow down? He was hurting her.

Haze. Blackness.

Eva could hear a man, feel him pushing inside her, grunting. It was all wrong. Illiah never sounded like a stag in rut. She wanted him to stop.

The veil muddling her senses disappeared with frightening clarity. The wrongness exemplified, Eva was lying on her back in a strange bed; a strange ceiling leered above her. The air was cold, her skin clammy. She tried to move.

Cotoch was on top of her. Inside her.

He shushed her, managing to grasp both her narrow wrists in one of his hands, pinning her to the bed. Eva's muscles bruised under his grasp. Her heartbeat quickened sickeningly in panic. The violation made her cry out. She squirmed against him, and he looked down at her with an amused expression. He took his other hand and pulled her by her long braid, effectively immobilizing her.

The door opened, and Cotoch turned his attention toward it.

"Cotoch, what are you doing?" A woman's voice. Eva managed to look around the bulk of Cotoch's naked body to see a woman standing in the doorway. The woman didn't sound upset, just tired.

"Just having some fun, my dear," Cotoch replied, returning his attention to Eva. His eyes were full of lust. And something else. For an instant, Eva saw a flash like a bright, fiery worm racing across the deep brown in his eyes. Anger flowed over her like stormy waves. She went limp and hoped Cotoch would relinquish his grasp on her, but he did not. He gave her no opportunity to strike out. The woman came into the room and regarded him - them.

"She doesn't look like she is having fun. You know how I feel about that." She crossed her arms over her chest.

"She was happy about it until you came in here and interrupted," Cotoch told the woman. He moved slightly, pushing into Eva, enjoying her reaction. "Leave us."

Cotoch's wife obeyed, but not without a venomous look aimed at Eva, as if Eva were to blame for her dismissal.

"You thought you could just pay with just a couple pretty stones?" Cotoch's voice was that of a lover, soft and breathy. "I have been waiting for you, Eva. For so long. I have watched you. Imagine my surprise and utter delight when you walked into my house. All these years, all the miles between us, and you walk. Into. My. House. And it is not often I get to test out my *candarii*." He said the strange word in a seductive whisper. The room, Cotoch's touch, turned smoky. Darkness hovered.

Eva fought it, but the darkness closed around her like a box, crushing her slowly, suffocating her senses. In her mind, she was screaming, shackled inside a body that would not obey her. Cotoch's magic was familiar, not unlike her own, but wrong and twisted, made of blood and hurt. And she knew that it was the same magic that had created the wanderer. The same magic that had taken the men in Dweller's Knoll and had corrupted Illiah's will. The same magic that her son was destined to defeat.

She strained against it with her mind, her magic, any scrap of strength she had. Slowly, the walls of Cotoch's magic constricted until she could no longer fight. The tenuous branches of her magic collapsed. She was left alone in the prison of her mind, wailing in despair.

CHAPTER 53

EVA

THE MURK from the strange magic grew faint. Eva's mind broke free first. The fingers of the blood magic trailed through her body, but she was no longer strangled by them. Cotoch's magic was still and silent, waiting for its master's command.

She didn't attempt to move or open her eyes. Her head felt thick and dizzy. And her body - she tried hard not to think about her body.

His voice. Cotoch spoke a decisive word, almost a command. It was not directed at her. The word was strange, almost slurred. She could not make it out. As Cotoch spoke, his lingering magic fell from her eyes, from her body. Her surroundings came entirely into focus. Anger and outrage rang in her ears. She fought the instinct to rise and fight. She forced herself to lie still, to take stock.

She was on the bed, the soft mattress cradling her naked body, her hands and feet bound with thin, yet unyielding rope. She dared to open her eyes, just a little.

The room was lit by candles. Cotoch was not far from the bed where she lay, sitting with his back to her. His skin was bare, exposing his strong muscles crosshatched by thin white scars, his long hair undone. Her loathing was like a hound slavering over meat. Eva shifted slowly, careful to not make a sound. She needed to see what he was doing.

His attention was entirely on the large, shallow gold bowl before him. The warm candlelight reflected the bright gold light around the room. A fear Eva did not fully understand clutched her heart.

He said the strange word again and leaned over the bowl slightly. The next time he spoke, it was in the same strange tongue, but the tone was different. He sounded annoyed and impatient. He was having an invisible conversation with an invisible person in a language Eva did not know. Eva could not make sense of it, but her mind formed around a word of her own - sorcerer.

Had Stone known? Had he led her to this man knowing what he was, what he would do? Her heart whispered no. Stone would not betray her. But where was he? He had sworn to protect her.

The strange one-sided conversation lasted hardly a minute. Cotoch went still. Then he moved, twisting. She closed her eyes hoping he would not notice she was awake. When she heard him speak again, she opened her eyes once more. He was still speaking into the gold bowl. This time she could understand his words.

"What news?" There was a pause while Cotoch listened. Eva felt the hairs rise on her arms. His magic was strange and deeply unsettling. "Soon. It will be soon." Another pause. "I have his wife."

Eva's heart lurched.

Whomever he spoke to, knew Illiah. Impossible. Unless … Tayeh.

"No, she will stay here with me. Have no fear."

Eva's anger radiated with such ferocity, it was a wonder Cotoch couldn't sense it. She forced her body to relax, to ease her straining muscles into a state of convincing sublimation.

Cotoch said another commanding word in the language Eva did not know. A sigh escaped the room. The tension in the air went limp. The magic was gone. Cotoch slumped where he sat before the bowl.

"Sandra," he called in a plaintive, weak voice. Eva knew he was exhausted. Like her own magic, his seemed to take his strength. He was left spent and empty. He stumbled to the bed where he collapsed onto the soft mattress beside Eva, asleep instantly. He would not wake for some time.

Time to escape.

Eva no sooner thought of escape when Sandra came into the room, hearing her husband's call. She looked at Eva. At her husband. She pulled the blanket over her sleeping man with a tenderness that made Eva sick. Sandra obviously loved Cotoch. She turned to Eva and frowned, her eyes glinting angrily.

Sandra took out a short dagger from the chest in the corner of the room. With her hands still bound, Eva struggled to find a defensive position among the pillows and blankets that wanted to swallow her. Sandra climbed onto the bed, straddling Eva like a lover. She was heavier than Eva and had full use of her hands and legs, and a weapon. Sandra's eyes were wild. The woman was not entirely sane. She pointed the dagger at Eva's throat, the steel tip pointy and ominous. Sandra tilted her head like a bemused dog. A slow, mirthless smile stretched her pretty lips.

"You are in my bed."

Eva had not spent her childhood idly dreaming of being a warrior. She had trained with a legend. She was married to a hero, the best damned swordsman and fighter in Jullayah. Eva quickly twisted her body away from the dagger point as she brought her head to meet Sandra's. The woman's nose cracked appreciatively. Eva's hands were bound, but they were in front of her, and she wrenched the knife handle from Sandra's amateur grasp. Eva pointed the blade at the woman's neck, digging into the flesh. It was Sandra's turn to squirm backward, glancing at her sleeping husband wistfully. Blood dripped gracefully from her nose.

"Calm down. I didn't come here to hurt you," Sandra said, her voice wobbling slightly. "I came to set you free."

Eva narrowed her eyes. "Prove it."

Eva allowed Sandra to retrieve a small knife from Cotoch's desk. It was no defense against the dagger Eva held in her hands, even bound as they were. Sandra cut the ropes on Eva's wrist and raised her brow.

"Your clothes are over there. Go. Leave this place and don't return. Cotoch is mine. I will not watch as he begets a son on you. I know it is what he desires. I will not have it," Sandra said sharply, her eyes flashing possessively.

There was nothing to say. Sandra was insane if she thought Eva wanted her husband.

Eva ordered Sandra to lie on her stomach, her hands behind her. Eva put her knee in Sandra's back as she tied her hands. She had learned knots from Illiah too.

Once Cotoch's crazy wife was secured, Eva tested the weight of the dagger in her hands. It was heavy, sharp, a good blade for killing. She wanted them both dead. Yes, Sandra said she wanted to help, but only after Eva had a sharp blade ready to release her lifeblood. Cotoch was a snake. He had violated her effortlessly. He deserved to die. Illiah would have killed them. Tarek would have killed them.

Eva could feel the cold tang of the metal in her palms, waiting, eager. Restless anger welled in her bones. Anger at Sandra. Cotoch. The betrayers Macyna and Tayeh. Her hate should make killing easy.

Indifference, not hate, is the soul of evil. You are not evil. Your hate is not an excuse to kill a man.

A voice was in her head. Or maybe it was in the whole room. In the stones. The air. Eva closed her eyes and could smell moss and damp and summer. She opened her eyes.

Don't kill him. Please.

She didn't know if the voice was hers, born from some deep recess of her heart that recognized the consequences of taking a life. Or something else.

She lowered the dagger. She was no killer. The realization made her feel sick, and cowardly. She was a poor excuse for a warrior.

Eva dressed with shaking fingers as quickly as she could manage. Her sword was still attached to her belt. Sandra watched her tearfully, her face pressed into the blankets, a red halo of blood soaking into the linens. Eva went for the door, keeping the dagger low, out of the torchlight.

There was a servant in the hall, slumped against the wall, waiting in complete boredom for his master's bidding. A guard stood by as well, but he hardly looked at Eva as she went by.

"How do I get to my room?" she managed to ask the servant, her voice weak, panic threatening her forced calm. The servant perked up and led her down the maze of hallways and corridors.

By the time she reached Stone's room, tears were streaming down her face.

CHAPTER 54

STONE

INHOSPITABLE AS THE TARM was, Cotoch sure knew how to live comfortably. Stone was reminded not to underestimate the man.

Cotoch seemed amiable enough, and Stone relaxed. Perhaps his former employer spoke the truth and held him in no contempt over the demise of one of his favorite henchman. It was possible Cotoch could be reasonable.

Stone enjoyed the meal. It was warm and delicious, as usual. He didn't know what corner of the Midlands Cotoch found his cooks, but they were skilled indeed in making a feast of such simple, late-winter offerings.

Stone had little to add to the dinner conversation. Eva and Cotoch's relationship quickly evolved from acquaintance to friend, to whatever name humans used for the person they had sex with, who they did not love or pay to perform the favor. Stone did not understand humans, but he did understand loneliness.

Eva laughed at Cotoch's stories, looking at Cotoch under her lashes as only a pretty human woman could do. Stone had spent enough time around the unpredictable, sometimes idiotic race to know the look. Eva had been alone for a long time - why wouldn't she welcome some companionship? Humans were not like Kitarrans. They did not mate for life. Not that Stone cared either way. Life was too complicated to hand out judgments.

Clearly Eva had succumbed, like many women before her, to Cotoch's flirting. Cotoch was considered a handsome man and rumor had it he was a skilled lover. Stone could not quite remember where he learned that tidbit of information.

Lady Sandra, Cotoch's wife, took no offense from his meandering nature. All of Mahlas knew she enjoyed taking her own lovers.

Cotoch made some subtle suggestions for evening entertainment; Eva made a less subtle suggestion of her own. And Stone knew his presence was no longer necessary.

"Is it all right, then, if I retire?" Stone asked Eva directly. She turned her blue-green eyes to him and patted his hand.

"Of course. Go - rest. I will be up later," Eva told him with a knowing smile.

"Much later," Cotoch added in his honeyed voice, stroking Eva's hand, sliding his hand up her arm.

"You're sure?" Stone asked again.

"Yes," Eva said, rolling her eyes with exasperation. He took the hint.

Stone nodded and left. He didn't like leaving Eva alone with Cotoch, but Cotoch was fair to his lovers. He wouldn't hurt Eva. And Eva was a grown woman, not some naive maiden in need of a chaperone.

He went to the kitchen and grabbed some bread, cheese, and a basket of apples that were not too wrinkly. He took anything that caught his fancy. The cooks were intimidated by his presence, as usual. He ignored them, as usual. Raiding the kitchen stores was a pastime of his. He took a ring of sausage as an afterthought.

The fire filled his room with lonely light. He was tired, more tired than he had been in a long time. If his veins had been pulsing with culla, as they had so many times in this very room, he would have paced restlessly and swung Mistura until his arms failed him. He would not feel the fatigue drowning him.

The desire for the drug pulled at his will. His mind remembered the relief of the culla's influence. His heart desired the comfortable numbness. But he had made a promise. A promise made with honor. A painful vow, but it gave him hope that he could stand in the shadow of the man he had once been.

As weary as his body felt, he wasn't ready for sleep. He sat on the floor and practiced the meditation he had learned many years ago as a youth learning the ways of the Kitarran warrior.

He closed his eyes and aligned his body, making his seat even on the hard floor. He crossed his legs and recrossed them, taking deep, even breaths, relaxing down into his body, imagining the separation of his skin from his bones, his eyes from their sockets. Deeper and deeper he went, keeping thought from his mind, memory from his heart. Only when a controlled peace came over his body did he lay down on the bed and let himself succumb to sleep.

He dreamed of sunlit passageways. Of summer breezes. Of blue sky so clear and vast, it lifted the spirits and the mind, and in the manner of dreams, suddenly it was not the sky that filled his vision but a pair of eyes. Her eyes. They were just as fathomless and peaceful as the summer sky. She spoke to him in a bubbling voice she reserved for times when she was exceedingly happy.

She had been away for a long time. She had missed him with her soul and her body. She wanted to tell him about everything. The waves of the ocean, the smell of the river, the people she had met. A human girl, barely a woman, a little adventurer bound to the duty of a courtier.

The dream was sweet. Stone didn't want to leave. He could almost feel her in his arms. Then something, someone, yanked him from that place. His warrior's instinct cried out. He felt the blow, expecting the piercing cold of steel to follow, a sensation not long forgotten.

But this blow was soft, not determined enough to cause damage or pain. His arms went up instinctively to stop whatever - whoever- was assaulting him. Stone found himself staring Eva in the eye, her hand caught in his. Her face was wet with tears. Her eyes burned with fury. Her breath was a sob. There were words too, but he couldn't make them out through her hysterics.

"Did you know? Did you know what he would do?" He finally understood what she was saying through her harsh voice, ragged with emotion. Stone shook his head, bewildered and groggy. His gut felt ill. He had made a terrible error.

She slumped against him, still sobbing. His arms were around her without him realizing it.

"You were supposed to protect me," she whispered.

He had failed her.

Eva trembled slightly in his arms. She had been hurt. But how? He opened his mouth to ask, but she had more to say. "We have to leave. Now." Her eyes met his once more, round and desperate.

"Why? What? I don't understand." Sleep made him slow - was he so out of practice?

"Cotoch doesn't want to let me leave." She didn't elaborate. "The horses - we must get them. We have to get out of here."

She was throwing things into her bag. She tossed Stone his weapons that he had laid meticulously in a line on the floor. Stone secured his weapons before helping her with the rest. His eyes flicked from packing to her shaking hands as she tried to tie her bag. Eva took a deep breath, her lip quivering.

He felt like someone had forced a rock down his throat. A sharp rock. It stabbed him from inside as it twisted and sunk toward his gut.

He went over it again in his mind and could find no other conclusion than what he had already deduced: he had seen no coercion. Eva had been willing, eager, to go with Cotoch.

The horses were cozy in their stables, munching hay. Eva saddled Sasha. Stone saddled Penn. Stone grabbed a bag of oats from the nearby feed room and tied it to his saddle. Stone looked at Eva, but she was intent on her task, which was taking longer as her hands would not stop shaking. He took over and finished tightening the girth.

He watched her wince as she sat in the saddle. The cold lump in Stone's stomach curdled and spread up his spine. Anger. Guilt. His duty had been to protect her. He had promised.

He allowed himself a moment of self-loathing before he mounted Penn and his warrior's instinct kicked in. It was not the time for internal debate; it was the time for action.

The gate would be barred from them, but there was another way out of Mahlas. Only a handful were privy to its existence, Cotoch and a few of his trusted men, so naturally Stone knew of it. Men did not keep secrets from him.

The path was narrow. The hill behind Cotoch's house rose sharp and steep, a foolish way for a person to attempt on horseback, a suicidal way for an attacker to come. The cat track - funny name

- wound up the hill like a vine on a branch. They would have to dismount and lead the horses. Eventually the track led back around and met up with the road, but they would go north, into the forest, into the mountains. The trees would help hide their tracks. He hoped they could avoid Cotoch's patrols.

Stone knew a place he could take Eva. It was not too far. A place of secrets, a place no one but he knew of. She would be safe there until they could think of a plan.

Eva didn't question him when he told her to dismount and lead Sasha. She said nothing at all, her face intent on the task he had given her.

Slowly, they rose above the village. Down below was the town square and Cotoch's house. It seemed quiet. Stone longed to ask Eva what had happened, but they needed to press on. It was safe to assume Cotoch would expect Stone to take the secret route into the forest where the patrols were few and far apart. The sooner they were under cover of the trees, the better.

Eva stumbled on a rock, sending loose scree down the hill. Stone could see her expression - Kitarrans had excellent night vision. She was crying, her face wet with tears.

Damn. Couldn't Stone do this one thing right? Why had he left her? Why had he let her out of his sight? He gripped the pommel of his borrowed sword tightly, wishing he could run it through Cotoch's wretched gullet.

A huge tree with black, leafless limbs adorned the top of the hill. It had been dead for as long as Stone had been in Mahlas. The tree felt like a warning, like impaled heads of a conquered enemy. A stupid notion. It was just a tree.

They stood beneath the dead branches and looked down below to Mahlas. It was still quiet. No alarm had been raised. Questions circled in Stone's mind.

"Let's go," Eva reminded him quietly, pulling at his sleeve.

As the land became more stable under the trees, they mounted up once more. They kept their pace as quick as they could. The horses were nimble-footed creatures and seemed no more perturbed in the forest full of roots and rocks than they were on the wide, open road.

In fact, the black stallion seemed to be enjoying himself.

They rode for the remainder of the night. Stone was thankful the snow had stopped, and most of what had fallen had already melted. The wind had picked up and blew the clouds away, leaving a sky full of tiny stars. There was no moon.

As the night sped to morning, Stone knew they could go no farther. He stopped and made Eva sit and take rest. She bit her lip as she dismounted stiffly. He gave her some food, thankful he had relieved the kitchen of some of its stores. He hadn't meant it to be their travel fare, but at least they had something. Eva nibbled like a bird on the bread he gave her. He handed her the canteen of ale. She made a face as she took a deep swig.

"I know a place, not too far from here. No other person knows how to find it. We will be safe there for a while." Until you can heal, but he didn't say it.

"How long?"

"Tomorrow, if we go quickly."

Eva made to get up, but he stopped her with his hands.

"Rest. Sleep."

She glared up at him, her eyes full of loathing. She shook off his touch. "Don't touch me."

He stepped back, trying to ignore how her words inflamed his guilt. He busied himself getting her a blanket, folding it around her shoulders with as much care as he could, careful not to touch her again. She pulled it close and curled in on herself. He hoped she would sleep.

As the day brightened, they pressed on. Winter hovered like a haggard crone. Hoarfrost encapsulated the trees. The ground cracked under the horses' hooves.

Several times Stone had to stop to take in his surroundings. There were landmarks that led to his hidden place, but they were easily missed. He had not been to the Vale in over a year. He didn't want to delay them by carelessly missing the marks. It was a fickle place; only those who knew its secret path could make it into the small valley. Other things kept visitors out, things Stone wasn't sure he believed in.

"Here we are," Stone announced, finally spying the mark he had been looking for. He almost rode past the rock. The moss had grown.

It still had some semblance of the head of a bull, indicating to Stone it was the right place.

The narrow path led gracefully down, and the rocky cliff rose on either side of them. Soon the rock surrounded them, towering over them, leaving just enough room for a horse to walk. Stone could easily touch both sides of the path with outstretched arms.

The way opened, exposing the whole of the small Vale: the creek running through the tumble of rocks, the trees clinging impossibly to the cliffs. Moss and ferns were still green in the Vale, untouched by winter. The secret of the Vale encouraged plants to grow year-round.

They crossed the creek and before them was the cave. The entrance was taller than Stone, wide enough for their horses. Thick steam swirled in lazy circles up into the air through cracks cut into the hill.

The cave was not dark or dreary. Plenty of natural light came in through the rifts in the roof. Stone dismounted and tethered the horses to the entrance. There was a flat area large enough for the horses to be comfortable. He helped Eva slide off Sasha and led her inside.

Her features were pale. Stone felt his gut turn over once more. She walked like a person hiding a wound. He could only hope the restorative qualities of the Vale would help her heal. She looked around with clouded eyes as if half asleep already. Exhaustion and pain were written in every line and gesture of her body.

The air in the cave was warm and pungent, filling the space with the smell of moss and minerals reminding Stone of his childhood. He pushed the memories away as quickly as they came.

A waterfall descended into a little pool at the back of the cave. After filling the pool, the water forced its way underneath the rock and only surfaced beyond the cave, joining the little creek that ran down the center of the Vale.

Eva exclaimed in delight as she touched the water. It was hot where it came out of the rock. Only when it met the cold water of the creek outside did the heat dissipate. Such was the magic of the place, the magic of the earth.

Eva didn't wait for another word. She shucked her clothes and left them where they fell. She walked carefully to the pool's edge, mindful of the slippery rocks and sunk into the hot pool with a sigh of contentment.

The ice of Stone's self-loathing thawed a little. At least he could do her this one kindness.

CHAPTER 55

COTOCH

COTOCH'S RAGE was unlike any he had yet felt, reminding him starkly of his father. And that just fueled his indignation.

He had been betrayed. By a woman. By his wife.

He had woken, his body stirring, remembering Eva's. Her curves, her skin, her bright hair and luminous eyes. What hardened him was not just her physical attributes, lovely as they were, but the way the *varing* wove into her magic, took her magic, coerced and molded it - her - to his whims. When she managed, just for a moment, to over-come the *varing*, her fear and anger and pain made the *varing* course stronger, filling Cotoch's body, making him invincible.

Ready and fully awake, he reached for her. She was not there.

Cotoch sat up abruptly. Her bonds were in tatters on the floor. Impossible.

Then he knew. It had been her. Jealous bitch.

"Bring me my wife," Cotoch growled to his guard outside his door.

When Sandra came in, she held her head high, her eyes level. She held a cloth over her nose, diminishing her noble bearing just a bit. The cloth was red with blood.

"Where is she?"

"How am I supposed to know?" Sandra replied innocently. Her voice was high and nasally from the cloth.

"You let her go."

Sandra's face shifted from sunny daylight to stormy sky in an instant.

"She cannot have you. You are mine!" Sandra shouted, her face ugly and contorted in her rage. "She would never have replaced me."

"Where did she go?" Cotoch asked. Sandra heard the lethal edge to his voice and melted under his anger.

"She broke my nose. My nose, Cotoch! She forced me to cut her bonds. I imagine she is somewhere with her Kitarran - I told you Stone was useless! She was certainly anxious to leave you. She tied me up, and I couldn't wake you. I had a terrible time getting to the door to get the guard to cut the knots. And my nose! Look at my nose!"

Cotoch narrowed his eyes at her. "My love. You have cost me more than you realize."

Sandra said nothing, folding her arms across her chest, daring him. Her nose really did look awful.

Cotoch turned to his guard.

"Tell the men to search the forest. Send word to Lord Eldin - search everywhere. Stone and the woman I need them back." The guard nodded tersely and left. Cotoch was alone with his dear wife.

He took her by the arm, and not gently. She protested, but she was a weak, little thing. Pathetic really. Barren, useless. She would never give him a son. Eva was the only woman Cotoch wanted. The only woman who could give him what he wanted, what the *varing* wanted. Next to her, Sandra was nothing.

"Where are we going? You're hurting me," Sandra whimpered.

Cotoch led her to a door she had not even known existed. Only Cotoch knew of it. Well, him and his ghosts.

"It's dark down there, Cotoch. I don't want to go. Stop. Let go."

Sandra tried to bolt, her panic turning her mad, but Cotoch was the master of the crypts. No one escaped.

CHAPTER 56

ILLIAH

"I SMELL smoke."

Illiah sat, swaying with the rhythm of the boat, turning his face into the sea breeze. The breeze, usually briny and benign, was thick with the smell of burning things.

Turk put down the line he had been untangling to do the same. To the north were islands, dozens of them. Some no larger than the boat, others so big it would take days to walk across.

"Aye, and it smells foul," Turk mused.

Illiah agreed. It wasn't the smell of burning wood brush or chimney smoke. Something about its smell was off. Something hauntingly familiar. He couldn't see the smoke - the clouds were gray and low, and many islands blocked his view.

They had gone north that morning, away from the other fishing boats out looking for the day's catch. They were going on a gut feeling Turk had woken with. Turk had been five days with no catch, two of those days with Illiah, so he wanted to try something new. Hence the path northward, closer to the Isles.

"There is something in the water, over there," Illiah said, spotting a pale form floating among the flotsam, but clearly not of the sea. He grabbed the long, pronged pole used for pulling in large fish and hung over the rail, reaching. As they grew closer, his stomach tightened.

"Turk!" he called. Turk was already at his side, a rope and prong ready. They watched in silence as they drew up to it. Illiah reached down and pulled it into the boat. The prong was not needed.

It was a human child. Her skin was pale in death, soggy from the water, her limbs stiff, but not wholly so. She was naked, perhaps eight years old, her hair a mass of slick tangles, stark against her pale skin. Her eyes were closed, pinched in death.

There were no words.

Illiah lay her body on the deck of the boat, arranging her in a position of respect. Turk brought out a blanket. He wanted to wrap her up, but Illiah put out his hand.

"Wait," Illiah said, looking over the girl's body. He didn't want to. He wanted to let her rest, protected, even if it was just with the pathetic blanket. But there were marks on her body that spoke ill. He needed to know what had befallen her. The bruises and other marks eluded to sickening violations. Her throat had been cut, draining out her lifeblood. Turk understood. He cursed, turning away.

Illiah's breakfast fought to make a reappearance. The anger he felt was not new. It was a lifetime old. Armeria came beside him and pushed her nose against his hand. He put his hand on the dog's neck, his fingers digging into her soft fur, grounding him.

He wished for something to say, some prayer for the girl's soul, for her parents. He didn't know any, so he wrapped the girl up carefully and placed her somewhere safe.

"We need to check out that smoke," Illiah told Turk.

"Aye, captain," Turk said, turning the boat in the direction of the smell. Illiah ignored the title. Turk liked to call him captain, mostly to tease him. Illiah had told him of his previous life in Jullayah. Just then, it didn't sound as if Turk was teasing.

Soon they saw the smoke. Great plumes rising from a fishing village became visible as they rounded the leeward side of the large island before them. The docks were gone, the houses mostly blackened, smoking husks. Only one boat sat along the shore, burning slowly. There was no sign of life, not even a meandering sheep or goat. Turk gave one small cry. Then he fell silent, his face white underneath his fur.

"We need to go ashore," Illiah said.

"What happened here?" Turk whispered, his voice filled with sadness.

"That is what we need to find out."

With the docks destroyed, they couldn't get as close to the shore as they would have liked; the water was too shallow for Turk's boat. Wet up to their waists, they pulled the boat in until the hull gently scraped the rocky bottom of the little bay. Illiah told Turk to make the ship ready for a quick departure, just in case.

Illiah waded awkwardly ashore. Armeria whined from the boat for a minute before Illiah heard a splash that meant she had joined him. He turned to see her swimming with the grace of a cow. She had never swum before.

"Good girl, Ari," he told his loyal dog.

Illiah walked up into the village. It wasn't far. He was quickly distracted from his wet pants and chafing feet. What he saw brought back memories from long ago.

The villagers were dead. But only the old and young, their bodies placed in a neat pile, as if they had been sorted and then dealt with. There were not many. It had been a small village. Illiah remembered similar scenes from the war in southern Jullayah, bodies stacked as high as a house. Always the old and the young.

There was no sign of any others. He was glad Turk had not come ashore. This, Illiah had seen before. The fisherman was not hardened to it. Neither was Illiah, not really. He had never grown used to it. He merely endured it better than some.

Armeria started to growl, and Illiah stiffened, heeding the warning. He had no sword, no vercuri, only his long knife, which was useful for gutting silver strikerfish but not the best weapon against a man - or men. Still, it was better than nothing. He unsheathed it, pressing himself up against a stone wall that escaped the worst of the devastation. Armeria's eyes were locked on a house at the top of the village, her ears forward in concentration. It was the only house that was not burnt or burning.

Illiah crept forward silently, crouched, his body pressed against the remains of the village. Armeria kept close to his heel, no longer growling, but still intent, her body low to the ground like a stalking wolf.

The wind changed and Illiah breathed in a cloud of smoke. His eyes burned and his body begged as he held back the cough that would appease his aching lungs. He moved out of the smoke as quickly as he could, taking a moment to clear his lungs.

He reached the low stone house. The shuttered windows were open to the sea air. The roof was thatch, set apart from the other houses just far enough that it did not catch fire from falling sparks.

Illiah crouched beneath the window and listened. He could hear voices, but he couldn't understand the words. Their voices were pitched low. Two, perhaps three men, he guessed. He wished once again he had his sword. He could get Turk. Another body would be an advantage, and the fisherman was a trained warrior. But no, there was no time. It was a mercy they had arrived unseen. Something was keeping the men distracted in their borrowed accommodations. Illiah needed to know what.

As he listened, Illiah realized they did not speak his language, but he had heard it before. He waited only long enough to ascertain the approximate location of the voices. The door had been broken off its hinges and lay useless on the ground. Illiah moved past it like a shadow and burst with speed into the room.

Surprise was an invaluable weapon. The first man didn't see the blade that slit his throat. His lifeblood pooled at his feet as he fell, his eyes bulging in surprise. Another man looked on with mute astonishment before pulling his dirk from his belt. Illiah leaped across the room and slammed his blade up into the man's stomach. The dirk fell with a thud to the ground. Illiah drew back. Hot blood splattered his hand, dripping down the handle of his fishing knife. There had only been the two men. Armeria stood calmly, the worried intent gone from her face. Illiah checked the second room of the house to be sure, but the danger was past.

In the second room, the hardened anger in Illiah's gut twisted into a knot, softened only by the feeling of satisfaction he had from killing the two men. Once Illiah would have been shocked by the scene before him. But now he knew this dance too well. He had expected it.

There was a bed, once neatly cared for with earthen linens and stuffed with feathers, now a mess of blood and other things. A naked girl was lying on it, her body covered in bruises and scrapes. Her hands were tied to the post with rough twine. She moaned and stirred, opening one eye a little; the other was black and swollen shut. She saw Illiah and panic overtook her features. She didn't make a noise, but it was clear she was terrified. Armeria jumped up on the bed and put her nose next to the girl's ear, her tail wagging low and reassuringly. A tear slipped down the girl's cheek, but not from fear. Illiah placed a dirty blanket carefully over her abused body and cut the twine with his knife.

Illiah doubted the young woman was older than fourteen. She cried as the blood rushed into her hands. It was painful, Illiah knew. He soothed her as best he could. He looked around for some clothes for her, but saw none. At least there was the blanket.

"What is your name?"

"Tani," she said clutching the blanket around her.

"We are leaving now. You are safe. I am taking you to Kilev," he told her, helping her to her feet. She nodded numbly but couldn't hold her own weight. Illiah scooped her up and carried her. "Close your eyes. Open them only when I say." Again, she nodded, placing her head upon his shoulder.

The girl opened her eyes when she heard the sloshing of Illiah's feet through the water. She saw Turk, ashen-faced, and held her arms up to him as he reached down for her. Illiah awkwardly helped Armeria into the boat, getting a face full of wet dog tail, the least of his concerns at the moment.

"What happened here?" Turk asked, his voice barely audible above the gentle waves. He wasn't actually asking the girl - he was just thinking out loud.

The girl answered anyhow, her voice devoid of emotion. "Three boats full of strange men came ashore yesterday. They killed Torac, our elder. They killed anyone who tried to fight. They saw me and took me into the house. I did not see the rest." Her face was a blank mask. Illiah had seen the look a dozen times. He had seen it on his own sister. Illiah told the girl she didn't need to say a thing more. He knew what had happened. The glance he gave Turk told his friend not to ask questions.

Illiah and Turk settled the girl as best they could and gave her some food. Armeria lay beside her and the girl put her hand in the dog's fur. The uandian closed her eyes and so did the girl.

"We need to get back to Kilev, right away. The boats will come back," Illiah told Turk. "I killed two of the men. They were not abandoned. They will come to get them sooner or later. We are no match for them.

I know their kind - these men, they are the same type that invaded Jullayah six years ago. They had the same look, the same manner of speech, the same cruel appetites."

Turk said nothing. His fingers shook slightly as he pulled the ropes. Bellah had not come along that day, so it took both men to get the ship back out into the open sea.

There was no other sign of the strange ships as they pushed out beyond the Isles, into the open ocean once more, making all speed for the great city. Illiah breathed a sigh of relief when they reached the mouth of the river.

As they traveled upriver to Kilev, all Illiah could think about was that Kitarra had fewer than two hundred Peace Guards spread throughout the realm. A mere handful of men and women trained and ready to fight. It was not enough, not nearly enough.

Illiah and the boys had joined the queen for breakfast, so it happened that Illiah was with Arrah when the messenger came.

The messenger looked exhausted, dirty, and profoundly sad as he entered Queen Arrah's atrium. It was Rangel, captain of the *SeaSwift*, one of the boats that had been sent out to scout the islands, to locate the enemy and help any survivors. Illiah saw his face and knew there had been none of the latter.

"Selene, take the boys out for a moment," Arrah asked the young woman. Rhyl and Talo obeyed, eager for some fresh air, their dogs trailing them. Arrah didn't ask Illiah to leave, so he didn't.

"My queen," the man said, kneeling before her. "It is worse than we feared. The Long Isles are lost. We trailed up through the Glen, around Shallow Peak, the Ridge Islands. There was nothing left - every village we saw was burning; the enemy's boats were everywhere. Pinnae … the city is in ruins, smoking. We couldn't get close. We just barely made it back. We had the weather gage, and the smoke helped keep us hidden," he added with distaste.

The queen's lips were a grim line. Illiah worried she would have an ailment. She was not a young woman, and such news … The queen did not - could not - speak.

"At least you are alive," Illiah said, turning to the messenger, gripping his shoulder tightly in what he hoped was an encouraging gesture. "Thank you for your report."

The man nodded.

"Go now, and rest," Illiah commanded. The man nodded his thanks and left, leaving Illiah alone with the queen.

"Illiah, the Long Isles were our heart, and they are gone. Deecon, his family, so many Kitarrans, gone." Arrah's queenly composure was replaced by a mother crying for her lost children. Illiah's chest tightened in sympathy. "We are a strong race, but we were so few, and now … a handful are left. The darkness has come." Her desolation gripped Illiah hard.

"There is always hope, your grace," Illiah told her, not sure if it was the truth. "But you must reach out to the dwellings along the sea, even along the river. The attackers could come up by night. They are cunning and ruthless. Merciless."

Arrah nodded sadly. "I need you, Illiah," she said in a quiet voice, not meeting his eyes. "I need you to lead us as First Defender of Kitarra. I have no one else."

Illiah nodded. He had been waiting for her to ask ever since he had returned with Turk and their terrible discovery. Over the last few weeks he had kept his mouth shut, watching Scytt make decisions Illiah would not have. More smoke had been spotted. Fishing boats mysteriously disappeared. Illiah would have forbidden any ships leaving the river other than those sent by the First Defender. Scytt had sent out a scouting mission, which hadn't returned, then another, and another. Rangel and the *SeaSwift* were fortunate indeed.

Perhaps Illiah should have said something, stepped up, but there was no indication his own decisions would have saved lives. Calling judgment to Scytt's decisions had been on his mind. He was not afraid of Scytt's wrath. A different fear had halted his tongue. War terrified him. He had lived through it, seen the havoc, felt the pain it wreaked. To lead these people, to be the one to offer them hope, was equally terrifying. And he no longer had the dagger. He didn't have the strength to ask for it.

"Arrah, swear to me that you have never used the vercuri on me,"

Illiah said, looking intently at the queen, pouring all his emotion into his voice. "Swear to me. I need to know that this decision is mine."

"I swear it. And if you knew more about the vercuri, you would know that a vercuri works differently for a Kitarran than it does a descendant of Crea."

"Oh?"

"Yes. It would take years for a Kitarran to learn how to use your vercuri."

Illiah nodded, content to accept her answer. Did it really matter, anyway? Vercuri or not, afraid or not, his fingers still itched with suppressed action.

Arrah was still waiting for his answer, her beseeching eyes full of that same hope. Illiah closed his eyes, mustering his courage. He knew what needed to be done. There was no other choice.

"I will do it."

Arrah's eyes brightened, and her smile held a sliver of relief. "You are a man of gold, Illiah. After everything we have done to you and your son."

"Oh, I know."

It was crazy, risking his life for a people that had caused him great, everlasting pain. But the last shred of his hatred toward the Kitarrans had shriveled and died when he pulled the girl from the water. The prophecy was correct - Kitarra was dying. And if his son was their only hope, then Illiah would do anything within his power to make sure Rhyl would succeed. The Kitarrans had become like kin. Talo and Rhyl were brothers in every way but blood, and Illiah could not deny that he cared deeply for the Kitarran child. He would do what was necessary to protect his sons.

"I will assemble the high council, and we will make it so," Arrah said, the glimmer of hope in her eyes growing like a spring flower. Illiah had sown that seed; he had given the queen something to cling to. The weight of that responsibility might drown him, but it was the right path for his wounded feet.

In his mind's eye was the dead child floating in the water, the terrified girl raped and beaten. Illiah could still feel the hot blood of his enemy spill onto his hands. The right choice was never an easy one.

The queen assembled her high council that same afternoon. Ten lords and ladies, old and young, the queen's most trusted and valued advisers. With Arrah and Illiah, it made for twelve seats around the queen's oval council table.

The others were already seated when Illiah arrived, following the queen's gentle footsteps. The assembly rose for their matriarch and sat when she took her seat in her throne-like chair at the narrow end of the table. Illiah took the chair next to her, a place reserved for the First Defender, the seat Scytt had previously occupied. The former First Defender negated to come, even if it was traditional for the queen and the entire high council to observe the change of seats.

Scytt took his demotion hard. Illiah was unsurprised. The man was arrogant and unyielding in nature. Scytt was likely drowning his sorrows slowly in a dockside pub somewhere.

"My lords, my ladies," the queen began. "These are trying times, to say the least. One of the scouts came back this morning, Rangel on the *SeaSwift*, with word that the islands are lost. There are no survivors to be found. Every city, village, and settlement are burned. The enemy patrols the ocean like sharks." Arrah could not speak without a slight tremor in her voice. The show of emotion did not make the queen appear weak. Instead Illiah thought it only added to the determined strength he had come to associate with the queen of Kitarra. The news brought silent shock to some, cries of grief to others, demands of action from several.

The queen put up her delicate hands, the chains between her fingers tinkling in the following silence.

"Lord Illiah has fought these monsters before. He has defeated them. Though he does not promise miracles, he has taken the vow of the First Defender and he will do his best to lead us in this war, this onslaught."

"You have taken the vow?" Lord Irion, an old Kitarran with wrinkled ears of twisted gray fur, asked him.

"After all that we have done to you and your family?" Lady Serys asked. She was no highborn woman but a merchant. She was rich and clever. She had risen through the ranks of the privileged by her own hand. The queen adored her.

Illiah nodded.

"Why?"

Illiah took a moment to gather his thoughts. His studied his hands. Hands that had killed and maimed and rescued. In Jullayah, he had chosen his path willingly, but at the time he did not know the evils he would face, the loss, the grief, the terror. He knew what lay before him and it terrified him to his core. He was just a man. He had no vercuri to make him into a hero.

He looked up, fixing his eyes on them each in turn. "You ask me why? The pain your Guardian has caused my family is beyond measure, but I have come to understand that Kitarra is a peaceful realm. Your people are kind and good - for the most part. I admit that I am terrified. To be at the forefront of war, facing this evil once more, is something that turns my vitals cold. It makes me want to run and hide, to scream and weep. But I cannot. I will not stand by and watch these monsters tear apart this land." Illiah spoke clearly into the room, his heart beating fast. "I pulled a child's body from the ocean. I smelled the stench of rotting, burning flesh. Innocent people killed and hurt for no reason. What kind of man would I be to ignore it, to not do my part? I know no other choice."

CHAPTER 57

EVA

EVA HISSED as the penetrating almost scalding heat enveloped her cold skin. She wished it could scald her memories.

The pool was deep enough to sit in comfortably. The bottom was smooth limestone. She walked under the waterfall, letting it fall onto her hair, her face.

The earthy mineral smell was the same as the hot pools of the Keep, born from the deepest places of the earth. It reminded her of countless nights spent soaking in the arms of her dear one. Sometimes she and Illiah would gaze up to the sky, searching for shooting stars, talking or arguing about nothing and everything. Other times they were too delighted and indulgent with each other to care.

Eva stared through the fissure in the cave above her to the pale sky. The brightness hurt her eyes.

Thinking of Illiah reminded her of her stained and soiled and hurting body. She didn't understand what had happened, only that it had involved magic.

The look in Stone's eyes when he soothed her hysterics, the worried glances he cast her way, told her how sorry he was. She didn't think he intentionally let Cotoch take her.

The chaos of her heart strangled her with its nonsensical emotions. Guilt. Shame. Her feelings of ineptitude infuriated her. She should have been able to stop Cotoch. But Cotoch had beguiled her and forced her into his bed. He overpowered her, both physically and with his strange magic. He was a sorcerer, and she knew nothing of their ways. She had believed them extinct, existing only in frightening fables told to errant children. She should have known better; the evil magic was leaking into the world, why wouldn't there be someone to claim it and make it theirs? Logically, she was not to blame for her circumstance, but why then the festering guilt?

She scrubbed at her skin as if she could wash away the awful, gut-wrenching feeling. Stone tossed her some soap that smelled of honey and lavender. She wondered where it came from but didn't ask. Questions were for later.

Finally, her skin almost raw, her hands aching, she sank into the pool, keeping only her face above the water. Her hair fanned around her like some living thing, a pale weed. She watched the water meditatively as it fell from a dark chink in the rock, a place of unimaginable depths and queer, sightless creatures. Something sparkled in the rock. She put her hand up to deflect the water. The rock was flecked with gold, some pieces as large as her thumbnail. She let the water go back to its natural course and looked into its depths.

The vision was instant. Before Eva was the towering city of Kilev, the queen's palace perched atop the city, its back against the formidable mountain, the forest begging at its walls. Eva was like a bird circling the city from afar, finally coming to roost on a palace window left ajar.

The sunlight was warm, full of spring's warmth. A man stood in the room, looking down at a table littered with maps, his fingers tapping tunelessly on the table. He was thinking hard, his face furrowed into a frown, a rugged beard covered his strong jaw.

"You look tired, my lord," said a woman sauntering into the room carrying a tray of food and a jug of wine. Not a servant - her dress was too elegant, immaculate. She moved maps aside as she placed the tray upon the long table before brushing a long strand of auburn hair from her face. A light-gray dog was lying on the floor under the table, its nose close to the man's boot. It didn't move, but its eyes followed the movement of the woman. "Illiah?" the woman said less formally. He hadn't acknowledged her.

Illiah looked up at her, his eyes unfathomable. If he regretted the intrusion, he didn't show it.

"My thanks, Selene," he said, yet he didn't move to partake of food or drink.

"Rhyl is asleep. Talo too. Their hike this morning created little monsters crying out for naps. The fresh air was intoxicating."

Illiah smiled, a wan, tired smile. His eyes were still on the maps, his hand on his chin, absently smoothing his beard.

"They certainly know how to make the most of every moment. Even when he was a baby, Rhyl hated to go to sleep. He would be on the brink of exhaustion and still fight it," Illiah said with a rueful laugh that didn't quite reach his eyes.

The woman named Selene looked at him, her eyes warm and concerned. She didn't say anything but pretended interest in the map he was examining. She sidled close beside him. She was short; she tucked herself neatly against the hollow of his ribs. Illiah didn't move away from her as she leaned against him, pushing her body against his. One of her arms came around his waist. The other took his hand down from his face, forcing him to look at her, which he did. Her lovely eyes were no longer concerned. They sparkled with excitement. She pushed her curve-hugging, embroidered bodice against him gently and leaned up to kiss his lips.

The *simul rami* fell from Eva's eyes, from her touch, leaving her hollow. So, so hollow.

She must have cried out, because Stone was beside her, ankle deep in the water, ready to pull her out. She shook her head when he tried. Her breath came in shallow gasps. Her heart pounded so hard it hurt. Stone mumbled colorfully and pulled her out of the water despite her protests. He wrapped her in a blanket like a little child and set her before the fire, his yellow eyes overflowing with concern.

Eva clutched the blanket to her wet body, trying to comprehend the vision. Illiah in Kitarra, tired and stressed, a beautiful woman offering to comfort him, her face filled with wanton desire. Would Illiah be adverse to it? What lonely man was strong enough to withstand that kind of allure? Eva hadn't been able to hold onto the vision long enough to find out. Eva tasted blood. She had bit her lip.

"Okay. Tell me what in the three fucking realms that was all about," Stone demanded. He had a furious look in his eyes, furious that she dare startle him.

Eva found herself smiling, just a little, at that look. As if he could command her.

"The way I see things in the air, I can see things in the water, in the earth, if it is the right kind. Pure ore is the best. The gold here helps. I also see things in the fire."

"A true elemental *sanarii*, then. I did wonder," Stone said sitting back on his heels. "What did you see that was so terrible?"

"That is private." Emotion made her voice sharp.

"Did someone die? Someone you care about?" Stone's voice was soft. "You sounded - you sounded like you were being flayed or something."

"No. No one died. It was alarming, not what I expected. What I saw hurt deeply, but I must move past it."

Stone was silent a moment, assessing her.

"Can you tell me what happened with Cotoch?" he asked in a tone one would use to tame a wild creature. "When I left dinner, you two seemed to be on very amicable terms. I felt no concern for you. You seemed happy, welcoming of his affections."

Eva cringed, and Stone looked like a faithful pup who didn't understand its reprimand.

"I don't know what happened." Eva's voice rose in pitch. She put her head in her hands. "Can you make me some water for tea? I have an infusion I need to make." Stone nodded and within a minute had the little pot on the fire. "I don't really remember anything after I took out the sapphires. My perception went hazy - I had dreams, but they were not reality."

"You and Cotoch talked about the stones. You came to an agreement. Then you started talking of other things, not important things. He made you laugh. Then you two were alluding to things that certainly didn't require me, so I left. You told me to go."

"That's impossible. I would never flirt with a man like that. I would never have chosen to - to bed him," Eva said, her stomach sick. "After -" Eva took a deep breath. "After, Cotoch made reference to something - *candarii* was the word he used. I could feel his magic. He is a sorcerer. He used a gold basin to speak to someone. It was very strange."

Stone's eyes widened slightly, then narrowed angrily. "*Candarii* are sorcerers, people who use the *varing* - the magic that comes from the dark river - the dark energy of the world. *Candarii* are said to be able to control Allati with *sanarii* blood, royal blood, to force them to do whatever they want, like puppets. That is why the Allati Shadow Guards have hunted them for hundreds of years. I didn't think there were any left."

"You sound like a scholar," Eva muttered. For an instant, the corner of Stone's mouth twitched into a smile.

"That is why he is on such amiable terms with the Allati north of here," Stone continued. "He has been manipulating Lord Eldin, who is of royal blood. Foolish man. I thought he was smarter than that. If Eldin knew Cotoch was a *candarii*, Cotoch would be a dead man."

Eva took a deep, shuddering breath. Tears trickled down her cheek. She wished selfishly of home. Illiah walking the battlements, little Rhyl holding his hand and looking grave and serious at being included in such a task. Rhyl feeding Calypso a scrap of his lunch he had saved in his pocket. Rhyl hugging her neck tightly, planting wet kisses on her cheek.

"Did Cotoch rape you?" Stone asked quietly. The image of home dissolved instantly, both blessing and a curse.

Eva didn't know if she wanted to talk about it, but it came out despite herself. She told Stone all she remembered. Stone listened, his expression full of compassion and yearning to make it right. Not that he could. The grimness about his features spoke of death and violence. He obviously cared for her, to have such a fierce look in his eye on her behalf. When she told him how she overtook Sandra, Stone's brows arched with appreciation before resuming their position around his grim eyes.

"I am sorrier than you know. I have failed you. Such an ill to the body affects the mind, the soul. I would do much to salve it." His words sounded like an oath as much as an apology.

Eva nodded. She believed him, trusted him. Stone would keep her safe. He wouldn't let it happen again. He might be an exiled warrior, but Eva could sense his compassion and goodness. Words deserted her, but Stone didn't need them.

"I could have killed them both, but I didn't," Eva said after a moment. She didn't tell him about the voice begging for Cotoch's life. She didn't even know what to tell herself about it.

"Killing should not come easily, even if it is your enemy," Stone said.

Strangely, his words settled some dispute inside her heart. She took a deep breath and exhaled slowly.

She pulled out her little bag of herbs Stone had fetched from her supplies and selected the ones she needed. It would be a bitter brew. The herb had many uses, but mixed with others in the right quantities, it made the brew she needed. She knew it was the reason she had brought it, unpalatable as the reason was. A woman traveling alone could face many perils. Rape was common enough. She didn't think, after years of trying for another baby with Illiah, she would get pregnant by Cotoch, but she didn't want to take a chance. She could not imagine carrying a baby that was not Illiah's.

Her hands shook as she poured the carefully measured amount into the pot. It bubbled, filling the cave with its pungent aroma. It didn't smell bad, but Eva knew it smelled better than it tasted. She had made the brew for other women before, not often, but every once in a while, a woman at the Keep did something they regretted.

"After I drink this, I will need to sleep," Eva told Stone, taking the pot off the fire to cool.

"There is an alcove where you can sleep. It is more sheltered than the open part of the cave. There is a bench for sleeping. Come," Stone said, watching her warily, as if she might disintegrate the instant the drink touched her lips.

The light was fading from the cave. The daylight left the narrow Vale quickly, though Eva didn't think it was that late. Sleep threatened to overwhelm her, and she hadn't even taken the draught. She took a tentative sip. It was hot but didn't burn her tongue, so she kept drinking, each sip making her face twist more and more from the bitterness.

"Argh, that's awful stuff," she spat.

"Here." Stone handed her some dried fruit.

"Thanks," Eva said, gnawing on the leathery piece of sweetness.

"You should eat something more substantial. I have some sausage."

Eva shook her head. "No, the draught is better taken without food. Tomorrow will be soon enough." Her eyes drooped and her head swam. "Where is the alcove?"

Eva stood on shaky feet. She felt so dizzy. Stone's hand lashed out to catch her arm, steadying her. In an instant, her blanket was wrapped tighter around her naked body, like a babe in swaddling. She was pulled off her feet as Stone carried her into the alcove. She couldn't find the energy to complain.

Stone placed her on a bed. It was rough, but not as firm as stone. Eva looked around groggily at the room she was in, for the alcove was just that - a room. The floor was level and smooth, the walls carved and round with shelves built into them that held an assortment of unrecognizable dust-covered items. Eva had questions, but sleep claimed her.

When Eva woke, it was morning. She was warm and comfortable. Several layers of blankets covered her topped with a thick fur. Underneath, she was still naked. Her hair was a tangled pile. Her stomach roiled uncomfortably as she sat up, pulling the blanket around her, assessing the strange room that had no business being part of a cave.

The room wasn't large, but there was a finely crafted table, a single chair. The bed Eva slept on was large and carved into the side of the cave. There was a mattress underneath her, stuffed with old straw. There were books, candles, and a large chest. A refuge of sorts.

She swung her legs over the edge of the bed, which was for a much taller person than herself. Before her bare feet touched the ground, her stomach went from roiling to upheaval. She made a run for outside, trying to hold in her vomit. The last thing she wanted was a sick mess all over their camp.

She barely made it to the cave edge where ferns and moss grew thick. She emptied the contents of her stomach, which was more than she thought. The brew tasted even viler coming up. Eva succumbed to her body's urgings. Her eyes watered and her chest hurt by the time she was done. Then she realized Stone was behind her. He took her blanket, which had fallen on her mad dash, and put it around her shoulders. She was already shivering from the cold and sick.

"Better?" Stone asked her.

She nodded.

"You don't feel feverish," he noted, placing a palm across her brow. The gesture almost made her smile. It was something a mother did, not a warrior with a scowl to curdle milk.

"It's just a side effect of the brew. At least I know it is working." She tried standing up straighter and found herself steady. She pulled the blanket tighter around her as a breeze came in. She was feeling better already, and hungry. "Do I smell sausages?"

Stone grinned at her. She liked how his grin stretched up to his ears and made his sharp teeth gleam with character. His yellow eyes looked less incendiary and more like flower petals in the sun. Buttercups, perhaps.

Eva could hear the sausages sizzling on the fire, making her mouth water. She stopped and patted her horses each on the nose. They looked at her with guileless eyes. "Good boys."

"I think you have sick in your hair," Stone mentioned as he followed her back inside. Eva sighed, spotting it.

Despite the delicious smell of sausages and her plaintive stomach, she went back to the alcove where she had spotted her pack. She pulled out some clean clothes. Once dressed she took her smallest knife and applied it to her hair. The strands fell at her feet like delicate slivers of ice. She didn't stop until her hair was only a finger-length long, brushing around her ears, tickling her neck. She had never had short hair before. Her head felt light and airy. She could vividly recall Cotoch pulling her braid, shackling her. Her heart beat fast remembering how helpless and violated she had felt. She could still feel him inside her.

The sausages were almost cool by the time she came back to the fire to eat. Stone was eating a chunk from the end of his knife, his large canine teeth clearly visible. His yellow eyes lingered on her hair. His spotted brows rose. Eva said nothing but imitated him, taking out her knife and stabbing it into a thick piece of the meat.

"I like it," he said, gesturing to her hair. "Smart too, since now we will have to travel through Allati to get to Kitarra. You will have to keep your hair covered. Easier to do with short hair."

Eva agreed.

"What is this place?" she asked after eating her fill of the sausages.

Stone offered her a cup of hot tea. She held it in her palms, feeling its warmth spread through her fingers.

"This is the Vale of the Warrior. It is said to be the home of the great warrior Tayeh, where he lived in exile for ten years before the war. The War of the Last King, as it came to be known. The war that would turn him into a legend."

"Tayeh, the Guardian of Kitarra?" Eva asked. Tayeh, who had loved her and betrayed her.

"That is the legend, yes," Stone said with a snort.

"You don't believe it?"

"I don't believe in Guardians."

Eva had believed Kitarrans had a healthier relationship with their Guardian than Jullayans. She thought they loved and revered Tayeh, not as a god, but as a Guardian, a mentor, a protector, though her information was now circumspect due to Tayeh's misdeeds. But then, Stone was not an average Kitarran. He was an exile himself, after all. His derision to the ideals of a Guardian was not shocking.

"Why was Tayeh exiled?"

"Legend tells that he threatened the king. One thousand years ago, Kitarra was ruled by a king, and succession was through the king's sons. The Last King was cruel, a tyrant, and Tayeh, who was no more than a petty warrior, challenged him, confronted him with his crimes and cruelty. Guess he wasn't too bright - barely escaped with his life. It is said he waited in exile, plotting the return of Kitarra's graceful monarchy. War came, as it usually does. The king had no sons, only one daughter. While he was in exile, Tayeh plotted with the rebels and secretly with the princess to overthrow her father. After the war, she married Tayeh and became the first queen. Kitarra found peace at last and thrived under her rule. Since then, it is the queen who rules with her consort, and her daughters who inherit."

"How did you find this place?" Eva asked, her mind still on the story of Tayeh. She tried to imagine her old mentor as a father and husband, but somehow could not. The place Tayeh held in her heart was black and rotten.

Stone was silent, thinking, looking around as if wondering how he had indeed come here.

"I just stumbled across it one day as I was returning back from

Allati on a mission for Cotoch. The path opened before me and the Vale showed itself. I have walked through this forest and these hills many times but had never come across it before. Perhaps there is some magic to this place," he admitted bitterly.

"Not such a bad place to live in exile," Eva mused. "You think we are safe here?"

"I know we are."

"How? How do we know Cotoch's men aren't combing the forest and hills at this very moment, poised on the edge of the Vale?" The sudden thought made her shiver.

"Trust me."

Eva narrowed her eyes at him. "You discount the Guardians, but rely on their magic to protect us? That is highly hypocritical."

"Okay, maybe I believe the Guardians exist, but not in the capacity most believe," he told her with an edge to his voice. "They have no power over us."

Eva couldn't agree, but she fell silent, once more wondering what Stone's story was and the secrets he held close to his heart.

"Tell me how we are going to get to Kilev from here," Eva said, changing the subject.

Stone chewed his lip, a long, pointed tooth making a brief appearance, his ears back. He stood up abruptly, gesturing her to follow him into the little room. Along the wall was a shelf full of parchments. He took one of the delicate rolls and unrolled it carefully on the table. Eva could see the neat lines of faded ink.

"We are here," he said, pointing to the map unfolded before her. "This path through the hills leads to Allati. We will follow the road to Little Fold. The mountain passes to either side are too dangerous, as I have mentioned before. This is the city of Little Hill, Lord Eldin's hold. There is a precept at Little Hill as well, best avoided - I have never met a precept who is not cruel. Seems to be a prerequisite for the position. I wish we could just avoid the place altogether, but we will have to pass through his lands. Unfortunately, we will be very conspicuous. I am well known in those parts, and you -" He shrugged, glancing at her hair. "Together we are an intriguing pair. But Eldin's men are cowards. We can buy them off - hopefully. If not, we have something to our advantage: we can use our knowledge of Cotoch's ability as a sorcerer. Lord Eldin will have to approach the king, and it will be Cotoch's death sentence. I would rather not do that, because Cotoch has a good-sized army, his men are well trained, and he will fight. It would be a bloody, long-winded war and many innocent men would die on both sides. There are good people in Mahlas. I would hate to see them suffer.

"So, we pass by Little Hill and go north, then west, until the mountains give way to the river plain. Then we follow the river to Kilev." He trailed his finger along the gray ink line that looked like it had once been blue. He tapped the map on the black dot marked Kilev. "Easy," he said with a great deal of sarcasm.

"When do we leave?"

"Seven days."

"That long?"

"In seven days, Cotoch's men will have searched long enough to know they won't find us. Then we leave with a better chance of not being discovered - a good thing, no?"

"How do we know Cotoch won't go to Lord Eldin and tell him to keep an eye out for us? What is there to stop Eldin from handing us back over to Cotoch?"

"It is more than a possibility. But Eldin has no love for Cotoch, and I don't know how easily he succumbs to Cotoch's *candarii* magic. There is always the chance he will see you for who you are and keep you."

Eva huffed. It was a redundant topic. "If he has no love for Cotoch, I can't imagine he holds you in high esteem," Eva remarked dryly, feeling the weight of their situation like an iron longsword.

"No, Eldin does not like me, but he does fear me," Stone said slowly. "Don't dwell on what happened, milady. You are free now. You are not a slave, nor a prisoner. And I will see you safely to Kitarra."

Eva's brows rose in surprise. Stone was adept at reading her moods.

"There was always the concern that Cotoch would decide to sell you to the Allati."

Eva glared at her amourii.

"I didn't know anything about Cotoch being a *candarii*. If I had, I would never have taken you to Mahlas," Stone said in a heavy voice. "And it would be over my dead body that I let him sell you to the Allati - that is not an easy thing to achieve, it seems. Besides, Cotoch's men wouldn't want to challenge me," he told her with a smirk.

"You succumbed to those bandits easily enough. Maybe you are losing your edge," Eva told him with a smirk of her own. "Cotoch would not have sold me. He wanted me for his own."

Stone looked down at his feet, his expression somber, ashamed. Eva had hit a nerve. Or two.

"I was not in a good state when those bandits found me. I ran, but really I cared for nothing, not even my own life," he said in a small voice, the voice of a lost child crying for help, calling to Eva's wounded soul. She took a deep breath and ignored it.

Eva gave the map one last look, committing it to memory, at least the less faded bits. She stretched her arms up over her head, feeling the stretch in her ribs. Her body was sore, full of tender places reminding her of things she couldn't - wouldn't remember. She understood the desire to rid one's mind of hurtful thoughts and feelings. She could better understand the pull and promise the culla must have had for Stone. She must have cringed outwardly, because Stone cast her a worried look.

"I'm fine," she lied.

Stone rummaged through one of the large storage chests and pulled out a dusty glass bottle. He opened it, smelled it, and took a swig before handing it to her.

"Kitarran blackberry fire wine, the late Prince Arrain's favorite. I stole it from an envoy traveling from Kitarra to Allati last year. It has aged nicely." His mouth lilted with a mischievous smile.

Eva took a swig, enjoying the rich, fruity taste.

"That's pretty good."

"Damn straight. What are you doing?"

"I'm stretching." Eva took advantage of the flat floor of the alcove and began her routine. She hadn't done it since before she found Stone. She didn't take out her sword; she would start slow. She had learned the routine from Tayeh and later she and Illiah had perfected it together. Thinking of Illiah made her knees buckle; she adjusted accordingly. She closed her mind and concentrated on her breathing and her muscles, keeping her body relaxed but still working.

"That is a Kitarran routine. Or at least a variation of one."

"I know."

"Where did you learn it?"

Eva smiled. "Never you mind where I learned it."

Stone grumbled. "There are no Kitarran masters in Jullayah?" It was stated as question and fact.

Eva said nothing.

"Fine. Never mind," Stone said, stalking out of the cave.

Eva was thankful Stone gave up his questions. She had no desire to lie to him, even less desire to tell him the truth. The truth she held close to her heart with her memories of home, of times past. Of glorious days and evenings spent in the simplicity of being with the ones she loved.

To talk about Illiah and Rhyl was to open those safely stored thoughts and memories. Acknowledging the distance and danger between her and her loved ones gave wings to a superstitious fear that they would be more vulnerable, and her path more perilous and difficult. Their names on her lips would allow her greatest fear to take root within her heart: the fear that she would never see them again.

☾

Stone was stubborn and controlling, but since he had Eva's best interests in mind, she was willing to forgive him, at least a little. The days spent in the Vale were long. Stone went out to hunt but forbade her from joining him. And there was no telling if she would find her way back into the Vale without him, if what he said was true about it being enchanted. She would be a fool not to believe it.

She spent most of her time strengthening, as she had over winter. She practiced and practiced. She did all of Illiah's drills she could remember, even the ones she detested.

Stone insisted on sparring with her. She hadn't sparred with a Kitarran since before she was pregnant with Rhyl. Remembering her bouts with Tayeh sent a cold, angry shiver through her. Stone insisted, and Eva relented.

Eva was pleased to discover Stone as a sparring partner was no comparison to the Guardian of Kitarra. Stone was leaner and taller than Tayeh. He laughed at himself, something Tayeh never did. His style was different, his skill close to impeccable, even with the borrowed blade, but he wasn't arrogant. He laughed at his follies and was downright silly at times. Sometimes their matches devolved to the point where Eva found herself laughing with him. She hadn't laughed in a long time. It felt good - they both felt lighter for it.

"Tomorrow, we leave here," Stone told her as he sheathed his sword and threw more wood on the fire. Eva nodded, putting her own sword away, and bent over to stretch herself out. "I am going hunting at twilight." Kitarrans and their night vision - another reason Stone insisted she stay behind. She couldn't hunt past sunset.

"I'll be ready," she assured him.

They ate a simple dinner. After, Stone fastened the quiver and picked up the bow and left the Vale. Eva tidied up and packed her things away. The saddles had been oiled, her blades had been sharpened. The cave was full of supplies and tools for such things. There had even been extra leather to fix the wear in her right boot.

Eva stripped to bathe. It would be the last time in she didn't know how long, and she would miss it. She slipped into the pool and relaxed, running her hands through her short hair, still a strange sensation without her long locks. Every time she looked into the water, she found her visions easily.

She had seen Illiah, yet nothing to tell her more about the beautiful woman who seemed set on stealing his heart. Rhyl looked content, always in the company of the Kitarran child with the strange light-blue eyes so pale and clear, it was like looking into the dawn sky. She wondered if Rhyl missed her, if he had forgotten her. She saw Illiah talking to a Kitarran woman who could only be the queen. They talked in hushed voices, and the queen's face was writ with worry and grief.

Eva sought out Cotoch. He was angry, surrounded by dark and pain. Eva lurched out from the vision like she had been stung. She did not seek him again.

Finding a vision in the present was easier using the wind; the water was best to find the past. After Eva bathed and dressed, she climbed to the top of the cave where the steam rose from cracks lined with green moss and lush ferns. She stood and reached up into the fading daylight, following the steam up and up, careening over the world like a bird, above the trees, connecting to the wind, the air. The setting sun kissed the horizon, casting a red glow over Stone's silver fur where he stood looking out of the forest. He had a strange look on his face, grief and longing and fierce determination.

She moved past him to the west. The wind showed her a troop of men, around fifty strong, two companies that had just united. Their leaders conversed, shaking their heads. They turned and headed back to the southwest, back to Mahlas and Cotoch. Stone was right. It had been seven days and they were giving up.

Riding the wind was tiring, so with the last of her strength, she sought out Kilev. Passing over the long distance was like dreaming, one image shifting to another without care or notice. The wind was at her command and brought her to Kilev in an instant, to Rhyl's room. He appeared asleep, the Kitarran child in the bed next to his. Rhyl's eyes were closed, his long lashes outlined against his fair skin. He looked so perfect, so sweet. Illiah's strong features were echoed in Rhyl's face - his nice straight nose, his well-shaped lips. Eva was merely the wind, but she used it to caress his small cheek. She imagined kissing his forehead. Rhyl's eyes flew open, glinting in the dark.

"Mummy," he whispered into the night.

Eva drew a surprised breath, and the *simul rami* slipped through her fingers like rain. She was not the wind. She was not the light or air or water. She was solely herself once more.

Her body was heavy, confining. She sighed deeply, wondering if Rhyl had really sensed her. She tried to reach out to him again, but she was tired. Her magic had become tenuous, and she had already traveled with the air a long way.

Stone came back late with a skinned carcass over his shoulder. It looked like a small mountain goat. He began cutting it up and putting the meat to cook on the hot rocks Eva had prepared.

"Tea?" Eva asked when he was done.

Stone nodded and thanked her as she handed him a hot mug.

"Cotoch's troops are heading back."

Stone nodded again. He had expected that.

"Last night in relative comfort," Stone noted. "Best enjoy the soft bed while you can."

"Soft is a bit of a stretch, but I intend to," she told him with a smile.

Stone grinned back. "Nice to see you looking a bit happier."

"This Vale is safe and cozy, but I am happy to be moving on tomorrow."

"Kilev is still a long way away."

"You have mentioned that, once or twice."

CHAPTER 58

EVA

THE FOREST THINNED at an alarming rate. Eva and Stone were riding through dense evergreen trees one moment, and the next, bright sun was in their eyes, dancing between the leafless branches of sporadic oak trees.

They crested a hill; below was the thin, winding road leading to Allati and Little Hill. To the northwest were the ever-present, towering mountains. Their rocky, jagged peaks clothed in fresh snow, blazing in the spring sunshine. They looked angry and menacing, and Eva was glad their path did not lead through them. North would lead them around the mountains to the Ilba river. The Ilba would lead them to Kitarra and Kilev.

Eva shivered, feeling exposed. The tall, glossy evergreens had felt comforting, enclosing them with bough and limb, keeping away the eyes of potential danger. Now only Eva's magic kept them from encountering those that would wish them harm.

Once on the road travel was easy. Spring was tardy, and there was little traffic. The road branched and forked, each way marked by an old signpost. At the top of each post was a carving of a single rose flower. The Rose Road, Stone told Eva. The name of their route.

The road threaded through all the major cities of Allati, the fastest way to traverse the realm. The Allati were a nervous, careful people, Stone explained. Better to stick to the main road than to traverse the smaller roads and fields beyond it. The people would be more suspicious of someone crossing their land without permission than a person on the road. Not the most hospitable people, he told her. Eva kept her hood up, even when the warm spring sun made an appearance.

"Isn't it suspicious if I have my hood up in such warm weather?"

"Yes," Stone agreed. "Better the alternative. They will know what you are and will insist on escorting you to the nearest lord or precept."

Eva remembered Felis's warning. It seemed like an age ago that she had left him.

"A friend told me he was exiled because a precept decided to take the woman he wanted to marry, the woman he loved," Eva said.

"Who is this?"

"Felis of Stonyhill," Eva replied.

"Ah. I have not heard that tale."

"You know Felis?"

"No. I have heard of him, though. Sounds like a likely tale. There are dire punishments for boys and young men. Many men are banished from Allati with barely an offense, for glancing at a woman destined for another man. They often end up in Kilev, or more likely with Cotoch, or wandering the Midlands, angry, starved, and bitter. Cotoch scoops those ones up and adds them to his army. Not really the smartest thing for the Allati to do."

"What I told Cotoch was true - my mother fled Allati," Eva said absently. "She made it all the way to Jullayah, where she met my father."

"A brave woman."

"Yes. She never got a chance to tell me why. She died when I was seven."

"Was she a *sanarii* like you?"

Eva shook her head. "I don't think so. Though perhaps she didn't have anyone to teach her." Eva closed her eyes against the warm sun. It felt so good.

"Who taught you?"

"I have my secrets, Stone, as you have yours."

Stone growled low in his throat. He didn't like secrets. She could tell his curiosity was nagging him.

"You don't trust me?"

"I do," Eva said, knowing it for the truth. "I just can't speak of it. It hurts too much."

The day wore on, and the sun settled below the horizon filling the sky with a faint blush. Stone was on the lookout for a good place to stop for the night when his ears flattened and a scowl came across his face.

"Riders," he said in a hush.

Eva strained her ears. She too could hear the faint clinking of mail, the faint plod of shod horses. Her sight had not given her warning. There were too many intertwining roads and paths before them. She couldn't watch them all. Her body stiffened with anxiety. She had to be calm and collected if she were to face this trial and get to Kilev.

"What do we do?" Eva's voice sounded scared even to her ears. Damn. She thought she was braver than this. Cotoch had weakened her. She felt like a rabbit ready to dart into the hound's mouth.

"Don't worry." Stone drew himself up tall in the saddle. He didn't draw his sword or knife, but he was poised to.

The last rays of sun shone upon the riders, a troop of men. Eva counted twelve. Their cloaks were midnight blue with three yellow roses upon their shoulders. Their helms were fine steel. The leader had a ridiculously tall yellow plume upon his helm.

"Lord Eldin's men," Stone told her.

"Ho, ho," came a loud voice. The yellow plume wearing man pushed his horse into a canter, closing the distance between them. His troop followed, and for a minute there was nothing but dust and the sound of horses and clanking armor. Penn snorted and tugged on his rein. He did not like the hoard coming into his space. Stone turned him in a tight circle to keep him from charging.

"Just who we were looking for, Cotoch's lost warrior and Cotoch's lost whore," the leader said, looking them over.

"Watch your tongue, Cedris," Stone warned, unmoving. Even Penn quieted under the commanding calm of the Kitarran. Eva looked from Cedris's plume to Stone and finally to Cedris's face. He was smiling arrogantly, but his eyes glinted with unease. Stone was right - they feared him.

Cedris swallowed. "Cotoch is looking for you. He wants Lord Eldin to turn you over once you are found."

"I know," Stone said simply. "But you won't. You are too greedy. Eva, give him the bag."

Eva reached into her pocket and took out the little sack that held two red rubies, perfectly cut and worth a good price at any market. She gave it over to the plume.

He emptied them into his hand, rolling them between his fingers. "My silence?"

Stone nodded deliberately.

"All right, men, onward. These are not the ones Lord Eldin is looking for," Cedris said, kicking his horse into a canter. His men followed without question.

"Come. We need to press on," Stone said. "Cedris is a coward. I don't know how his men are so loyal to him, but let's hope they are."

That night, they did not risk a fire. Despite Cedris's lack of loyalty to his lord, Stone felt it would be foolish to attract unwanted attention, just in case one of Eldin's men spoke out against his captain.

They took turns on watch. It was cold and lonely. Eva shivered thinking of the warm cave of the Vale. Stone stirred in his sleep, turning toward her. She leaned into him, and he curled around her. He was warm and soft, like a big dog. What would she do without Stone? She would surely be at the mercy of Cotoch, bent to his will, dying a slow death.

If Stone got her safely to Kilev, she would owe him a debt of gratitude. His debt to her would surely be paid. What would he do then? Would he go back to Cotoch and succumb once more to the evil of the culla? The dark shadows that had brought him to the culla still lingered in his heart. He was trying, but Eva sensed a battle within his will, despair warring with his fealty. He stirred behind her, no doubt sensing her foreboding thoughts.

It had been raining for three days. Eva did not complain about keeping her hood up. The rain was warm, but still unpleasant. No one looked up from the road as they passed. The other travelers were too immersed in their wet misery to take in their fellow travelers, not even to spare so much as a glance. Only Stone braced the rain uncaring, ever watchful, his fur wet and tousled, his ears drooped slightly.

Finally, they were free of the bustling Rose Road. They turned onto the smaller road that led northwest to the Ilba river and Kitarra. If they followed the Rose Road for one more day, Stone explained, they would be in the great Allati city of Attingard, the king's city.

Eva scanned the new road with the wind for miles and saw no one. It was early in the season for merchants to make the trek to Kitarra, and vice versa. Stone expected little traffic. The track they followed led nowhere but the river, to a little town that was just one inn and a farm.

Stone was a humble authority on many things and explained that the innkeeper was also the ferryman. He had a small barge that would take them and the horses across the river, for a fee. He would be eager for business, Stone noted. Generally, no one visited Kitarra until midsummer when the river was calmer. Even then it wasn't used much. Allati and Kitarra were on tenuous terms, as usual. The Allati king was ever angry with the Kitarran queen because she harbored Allati runaways and refugees. Allati would never have the power to overthrow Kitarra, so the king merely purchased the rich ores from Kitarra and pretended they were on friendly terms.

"How is it you know so very much?" Eva asked of Stone after a paraphrased lecture of the history of Kitarra and Allati.

Stone hunched down, a little sheepishly. "I have a good memory for mostly useless facts. Look, there is funnel grass. Remember how I mentioned it was once used as a - ?"

Eva was laughing so hard, she could not hear the rest of his fact.

"See? Useless facts." Stone's sheepish smile grew and he was laughing too.

The land turned rocky and uneven as they neared the river. The hills rose higher and steeper. The road was all twists and turns and blind corners. Stone became even more watchful, if that were possible. He told Eva that in summer it was a favorite route for raiders and thieves, but being spring, perhaps they would be safe yet. He bade Eva to keep looking, to be ever watchful, just in case.

Eva was beginning to suspect every time she reached for the *simul rami*, the magic became more and more stretched, her sight shortened, and after she was fatigued. Eva didn't tell Stone, but she worried the strength given to her by the creatures of the Great Forest was wearing thin. Soon she would have only the skill she was born with. They were almost to Kitarra. She hoped it would be enough until then.

Two more wet days passed and finally, the wind picked up, and the sun came out once more.

"We are getting close. We should reach the river today," Stone told Eva.

The breeze brought the smell of smoke and burning wood. Stone pressed his face into the wind, his ears back, his mouth set.

"I do not like the smell of it. There is a foulness to the air. What can you see?" he asked her.

Eva saw ashes. And smoke.

They cantered down the road, and the smell grew stronger, the air thicker. Around a bend, a great plume of smoke rose thick and forbidding above the willow trees. The rising column spread ash in a thin layer all over the road.

The place was unrecognizable. What had been an inn and farm was either ash or blackened ruins beneath the thick smoke. Stone circled the site and came back shaking his head.

"All the buildings are burned and smoldering. There is no sign of the innkeep and his family, nor their livestock. This couldn't have happened long ago. The rain would have quenched the fire, at least somewhat, yet it gutted everything." His jaw was set. "Come, let's go down to the river and hope there is a boat. Be wary. This speaks of foul work."

Beyond the smoke, the river stretched out wide before them. Its banks were sandy and lined with willows and poplars. New, bright shiny leaves shifted in the sunlight. The water was muddy and lazy with the spring thaw. Eva could see a dock, untouched, but no boats, no ferry. Her gaze traveled across the water to their destination, Kitarra. The distance between her and the far shore seemed fathomless. Too far to swim. The gentle current could be deceptive, laying trap for strong and dangerous undertows. Downriver another plume of smoke rose into the air. Eva turned to Stone.

"The other side is burning too. What happened here?" Eva stated, goose prickles rising along her skin.

Stone echoed her unease. "I don't know."

"And this is the only way to get to Kitarra?"

"Without spending weeks in the mountains? Yes."

A movement, a shift in Eva's peripheral was all the warning she had. There was no time to hide, no place to run. A horde of men materialized from the smoke-ridden forest, ominous in their stealth and numbers. Their weapons were crude implements - serrated blades, axes made of thick metal. Eva couldn't count them. Not that it would have been any use as there were too many. She called out a useless warning to Stone. He had already seen them. He already had his sword in hand, waiting.

It was too late to run. The men, if they could be called men, were circling them with intent. Their eyes were feral, their long hair unkempt and matted. Their faces were craggy and scarred. Not the random scars of battle; theirs were self-inflicted. They decorated their skin with their pain like a carver embellishes wood. They wore skins of animals Eva had never seen, and even those were ragged and matted. Worse were the thoughts they wore like masks on their etched faces. Thoughts of blood and gore and depredation and lust and taking.

Sasha whinnied in alarm, desperate to bolt. Eva wanted to bolt too, but she couldn't. The men were behind her, between her and escape. And she refused to leave Stone alone to face them. Her sword was in her hand. She didn't remember drawing it.

Stone dismounted and tossed her Penn's reins. Eva couldn't hold the destrier; Penn wanted a fight. Eva hopped from Sasha onto the war horse's back, a trick she was pleased to put to good use. As soon as she abandoned the gelding, Sasha did his best to bolt through the horde of men. He had not been trained for battle. Eva couldn't blame him. Penn reared and Eva held on with rein and mane. Her free hand held her sword, and she thanked Illiah for teaching her how to fight from a horse.

"Eva, get out of here!" Stone roared as he took a man in the gut with one easy blow. Stone cut through the line of men as if he was cutting through brush. He made it look easy. And he was fast, incredibly fast, a blur in the sea of wretched men. His reach was long, his aim exact. The attackers were intent on Eva and sped toward her, creating a line between her and Stone.

Penn reared and brought his hooves down upon the men. Someone cried out in anger and pain as his teeth found flesh. Despite her valiant horse, the circle of monsters tightened around Eva. She couldn't heed Stone's command, even if she wanted to. Eva's sword found flesh. Blood and gore rained.

Eva spun Penn around, using her sword where she could. Her reach was nowhere as long as Stone's, but she found arm after arm as the men tried to reach her. One of them managed to grab Penn's reins and yanked hard, nearly pulling Eva from the saddle. He earned a bite from the horse and faltered, but another man took his place.

Eva tried not to think about the sickly texture of rent flesh beneath her blade, nor the man whose lifeblood drenched his comrades as it dehisced from the slash at his neck. Another man howled in pain as she cut off his ear. With both their lives at the edge of the precipice, Eva did not hesitate. Death was hers to wield and she did not deny it.

A fierce grip on her leg pulled her from her saddle. Her leg burned like it was torn. She cried out instinctively as the ground rose to meet her, but she didn't hit it. They grabbed her, carrying her. She wiggled and strained, but she could not get free. They were too strong. The smell of rank, unwashed bodies assaulted her nose. Her sword was useless in her immobilized grasp. Her wrist was wrenched painfully, making her drop her sword.

A roar of desperation ripped through the fight. It sounded like Stone.

She went limp. The dead weight startled them, their grip slackened. She used the instant to regain control, managing to free herself from their grasp long enough to land a blow with her feet, an elbow. A fiery pain lanced into her shoulder and neck as she heard a sickening crack as her bone broke under the impact of something. Something else hit her stomach. The sharp, twisting pain crippled her senses. A sudden warmth on her tunic was her own blood. Her voice was lost under the weight of pain as her body cried out. The sky was gone, blocked by the press of monsters.

She heard another roar that sounded like her name.

The seconds passed like hours. The dirt below Eva's face was wet and smelled wrong, like blood and death instead of earth. She couldn't move because her body was on fire. Her arm. Her gut. The sharp, slicing pain spread deeper and deeper. Every breath was a struggle against it. She could open her eyes, but all she could see was the grass that grew along the river bank. It was crushed and painted red with blood, dusted with gray ash. She heard the sounds of battle, but she had been forgotten.

The sounds of clashing steel were gone, finally, leaving behind grunts and groans. Eva waited. She tried to move and failed. She couldn't think beyond the pain engulfing her fear. All she wanted was peace, numbness, but it didn't come.

A face filled her vision. Stone was beside her, his yellow eyes an endearing, reassuring sight. Eva whimpered in relief. He helped her to sit up. She vomited.

Stone silently inspected her from head to foot. He looked at her stomach for a long moment, not meeting her eyes. Eva couldn't assess herself; to move at all increased the waves of pain through her body. Stone took off her boots, making her wiggle her toes in turn. She could do that. Her legs were okay, sore where the man had pulled her, but not broken. She didn't let him touch her arm. She cradled it protectively against her torso.

Stone helped her lie straight on her back. He rummaged in her pack for her healing bag. Eva could see he was mostly unscathed, which was remarkable.

"How bad is it?" Eva asked him, weak and shaky. "I can't heal myself."

Stone's face remained expressionless as he ripped her tunic, exposing her skin. He placed a wad of bandage on her stomach tenderly.

"It's not nothing," he said at length. "We need to move you. Come on, hold on to me." He picked her up as if she were nothing. But the pain was too much. She retched. Spots danced in her vision. Her head swam. She was drowning in a sea of pain. As she concentrated on not passing out, she saw one last glance of her surroundings.

Bodies. Everywhere.

Bodies and blood. Eva could hear the grunts of men not yet

succumbed to their injuries, but they would, and soon. Eva could not believe one man could accomplish so much death in such a short time. It was hard to tell how many men lay slain. Stone was a force to be feared.

The horses had not gone far. Sasha had made his way back already, the battle being over. Eva cried out as Stone lifted her into the saddle. She couldn't help it. The cry came as the searing pain riddled her body. She vomited again. Stone mounted behind her and held her steady so she wouldn't fall from the high horse. The uneven gait of the horse was agony. As Eva cried, the tears rolled down her cheeks.

She didn't know how long they rode. A minute, an hour, an age of men. She gripped Stone's hand tightly as the pain came in waves, reminding her of another pain years ago, the hours of long labor she spent delivering Rhyl. That had been for her baby; this was torture. She wondered if death lingered over her. Her cheeks were so hot with tears.

Finally, Stone pulled her onto the soft grass and she could lay still. She breathed deeply, calming her body. It helped a little. Then she started shivering. Stone's gentle hands lifted her, placing a cloak under her head. He piled her with blankets and kept her legs up above her heart. He checked her stomach again where he had wrapped her tightly. Eva could see through his fake calm.

"I need to make a fire. Just lay still and press down if you can," he told her, placing her undamaged hand upon her side where the bandage was. Eva did as she was told, closing her eyes, listening to the sounds of Stone making a fire. The crack as he broke sticks. The sound of the first timid flames. The smell of wood smoke in her lungs. It helped distract her from the pain, from the throbbing of her arm and gut, the itch of blood drying on her stomach.

"Throw some dried comfru, from my bag, on the fire." She despised the shaky quality to her voice.

Stone got the herb. The pungent smell filled the air, and her breath came easier.

Stone was back at her side, pulling away her shirt and bandages to expose her wound once more. He poured something on it that smelled like wine. Eva wondered where he had gotten it. It stung. She cursed him.

"Save your breath, milady," Stone said unperturbed. "I need to stitch you up."

He rummaged through her bag for the needed supplies. Eva fought once more to regain control of her calm at the thought of her skin being sewn back together. "It's not bleeding too badly. How do you feel?" he asked.

"Not good."

"Hold still."

The first pinch as Stone began his work to repair her broken body was just one more layer of pain above the others.

"I have seen that kind of man before," she said in a weak attempt to distract herself.

"What do you mean?"

"They are invaders, from the sea. I saw them in Jullayah. Six years ago, they came and attacked, killing, raping, stealing women and children. They came from across the ocean. They were defeated from our shores, but not for good, it would seem."

Stone did not stop his careful stitching, but he bit his lip, his eyes pinched in distress.

"That is unnerving. They likely came up the river, from Kitarra. They attacked the Kitarran ferry first," Stone mused.

Eva had no more to say about it, but she was sure she was right. It was evident from their strange garb, the designs in their skin, the fierce eyes and matted beards, and their weapons, crude and cruel, but effective, matched by their obvious battle lust.

It took a long time for Stone to stitch her up. Eva was scared to know how badly she was hurt. Stone applied an herbal paste to the wound at Eva's instructions and wrapped her tightly back up. Then he turned to her arm, which she still held against her.

"Your left arm at least. You will wield a sword once more," Stone assured her. "I am no healer, but I think this might be broken." He was gingerly probing her arm up and down. Right above her wrist was already swollen and turning vivid colors. The pain was lancing. She begged him to stop. "I think it is a clean break and won't need to be set, but I am not sure." His yellow eyes lingered over her. He wrapped her arm securely and made a sling from her bloodied tunic.

"Did you know your eyes look like buttercups?" Eva told him absently.

Stone didn't smile.

Eva was so tired, but the pain made it hard to sleep. Stone cooked a simple meal, but she could barely stomach the thought of eating.

He worked hard to distract her and told her stories - Kitarran legends, apparently he knew plenty. Eva finally fell asleep listening to his soft voice. He was a good storyteller, his voice fine and sure.

CHAPTER 59

STONE

STONE WAS NOT A HEALER. He watched Eva as she slept. Her breath came easy, steady. A good sign. Still, she looked wan and pale, and her skin was clammy. She had taken a hard blow. The enemy's blade had plunged deep. Besides losing a lot of blood, she was at risk of infection or internal bleeding.

Eva's eyes had been sharp with fear. She knew the fine line between life and death she walked. Stone chewed his lip. Her wounds were as much from him as they were from the foreign raiders. If he had been quicker, he could have reached her before she was pulled from her horse. He had failed her again. He could hardly bear it.

And now Stone had a terrible choice to make. If he did not get Eva to a healer, someone skilled, there was a good chance she would die. Attingard was not far away, and a healer could be hired for a price. But what then? There was no healer in Attingard that would not know her for what she was and alert the king. They would claim her as their own and imprison her in a loveless marriage to one of their highborn lords. There was no hope getting to Kitarra quickly without a ferry. The way to Kitarra was now a long trek with the steep mountains on one side and the unpredictable river on the other. He would have to ask her when she woke.

As it turned out, there was no chance to ask her. When Eva woke, she was feverish and incoherent. Her brow was warm, her eyes faded. She barely spoke, and when she did, it was weak and garbled. Her wound was ugly and possibly infected. He gave her water, but there was not much else he could do for her. He had to move her. He was out of options.

Three days.

It would take three days to get to Attingard.

Stone grit his teeth. He didn't know if she would make it.

"You must, Eva." He told her. She didn't answer. Her eyes were closed, but he suspected the barest of nods.

He wasted no time and saddled up Penn, loading their supplies onto Sasha. The gelding would follow even without a lead. He was a good, loyal horse.

Stone cradled Eva to him like a small child and mounted up. It was beyond awkward, but somehow he managed it without causing her undue pain and discomfort, at least as far as he could tell. She had slipped into a nearly unconscious state.

He pushed Penn into a canter. Luckily his stride was smooth, for a horse, although Eva did give a cry. Stone could only ignore her. It was the only way.

By nightfall, Eva was worse. She didn't wake when Stone tried to give her something to drink. Her skin was hot as glowing coals. Her abdomen was red and swollen and the stitched puncture bled more than Stone felt was good. He made a fire and prayed to whatever Guardian might be listening to help him get her to Attingard. He even prayed to the Allmakers, the spirits of legend and stories.

If Eva died, Stone knew he was not strong enough to live with her blood on his hands.

She will live, coward.

The voice was an old one. It gave him the kind of strength a slave musters from a whip.

He lay beside her at night. Her skin burned but she shivered as if a great chill was upon her. She did not wake. He poured tiny amounts of water in her mouth and hoped her body could absorb it.

Stone spent the night thinking of her strange quest to get to Kilev. She never told him why she was traveling there, what she had been seeking. If she died, her quest would die with her. There would be no way for him to redeem himself.

Selfish bastard. He did not deserve redemption. Never had.

Something bad would happen if Eva did not make it to Kilev. Stone didn't know why, but the feeling was strong. Whatever reason she had to get to Kitarra, it was of great importance. He knew it from the desperate look in her eyes at times, the grief, the longing. But most of all, from the hope that broke through her stony countenance lifting her spirits and making her smile. He regretted with illimitable anguish that he had not asked her about her plight. But he refused to believe he would never know.

Buttercups. Eva told him his eyes looked like buttercups.

It was a long night. He fed the fire as much as he could with his limited supply of wood. He wouldn't leave her again to find more. He made the tea from her herbs she had requested before her wounds robbed her of her lucidity. He would give her some in the morning.

The darkness crept around him. Stone strained his senses, listening for any change in Eva's breathing. The road was not far beyond the swath of poplars where he made camp. He dared to hope for the sounds of a wagon, knowing in the dead of night, in the middle of spring, it would be unlikely. He also listened for any sound that was not natural. Any sign more monsters were lurking in the forest.

He doubted it. It had been a large group he had slaughtered. A larger group would never have passed through Kitarra unseen and unhindered. He wondered where they stashed their boat. There had been no sign of it by the burned-out inn. If Eva had not been injured, they could have sought it out. But now there was no time. Eva was out of time.

Eva had seen those men, or their ilk, before in Jullayah, invaders from beyond the sea. They were not so far from the sea now. With a swift boat, they could reach the sea in five days traveling downriver. Upriver would be more of a challenge, but with enough rowers and a streamlined craft, it wouldn't take long. The stench of death and cruelty hung about them, transforming them into a tangible nightmare. He felt no guilt from killing them.

He wondered, not for the first time, if they had poison on their blades. It was cruel and dishonorable, but such men would not care. Eva's wound had not been mortal. The bleeding was not uncontrollable, yet she had sickened with infection very quickly.

Stone's lip hurt, and he realized he had bitten it again. He tasted the iron of his own blood for an instant before his body healed it. He wished Eva had the Kitarran gift for fast healing. Kitarrans rarely fell to infection. They died from broken hearts, but not infections.

The sky gradually lightened and the stars slowly melted into the coming dawn. Stone turned his thoughts to preparing for the day ahead. They must press on and yet he was loath to move Eva.

He gave her some of the tea, dribbling it down her throat. His hope blossomed as she seemed to swallow it. She opened her eyes feebly, and Stone smiled in relief, but her words were unformed, and she could not focus. Within moments she closed her eyes and was silent and still, and Stone's hope withered.

Stone cleaned up camp, packed their things, and saddled and fed the horses, all the while keeping a watchful eye on Eva and the road. Then he lifted her as he had done before. She cried out in pain and retched all the tea upon the grass. Stone put her back down. His heart pounded in desperation and his thoughts swirled, overwhelmed with his inability to fix her.

"If I don't move you, you will die," he told her in a desperate, pleading voice. And yet he didn't try again. He couldn't bring himself to pick her up. He sat down beside her, his hand on hers. He pondered his options and cursed. He prayed and cursed.

He wasn't sitting long before he heard the unmistakable sounds of horses from the road. In harmony with the horses were also the creaking of wheels and voices.

Stone's heart leaped. He grabbed the bag of jewels out of his waist pocket as he ran through the brush.

"Wait!" he called out. The wagon, which was not moving fast, came to a halt as the driver pulled in his pair of horses. It was a big wagon, the back covered with a canvas frame. A woman popped her head out, a questioning look on her face. The man, the driver, looked down at Stone with a scowl that was part fear and part annoyance. "Please," Stone said in a calmer voice, trying to look less threatening. "I need passage to Attingard for my friend and me. She is badly hurt and will surely die if I don't get her to the master healers there."

The woman climbed onto the driver's seat beside the man and they looked at each other.

"We just came from there. We have a load to take to Kitarra. It will put us behind schedule if we deviate," the man said in a deep, crackly voice.

Stone approached the wagon. He thought briefly about the burnt ferry, wondering whether to tell them. The road there held nothing but death and carnage, a feast for crows and ravens.

"I can pay you." He held out his hand, deciding against the truth. There were too many questions in it. In his mind he was already thinking of a story - he had to go with it. The driver looked at the pool of glossy gems and his eyes widened. The woman gave him a smack on the shoulder.

"I think we can arrange it," the driver said.

"It's only a couple days longer," the woman said, her eyes greedy as she snatched up the gems.

"There are more if you get us there safely and quickly," Stone offered.

They both nodded.

"Can you help me? I have two horses as well that would do well tied to the back of the wagon."

Another solemn nod as the driver handed the reins to the woman and hopped down. He stood next to Stone, looking up and up at Stone with unease.

"I've seen many Kitarrans in my day, but you got to be one o' the biggest," he remarked in a dry voice. "I'm Granger. My wife here is Flora." He pointed to the woman who sat in his seat, an unremarkable creature.

"My name is Stone, and my friend is Eva. Here, take Sasha and Penn and tie them to the wagon." Penn pulled his head as the strange man took his lead. Stone hissed at him, and then smoothed his neck, telling him to be a good boy. In the back of his mind, he heard Eva approve. She was particular about the horses' treatment.

Stone lifted Eva once more, knowing it would be a short walk to the wagon. She was not really awake, but she whimpered in pain, making Granger look back at them. The furrows of his face deepened as he saw her pale gold hair, but he said nothing. Cut short as it was, Eva's hair was still remarkable.

Eva's eyes were open and feverish. Stone would have done much to hear her speak his name or show any sign that she was trying to stay with him.

Granger tethered the horses to the wagon and quickly made a place for Eva inside under the canvas cover. There were blankets aplenty. Granger and Flora were nomads and lived mostly out of their wagon. Stone laid her down and sat beside her. Granger gave a call to his horses, and they pulled ahead.

They had to go forward until there was an area suitable to turn the large wagon around, but soon they were headed back toward Attingard.

Stone felt a great relief wash over him, accompanied by a great weariness. He lay down beside Eva and was lulled to sleep by the bumps and rocks of the wagon's gait.

"I know you said quickly, but we must stop on account of the horses," Granger said. Stone woke up as the wagon lurched to a stop. Stone didn't know how much time had passed, but the sun was high in the sky, past its zenith. He nodded, feeling groggy.

Eva was unchanged. After dripping more water down her throat, Stone saw to Penn and Sasha. He led them to the creek to drink. Granger had stopped there for that reason - a creek ran beside the road, making it a perfect place for the horses to drink their fill.

Eva's horses were hardy beasts. They had proven themselves capable many times over. Stone wondered if they hailed from Jullayah or if Eva had picked them up along the way, paid for by more kingly jewels. He had never asked her. The things he didn't know about her could pay a ransom. What surprised him was that he wanted to know, that he regretted not knowing. Stone wanted to know where she came from, how she had been raised in Jullayah when she was marked as a royal Allati, why she was skilled in the ways of a Kitarran warrior, and mostly why she had traveled across the wild country of the Midlands.

From long-neglected memories Stone thought he found the answer. He thought he could guess the reason for Eva's strange quest. He vowed to ask her everything. She would wake and assuage his curiosity. Then he would have to tell her about his own past - a thought that was less than pleasing. But perhaps she deserved it.

Something tickled his fur, unseen and unexplainable. A chill spread through him. Not a foreboding, fearful sensation, but one of hope and meaning. It could not be a coincidence that she had found him, saved him, bound him to her with honor. Maybe she was sent to guide him home and help him atone for his cowardice. Unmistakably, their lives were intertwined. If it was true that they were destined to journey forward together, then she couldn't die. Not with their path still stretching so far ahead.

When he was back in the wagon, trying once more to get some liquids into her, the hope and optimism left him. She was so ill. How could she survive the journey? Flora was gazing at Eva with a frown, asking if she could help in any way.

"Do you know anything of healing?" Stone asked her, not expecting a heartening response. Flora shook her head.

"Not for this kind of wound," she said, musing over Eva's sick form. "Granger told me not to ask, but how did it happen? How did she get hurt?"

"We were on our way to Allati, from Kitarra. A madman jumped us - her," Stone lied. "I didn't get there before he stabbed her and broke her arm, pulling her down from the horse."

The wagon began moving again as Granger called the horses to order. Flora was studying Eva as if she were an exotic flower.

"She is so beautiful, like a princess in a story," she said with child-like fancy. Stone wondered how old Flora really was. She looked weathered and worn down by life, but he doubted if she was older than Eva herself. "Why are you going to Allati?"

Stone didn't see any reason not to breathe life into his lie. "She grew up in a part of Kitarra that is very isolated. She was married, and her husband was cruel. He beat her and cut her hair. She did not know who she was. When she found out she was of royal Allati blood, the child of a runaway, she escaped her cruel husband to come to Allati. She is hoping to marry well, to shed her life of poverty."

Flora nodded as if that make a strange kind of sense, although Stone could tell she did not approve. "She is royal blood, but only a fool would think marriage to an Allati would be better. They are pigs to their wives - most of them, anyway."

Stone said nothing.

"So, are you her bodyguard or somethin'?" Flora asked, and Stone wished she would quit nagging him with questions and leave him and his worries in peace.

"Yes. She paid me to take her safely to Allati," he said with a great deal of self-loathing.

"I have never met a Kitarran hired sword before," Flora ventured. "You are as scary as they say," she added in a whisper, moving away from him. Stone was thankful the girl had some sense. He had been emitting irritable vibes for some time. An annoyed Kitarran was a dangerous Kitarran.

They stopped again to eat, and the couple made Stone a meal that he was surprised to find appealing. Flora was a good cook, Granger boasted, the thing he liked best in a wife. Flora beamed, as if that was all the praise she needed from her husband. Flora made some broth for Eva. Stone took it, and drip by drip managed to get some into her. He watered it down, doubting she would be able to keep it down, rich as it was.

Eva woke as he propped her up carefully. She opened her eyes and looked directly at him.

"Tayeh?" she said. "What - are you doing here?" The sentence was weak, and Stone almost didn't catch it. She took a sip of the broth and fell into oblivion.

Tayeh?

By the tree spirit's good graces, what was she talking about, mistaking him for the Guardian of Kitarra? It was unnerving.

Stone remembered his lessons as a child. Tayeh, Crea, Attin - the Guardians of the three realms. There was another one too, but Stone couldn't remember the name. The Guardian of beasts and trees and the deepest magic. He shook his head. It had been long ago.

They stopped for the night. How could they not? The horses were exhausted. Stone hated the inconvenience, but there was no bribe, no threat that would make a horse hold out all night without falling to its death from exhaustion.

Eva still burned with fever and shivers. Stone didn't sleep for fear she would slip away without his permission. He wondered morosely how long a person could burn with fever, take in hardly any water, and live. Not long, he thought. They needed to get to Attingard tomorrow or, something whispered darkly to him, it would be too late.

☾

Stone urged Granger to make all haste. By morning, Eva's breathing was shallow and uneven. At times, she fought for breath, and when Stone placed his hand upon her heart, it beat rapidly and irregularly. Every time he replaced her dressings, the wound looked nastier and smelled worse. He began to despair that not even the great master healers of Attingard could heal such a wound.

"How much farther?" Stone growled as midmorning came and went.

"A while yet," Granger said regretfully. The Rose Road was busier as they approached the royal city. There were wagons, carts, and foot travelers. Stone could barely stand it. If he could have taken Eva on horseback and raced to the city, he would have. But he couldn't.

Eva's cheeks were hollowed, her eyes sunken. The fever was whittling her away to skin and bones. Her fragility terrified him. He could sense her slipping away. Any breath could be her last. He begged her to hold on, a little longer, they were almost there. He pleaded with the spirits of destiny, hoping there were such spirits.

Attingard was a gated city, but the large gates never closed. The wall and the gates were a symbol of forgotten times. It was guarded, but travelers went by unchecked. With a wave of relief, the shadow of the arch fell over Stone as they passed beneath.

Granger knew where Stone wanted to go, but Stone told him again anyway. The Hall of Healers was situated next to the Royal Keep. And the Royal Keep was at the top of the hill that was the city of Attingard. Attingard had been built to resemble the great Kitarran city of Kilev with its lofty buildings and tiered walkways. But Attingard sat upon a hill; Kilev was at the foot of a great mountain. There was little to compare.

Kitarran architects had been commissioned generations ago to build the great buildings of Attingard. The master builders had spent nearly a generation completing the Royal Keep, Attin's temple, and the wall surrounding the city. Stone had seen his fair share of grand

Kitarran architecture, and Attingard was a fair likeness. It was grand and graceful, beautiful and secretive.

The Hall of Healers was no exception, echoing the greatness of the royal building beside it. But Stone would have found a hovel prettier if there was a person inside who could save Eva's life.

Granger pulled the wagon alongside the tall entrance. Stone leaped out and knocked on the door. A young woman opened it, dressed in a deep shade of red. Her eyes widened to see a Kitarran glaring down at her with feral desperation.

"Can I help you?" she asked nicely enough.

"My friend is very sick," he stated.

The woman opened the door wider. "Bring your friend in. I will get a master."

"I can't move her. She is in the wagon."

Another nod. "I will get the boys to bring a carrier." She went off into the building.

Granger and Flora promised to find stables for the horses and an inn for Stone, but Stone had no intention of leaving Eva's side.

Stone waited at the door anxiously. Each second Eva was alive was a small victory. Finally, the girl reappeared with two men. They carried a sling-like bed between two poles. Behind them came a man Stone assumed was a master. He was wizened with black hair heavily streaked with gray; his face looked slanted like all his features dissected toward his small, pursed mouth. He wore a frown as impressively as a king wears a crown.

"You have funds?" he asked as they went to the back of the wagon.

"Of course." Nothing was free in Attingard, although the master wouldn't care about money when he saw his patient.

The Allati's reaction was as Stone predicted. The master came around the back and saw Eva with her silver hair, her fair face. He gave Stone a look of astonishment before inundating "the boys" with his expedient orders. He put on an expert face and began to examine Eva. He said nothing, his frown deepening, if it were possible. He told "the boys" to move her, but Stone growled at him and lifted Eva himself, placing her on the carrier as carefully as a feather. The master nodded in affirmation at a job well done.

"Her name is Eva," Stone told him.

"Her wound looks poisoned," the healer told Stone as they followed the men inside. "What happened?"

"We were attacked. She was struck. Her arm is broken as well."

"There are some things to try, but I don't know if they will work. She is quite far gone," he mused almost to himself. "A woman of pure, royal blood! The king will be most intrigued. Pity he is in the east at the moment. Tell me her story."

Stone repeated the tale he told the nomads. Thankfully, the master accepted it. He looked like he had just found a treasure beyond compare. Stone sighed. Allati and their possessiveness. They collected women like crows hoarded trinkets.

The Hall of Healers was an actual hallway. Small rooms punctuated the wide corridor with practical closeness. Women in red walked on soft, slippered feet carrying everything from bowls of clear water to trays of strange implements.

They placed Eva on a bed in the first empty room. The master drew the thick red curtain across the opening. Another young woman appeared with a bowl of hot water that smelled of some strange herb.

Stone leaned against the wall and folded his arms across his chest, watching the healer at work. His heart was in his throat as Eva whimpered, almost soundlessly, when the healer removed her bandages and washed her wound with the hot water. The master used a thin metal tool to carefully inspect the wound.

Stone turned away. He couldn't watch Eva being poked and prodded. When he looked back, the master had placed a poultice over the wound and was wrapping her back up. Then the healer inspected her arm, touching it carefully, closing his eyes as he examined it under his fingers.

"The salve?" he asked the girl. She handed him a jar of a reddish balm. He rubbed it on her arm and wrapped her arm up tightly.

"The arm is not critical. It was cleanly broken. It will heal fine if the rest of her does," the healer told Stone. "Jesa here will feed her some broth and water if she can, and bathe her. You come with me and have a meal yourself and tell me more of her story."

Stone bristled at the command in the healer's voice but decided to ignore it. He nodded wearily. He couldn't remember when he last ate.

As they walked, the healer introduced himself as Master Whenting. He led Stone past more alcove-like rooms. Some were occupied; some of the patients were in obvious pain and discomfort. Some were sleeping. Some rooms had heavy red curtains drawn. Past that long, miserable hallway was a large kitchen with an area for eating with several sturdy tables. Whenting applied himself to washing in a large basin, scrubbing his hands up to his elbows. Another servant brought them soup. Stone washed and ate the ample meal. He thanked Whenting.

Whenting did not eat. He did not speak. He waited, gazing at Stone until Stone grew irritated with his passive-aggressive attitude.

"We came from Kitarra via the river ferry," Stone told him. "We were almost to the Rose Road when we were ambushed. I killed the men, but not before they struck Eva. I don't know who they were. Luckily, I ran into the nomads and bargained for a ride here."

"She should have been dead already. She must have a strong will." The cogs in the healer's mind could be seen turning. "She was clever to hire a guard like you. Tell me, how much do you charge for such a job?"

"Not much. She is a friend. That is why I am so anxious to see her well." It was another way of telling the master that he wasn't going anywhere.

"Excuse me. I must send a message," Whenting said. "Her arrival here will cause a stir. I would like to ask her after her parents. Hopefully I get the chance," he mused as he stood up. He hadn't taken a bite of his meal. "I will check in on Eva once more before I leave for the King's Keep."

"Thank you," Stone said again.

Stone finished another helping of soup. He checked in on Eva quickly. She was still under the ministrations of the healer folk. He headed out into the street to see if he could find what had become of the horses and pay the nomads. Eva had looked a little better. Her breathing was more even, at least.

Granger and Flora were waiting for him. They told him where the horses were stabled, and Stone thanked them with kind words and another three green gems. He had five amber gems left, less valuable, but still beautiful. He hoped it would be enough. Enough for what, he wasn't quite sure.

"Good luck to you, Kitarran. I hope your friend will be all right," Granger said. Flora nodded gravely from her seat beside him.

Stone bowed to them. The old Kitarran farewell came from his lips out of a deep memory, for he had not spoken the words for years. "May your path be clear but ever winding."

CHAPTER 60

ILLIAH

THE DEEP STILLNESS of the morning was as welcome as the warm sunshine pouring through the glazed window, infusing the map room with light. Located in an ancient wing of the palace, the map room's stone walls were thick and pitted, the mortar crumbling in places. The only sounds were the dust settling on the large table and Illiah's breath and every so often, the faint groan of Armeria as she resettled herself on the floor at his feet.

The stillness and silence were his own making. He had locked the door and ordered his guard to make sure he was not disturbed.

He had had the archives scoured. The map room was littered with the spoils: old documents, maps, bits of scrolls and books. He was relatively unfamiliar with Kitarra, and his new post necessitated he inform himself - quickly. He couldn't read, but then there were none left who could read the ancient Kitarran writs. He spent much of his free time pouring over maps and was rewarded with a clear picture in his mind of Kitarra's coast and the Islands.

His first orders as First Defender had been to evacuate the coast.

Every house, farm, and village along the ocean and inlet of the river had been abandoned. They had been replaced by watchtowers, hastily built, but sturdy enough to house a small contingent of guards. Each watchtower had the means to light a signal fire big enough to see from miles and miles away.

Interim homes were found for the people and their livestock. No one complained; no one wanted to contend with the raiders. As a result, Kilev was brimming with refugees. The Peace Guards were hard put to settle disputes among the worried and upheaved citizens.

The queen would often walk the city to reassure her people as best she could. They were thankful for it - just the sight of their sovereign calmed troubled minds and tongues.

As Illiah pondered the maps, acquainting himself with the dozens of tiny islands, named and dotted by homesteads and villages, some dating back hundreds if not thousands of years, hope began to grow and bud within him. It seemed impossible every one of them was ravaged and destroyed. Surely a handful, at least, would have escaped the carnage of the invaders.

Illiah's ships had come back. Their report had been dire. All his hope shattered.

He had sent out an armada. Any remaining vessel that could sail at speed was acquired by the queen and added to her growing navy. Many Kitarrans had been volunteered, including his friend Turk.

He nominated Turk as his sea captain and sent him out with the large fleet at his back. Any lingering raiders wouldn't dare attack such a force.

The Kitarran fleet flooded the islands and saw no sign of the enemy. But there was also no sign of any village or house left undamaged. Not one person found alive. Not. One.

It was heartbreaking. All of Kitarra reeled from the loss. Illiah's ships had been too late.

Illiah cursed the drunkard Scytt who had not compiled the armada immediately. Perhaps they could have scared off the raiders before they finished their plunder. Scytt had claimed he had too few soldiers, too few boats. And that was true. His men were few. The Peace Guards spread out over the realm.

But still, Illiah knew Scytt could have wielded the iron law of the queen and taken what ships were needed, along with able men and women to sail them. Scytt had lacked determination, or courage, or common sense - Illiah would not waste any more thought on the man.

Once the tragedy of the islands was known, the palace was overrun by people, young and old, wishing to help, to fight. Illiah didn't turn anyone away. Many Kitarrans learned to fight and wield a sword as youngsters; Kitarra was a realm of warriors, after all. And many excellent archers volunteered. Most were shepherds who honed their skill protecting their livestock from the big predators of the mountains.

Kitarra's army grew.

When Illiah was not overseeing the accelerated training of the new recruits, he was in council with the queen, or her councilors, or meeting with his captains or scouts. He had messengers running and riding all over Kitarra, trying to keep the realm updated. He summoned most of the Peace Guards to help train others or captain under his rule. He wished fervently for a handful of his foster father's fast, long-legged horses.

Then there was his son and Talo. The boys were patient with him, but he felt guilty. He had little time for his own child.

Rhyl and Talo were inseparable. Illiah was both thankful and guilty that Rhyl had someone to keep him company. The boys didn't ask why he was kept busy, kept away from them and their games. They sensed the disquiet around them. They spent most of their time with Mehmet, who was content to teach the children.

Aisha was not. The young Kitarran warrior had begged Illiah to let him join the army. Illiah was not foolish enough to say no - he needed Aisha. He needed any leader he could find, even if he was only sixteen. Aisha was a capable young man. So, he robbed his boys of another friend. At least the boys had Mehmet and Selene.

Illiah sighed.

Selene. He had been avoiding her company for the last few weeks, ever since she had flattered him by kissing him. At least he thought it was flattery. Maybe that was his pride speaking. Since that day, she had attempted to get him alone again, but he never allowed it. He made sure there was always something, preferably someone, between them.

Yes, Selene was beautiful, sweet, and smart. Illiah appreciated her as a friend to his son, a loyal servant to the queen, but it was impossible and distasteful that she would kiss him. He didn't want her. He didn't need her. He had a wife. He would never betray Eva, even if miles and years lay between them.

Eva was watching him, not always, but sometimes. Rhyl felt it strongly as well. If Eva saw him with another woman, it would break her heart. He would never do that to her. Never. Besides, the stirrings of the body were nothing next to the turmoil around him, nothing compared to the challenge ahead. Keeping Kitarra - and his sons - safe was foremost in his mind.

The map room was where Selene had come to him under the guise of hospitality. Part of him sensed her desire from the first but chose to ignore it, thinking her too shy, too innocent to act upon it. He had been wrong. He wasn't sure why he allowed her to get so close. He had been distracted and lonely. She was a friend - had been a friend. Now he didn't know what she was. He couldn't allow it to happen again. He didn't know how to tell her of his apathy without breaking her heart, so he avoided her. It wasn't right, or mature, but he had enough on his mind without fretting over the delicate emotions of a young woman.

Illiah straightened his back. His bones snapped and creaked. Armeria was instantly alert, beseeching him with her amber-brown eyes, her tail thumping against the stone floor with pleasure from the simple contact. She rolled onto her back in submission, a doggy smile on her face. Illiah rubbed her tummy with his foot.

The map before him was not of the Islands or any part of Kitarra. This one was older, more faded, and had not been crafted by a Kitarran guild master.

The Tarm. A place he hadn't even heard of before coming to Kitarra. The queen assured him the Tarm had been growing on her mind over the past few decades. The piece of no-man's-land lay between the Southeastern Ridge and the sea. It was grassy and nearly flat, home to a single city built around an ancient temple from a time long forgotten.

The story went that around fifty years ago, a man birthed the city. An exile, a criminal. He gathered other forgotten and castaway souls and built a home for himself. Other outcasts were eager to follow him, eager for leadership. They came from Kitarra, Allati, the Midlands, even Jullayah. The leader bartered for supplies as best he could with both Allati and Kitarra and began farming the brutal land in the Tarm - no simple task. It was a place of harsh winds and cold winters, the ground rocky and unpredictable. But he kept to himself, causing no trouble, so Kitarra ignored him. The place was now run by a man named Cotoch, who claimed to be this man's son. Arrah had met him some years ago.

She described Cotoch as a man of middle years, ambitious, and clever - a leader. He had visited Kitarra eight years earlier and came well dressed and well spoken, surprising the queen and her councilors. At the time, he wished to trade with her for weapons, offering all Kitarrans safe passage through his lands. She had asked why. He spoke of the need to protect his people from the wandering folk of the Midlands who preyed on the weak. He claimed his people were the ones keeping the riffraff from Kitarra's borders.

At the time Arrah thought it a small price to pay for a truce with the Tarm and to keep the southern border of Kitarra free from the wandering folk. Trade and truce were not the only things Cotoch took away from his visit. He also found himself a wife, the daughter of a well-connected Kitarran merchant.

Arrah had agreed to the trade but sent some of her most trusted men to spy on the self-proclaimed lord. Her spies reported, to her surprise, that Cotoch had amassed a considerable army, even several Kitarran warriors. It had been disquieting, but she had not the means to stop him. He never lifted a sword against her people, claiming a desire for peace. She had no reason to doubt his truce.

After word of the lost islands spread through Kitarra, a message arrived from Cotoch. He sent his concerns and condolences and wished to meet with an interesting proposition for the queen.

"Cotoch has offered five hundred men," Arrah told Illiah, waving the letter under his nose. "Five hundred men! My sources tell me they are well trained and disciplined."

"But can you trust this man?" Illiah asked.

"I don't know if we have any other choice. Your recruits are willing, but they are bakers, farmers, smiths. They are not warriors."

"They will be."

"But when? A year from now? We need men now."

"A man who fights for his home is worth ten that fight for money."

Queen Arrah nodded but looked unconvinced.

"We have riches, but not warriors. Cotoch wants gold and steel, and he has the fighters we need. He wishes to meet at the Kitarran border in six days with an example of what he offers. I need you to meet him and tell me what you think."

"I have told you what I think," Illiah retorted, annoyed. Migel, one of the high councilors, was listening and growled, his ears back. Illiah ignored him and kept his eyes on the queen.

"Illiah, I need you to do this."

Illiah crossed his arms, giving the queen a level look. "I don't think this is a good idea."

"Can you at least meet with him? I beg you to consider. And I am the queen - I do not beg," she added with a touch of her usual fire, her eyes flashing.

Illiah sighed. "Fine. I will meet him, but I offer no promises. You have trusted my judgment so far."

"I know."

Migel glared as Illiah stalked off to make preparations. No one spoke to the queen the way he did. It wasn't discourtesy exactly. It was just that when Illiah knew he was right, he wasn't easily swayed. And his gut was telling him Cotoch was not a man to be trusted.

That had been three days ago. The map of the Tarm didn't offer Illiah wisdom or answers. Illiah wished he had a better way to educate himself about a man whose history was mostly rumor and conjecture. Illiah had no idea what to expect, but he would prepare for anything.

Illiah had Aisha select his best men to accompany them. The Lord of the Tarm assumed them weak and undermanned, under attack and desperate. He planned to show this man that Kitarra was not without resources.

Preparations were being made to leave that afternoon. Illiah hoped they would only be gone for five days. Five days was five days more than he wanted to be away from Rhyl.

He had spoken with Rhyl that morning as he spent time playing with him and Talo, a rare occasion of late. They had played blocks and swords, dragon hunt, and a special game using an ornate set of decorated players Mehmet had given the boys. A game beyond their years, though they played it well for youngsters. After lunch, Illiah secluded himself in the map room, more to gather his thoughts than anything else, and now the boys would be waiting for him to say goodbye.

Selene stood in the cool, empty corridor on the way to his chambers, her hands clasped together nervously. It was dreadfully apparent she was waiting to speak with him. Illiah had no desire to speak to her with his thoughts swirling about his upcoming journey and the self-proclaimed lord's offer. But he didn't want to be an ass.

He stopped beside her. Armeria came to sit right next to his feet, one of her paws on his boot.

"Lord Illiah." Selene's voice was small, her pale skin flushed. "The queen tells me you are riding to the Tarm to meet with Lord Cotoch."

"Yes. I am leaving right away. I was just going to wish the boys goodbye."

"You shouldn't go," Selene exclaimed with none of her usual demure politeness.

"The queen bids me, and I go."

"Ha! You scorn the queen on every occasion. She loves you for it. But Illiah, please, send someone else. Aisha, Turk - not yourself." She took his hand in hers and kissed his palm. Illiah wanted to snatch it away, but couldn't bring himself to do it.

"Selene, I will be back in five days. Please watch over the boys for me. Keep them busy."

She nodded, and a deep frown settled over her fair features. She kissed Illiah's hand again and dropped it, walking off into the silent corridor without another word of protest.

Illiah ground his teeth as he followed the corridor to his chambers. The last thing he needed was a love struck girl questioning his decisions. He had enough on his mind besides the fragile heart of a misguided, infatuated woman.

The boys were surprisingly quiet when he entered the chamber. Then Illiah saw Mehmet was with them and it made sense. The old Kitarran had a knack for bringing calm to the boisterous boys. The boys knew Illiah was there to say goodbye. They came over to him with sober expressions.

Rhyl wrapped his little arms around Illiah's neck and kissed his cheek, murmuring words of love and promising to be good. Illiah squeezed him tightly making Rhyl giggle. It was harder than he expected to let go.

"I will be home in five days, Rhyl," Illiah said to his son, but he was looking at Talo, who stood silent and brooding. Both boys were unhappy about his upcoming absence. Nothing Illiah could do or say would appease them.

Talo didn't say anything or offer an embrace. Illiah recognized the longing in the boy's face, so he knelt beside him and embraced the tall boy. Talo's arms came up around him. Illiah gave him a little squeeze, and when he released him, Talo was smiling, just a little.

"Be safe, my lord," Mehmet said. Illiah nodded and stood tall. Rhyl went and stood beside Talo. The two boys looked identical in their unease. Illiah resented the necessity of leaving them.

Illiah's troops awaited him in the main courtyard. He looked on them with pride. Thirty mounted men and women, another thirty foot soldiers. They all wore forest-green cloaks. Each had a brooch of the Kitarran cendari flower in gold pinned upon their shoulders. Their helms were simple in design but made of strong Kitarran steel. Illiah wore the same green cloak, the brooch upon his shoulder that of the First Defender, a sword through a cendari flower.

The banners of Kitarra flew from the standard bearers, the gold unfurled in the spring sunshine, moving gently with the breeze. The camp wagons would follow with supplies. It was only for five days, Illiah told himself. Five days was not a significant amount of time, right?

Aisha held his reins ready for him. Illiah mounted up onto his mare and kicked off. His army followed him.

As they rode through Kilev, winding down the hill, people came out to greet them, waving golden scarves, grinning, shouting encouragements. Pride shone in their faces - and hope. They called Illiah's name.

It made him queasy.

They wanted so much from him. They wanted him to bring peace, victory. They looked to him to salve their wounds, and he knew he would fall short. They loved him, and Illiah found that he loved them too. He loved the city, the people. He cared about their hurts, their lost souls and comrades. He would do everything he could to help them. Guardians help him, he would. He just hoped Rhyl would not pay the price for his gallantry.

A line of standing stones marked the border of Kitarra. The stones were impressive, taller than Illiah, broad as three men. They made a curving, uneven line as far as he could see. Illiah wondered who had decided where the line fell, for on either side the land looked identical. It was grassy and flat, the foreboding mountain range rose to the northeast, and to the south, the knobbly, rocky hills led to the cliffs at the sea. His time studying maps was paying off.

Cotoch was already waiting. His camp stretched along his side of the line. Red-brown tents, made of heavy canvas, were emblazoned with his chosen symbol, a black bear. The largest tent was surrounded by five guards, dressed in dyed leather armor to match the tents. The sharpened heads of their spears glittered in the noonday sun.

Illiah gave the order for his men to set up camp. He signaled for Aisha and seven guards to attend him as he went to meet the Lord of Mahlas. He saw no reason to wait.

"I am Lord Illiah, First Defender of Kitarra. I have been sent by Queen Arrah to meet with Lord Cotoch," Illiah spoke to the guards. He didn't dismount; let them look up at him.

Two guards disappeared within the tent. Illiah was forced to wait. He didn't like waiting. And he was tired from two days of travel. Was he so soft that two days on horseback was such a terrible thing? He remembered the months during the war he spent without bed or roof. Sometimes the war felt like a lifetime ago. Sometimes it felt like it had happened to another man.

The tent door shifted, and a man stepped into the sun. Illiah could not determine the man's age. Fine lines haloed his eyes as he squinted in the bright light, though there was no gray in his dark hair. His clothes were as fine as any scrupulous Kitarran merchant. He smiled up at Illiah in greeting.

"Lord Illiah, welcome," Cotoch said. "Please join me for refreshments."

Illiah accepted and swung down from his horse. His primal instinct decided it was a good thing that he stood taller than Cotoch.

Illiah took a deep breath to settle his animosity. He had no reason to distrust this man, yet his intuition was screaming at him.

Aisha stayed at Illiah's side, Martel stood by the door. The others arrayed themselves just outside. His men knew what he wanted of them. Illiah did not need to bark commands.

Inside the tent, Illiah instantly deduced several things about the Lord of the Tarm. First, he enjoyed his comforts. Furs lined the ground. Furniture transformed the tent into a palace: a well-fashioned table and chairs, a cushioned couch, and a large bed for sleeping. Illiah's own tent would hold a tiny fraction of Cotoch's luxury. Not that Illiah needed such cosseting. Second, Cotoch had wealth, and he wanted Illiah to know it. Wealth was another kind of weapon. Cotoch was ambitious, that was also clear, his smile arrogant. Illiah had no reason to believe Cotoch was charitable in his offer of five hundred men. He wanted something.

Cotoch led him to the table and poured them both wine. He sat, and Illiah followed suit, placing himself opposite. They studied each other, taking a sip of the wine - which was really very good.

"My Lord Illiah, I knew it was too much to hope that the queen would come herself. I would have been honored to receive her," Cotoch began.

"The queen cannot leave her city, as you can imagine."

"Yes, of course. My condolences. The state of Kitarra grieves me deeply, so many souls lost." Cotoch sounded sincere. "As I said in my message to the queen, I have five hundred men ready. They are highly trained, highly disciplined."

"For a price," Illiah added bluntly.

Cotoch winced. "I cannot sacrifice my men without recompense."

"I would see these men, and then perhaps we can discuss more," Illiah said, knowing Arrah wished for him to see the merit of the deal. Illiah couldn't yet - not nearly - but he wanted to see for himself what kind of fighting force this man had, be him friend or foe.

"Of course!" Cotoch said, clapping his hands in delight. "They are awaiting my command to begin the demonstration. Would you care to follow me? Our refreshments will find us, I assure you."

Illiah allowed Cotoch to lead him beyond his tents where a large field had been prepared for his men's demonstration. The grass had been trampled flat. The men lined up at attention, five hundred strong. An army. They wore leather armor and stoic faces. A man stepped forward and knelt before Cotoch.

"This is Captain Thire. He commands this host."

Captain Thire rose and gave Illiah a polite bow. Something in the man's eyes was unpleasant. Illiah couldn't pinpoint what it was, but it sent another warning through his body. He was aware of his longsword at his hip, a Kitarran weapon, of strong Kitarran steel. Not a latha, not yet, but it was still reassuring. He was also aware of Aisha at his back who bore a long, powerful latha with the skills to wield it. And his other guards were nearly as ominous. He left Armeria at camp thinking it best not to have her at his heels, but now he wished he had brought her.

Cotoch told the captain to begin. Table and chairs were set up, and Illiah took a seat to watch Cotoch's army perform. Cotoch ate from the dishes provided. Illiah did not. He was growing uninterested in his host's hospitality.

The five hundred men took up a considerable amount of space. Twenty disciplined lines, twenty-five men per line. Line by line they advanced. Performing first with swords, then bows, then spears. They were capable, fast. Not one missed a target. Illiah could not find anything amiss about them. They were what Cotoch had promised: five hundred well-equipped, schooled warriors.

"Who trained your men?" Illiah asked, his first question.

"Thire, for one. I have several other captains in my city who are equally exceptional instructors."

Illiah nodded.

"How old are they?"

"The youngest is eighteen, the oldest three and thirty. Young, strong, in their prime." Cotoch smiled smugly.

"Do they have families, wives?"

"No. Sweethearts, perhaps. But no families. You will make no widows or beggar children if they die at your command."

Illiah rose and walked through the contingent of men. He didn't ask Cotoch's permission. Cotoch hopped up and followed him, showing no sign of irritation at Illiah's presumption. Illiah wanted to look into their faces, measure their character as best he could. It was mostly futile. They stood still and resolute under his circumspection.

"Well, my lord? What do you think?" Cotoch asked as Illiah made his way from the warriors.

Illiah paused at the table and took a sip of his wine before turning to face Cotoch.

"No."

Illiah watched with a certain satisfaction as Cotoch's congenial mask slipped away, exposing his irritation. "I do not trust you or your men," Illiah told him.

Cotoch raised a brow in surprise, trying to look disappointed, but Illiah could see his rage. This man did not like it when things did not go his way.

"All I want to do is help Kitarra in its time of great need."

A lie. Illiah was sure Cotoch had other motives. He couldn't guess what they were exactly, but his intuition told him they were far from noble.

"I know Queen Arrah wants these men. She will be displeased with you," Cotoch said, his voice holding an edge of dismay - and warning.

"The queen defers to my good judgment," Illiah assured him amiably.

"Your good judgment? The opinion of a foreigner? I know who you are." Cotoch's voice turned scathing, mocking. "You are the queen's prisoner, her slave, not her confidant. You are a fool to think she cares about your safety. She is using you like she will use your son."

Aisha stepped forward in anger, eager to put Cotoch in his place. Illiah put his hand out to halt the hasty youth.

"We are alike, Illiah. You and I. We just want our people to be safe, to find justice in a world run by tyrants and mystics. We are the men who are fearless, unafraid to do what is necessary. We are the grit under the fingernails of life. Why should we let our lives be used and cast aside by those who claim power and knowledge? The queen does not own you."

"And that is supposed to make me trust you?" Illiah responded. It was time to go before tempers ran hot. "My lord, thank you for the demonstration, but the answer is still no," Illiah said, giving Cotoch a shallow bow. It was half in mockery, but Cotoch might not perceive that.

"I am disappointed in you, Illiah. Your wife was easier to convince."

Illiah swung back toward Cotoch. Gone was any sign of geniality. Cotoch's eyes were cold, his mouth set in a hard line. A chill rippled through Illiah even as he was confused by Cotoch's words.

Ignore him. Keep walking.

"She is beautiful, by the way - your wife," Cotoch said loudly as Illiah walked. Illiah halted, even though he knew a bait when he heard one. Why would Cotoch speak of Eva? The man could gain nothing by it. Illiah was right not to trust him. Illiah wanted nothing more than to keep walking, to ignore the worry Cotoch's words invoked.

He couldn't.

"You know nothing of my wife."

Cotoch smiled. A sly, evil expression that made Illiah flex his restless fists. Cotoch was playing him, and Illiah knew it.

"I met your lovely wife about four weeks ago. Eva came my way looking to barter passage to Kitarra. She carried a small fortune in gems, but she still preferred to pay with her body. How could I say no? She is a beautiful woman. I fucked her, Illiah. And she liked it - most of it anyhow."

Illiah was rooted to the ground. His feet had turned to stone, but his hands had not. He didn't remember drawing his sword, but he heard the harsh sound of the metal sliding from the sheath. Aisha muttered something and more weapons were drawn. Cotoch was grinning in pure satisfaction. He wanted a fight.

Lies. It was all lies. Illiah forced his mind around the concept. It couldn't be true. Eva was in Jullayah, safe, in the Keep.

At least he wanted to believe she was.

He had enemies in Jullayah. Had Eva been forced to flee? Had Serac dared to hurt her again? He knew his wife. She would never lay with a man like Cotoch, not willingly. Cotoch was a crazy, slighted man. His lies were Illiah's perfect poison.

He forced himself to sheath his sword. Cotoch had five hundred men at his back, Illiah had a handful in comparison. He would not fight on threats and lies. It took all his strength, but he turned his back on the Lord of the Tarm. Cotoch laughed as he left.

"We are leaving," Illiah said quietly to Aisha as they walked. "Now."

What a complete waste of his time. Next time the queen would heed his judgment.

The Kitarran camp was not as elaborate as Cotoch's. His men were still setting up when Illiah called the order to dismantle. His soldiers tried to hide their discouragement. They would be camping under the stars that night. The sun had already set.

Illiah wanted to put as much space between them and Cotoch as possible. He would not be able to sleep knowing Cotoch and his mocking words were close. And Cotoch's five hundred men. He fought the impulse to stalk back over to Cotoch and put a sword to his throat - he wanted to know with certainty what Cotoch said was a lie. It had to be a lie.

It was full dark before Illiah called his company to halt. His men were tired, their horses weary. They built fires and hoped there would be no rain. Illiah planned to sleep under his cloak like he had many and more nights in the past. Aisha set the watch and came back to join Illiah at the fire.

"At least we know the measure of the man, sir," Aisha said quietly. The others nodded and grunted in agreement. "He is less than honorable to speak such lies."

Illiah didn't say anything but nodded in agreement. He prodded the fire with a stick. His heart was in the process of being crushed, suffocated, and squeezed into a shape so unrecognizable, a meat grinder would do less damage. Images ravaged his mind. Eva and her pale hair, her fair skin, Cotoch rearing above her, his long black hair masking out hers. His cruel mouth on her body, on the very places Illiah loved best. He lay down and tried to sleep, but the images were haunting. His mind was relentless in its torment.

Not surprisingly, Illiah slept poorly. He roused his company with the dawn.

Illiah saddled his young mare, chosen from the queen's stables. She was a beauty of a horse, with a glossy chestnut coat and a white blaze on her nose. She was as fiery as her coloring and stamped impatiently. Illiah crooned to her, his full attention on the horse.

A feral growl rattled Illiah's spine, breaking his concentration. The sound reverberated through Illiah's skull into the recess of his brain reserved for nightmares. The snarling, choking, rasping noise came from his uandian. The dog's hackles were mountain ridges, her ears flattened plains. Armeria had her teeth locked on a man's arm. The man wore the green cloak all Illiah's men wore, the same dyed leather jerkin, but Illiah did not recognize him. Illiah made it a point to know all his people, be they cook or warrior or scout or blacksmith.

This stranger was still upright, even with Ari trying to take him down. The man had a long, lethal dagger in his hand - the hand firmly lodged in Armeria's teeth. His other hand aimed for Ari's head. The blow fell wrong as Illiah used his weight to pin the impostor to the ground, his own long dagger pressed into the stranger's throat. Armeria dropped her burden and backed away. Aisha was there in an instant, as were most of Illiah's guards.

"Who are you?" Illiah asked the man through gritted teeth. Aisha assessed Ari. With a nod, Aisha told Illiah his dog was all right. She whimpered, her ears still pinned.

The man didn't say a word. His hand was bleeding where Ari's strong teeth had punctured his skin. Illiah pressed his boot firmly on the wound, and the man cried out in pain, but still wouldn't talk. Two of Illiah's men took the captive by the arms. Illiah was free to stand.

"He was sent here to kill you, that is clear by the dagger in his hand," Aisha said, coming to the same conclusion as Illiah. "He would have succeeded if Ari hadn't stopped him."

"Yes. Good girl," Illiah said, leaning down a little to scratch his dog's ears. Her tongue came out, and she gave him a doggy smile.

So Cotoch wanted him dead. Illiah wondered if that had been his desire all along. Or only after Illiah had turned down his offer. A dangerous man, indeed. Illiah shook off the feeling of cold dread. Without Ari, he would have a dagger in his heart.

"Search the camp. Make sure we have no more visitors," Illiah commanded. "I am afraid we will find one of our watchers disposed of," he added, his stomach churning.

"What of this one? Should we put him to the sword?"

The captive glared up at Illiah with a look of venom. If he had suc-ceeded in assassinating Illiah, Illiah's men would have cut him apart. This man had been willing to die following Cotoch's orders. Illiah looked at the man, pondering, thinking of Cotoch and the man's lies.

"Hold him down," Illiah instructed. His men did. The captive's eyes widened, but he looked prepared to accept his fate. "Death is too quick for you," Illiah told him. The man struggled then, pleading. Illiah was deaf to it.

Illiah pulled his great sword from its sheath.

"Hold out his arm."

Illiah's men were loyal and obedient to a fault. He raised his sword and brought it down on the man's bitten hand with great force and precision - he didn't want to harm his men.

The captive screamed as his hand was hewn. Illiah's blade was sharp, the force strong enough to cut through the thin bones of the wrist. Illiah's men winced at the horrifying sound of the man's pain.

"Bind the wound. Send this scum back to his master."

The blood did not sicken him. Grit of life, indeed. Was that all he was? The queen's henchman? Her sword? After everything, his blade was still drawing blood, and it didn't bother him anymore.

CHAPTER 61

EVA

EVA dreamed.

She dreamed of a little boy playing in the sand with hair white as snow. The silty river water lapped his ankles, and he cried out in delight. He chased waves and built cities in the sand, he found precious treasures in perfect round, smooth river rocks. There was another boy too. A brother who was not a brother. He was as different from the other as sand is from water.

They drew in the sand together. They walked unspeaking. They laughed and pretended they were each other's greatest adversary. A woman watched over the children with a little smile, walking barefoot in the sand. Seeing her was a persistent ache in Eva's gut. The woman was sweet and pretty with long, brown hair, tussled from the river breeze.

As Eva dreamed, the constant, agonizing pain diminished slightly - until the woman. She couldn't breathe. She was suffocating under the pain. The pain lived in her side, spreading to her heart until it was ready to burst. Eva could not command her breathing to slow. She could not contain the agony of her body and her hurting soul.

And the thirst gnawed at her, competing with the pain. Sometimes, water dripped into her mouth, and it was like honey, but sometimes it made her cough and her stomach spin.

When Eva managed to open her eyes, Tayeh was waiting for her. Why did he care? He had betrayed her, tossed her aside like the spent pawn she was. His yellow eyes were brimmed with concern, wet with fear. She almost begged him to tell her that he still loved her.

He was afraid because she was dying. Eva knew it, and it made her angry. Sometimes she couldn't remember why. The pain was every-thing, her whole existence. But she knew she had to keep breathing. She had to try to calm her raging body.

Sometimes a man visited Eva's dreams. He looked sad, lost, and oh so lonely. She yearned for him to reach out for her so he could hold her secure in his love. His hands were strong - if she could just reach him, he could pull her from her pain, and they would both find comfort and solace.

He was so far away. In a boat filled with grim warriors, rocking among the waves, watching the shoreline with intensity. Eva saw him in a seaside village that was more a burnt husk than a dwelling of people. The dead were everywhere. Men, the elderly, little children. No women.

Even in her dream, the inescapable loss trapped her like iron chains. She knew where the women were, but she could not save them from their cruel fate any more than the warriors could. She wept dry tears for them. Her body would not give her more.

A time came when there was nothing, only pain. Her body begged her to give in, to die, to banish the pain forever. Only the little voice inside her heart held her back. Not yet, it said. You haven't found them yet.

Then she felt something change. There came a coolness, the pain lessened. She thought, perhaps, she was really asleep.

Eva opened her eyes. It was nearly dark, only a small lantern faintly illuminated a small room. She sensed another person in the room, but she couldn't even move her head to see. Her body ached, gripped by shivers.

"Evangeline," a soft, feathery voice spoke. Out of the darkness came the form of a man looming over her. His face was close to hers. She could have reached to touch him if she had been able or inclined.

The man was young, she supposed. He had long, wavy hair that contrasted against the night, the same shade as her own, moonlight over midnight water. He wore a white shirt, unlaced in a lazy fash-ion, a hint of the muscular form exposed. He was very handsome.

His eyes were like liquid sunshine, pale yellow and orange. Eva took a breath.

"Attin." She wasn't sure if she managed to whisper the name of the Guardian or if it was her mind's voice that spoke.

He smiled and nodded.

Above him, above both of them, fanned a great pair of white wings. They filled the room and came down to encapsulate them both in a feathery cave. Attin moved his frame and sat on the edge of her bed, his wings fanning out behind him. He was a striking creature.

"You are in Attingard. You were brought here to the Hall of Healing, but they can't cure you. Your guard will find out in the morning, and it will break his heart. The master gave you something that will help for a time, but the poison is too strong." Attin gestured to where Stone lay sprawled and asleep on the floor. Eva felt a pang of gratitude toward the Kitarran. He had brought her here, to save her, and she would die anyway. A single tear slid down her face, hot and real.

"Sshh," Attin said catching her tear with his finger. His touch was strange, less tangible than Tayeh, less menacing than Crea, not quite real. "Do not cry. I am here. You are special, Evangeline. I know you, daughter of my body. I will heal you, but you must stay here in Allati. We need you here. Your people need you here - the magic in your blood runs clear and strong. Your gifts cannot be wasted. I can train you myself, and your sons after you."

Eva opened her mouth to ask a question, but no sound came out of her dry throat. Did he know she was a *sanarii*, but not that she was trained by another Guardian?

"We will talk again. You will need rest. Many days of rest, there is plenty of time. Perhaps after the king finds you a husband, I will find you again. Sleep now."

And Eva learned what it was to receive a healing gift.

Attin placed one hand upon her brow and the other upon her wounded side and the poison left her body. The pain disappeared, drawn out through his hands. Her arm stopped hurting. Her side felt numb with the lack of pain, and her breath came deep and easy. Her shivering was gone. Her heart slowed, and she closed her eyes. Sleep. Real, nourishing sleep followed.

A child was crying. At first it was distant and hazy, then loud and insistent, bringing Eva fully from the edge of sleep.

A child, crying out in pain: the most piteous sound imaginable, urging Eva's maternal instincts into action. Rhyl's name was on her lips before her sleep-addled mind remembered it could not possibly be her son. Rhyl was far, far away.

She couldn't help the child. She could barely move her body, or lift her arm to wipe a greasy strand of hair from her eyes. Her arms were stiff. Her legs were stiff. Her back was sore from being wrought with shivers and convulsions. For a moment she forgot the child and remembered Attin's gift. She smiled. She was alive. She would live. She would get to Kitarra.

The child's cry continued, becoming hoarse and desperate. Her heart hurt in empathy.

The room she was in was small and dim. The door was a curtain, and beyond it, somewhere, was the child. The Hall of Healers, Attin had told her. In Attingard, the heart of Allati.

She could move her head. Stone had stirred, looking beyond the curtain, his gaze following the sound of the crying child. There were shouts and the patter of feet. Stone's expression mirrored Eva's feelings about the suffering child.

"Stone?" Her voice was not even a whisper. But he heard it.

His expression shifted from stormy sky to summer sun, his yellow eyes brightening. He was at her side in an instant with a cup of water, which she wanted more than anything.

She took it and held it to her own lips with shaking hands. Stone helped her in the end, she was so weak.

"You look better," Stone said as a great sigh of relief.

"I am better, mostly, just weak. Attin came to me last night. He healed me," Eva told him. Stone narrowed his eyes, assessing her for signs of fever madness. Then a smile across his face. He wrapped his great furry arms around her and gave her a squeeze, gently enough.

"Thank the Guardians - Guardian, I guess," he said into her ear. He put her at arm's length, looking serious again. "We are in Attingard.

You were dying - I had no choice but to bring you here," he whispered severely. "I have told them you are escaping Kitarra from your abusive husband to come here to make a new life, which means finding a new husband. You hired me as your bodyguard to see you safely back to the land of your mother."

Eva couldn't help but roll her eyes.

"So, when they talk to you, that's the story. Pretend to be interested in finding a husband while I find a way out of here. If they suspect you want to leave, they will make it impossible for you to do so. You will be a prisoner." He cringed as another round of heart splitting wails came from down the hall. "It must be soon. They will expect me to leave once you are better, my job being finished."

"Can't I insist you stay here to protect me until my husband can do it for me?"

"That might work, but still, sooner is better."

Eva sighed. She didn't know how long it would take to get her strength back. It wouldn't be overnight.

"I'll get you something to eat," Stone told her.

She nodded, feeling tired already. But those cries, she didn't know if she could ignore them. They rattled her deeply.

Before Stone returned with some food, a man pulled back the curtain. He had a sharp look about him. He was shadowed by a young woman dressed in red. He saw Eva's alert state and looked startled, then pleased.

"Ah, Eva. I am Master Whenting. You are looking better. How do you feel?" He began to pull up her shift to check her injury. She started at his forward approach, but he didn't seem to care. His hands were cold against her skin as he peeled back the bandage. His eyes furrowed as he saw her wound, now a thin, neat red line.

"You are healed," he mused, then he turned a smile up at her, a strange smile. She had never met a man less suited to smiling. "Is it possible?" His eyes were alight, his voice barely more than a whisper. "Is it possible this is the work of Attin? It must be. It must have been Attin himself. There are stories that he still walks among us and heals those who are worthy. Praise be to Attin! The king will hear of this immediately," Whenting went on. "Let us just take those threads out.

They are not needed anymore." He pulled a tiny pair of shears from some deep pocket and snipped the threads that had once held her skin together. The sensation of the threads being pulled out made her shiver uncomfortably, but it was over quick enough.

"Where is your guard?" Whenting asked.

"He went to find me something to eat."

"Most excellent. He is an honorable servant. He can return to Kitarra, now that you are healed," he mentioned. Eva had the feeling Whenting disliked Stone. Not surprising, Stone's presence would be intimidating for anyone.

"I have asked him to stay here with me until I am settled, until my new husband can assure my safety," Eva told him. Whenting nodded as if that made sense, but he didn't look pleased about it.

"We will move you to the upper level of the Healer Hall. You will have an elegant room and attentive servants. It is close to the Royal Keep, and I know the king will want to meet you as soon as he arrives back from the east. You must know how excited we all are to have another female of such pure royal blood. One touched by Attin himself!" His face was flushed with excitement. "Tell me about your mother."

"My mother? She died when I was small. I don't know much about her, except that she was from Allati. Her name was Jaia. It wasn't until recently that a traveler came to my home, an isolated island community, and told me what I really was. My husband was unfaithful and cruel, so I decided to leave Kitarra and come here."

"A wise choice. You will be loved and prized above all others. Soon a husband will be selected for you and you will be happy." He patted her hand. "Jesa here will help you with your ablutions. You will be weak from your sickness."

"Master?" Eva asked him as he turned to leave. "The child, the one who was crying? Is it okay?"

Whenting sighed heavily. "Lord Pruit's young son. He was burned badly, over half his body. I don't know if he will live. He is only three, so young for such a terrible injury."

Eva's eyes pricked, the poor child. Burns were terrible. The pain of healing was atrocious and excruciatingly slow. The boy was close in age to Rhyl. She could not imagine if it were her own child suffering. It would be unbearable.

Jesa, the young servant woman, helped Eva stand and make her way to the privy.

It was as bad as Eva feared. Her legs were wobbly. She had to lean on the girl, relying on another's strength. Stone met them on their way back, his brows furrowed to see her slow progress. He held a tray of steaming food.

"Milady, let me put this down, and I can carry you," he suggested after waiting a few patient minutes.

"No! I need to do this," Eva replied, glaring at him, breathing hard. She made it to her bed without taking advantage of Stone's offer, a small victory.

The food Stone brought smelled delicious. Her stomach rumbled appreciatively. She was suddenly ravenous. She ate everything. Stone watched with the smug expression of a mother hen.

"Where are the horses?" Eva asked, settling back into her bed, her eyelids heavy.

"They are stabled nearby, never worry."

"Good. Thank you, Stone," Eva told him. "Does this mean our debt is even?"

"Hardly. I did not heal you if you recall."

"You did get me here."

"Barely."

"Hmm," Eva mused. "I don't know if I accept that reasoning. But I do need your help, so I won't argue." Her stomach was full. Her pain was gone. A great drowsiness came over her. She lay against the soft pillow and closed her eyes.

"I won't abandon you," Stone vowed.

Eva's eyes were closed, but her mouth pulled into a genuine smile.

(

Eva was weak as an early born lamb. She could walk by herself, but she was out of breath quickly. It was not hard to feign the meek, dutiful maiden when she could barely entertain the thought of walking, much less escaping. But she was alive.

The healer folk took her to a new room, up a flight of stairs Eva couldn't yet master on her own. Stone carried her, but she was not happy about it. The room was grand, not huge, but certainly the kind of room meant for ailing or recovering royalty. Tall, glazed windows overlooked the gardens surrounding the palace. Eva could see the king's flag was not flying from the tallest tower. The gardens were alive with the first flowers of the season, but the mountains leered at her from a distance, dusted in fresh spring snow.

They gave her beautiful clothes and soft slippers, as befit her royal status, and a spring cloak made from a soft fabric dyed pale gold, the color of Attin's eyes.

A knock came at her door, and Stone answered. He refused to leave Eva's side, not that she wanted him to.

Two women begged an audience. They were courteous enough; Eva saw no good reason to deny them.

The first woman held her head high, her arms lightly folded before her. Her gown was azure, and her long, white hair fell down her back nearly to her toes. The second woman was younger, but still of middle years, her silver-gold hair pinned high upon her head. Both women were of pure blood, like Eva. So this is what the treasures of Allati looked like.

Two guards wearing silver helms and greaves followed the women. They stood to either side of the door, ignoring Stone as best they could. A difficult task, as he towered over them, eying them closely.

"Lady Eva," the older woman said coming close to Eva's chair. Eva's strength was still far from recovered. Her cushioned chair and plush pillows were her favorite companions, besides Stone.

The woman's face was aged and lined, but still beautiful. Her eyes were clear and sharp, her mouth curved slightly at the corner.

"My name is Lady Talia," the woman said. "I am the third wife of the king. Lady Jaia was my daughter. This is Lady Tersia, my daughter, Lady Jaia's sister."

Eva was shocked into silence. Her gaze shifted to the younger of the two women, her aunt, sister of her mother. Old memories surfaced. Tersia's face was almost Eva's mother's face, the similarities obvious, but aged. Suddenly, Eva felt the absence of her mother like she had as a young child. Her parents had been dead a long time, but the grief never really disappeared.

"You look so much like her," Eva said in a small voice. Lady Tersia smiled a little, a ghostlike smile that did not reach her eyes. Eva turned from her aunt to her grandmother.

"I see her in your features, child, your eyes, your chin." Lady Talia put her hand over her quivering mouth, her eyes brimmed with tears. "To think you have come back to us! Your mother?" she asked hopefully.

Eva took her grandmother's hand. Her skin was soft and thin. "My mother died when I was little," Eva told her grandmother. Talia's tears fell then. She pulled a silken handkerchief from her sleeve and dried them, nodding. Tersia did not cry. She watched her mother silently.

"I feared it. A mother knows. I felt many years ago that she was gone."

"Do you know why she left Allati?" Eva asked.

Talia took a deep breath. "Your mother was not well - not well in the mind. She was given everything, yet she found no happiness. She had a handsome husband, a beautiful son, yet she left them. We searched for her for a long time, but no one could find her. In the end, I thought perhaps she had thrown herself into the Deeping."

Eva tried to remember everything about her mother. What her grandmother said didn't match. Her mother had been gay, Eva remembered her singing, her voice full of joy and adoration. Not addled or mad.

"A son? I have a brother?" Eva found the thought comforting.

"Yes, a half brother. He will come. He has been notified of your arrival. Lord Vagar is on the king's council. It is two days of hard riding from Windekeep. But he will be here to help the king select a husband for you. Now that we know you are his sister, he is no longer a good candidate, but they will find someone worthy, never you fear," Talia said with a pat on Eva's hand.

"Can you tell me about him?" Eva asked eagerly. She looked to her aunt, who remained stoic and silent. Her grandmother seemed to prefer to do the talking.

Talia's lips formed a thin line; fine wrinkles hemmed her mouth.

"Lord Vagar is a particular man. He came into his inheritance early, after his father's father passed away. His father died at a young age in a hunting accident. Not too bright was Lord Conely, your mother's husband. But Vagar is different. He is ambitious, smart as a whip, cunning, a man not to be crossed." There was pride in her voice, but something else as well, trepidation, perhaps. Eva wasn't sure.

"My husband, his Highness, is away east at the moment. He will be back soon. We have had disturbing news from the west, from Kitarra. We were hoping you could shed light on what we have heard," Talia said in a grave voice. Eva dared not glance at Stone, though she wanted to see his reaction.

"What kind of news?" Eva asked.

"The ferry inn and farm are burned to the ground, the ferryman and his family nowhere to be found. A host of strange men were found dead, slaughtered," Talia told her, eying her intensely. Eva hoped her face was properly schooled. "Tell me how you received such a heinous wound?"

"Bandits. We crossed the ferry. It was not burned," Eva lied. "We were almost to the Rose Road when they attacked. Stone drove them off, but not before they pulled me from my horse and stabbed me."

Talia looked to Stone, her face lined with displeasure. "It seems to me you should have hired a more capable guard. Bandits? I suppose they could be traversing the country this time of year. You saw nothing of these strange men? It is said they had long hair, braided and matted with vile faces. They cut designs into their own skin," Talia said with a delicate shiver. Eva had the feeling it didn't bother her grandmother as much as the older woman pretended. "And is it true Attin himself healed you?"

Eva nodded, thankful to tuck a shred of truth in with her lies. Talia shook her head in wonder.

"You must truly be special. What was the Guardian like?" Talia asked in a daring whisper.

"He was beautiful," Eva told her honestly, thinking of the Guardian's feathered wings the color of fresh snow, his long hair and startling gold eyes. Talia smiled and bowed her head.

"The Guardian has no idea how thankful we are - I am. I thought our line almost extinct, Vagar being the last - and his children are not pure. They have black, muddled hair. Tersia here has no children - barren," Talia said with some scorn. Eva didn't miss the crestfallen look on Tersia's face. "But you! And look at you. It's unfortunate about your hair, but it will grow back, and Attin would not have healed you if you did not carry the purest blood in your veins." Talia looked flushed with the thought.

Talia and her daughter left then, telling her to rest, reminding Eva that soon the feasts and banquets would begin in her honor. She could expect gifts from potential suitors or others who wished to earn her favor. Everyone wanted to meet her. Eva smiled and thanked her, hoping she sounded sincere.

Stone turned the lock in the door after the two women left, taking the two guards with them. He turned to Eva and gave her a discerning look.

"What do you make of that?" Eva asked him.

"I can tell that they are indeed your kin. You have the same look about you. The same sharp tongue," he added with a grin.

Eva rolled her eyes.

"I don't trust the Lady Talia, not too surprising," Stone continued. "I don't trust any of these Allati. Your aunt seems harmless, beaten of any will she might have once possessed."

"You're right - on both accounts."

"And this brother of yours doesn't sound too good either. I have heard of Lord Vagar before, nothing good, I am afraid. I wish we could get away before he arrives," Stone muttered. "Though I doubt it. We will have but one chance and I am not ready, not yet."

Eva nodded. Part of her was curious about her brother. What he looked like, would he remind her of Rhyl, did they share any of the same gifts? But how could her mother leave her son? She must have been in dire circumstances to leave her child behind.

Eva thought of Rhyl. Her longing was painful. She didn't dare use her magic to find visions of him. She didn't know what Attin would do or what power he held if he discovered her plans to disobey him. She didn't need Stone to remind her for the umpteenth time that if the Allati learned the truth, they would imprison her.

The next day, she was invited to dine with Lord Pruit, whose child had been so badly burned. Pruit was on the king's council, a man of immense status, the nurses told her.

A man of status he might be, but Eva found him lacking.

Lord Pruit was a round man with balding white-gold hair that looked less than noble upon his shiny head. His eyes were small and didn't fit well with his narrow features outlined by an extra layer of fat. His cheeks were rosy but not charming. He insisted on escorting her to his fine house just outside the palace.

Eva took his proffered hand, despising how it felt clammy and limp. She did her best to ignore the possessive glint in his small eyes. She was determined to not think ill of him without giving him the benefit of the doubt. Perhaps he was kindly and gentle. She thought of his son, his heir she was told, lying mortally injured in the healing halls. His heart would be grieving.

As they walked down the street to the lord's home, not a hundred paces from the Healer's Hall, Pruit kept glancing over his shoulder to where Stone stalked behind them. Eva's amourii wore Illiah's longsword at his hip, his hands folded behind his back. His tail twitched with agitation, at odds with his calm demeanor. Pruit didn't bother to hide his resentment at the presence of her guard, but Eva wasn't going anywhere without Stone.

Lord Pruit's house was built of gray and white marble, rising tall and stately from the cobbled streets. Two tall trees flanked the grand front doors. Eva felt sorry for them. They were heavily pruned, only a pathetic handful of leaves had opened, the others left struggling on the chastised branches.

The wood doors were beautiful, oiled and smoothed until they shone. Two servants stood waiting. As their lord approached, they opened the doors in unison for the small processional.

"My lady, welcome to my home," Pruit said, guiding Eva inside.

"Thank you, my lord."

Inside, the house was warmly lit by ornate lanterns. The hallway was wide, and a thick, colorful rug lined the floor. The walls were decorated with paintings and tapestries, too many to take in at once. What did hold Eva's attention was the line of women standing along the wide hallway like statues.

"Come, let me introduce my wives," Pruit offered in a smug voice, leading her to the first woman.

Eva knew Allati men took more than one wife, especially wealthy men of pure blood, but it was one thing to think of and another to see all the women who belonged to one man. Eva counted twenty women in the line. The youngest, the first wife she was introduced to, was barely older than a child, and she was pregnant. The oldest was older than Lord Pruit by some years - she had plenty of gray threaded through her brown hair, but her gaze was sharp and piercing. The thought of Pruit bedding all these women made Eva feel sick.

"Where is Essi?" Pruit asked the gray-haired woman, introductions concluded. Eva couldn't recall their names. She was surprised Pruit did.

"She is still in confinement," the oldest wife told her husband.

Pruit gave a nod of affirmation.

"Essi was watching my son when he had his accident," Pruit mentioned to Eva as they continued down the hall. His voice was severe with grief. "If he dies … His mother Lira is most distraught." He shook his head sadly. "He is my only child born with the pure blood of my royal heritage. If he dies …" he repeated.

"How many children do you have, my lord?" Eva asked with what she hoped was a convincing smile. She didn't want him to sense her intense disapproval.

"Thirty-six. My eldest boy, Dartin, just bought his first wife. A beauty of a creature, with not much breeding, but still she will make pretty daughters," Pruit said with a laugh. Pruit had thirty-six children, but only one with true royal blood. One.

Eva thought she heard a soft growl from somewhere behind her and wondered if Pruit kept any dogs, or had she really just heard Stone's inability to keep his opinions to himself?

Pruit didn't seem to notice. Eva discreetly flashed Stone a look. Everything about Stone's face was pointy. Thankfully, he was in the shadow and Pruit was not an observant personality.

Eva was led into a beautiful dining room where Pruit's other guests had already assembled. Three of Pruit's wives followed them. Pruit introduced the men as lords, members of the king's council, or close kin. Eva wondered if that made them her kin as well. She had no idea how wide the branches of the royal family tree spread. They all had wives draped across their arms, dressed in fine velvets and jewels. Eva was introduced to them as well, the favorites they were called. Pruit laughed lightly as his three favorite wives joined them. He smiled his smug smile.

"Are we still waiting for …?" Pruit did not finish his sentence, but the others nodded as if they knew to whom he was referring.

"Lord Vagar is not here yet. He should be here shortly. I was told he arrived at the palace this afternoon," one of them answered. "He has a Shadow Guard with him." The announcement was welcomed with a hushed silence. Was it fear, or reverence, shadowing their expressions? Eva managed to catch Stone's eye, and he shared her uneasy look.

Pruit's face pinched as he nodded in acceptance. They were forced to wait for the absent lord. There was no talk of starting without him. In fact, they avoided mentioning anything more regarding Eva's half brother.

They fawned over Eva and told her how pretty she was, and young. They asked after her previous husband and how she had run away. Some of their questions were pointed and intimate. She tried to hide her annoyance and act demure and shy. It seemed to work. They declared her as innocent as any maiden and wine was poured.

There was no mistaking the arrival of her brother.

A silence fell over the room as a servant entered, shuffling over to beg his lord's attention, whispering in Lord Pruit's ear before shuffling away. Pruit nodded meaningfully, and everyone turned to give Lord Vagar their full attention. The doors were opened wide for his formidable presence.

Eva's brother entered the room with a piercing, hawk-like gaze that glazed over them and singled them out at the same time. His familial eyes of blue and green were inescapable. He was tall, with two of the most beautiful women Eva had ever seen, one on each arm. His boots were black, the leather polished to a shine. A longsword hung at his hip, the sheath made of black leather to match his boots. His coat was indigo velvet, a striking color against his eyes and his wavy starlit hair, which he wore long, tied loosely at his neck. His face was handsome, with a well-shaped nose and fine lips that neither smiled nor frowned. He moved with the grace of a predator.

Behind him, hooded and cloaked entirely in white, was a strange person. The Shadow Guard, Eva guessed. He was neither introduced nor welcomed. He came into the room like a shadow of white fluidity and remained slightly behind Lord Vagar, not dissimilar to Stone's position behind herself. She could not see the person's face, but she had the feeling it watched and was aware of everything.

"Lord Vagar," Pruit said, mustering his manners despite his obvious unease. "We are honored."

"My Lord Pruit," Vagar said with a slight bow, his voice like silk. "I am at your service."

"Of course, come! We must eat!"

They all sat. Eva was placed across from her brother, who had yet to acknowledge her. Stone stood silently behind her. Only once the feast was laid did Vagar meet her eyes, sending a chill down her spine. His gaze was disquieting. It held no joy, no kindness. There was no hint of softness about his mouth or features.

"My Lady Eva, I am told you are my sister," he said after a sip of red wine.

"And I am told that you are my brother, well met."

Vagar's fine mouth pulled into a smile, but there was no mirth in it.

"Elsa," Vagar heralded one of his wives. She had long hair as dark as night and straight as a north wind. Her eyes were living ocher. She was beautiful. She held a small wooden box. "Give it to Eva." Elsa did as her husband bid.

"A gift, from Lord Byros. He beseechingly asked me to bring this to you," Vagar told Eva. "He hopes to win my favor, and yours - he is a possible suitor. Tell me what you think of it."

Eva opened the box under the scrutiny of those assembled. It was a fine thing on its own, the wood smooth and polished, catching the light and shimmering like the sea. Inside was a golden torc, intricately wound. Eva wondered what response was expected of her. Her first thought was that it looked like a collar, a chain, but she thought it would be best not to mention that. She would never wear it.

"Lord Byros is kind," she said.

"Lord Byros is a fool," Vagar said pointedly, almost a growl. A murmur of uncertain agreement moved around the table. Vagar took another sip of his wine.

They are all afraid of him, Eva realized.

"Lord Pruit, do you not have a bard?" Vagar asked after several moments of awkward small talk.

"You threw a persimmon at my last bard, my lord, if you will remember. Broke his nose," Pruit said with a small degree of irritation.

"Ah, yes," Vagar recalled without a hint of remorse. "He could not sing a long note without lilting off-key - irritating." He easily ignored Pruit's pinched look of aggravation.

When the four courses were finished, Eva could not help the fatigue that came over her. She tried to contain a yawn but couldn't. Pruit saw and begged her forgiveness and suggested she return to the Healer's Hall immediately. The others concurred. Vagar watched Pruit with a closed expression as he offered his carriage.

"It is not far, my lord. My guard will see me safely back. He can carry me if need be," Eva reassured him, hoping Pruit would not offer to carry her himself.

Eva did not miss the quick glance exchanged between Stone and her brother, though she didn't catch the meaning. She passed the Shadow Guard as she left the dining hall. She could feel its eyes on her. She shivered, trying to dismiss the urge to run, to flee. Pruit saw her out the door and wished her well, promising to send some of his women to visit her, since she must get awfully lonely with only a Kitarran for company, and women do miss the companionship of their own kind, but not to worry, Pruit had her health and happiness in mind.

Eva managed to garble out a polite response.

Stone did end up carrying her. She made it half way and couldn't go any farther. Her legs burned, then wobbled, and she was afraid she would fall on the hard cobbles and hurt herself.

Stone scooped her up. She wrapped her arms around his neck and put her head on his soft shoulder. Kitarrans had a funny smell to them, not a bad smell, but strange. Like popped grains. Or a warm summer breeze. She remembered Tayeh had had the smell about him too, even though he was a Guardian and not wholly alive.

She wanted to ask Stone about the Shadow Guard, but she must have dozed as the next thing she knew, she was in her bed.

True to his word, the next day Pruit's wife Amela arrived with a group of women. A gaggle of favorite wives and daughters of the king's council and the king himself.

Six women descended upon Eva, bearing gifts from possible suitors and bolts of beautiful fabric for her to choose from. They wailed over her cut hair and offered her hair clips emblazoned with pearls and gems to pin it back. Stone backed himself into a corner, and the women ignored him.

"You are so fortunate!" one woman told Eva. "You will want for nothing. Your husband will buy you anything you desire!"

"Lord Byros is a handsome man," another said.

"Lord Heth is not," clucked another.

The women cackled like a gaggle of hens or geese and were just as nonsensical. Eva reminded herself she had a part to play. It was expected of her to be excited about her suitors, to value their gifts and discuss the merits of each match. Disgusting.

"Lord Heth is capable in the bedroom, though," another woman piped up. As a wife of Eva's suitor Lord Heth, her claim was credible.

"None of the suitors are as handsome as Lord Vagar," the youngest girl said in a dreamy voice. She was barely a woman grown and not yet married.

"Oh, Alyssin, Lord Vagar may be pretty, but he is so particular and cold."

"I heard he blindfolds his wives before he beds them. He does not like them to look upon his manhood."

"I heard he has insatiable desires."

"I heard he does not even like women - you know what I mean - that is why he has so few children."

"But why does he have so many wives, then? How many does he have now? Thirty?"

Eva could not imagine sharing a man with even one other. In her mind, she saw Illiah and the auburn-haired woman from her vision.

"How many children does Lord Vagar have?" Eva asked, hoping to distract herself.

"Two. A boy and a girl. Young things with hair the color of tar." The woman who answered was the loudest of the bunch and seemed to hold all the answers to Eva's questions.

"I could give Vagar another child," Alyssin spoke up once more.

"Hush now, child, don't be foolish. Some of his wives have disappeared. You know what that means."

"What does that mean?" Eva asked.

The woman shrugged. "Some men have severe punishments when their women error."

"What will happen to Lord Pruit's wife, the one who was involved in the accident with his son?" Eva thought of the disapproval in Pruit's voice as he spoke of her. Essi had been her name.

The loud woman tutted, her face souring. "No more than she deserves. There are rumors she did it on purpose. Cruel, ungrateful woman. If she is found guilty, she will be put to death. Pruit will decide."

"What if it was an accident?" Eva thought of the reasons that would drive a woman to hurt a child out of spite. She would be desperate, hurt, or mad beyond reasoning to sacrifice her life and the life of a child.

The woman shrugged. "She will probably be sold. She is young and pretty. Many men would take her to their beds."

Eva wondered angrily if Essi would be exiled after she was raped.

Soon Eva feigned exhaustion and begged them to leave. Once they were gone, she breathed out in a huff, rising to her feet.

"Stone. We need to get out of here."

"I know. Soon."

"Allati men are awful. Vile."

Stone regarded her solemnly, his arms folded. "You don't need to preach to me. Kitarrans mate for life, to one woman only - ever."

"And the women! I can't stand them. And I thought Jullayan courtiers were horrible. The young woman actually fantasizes about being wed to my brother, to be a thirty-first wife! She is less than half his age. Did you see the quiet girl with the bruise on her arm? She was trying to hide it, but I saw it. If I had to stay here, I would revolt. I would gather an army of forsaken and abused wives, and we would take the men with their pants down."

Stone gave a laugh, but not at her expense. "Maybe we should stay after all. Allati would do well with you as their queen."

Eva smiled. "They really would."

"So what is it to be? Kitarra? Or the sacking of Attingard?"

Of course, there was no choice, they both knew it. Eva laughed, and Stone joined her. They grew quiet. Stone's silences were always strangely comfortable.

Eva took a deep breath. She had such yearning for her family, for Illiah and his strong, loving arms. For Rhyl and his silliness, his exuberance, his sweetness. She rubbed her cheek and found it wet.

"Eva?"

"What, Stone?" Eva asked feeling the weight of fatigue pulling her down.

"Nothing … never mind. Get some rest."

CHAPTER 62

ILLIAH

"YOU DON'T LOOK WELL," Queen Arrah remarked dryly when Illiah approached her. She had sent for him immediately upon his arrival in Kilev. He had nothing promising to tell her.

"Yeah, it went that well," Illiah said, sitting down heavily at her table, pouring himself a cup of fruit juice. He had hardly slept in three days.

"Tell me."

Illiah gave the queen his report, leaving nothing out. He gave a full account of Cotoch and his dishonorable attitude. The near successful attempt on his life. Cotoch's lies. He didn't have to tell the queen how he felt.

"I fear that you have two enemies, one to the east and one to the south. I do not know what his plan is, but I fear he means Kitarra harm," Illiah told her gravely.

"We must consider it," Arrah said solemnly, looking out her window to her city below. Her hand fidgeted with the beads and jewels hanging from the web around her head. She looked sad. The queen was always sad.

"He told me you were using me. And that you will use my son," Illiah said.

Arrah pierced him with her gray eyes. Nothing. He felt nothing under her assessing gaze.

"I am using you. Does that make me evil?"

Illiah shrugged. He didn't know. He didn't know which way was north and which was death and which way would spare his child the pain of his father.

"How did Cotoch know my wife's name?" Illiah asked the queen. "Is so much of my life common knowledge?"

"I didn't think so. My people know you are from Jullayah, that you are the prince, but they do not know who your wife is, unless you have told them."

It sat ill with him. Cotoch knew exactly how to enrage him.

Arrah still looked troubled. There was something else, something she had not yet spoken of.

"What is it?" Illiah asked sharply.

The queen sighed, clearly torn between letting him rest and needing him to be the leader he had vowed to be.

"A boat was spotted heading upriver yesterday morn at first light. Not a Kitarran boat. It was like a ghost, they said, unnaturally fast. It faded around the bend upriver."

Illiah sat mute and horrified.

"I need to see my son first," he finally said.

"Yes, he will be very happy to see you. He has missed you."

The queen was right. Rhyl squeezed him tightly and didn't let go for a long time. Illiah didn't know how he would say goodbye again so soon.

CHAPTER 63

STONE

STONE FELT HIS FAILURE like a deep knife wound.

Yes, Eva was alive, a relief, a great comfort. The Guardians had a use after all, which was not really that comforting. Still, if he had been quicker and killed the man before the poisoned dagger stabbed her, they would be in Kitarra. Stone would be facing his own demons instead of wading through the dangerous yet idiotic culture that was the Allati.

Eva's tears didn't help his guilt. Perhaps it was the memory of rape that made her cry, or the fear and frustration of being trapped in Allati (twice Stone had failed her, the little voice would not let him forget). Or sheer exhaustion. The poison and fever had ravaged her body. She was still weak.

More and more he suspected her tears sprung from something else, a deepening of grief that had always been. Since the first time he laid eyes on her, he had seen the shadow in her eyes. Even haloed by pain and withdrawal, he had seen it behind her calm facade. Watching her cry, seeing her desperation, almost gave him the courage to ask what caused her shadows. But he couldn't. He was a coward. The question caught in his throat and his heart wrenched with an old pain.

"What do you think of the Shadow Guard?" Eva asked, distracting him.

"Ah yes, the Shadow Guard. There are only a few of them in all Allati. Once there were many, many more. They are an ancient line of warriors, trained in secret, high in the Wanderling mountains, servants of Attin, it is said. Once, they were trained to combat the *candarii*. I don't need to tell you why. Now they stay mostly in the mountains, but perhaps Attin sent this one to watch over you - his precious treasure," he added facetiously.

Eva smacked his shoulder.

"After every last *candarii* was destroyed - so it was believed, you and I know differently - and the royal line grew thin, the magic was passed down less and less. The Shadow Guards were nearly forgotten. Now, no one sends their sons to be initiated, so the numbers have dwindled. I heard they are eunuchs, mutilated as children, but that is just a rumor." Stone tried to remember where he had heard that fact and wondered if it had any credence.

"That would be terrible," Eva agreed. "And now we know that not all the *candarii* are gone." Her voice was icy.

"Aye. But they don't."

Eva turned her gaze to the window, deep in thought. Stone thought of Cotoch. The man was ambitious, but would he really try to take on Allati? Stone doubted it. The man's army was large, but not large enough. There were too few of the royal blood left, and only they were at risk from the control of *candarii* sorcerers.

"I am afraid of the Shadow Guard, Stone," Eva admitted. Stone moved to stand beside her, watching the sunlight play off the great marble city sprawling before them. "I am afraid he will see me and know my thoughts, my plans. There is something familiar about him. I know his kind. The Guardian of Jullayah has the same minions."

"How is it you know so much about the Guardians?" Stone asked.

"I have met all of them."

Her answer should have shocked him, but it didn't. It made sense. He ran over the names in his head. Tayeh, Guardian of Kitarra, whom he had dismissed as a myth - any Guardian of Kitarra who neglected his people was of no concern to him. Attin of Allati, whose blood and magic was passed down to his fair-haired kin, one of which was Stone's amourii. And Crea of Jullayah - he knew little or nothing about her. Why couldn't he remember the fourth? Eva claimed to have met them all. Impossible.

"You don't believe me?" Eva turned a piercing eye on him. She had an intense gaze when she wanted. Inwardly, Stone thought she looked very much like her brother.

"Do I have any choice but to believe you?" Stone countered. "It seems unbelievable, but you were healed miraculously. I have no choice but to admit they are real, and that they have some interest in you."

Eva took a deep breath. "We need to get to Kitarra."

"We should not speak of it lest the walls have ears," Stone reminded her.

The appearance of the Shadow Guard worried him as well. They were legend. He had never thought much of them until now. He felt the same unease Eva admitted, as if the creature was probing and all-knowing and under its hood were eyes that could see beyond flesh and bone, wall and rock. They needed to leave. Soon. Yesterday.

Stone had not been idle as Eva recovered, playing the dutiful Allati maiden princess. He spent time listening, observing. The nurses of the Healer Hall were gossips, as were the courtiers. He learned one of the king's wives was having an affair with a street boy in the city. He learned where their trysts were held and how they managed to remain undiscovered. Stone knew the girl's secret would be found eventually. The king would have her head for her insolence. Poor child.

He wandered the streets at night mapping the walled city in his mind, looking for a discreet way out. There was no good way out of the city. The main gates, which were always open, were always guarded. He thought about killing the guards in the dead of night to ensure their silence, but it was not without risk. Plus, he didn't relish killing men in stealth and cowardice. So far it was his best escape plan - which wasn't saying much.

They were running out of time. The king would be back within a week; already most of his councilors had arrived, and the potential suitors. As soon as the king was back in his royal city, there would be no delay. They would wed Eva as soon as possible. Stone was not going to let that happen. He would not fail Eva again.

The following day Stone planned to put everything in place. If they had to make a bloody exit from the city, they would. They had two fast horses. A head start was all they needed. They could follow their original path, then lose themselves in the hills above the river. The land was tricky, but if any horse could manage it, Eva's could. They would have to follow the river on the Allati side as best they could until they found a town with a boat, possibly for weeks. They would need provisions. Hunting would be difficult. But first they had to get out of the damned city.

He sneaked out after Eva was asleep. She slumbered fitfully. She never slept well. He heard her toss and turn, but he knew she wouldn't wake if he left.

The halls were usually still and silent. Stone's stomach lurched as he heard a keen wail permeating the hall from several doors down. It tore at his heart. A child, probably the burned child of Lord Pruit. The sound rose to a crescendo and then died to a whimper that was no less terrible to hear.

Stone paused in the shadows, waiting for the shuffling feet of nurses, but no one came. No one heeded the child's cry. No one came to soothe his pain. No doubt they had done everything they could to ease the little boy's pain. Stone knew enough about healing to know there was no cure for the pain of burned flesh. He hoped it boded well for the child that he had been moved from the critical triage below. Perhaps his pain would soon be ended as he recovered. Stone fervently hoped so. He turned away from the sound with an aching heart.

There were guards at the main entrance of the Hall of Healers, but the kitchen door leading to the lane was never guarded. He slipped out easily.

Sasha and Penn were stabled just down the street. Stone brought a bundle of supplies to stash, hiding them close to the saddles, covered with a layer of hay. He hoped no one would discover it before tomorrow. He needed just one day. The supplies were stolen. He didn't like being a thief, but he didn't need suspicious questions from prying merchants.

He prowled the city, taking care not to be seen, which, luckily, was not difficult. Attingard slept at night, unlike Kilev, unlike any city Stone had met. There were no brothels in Attingard that Stone knew of, strange as it was. Even Kilev could not get rid of the lure of the whorehouses.

The escape path he planned was the quickest and most discreet, keeping the horses in mind. Their shoes would be loud on the cobbles, so Stone had chosen back alleys where dirt and mud would dull the sound.

The sky was clear, but the deep purple of night was fading to gray as the dawn approached. Stone hoped for a couple of hours of sleep; the next few days he would have little. He worried Eva was not recovered enough for such an arduous journey, but there was no choice. They could not wait any longer.

The halls were silent as he crept back to Eva's room. Soon the servants would begin to stir, and the nurses would begin their morning rounds. Their routine was predictable enough to avoid them, to know when he needed to be back in Eva's room.

He slipped in quietly, as usual. Eva's bed was empty. Fear clutched his heart. He leaped across the room to check the bathing chamber, but it too was empty. Where was she?

The door latch clicked behind him. He whirled to see Eva in her night-robe. She jutted her chin out in triumph. And he knew. He knew where she had been. He should have known by the silence of the hall, the peace of the faltering night.

"I'm sorry. I know it was not a good idea, but I just couldn't listen to his crying. I woke, imagining he called my name," Eva said in a far-off voice. "I had to, Stone. I had to help him."

"I know," Stone told her. "We need to leave. Now. I don't want them to find out you have these abilities. They will sink their claws into you without hesitation." His mind tripped over his thoughts as he went over the changes to plan. The morning light seeped in the windows slowly. Stone tried to remember when the morning guard changed.

Eva nodded. Stone threw clothes at her. The clothes the Allati had given her were not practical for traveling. Luckily, Stone had found her some new things, discreetly, and kept her spares. Lastly, he tossed her her sword. She smiled as she clipped it to her belt.

"You okay?" Stone asked as she took a deep breath.

She nodded, the circles under her eyes stark against her wan skin. "I can do this - let's go."

The night was receding at an alarming rate. The cover of darkness would no longer be their biggest asset. The city would be stirring. Servants would be in their kitchens baking the day's bread, fetching water from the wells. They would need to be fast.

Eva grinned to be reunited with her horses. She crooned to them, helping Stone as best she could to saddle them and load up their supplies. Stone heard the stable boy climbing the ladder to the hay loft. He hoped the boy would not hear them. Soon the boy would discover the missing horses and tell his master, but there was nothing for it. The boy was a child. There was nothing Stone was willing to do to silence him.

The horses were restless. They paced through the streets swiftly. There was no point in secrecy - speed was their only option. As they neared the gate, they let the horses fly. There was no muffling the rattle of their shoes on the cobbles. People opened their shutters to look.

The guards at the gate came out of their houses, barring their weapons, shouting for them to halt. Stone drew his sword and Penn reared, his hooves threatening.

Something white coalesced before Stone as if from the dawn light itself. The Shadow Guard. His hood was thrown back to reveal a shaved head, round and polished like a fine gem. His eyes were like obsidian, but it was the long dagger in his hand that held Stone's attention.

The warrior was fast and daring; he lunged and sliced the war horse across his forearm. Penn screamed and collapsed on his useless leg. Stone tumbled off, landing on his feet, thankful for his quick reflexes, turning to face the warrior in white.

Eva held the guardsmen at bay from atop Sasha. The horse handled two men better than thirty it seemed. He didn't spook this time.

"You cannot take her. She belongs to Attin," the Shadow Guard said in a strange voice, crackled and deep with age, though the man looked youngish.

"Ha! You can't own a woman, maggot," Stone told him as he lunged forward and met the warrior's dagger. Another flashed in his peripherals. The warrior held one in each hand, each equally quick and long and deadly.

Stone's borrowed longsword was lethal in its own right, but not a good match for two slicing daggers. Stone had trouble blocking and felt a sharp slice on his hand, but he ignored it. He managed to push the Shadow Guard with his foot, backing him into the shadow of the wall.

Something else moved from the shadows, something alive. The shadow materialized and became a living creature of flesh and bone and steel. A glint of steel flickered, the Shadow Guard gave a grunt, his white cloak stained with blood. He collapsed onto the ground in a heap.

Stone had no time to be shocked or to ponder who their rescuer was. He left the dead warrior where he fell and went to Eva's aid. He took down the two guards Eva had kept distracted. The shadow followed. It seemed to be on their side.

"Come!" the shadow hailed.

"Wait!" Eva dismounted and bent over Penn. Stone couldn't stop her; she placed her hand on the horse's leg. The stallion struggled to his feet with a snort as soon as she rid him of his pain and panic.

"Better and better," the shadow drawled.

Stone knew that voice. So did Eva.

"Vagar," Eva whispered.

The man in the dark cloak didn't remove his hood but nodded slightly. "We need to leave, now!"

They followed him without hesitation.

"The Rose Road is not safe. Soon it will be swarming with armed men looking for you. There is a better way. Allati are unimaginative, trust me - they will not suspect you to retreat into the city," Vagar explained with a fox-like grin.

Vagar led them through what seemed to be an unused part of the city. Stone had noted it himself and planned to use it in his original plan, but what he hadn't known was that there was another gate. It was locked, but Vagar had the key. Of course he did.

It opened into a forest. The morning sun was just rising as they left the city behind, sending bright shafts through the new leafs. Not far into the forest, Vagar called a halt.

"My sister is faltering. We can afford to rest, I think."

It was a sign Eva was indeed on the brink of exhaustion that she allowed Stone to lift her off her horse and place her on a cloak to keep the dew from soaking into her clothes.

"Why are you helping me?" Eva asked her brother. Vagar handed her a skin of water, which she took gratefully. Stone rummaged for some bread and cheese while they waited for the man's answer.

"Most of the Allati are fools. They are willing to believe a young, scared woman would run home to Allati to find a husband to keep her safe from the horrors of the world," he began. Then his face stretched in a mirthless half smile. "I know that is not true. One look at you and I could tell you were false. You hid your disgust and disdain well, pretending to be demure and pathetic, but not well enough." He laughed. "You didn't fool me. And you -" He turned to Stone. "Bandits were a poor excuse. Only a great warrior could have caused the massacre at the ferry. Kitarra has few of them left, that is true, but still it made more sense that it was you. Incredible."

"Thanks," Stone said at his most sarcastic.

"Also, you would have a different tale to tell if you were really from the Kitarran Islands," Vagar said. Stone thought he almost sounded sad. "You are an exile?" Vagar asked Stone.

"I am."

"Why are you going back?"

"I am Eva's amourii. She commands it."

Vagar gave a sharp nod as if it was what he expected.

"Eva, you and I share a gift - although yours is much better honed," Vagar said, turning to his sister, placing his hand on her cheek. "Allow me."

Eva closed her eyes. When she opened them they were lighter, stronger.

"You are a *sanarii*," Eva said.

"Yes, but not a very strong one, I'm afraid."

"How did you know where to find us?"

"The Shadow Guard."

"How did the Shadow Guard know?"

"He has been watching you," Vagar said. A shiver of revulsion crept down Stone's spine. "And I have been watching him - I don't trust the

Shadow Guards. I followed him, knowing he was going to stop you from escaping."

"Will anyone suspect that you helped us escape?" Stone asked. Clever as Vagar seemed to be, Stone was reluctant to bet Eva's safety on the man.

"The king's court will not miss me. Yesterday, I told the council I had pressing business at home. It was abrupt, unexpected, but they expect that from me - the unexpected. I keep them on their toes." Vagar spoke with a sideways grin that left his face as suddenly as it came. "I will take you to my estate. There you can get more supplies for your long journey. Eva, you can meet your niece and nephew." He gave Eva another smile, his face softening as he spoke of his children. Stone liked the man a little more for it.

Stone looked at Eva. She nodded and said, "We will come with you. Thank you, Vagar."

They pressed on. Eva let her brother ride Sasha and she rode behind Stone. Penn didn't mind the extra weight. Kitarrans are light for their size and Eva was still a featherweight from her sickness. Stone liked having Eva close. She trusted him, and that was good. Stone was reluctant to trust the Allati lord, but there was no choice. And Vagar did kill the Shadow Guard. No faithful Allati would dare attempt that.

CHAPTER 64

EVA

THEY REACHED VAGAR'S ESTATE AT DUSK. The sun had vanished below the horizon, and already great shadows lay about his land. Eva could see newly tilled fields and smell the good earth. Vagar's villa was nestled in the trees beside a long, narrow lake, its waters a deep blue, almost black in the failing light. To the north was the unbroken line of the Wanderling mountains, their tips glowing with the day's last light. The barrier of the realm.

Vagar's main house was huge, sprawling and elegant, coiled around the hill like a snake. He did not lead them to it but skirted around the main dwelling to a smaller house at the side. It was no less elegant but separated from the main house by a garden of high trees and flowering shrubs. The air was thick with the sweet fragrance of early blooming flowers. Eva recognized some of them; others were new to her.

"Elsa loves flowers," Vagar whispered.

The house was no larger than the servants' quarters. The door opened as they approached and Eva recognized one of Vagar's wives, Elsa, whom she had met at court. Elsa who apparently loved flowers.

"Vagar," Elsa said, greeting her husband with a kiss. "I see your suspicions were correct?" She raised a delicate, black brow at her husband.

"I am never wrong." Vagar turned to Eva. Stone asked where the horses could be stabled and Vagar went to show him, leaving Eva with Elsa.

"Come in. There are eyes and ears in this place. Vagar's other wives are not likely to pry. They know Vagar has his secrets, and they are happy to keep them for him. But still, best not to risk it. Come in."

Eva followed her inside. From somewhere within the cozy house, children's laughter echoed loud and raucous.

"Your father is home, my little wildlings!" Elsa called out. The shouts grew louder and two children tumbled into the room. They were lanky like their father, but dark-haired like their mother. They saw Eva, a stranger, and stood quietly.

"These are our children, Matas and Ella," Elsa said proudly. "This is Eva, your aunt."

Eva guessed Matas's age at about nine, Ella a bit younger. They watched her solemnly, all sign of their loud behavior extinguished. Eva smiled at them.

Stone and Vagar returned, filling the room. The children looked at Stone before turning to their father with shrieks of delight. Vagar embraced his children, his face transforming with joy. Stone looked away, his expression mirroring Eva's pain at watching the heartwarming scene. Vagar noticed her unease and sent the children on their way to their beds with their mother.

"You only have two children and thirty wives?" Eva stated.

"I have one wife," he answered. "The others are for show. I love Elsa. I will have only her. Come, I will tell you my story, for it concerns our mother." He poured her some tea and fetched them all some soup that was simmering on the kitchen fire before leading them into the comfortable sitting room.

"Our mother was married to my father at a young age. My father was the only son of Lord Fishur, a bitter, callous man who had many wives, but few children, and only one son. He blamed his wives, but of course, it was likely his own impotence that betrayed him." Vagar spoke of his grandfather with an emotion close to loathing. "He treated his wives with cruelty and contempt - theirs was not a happy existence. His heir and only son took Jaia, daughter of the king's favorite wife, as his wife and sired a son of royal blood - myself, of course. Grandfather, who had suffered a lack of sons, took me from our mother's tit and vowed to raise me as he saw fit. My father couldn't or wouldn't say anything against it, so it was done. My father died a few years later in a ridiculous hunting accident. I grew up with no real mother, only Fishur's wives, who were essentially bitter, resentful servants. When

I was old enough to understand such things, I asked about my birth mother. No one would speak of her or tell me where she was. One of Grandfather's wives, Lucilla, took pity on me and loved me in a way that was close to a mother. When I was nine, she was sold. I was furious with my grandfather - I cried and begged him to bring her back. He beat me for my insolence, for my attachment to a woman. Women were currency to him. He saw my tears as weakness. My hatred ran deep because of his mistreatment of Lucilla, who was a kind-hearted soul.

"When I was thirteen, I ran away to find her, the only person who ever really loved me at all. I found her. It wasn't hard. I was shocked to learn she was happier in her new life. She had been bought by a decent man whom she much preferred as a husband to my grandfather. Lucilla told me the true story of my mother, how Fishur refused to let Lady Jaia see me, that Jaia begged and pleaded until she was chastised by my father and forbidden to speak to my grandfather. It broke my heart to hear then, and now I cannot imagine being forced from my children, and I am not a mother. Lucilla didn't know what happened to Lady Jaia. There were rumors that she died in childbirth, that my grandfather had her sold as a whore, that he beat her to death himself. All she could tell me was that she hadn't been seen since I was two. Our grandmother Talia, whom you had the great pleasure to meet," he added sarcastically, "was so ashamed, she pretended her daughter didn't exist. It took some time, but finally I learned a little more of the truth - from Tersia, actually, another sad story - she told me that her sister ran away. I didn't know if Mother was alive or dead, if she found a new place to call home. I just hoped she had found a place where she didn't have to suffer like many Allati women do. I hoped she was happy. If my grandfather hadn't died when I was seventeen, I might have run away myself to search for her. At the time I had no wish to be this." He gestured to himself, his fine clothes, the sword at his belt. "But he died, and I was his heir. I saw an opportunity, a chance to help my people."

"She died," Eva told her brother. "Both my parents died when I was seven."

"I am sorry to hear that."

"But she was happy. She loved my father very much, and he loved her."

Vagar nodded. "I met Elsa when I was seventeen. I bought her. It went against everything I wanted to be, but they wouldn't let me be who I wanted to be. I have to play a part, a role. I am sure if I wasn't of royal blood, they would have banished me long ago, but they have to put up with me," Vagar said with a grin. "Elsa loved me, even then. I promised her she would be my only wife, the only woman who would share my bed and bear my children."

"That is why you helped me?"

"I help a lot of women get out of unfortunate matches. Why do you think I have so many wives? You are my sister, my blood - that means something to me."

"Thank you."

"Someday, when the king dies, I will put my name up for succession. If I am appointed, Allati will never be the same," Vagar said with eagerness, then he shrugged. "So, why are you going to Kitarra? They are at war, or will be soon." He turned to see Stone's reaction.

"War?" Eva's gut clenched. Of course. That was why Illiah's face was drawn and pained, why his eyes were haunted. He would not stand by and watch the suffering of others when he could help. Illiah the hero. She loved him for it, but what of Rhyl?

"I have contacts in Kilev, discreet ones - the rest of Allati are ignorant to what is happening in Kitarra. Though I have not heard anything since the ferry burned." Vagar met her eyes knowingly. He knew about Rhyl, she was sure of it. "The Isles have been lost."

"What?" Stone's voice was sharp with unmasked pain.

"Yes, exile. They have been eaten up by raiders, looted and burned. I cannot tell you what you will find in Kilev, with the invaders as far up river as the ferry."

"Kilev is safe," Eva told her brother. She had used what little strength Vagar had given her. As they rode under the spring sun, she had floated with the wind and sought her little son. He had felt so far away and the journey to find him was hard, the hardest yet. Still, she had found him, safe and sound, playing with the young Kitarran child and two large puppies. The queen's city looked the same - it was not ravaged by the enemy, but still and silent. Now she understood the city's grief. She had not seen Illiah. She couldn't find him anywhere within the city walls. She didn't have the strength to search for him again, but if he was playing the hero, he could be anywhere. It worried and angered her that he was not with their son.

"You have the sight?" her brother asked, pulling her from her thoughts.

Eva nodded. Stone growled at her.

"You shouldn't be using it," Stone barked at her. "You are weak and we still have a long, hard way to go. You must keep what little strength you have."

"Don't cluck at me!" Eva told her amourii with a sharp laugh.

"You almost died, then you used up what scarce energy you have for the child, then the horse, and now again you use your energy to manipulate your strange magic. I can still see the shadows under your eyes, milady. Even your brother couldn't erase them. I forbid you to use your gift until you are healed."

"By the Guardians, you are bossy! I thought you had to obey me, not the other way around?" Stone's regard for her was heartwarming, but mostly irritating. She could take care of herself. She turned back to her brother.

Vagar whistled. "No wonder Attin healed you. No wonder the Kitarran's have taken such an interest in your life. I can only heal. A full elemental *sanarii* has not been heard of for many generations. What child do you speak of?"

"Lord Pruit's son. He was badly burned. He will still have scars, but not many."

"Ah, your heart is gracious."

Eva's heart was hard and cracked. Lord Pruit's son had looked so much like Rhyl - the same shaggy pale hair but his face had been different, his little features obscured by pain and raw, barely healed wounds.

But Vagar was right about her gifts. She had been ignorant. She never heard the truth and warning in Tayeh's words. He told her she was special, that she was destined for something more. She should have known the Guardians would not let her live a quiet life in the Keep. They had contrived for her to marry a prince and bring his son into the world, a boy born with the blood from two realms, two thrones, filled with magic. She should have guarded Rhyl better, kept him away from Tayeh. She remembered Tayeh's amber eyes, thoughtful and knowing. She had been tricked. She had been a young, lost girl and he had offered her solace. It had been a trap she could never have foreseen or escaped.

With a shake of her head, Eva tore herself away from her thoughts. They were of no use to her now.

Beside her, Stone was pensive, his mouth a hard line, his hands clenched. He watched the fire, but Eva wondered what visions and memories stirred within him. She could sense his pain, lined and etched through his whole person. She reached over and squeezed his hand. He came from some dark place and met her eye. His yellow eyes were like honey in the firelight.

"You can both stay here for tonight," Vagar said. "But tomorrow you must move on. My other wives must not know you are here. Some of them cannot be trusted, unfortunately. You must not be seen."

Stone agreed without hesitation and insisted Eva be given a bed. Eva rolled her eyes but allowed her brother to lead her away to the innards of his house where he had a small but comfortable room ready for them. Stone lay on a pallet on the floor. Vagar had plenty of extra blankets.

Night enveloped the room as Stone extinguished the lamp. A pale shaft of light came in through the window from the moon. The last place Eva had felt so secure was in Tayeh's Vale. The cave, warm from the heated water, the trees and cliffs an impenetrable wall around the valley, magic steeped in every leaf, stem, and root. Vagar's magic was not the same, but his house felt just as shielded. He was a force - the other Allati feared him, and he had cut down the Shadow Guard ruthlessly.

"Stone?"

"Yes?" He didn't sound sleepy at all. In the darkness, Eva didn't bother trying to read his face. She spoke to the ceiling.

"How many people lived on the isles Vagar spoke of?"

Stone was silent. Eva wondered if he had heard her. Then he answered, "There were dozens of settlements, some large enough to be called cities - many people."

Her imagination didn't need to stretch far to envision what those islands looked like now if what Vagar said was the truth. Years had passed since the raiders struck south Jullayah, but the smell, the evil, were burned forever in her mind, waiting, lurking, never forgotten.

"Vagar said there weren't many warriors like you left in Kitarra."

"That is true."

"Why were you exiled?" Eva held her breath for an answer she wasn't sure was coming.

"Because I am a coward," he said in a quiet voice that was perhaps full of grief, or maybe repugnance.

"You are not a coward." Eva was sure of that.

"I do not fear death, but there are other forms of cowardice."

"You are wrong. You do fear death. You fear it with all your being. I saw you when you woke from your death sleep. You were relieved, almost joyful. Don't deny it."

"I wouldn't dream of contradicting you, milady," he said at his driest. "Good night, Eva."

CHAPTER 65

COTOCH

"DO YOU KNOW what you have done?"

The voice was crackled as dry leather. Like it hadn't uttered a sound in a thousand years. Which was not an impossibility. The prisoner had never spoken to Cotoch before. He didn't even wonder why it decided to break its silence now, after so many years. He knew.

Cotoch sat at the edge of the pit. Beside him was a lantern, the only light, just enough to keep him from falling into the pit himself. That would be too ironic.

Rats and other vermin dwelled in the pit, feeding on the remains of Cotoch's work. It stank. The pit extruded a smell so thick and pungent and forsaken, Cotoch wondered why he bothered with the lantern at all. The smell was enough to see by. Somewhere at the bottom of the dark hole was his wife's body.

Cotoch wanted to ignore the voice. To pretend it didn't exist, that the prisoner was too old, too frail, too other to speak to him. But he couldn't. The emptiness in the crypts was too vast, the emptiness in his blood too lonely. He had been a child when he first touched the *varing* and felt it sing inside of him. The *varing* had given him strength when his father beat him, and nourishment when left alone in the crypts with nothing to eat but rats. And now, after so many years, the *varing* had abandoned him. Now, after so many years, he learned the *varing* was never his.

Mistakes were blaring after the fact, the curse of the foolish. And there was no question Cotoch had made a mistake.

He had taken Sandra and used her love for him and his anger at her to reap the *varing* from her pain. Afterward, the *varing* hummed and pulsed like never before. And he thought it had been worth it.

As Sandra's last breath exhaled from her dismantled body, Cotoch, half blind by the humming magic in his blood, didn't notice the change at first. The *varing* rose like the peak of a wave, but as it descended, it left his bones, his blood, like water slipping through a cracked chalice. Then a summer-hot breeze rustled through the stone chambers, an impossible breeze since the crypts were sealed and locked, deep underground. The wind came with a sharp smell of heat and metal. Then the air stilled and grew cold once more. The room was empty. Cotoch was empty. He had never felt such emptiness. He stood, numb and disbelieving. For how long, he didn't know.

Then he picked up his wife's body, slippery with blood and stiff in death, and dumped her into the pit. To feed the rats.

Tears pricked his eyes. Cotoch had loved her. Even after her foolishness, he had loved her. And he had killed her. Horribly. Slowly. She had been a prisoner of the crypts for a long time.

Her screams still rang in his ears, but worse was the weak plea that came at the end. So quiet and scared and real. And for what? Nothing. He had never been the master of the dark.

A sob broke from his chest. A sob birthed in a recess carved long ago by a pant-wetting child lost in the crypts.

"You have given it the strength to break free of its cage." The cracked voice rose in volume and penetrated Cotoch's skull like an ax. The sadness of it made Cotoch's eyes brim over. "Crea wants this, you know. She wants the *varing* to spread chaos throughout the realms once more. This time, I don't know if it can be stopped."

CHAPTER 66

EVA

THEY LEFT VAGAR'S HOUSE under cover of dusk. They would only travel at night until they were beyond the border of Allati. Vagar urged them to follow the little river through his lands. Eventually, it would lead them past the burned ferry inn to the river. A difficult way with no roads or paths, filled with dips and ravines and loose rocks among tall trees.

Eva said farewell to her brother, his favorite wife, and his two children. She had nothing to offer them, and that made her sad. Vagar gave Eva a nod of acknowledgment, his cool eyes lightly tinted with some of the same warmth he reserved for Elsa and his children. Then Eva was alone once more with her amourii.

Beyond the lights of the houses, the shadows welcomed them, ushering them into the folds of night's bosom.

They rode until daybreak. The little river, which was their guide, was often hidden in a shallow, rocky valley. It was easy to find a hidden nook or overhang in which to hide for the day. They were careful to stay away from the many paths that wandered in and out of the little river valley where people came to fish.

With every day, the weather warmed considerably. The trees held timid new leaves of bright green or even yellow. Insects and birds canvased the sky, filling the air with their small sounds.

Every pore of the ground exuded spring energy. Eva wished it would seep into her bones. She couldn't shake the fatigue that had plagued her since she had taken ill from her wound. She was exhausted, yet she couldn't sleep. At night she found herself dozing in the saddle. Her magic was almost nonexistent. The effort to find a vision was immense. She could no longer search ahead of them on the road. They rode slowly and cautiously.

Days passed.

"I'm tired, Stone," Eva said as they sat under a rocky overhang, hiding from the spring rain that was doing its best to fill up the little river.

The horses didn't mind being out in the weather. Eva did. She sat beside Stone, their shoulders touching, the silence between them companionable. "I knew it would be a long, tiresome journey to Kitarra, but it feels endless. Like I am doomed to travel this valley for eternity, never to find a way out."

"Soon, a day or two, and we will cross over the last of Allati. We will see the Ilba, and then you will feel like we are finally making progress," Stone told her encouragingly.

Eva sighed, putting her head on his big shoulder. "Stone, what do you know of the Guardians?"

"You are the expert - you have met them."

"I have. But there is so much I don't know about them." Eva stumbled for the words. "I don't know why they do what they do." She wanted to tell Stone about Rhyl and Illiah, and the prophecy. But Tayeh's betrayal was like a knife in her throat, making it impossible to form the words.

Stone took a deep breath. "I only know the legends. I learned them as any child does in Kitarra."

"In Jullayah, we are only taught about Crea, and she claims to be a goddess with the power to change a man's destiny. She does not call herself a Guardian. And no one ever speaks of the others, except in the odd story."

"In Kitarra, legend says the Guardians were created by the Allmakers, the old spirits of the earth, to guide the errant half-mortals. When Kitarra was the only realm in this land, there were no Guardians, just the Allmakers, but when humans came, the Allmakers created the Guardians to protect the realm and bring unity to the land. To keep their people from being forgotten or destroyed. To protect the old magic."

"Their people? You mean the Kitarrans?"

"No. I mean the Shiftlings - the *velidar*. They are the first people, the real children of the Allmakers. It is said the Allmakers created Kitarrans from the Shiftlings, brought them out of the Forest, but in doing so, took away almost all their magic. Kitarrans are able to regenerate quicker than humans, but we have no talents such as yours. We cannot harness the energies of the world through the elements. That is the Shiftlings' gift to the humans."

"The Shiftlings," Eva repeated. In her mind was a man that looked like a mountain cat, his feral eyes capturing the wild in his human-like body. She thought of Lula, the white fox.

"Don't tell me you have met them as well?" Stone asked, almost sarcastically. Her non-answer was admission enough. He guffawed. "Guardians, Shiftlings. You are like a lady from some old song or ballad, from the days before the humans came to this land. A time forgotten but in the deepest roots of the trees and darkest caves."

"When I traveled through the Great Forest, they came to me and lent me their magic, infusing mine with their own. That is why I could see so far and so clear. They warned that it would not last forever, and now their strength has left me. I still have my own gifts, but I am so tired, I can hardly use them." Eva didn't like to complain, but her voice sounded bereft even to her ears. She pressed her face into the leather of his jerkin and took comfort from his Kitarran smell. He was silent beside her, offering her no words of pity or promise. His presence was enough.

The next day, as Stone had promised, they left the little river behind and traveled through the last stretch of Allati. They crossed the road cautiously. Eva knew it should look familiar, having traveled down the road some weeks before, but she couldn't recall it. The hills beyond were thickly treed and steep. The terrain would be a test for the horses, but they would pass it. The hills around the Keep had been difficult too and the horses had never balked at root or hill or rock.

Leaving the Allati road behind was a relief. As the night waned to day, the Ilba river showed itself, pale in the dawn light, stretching out to the south, curving gently to the west. To the south were mountains, beyond them lay the Tarm, and nestled among them to the west was Kilev and her family.

Stone was wrong. The mountains - Kilev - were a lifetime away.

CHAPTER 67

STONE

STONE TRIED NOT TO THINK about the possibility that the river
was overrun by the raiders. Kitarra would fall before the queen would
allow the waterways to be polluted. The river looked quiet, untouched.
Stone was just paranoid. Optimism was a luxury. The closer he came to
his old home, the more bravery his demons leeched and used for their
own devices.

The river was swollen with spring floods, but the water was not too
high - they could still ride along the clay and gravel shore. It would
hasten their journey. They would be exposed along the bank, but he
hoped a Kitarran boat would pass by and they could barter passage.

Stone had worried about the horses over the rough, untamed terrain,
but he needn't have. For their size, they had the nimble footing of the
stoutest hill ponies.

Stone studied Eva's back as she rode ahead on Sasha. Nearly forgotten memories from a lifetime ago circled in his mind like carrion birds.
He couldn't quite remember all the words, but what he could remember
fit her. Almost fit her. She was of royal Allati blood, raised in Jullayah.
She had never admitted it, but he knew she was a noblewoman, perhaps
even royalty.

If he was right, he knew what drew her to Kitarra.

He opened his mouth to ask, but no words came out. He could not
phrase the question. Once he asked, Eva would ask him how he knew
about Tayeh's prophecy. He would have to tell her. It would hurt. Too
much. And then she would know he was a worthless cur.

When did her opinion matter so much to him?

"Look! We are almost to the river!" Eva exclaimed.

Sure enough, through the thick swath of poplars, he could see the shimmering river as it flowed on its silent course out to the sea. He could smell the tang of the water and earthiness of the clay. Old smells he had known as a babe, familiar and distinct.

They followed the high bank until there was a suitable spot to take the horses down. The shore was cut away in many places from the last high flood. The sand mixed with knotted roots and reeds made the terrain difficult for horses. Eventually, they came to a place where the land was less steep, where the river had worn away at the shoreline gradually, softening the drop to the sandy beach stretching out before them.

Stone assessed the river up and down, getting his bearings, scanning with his keen eyes. He could see as far as the bend in the river below. They would be able to travel some ways before the beach gave way to rock and hill.

The sun came out from behind a cloud and the landscape warmed beneath it. The new leaves of the poplars turned green and golden, flickering loudly in the river breeze. The sand sparkled with flecks of mica.

Eva dismounted and scooped the fine, sandy dust into her hand, watching the sparkles run through with the rest, a small smile playing on her lips.

The river transformed under the sun. It had been gray and lifeless, but now it shone with a green glow, and the ripples and waves glinted white and golden. Shorebirds swooped down into the waves. Two dark shapes flitted across the sun, followed by a sharp keel. A pair of huge eagles glided across the river, dipping their wings with some secret pleasure or message shared between them. It was beautiful and peaceful. Eva begged a moment to sit and rest. Stone smiled as Eva discarded her boots, letting the sand spread beneath her feet, between her toes.

Stone's half smile faded quickly. The river was captivating, but the sun fell away as quickly as it came and the clouds were thick and ominous. Stone doubted it would appear again. A cool wind came off the water. Eva asked if they would be able to build a fire.

"Not tonight, perhaps tomorrow. I would feel better if we put a little more distance between us and Allati," Stone said, looking the way they had come. He couldn't see it, but several miles upriver was the burned husk of the ferry inn. He turned his eye on the opposite bank, half expecting to see Kitarran farmers taking their flock to the river to drink, or a barge heading upstream, or a fishing vessel. But there was nothing. It was silent and wild. They might be the last people on earth. A wandering magical girl and her cowardly amourii. He wondered how the story ended.

"We can camp in the shadow of those rocks at the bend," Stone suggested, pointing. "It's not far."

Without the sun, the optimism that warmed Eva's features disappeared. She looked haunted and haggard. Stone thought it was more than just her tired body; her mind and heart were rent.

The following day, Stone judged they had put enough distance between them and Allati to warrant a fire. If anyone were to see it, there was a good chance it would be Kitarrans, and he knew they would help them. His people were generous, cautious enough, but kind. They would help if they asked.

The nights were still cool enough that a fire was welcome, if not necessary. Eva made tea and Stone watched her shoulders relax as the herbal brew seeped into her bones and lifted her spirit, if just a little. It was easier traveling by day rather by night. They both found it easier to sleep, succumbing to their natural patterns once again.

The days passed slowly. Stone found himself watching the river more and more, looking for boats, any boat that could carry them downriver under swift sails. Riding over the sand was slow, and when the banks grew steep and unstable, they were forced to climb high into hills or backtrack away from the river. It was frustrating.

They both preferred to camp along the river, just under the shadow of the river trees, within spitting distance of the sandy shore. The breeze in the night from the river was cold, but the trees sheltered them from the worst of it. Eva liked to walk along the sand in the morning. Sometimes the sun came out, and she took off her shoes, walking barefoot for a time.

Eva's bare feet in the sand reminded Stone of countless childhood memories. The river had always been part of his life. He realized that he had missed it. He realized the memories didn't hurt quite so much. He found himself smiling as he felt the smooth sand run through his fingers.

Still, the river had betrayed him in the end.

The daylight was fading. Stone discarded the sand and stood to use the last light of the day to find suitable firewood and build a fire. Dry driftwood was plentiful from previous spring floods. It didn't take long to have a stockpile that would last until morning.

"I wish we had something else to eat," Eva mused, settling down in her blankets before the fire, tucking them under her chin. Stone followed Eva's gaze up above them to the stars peeking out behind a rustling curtain of spring leaves.

"Yes, some fresh meat wouldn't go amiss," Stone drawled.

"Back home, the cook used to make these honey cakes that would melt in your mouth," Eva said wistfully. "He always made them for me when I came home."

"Home from where?"

A wary veil instantly came over Eva's expression. He felt like she had slammed a door in his face. Stone wished she would tell him more, that the openness had not left her face. They were friends, yet she looked at him like a stranger. He didn't like it.

"When I was sick, I saw you," she told him, changing the subject. Cheater.

"I remember. You thought I was Tayeh." At the time it had been mystifying, but now that Stone knew she had been close to the Guardians, it made a kind of sense. "You also told me my eyes look like buttercups." He couldn't help but grin at her.

"They do." Eva leaned forward, her eyes intent on his, as if by searching his face she could recall the vision. "That was different. No, I saw you, but you were different. Your fur was darker, tawny, the spots not so vivid, barely visible, really."

His body stiffened.

She continued, "You were standing at the top of a great cliff above the river - it was like a tower. A very old place, surrounded by old, gnarled, wind-bitten trees. You were fearless. Next to you stood a Kitarran woman with fur as black as night - Emri." Her voice was almost lost, but Stone was sure he had vanished under the pounding of his heart. "Then you fell. She watched you. It was a long, long way down. The fear in her eyes was terrible. I could see them because she focused them on me. Her fear became my fear. 'Catch him!' she told me in a strange, calm voice, but she was anything but calm. 'Catch him, for I cannot.' It was a command. I don't know what happened after that. I don't remember anything else. If I woke up, I was not coherent, and if I dreamed more, I cannot remember. I didn't remember this dream until now." She looked back up at the stars. "She is dead, isn't she?" Her voice was sad, aching, and Stone knew he had been right about her.

Stone could not breathe. His claws bit into his palms as he clenched them hard. Her dream evoked his terror. Suddenly the cliff was below him. The wind pulled at him. The river below waited, whispering promises it did not intend to keep. Alone. Achingly alone.

"What do you think it means?"

Eva's question lifted him from his memory. He focused on her summertime eyes. Even in the dark, he could see their beauty. Her eyes were knowing. She already knew what the dream meant. Her words were a test, a question.

But he was a coward, and he still could not speak the truth to her.

Stone drew a long breath and shook his head. "I do not know."

CHAPTER 68

EVA

THEY DIDN'T SPEAK of Emri or the cliffs or the river. Stone went to sleep in silence, and Eva could not find the words or the strength to pry the truth from him.

Sometime during the chilly night, Eva pulled her cloak over her face to keep warm. She then pulled it off, her eyes still closed against the bright, filtered sunlight. There were voices - at least it sounded like voices, loud, yet far away, but maybe she was still dreaming.

"Those horses, where did you get those horses? Are you alone?" a man demanded.

"They are my horses, and yes, I am alone." Stone's reply was terse.

Then Eva remembered there was no one but her and Stone, so who could her amourii possibly be talking to? Her sleepiness dissolved. Had the Allati caught up with them in the night? Had they seen the fire? Panic germinated in her gut.

Stone and another man were just beyond the trees, not ten paces from where she lay. Stone just lied about being alone; it must be the Allati.

"Sir, let's move on. A rogue Kitarran is no one to antagonize," a third, hesitant voice said.

"Best listen to your man, captain," Stone growled.

"Not until I get some answers." The first man sounded strained, desperate. The hiss of metal forced her to sit up, grabbing for her sword.

Eva could just make out the forms of several man-sized shadows through the leafy undergrowth. She didn't want to draw their attention and make a liar of Stone. She kept low, holding her sword close as she edged toward them.

Stone was on the beach, his head level with hers as he stood on the lower bank. His back was to her. Beyond him stood three men dressed in obscure gray-green cloaks that blended like shadows into the forest and the gray of the sand, making their faces and forms hard to discern through the leaves.

Eva breathed a sigh of relief to identify two tall, imposing Kitarrans - though they were not as tall as Stone. Kitarrans were better than Allati. Still, Stone seemed wary and swords were drawn. The human leader, whom Stone had addressed heatedly, was obscured by the rigid form of her amourii.

Something whitish and fluffy moved silently in the underbrush toward Eva. She froze. A dog. It had long legs and a pointy, wild face. Its amber eyes were fixed on her as it approached purposefully, sniffing at her hand, her face. After a brief moment, it started wagging its tail, and Eva relaxed slightly. The dog bounded off again with a yip, no doubt alerting its master to her presence. Not good.

"Ari! To me!" Eva heard the sharp command. "I don't believe you are alone. Tell me again where exactly you got those horses and we can put these swords away. I have no wish to shed blood. I just want answers."

Eva stood up slowly. The deep sleep had done her good, but she was in no shape to fight any battles. Her head was still fuzzy. As she stood, she felt dizzy. She was forced to steady herself against a tree. She could see the captain now where he stood facing Stone.

Eva forgot to breathe.

Her knees almost buckled; she was thankful for the tree. Her voice was almost lost in her surprise. Almost.

"Illiah!"

She forced her despondent legs to walk forward through the underbrush. Ten steps or one hundred, there was no way to tell. Eva tried to run but got caught on a root. Stone, with his astute reflexes, caught her before she tumbled down the bank.

She squirmed from Stone's grasp as quickly as Illiah pulled her out of it. Illiah held her at arm's length for the briefest moment before crushing her against him.

Eva forgot to breathe.

Illiah was strong. He held her tight, employing that strength. Who needed to breathe anyhow?

Her relief was like the warmest sunshine, the perfect moonlit night, the first singing birds of spring. All the hope and longing she had bottled up for months and months was poured into that moment. It was real. Illiah was real.

Eva realized she was sobbing against his chest, but she couldn't stop. Even when Illiah released her, just enough to look into her face, cupping it gently with his hands, she couldn't stop. Behind her tears, Eva could see his beautiful face, the deep emotions in his forest-green eyes, the softness of his mouth. Her sobs were not all joy - there was so much that needed to be said between them. Questions to be asked, answers to be given.

Suddenly Eva ripped herself from Illiah's arms, backing away from him. Anger was easier than the other emotions coursing through her. It blocked her fear, her confusing shame.

"Where is Rhyl?" she demanded. "How could you leave him?" She didn't wait for his answer. "You are his father! What if something happened to him? What if you were killed? By the Guardians, what if he had no parents? What were you thinking?"

Illiah looked guilt stricken, silent, hurt. He reclaimed his sword from where he had discarded it and slipped it into its scabbard. He had no quick answer for her.

"Many things need to be spoken of, Eva," he said slowly, his voice calm. The hurt in his eyes was crystalline. Eva wanted to wrap her arms around him again, but something held her back. She was damaged. Raped. She remembered the woman, the beauty who was no doubt at that moment playing mother to her son. The woman who dared to try and steal part of her husband's heart.

"Let us make a fire. Eva needs to eat, and explanations can be made," Stone said, stepping up protectively beside Eva as he spoke, towering over Illiah by almost a full head. Illiah turned a scathing look upon her guard.

"I was right about the horses," Illiah muttered. He turned to Eva, reaching out and twisting a short lock of her hair in his finger, a smile tugging at his sad lips.

The rest of the men immediately set about to collect wood and organize themselves, eager for some chore to ease the tension. Eva recalled Stone calling Illiah "captain."

Illiah gave orders to prepare breakfast on the beach in the morning sun. His men had been on foot - Eva knew the look of a scouting party when she saw one. The dog stayed close to her husband. It sniffed Stone's outstretched hand with a wag of its tail and then gave it a lick. Illiah followed Stone and Eva to their small camp.

"Illiah, this is Stone," Eva said making formal introductions. "Stone is my amourii," she said, not guessing Illiah would know what that meant. Apparently, the title did mean something to him. He gave her an incredulous look, one brow raised. His expression was so like Stone's, Eva felt dizzy, like two worlds were colliding resulting in her chaotic emotions.

"You know what that is?" Eva asked.

Illiah nodded, gathering up her things for her, setting her cloak about her shoulders.

"I have been in Kitarra over two seasons now. I have learned a lot about their ways," he told her with a smile. Eva felt herself smiling back. Illiah's smiles always had that effect on her. Until her stomach turned at the thought of the things she must tell him and her smile faded. His did too. It was replaced with worry.

"Illiah is my husband," Eva told Stone a little sheepishly.

"As in Lord Illiah of Jullayah, brother to the prince?"

Illiah's eyes narrowed thoughtfully. "Prince Illiah. My brother is king now."

"And this Rhyl you spoke of is your child?" Stone asked, turning back to Eva.

Eva nodded, feeling tears close. "My son, yes."

"Why didn't you tell me?"

Eva opened her mouth, but the words stuck like mud. "I - I couldn't. It hurt too much. I think you can understand that, can't you, Stone?"

Stone looked at the ground, avoiding her gaze. "Your son and husband in Kitarra," Stone mused. "The son of a woman of Allati royal blood and a man with the blood of royal Jullayah," he said, turning to Illiah. He opened his mouth. "Well -"

"Don't swear on Attin's nipples again. Just don't," Eva warned Stone, ruthlessly interrupting him.

Stone rolled his eyes. "The child of the prophecy."

"Yes," Eva said.

Illiah was nodding.

"Why did they take you and not her?" Stone asked Illiah.

"The Guardian's orders, so the queen tells me."

"You are a captain of Kitarra. You wear the Queen's Flower upon your sleeve." Stone pointed to the six-petaled, star-shaped flower etched in gold with a sword through the center.

Illiah shrugged.

"You have an uandian."

A what?

"I am the First Defender. Unfortunately the queen didn't have a better man for the job," Illiah said.

"So, you risk your life?" Eva started again.

Illiah gave her a level look. Eva hated that look. It was often followed by Illiah proclaiming something irrefutably righteous.

"A friend and I were fishing. We pulled a dead girl out of the water. She was about eight years old, and hers was not an easy death. Entire villages, island communities have been destroyed by these monsters - the same invaders from Jullayah. The people are missing or dead. We heard reports of strange boats so we were tracking them up the river. We found a boat downriver two days from here with a small guard. We slaughtered them and are on the hunt for the rest - perhaps twenty men," Illiah told them, standing up to move back toward the beach. Eva followed, taking his outreached hand. Stone walked behind them moodily.

"Eva," Illiah continued, "the Kitarrans have lost their islands, homes, thousands of people. They need me. I have fought these monsters before - I am the best man for the job, the only man for the job. The Kitarrans are not an evil people. What they did to us, they did because they believed there was no other way." He squeezed her hand. Eva squeezed back.

Eva nodded. Her heart filled with pride and fear, yet she could not quite forgive him for leaving Rhyl.

"But?" He could still read her silences.

But Eva could not form the words. Illiah waited, knowing there was something she wanted to say.

"Here, captain, I believe this belongs to you." Stone filled the silence for Eva. He undid his buckle and handed Illiah his borrowed sword. Illiah grinned and took it, trading it for the blade on his back.

"It's really too short for you anyhow," Illiah said, looking up at the lofty Kitarran.

"You were right. It was twenty or so men, by the way, that were raiding up north of here. They are dead," Stone told him, sitting down in front of the fire. Illiah's men were already making breakfast. A pot of hot water was already steaming. One of the men tossed in some herbs. The air soon smelled sweet and refreshing. They all looked at Stone, or tried not to, with questioning looks, or blatant unease. It was strange that Illiah's men, Kitarrans, would be afraid of one of their own.

Eva sat between Illiah and Stone; the latter kept close. Eva caught him looking at Illiah with speculative interest. Meager rations were passed around. Stone handed Eva a cup of tea. She ate while they talked.

"It is a bit of a strange tale - we were headed to Kitarra," Stone began when Eva didn't. "We were passing discreetly through Allati. We came as far as the inn and ferry, but it was burned, not a boat in sight. We could see across the river - the ferry inn on the Kitarran side was burning too. It had been recent, not more than a day or two. The air was still thick with smoke. We were about to turn back when they surprised us, twenty-odd men, with monstrous faces and an evilness about them that made them easy to kill. They attacked, and we fought. Eva was struck and pulled from her horse. I killed them, but Eva was hurt badly. She almost died."

Illiah paled. His arm was already around Eva, but he pulled her closer, kissing the top of her head.

"I had no choice but to take her to the healers in Attingard." Stone didn't mention Attin, or Vagar. "I'll just say that Eva is healed, but still weak. We have been riding hard for days. The Allati might still be looking for us. They want Eva for their own."

"You killed twenty men?"

"Eva got a couple," Stone said with a shrug.

Illiah laughed softly. "So, you came through Allati, probably safer." Was that relief in his voice? Eva couldn't be sure. "The Tarm has been compromised to Kitarrans. Cotoch is up to no good there."

Eva's heart pounded. Her hands felt clammy. Stone looked coolly at Illiah. How was it that Illiah knew so much about this new land, a land that was not his own? Or was it? Eva wasn't sure anymore.

Stone cleared his throat. "Eva, I think you and Illiah should take a walk down the beach. Surely a husband and wife would want some time alone. I will make sure you are not disturbed," he said, glancing at the other men who were covertly listening.

Eva glared at Stone, the meddler. Illiah chuckled.

"Come, dear heart. Your Kitarran is right."

Eva glared at her husband but allowed him to take her hand and pull her up. He had never been one for endearments, "dear heart" was a new one. Illiah put his arm around her waist as they walked and she leaned against him. He waited until they were out of earshot before speaking.

"I can't believe you are here, Eva. I have missed you more than I can tell. I thought I might never see you again. Yet something is amiss, I can sense it." Illiah's voice was grave, his green eyes bright. Eva hadn't noticed how hollow his face looked. He had lost weight from his already lean frame, but then, so had she.

"They told me you and Rhyl were dead. They found your bodies." Eva shuddered, remembering the few days she had almost believed it.

"A trick." Illiah's jaw was set with anger. "I knew - I hoped you would see the truth. I didn't know you would come all this way. Eva, it is dangerous country - what were you thinking?" Eva raised her brows at her husband's daring reprimand. "I'm sorry."

She told him her tale. Tarek and his band of rogues. Stone, lying in a pool of his own blood, dying, for even Kitarran's quick healing would not have saved him.

Illiah glanced back where Stone was watching them, but not watching. "He guards you even now, from me." He took a long, deep breath. "He is the scariest Kitarran I have ever seen."

Eva found herself smiling. "He is, but he has a kind heart." Her smile vanished as she told Illiah about Stone, or what she knew of him. That he had been addicted to culla. He had worked for Cotoch. She told him how they planned to barter with Cotoch for passage across his territory. "Stone believes he failed me then." She certainly had Illiah's attention. His grip on her hand was tight, his eyes intense. "Have you ever heard of the *candarii*?"

To her surprise, he nodded, eyes clouded with rage, and he looked more fearsome than her Kitarran.

"I have." He choked on his words.

"Cotoch," Eva said, unable to look him in the eye. Her skin crawled with the memory of him. She could almost smell him, feel him moving inside her. She took a step away from Illiah lest she somehow infect him with her foulness.

"He raped you." Her husband's voice was iron on a midwinter night.

Eva's throat constricted and tears welled behind her eyes. She nodded and let him gather her in his arms. He crushed her to him, vibrating with rage.

They stood that way for a long time, neither of them able or wishing to speak. There were no words to salve their wounds, no actions that would make it easier, more bearable. He sat on the sand and pulled Eva into his lap, cradling her like a small child.

"He will pay for this. Cotoch will pay. How do you know Stone is trustworthy?" Illiah hissed.

"I know. His reaction was much like yours, and I am not his wife. If Stone sees Cotoch again, Cotoch will die."

"Not if I kill him first."

"He is a dangerous man," Eva reminded him. "After we escaped, Stone took me to a place, a magic place, Tayeh's place."

"Did you see him?"

Eva shook her head. This was not about Tayeh. "There was a hot pool of water that flowed through the cave. I saw visions." She took a deep breath. "I saw a woman kiss you."

And Illiah laughed. Eva wanted to punch him.

"Selene? Yes, she did kiss me. She tried to warm my cold heart," Illiah told her honestly. "But I would never consider it. Never. You are the only woman I want, ever. If I can't have you, I shall not have anyone." He put his head against hers. "Selene is used to getting what she wants. She will not be happy to have you around. She enjoys playing mother to Rhyl and Talo." His omniscience surprised her.

Eva growled. "You and Rhyl are mine - mine. Can she use a sword?"

Illiah laughed again. "No, you could take her easily. Plus, you have your scary henchman to do your dirty work."

"Talo is the Kitarran boy? I see him sometimes in the visions. He and Rhyl are like brothers, are they not?" Eva recalled the image of the Kitarran boy, his lanky frame, his tawny fur, his liquid blue eyes. The memory of those eyes stayed with her. She knew them. Emri, her old friend, the woman from her dream, had the same eyes.

Illiah was saying something, but she could not hear him - two pieces of a broken puzzle were almost coming together.

"Talo's parents are both dead," Illiah was saying, his fondness for the Kitarran boy clear in his voice.

"Dead?"

Illiah nodded. Eva settled back against her husband and closed her eyes. The sun was warm, and she felt safe and almost whole for the first time in many months. She had questions. Questions she didn't even know how to voice or whom to ask. In her mind, she pushed the questions into a box for later.

"I can't wait to see Rhyl," she murmured.

"Soon enough. You'll like Kilev."

"The queen will never let you leave, will she?"

"She will never let Rhyl leave, and we can't leave him. Not before he is a man grown."

Eva nodded. She had accepted long ago that she wouldn't be going home to the Keep. Her family was her home. She would miss Mila and Illiah's brothers. She would miss watching Tarran and Murryn wed and the rambunctious children they would have. Someday, perhaps, they would go home to a home that was no longer theirs.

Eva told Illiah everything. She had forgotten the ease of conversing with someone who was not just her closest friend, but a part of her soul. She had missed the wrinkles at the corner of his eyes, his mouth as it lifted in a half smile. The curve of his throat, one of his many perfect places to kiss.

They fell into silence, their thoughts drifting away from memories back to the present. To their bodies touching after so many lonely nights.

"Our boat will meet us in two days," Illiah told her lazily.

"We won't have very much time alone will we?" Eva said wistfully, slipping her hand under Illiah's shirt to feel his smooth, warm skin. Being close to him roused the most precious memories she had submerged for the past months. Memories of laughter, closeness, ecstasy. She had feared being raped would make such feelings impossible, but the memories of countless nights with Illiah almost eclipsed that one terrible night. Her heartstrings were tied to Illiah's. Her body would never forget the music Illiah pulled from her flesh. Light would always dissolve shadow.

Illiah kissed her then, tentatively, as if expecting her to back away, but she didn't. He pulled up her shirt, his fingers working her laces gently.

"Show some decorum, captain!" she exclaimed with a peal of laughter.

Illiah grinned and kissed her again. She took his hand, pulling him toward the tree line. Past spring floods had carved away the bank, creating an alcove, and a fallen tree also provided some privacy. It was there Eva led her husband.

There was no need for words. Words were too tedious. They moved into the bright leafy shadows beyond the beach. They were alone, forgotten. Time could have stopped, and they would have never noticed or cared.

They kissed and touched and moved in a rhythm not unlike the irrepressible waves of the river. Illiah's fingers found the places they loved best, and his tongue and his lips traced his desires on the contours of Eva's skin.

Eva could not count the nights she had spent in Illiah's arms, the countless nights they had joined and become one. And still it was not enough, never enough. Eva took him in her hands, in her mouth, and finally in her body. She forgot the dark and the doubt. All she wanted was the day, what only Illiah could give her. He chose her and she chose him and together their love was the current and tides and the moon. Natural, unchangeable.

The sharp sound of a dog's bark made Eva and Illiah both stir abruptly. Armeria hunched, her hackles a sharp ridge down her back, her barks of desperate fear echoed through her frame.

A man stood before them. The harder Eva tried to distinguish his face, the more impossible it became. The sun was shining, but its warmth, its light, had vanished. The beach was in man's shadow as if he stood a hundred feet tall.

Illiah's cloak, their blanket, dropped to the sand as he grabbed his sword. He was naked, as was Eva. Eva dove for her sword.

The man - or shadow - was fast, incapacitating Illiah with one hand around Illiah's neck. Eva lunged with her sword. The man grabbed her arm with his other hand, pushing her to the ground. The force of the shock rippled through her body. She tried to stand but fell back, blinking hard. She opened her mouth to shout, to scream, but couldn't.

The man opened his mouth and breathed into Illiah's face. Something went into Illiah's mouth with the breath. It was dark and thick and reminded Eva of rotten leaves. Illiah choked on it.

Illiah was placed back onto his feet. He was no longer choking, but Eva's relief was short-lived. His green eyes were cloudy. He did not put down his sword. He didn't look like he had the strength to use it. He was diminished - gone. He was a husk. He was taken.

Armeria barked and barked.

Eva tried to stand again, this time successfully, but her feet were shaking. Eva lunged at the man again. He smiled as he caught her easily in a grip as strong as roots, impervious as rain. He smelled of metal and heat. His breath was a fire against Eva's neck.

"So pleasant to see you again, Eva."

His face solidified. Eva knew his face. She knew his voice.

"Impossible," Eva breathed.

Ari was still barking. Stone would hear her. Illiah's men would hear her. Wouldn't they?

"Oh?" said the man who looked and talked like Serac. "You can see visions, you can heal the weak, the dying, but you don't believe that magic can take other forms?" His mocking cadence was mnemonic.

"What are you?"

Serac grew and stretched. He smiled, but his face looked wrong, like he knew how to smile but he did not know what to do with it. His eyes shifted, and Eva saw what was in them. They pulled her in, devouring her.

Magic. The *simul rami* was a river of time and energy and light. Inside his eyes, she dove down through the clear, perfect water; at the bottom was neither rocks nor sand nor clay. It was dark. Smooth. Another river. Only black. But not the black of nothingness - this was the black of everything pooled and mixed together. Every color, every thought, every emotion. The *varing*. She touched the black river and suddenly it twisted and rose, mingling with the *simul rami*. The waters of two colors didn't exactly mix; they swirled around each other in a strange, intoxicating harmony.

"Eva."

Eva was called back - no, she was summoned. Her stomach roiled with haunting familiarity, the magic tightened around her mind and body, constricting her will, just like with Cotoch. Panic rose up her spine with sickening speed, squeezing her breath from her lungs.

The man resembling Serac was changing. Roots wriggled out from his ears, his eyes; black, rotten leaves mottled his skin.

"You see? I am Serac. I am Cotoch. I am everyone the *varing* has touched. I am the center of the *simul rami*. I am the Black Goddess. I come from the depths of time and this world, coalesced into being to -"

The thing resembling Serac paused, its face distorted, its eyes rolled back into its head. Blood crawled from the gaping mouth. Crawled - not dripped - black and sticky, a separate entity, reminiscent of insects abandoning a burning log. The body slumped against Eva, knocking her to the ground by its dead weight. A dagger was lodged in its head. The dagger was crude, reddish-brown and made from wood. A vercuri.

The escaping substance dissolved into the ground like a thousand tiny worms. The *varing* fell from Eva's mind, shed like water from a leaf. Eva slithered out from under the corpse. Stone stood behind it, his eyes blazing and wide and utterly shocked. Behind him, Illiah's men ran up the beach.

Illiah groaned, and Eva watched apprehensively as her husband's eyes became green and his once more. His body slumped before he stiffened, ingesting the sight of the thing before them.

The corpse was indeed dead, but not dead like a person. It melted before their eyes, turning black and wet. The clothing and skin and normalcy dissolved, seeping into the sand. A smell filled the air like putrefaction, but bitterer and more awful.

"Sweet Attin's nipples, what the fuck was that?" Stone asked in a ragged voice.

Eva didn't answer. She ran to Illiah. He cradled her face, and they took a moment to inspect each other's eyes for bits of lost soul. Assured Illiah was himself once more, Eva kissed his lips briefly.

Stone put the cloak about Eva's shoulders. Eva turned from Illiah to her amourii and Stone's arm came around her. The contact was mutually comforting.

"I don't know what that was. But it is not good," Eva whispered.

Illiah had dressed quickly, his pale face almost hidden behind his mask of leadership. He reluctantly retrieved the wooden dagger from where it lay on the darkened, wet sand. It was smaller than Illiah's and shaped differently - fatter, shorter. He gave it to Stone, who put it back into his pocket. Eva shivered.

"Where did you get a vercuri?" Illiah asked.

"At the Vale."

"How did you know it would kill it?" Eva asked Stone.

"I didn't."

"Stone, that thing was too easy to kill."

"Agreed."

No one knew what to say about the attack. No one mentioned the possibilities and what-ifs had Stone not had a vercuri and the intuition to use it. But they all were anxious to put distance between them and the place where it had fallen, where the sand was blackened. Illiah informed his men that they were going to make all haste for Kilev. No one complained. Eva tried not to think about *varing's* mysterious effect on her husband. It called to him, consumed him. She wanted answers but had no one to ask.

Illiah took his men aside to debrief them on their new circumstances. He introduced them formally to Eva, his wife, and Stone, her amourii. The humans were Alec, Vayn and Harol. The Kitarrans were Rourke and Bolyn. Their ages and looks were mixed, but they all wore the same drab clothing best suited for blending in with their surroundings.

They looked pleased with Eva's acquaintance but kept a respectful distance from Stone. It was unfair - Stone had just saved Illiah's life, and possibly Eva's. He didn't deserve their derision. But Stone kept his distance as well. Eva noticed his reluctance.

Illiah greeted his black charger with enthusiasm. Penn tossed his head and butted Illiah with his nose. Illiah laughed softly. The dog reappeared on the sand and trotted over to sit at Illiah's heels. Eva let her sniff her hand, and Ari's tail began to wag slowly.

"Kitarran horses don't have the quick, graceful quality of these southern beasts," Illiah said as his men took an interest in the horses. Illiah went on to explain where they came from.

"You can ride Sasha, Stone, if you like. I will ride with Illiah," Eva told her amourii. Illiah gave her a raised brow. "I can barely get in the saddle by myself. I am still weak from being ill," Eva admitted.

"That must be embarrassing," Illiah teased. Eva stuck her tongue out at him. He mounted up on Penn and breathed a sigh as he patted the horse on his neck. "When we get back, Penn, we shall breed you with the finest Kitarran mares, and a whole new fleet of fast Kitarran horses with be born."

"Your heritage is catching up with you," Eva told him.

Illiah nodded with a grin. "My father would be proud. If he didn't think I was already dead," Illiah added with a frown.

"Illiah's foster father bred horses. These two are from the south of Jullayah. You will not find their like anywhere else," Eva explained as Stone waited with a question in his eyes.

"Foster father?" Stone asked, helping Eva up so she could sit behind her husband. She locked her arms around Illiah's middle.

Eva smiled. "There is a tale there, perhaps later."

Riding was easy sitting behind Illiah. They kept a slow pace. Illiah's men were on foot, and some of them were human, so there was no use going faster than a walk. Stone acted as guard, keeping to the back of the small host.

The day passed and the time came to make camp for the night. Illiah's men made a fire. Eva watched the river wistfully, wishing Illiah's boat was coming up the bend. Only one more day, Illiah had promised.

Rourke had gone out hunting and brought back a set of rabbits. Vayn was quick with a knife and set to work making a stew. As the sun disappeared the chilly night air blew in, Eva sat close to the fire, wrapped in her cloak.

Illiah tended to his horses, a task which apparently he had missed. Stone offered to help him, and Eva watched the two men rubbing down the horses and feeding them some of the oats Vagar had sent with them. Eva couldn't hear what they talked of, but Illiah was smiling, a good sign, even if Stone was not.

"My lady." Vayn handed her a mug of tea with a crisp smile. She took it, nodding her thanks, letting the warmth seep into her. She couldn't help but smile at the thought of sleeping with her husband's warm body beside her. Vayn caught her eye and gave her a wink, making her blush like a maiden. Vayn's smile faded as Stone came into the firelight and sat beside Eva.

"Why are they all so afraid of you?" Eva whispered to him.

That made Stone laugh - a mirthless, deprecating sound. "They are not just afraid of me - they dislike me. A rogue Kitarran is a Kitarran who has abandoned his people. They are a loyal people. I would expect nothing else."

Eva frowned, wishing she could ask him more about her dream, his past. But she couldn't, not in front of the strange men.

Illiah sat down on Eva's other side after taking a bowl from Vayn.

"Will you tell your tale now, my lord?" Stone asked of Illiah. "I thought you were a prince - how did a prince have a foster father who bred horses?"

Illiah grinned. He told the tale of the twin brother, the stolen baby, and his upbringing in the large family of Devlin Horsemaster. He told how he had trained as a warrior under the tutelage of a nomad, and went to win a war. He always spoke of that time with reverence and grief, never boasting. Eva respected him for it. He didn't mention the vercuri. He never did. Eva wondered where it was.

Eva looked around the circle, missing only Alec who was on watch. Respect and devotion shone in the eyes of her husband's men. They loved their foreign captain. Illiah still had a great capacity for capturing loyalty, even without an enchanted dagger.

Illiah ended his tale after telling how he met Caeris for the first time.

"Twins are a blessing from the Guardian," Rourke said, smiling. "Kitarrans do not bear children easily. They are fortunate to have one child in a lifetime, but often that is not so. Too many of our babes are stillborn. One of the reasons there are so few of us."

Eva's heart ached with compassion. She thought of all the poor women who birthed beautiful, eternally still children who would never cry or laugh.

"That is one of the lines of the Guardian's prophecy," Illiah said, throwing another log on the fire. "It speaks of a boy with magic blood that will save the children of Kitarra."

Stone's voice filled the space left after Illiah's words,

"Those who were strong are now weak,
With healing hands, the babes will speak
Light turns to dark and colors shift,
Two rivers join when two lovers rift,
Watch for the child of two thrones,
Born with magic in his bones,
A child lit by the stars,
Watch for him, for he shall be ours."

Stone finished the verse into stunned silence. The hairs on the back of Eva's neck bristled. She was torn between anger, sadness, and a desperate longing to hold her son in her arms. Rhyl was hers, not Kitarra's. Two rivers. She had seen them in the creature's eyes. The *simul rami* and the *varing*. Light and dark. *Sanarii* and *candarii*.

The madness of the men in Dweller's Knoll years ago. The invaders Illiah had destroyed. The bestial thing that had hunted Illiah. Cotoch's dark magic. The thing that took the shape of Serac and died on the beach under Stone' vercuri. They had all been tainted by the *varing*. And the vercuri had the power to stop it. Tayeh had told her once that there were nine vercuri; it gave Eva hope.

"Rhyl is already the light of Kitarra," Boyln said, breaking into Eva's thoughts, his green eyes bright. "Him and the little prince. They will be great leaders one day. All will follow them."

"Little prince?" Stone asked in a flat voice.

Rourke's eyes were warm with love and devotion. "Little Prince Talo, Arrain's boy. You remember what happened -"

"We don't speak of it," Bolyn interrupted with a stern look at his comrade. There seemed to be a silent understanding between the Kitarrans, a story well known, but no one wished to repeat it.

Next to Eva, Stone's body was still and taut, gripped by some strong emotion. She put her hand on his, but he moved away as if hers burned. Eva turned back to the fire, consumed with the desire to help her friend. But she didn't know how.

"The lights of Kitarra," Illiah mused proudly, taking a drink.

Stone stood and left the circle of firelight, stalking off into the darkness. Eva watched him go. Her poor friend. Her defender. She was beginning to have a picture in her mind of who he had been. His emotions betrayed the secrets of his past.

The flickering firelight blurred Stone's expression, but Eva had seen ghosts in it. Something terrible lurked beyond the yellow depths of his soul. Part of her wanted to follow him, but her whole body protested the idea of moving. And Stone would be all right. The cruelty of life was inevitable, but life was also kind, Eva knew that now. Stone didn't believe he was brave, but he was. He would find his way.

Eva's head was heavy and she laid it on Illiah's shoulder, closing her eyes. He gathered her close, and she fell asleep sitting up, curled next to her dear one.

CHAPTER 69

STONE

STONE HAD DROWNED ONCE. He would never forget the crushing, burning ache before oblivion. But the night was not the river and there was no oblivion to consume his anguish. The darkness overwhelmed him but gave him little relief. It was not enough to obscure his senses ablaze with guilt and grief.

A child. A little prince. How could that be? A lie perhaps. A misconception. Stone had seen the babe with his own eyes - still, lifeless, its blue lips, no trace of a heartbeat. It was not his first child to be born dead. The blood - so much blood - the awful stillness of the mother. His wife. His love.

And yet an awful doubt crept like icy fingers into his memories. Talo was the name of his father, the name he and Emri had chosen for their unborn child. If it was a boy. If, this time, it lived.

Emri …

The cry was unbidden, silent, but it tore from his heart, from the deepest recess of his hurting soul. If it was true, if somehow the child survived, then he had betrayed those he loved more than he had thought possible.

He had abandoned his child. Her child. The child of his soul and his heart, the child born from a love that came only once in a lifetime. He had left his son an orphan, lost and hurting.

The pain of losing both child and wife had been more than he could bear. His choice to seek out the cliffs had hardly been a choice. The cliffs had called to him. The void had called to him.

The realization that his son lived despite the odds made Stone fall to the sand.

His son … his son whom he had loved before he was conceived, whom he had loved even after he believed death had claimed him. Arrain, the man he had been, could not imagine a world without his son and his wife. He didn't want that world. He had left it willingly, eagerly. But he had been wrong. He made the choice of a coward. Arrain had abandoned his son, his babe, his love. He had gone looking for death, but death did not want him.

When he had washed up on the shore like driftwood, he had believed the second chance at life was merely penance. Then Eva offered him a third chance, a chance to atone for his cowardice, a chance to earn back some of his honor.

It was all meaningless. Stone's - Arrain's - inability to die was not ordained to urge his soul into the light. He would never regain what he had lost. His pitiful honor would not patch back together. There was only life. Ugly, painful, futile life.

A deep, heart-tearing guilt filled the space left by grief, and to his shame, one desire overrode all the others. The all-possessing need to obscure thought and emotion. He had never felt the need for the culla so badly as he did at that moment, in that realization. The need eclipsed all else, or almost all else. Far in the dark recesses of his mind was a child with tawny fur and large blue eyes.

He pushed it away. He was unworthy of that child. He was unworthy of being Eva's amourii. He was the scum of the earth, and he was a betrayer.

Stone rose slowly and was soon surrounded by the forest. He could move as silent as death. It was natural to him. He was past Illiah's lonely guard easily. He went southeast.

Illiah. Noble Illiah. A leader, a good man. He would take care of Eva. Eva wouldn't care if Stone left. She had her captain, her companion of the soul. He had seen the looks that passed between them, one being of two souls. They would be reunited with their child and forget about their troubles. Their love would shine upon Kitarra and help mend the hurts of his homeland.

Eva had a child, a son. A son, taken from her by Stone's own people. Yet she had saved him, brought him back to life. Would he have done the same if it had been her people who took his loved ones from him?

Prince Arrain might have, but not Stone. Stone was empty. Empty except for the urge to drown in the oblivion of a drug that made him a slave to a rapist.

He stifled a sob. He knew where he would wander. He would find Cotoch. He would beg and lose himself as he had done years ago. He would break his vow, his promise, his honor. There would be no magical girl from Jullayah to save him. Surely, he would find some kind of rest, if not forgiveness - no, never forgiveness. One had to forgive one's self before one could gain forgiveness. Stone would never forgive himself. He was too weak.

The other Kitarrans were right to despise him. He despised himself. He had ever since the day Arrain leaped from the cliffs, and the spirit of his dead wife would not let him die.

ILLIAH

"ILLIAH."

His name on her lips was the sweetest sound he had heard in a long time. Never would Illiah take it for granted again. Eva held her hand out for him to clasp, inviting him to join her where she stood at the prow of the ship, watching the peak of Kitarra as it came closer and closer.

The north side of Kilev could be seen before them, spiraling up onto the mountain. Young Olrin was perched, ready, along the edge of the ship, an eager grin on his face. Everyone wanted to be the messenger of good news. Illiah instructed him that the instant their boat touched the dock, he was to run up to the Queen's Keep to inform the queen of their arrival and fetch Rhyl.

Orlin was not the only one jittery with excitement. The mood on the boat echoed Illiah's happiness. Eva's elation to be reunited with Rhyl was catching, and there was not one man who wore a gloomy expression, not one woman who didn't go about her task with enthusiasm.

Illiah squeezed Eva's hand. Her hand was lovely to hold, but he dropped it so he could wrap her in his arms. She leaned against him, still watching the approaching city. He bit her neck, and she squealed, laughing a little. The sound died quickly. Illiah knew she was overjoyed at the prospect of seeing Rhyl, but she carried a deep sadness in her heart. Illiah was a clever man, so he kept his mouth shut on the matter of her amourii.

Stone had abandoned them. Abandoned Eva. She was devastated.

She feared for his safety. Illiah wasn't sure the Kitarran was worthy of her concern, even if he had been a prince. Eva had confided in him about her companion. She was sure the reason for his abrupt departure came from him learning that his son was alive.

Eva guessed that Stone had been hurt beyond imagining when his wife and son died, or so he believed. Eva tried to explain to Illiah the shame Stone carried with him from trying to take his own life, the shame in the years that came after. He called himself a coward, but in truth, he hated himself. Eva said it was because he was lost and didn't know how to find his way forward. Stone blamed himself for failing to protect Eva from Cotoch and later from the blade that nearly killed her.

Illiah didn't know what to think. He had liked Stone. From the little time he had spent with him, he had begun to accept he was worthy of his wife's respect, even her love. He wished they could have found him, convinced him to come to Kilev, to face his demons and know his son. But they couldn't. He was gone, and Eva had no way to track him. Her magic was no use to her. She had an idea of where he went, and if she was right, there was nothing more they could do.

Their boat had been spotted. Illiah's watch guards did their duty well. Men waited on the queen's dock, ready to help them ashore. Illiah had been gone longer than planned, searching the river for the enemy, visiting towns and reassuring the people, following clues and witnesses that might have seen strange boats. The guards would have been watching for their return for some days.

The ship's hull bumped against the wharf gently, and before the ropes could be tied, before the gangplank was secured, young Olrin took off with a grin, jumping the closing gap, running up the winding road to the Queen's Keep. Eva laughed, but again her mirth was short-lived as she stepped off the boat to see who else awaited them.

Selene stood on the dock with the guards. She tried unsuccessfully to hide her dismay. Eva did not bother to hide hers.

"May I introduce my Lady Wife, Evangeline," Illiah said in a ringing voice to those assembled. They all stood at attention as Eva walked down the gangplank. They knew who she was even without Illiah's introduction. Her resemblance to Rhyl, their chosen one, was distinct.

They all smiled and swooned, offering her their warmest greetings. All except Selene, who stood mute in astonishment. Illiah felt a pang of pity for her.

Eva lingered before the other woman.

"Thank you for watching over my son. But I will not thank you for trying to steal my husband's heart."

Illiah swore not a soul breathed. He could almost see the river freezing over from Eva's words. It was harsh. He should really say something, but Eva's possessiveness was like a warm, fur-lined cloak of smugness. The moment passed, and Eva was pulling him up toward the palace.

The guards followed behind them, as did most of Illiah's crew, eager to see the reunion of mother and child. Illiah did not have the heart to dismiss them.

Under the gate, before the road grew steep, the queen awaited them. Arrah was short of breath; she must have run from wherever she was to greet them. Her face was alight with joy and worry both. She held her hands out to Eva. Eva clasped them without hesitation.

"My lady, may I welcome you most graciously to Kilev," Queen Arrah said, bowing her head, her chains tinkling, her jewels catching the light like little rainbows.

"Thank you."

"And may I offer my humblest apologies?" the queen asked softly - no, she was pleading.

Eva took a steadying breath. Illiah wondered what Eva would say. The hurt the queen had caused her was exquisite.

"Queen Arrah, what your people did to my family and me was cruel, heartless. I have an inkling as to why the Guardian asked it of you and what he wanted of me. I do not blame you. I know you love your people. Illiah speaks highly of you," Eva said, still holding the queen's hands in hers, though she looked at Illiah. He thought of the secret they shared, the truth about the queen's son, Eva's dear friend. They would not tell Arrah, not yet, perhaps never. Eva knew Stone would want it that way, not that she owed him that or anything. But Eva did not see it that way.

Illiah was surprised to see tears of relief glinting in the queen's eyes.

"Mummy?"

Those gathered became living statues. Even the breeze held its breath. Every bird, every whispering insect paused. Rhyl appeared in the courtyard with Pudding at one heel, Talo and Crackers at his other, his eyes vast pools of disbelief.

Eva went to her son and gathered him up. She was shaking, clutching Rhyl to her heart, to her soul. Rhyl began to sob, overwhelmed by the intensity of his emotions. He was a very young child, after all.

Something hugged Illiah's leg. He looked down to see Talo encircling his leg with his little furry arms. Illiah put his hand on Talo's head and ruffled his fur before holding him close as they watched.

No one watching Eva and Rhyl's reunion could say it did not touch them, that it was not a testament to the love of the heart, that they did not feel a hint of the longing and love a mother has for her son.

Finally, Eva put Rhyl down. Her son beamed at her with a smile of pure radiance. His world was fixed, complete. Rhyl turned to Illiah.

"You found Mummy!"

Everyone laughed. Illiah nodded, for he could not speak.

Eva held Rhyl's hand firmly. She walked to Illiah, to Talo, and knelt before the Kitarran child. The son of her friend, her amourii, her lost warrior.

"Talo. You look so much like your mother, and your father. Dear child, I am so happy to meet you," Eva said to the boy. To Illiah's great surprise and the delight of the queen, Talo unlinked his arms from Illiah's leg and put them around Eva's neck. She gave Talo a hug, kissing his furry brow, and the boy was nothing but smiles.

Then Rhyl burst into a litany of all the things he was going to show his mummy. They were going to play dragons with Aisha and listen to Mehmet's stories and - and … He went from one thing to the next with the audacity of a squirrel, and everyone laughed.

Illiah sighed and let his heart absorb the contentment of a perfect moment. The contentment of home.

Tayeh sat at the base of the cendari tree. The lifeblood of the tree hummed at his back. A tree so branching and old and wise even the Allmakers listened to its words. It was almost blooming. Its large, white blossoms would open on the next warm, spring day. As they should.

Kitarra would not die. Not yet.

He had given his people hope.

But if hope was all the Kitarrans needed, Tayeh would consider his task accomplished. Hope was essential, but not a solution.

The child. The warrior. Their path lay ahead of them, twisting and forking. Choices were the burr in Kitarra's future. Choices led to action and reaction, what rose would fall, what was lost might not be found.

Eva had done her best to absolve Arrain of his turmoil. She had made the right choice, planting the seed of love in his chest. It would grow and fester in his thoughts. He was an essential piece, Tayeh knew, just as Illiah and Eva were. Just as the two boys were. Three boys, Tayeh corrected himself.

Abandoning Eva to such an impossible task had been hard. Her suffering was Tayeh's greatest shame. Every tear she had shed had been echoed in his heart.

A Guardian should be beyond such grief, but somehow death and immortality were no release from the pain of his soul.

The tree whispered peace into his heart, and Tayeh knew he was not alone.

The world spun, time tumbled forward. Tayeh knew, for good and ill, ancient forces were at work other than evil men, *sanarii*, and the Guardians.

Lulanan watched the raven. He was oblivious to her, but he was learning. There was time for him to grow up, time for him to master his wings. The darkness had left the Forest, for now. But it was not gone, not nearly. It would wait. The *simul rami* had lost its grip and the *varing* poured through a chasm made of blood and pain and fear.

Lula watched the raven.

ACKNOWLEDGEMENTS

This book. This moment. This everything has been a long time in the making. A lifetime, really. As a kid, I wrote poems and scraps of stories and drew pictures of my characters. As a teenager, I thought it would be wonderful to write novels. I filled a dozen notebooks I didn't let anyone read (and probably never will). As an adult, other things got in the way. Careers. Time. Projects. Oddly, having a baby, the busiest, most exhausting thing a person can do, was what switched something inside me, made me write more. My writing was my exhale after a long day. My reprieve in a busy, exhausting world. And if you are wondering how I managed to squeeze writing into a busy mom life - well, I had a messy house and piles of laundry and I was quite tired. Also, that was eleven years ago, so … yeah. Let's not think about that too hard.

Writing fills my soul. Writing makes me - well, not sane - but balanced. My hope is my stories find their way to fill someone else's heart too.

Writing a book is not easy. And it is not always fun. This book's path has been riddled with doubt (self-doubt you are one tough Mother Fucker) and hard work and sweat and yes, even some tears - the good kind, and the bad. (Eleven years, remember?)

But I couldn't have done it without some help along the way. Well, maybe I could have, but it wouldn't be any good.

Thank you to my first beta readers who read the original very terrible and very long version. Carol, Sonya, and Mom, you have no idea how much I appreciated you just wanting to read it. Sending your work out for someone else to read for the first time is terrifying, to say the least.

Thank you, Amy H., for being in my corner and all the feedback.

Sonya, thank you once again for the re-read, and for believing in me and this story.

Jennifer Sommersby, my editor, thank you for telling it like it is and helping me get this book done and for all the amazing, helpful advice.

Thank you, Donald Maass, for writing some outstanding books about fiction writing. They changed everything for me.

And thank you to my husband Quinton for being the first ear to listen to the adventures of Eva and Stone. And for the brainstorming sessions which were not really helpful plot-wise, but made me laugh. Thank you for being the earth to my air, and the night to my day. I have a lifetime of novels to write, and someday, perhaps, I will be able to express exactly how much you mean to me.

And last but not least, thank you to my two boys, Robbie and Ben, for threatening (after learning my book was for adults) to sneak onto my computer to read my manuscript - it's the best compliment a writer could receive.

All mistakes are mine.

ABOUT THE AUTHOR

Andrea Gibb lives on Sumas Mountain, in British Columbia, with her family. She is an artist and book designer. And when not writing, enjoys long, misty hikes in the forest with her dog.

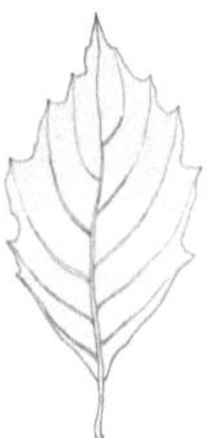

www.andreagibb.com

@andrea_gibb_author

THE SANARII CHRONICLES

BOOKS II AND III OUT NOW!

Available in paperback and ebook.